'LIVELY' AND OTHER STORIES
BY
BORIS MOZHAEV

&

A MEMOIR
BY
ALEXANDER SOLZHENITSYN

TRANSLATED WITH AN INTRODUCTION AND NOTES
BY
DAVID HOLOHAN

David Holohan read French and Russian at Queen Mary College, University of London, and subsequently was awarded a PhD at the University of Bath on the writing of Boris Mozhaev. He also studied at Moscow State University and other universities and institutions in Russia under the auspices of the British Council. He has taught Russian in schools and at the University of Surrey, where he was head of Russian. He has written on Mozhaev and other contemporary Russian writers, and he is currently preparing the first comprehensive study of Mozhaev's life and career. He is also translating more of Mozhaev's works.

He lives in London with his partner.

'LIVELY' AND OTHER STORIES
BY
BORIS MOZHAEV

&

A MEMOIR
BY
ALEXANDER SOLZHENITSYN

TRANSLATED WITH AN INTRODUCTION AND NOTES
BY
DAVID HOLOHAN

Hodgson Press

First published in Great Britain by Hodgson Press 2007

Hodgson Press
4 River Court
Portsmouth Road
Surbiton
Surrey
KT6 4EY
United Kingdom

enquiries@hodgsonpress.co.uk

www.hodgsonpress.co.uk

A CIP catalogue record for this book is available from the British Library.

ISBN: 978-1-906164-00-3

Printed in Great Britain by Lightning Source Ltd.

Typesetting and layout by Bernard Lowe

Dedication

For Phil Armitage (1960-2006), sorely missed by all who knew him.

Preface

The purpose of this book is to make available, for the first time in English, a selected sample of the prose of the Russian writer Boris Andreevich Mozhaev (1923-1996). Mozhaev was a thorn in the side of the former Soviet regime because he insisted on writing the truth about Soviet life, and particularly about rural life in Russia. Rural folk were badly treated by the state in the former Soviet Union, where they were regarded as second-class citizens. Nevertheless, Mozhaev's characters do not passively bemoan their harsh lot, but they show remarkable tenacity and wit as they battle against life's vagaries – not of the harsh Russian climate – but of the bureaucrats and officials who oppress them.

Mozhaev was a great satirist with a wicked sense of humour and he turned his satire frequently against the Soviet system, showing how ludicrous so many aspects of life in Russia were – and still are. He lambasted those leaders, and their officials who blindly did their bidding, who wanted to direct every aspect of life by fiat in a society where to dissent and express a different opinion was dangerous. He was terribly critical of people who would not think for themselves, or be prepared to stand up for what they knew to be the truth. And, as a writer, Mozhaev paid dearly for his outspokenness: many of his works were not published for many years after they had been completed, and he became an outcast within society and particularly within the writers' community, like Alexander Solzhenitsyn, who was his closest friend. Fortunately for Mozhaev, however, he was not expelled from the Soviet Union, unlike Solzhenitsyn. He remained in his beloved Russia, but he had to battle all his life to get his stories and articles published.

The Soviet Union collapsed in December 1991, and life in Russia changed outwardly, but many aspects of society, and in particular the Soviet mind-set and ways of thinking, have changed little: so much of what Mozhaev wrote about is as fresh and relevant today, as it has ever been. His works are still printed and appear in new editions regularly in Russia. Mozhaev wrote his story *Lively* in the late 1950s, but it was published only in 1966 and later adapted for the stage. The play was subjected to several bans and it took another twenty-one years before the censor would allow the play to be performed in public. When it was performed, audiences and critics alike were amazed how poignant and contemporary the subject matter still was. The same is true of all his other stories today.

By reading these stories, the reader will gain an insight into some of the most tragic and darkest moments of contemporary Russian history – War Communism, the campaign for the full collectivization of agriculture, the paranoia and ruthlessness of Stalin's purges, the rooting out of so-called 'enemies of the people', and a life of bondage to the state on the collective farm… But this is not narrated as bald, historical fact: it is told from a personal perspective with great humanity and passion. However, amidst all the pathos, Mozhaev manages to entertain and move the reader by his characters' charm and vivacity, all narrated with a sincere and profound love for his native Russia, and particularly for its rural folk, whom he knew would survive, come what may.

This is the story of an indomitable people.

Illustration 1. Boris Andreevich Mozhaev (1923 – 1996).

Contents

List of Illustrations

Acknowledgements

I have been so very fortunate in having help and encouragement from many people while preparing and working on these translations. Mozhaev is a difficult writer to translate because his language is riddled with dialect and specialist terms, chiefly from the sphere of agriculture and rural life, and his characters revel in making witty comments, which are hard to put over in English without lengthy explanations, which can kill a pun stone dead! Humour from an alien culture is notoriously difficult to convey.

A number of former colleagues, friends, and native speakers have been very generous with their time and sharing their considerable knowledge with me, by answering my questions and helping me to understand the subtle nuances of countless words and phrases. My grateful thanks go to Martin Dewhirst and his Russian wife Marina, and likewise to Mervyn Matthews and his wife Ludmila Bibikova. Above all, I must single out my friend Natalia Bulgakova, who has spent an enormous amount of time, tirelessly and patiently considering many difficult passages with me.

Huge thanks go to Milda Emilevna Shnore, Mozhaev's widow, for her kindness and generosity in granting me a lengthy interview and answering so many questions about her life with Boris Andreevich, and not least for granting me the permission to translate and publish Boris Andreevich's work. I am grateful also to Alexander Solzhenitsyn for his interest and encouragement in these translations.

No fewer grateful thanks go to many kind friends for reading the translations in their early drafts and making useful suggestions, without which these translations would be the poorer: they are Jim Riordan, Dave Hanrahan, Philip Taylor, and, of course, my partner Berni, whose patience is without limit, not to mention his inexhaustive computing skills.

Many other kind people have answered individual queries and they have sometimes gone to great lengths to find out information for me. Grateful thanks go to The Royal Botanic Gardens at Kew for help in tracing a rather unusual plant mentioned in Mozhaev's story *Lively*. One hesitates to approach so august an institution as Kew, with a request to find out the botanical name of a plant, popularly called a 'bollock cutter'. (When the reader reads this story, all will become clear!) But I did approach them, and I am particularly grateful to Craig Brough, Mark Nesbitt, and Maria Vorontsova. Maria Vorontsova forwarded my query to a professor at a university in the Urals, and I received an email from him with an identification of the plant in question. What a wonderful thing the internet is! So my thanks go to Professor Alexander Petrovich Diachenko of the Urals State Pedagogical University. Faith Wigzell of the School of Slavonic and Eastern European Studies kindly helped me with some Old Russian, and Birgit Beumers at Bristol University generously provided me with information about Mozhaev and the Taganka Theatre.

I also thank my former students at the University of Surrey, who read my translation of *Sania* many years ago and gave me some very useful feedback and encouragement.

Thanks are also due to the Society for Co-operation in Russian and Soviet Studies, London, for their help in finding and providing me with photographs, which are reproduced in this volume. Similarly, thanks also go to Tracey Alena Brett for her patient and friendly help in going through piles of old newspaper sketches at her antiquarian bookshop in London.

My heart-felt thanks go to two very special people, without whose kindness and skills – though very different – these translations would never have been accomplished: they are again, my partner Berni, and David Asboe. The debt I owe them both can never be repaid.

I am touched by the generosity of spirit all these people have shown me.

David Holohan

March 2007

A Note on Transliteration

The system of transliteration I have used in this book is a simplified version of the system used by the US Library of Congress. I have dropped both the diacritical mark and any indication of the soft *i*. I have indicated the *yo* sound as *ë*. Hence, I have written Khrushchëv, and not Khrushchyov, or the common spelling of Khrushchev.

I have also not indicated any soft signs, whether within a word or at the end, so *oblast'* appears simply as *oblast*. My purpose in simplifying all these spellings is so as not to make the text too fussy in appearance for the general reader, who does not know Russian.

By and large, I have observed the system of transliteration as stated above for proper nouns, but, again with the general reader in mind, I have used Anglicized forms of names when they would otherwise look strange. Hence, I have spelt *Aleksandr* as *Alexander*, and I have kept to accepted Anglicized spellings of common names like *Gorky* and *St. Petersburg*.

A Note on Proper Names and Modes of Address

Many general readers of Russian literature, who do not have a knowledge of Russian, find Russian names extremely confusing, because they can be altered by truncating them and by adding various diminutive forms. In order to save adding a footnote every time such variations occur, the reader might find a short explanation of this convention useful.

The usual polite mode of address amongst Russians is to use their first name and patronymic, i.e. the name a person inherits from his or her father. This is tantamount to using '*Mr*' or '*Mrs*' in English. Hence, on meeting a person for the first time, or when on formal terms, it is perfectly polite to refer to someone as '*Boris Andreevich*', and omit their surname. '*Andreevich*' means '*son of Andrei*'. A woman, whose father was called '*Andrei*', would use the patronymic '*Andreevna*', i.e. 'daughter of Andrei'. Patronymics are often shortened by a syllable in everyday speech for the same reasons that speakers find it easier to call a person 'Nick', rather than 'Nicholas'. Hence, '*Andreevich*' is often shortened to '*Andreich*'. When pronouncing Russian names, such as '*Andreevich*', each vowel sound should be enunciated separately, i.e. *Andre-e-vich*, and not elided as one syllable.

However, peasants and rural inhabitants are much less formal over modes of address, and they usually use familiar forms of a person's first name, or, even more commonly, they use a nickname. As Mozhaev often points out, they would only use a first name and patronymic for people they felt they ought to address formally, because of their elevated status or as a mark of respect. Hence, in the story *Sania*, the elderly lady with whom Sania lodges is referred to as '*Nastasia Pavlovna*', in deference to her age and wisdom. That is not to say that anyone who is not addressed in such a way is not worthy of respect.

Many of Mozhaev's rural characters have nicknames and usually these are derived from their job, or from some physical characteristic, or from a quirk in their character. Where such nicknames have an actual meaning, I have explained them in a footnote so that the reader does not miss out on any significance a name might carry. Often nicknames are a source of comedy.

First names are subjected to many variations in Russian, wherever a person might live. These variations go far beyond the familiar forms English speakers will be used to using, such as '*Dave*', instead of '*David*', or even '*Bob*', for '*Robert*'. Russian names, and even ordinary nouns, can be altered with suffixes to add emotional overtones, such as an expression of affection. Hence, the conventional way of shortening the first name '*Mikhail*' (Michael), is '*Misha*', but the name can be altered to indicate a greater degree of affection by calling him '*Mishenka*', which in English would be akin to saying '*dearest Misha*', or '*darling Misha*'. Many other variations are also possible, each conveying a nuance. Whenever variations of characters' names become unrecognisable or confusing in these translations, I have added a footnote by way of explanation.

Readers may also be confused by Soviet modes of address, such as '*comrade*' and '*citizen*'. These were forms of address imposed upon Soviet society by the Bolsheviks after the Revolution of 1917. Bolshevik activists were, by and large, urbanites, and it took some considerable time before the more informal rural population understood the conventions of when to use which mode of address. Basically, '*comrade*' was used very much like an English speaker would use '*Mr*' or '*Mrs*' in everyday speech. It can also be used in conjunction with a person's rank or position. Hence, a Russian might hail a doctor as, '*Comrade Doctor*'. The word '*citizen*' was used less than '*comrade*' as a form of address, but it was always used in certain formal situations, such as in a court room. Persons who found themselves in the dock were not accorded the honour of being called '*Comrade*'. In Mozhaev's stories, rural folk frequently confuse these conventions, which they found alien to their culture and way of life – just one of many aspects of Bolshevism they found bewildering. Mozhaev uses such confusion partly for comic purposes, but also as an indication of how remote Bolshevik ideology was from their understanding and sphere of experience.

Today, of course, in post-Soviet Russia, the words '*comrade*' and '*citizen*' as modes of address are now a thing of the past, except amongst the dwindling party faithful, who now seem like political dinosaurs. Russians have reverted to pre-revolutionary modes of address.

Finally, the Russian word for '*uncle*' (*diadia*) is used a great deal as a mode of address, other than to a person's actual uncle. Small children and young adults commonly address older adult males as '*uncle*', as a mark of some formality. Hence, if an adult man were to give a sweet to a child, the mother might prompt the child and say, 'Say thank you to the *gentleman*': a Russian would use the word '*uncle*' here. Similarly, when Sania addresses the elderly Nastasia Pavlovna, she may use the word '*aunty*', and conversely when she addresses the elderly Vasia as '*Uncle Vasia*', who accompanies her to the Comrades' Court.

Introduction

The general reader is unlikely to have heard of the Russian writer Boris Andreevich Mozhaev (1923-1996), because this is the first time his work has been translated into English. There is little at all written about him in English, apart from specialist works on Soviet and Russian literature, although his work and career have been extensively discussed in Russian publications and in the media. Hence, the reader might find it interesting to learn something about his career and literary activity in the brief survey below.

As will become clear while reading these stories, Mozhaev's writing and life were inextricably linked with the Soviet literary scene and rural Russia. For this reason, I have added a brief survey of the Soviet literary establishment and publishing protocol since it affected Mozhaev and all other writers, particularly those like Solzhenitsyn, who clashed with Soviet censorship. Similarly, I have written a short account of how the Soviet collective farm system worked and how the state treated rural workers on these farms, since much of Mozhaev's writing has to do with that milieu. In order to aid the reader to understand more fully the society and its institutions in which Mozhaev sets his stories, I have covered the salient points with quite a broad brush, and these surveys appear as Appendices I and II. The reader is recommended to read these Appendices first, before the stories, to understand them all more fully. The Appendices serve to limit the number of footnotes, which might appear daunting to some readers. To the same end, I have also compiled a Glossary of terms and names which crop up regularly in these translations. Glossary terms appear in bold type in the text, and the Glossary is at the end of this volume.

Boris Andreevich Mozhaev was born on 1 June 1923, on a day traditionally strongly associated with inspiration – 'Holy Spirit Day'. The Russian calendar was crammed full of saints' days, high days, and holidays, all of which had a festive and a religious significance, but each day also had a firm link with agricultural practice. Where Mozhaev got his inspiration as a writer is probably more to do with his own near relatives than with any form of extra-terrestrial influence. He was born into a family which had ties with the Russian peasantry over many generations. His native village was Pitelino, a small settlement in **Riazan oblast**.[1] Before the Revolution of 1917, Mozhaev's grandfather (on his father's side) was an Astrakhan river pilot, ferrying goods along the **Volga** Canal to the Caspian Sea: fish, wool and footwear were among the many goods transported to and fro through this area of Central Asia into Southern Russia.

As was common in rural communities, the family was a large one. Mozhaev had five brothers and sisters, and countless cousins and second cousins, and on his father's side alone, he had three aunts and five uncles. Mozhaev went to war with one of his uncles, Nikolai Ivanovich, in September 1941. Six members of the Mozhaev family went to war in the Second World War, just as six had gone to war from the family during the First World War. Luckily, all came back home, although some were wounded. During the First World War, his cousin, Ivan Mozhaev, was so wounded in the head by a piece of

---

[1] Mozhaev's native village of Pitelino is situated in the **Riazan oblast** at 54°34'N and 41°48'E. It has a population of around 2,700 people.

shell, that it made a permanent dent in the parietal bone on the top of his skull: as a 'party piece', he used to place an egg on his head, in the hollow, and it did not fall off. This phenomenon is referred to by the narrator of the story *A History of the Village of Brëkhovo, Written by Pëtr Afanasievich Bulkin*.

On Mozhaev's maternal side of the family, his great-grandfather and grandfather were sailors, and the latter took an active part in the revolution of 1905, serving in the Black Sea fleet. After the amnesty of 1908, he returned to his native village, which he had not seen for twenty-five years, with an astounding amount of luggage. His wife, Mozhaev's grandmother, thought that he had brought back a huge number of presents and valuable items for the family, but it turned out the cases and trunks contained the full library of the communist party cell with which he was associated. Mozhaev remembered these books in his grandfather's home. At the beginning of 1918, his grandfather set off again from his native village for Moscow and Petersburg, to play an active part in the Revolution, but he never reached his destination, having caught typhus on the way. He was brought home barely alive and died soon after.

Mozhaev's uncle on his mother's side of the family, Pavel Vasilevich Pestsov, graduated from the Nobel institute in 1912 and worked as a ship's pilot until the autumn of 1918 when, on a voyage from the Caspian Sea to Kazan, he unexpectedly died in March or April the following year.

Going back still further in his family history, Mozhaev knew about a great-grandfather, on his mother's side of the family, who used to be in the service of a Russian landowner, or **barin**, who lived in the Meshchëra area of Russia (to the east of Moscow). Mozhaev gives his name as Trofim Selivanovich Pestsov, whom his mother described as a soldier in the army of Nicolas II. He was murdered for reasons unknown, but it is suspected that it was because of a romantic liaison, of which he had many. Mozhaev's mother had described his grave in a local church yard to her son, but, despite a long search, he never found it.

Mozhaev asserted that all the Mozhaevs in the village of Pitelino were direct relatives of his. He also mentioned other distinguished relatives, such as his ancestor Maksim Korotkov, who fought in the Patriotic War against Napoleon in 1812, and who, after the battle of Borodino (2 September 1812), remained in the army and covered the forces of the famous Kutuzov from the attacking French army. Borodino was a village in the **guberniia** of Moscow (one hundred and sixteen kilometres to the west of Moscow), in the **uezd** of Mozhaisk, and the members of his family who defended Russia at that time were given the name '*Mozhaev*'. Hence, this name entered his family.

Thus, several seminal influences upon Boris Andreevich's life can be traced, which had their origins in his ancestors and background. He was proud of his roots, especially his peasant origins, from which he retained a deep, life-long interest in the Russian countryside, with its traditional peasant ways of life and language. He developed a great passion for reading, and it is significant that he had such a vivid memory of his grandfather's library. His interest in, and love of, the area around his native village and the waterways of eastern Russia, on which his ancestors worked, were also to remain with him throughout his life: they feature in his writing, from his earliest works to the last.

Mozhaev followed in the steps of some of his ancestors, when, after completing his secondary education in a local school, he enrolled at the **Gorky** Engineering Institute of Water Transport in the ship-building faculty, in the autumn of 1940. As a younger man, he was to have gone to study at the industrial technical college in the nearby town of Kasimov, but his family could not afford to send him because of the distance from his home, which was fifty **versts**: it was too far to travel on a daily basis and it would have meant that he had to take up lodgings there. The family simply could not afford such expenses. While studying at the **Gorky** Institute, Mozhaev managed to get a job loading boats and ferries on the River **Volga** to pay his way, but when winter set in and the river froze, he took leave of the institute with the right to return, and he applied to join the armed forces. His initial application was rejected because he was officially dubbed the 'son of an **enemy of the people**': his father had been classified as an **enemy of the people** because he refused to join the **kolkhoz** in the 1930s. This epithet was conferred on all people who would not submit to **kolkhoz** membership.

At the end of 1943, Mozhaev was sent as an officer cadet to a naval college and he ended up at a higher engineering and technical college in the navy, from which he graduated at the end of 1948, as a lieutenant engineer. He followed courses in Moscow on film script writing, before he was sent to the Pacific Ocean fleet. He also managed to pursue literary studies in the philological faculty of Leningrad University, under a number of eminent academics. It was at this time that he developed an interest in folklore and history, two strands in his writing which are core elements of many of his works.

Mozhaev lived in China from 1949 to 1951, as a naval engineer. He left the navy after Stalin's death in March 1953 and became a journalist and writer. All the training and wide-ranging education he had received can be seen in the varied output of his *œuvre*. His script writing studies led him to produce works for the theatre and cinema, and many of his films featured famous, popular actors. The renowned Vladimir Vysotskii played the main role in many productions. He was an actor and 'bard', or *chansonnier* – a Soviet *enfant terrible*, who drank and smoked to excess, and composed and performed many dissident and anti-Soviet songs, which circulated in secret recordings. Vysotskii dedicated one of his songs to Mozhaev. Mozhaev wrote plays specifically for the theatre and he adapted others from his prose, which brought him into contact with the internationally renowned theatre director, Yuri Liubimov at Moscow's leading Taganka Theatre. Many of these works would bring him, and those who worked with him, into direct confrontation with the Soviet censor.

Mozhaev began his writing career while still on active service in the navy, initially writing poetry and short pieces, some of them for children. It was while he was living in the Soviet Far East that Mozhaev's former studies in folklore led him to become interested in the local culture and way of life of a small group of people called the Udegei. They are a people of Chinese and Mongolian origin, who speak a dialect which has been broadly classified as one of the Manchu-Tungu languages. As characters in Mozhaev's stories, they feature as guides and fishermen in the taiga, high up in the mountains of the Sikhote Alin. Their villages are scattered far and wide, over a large area of Russia's Maritime Province. Today they number a mere 2,000 people, only 500 of whom still speak their native language. The province used to belong to China, but in the 1860s the territory fell under Russian control and the Chinese were gradually replaced by Russians. The Udegei people live primarily by fishing and hunting, as Mozhaev's stories describe, but they also trade in ginseng root, furs, and other natural products for traditional Chinese medicine. However, the tiger is sacred to them and it is only to be killed in self defence. They also have a strong tradition of shamanism and belief in natural spirits, and they have a rich folkloric tradition, expressed in story-telling. Mozhaev wrote down some of these tales and published them under the title of *Udegei Folktales* (1955). Mozhaev describes the Udegei people and their respectful approach to conservation, nature, and natural resources, by way of contrast with the ruthlessness of local Russian authorities, who plundered the natural resources of the area in a cavalier way, not caring for the future or for the well-being of the local inhabitants. Through his depiction of this people, he made a strong statement about the Soviet Union's disregard for ecological issues.

Mozhaev's interest in the Udegei people never left him: he returned to the Udegei people in his detective novels, published between 1969 and 1974, and he also made references to them in his final (unfinished) novel *The Outcast* (1990). Solzhenitsyn so admired Mozhaev's knowledge of the Far East that, on his return to Russia in 1994, he insisted that Mozhaev be his guide on a trip around the region.

Mozhaev's interest in native Russian folklore can be clearly seen in his highly controversial novel *Peasant Folk*, published in two separate books in 1976 and 1987, which feature the fictional villages of Tikhanovo and Gordeevo, amongst the real settings of the Oka River and its tributaries. For Mozhaev, folklore serves as a poetic background to events going on around the characters and it is not recorded as an end in itself: the folkloric element encompasses local history and the peasants' apocalyptic vision, as they see their way of life being gradually destroyed during the campaign for full collectivization in 1929-30. The inclusion of such a folkloric element enhances the dramatic impact of the work and conveys the traditional peasants' outlook, which is rooted in both Christian and pre-Christian religious traditions.

In the late 1950s and early 1960s, Mozhaev travelled extensively throughout the former Soviet Union as a journalist and writer, observing, discussing, and examining rural issues, particularly the issues of agricultural organization and practice within the **kolkhoz** and **sovkhoz** systems. On his travels, he met a number of **kolkhoz** chairmen and directors of **sovkhoz** farms, several of whom he kept in contact with for many years, visiting them on more than one occasion to learn of their concerns and problems. He used this information to write essays and articles, which regularly appeared in the Soviet press, and he firmly believed in the need to see the situation as it really was, with his own eyes, before he wrote about rural issues. Some of the chairmen and directors he met featured in several of his essays, which began to appear regularly in leading publications with a huge readership, such as *Literaturnaia gazeta* (Literary Gazette). Some people he met had to be given changed names, or no name at all, to protect their anonymity, because their views, which Mozhaev reported faithfully and honestly, were highly controversial.

It was in the early 1960s that Mozhaev really started to make a name for himself, first as a publicist, with the publication of a highly controversial article on Soviet agricultural organization, and later as a writer of fiction, tackling subjects which the Soviet censor would rather he had left alone. In the late 1950s and early 1960s, Mozhaev had travelled to the Khabarovsk **krai**, and to the Amur **oblast**, where he had met senior figures in Soviet agriculture – Overchenko and Dugintsev – who had expressed their deep disquiet about the whole Soviet farming system. They both believed in allotting small areas of land to family groups, or to small groups of people, who felt they could work together. They were given technical assistance, but with that came full responsibility for the crops they undertook to grow, and they were expected to produce good results. Their remuneration depended on good yields, but, exceptionally, they were given a free hand to sow what they wanted, when, and where, as their experience and knowledge of local conditions demanded. All this flew in the face of the monolithic Soviet command structure, which Mozhaev and all his interlocutors believed mitigated against good productivity and a personal incentive to work well. Essentially, what Mozhaev was advocating was freeing **kolkhoz** workers to allow them to work in small, independent groups within the **kolkhoz** system, which, to conservative ideologues and planners, flew in the face of the collective spirit. This experiment did indeed produced impressive results, and Mozhaev became a firm believer in the 'independent farmer', a position which he defended to the very end of his working life. Mozhaev wrote up his impressions in an essay entitled 'The Land Awaits an Owner', which was published in the **thick journal** *Oktiabr* (October) in 1961. The editor of the journal was the renowned Fyodor Ivanovich Panfërov (1896-1960), a writer on rural themes in his own right. The censor instantly took a dislike to the title of the piece, which smacked of 'private property' and 'independence', which the Bolsheviks had tried so hard to eradicate by imposing the **kolkhoz** system upon the peasantry. Panfërov had to get the personal sanction of Khrushchëv himself to publish the essay, so radical was the content. However, it was officially insisted that the title be changed to the more bland 'The Land Awaits…', ridiculously not stating what it awaited. This was not the first time that Mozhaev would have to change a title in order to tone down the sharpness of his criticism. It was also not the first time that such a high-ranking person within the Soviet government was to notice Mozhaev: much later, both Andropov and Suslov criticised Mozhaev for 'desecrating our present-day life' by his writing.[2] Mozhaev insisted that all he had done was tell the unvarnished truth about what he had witnessed with his own eyes.

As a result of his article 'The Land Awaits…', the journal *Oktiabr* was inundated for the next three months with letters and criticisms of Mozhaev's ideas on agricultural organization, and others, yet to be written in the same vein, were ultimately to set Mozhaev on a collision course with Soviet censorship, which eventually led to a long, enforced silence, as newspaper and journal editors refused to publish his writing.

While working on a film adaptation of his story *Narrow Gauge Trees* (1956) in the early 1960s in Sverdlovsk, the director of the film, Ivan Konstantinovich Pravov, brought Solzhenitsyn's story *One Day in the Life of Ivan Denisovich* to Mozhaev's attention. The director was so excited about the story because it was about a political prisoner who had spent a number of years in Stalin's camps, just as Solzhenitsyn himself had. Nothing had been published like this before: the very publication of the story was tantamount to

---

[2] Yuri Vladimirovich Andropov (1914-1984) was head of the KGB (State Security Committee) from 1967-1982, and subsequently General Secretary of the Communist Party's Central Committee, from November 1982 to his death, just fifteen months later.
Mikhail Andreevich Suslov (1902-1982) was a leading Communist Party ideologue of an extremely conservative persuasion, who exerted a great deal of influence on political ideology and policy. He was the chief organizer of a group of politicians who ousted Khrushchëv in 1964, whom they believed to be too liberal.

admitting that such places existed – a fact that had never previously been officially acknowledged, though everyone knew of their existence. Pravov told Mozhaev that he himself had been a prisoner in a camp. On returning to **Riazan** a short time later, Mozhaev went to the secretary of a local branch of the **Writers' Union**, Matushkin, and asked what he knew of the author. To Mozhaev's great excitement, he discovered they were neighbours, and he was taken by Matushkin to meet him. This started a friendship which was to last for the rest of Mozhaev's life. An account of how Mozhaev and Solzhenitsyn met is given by Solzhenitsyn himself in his memoir translated in this volume.

The **Writers' Union** was not a union in the traditional sense of the word. It was rather more like an elite club, membership of which was virtually essential in order to publish literature in journals and books. Also, it had in its power to hand out privileges to its members, such as access to elite social clubs and restaurants, the use of country houses (known as '*dachas*'), and cheap trips to luxury, exclusive seaside resorts. In essence, it was a body which played a major role in controlling authors and their writing by exerting pressure on them to do the state's bidding, either by putting a rosy tint on their depiction of everyday Soviet life, or by keeping quite on issues the state would rather not have discussed. Many writers of conscience, like Mozhaev, refused to do this, which meant that their membership was rather precarious: they were often expelled from the organization whenever it was deemed that they had overstepped the mark, thus closing journals, newspapers, and publishing houses to their work. Sometimes this membership was reinstated. Amongst union members was also a large cohort of writers of modest talent, or even of none, who were more than willing to toe the official line in return for assured publication in large print runs and the usual privileges. Soviet bookshops were piled high with such volumes that few people wanted, whereas quality literature was on sale in limited quantities and generated long queues amongst book-lovers and avid readers. There was also a buoyant 'black market' in quality literature of both the pre- and post-revolutionary periods.

When Mozhaev first met Solzhenitsyn, he was having considerable success with his own writing, publishing frequently in the *Oktiabr* and the popular, but serious, weekly newspaper, *Literaturnaia gazeta*. He offered Solzhenitsyn help in getting something published, as narrated in the memoir. This was at a time of liberalization, when it looked as though more works of a controversial nature might be published, especially in the prestigious **thick journal *Novyi mir*** (New World), under the editor **Alexander Tvardovskii** (1910-1971), himself a respected writer. It was **Tvardovskii** who had personally negotiated the publication of Solzhenitsyn's *One Day in the Life of Ivan Denisovich* with Khrushchëv. **Tvardovskii** believed that under the 'liberal' ideological climate of that time – the end of 1962 – there would be ample opportunity to publish contentious works. Khrushchëv was engaged in an anti-Stalinist campaign, unmasking the 'mistakes of the past', as they were officially known, and a number of works critical of Stalin's regime were allowed to be published in order to further Khrushchëv's own policies. **Tvardovskii** was optimistic that this door of opportunity would remain open for some time, but Solzhenitsyn was much more doubtful. The clamp-down came as early as March 1963, proving Solzhenitsyn to be the more astute of the two.

In the meantime, Mozhaev and Solzhenitsyn continued to develop their friendship, as Solzhenitsyn regularly met up with both Boris Andreevich and his new wife, Milda

Emilevna Shnore. Milda Emilevna had inherited a country house in the Gulf of Riga from her family – she was Latvian, and the Mozhaevs spent a considerable amount of time there, as Boris carried out extensive repairs to the house. However, he found it difficult to settle there: he was much more at home in his native village and region – a feature of his character which was to stay with him for the rest of his life.

What impressed Solzhenitsyn about Mozhaev was his depth and breadth of knowledge of the Russian peasantry, the countryside, its flora and fauna, and his love of the Russian language, as spoken by rural people. He was passionate about all things rural – small villages, beautiful homes, local churches, manor houses built by former rich merchants, carving, and pieces of folk art – all the products of skilled, local craftsmen. He admired the industry and the proud independence of farmers and peasants, when left alone to do their work as they saw fit, free from state interference. He was passionate about the local ecosystem and the delicate balance of nature, and he was incensed at the indifferent and cavalier way that Soviet bureaucrats wrought devastation upon the landscape of his beloved **Riazan oblast**, and areas of the Russian taiga. Mozhaev adapted several of his stories for the cinema in which he made severe criticisms about the Soviet forestry industry and other types of activity, which recklessly plundered the natural resources of the north and Far East of the Soviet Union, leaving in their wake large-scale ecological devastation. The stories got through Soviet censorship unscathed, because he had made his criticisms within the popular genre of the detective story. Less critical attention was paid to detective stories by the authorities, because they were not regarded as terribly serious literature, despite their wide appeal.

The ideological clamp-down in March 1963 directly affected Mozhaev and work on a film, which was based on one of his detective stories. Khrushchëv had turned against writers and artists of all types at a meeting which took place in Moscow only three months after the publication of *One Day in the Life of Ivan Denisovich*. Khrushchëv's outburst was a truly extraordinary event, since his rant against contemporary art and writing was expressed badly and coarsely, in uneducated Russian. He singled out specific artists and writers as targets for his ire, but he did not recognise other prominent figures at the meeting, thus showing his ignorance of contemporary Russian culture. It was a disgraceful outburst by a major head of state, akin to the stream of foul language and banging his shoe on the table at the United Nations in 1960. The outcome of this meeting with artists and writers marked a return to the severe restrictions which had dogged Russian *belles-lettres* before the ideological relaxation, or 'thaw', as it is known. For Mozhaev, the effect was disappointing to say the least. The work on his film, which had started on 10 March 1963, was interrupted by the authorities after only four days. Work on the film was resumed much later, but his criticisms on ecological issues were severely toned down, to the extent that Mozhaev was very unhappy with the completed film. He remarked, fittingly using vocabulary derived from the forestry industry, that by the time the censor had finished hacking away at the piece, 'there were only chips left'. The film was given a bland title and another two years elapsed before it was released. The film, *Lord of the Taiga*, starred the great Vladimir Vysotskii in the leading role.[3]

Mozhaev and Solzhenitsyn made two memorable trips into the Russian countryside, with Mozhaev as guide, and Solzhenitsyn recalls these trips with great affection in his

---

[3] *Xoziain taigi*, directed by V. Nazarov (Mosfilm, 1968).

memoir. Both writers were planning and researching important future works, but the subject matter was so sensitive that they dare not let anyone else know but each other.

In 1966, Mozhaev had one of his most important works published in *Novyi mir*: it was his novella, *Lively*. He had offered the manuscript to the editor **Tvardovskii**, who had already published Solzhenitsyn's *One Day*. However, since the publication of Solzhenitsyn's piece, the political climate had changed, and by 1966, the forces of conservatism had regained some of the ground won by liberal reformers. Later, Mozhaev was to complain that **Tvardovskii** held on to the manuscript of his story for a long time before doing anything with it. Mozhaev was also subjected to severe criticism in the national press, in articles published by *Pravda* in the same year *Lively* was published. The critics accused him of a 'selective approach to the depiction of reality', and also of a 'superficial approach to life', standard phrases used by critics who wanted to aim a warning shot over the writer's bow. He was also accused of not writing within the confines of socialist realism. Mozhaev started writing *Lively* in 1956, but it took him ten years to get the story published, and even then it was not reprinted in a separate edition for a further six years.

When **Tvardovskii** saw the manuscript of *Lively*, alarm-bells rang in his head, owing to the very title: Mozhaev had called the main protagonist of the story 'Zhivoi', which means 'lively' or 'alive', in Russian. Solzhenitsyn remarks in his memoir that it was a miracle that any peasant could still be regarded as 'alive', after being subjected to the serfdom of the **kolkhoz** system. **Tvardovskii** insisted on changes and cuts be made to the work, in order to get it published, and he started with the title, which was changed to the much more bland *From the Life of Fëdor Kuzkin*. However, the changes did not stop at the title: many cuts were made, ranging from odd words or phrases being deleted, to whole passages being cut to tone the work down. **Tvardovskii** took a whole year over the manuscript, negotiating the 'corrections' with Mozhaev, who had no choice but to go along with his suggestions, otherwise the work would never have been published. **Tvardovskii** subsequently expressed his doubts that a number of Mozhaev's other works would ever be published in the Soviet Union, namely his story *Old Mother Proshkina* (1966), his *A History of the Village of Brëkhovo, Written by Pëtr Afanasievich Bulkin* (1968), and his *One-and-a-Half Square Metres* (1970). Fortunately, he was wrong, but Mozhaev had to wait a long time before he saw them in print: some of his works had to wait twenty years before publication.

As you will see in Solzhenitsyn's memoir, in 1968, the director of Moscow's Taganka Theatre, Yuri Liubimov, expressed his enthusiasm for Mozhaev's *Lively*, and work was started to produce a stage version of it. Liubimov and the Taganka theatre, where Mozhaev was on the board of artistic directors for many years, had a reputation for staging works which were politically sensitive and daring. Liubimov tried several times in 1968 to get permission for the stage version of *Lively*, but it was refused. They both had to fight high-level opposition while rehearsals for the stage version were already under way. Liubimov gives a detailed account of how the Minister for Culture herself, Furtseva, became directly involved in the controversy, and how Mozhaev defended the subject matter of the play in the strongest terms, involving him in a shouting match with the minister's entourage. The performance was closed and Liubimov lost his party membership as a punishment, although it was later re-instated. The play was banned again in the years that followed, and it received its public performance only in 1989, twenty-one years after the first attempt, by which time Liubimov had been forcibly exiled in the West by the Soviet authorities. Mozhaev stated that Liubimov 'suffered personally' for his constant battle with the censor over the production of *Lively*, but they became close friends. Liubimov returned to Russia in January 1989 specially to direct the production of Mozhaev's play, which featured a number of the original actors. The work was also turned into a film, directed by S. Rostotssky in 1989, and it was eventually shown on central television on 1 January 1990, and in cinemas. It caused a huge amount of interest and discussion on television and in the press.

All his early short works brought him criticism from critics of the literary establishment, who called him a 'slanderer with a long service record', and the furore caused by the publication of such early works as *Sania, Thin Ice*, and *Narrow Gauge Trees* culminated in his being expelled from the **Writers' Union** in 1959. He was reinstated six months later, but only after considerable debate and by the direct intervention of other writers, who defended him and lobbied influential people on his behalf. Mozhaev always insisted on the individual's right to follow his own path in life, be he **kolkhoz** worker or writer, and this is a central theme of his writing.

Just after the publication of *Lively*, Mozhaev had to suffer more public censure: this time it was at the Writers' Congress in 1967, by the 'official' writer and Secretary of the **Writers' Union** of the USSR, Georgii Mokeevich Markov (1911-1991), whose condemnation of Mozhaev effectively closed all official presses to him, meaning that he could not publish at all. This was not the first time he and the **Writers' Union** clashed over his work not being published. True to the usual Soviet practice, Mozhaev's own family also suffered obstacles and difficulties in their lives, just as Mozhaev's own father's resistance in joining the **kolkhoz** caused him problems: despite Stalin's statement to the contrary, the regime believed in the quasi-biblical ethos of 'visiting the sins of the fathers upon the children'.

In 1971 to 1972, Mozhaev bought a rural house in the village of Drakino, which he used to escape to when writing. Solzhenitsyn went out to visit the house in Mozhaev's black **Volga** car and it was there that he met Mozhaev's mother, Maria Vasilevna. Solzhenitsyn's keen ear for language and his interest in Russian dialect were instantly enchanted by the stories the old woman had to tell of her past life and the Russian countryside. She made a great impression on him and he could then see where Mozhaev's expressive vocabulary and love of story telling had come from. Solzhenitsyn narrates this meeting with great affection in his memoir.

Shortly after this time, Solzhenitsyn spent two very busy years writing and Mozhaev and he did not meet for quite some time. Solzhenitsyn had settled in the *dacha* of the Chukovskii family at Peredelkino – a writers' colony not far from Moscow, where Pasternak and many other writers had resided. He became the target of increasing hostility from the official press, and it was clear that the Soviet authorities were preparing to take drastic steps to silence him. He was followed constantly and his telephone was tapped by the KGB (the Soviet secret police), but Mozhaev and Liubimov bravely broke through the KGB cordon and visited Solzhenitsyn shortly before he was deported and stripped of his Soviet citizenship. Again, Solzhenitsyn narrates this incident in his memoir with great affection and admiration for the boldness and courage both men showed. Liubimov also fell foul of the Soviet authorities and he was also stripped of his Soviet citizenship in 1984. When Solzhenitsyn was deported on 13 February 1974, it was the last time Liubimov was to see him for fifteen years, and Mozhaev did not see him again for eighteen years. Mozhaev managed to visit Solzhenitsyn in the spring of 1992 in the United States of America.

Mozhaev's prose and writing for the theatre were constantly dogged by the censor and editors who were unwilling to take the risk of publishing his work, which would result in invoking the wrath of the authorities upon them and their journal. In the preface to his 1978 edition of *Old Stories*, amongst which 'Old Mother Proshkina' and 'The Saddler' feature, Mozhaev complained that the stories had lain unpublished for years. In an interview with the literary critic, Saraskina, he said: 'A whole volume of *Old Stories* (500 pages) languished for over fifteen years in the editorial offices of various magazines and publishing houses.'[4] He had similar problems with his play *Cry Wolf*: it was due to be performed in the Moscow Arts Theatre, but it was banned in 1968, and it was not published until 1988. A similar fate befell many other works. Obstacles were put before all his works – prose, plays, film scenarios, etc., but the biggest hurdle was yet to be overcome by him – the publication of his novel *Peasant Folk*, the very pinnacle of his output and his most contentious work of all.

Mozhaev had outlined the idea for his novel *Peasant Folk* to Solzhenitsyn on one of their trips around rural Russia, and work on it was finally started in September 1972. By June 1973, Book I was ready for publication. The novel describes a fictional rural community which has benefited from the ideological and trading relaxations of the NEP period (New Economic Policy). (See Appendix II, p.440.) The community is shown to be hard-working and independent, the epitome of the peasantry when left to their own devices and not crippled by state quotas and excessive taxes. Cooperatives of craftsmen flourish, as do millers and independent farmers, who work within the communes. Then, dark rumblings of an ideological clamp-down are detected, as preparations are made to end the NEP, and ultimately the whole rural community is herded into the **kolkhoz** system. In Book II, the most devastating and ideologically sensitive of the two books, activists first try to use persuasion to get the peasantry to join the **kolkhoz**, but when this proves to be an unmitigated failure, a campaign of physical coercion and intimidation is unleashed upon the community, which in turn engenders an orgy of violence. So-called '**kulaks**' are dispossessed in the most arbitrary fashion, and peasants lay their hands on their own property to destroy it, rather than let the state confiscate it. The activists, who do the bidding of the state, give rein to their own spite and prejudices, committing the most horrific acts of barbarity, even to the extent of harming women and children. The traditionally passive, long-suffering peasants arrive at a point where they can take no more and they revolt against the officials. Such riots actually took place – they were not a figment of Mozhaev's imagination – but they were suppressed in the official media and their very existence was denied even by historians. The insurgents were mercilessly repressed and many were actually shot by local authorities.

The editorial board of *Novyi mir* was experiencing some problems, which meant that, although the manuscript of Book I of *Peasant Folk* had been approved for publication, it 'hung in the balance', as Mozhaev said. However, when Editor-in-Chief Kosolapov, who had approved the novel, was replaced by the more conservative Narovchatov, the novel was unceremoniously banned. Only six months later, the nationalistic journal, *Nash*

---

[4] Interview with L. Saraskina, 'People of the Resistance', *Moscow News*, 31 (1988), p.10.

sovremennik (Our Contemporary), also imposed a ban on Mozhaev, who tried for a further three years to get the novel published, doing the rounds of the **thick journals**. Alekseev, Editor-in-Chief of the journal *Moskva* (Moscow), refused even to read the manuscript, despite the fact that it bore the censor's stamp, saying 'Publish'. It was the publishing press 'Sovremmenik' (Contemporary) which finally agreed to publish the first book of the novel, without it ever having appeared in a **thick journal**, which was unusual within Soviet publishing protocol. Such delaying tactics were designed to wear Mozhaev down and hinder publication of the harrowing and sensational nature of the subject matter.

Book II of *Peasant Folk* had to wait even longer before it was published, mainly because of the vivid description of the peasant uprising. Mozhaev had to wait for *perestroika* and much more liberal times, initiated by Gorbachëv, before it was published in full. Book II finally appeared in the **thick journal** *Don* (The Don) in 1987, seven years after its completion.

In an interview in 1988, Mozhaev admitted that the novel had been received with critical acclaim, but that it had been deliberately marginalised to one of the 'peripheral journals', i.e. *Don*, which had a much more restricted circulation than any of the other **thick journals** to which it had been offered. This amounted to another tactic to minimize the spread of such sensational material: the literary establishment marginalized controversial works and surrounding them with critical silence. However, *Don* published a whole collection of letters from older people who had had first-hand experience of the campaign for collectivization, attesting to the veracity of Mozhaev's narrative and its historical accuracy.

Mozhaev commented publicly on this conspiracy of silence, and he used the opportunity afforded him by the Eighth Writers' Congress in June 1986 to draw attention to the problems he had in getting his works published.

In 1993, Mozhaev's last and unfinished novel, *The Outcast*, was published in the journal *Nash sovremennik*. The setting of the novel marked a return to his beloved Far East, and there are many autobiographical details associated with the main hero of the novel, Sergei Borodin, the son of the hero of his novel *Peasant Folk*. Mozhaev wrote only the first part of the novel, as his last few remaining years were taken up with editorial duties of various journals.

One notable event of Mozhaev's last years was the return of his friend Solzhenitsyn to Russia in 1994, and Solzhenitsyn's request that he personally accompany him on a trip round the Soviet Far East, which Mozhaev had come to know and love whilst serving in the Soviet fleet. Solzhenitsyn again recounts this trip in his memoir, but it is tinged with great sadness, since this was to be the last trip they would ever make together. Mozhaev was to die of cancer a short time after that.

Why is Mozhaev not known in the West? The simple answer is that he has not been translated into English. Some of his works have been translated into several languages of the former Soviet bloc during an era when funding was readily available to undertake such work. A translation into French was made of *Lively* to critical acclaim, but it was made from the original *Novyi mir* edition, with all the original cuts and changes to the text and title.[5] But given that Mozhaev was not in favour with the regime as a writer, one can hardly expect that his works would be readily translated. As *glasnost* proceeded apace under Gorbachëv, and a great profusion of literature was printed in the **thick journals**, and as the Soviet economy fell into serious decline, all funding for translating works of literature from Russian into foreign languages seeped away. In fact, funding for many jobs and professions became unreliable: teachers, lecturers, and other professionals were not paid for months on end, pensions went unpaid, to name but a few problems, and there was wide-spread poverty and hardship. There was an orgy of publishing in journals of so-called 'held-up literature', i.e. novels, plays and poetry of all types, which it was thought would never be published in the Soviet Union, but which writers had written 'for the long drawer', as such literature was dubbed. But after this flurry of activity, apocalyptic essays started to appear on the death of literature as Russia had known it: **thick journals** went bankrupt and the **Writers' Union** disintegrated. People turned away from reading literature, partly out of necessity – they were not being paid for an honest day's work and they literally did not know where their next meal was coming from. Reading was not uppermost in people's minds. All these factors played a part in Mozhaev not being translated.

There has also long been an attitude in the West – an attitude often promoted by émigrés and those who suffered terribly within the Soviet system – that any literature published officially in Russia was unworthy of serious attention. Critics of writers who did not emigrate considered that the compromises the writer had to make within the Soviet system were too many, and hence, the 'truth' of Soviet life, as reflected in officially published literature, was watered down to an unacceptable level – like their beer! This was far from the truth: some wonderfully powerful and moving literature was officially published *despite* Soviet censorship. Like their tractors, the censorship colossus faltered and failed to perform as intended, and a number of editors were courageous enough to fight for what they knew to be the truth.

Another factor for Mozhaev's works not having been translated is the difficulty of his language. It is full of specialist vocabulary to do with agriculture and rural life, but more challenging than that – the speech of his peasant characters is full of dialect and witty turns of phrase, that challenge even the most well-read native speaker. These features amount to a daunting prospect for the translator. Imagine translating Yorkshire dialect into French, or any other language!

However, this translator thinks that the exercise has been well worth the effort. I hope the reader does also! The help I have had from enthusiastic, knowledgeable native speakers has been enormous and has been acknowledged in the appropriate section. When in the text sayings, proverbs, and witty quips in the original Russian have a close parallel in English, I have used them. However, where it was felt that simply to substitute an English set phrase removed all the colour and interest from the original Russian, then the original has been translated and/or a footnote has been added to elucidate: sadly, sometimes these (hopefully!) brave attempts are a mere shadow of the richness conveyed by the original. Russian is one of the most expressive and rich languages of the world with a long literary and oral tradition. Luckily for this translator and the reader, English is equally rich, though very different as a language. Boris

---

[5] *Dans la vie de Fédor Kouzkine*, par Boris Mojaïev, translated from the Russian by Jean Cathala (Editions Galimard, 1972).

Mozhaev did not know English, but I like to think and hope he would have been pleased with these translations after all the many hours I spent talking to him about his work and trying to get to grips with the author, as well as his writing.

I first came across Mozhaev's writing on a visit to Moscow. I was in a foreign currency shop, the old 'Berëzka' chain of the Soviet regime, which was designed to part the foreigner from his precious convertible currency. These shops – closed to ordinary Russian citizens – sold the best of Soviet goods to tourists for foreign currency, behind closed blinds. Many of the best contemporary writers' works were on sale and amongst them was a two-volume set of Mozhaev's, a 1982 edition. As a graduate of Russian with a keen interest in contemporary Russian literature, I had never heard of Mozhaev. I bought the volumes 'on spec' and I settled down to read through them with a pile of thick dictionaries close at hand. I was bowled over by the quality of his writing, which I found rewarded in every way my painstaking efforts at understanding the text. My enthusiasm for this new discovery led to further research and ultimately to a doctorate in his writing, and my interest in him continues unabated, to this day.

I was in Budapest in August 1991 and I visited the Russian bookshop there. Mozhaev's four-volume collected works had just been published, and I managed to get the first three volumes, but the fourth volume was not available to buy in that shop. In April 1992, I arranged to meet Mozhaev in a writers' club in Moscow to interview him at length, and he turned up with a gift for me, which he inscribed. It was the fourth volume. We both light-heartedly agreed that it was fate!

Meeting Boris, talking to him and his widow on the telephone, and interviewing his widow by proxy, through the kind auspices of my friend Natalia Bulgakova, who recorded the whole interview on video, have only enhanced my enthusiasm for his writing. Most of all, I admire him as a truly honest and courageous man with not the slightest hint of any pretensions or insincerity. To these rare qualities, add his wicked sense of humour and his magnificent physical presence, and you have one of the most unforgettable human beings that ever lived. I think these qualities shine through in his writing and I hope that the reader appreciates and enjoys them too. Should that be the case, I shall feel that I haven't done too bad a job!

David Holohan, London, 2007.

The Solzhenitsyn Memoir

Illustration 2. Riazan from the Oka River, 2005.

Foreword to the Solzhenitsyn Memoir

This memoir was written by Solzhenitsyn and printed in the popular literary newspaper, *Literaturnaia gazeta*, to commemorate the first anniversary of Mozhaev's death. It is translated into English here for the first time.

Alexander Isaevich Solzhenitsyn (1918–) was born in Kislovodsk, a city in the Stavropol **krai**, in south-western Russia. His mother was from a family of gentry stock, but his father was of peasant origins. Solzhenitsyn grew up in Rostov-na-donu (Rostov-on-Don) and he studied physics at the university there. After finishing university in 1941, he taught mathematics and astronomy for a short while, before enlisting in the army and going to the front in November 1942. He was promoted to the rank of captain and he was twice decorated for bravery. However, he made a disparaging remark about Stalin in a letter to a friend, which was intercepted, and he was sentenced to eight years in a prison labour camp. The camp he served in was near Moscow, where he worked as a mathematician in radio telecommunications research, which was to become the setting for his novel, *The First Circle* (1968). Solzhenitsyn's incarceration was followed by a further period of internal exile in South Kazakhstan from 1953 to 1956. He worked as a school teacher for about ten years after he had served his prison sentence. He taught mathematics, physics, and astronomy, and he was a brilliant teacher, by all accounts.

His story *One Day in the Life of Ivan Denisovich* was published in the influential literary journal *Novyi mir* in 1962. This work caused a literary sensation and it also launched the career of Solzhenitsyn as a major writer, historian, and commentator on Soviet life. Subsequently, he refused to conform and write works which would please the Soviet authorities, and his manuscripts were confiscated by the KGB in 1965. However, some of them were successfully smuggled out of the Soviet Union and published abroad, for which he was arrested in 1974. He was found guilty of treason and was forcibly deported to Frankfurt, having been stripped of his Soviet citizenship. After a brief sojourn in Zurich (1974-76), he eventually settled in Cavendish, Vermont, USA, where he lived until 1994. After the collapse of the Soviet regime, his citizenship and **passport** were returned to him and he decided to resettle in Russia. On his return to Russia via Khabarovsk in the Russian Far East, he insisted that Mozhaev meet him there, and together they made a tour of the area, as he describes in this memoir.

The publication of Solzhenitsyn's *One Day in the Life of Ivan Denisovich* continued to be a literary phenomenon for many years after it had appeared, and when conservative elements within the Soviet regime gained the upper hand, and writers were censored and repressed with increasing severity during the Brezhnev era, it was clear that those in power, after the fall of Khrushchëv in 1964, regretted that the work had ever been published in the first place. When I was a student in Moscow in 1975-76, I looked up the appropriate volume (number 11 [November], 1962) in the catalogue at the Lenin Library: it was the only edition of *Novyi mir* not listed for that year. I tried to order the volume and it was refused – the reason given was that it had gone missing! This is a typical example of how the Soviet regime constantly tried to rewrite its own history.

Solzhenitsyn's novel, *The First Circle*, was written in the vain hope that it would be published officially in the Soviet Union. The novel was published in the West in 1968, but it was published in Russia only in 1990, in *Novyi mir*.

In his memoir, Solzhenitsyn makes reference to two other of his own works:

(i) *The Red Wheel*, which is the general title of Solzhenitsyn's *magnum opus*, written between 1971 and 1991. It is a tetralogy, i.e. a series of four related novels, each with their own title, which span historical events from the collapse of Russia during World War I, through to the Revolution and the origins of the Bolshevik state. The separate novels themselves comprise several volumes, and the whole work is some 6,000 pages of narrative, which is a mixture of history (as seen from his own idiosyncratic viewpoint) and fiction

(ii) *Arkhipelag GULag*, which is his vast survey of the Soviet prison-camp and forced-labour system, comprising some 1,800 pages. It was published abroad on his personal authority in three volumes between 1973 and 1975, after the KGB had confiscated some of his other manuscripts. After the first volume appeared in Paris in December 1973, a virulent campaign against him was initiated in the Soviet Union and it culminated in his arrest and deportation. When he left the Soviet Union, he had no hope of ever returning to Russia at that time, but on the collapse of the regime in December 1991, and when his works had been published in his homeland, he decided to return. His citizenship was restored to him in 1991. He was formerly reinstated to the **Writers' Union** in 1989. He was officially greeted by President Yeltsyn, and he addressed the Russian Duma in 1994. A literary prize, the Solzhenitsyn Prize for Russian Writing, was inaugurated in 1997 in his honour.

The following memoir has been translated from Solzhenitsyn's original, highly stylized prose, as published in **Literaturnaia gazeta**. In keeping with its stylistically idiosyncratic nature, I have retained all the emphases of the original text, which are indicated by italics. The original paragraph format and his occasional strange mixture of tenses and off-the-cuff remarks, have also been kept. I have added a few comments to elucidate Solzhenitsyn's remarks, and these are indicated by square brackets.

"With Boris Mozhaev"

By

Alexander Isaevich Solzhenitsyn

Just a few days after the edition of **Novyi mir** had appeared with *Ivan Denisovich* in it, I was in **Riazan**, and I had already repelled a direct attack from a journalist from the Novosti Press Agency, who had wanted to write about me and my way of life; then there was an invitation from the agitation and propaganda section of the **oblast** section of the Party, to come along and get to know them, which I declined; and a request from the Telegraphic Agency of the Soviet Union in Moscow (TASS), to express my opinion about how Khrushchëv had handled the Cuban missile crisis (I could have told them straight, in no uncertain terms!) – and now, there was another ring at the door – yet someone else turning up. This is becoming a habit!

I open the door. It's a fat, squat man with a gentle voice:

'I am from the **Riazan** section of the **Writers' Union**, Vasilii Semënovich Matushkin.

And just behind him stood a strapping, young-looking, handsome man. Well, I couldn't just keep them on the door-step. They took their coats off. The tall chap had a warm, wide palm when he shook my hand, and he gave a broad smile. He mumbled in a semi-bass voice:

'Mozhaev, Boris Andreich, also from **Riazan**.'

I took them into the sitting room and sat them down on our tatty settee. I myself sat down on a chair in front of them. Our floors were cold and it wasn't very warm in the room, so I still wore my felt boots (my pair from the camp), which came right up to my knees. I was on my guard, so as not to blurt out anything too hastily.

Matushkin spoke in his smarmy, gentle voice, telling me that I should apply for membership with the **Writers' Union**: 'Could you write a personal request?' I dragged my feet as far as this matter was concerned, saying, 'Well, in a while. We'll see.' (I knew that they would jump at my application: they'd accept me in any case, but I reckoned that I wouldn't put in an application to see how they would cope with getting round it, just for my amusement. In December, a form had been hastily sent off to Moscow, without a personal request from me. Moscow had rung them up in **Riazan**: 'Where is his personal request, you dopes?')

This curly-haired Mozhaev, his head set upright, looked at me with his penetrating eyes, a look I've seen a thousand times. How is it that, right from the very first glance, one can determine so clearly the most important thing about a person: is he pure in soul, is he reliable, haughty, or natural with people? I instantly recognised Mozhaev's straightforward character, his guilelessness.

However, he asked me a question which struck me as being dangerous. He'd come from **Literaturnaia gazeta** to offer me the opportunity of having something published with them, any short story or long extract, anything at all. 'You must have something or other, don't you?' He looked at me with kind suspicion.

That 'something or other' was just a couple of paces away, in the form of a record player on the floor, under whose turntable my manuscripts were crammed. A long poem of twelve thousand lines, written while I was still in the camp, some other prison camp poems, four plays, and *The First Circle*, with its nuclear subject matter. What could I give him out of that lot? And I would have to think long and hard what I could take out that wasn't dangerous, and even so, **Tvardovskii** had closed all these avenues to me. He had said, 'There's no point in rushing... the door [i.e. the opportunity to publish officially] is now open to us for a long time.' (I knew from bitter experience that it would suddenly slam shut, and that all my stuff could only be published with his approval.)

I sighed and said that I would find it difficult.

Mozhaev looked at me kindly, but with obvious scepticism. (Later he told me: 'I soon caught the measure of you in those felt boots right up to your knees, and your "guarded peasant" manner.')

He told me that he himself was a native **Riazan** man, from way back, from around the River Moksha, but he had only just got a flat in **Riazan** itself. But whereabouts? In our own Kasimov Lane, just round the corner from our decaying, wooden house, in a new five-storey block – I'd walked right past this block every day to school, and I had seen it rise from nothing in front of my very eyes.

Just a week later, he invited me over to meet his wife – he'd only just got married. Two steps and we were there. It was a three-roomed flat, empty, and newly painted, just as it was when it had been finished, and almost no furniture or sign of permanent residence. Boris Andreevich and Milda Emilevna explained that they'd bunked up together in various flats in Moscow and hadn't managed to get one together. (Some time later B.A. told me that the secretary of the **Riazan oblast** committee, Grishin, had wanted to hang on to such a writer as him in the area – he, who was a first-class authority on farming – and so he had given him this flat.)[1] As things turned out, he was not to live in

---

[1] In the former Soviet Union, flats were allotted to a person by the state, and a low rent was charged. It was often difficult to get a flat and, as with many other things in Russia, it was a huge advantage to have the support

Riazan for long. The Mozhaevs managed to pull off a mind-blowingly complicated flat swap in Moscow, and they moved into a poorly appointed old house in Balchug Street. I went there a couple of times during my short visits to Moscow.

Milda had also inherited her father's log house, built as strong as a ship, on a farm called Uki, on the shore of the Gulf of Riga, but it was a fair trek from Moscow, and you couldn't just nip to and fro. My wife and I were once in Riga and we visited them there. The waves of the sea roared right near to it. Boris had spent his entire early working career with the Far Eastern fleet and he was trained as a marine structural engineer. When he was there in Uki, right by the sea, with his long legs set apart, he stood very sure of himself – yet it wasn't the same sea for him: he had given up his seafaring career, his native region, and the wide expanses of the fields of Russia – but they all still lured him, calling him back to return to them.

I took a keen interest in Soviet village life and in the history of the Russian peasantry – both recent and distant: Boris lived and breathed all this, and he knew it inside out. It was this that drew us so closely together, apart from the deep friendship we were developing. Boris's sincere straightforwardness engendered an expansiveness of spirit. Of course, I did not involve him directly in the shenanigans in my life as a writer, but our political opinions and views about daily Soviet life, and everything about the Soviet era, could not fail but coincide. The simple sobriety of his informed assessments left no scope in him for political aberrations. And he got that from his father, who was a man of remarkable, sincere determination. His kin were **Volga** river pilots: his father was also a pilot, but in Soviet times he settled amongst the peasantry. When **dekulakization** came, although he wasn't actually dubbed a **kulak**, Boris's father refused to join the **kolkhoz**, whereas his whole village joined it, cursing and swearing, but he resisted with the most amazing tenacity. He stood his ground as the only independent farmer in all the village, and he did not submit to the **kolkhoz** yoke amidst that atmosphere of malevolent jealousy, which came from **kolkhoz** workers. Nevertheless, in time, he was imprisoned, but as an '**enemy of the people**', and not as a '**kulak**' – and these things were all part of Boris's early, formative years.

However, Boris was not influenced by politics as he lived his life day to day – they never created any tension within him, and they remained on the periphery of his life. But then Khrushchëv idiotically ruined grasslands and meadows throughout the whole of Russia, and even more outrageously for Boris – the meadows around his native Oka River...! Khrushchëv ordered the grasslands to be ploughed up to grow maize, and in so doing, we lost that rich, golden pasture land for many years to come, and in return, we all got corn on the cob – it was this villainy wrought upon the earth that threw Boris into a rage. He tore around, looking at the ruined meadows, then on to the **Riazan** and Moscow editors' offices to get his articles about it published, but they were suppressed, as if they were bitter, counter-revolutionary material. At that time, all you could do was go around and try to win over and convince real people against the policy: surely, not everyone could have fallen under this spell and had gone out of their mind *collectively*?! But outwardly,

---

and influence of an official or someone with good personal connections in order to succeed in getting what one wanted.

Illustration 3. Khruschëv examining maize at the "New Life" collective farm, 1963.
(Photo courtesy of The Society for Co-operation in Russian and Soviet Studies, London.)

it looked as though everyone had – the whole lot of them, and all at the same time. How much effort he put into this issue! How much resentment he invoked towards himself from those in charge! He took upon his own shoulders the whole weight of this burden, without even giving a thought to its magnitude. And he shouldered it in its entirety, without paying heed to the enormity of the task.

That struggle to save our agriculture was not his first and only battle. He had even travelled as far away as the Far East, which was familiar to him from his navy days, and he looked into the innovative regeneration going on there: without changing the **kolkhoz** system *per se*, active participation in farm labour was nurtured by the 'link' system – small groups of **kolkhoz** farmers, who knew and fully trusted each other, were allotted land and agricultural equipment to work semi-independently: and they worked earnestly, not like **kolkhoz** workers. As far back as 1959, he came across a certain Overchenko in the Khabarovsk region, Dugintsev in the Amur **oblast**, and later Lozovoi in Kazakhstan, and Khudenko (who unluckily ended up in prison for his zeal) – and he published imprecatory articles about them, especially in the journal *Oktiabr*, causing a tidal wave of comments and passionate discussion – and in several parts of the Soviet Union, people thought that not all had been ruined through idiotic stupidity, and they were asking whether it might yet be possible to save Soviet agriculture.

No! Time was limited for these pioneers. The heavy hand of power slapped them down: 'Do we really need harvests at all? What we really need is the correct ideology.'

Boris campaigned for years like that. Not with great success. Still, he never lost heart. Despite the failures, he carried on regardless.

From the spring of 1963, on leaving school teaching, I got permission to use my freedom as a writer for the first time. During the spring thaw, when the ice breaks up and spring melt-water abounds, I lived and wrote in a remote area beyond the Oka River, in Solotcha. When the water level had fallen, and just after Boris had returned from one of his usual far-flung trips – it was like the earth was burning under his feet, he felt he had to go everywhere around the country, to see everything for himself – he visited me there. The little house stood on the edge of an oak and pine forest, set aside from the settlement. On the way to visit me, Boris had found a horseshoe. He brought it with him:

'Sania, look! This will bring you luck!'[2]

He had a child-like faith that a horseshoe brings you luck, and he was right: there are not many of them lying around. I fixed it to the porch wall. Conversations with Boria were always interesting and practical, full of lots of information, be it the latest news, or rural wisdom from time immemorial, or the differences between each plant or bird – the

---

[2] Sania is a familiar, shortened form of the name 'Alexander', i.e. Solzhenitsyn, and similarly, Boria is a familiar form of the name 'Boris'.

main thing is that he talked about all these things with such ease, whilst remaining totally receptive towards his collocutor. What a child-like purity shone within him!

From that year on, he no longer lived in **Riazan**, but he dropped by. In almost every **oblast**, and all the more so in his native **Riazan oblast**, he had his rural 'clients' – an agronomist here, a chairman of a **kolkhoz**, or chairman of a regional executive committee there... Boria visited them all occasionally, to find out how things were getting along, and he conveyed this information in his subsequent articles. At this time, I got down to gathering material in earnest for *The Red Wheel*, and I even got access to a special archive of the Petrograd Public Library: I'd already found out a fair amount about the Tambov peasant uprising of 1920 to 1921, over which I had agonized – but even then, I had too little information. Now, I definitely needed to visit the very places where the uprising happened. But how? My caution, typical of that of an ex-prisoner, stopped me from going on this trip candidly, with my real purpose out in the open: in 1964, I was still regarded by the authorities as a 'dodgy bloke', and the subject of the Tambov uprising would just add insult to injury... That would just be the limit! But, if I were simply to go anonymously, as someone who is totally inept in these things... I already knew from my previous bike trips around Central Russia how difficult I would find things: I would not be allowed to stay the night in a peasant house unofficially, then people would want to see my **passport**... 'Who was I?' and 'Why was I there?' At that time, everyone was ulcerated by suspiciousness.[3] And it wouldn't do to put the trip off, since I knew that, in the future, I would inevitably fall foul of the authorities, and I was sure that things could only get worse.

I once happened to share with Boris my dream about the trip, and also my forebodings. Without a moment's thought, he instantly suggested with the greatest of ease: 'Let's both go together, and I'll arrange everything for you.' How? He would get *Literaturnaia gazeta* to grant him a business trip, for the purposes of research on agricultural matters, to those places I was interested in (at that time, he used to manage to swing things the way he wanted), and I would go along, just as his mate. He really helped me out! He had provided the perfect alibi and had managed to cover all the expenses involved. That kind of dependability – his always being ready to help – was an unshakable feature of his character... And he was like that with others, not just with me.

So, in June 1965, we got on the train in **Riazan** and travelled along the Michurinsk-Tambov railway, the Balashov branch – along the very route where, in 1921, Tukhachevskii darted about with his armed flying squad.[4] I had a map of the Tambov

---

[3] As a former convict, it would have been recorded in Solzhenitsyn's internal **passport** that he had spent some time in a camp, and people would have been naturally suspicious of having anything to do with him, let alone put him up for the night.

[4] Balashov is a town in the Saratov **oblast**, situated on a tributary of the River Don, and it is an important railway junction for a branch line with leads to Tambov, where the peasant uprising took place. It was a town of about 76,000 inhabitants in the late 1960s. Tukhachevskii, Mikhail Nikolaevich (1893-1937), was a military commander and a Marshal of the Soviet Union. He had a distinguished military career and some of his most notable achievements were the recapturing of Siberia during the Civil War, heading Cossack forces against Denikin, and the crushing of the Kronstadt mutiny of 1921. He was a driving force to modernize the Red Army

oblast with me (in those years in Moscow, on Kuznetskii Bridge, **oblast** maps used to be on sale from time to time, and I didn't miss the chance to pop in there), and I studied it as much as I could beforehand.[5] We had to start from the right-hand side of the track, from Kamenka, and then dash over to the left side, into the thick of where the partisan hideouts had been.

We got off the train at Rzhaksa Station, which was also an historical station: every house had its witness.[6] We hitched a ride in a passing car which was going towards Kamenka: there was a feast for the eye at every crossroad – some historical event had taken place everywhere. We drove into Kamenka – our desired destination – and... What a coincidence! It was actually listed on the business trip permit, but it was not at all what the local **kolkhoz** chairman wanted! He started making a fuss, wondering what he had done wrong.[7] Naturally, we started on an official note: Boria had a serious conversation with him, bombarded him with questions, covering a wide range of issues about agriculture, and we went into the office. (I am no one – just a mate, no one pays any attention to me.) Their conversation was really interesting and I needed to get to grips and learn about rural life, since that heritage, which I should have been told about from my forbears, was lacking in me. But right at that time, my mind wasn't focused on that and I looked forward to getting out of the office. However, Boria could assume an important look and tone. So, it emerges from their discussion that things on the **kolkhoz** are in a very serious mess, and so we had to stay there for another couple of days. It was summertime: the school was empty and a couple of beds were set up for us there (the school was a former *zemstvo* school and it will feature in my novel!).[8] Well, in the evening it's a shame to do any work – the June day is long, and so we went along the steep slope, the whole length of the main street in Kamenka, first of all towards the north, right up to the Davydov manor house... And there it stood![9] Assuming a casual attitude, we talked with some old people about the past, and they remembered Iuri Vasilevich and his brothers, and what was all around his house. We ourselves didn't mention Pluzhnikov (the civil head of the Tambov peasantry), but by the way we manipulated the

---

after the Civil War, and yet he fell victim to one of Stalin's purges in 1937. He was rehabilitated and pardoned in 1988.

[5] During the Soviet era, it was difficult to obtain accurate maps of the Soviet Union: whole towns and villages did not appear on maps if they had any political or military significance, i.e. if there was a weapons factory or military installation there, or any form of prison camp. Also, independent exploration of cities, towns, and regions was not encouraged, even for Soviet citizens. The movements of foreigners were even more tightly controlled, and many places and routes were 'closed' to foreign visitors and tourists, and some were closed even to Soviet citizens, if they were of strategic or military importance.

[6] Rzhaksa is a small town of some 5,200 inhabitants. It is situated at 52°08.5′N and 42°01.6′E and it is part of the Tambov **oblast**, where the peasant riots took place.

[7] **Kolkhoz** chairmen were very suspicious of journalists, because they feared any subsequent critical reports or articles that might appear in the press, for which they would possibly suffer. Any deviation from official policies or practices could lead to anything from a mere reprimand to demotion, sacking, or even imprisonment in extreme cases. Mozhaev's story *The Saddler* exemplifies this fact.

[8] A *zemstvo* was an elective district or provincial council in pre-revolutionary Russia. It was set up by Alexander II in 1864, and it existed until the Revolution of 1917.

[9] The Davydovs were an ancient, noble Russian family, who could trace their ancestry back to the fifteenth century. As a group, they were scattered far and wide in the Central Russian region. Tambov is an ancient Russian settlement, which was founded in 1636. A serious peasant uprising occurred in late 1920 and early 1921, when peasants rioted on account of grain requisitioning, and there were further disturbances in the early 1930s, when activists tried to close their churches.

conversation, they themselves mentioned his name. 'But where did he live?' 'Just down there, right by Savala, where you'll find his stone house.' Fine. Now we go down the steep slope, and we looked over the Pluzhnikov house, and quite unexpectedly we managed to get inside (it would all go just perfectly into my novel!). And on the next incline, beyond the village, high up in the forest, there was the dug-out where Pluzhnikov hid after the rout.

Boria made a strong impression on everyone: he was tall, his chest stuck out, he still had his naval demeanour, and his shock of hair, ruffled by the wind – he hadn't a single grey hair then – and his playful, shrewd eyes… At that time he had neither a moustache nor a beard: he was a down-to-earth man of the soil at the dawn of his life.

Our inspection of the **kolkhoz** lasted two days, but we managed to fit in many walks, during which time we found out about the history of Father Mikhail Molchov, who was cut down by the Reds [i.e. the Bolshevik forces] right on his porch, and on that very spot, we found an old man who was still alive, Semën Paniushkin, a former **volost** clerk there.[10] What an exceedingly cautious old man he was! He was the only one who was suspicious of us, to such an extent, that he wrote down our names and addresses (I gave him a couple of false ones), but it was through this caution that he had survived all powers, both 'red' and 'white' [i.e. tsarist forces], and that he had got through them all, but, as he was, he did not tell us anything we could follow up (however, as a character, I'll put him into the novel!). On another day, we also got the use of the chairman's car, so we went to look at the rebel stronghold village of Tugolukovo, further down Savala River, where, beyond Kamenka, the rebels had dug trenches just once during the whole rebellion: subsequently, they vowed never to do that again, as it wasn't their way of fighting – they suffered heavy losses. We also visited the totally devastated site of the estate of the Vysheslavtsevs on a hill near Volkhonshchina – even something so ransacked speaks volumes to me. The chairman of the **kolkhoz**, who was extremely anxious, insisted that we went to a particular pond where, in our presence, some crucians were caught with a dragnet and, right there and then, someone made some fish soup for us. It was clear that the **kolkhoz** chairman had a lot to hide, but then it wasn't up to Boria to shop him. Once Boris had already left, I delved around in Tambov itself for a few more days, and then, at the station, a peasant man caught sight of me, dashed over, and poured out his heart to me, without keeping an eye out for the authorities, telling me what a crook of a **kolkhoz** chairman they had, and that 6 **centners** of good meat had been written off, that 180 hectares of peas had been sown but not harvested, – and that *I should tell* Moscow all about it and get it sorted! Oh my God! And to think this kind of thing was going on everywhere!

Boris and I also went east from Rzhaksa, into the depths of the countryside, where the rebellion took place – to the two Pandas, Karavaino, Kalugino, and Treskino:[11] we managed to get to some places by bus when we could, otherwise we went on foot. I remember the vast water-meadows around Karaul, raised up on a steep hill (Karaul was

---

[10] Solzhenitsyn refers directly to Paniushkin in his 'Author's Note' in *The Red Wheel: November 1916*: see A. Solzhenitsyn, *The Red Wheel: Knot II. A Narrative in Discrete Periods of Time. November 1916*, translated by H.T. Willets (New York: Farrar, Straus and Giroux, 1998).

[11] All these places are small villages in the Tambov **oblast**, about 13-20 km west of Inzhavino, the nearest settlement of any major size (pop. 11,500), which lies at 52°19.8'N and 42°28.4'E. Inzhavino has a railway station. Many villages like these have no metalled roads and they are linked merely by dirt tracks, which are impassable in the winter and rainy seasons.

Chicherin's, stamping ground, and later on he was a Leninist People's Commissar, but in those times he didn't come anywhere near here) [12]. Boris trekked around these fluvial, boundless lowlands with his rucksack, with such a joyful, natural expansiveness, as if he were in the midst of his native area, and he knew every inch of it. There was not a soul for miles around, and he sang songs at the top of his voice. He poured forth a stream of stories. He would pine away in the stony agglomeration of the capital, but here, the Russian expanses welcomed him, and he could recover his breath. Wherever we ended up, he would teach me how to tell the difference between bird calls: the buntings, who went, 'carry-the-hay-but-don't-shake-it!', the crackling of the corn-crake in the grass, the burbling of the goatsucker and the 'kvik-kvik' sound it made on taking to the air, and the call of the obstinate river cricket. We also visited the woods along the river, which were impenetrable riverside thickets along the Vorona River, where Antonov ended up hiding. I was staggered by how Boria, without making any notes, remembered signs of our trails, either in the meadows, or in the river-side thickets – always confidently leading us back. Sometimes he would test me as a joke; 'Where to now?' But I couldn't always tell him, I was lost. Finally we got to Inzhavino, from where we took the train, and I went off towards Tambov.

Boria gave this week to me as an unforgettable present: he helped me out, he showed me the opening for my novel. And how easily and guilelessly he could carry on a conversation on the topic of the rebellion, but my torment was that I could not note anything down of what was said in the presence of the speaker. I would commit to memory as much as I could, and then, at the end of my tether, I would make myself scarce, fleeing round the back of a barn or somewhere like that, make hasty, new notes, and then dash back. I went out a second time, and then a third, and my collocutor would look surprised. Boria covered for me and said good-humouredly, 'He's got stomach trouble.' Then he himself would later dictate as I took notes on what I had missed. He then showed me Tambov: I went to the **oblast** archive and asked for some old *zemstvo* newspapers, but my name had been reported to the man in charge – he forbade me to be issued with the most important years' editions. Even then, the authorities were all snapping at my heels. And the party archive in the town was like a fortress... Don't even think about getting in there!

For about the next three years, Boria and I saw little of each other. After the seizure of my secret manuscripts by the KGB in 1965, and my being left with my unfinished *Archipelago*, I looked for a distant hideaway to finish it off. Boris had finished his story *Lively* (a peasant man who was still *alive*, despite so many years of **kolkhoz** bondage! But no, in *Novyi mir* it had been euphemistically renamed as *From the Life of Fëdor Kuzkin*), and Mozhaev was enjoying a promising, but fragile, ascendancy. In *Novyi mir* '*Kuzkin*' was subjected to inflexible corrections by editors and opposition by censors, but even so it got through. Then Yurii Liubimov energetically turned all his energies to turning it into a play. This engendered a long, gruelling battle with the highest censorship authorities, with the Secretary of the Central Committee Demichev, and with

---

[12] Georgii Vasilevich Chicherin (1872-1936) was born in Karaul, where a number of this noble family had lived for generations. He was a Communist Party member from 1918 and, after numerous trips abroad, he returned to Russia. Then, in 1918, he was appointed assistant People's Commissar for Foreign Affairs, and from 1923 to 1930, he worked as People's Commissar for Foreign Affairs.

the Minister for Culture, Furtseva herself, both of whom had attended supervisory rehearsals of the stage version and had banned it. But then, there was a glimmer of hope on the distant horizon, but once again another sudden, crushing ban. All attempts to get the play through, to get it onto the open stage, ended up in bans – five times: 1968, '69, '71, '72 and '75! It *was* eventually performed in 1989... but twenty-one years after the initial attempt. These repeated attempts cost the author and the theatre director dear. (By the way, Liubimov wisely used this interim period for a string of 'public' performances, to invited audiences, and so a considerable number of the Moscow intelligentsia managed to see this 'banned' play, which didn't even make it to its official, public première.) As for the pernicious Mozhaev, who was pulled to pieces in *Pravda* before this theatrical sabotage – well, the door of every publishing outlet was slammed in his face for a long time to come, at the instigation of Georgii Markov at the **Writers' Union** Congress in 1967.[13]

In the summer of 1969, something long-promised by Mozhaev came to pass: isn't it about time we went for a trip in my 'Moskvich' car, to my native lands in the **Riazan oblast**, in the Pitelino **raion**? However often he went there, it was too little for him – the sweet earth beckoned him there, and he relished the opportunity to discuss things with peasant folk – both about the present and the past. Now, he wanted to show me his smart Kuzkin in the flesh.

Boria's mother no longer lived there in the village of Pitelino:[14] in the hungry years after the war, she had sold her house and possessions and had gone off to her sister's in Almaty.[15] However, she was very homesick for Central Russia. And in so far as Boria was getting on his feet, he promised her that he would bring her back from those foreign parts. Boris was already getting on for fifty, and he was born and bred on the Russian land, he had grown up in it, and he had seen it in all its manifestations during his many-thousand-**verst** wanderings – but he had not managed to find the right place for himself in this land. But, within him glimmered a definite instinct to build a home. Somehow or other, he would find for himself a hard-earned patch of genuine earth.

For me, this was to be another trip with Boris – it was a refreshing communing with Central Russian nature and everyday rural life, where you wouldn't venture under your own steam. As it happened, six years earlier, before we had even met, I had, unknowingly, almost got to his native Pitelino from Kasimov on my bike, to the **Old Believer**s' settlement of Vysokie Poliani, just twenty **verst**s away.

So we travelled from **Riazan** along the Shatskii highway, then we turned off towards Sasovo, where he showed me places further on, through overgrown side roads and meadows, where we splashed through mud on the way, in constant risk of getting bogged down. He took me towards Moksha River to witness haymaking, saying, 'Whoever has not seen haymaking, does not know rural life.' There, in the hurly-burly of haymaking,

---

[13] Georgii Mokeevich Markov (1911-1991) was a prose writer of conservative political views and he rose to occupy an influential role within the **Writers' Union** of the Soviet Union, initially as secretary (from 1956), then subsequently as First Secretary (from 1971). He was removed from his post and replaced by a more liberal First Secretary under Gorbachëv, as part of the process of liberalization in the arts, during which many influential veteran conservatives of film-making, literary, and artistic unions were replaced by more enlightened, progressive officials, who were vital to the process of *perestroika* and *glasnost'*.

[14] See footnote № 1, p.xix.

[15] Almaty (whose Russian name is *Alma-Ata*) is a city in south-eastern Kazakhstan.

we spent the night in a straw hut, and he took me to lie down on the earth and listen to the quail, which yelled, 'Time to be on your way! Time for the road!' Another night caught up with us in a forest clearing, at a beekeeper's. During those years, I slept badly because of stress. Boria gathered some leaves in a bucket from currant bushes and dogrose stalks, amongst other things, and he put the bucket to boil on a camp fire. We'd become parched during the day, and it was so delicious that, without stopping, we saw off five mugs of this *tisane* each. We slept the sleep of the dead, as I had never experienced it before – we might have been hacked to little pieces in our sleep, but we wouldn't have known!

As frenetically active as Boria always was, he was all the more so when in his homeland, becoming even more active than I had ever seen him at home: he could not catch his breath for joy, and he wore a constant broad smile – he himself grew up there, along with everything else that was growing, running around all the time, and flitting around in constant animation. And with everything that he showed me, he amazed me with his perceptive explanations, with his knowledge, and with his enviable powers of observation. How much he added to my knowledge about grasses! How I should recognise horse sorrel, shepherd's-purse, the tassel of bluegrass, and the cutting, triangular grass of the flowering rush, and the goose-foot (when you tear them off, they curl themselves up).

It was on this trip that he told me about his plans for *Peasant Folk* – set in a village initially flourishing in the 1920s, then came collectivization and the famous peasant mutiny, which had taken place in 1930 in the Pitelino **okrug**

I was all ears and I noted it all down. I couldn't tear my eyes away from Boria: he was the very embodiment of the Central Russian peasantry, and now of the insurgents – and I could never have had the least inkling that he was the embodiment of a writer's law: the formation of one's concept of a work comes most often after a delay, even after a very long delay. And it was only months later that I realised, that it was Boria, whom I would describe as my main peasant hero of *The Red Wheel*! Naturally, he went as a character into the body of serving soldiers with his readiness to fight, with his agility, and into characters of a peasant mindset, with their ordered ritual and finesse – but also his influence can be seen in that explosion of the Tambov mutiny. Hence, my character Arsenii Blagodarëv was born and described (and not finished off, like the whole of *The Wheel*, right up to the commander of the partisan regiment). I found it was easy to write from such a living example. Only I never told Boria himself about this, because I didn't want to impinge upon his naturalness. And when he read *August*, and then *October*, he praised the character of Blagodarëv, but he never guessed the source of his inspiration.[16]

For a short while around the time of our trip, Boria enjoyed a brief period of being in the good books of the Secretary for Agriculture to the Central Committee, Polianskii, on account of his rural observations and suggestions. By the way, it was in his compass to arrange for Boria to be sold a **Volga** car, and Boria had the cheek to ask him for a black model. It shouldn't have been allowed – black ones were only for the top brass, and Boria had asked for it more out of mischief than anything else, but suddenly, he was sold a black one. Then in Pitelino, he pulled off quite a *tour de force*: he drove up to the

---

[16] The references to *August* and *October* are to Solzhenitsyn's epic novel *The Red Wheel*. *August 1914* is part of *The Red Wheel I*, which was published in Paris in 1971. *October 1916* was published in two volumes in 1984.

regional executive committee offices, but stopped a little way off – about twenty paces, locked the car and went off. All hell broke loose in the regional committee! They thought some unknown bigwig had obviously turned up. But where was he?! Oh, what a disaster! Had he come straight along, in person, to check things out for himself? The regional committee members ran around like scalded cats![17]

The following winter, Boris got drawn into my clandestine life. In Moscow, a Slovakian communist journalist, P. Ličko, had approached him with a request to get in touch with me on an urgent matter – he wanted me to sign a contract for *Cancer Ward*.[18] (Ličko's wife was translating Boria's work into Slovak.) At that time, I was in my usual working hideaway. Boria informed me of this, and I gave him a categorical, resounding refusal. With that, Ličko went off. (It was a dodgy business, more of which elsewhere.) But the stubborn Ličko arrived again, around springtime, with a contract all drawn up, and once again he importuned Boria – and it fell to Boria, at an inconvenient time, to hare down to me in Rozhdestvo-on-the-Ista, only to return with yet another refusal for Ličko.

In the following autumn of 1969, immediately after my expulsion from the **Writers' Union**, we met near the *Novyi mir* offices, where I secretly showed Boris my angry, hot-off-the-press reply to the Secretariat of the **Writers' Union** of the RSFSR[19] – and although perturbed, he delighted in it: its broad, **Volga**-like scope appealed to him, it was right up his street, but he feared for me and made a lame attempt to dissuade me from submitting it.

But two months later, the pulling apart of *Novyi mir* started, and again we met at the same place: Boria was among the leaders of the group of writers of that journal who were brave enough to go direct to the Central Committee and protest. (It was in vain, of course.)

The truth of a rural person was intolerable for the powers that be, and it led to a block in the press, not only of his articles, but also of his novellas. He was reduced to having empty pockets. His friends asked him: 'What are you living off, Boria?' Boris would quip, 'On interest!' 'On what interest?' they asked, in amazement and incomprehension. Someone in Mosfilm had done him a favour and, quite legally, had commissioned a screenplay from him, for which they paid a 25% advance of the fee (many people lived

---

[17] This incident is highly reminiscent of Gogol's play *The Government Inspector*, which is branded into the psyche of every Russian rural official, especially in Soviet times. In Gogol's play, written in 1836, an unsuspecting and rather feather-brained young man, who is down on his uppers, blunders into a provincial town and is taken for an important government inspector. All the officials of the town believe he has arrived incognito, and they wine and dine him in an effort to humour him and win his favour so that their own bureaucratic incompetence and fiddling will not be noticed. It takes some time before the 'inspector' realises how he can turn this situation to his own advantage, resulting in the regional 'dignitaries' making absolute fools of themselves, as they are duped into parting with their own money. Some even offer up their nearest and dearest to him! By the time they realize they have been fooled and the false inspector has gone, suddenly, a genuine government inspector arrives.

[18] Solzhenitsyn mentions this incident again in his biographical memoir *Invisible Allies*, translated by Alexis Klimoff and Michael Nicholson (London: Harvill Press, 1997), p.159, where he writes: 'Later the Englishman Lord Bethell managed, through the Slovak journalist Ličko, to draw Mozhaev into his escapade, involving secret contacts that could even have landed him behind bars. Boris Mozhaev behaved with firmness and dignity, never losing his nerve for a moment, as if he were quite used to this kind of thing.' Ličko wanted to get Solzhenitsyn's *Cancer Ward* published in Bratislava in 1968. He was acquainted with Nicholas Bethell, who subsequently brought a copy of the manuscript from Czechoslovakia to the West.

[19] The acronym means the Russian Socialist Federal Soviet Republic, subsequently changed to the Russian Federation.

off Mosfilm in that way). Mozhaev presented them with a screenplay. It was usually on a rural theme and the content would turn out to be unacceptable for the censor. Then they would commission a rewrite and pay another 12½%. The author would make changes, but the screenplay remained unacceptable. Then it would end there. But later on, they would commission another one, on a different theme.

A long-standing argument arose between Polianskii and Mozhaev, which happened long before the future plan to 'liquidate economically unviable villages' – yet another enormous *Catastrophe* for the Russian peasantry: the destruction of rural life on Russia's expanses, where, after the steam-roller of Collectivization, depopulated villages still held on in their final death throes, where new, abandoned peasant homes were becoming overgrown and their windows boarded up. Boria found out about the plan – and he entered the troublesome argument, crossing yet another rural line, fearing it might be the last. Polianskii's arguments were those of the Central Committee: we are not rich enough to maintain roads, lines of communication, and electricity supplies to every peasant house. (Where are you now, 'Ilich's light bulbs'?)[20] We shall relocate people closer together and move peasants into four- and five-storey blocks of flats, which will work out much cheaper. In vain Boris hammered his point home, that a peasant on a floor in a block of flats, without his outhouses and his domestic animals, would cease to exist forever, unappeased by these urban 'mod-cons'. It didn't work. He showed that, as well as the remnants of the Russian village, we are losing a huge area of fertile, viable land, and no amount of Kazakhstan Virgin Land would compensate for that. We are abandoning Russia herself! They didn't buy it. The blind-deaf members of the Central Committee (while proclaiming themselves to be 'Russian patriots') put rural Russia under the steam-roller for one last time.

In 1970 to 1972, I holed up with Rostropovich in Zhukovka, and I almost never got to Moscow. However, Ermolai [Solzhenitsyn's son] was born and I invited Boris to his christening in the church of Ilia Obydennyi in Moscow, where I introduced him to Rostropovich, Ermolai's godfather, and we went off to his place 'to wet the baby's head'.

At the end of the same year, 1971, we were to sit down together at table, along with Liubimov, but this time it was for the bitterly sad wake of **Tvardovskii**, at Maria Illarionovna's, on Kotelniko Riverbank. Late in the evening, Liubimov gave us a lift to our homes, driving through Moscow in his car, which skidded severely and got bogged down in the snow-bound roads, and our conversation and the vision of what was going on around us were so very grim, like all the events of those recent years – from the banning of the Kuzkin performance to the present death of the persecuted Alexander Trifonovich **Tvardovskii**.

---

[20] 'Ilich's light bulbs' refers to a statement that Vladimir Ilich Lenin made about electricity and the electrification of the whole of Russia. He said that, 'Communism is Soviet Power plus the electrification of the whole country'. This statement reflects that Lenin had a promethean fixation with light and electricity, which epitomized progress and modernity: his idea was of a city in which light shone at night, and symbolically this contrasted markedly with the 'darkness', which was akin to 'ignorance' (same word in Russian), of rural life. Lenin's slogan about electricity was displayed large on the top of a prominent electric power generation plant on the banks of Moscow River, near the centre of the city. This juxtaposition of urban light and rural darkness was a corner-stone of Bolshevik utopianism. Ironically, when his vast display board advertising his ambitious, nation-wide network of electricity was switched on, power had to be cut to the rest of the city of Moscow, in order to provide the power for it. See Richard Stites, *Revolutionary Dream: Utopian Vision and Experimental Life in the Russian Revolution* (New York, Oxford: OUP, 1989), p.48.

That winter, Boris called me up to go and look at his recent purchase, something he had finally found – a rural house in Drakino, on a high bank of the Oka River, at the intersection, as it happened, of three **oblasts** – the Moscow, Tula and Kaluga **oblasts**.[21] We went there in his trusty black **Volga**, along the road that everyone takes to Tarusa. It was there that I met Maria Vasilevna, Boris's mother, a wonderful old lady: true to his word, he had brought her back from Kazakhstan in her old age. I went there, but not without an ulterior motive: Senia Blagodarëv was already written in my *August*. But now, in *October 1916*, I had to describe his homecoming, when he came home on leave from the front to his home village, right there to our own Kamenka in the Tambov **oblast** – and now I wanted to see and appreciate my hero in the midst of his own rural life, doing the rounds of his outhouses, where he kept the feed and his cattle. Boria willingly showed me all that, although most of his outhouses were empty and devoid of animals, but he explained it all wonderfully – this filled one of my core chapters, and Maria Vasilevna told me many of her own rural stories in addition, in the most evocative Russian language, just begging to be noted down.

Then, two of my most frenetic years started, and Boris and I did not get to see each other at all during that time. On Friday, 8 February 1974, while at the Chukovskiis' dacha in Peredelkino where I was working, I was told by my wife on the telephone that I was being summoned urgently to the General Public Prosecutor's office.[22] I didn't go. I decided I would sit it out in Peredelkino until Monday. KGB agents in disguise had already forced entry into the dacha itself to check that I was there. They had besieged the whole plot with a cordon of people to shadow me. That Saturday and Sunday, those people did not afford me the slightest chance to enjoy a genuine breathing-space. Suddenly, on Sunday 10 February, there was a knock at the door: it was Boria Mozhaev and Yurii Liubimov! They had not been afraid to break through this cordon and they were themselves photographed a dozen times, and their presence was noted by the KGB. What brave chaps they were!

I was very touched by their breaking this blockade. They sat with me for half-an-hour, then we said farewell: I knew I had no reason for optimism.

We said farewell – my separation from Yurii Liubimov was to last for 15 years. (He came to see us in Vermont, also deprived of his homeland.)[23] And with Boria – it lasted 18 years: he came to see us in Cavendish in the spring of 1992, with some delegation visiting the States. Ermolai brought him from New York (Boria hadn't seen him since his christening).

---

[21] Administratively, Drakino comes under the jurisdiction of the Moscow **oblast**. It lies 54° 51.6 N and 37° 16.8 E.

[22] Chukovskii, Kornei Ivanovich (1882-1969) was an important literary figure in Soviet *belles lettres*: he was a literary critic, poet, translator, linguist, and an eminent author of children's stories in verse. He was also the father of an esteemed literary family, whose son and daughter were active in Soviet literary circles after his death. Peredelkino is a writers' settlement a short distance from Moscow, where writers were loaned country houses (*dachas*) to live in by the state. There is a beautiful little church there and famous writers such as Pasternak lived there. Some writers are buried there, including Pasternak.

[23] Liubimov was stripped of his Soviet citizenship by a decree of the Presidium of the Supreme Soviet on 11 July 1984, which was announced by Chernenko – similar to the way in which Solzhenitsyn had been treated some years previously. Liubimov continued to work in the West, but he returned to the Soviet Union in 1988, during the period of *glasnost* and *perestroika*, to stage various productions which had been banned while he worked in Moscow previously.

Boria's beard and moustache were grey, as was his hair, but they were just as thick and bushy on top, not combed in any form of a smooth hair-do. And how handsome he had become! There is a law – a psychological or physiological one: from those people who have a pure conscience and pure life, a spiritual purity emerges in their advanced years, to express itself externally on their face. Boria was now sixty-nine. His *Peasant Folk*, which had first occurred to him while I was there, was now all behind him (and I had already received a copy from him and read it, and now we discussed it). He had endured a great deal over this two-part novel. The editor of *Novyi mir*, Norovchatov, took it, promised much, dragged his feet, and then abandoned it. Alekseev, the editor of the journal *Moskva*, wouldn't touch it with a barge-pole. Boria approached *Nash sovremennik*, the editor of which was Vikulov, then the ever-strengthening bastion of Russian nationalistic thinking.[24] He was unexpectedly subjected to brutal criticism in it and so *Nash sovremennik* also refused to publish it. It makes you think: wasn't Mozhaev just as much a 'village writer', as they were, since, who more than him had dedicated his life to the Russian village? But evidently there was an undercurrent between them: Mozhaev never turned his defence of the countryside into any kind of ideology. The 'Sovremennik' publishing house had the courage to publish the first part of his novel, despite vociferous demands from all quarters – and particularly from the Moscow writers' organization – to destroy the printing plates. For the second part of the novel to be published, with its description of a peasant uprising, courage was needed even during the *perestroika* era. It was the journal *Don* that took it on and published it. 'You won't go back on your word, will you?' asked Boris, hopefully. The then editor, Voronov, replied with his historic formula: 'There's no going back with the *Don*!'

Boris and I exchanged two or three letters over the years that had passed – unofficially – we never wrote anything openly under official Soviet gaze. His mother, Maria Vasilevna, died. Now, he said, he was planning to pass Drakino-on-the-Oka to his son Petia, and during these years he had had a great deal of difficulty in getting a plot on the Lopasna River, where he had been building a house for four years, singling out each and every timber with his eye and his hands. 'I made twenty trips in "KamAZ" lorries', he said.[25] He was proud of his building. He loved building and this passion never waned in him. He was, after all, an engineer, a builder, and that was his job in the navy, on our Far Eastern bases. Now, in Vermont, he walked around the wooden house where we resided, and around my stone house where I used to work, looking at the buildings with the eye of a builder, observing the American structures and appliances with an eye to wondering whether I would need them for much longer.

---

[24] Sergei Vasilevich Vikulov (1922–), himself a poet and publicist, became the editor of the literary journal *Nash sovremennik* between the years 1967-89. The journal had published some works by Solzhenitsyn himself, but it was known for being a journal with a nationalistic, right-wing stance, because it had published a number of works by 'Village Prose' writers, many of whom looked back to old, peasant Russia with extreme nostalgia, rejecting all things Soviet, and in so doing, some writers expressed open hostility for the West, as having been the source of Marxist and Bolshevik ideology. They saw Russia as a purer, more untainted repository of culture, imbued with the wisdom and sanctity of the Russian Orthodox Church, the one remaining bastion of the true Christian tradition. Some of these writers, whose work appeared regularly in *Nash sovremennik*, openly expressed anti-Semitic views, such as the writer Vasilii Belov, who was also one of the leading Village Prose writers. (See Appendix I for more on Village Prose.)

[25] KamAZ is the name of a certain type of lorry made at the Kama motor-vehicle factory, which was situated in the Tatar Autonomous Republic of the former USSR.

And quite right too: around this time, my and Alia's return to Russia had already been decided, and we had resolved also when it would take place – the spring of 1994. I disclosed to Boria what no one else knew at that time – that we would return via the Far East. Vladivostok and Khabarovsk were, as far as he was concerned, his home towns: he had spent his navy career there, a total of thirty years, and he began his writing career there also; he knew the whole seaboard very well. And I asked Boria to come and meet me in Vladivostok, and to think where we might go on a trip together. I asked him to make arrangements with the Oceanographic Institute, so we could have a look at rural life over there, and it would be even better if we could see some Udegei people...[26] Ermolai took Boria off to Boston – they'd become good friends also. They were to meet up again in Vladivostok, before my arrival. Ermolai flew there from Taiwan.

Boria made a trip to the Far East in 1993, a year before I was due to arrive, to have a good look round and prepare for our trip. In 1994, in the whirlwind of my first few days in Vladivostok, Boria and I were practically never apart. We went to visit oceanologists, he guided me to the Ussurii region, where I found wonderful experts, who knew all about the terrain and villages – it would have taken me ages to find them all myself: we went to a hospital, a university, and to some Udegei people, but then a sudden flood prevented us from going any further. In Khabarovsk, we once seized the moment, the three of us (we were with my son, Stepan), to slip out of the hotel secretly, through the back door, and so we got away from journalists and had a great time walking around Khabarovsk. Without Boria, I would never have managed to take in a trip like that. He pointed out how the planning of the city was conceived, how it was built, and where things were, and who lived where, starting right from the time of the Civil War, and where, returning from Manchuria, our writer Vsevolod Nikanorovich Ivanov lived and died – a marvellous individual. I heard about him initially from Boris.[27] Yes, our Far East always had its own particular fate, just as it had during the Civil War, and if we do not wake up now, it will slip from our grip for ever, as it follows its own path.[28]

Boria flew off to Moscow from Khabarovsk, and now our parting would not be for long. But it was so unforeseeable, so impossible to guess, that we would have so little time left to see each other.

---

[26] For the Udegei people – see Introduction.

[27] Vsevolod Nikanorovich Ivanóv (1888-1971) was a writer, poet, and publicist, who was a native of Khabarovsk. He served in the army as a company commander during the First World War and he wrote about his impressions of the Civil War in a work published in 1922. He published a number of philosophical works on the thinking of Dostoevsky, Tolstoy, and others. Many of his works of fiction have, as their inspiration, historical themes and the beauty of the countryside in which he lived.

[28] Russian expansion eastwards towards China and the Pacific coast had been a feature of Russian colonialism since the 16th century, but it intensified in the 19th century. Russia gained the Amur Province in the 1860s and special privileges in Manchuria, and from there it was a small step to taking over the seacoast north of Korea, where the town of Vladivostok was founded. Subsequently, relations between China and Russia were very delicate in the Far East, particularly as ideological differences appeared between these two rival communist regimes. As the Soviet Union fell apart, and the armed forces were no longer favoured and maintained by huge sums of money, many people of Mozhaev's and Solzhenitsyn's generation became deeply disturbed by the prospect of losing their distant seaports, and particularly those of the Soviet fleet in the Far East and the Crimea. Some of Mozhaev's last articles were written on this very theme, as Solzhenitsyn goes on to mention in this article.

In October 1995, we were planning to meet up to go to our **Riazan** and to Konstantinovo, for the Esenin centenary celebration, but it didn't work out, owing to my being ill, and we were only together for the unveiling of the statue on Tverskoi Boulevard.[29] In the summer which had just passed, Boria, full of energy, took up the position of editor of the new journal *Rossiia*, and he immediately submitted an article on agrarian reform in the Nizhnenovgorod **oblast**: he pressed me to give him something to publish. But then, I suddenly heard by telephone that he had torn something *internally* while lifting a fridge on his own. Despite this, he didn't go to see any doctors, not having the time, and, as was his wont, he flew off to Sevastopol, which was tormented and abandoned by us. He lived there for a week on a ship and returned with an article burning in his breast – but almost immediately he ended up in hospital. I was the first person to find out about the secret of his condition from the doctor: it was the old Soviet tradition of lying, of not telling a patient the truth about his own illness. I found out that Boris had an 'undifferentiated cancer' of his abdominal organs. From my own experience of cancer, which had forced itself upon me, I knew that it meant that a large area was affected, and that the cancer had spread.[30] With all his hectic rushing around and his hurried pace of life, Boris had not noticed the illness: he had not gone to see anyone in time, and the incident with the fridge was nothing to do with it.

However... However, if the doctors hid it, and Boris himself was convinced of the transitory nature of his indisposition, he would overcome it and throw himself into his work – for my part, contrary to my ingrained, tried-and-tested conviction that a sick person should know the full extent of his illness and then apply the full force of his spirit against it – I did not have the heart to shatter his hopes.

It was difficult to talk to him about such a delicate issue: if only some herbs could be found, or a rural sage, who could sometimes get hold of things that doctors couldn't...

In fact, traditional medicine could do nothing for him. One hospital did not even keep Boris in. He discharged himself, hoping to return to work, and he spent the whole of January going to work at the journal. But then he ended up in hospital again.

Alia and I went to see him there on Saturday 24 February. Milda had already been keeping vigil by his bedside for several days, almost not sleeping, not eating, in his single room with him. She had warned us on the phone that he was in a very bad way, but he didn't understand this, and he did not want to face the truth of his illness. He lay on his back on raised pillows, but as we came in he raised himself, trying to put his legs out of the bed – we could hardly get him back into bed.

---

[29] Sergei Alexandrovich Esenin (1895-1925) was a poet, who was born in the **Riazan guberniia**, in the village of Konstantinovo. He was something of a hell-raiser and he wrote many poems about the Russian countryside and rural living. He travelled to western Europe and the United States with his wife, Isadora Duncan, the dancer, and he wrote a number of pro-Soviet verses before becoming increasingly disillusioned with the regime. He drank heavily and he eventually committed suicide in a Leningrad hotel on 28 December 1925. Despite being married, it was widely rumoured (and not without foundation), that he was homosexual. The Soviet regime published his verse, but only rarely and in small collections which were not widely available to the general public. Through censorship, his later, overtly anti-Soviet verse was suppressed. It was only after the fall of the Soviet Union that a really frank assessment of Esenin as a poet and a person has been made, and he has been honoured with a statue on Tverskoi Boulevard in central Moscow, and also with one in his native region.

[30] Solzhenitsyn himself had suffered from cancer while serving his time in the prison camp. The cancer was surgically removed – it manifested itself as a large lump in his groin, and when it was diagnosed, the prognosis was very poor. However, he made a full recovery.

His appearance was shocking. Over the weeks of his illness, his hands had become emaciated to the point of boniness, they were hardly even sticks, as if devoid of any flesh, just skin – and the skin was somehow all yellow, full of bile. And how yellow the skin was on his face, which was unrecognisably emaciated. And what yellowness there was around those light-blue irises.

But here's the amazing thing: he had become even more handsome than before! How powerfully his spiritual beauty had permeated his face. On his head, his thick, uncut, grey ring of curls crowned this beauty. The expression on his face was striking by the fact that he was already, indubitably, *not in this world*. It was even more amazing because Boris surely *did not know* the truth of his condition, and he did not want to know: he had distanced himself from it. He complained, without a hint of malice, about the doctors: Why had they let things get so bad, so that his intestinal tract was so sluggish?

And his voice, which had lost its former vitality, weakened to a gentle kindness, which further heightened the impression of saintliness, which had become apparent in his visage. He found it difficult to speak, but he wanted to converse. At that time, he didn't finish his phrases. Sometimes his speech melted into a mere whisper.

And what did he talk about? What the country had been *reduced* to... by those same people, who had always been in power. How they had consigned to oblivion and had betrayed the whole Sevastopol population. He spoke about the fleet with the passion of a person who belonged to the fleet, because he had felt acute grief for it there. And the last thing he managed to write in life was a passionate article about the Sevastopol calamity, about the humiliating rent for Sevastopol, and about the impetuous concessions over ships and bases. And the owners of the *Rossiia* journal – where he was the editor-in-chief! – refused to print the article after Mozhaev's death, mindful of wrath from above – that's our 'freedom of speech' for you – one has to exercise a great deal of circumspection. And again, it was the journal *Don* that came to the rescue and printed it.

Throughout his life, how he had got worked up! How he had fought for what was right, for what we needed, and for what was to our mutual benefit! But who listened? What did he save? The people we had in power remained just the same.

Alia took some photos of me and Boris, and Boris with Milda. He even clasped his hands on his chest, unconsciously, just like a corpse.

He died during the night of the 2 March.

On the 6 March, his funeral took place in the Church of Filipp, the Metropolitan of Moscow (in the Meshchanskii quarter). His forehead was covered with the traditional paper band, but his face was no longer yellow – it appeared no longer thin, having taken on its peaceful, sculptural form.

It would have been preferable to bury him in a rural cemetery, amongst the well-trodden expanses of his native lands – but who could have undertaken such a trip at that time of year? What effort would it have taken, especially in winter, and in our present bitter, emotional state?! Isn't it easier to die, than to remain behind?[31]

1997.

Published in *Literaturnaia gazeta*, No.8, 26 February 1997, on the first anniversary of B. A. Mozhaev's death.

---

[31] Ironically, Mozhaev had written extensively on the state of roads in rural Russia and on the need to develop a good infrastructure to facilitate transportation and to improve the lot of rural dwellers. Alas, in some ways, he had fallen victim to such a lack of public highways. Solzhenitsyn's words at the end of this memoir are also evocative of a poem written by Maiakovskii on the occasion of Esenin's suicide. Maiakovskii, a poet much promoted and lauded by the early Soviet regime, had written a somewhat critical poem when Esenin committed suicide in 1926, due to his disillusionment with the Soviet regime and personal problems. The last lines of Maiakovskii's poem were: 'In this life, dying is not difficult. Building a life is much more difficult.' Tragically, and ironically, Maiakovskii himself was to take his own life, partly due to disillusionment, just four years later, in 1930.

Sania

Illustration 4. 'Soldiers' Wives Accompanying their Husbands to the First Station on the Road', *The Graphic*, December 30 1876.

Foreword to Sania

Mozhaev called his story *Sania* a '*povest*', which is a 'long short story' or 'novella' – a literary form which has no direct translation in English. The *povest* in Russian literature is similar in form to a short story, but thematically it has a wider scope, and consequently more characters than in a conventional '*rasskaz*', or short story. It was written in 1957 and it has been reprinted a number of times in many collections of Mozhaev's stories. It is one of his best early works, and Sania herself is one of his most memorable heroines.

The setting of the narrative is the Russian Far East, much loved by Mozhaev, and it was an area he knew well from his time serving in the Soviet fleet. Many of his stories are set in the vast expanses of this volcanic area, which Russians saw as akin to the American Wild West. The setting is an isolated settlement which represents a microcosm of provincial Soviet life, far removed from Moscow and other large cities, and it seems as though the settlement and its inhabitants have been forgotten by the powers that be. The community is left to their own devices in what is, essentially, a desolate place. The story contains a range of characters, each of whom has their own quirks, problems, and aspirations. The individual quirks of some of the characters in the work inject a comedic element, which lends the story a light mood in places, and it shows, for the first time in his early stories, that Mozhaev had a wonderful sense of humour. This comedy is highly reminiscent of Gogol's writing, in which the reader is presented with the absurdity of life, yet this humour does not mask or trivialise the serious points being made.

Sania arrives to a scene of utter mayhem and a total breakdown in discipline and order. Many of the characters have lost their sense of community spirit, if they ever had it in the first place, and they have become selfish and self-seeking. It is Sania who inspires the community to better themselves and not wait passively for the state to improve their life for them. She is spurred on by her youthful exuberance and optimism, and the sage advice of Nastasia Pavlovna, one of the village matriarchs. Several of the locals have turned to drink for lack of anything better to do, and Mozhaev does not shy away from showing this serious social problem in its true light. In fact, alcohol plays a central role in this novella. The very first line of the story describes the former stationmaster being drunk, and Nastasia Pavlovna tells Sania that, whenever they receive their wages, the workers drink and brawl, which Sania was to witness for herself.

Mozhaev includes some beautiful descriptive passages of the Amur estuary as Valerii takes Sania for a boat ride, during which a romantic liaison is formed. It is through this relationship that Mozhaev shows Sania's immaturity and lack of experience in affairs of the heart. Unwittingly, Sania becomes embroiled in bureaucratic irregularities, partly because of her *naïveté*, and partly due to the spite of a work colleague, which sets in motion an avalanche of sheer officiousness from a local investigator. Sania goes before a **Comrades' Court** – one of several such sessions referred to in these stories – which was a particularly nasty aspect of Soviet life. Though conceived to enforce discipline and censure minor offences, their real goal was the humiliation of the victim by their peers, who seemed to derive a rather sanctimonious pleasure from their 'duty' of sitting in judgement. Despite the unpleasant nature of the **Comrades' Court**, Mozhaev manages to inject a moment of humour and farce, which lightens the mood of the event.

The official investigation into the station fire was a daring piece of writing: Mozhaev shows how the investigator, Sofron Mikhailovich Kosiak, who, we are told, has a reputation for scrupulous fairness, is, in fact, anything other than fair. He is a typical Mozhaevan official, puffed up by his own self-importance and rhetoric, which has its roots in his own smugness and misplaced conviction that he knows the truth. He is prepared to see subterfuge and malicious intent where it never existed. He is, in fact, a product of the Stalin era.

Mozhaev also pulls no punches when he describes the poor living and working conditions of people in the novella. He describes the home of Krakhmaliuk's family, when Sania and Nastasia Pavlovna go to his wife's aid, because his wife is seriously ill: there are no sheets on the bed, the floor is dirty, as are the children, who are not even wearing trousers. Mozhaev refused to paint a rosy picture of bucolic happiness in this community. Workers live in barracks and there are no recreational facilities – the cinema at the **sovkhoz** has ceased to operate, and medical assistance is far away – in some of his stories, people die of such trivial conditions as appendicitis.

There is a rather curious passage in the *povest*, which is typical of an esoteric aspect of Mozhaev's writing. Sania sees a man working in a field and the description of him is quite significant: Mozhaev calls him 'elderly', which would make him a traditional peasant at the time the novella was written. He speaks in romantic terms about 'Mother-Earth', an epithet straight out of Russian folklore, and only a true, pre-revolutionary peasant would speak in these terms. He comments that the soil has become clayey, and Sania asks him if he will have to work hard like this all his life. He replies to her question with a wink, and says, 'Mother Earth will soon dry out and get into shape. She's gone to pot, been neglected. It can't be much fun for you, can it, being neglected?' Sania is annoyed at his temerity and it is clear he has touched a raw nerve in her. She asks him how he knows about her, and he replies in all seriousness, 'The earth whispered to me as a friend', and then he laughs. It is only the traditional peasant in touch with his roots, who has such insight into life in Mozhaev's works, and his words are full of wisdom, if somewhat idealized at times. Still, it is a rather touching moment in the work.

Were it not for Mozhaev's sense of humour, this tale would be rather gloomy. However, it does not leave a lasting, pessimistic impression, because of the Gogolesque incidents. The reader is alerted to Gogol at the very beginning of the work when Sania arrives, and Sergunkov asks her, 'Are we to have another government inspector?' Just to make the point, the word 'inspector' is repeated. No one with any knowledge of Russian literature could hear such a noun and not think of Gogol's play *The Government Inspector*.[1]

The *povest* contains several points of contact with Gogol's play: the setting is remote, and the line-up and inspection of the staff on the first day is highly reminiscent of Khlestakov's 'interviews' with each official in Gogol's play. The Gogolian ethos of 'nothing is what it seems' extends to Sania's first meeting with her staff: officially Polia, Sergunkov's sister, is on the staff rostra as a cleaner, but it is Sergunkov himself who does the work; Verka, the cashier, is really a milkmaid; Krakhmaliuk is really a stableman, who never washes his hands after grooming his horses, before serving customers in the station buffet; Verka was never really an officer's wife, despite her

[1] See footnote № 17, p.16.

claims to having been so; the pointsman, Kuzmich, is not really called Kuzmich at all, but Pëtr Ivanovich; and Sania herself looks like a young man, rather than a woman, which openly amuses the cleaner, 'Deaf Polia'.

Mozhaev also introduces into his story some popular songs, which were to become a regular feature in all his subsequent writing. Some of the songs are folk songs, such as **Stenka Razin**, and others are songs composed in the Soviet era, which glorify work and the pioneering spirit.

Sania is a beautifully crafted piece, full of interesting and entertaining characters, and it has a well-developed, carefully constructed story-line. It is full of small, almost throw-away, remarks and clues as to how the story will develop, which are only revealed on careful re-examination of the text. In terms of the length of the work, the issues it raises, and the range of characters and their development, it is a perfect example of the novella form. The narrative style is concise, beautifully balanced and paced, containing lyrical passages describing the landscape of the Far East, and the songs and comedic devices add a variety to the piece, which make it an extremely polished work. It shows Mozhaev as a master story-teller.

Sania

Chapter One

The stationmaster of the third-category station, Kasatkino, had taken to drink. While on duty in his office, people said, he would dance the '**Barin**'s Wife' to the signalman's balalaika and end up sleeping it off where he had fallen. Once, when the train arrived, he could not be woken for some time and so it had to be delayed.

Finally, the head of the railways board urgently sent Alexandra Kurilova (or simply Sania, as her workmates called her) to Kasatkino. Sania had graduated from the technical college in railway operations and came to the Soviet Far East from the Minsk region. She was an assiduous girl, strict in matters of work, and she quickly worked her way up to stationmistress. Now, suddenly, she received this unexpected promotion.

'You'll need to be a bit strict there, Kurilova. You know, the people there have let themselves go, so you go and sort them out,' insisted the boss. 'You're one of our real, steady girls, a youth organiser – you've got what it takes.'

Sania decided to put on her uniform shirt and her red-topped cap for the journey, to make a more official impression. In each of the tabs of her shirt she pinned three stars, as the position of stationmistress of a third-category station warranted. Walking past the station mirror, she unconsciously looked at the stars, and, for some reason or other, she remembered the jokes of the station policemen on duty, who kept on inviting her to transfer to the police service.

'You've got a manly look about you, and a voice to match!' they joked.

When all was said and done, she could not give a damn that she looked like a sharp-nosed, young lad. It was true that her voice was a little hoarse, and that, of course, wasn't so good. But you can't change your voice, so there's no point in worrying about it.

It took Sania a whole day to get to her new place of work. How far away this Kasatkino is! From the trunk line, along which Moscow trains travel, she had to change onto a freight train and travel on and on, in some direction or other, towards the frontier. Sania found a spot on the brake platform of the rear carriage, having refused the train driver's invitation to travel on the engine itself: it was noisy and hot there. Sitting on her case, she looked all around her. Wherever you looked you could only see the steppe, the featureless steppe, turning brown in the long summer sun. Pointed hillocks, scattered about the steppe like haystacks, drifted past, thickly covered with clusters of oak trees and hazel, looking as if they had all had a crew cut. In the distance, they looked quite small and made you want to stroke their green fleece. The stations here were small and empty: she saw no one apart from guards on duty who, like Sania, wore peaked caps, and pointsmen, carrying flags.

'Surely, even Kasatkino can't be as deserted as this,' thought Sania. 'You could die of boredom here!'

She was still dreaming of going to the large **Komsomol** construction site and operating an excavator. In the evenings, there was the youth club, and dances and parties... But of all the places, she had to end up in Kasatkino, where there wasn't even a **Komsomol** organization. But what could you do? Working on the railway is like working in the army – you have to work wherever you are sent.

Towards evening, the sky clouded over and the shadows of the distant steppe thickened, turning a dark blue. And now, in a gap between the clouds, the setting sun shone, illuminating a solitary, distant hillock. The hitherto invisible mound, merging with the horizon, suddenly flared up with the flickering flame of a torch and burnt long amidst the sleepy, blue steppe. Sania kept on looking out at that solitary mound until sundown. She felt miserable.

The train arrived at Kasatkino before dawn. Around the station Sania counted five squat barracks, their dimly lit windows looking mournfully onto the ground, along with four or five peasant houses. 'There's not much here,' she thought.

People milled around the duty office, which was just a small, wooden hut perched right beside the track. In the yellow light of a wall-lamp, people talked noisily and danced to a balalaika. Someone was trying to sing in a thin, faltering voice:

> *Oh, the one whom I love...*

'What's going on here?' Sania asked a short guardsman, whom she first took for a woman.

'They're seeing off the conscripts. They're from Zvonarёvo,' he replied, glancing sideways at Sania's case.

'Who d'you want, Citizeness?' he asked.

'I have to find the stationmaster.'

'Oh! Go in and have a look. He's somewhere around,' the guardsman advised indifferently, waving a green lantern as he went to the front of the train.

Sania went towards the crowd. No one noticed her, everyone was preoccupied with their own business. A fat, broad-shouldered woman towered up in the middle of this noisy crowd – in one hand she held a bottle of vodka at her breast, just like a candle, and in the other hand, a glass. From time to time, she poured out a glass to the very brim and shouted in a staccato, bass voice, 'Eh, Kolia! Have a drink!'

A young lad broke away from the dancers, drank the vodka in one gulp, and the woman took a piece of something black from her pocket, and, stuffing it into his hand, said, 'Get that down yer!' Then she started shouting again: 'Ivan, you have a drink!'

A short distance beyond the crowd, a small, elderly woman with a knotted kerchief tenaciously held a thin young lad by the jacket, and insistently burbled something to him: 'Brr, brr, brr,' was the only sound Sania heard from her rasping voice. The young lad could barely hear her and kept on looking sideways at the dancers.

'Okay, Mother dear! I already know!' he said, interrupting her and becoming embarrassed. 'Oh, what are you like...?!'

'And just you wait, just wait,' said the woman hurriedly. 'I'll be back in a moment. Just a moment...' Again, she made her regular 'brr, brr, brr' sound. A tall lad in a military peaked cap danced something like a two step and sang lazily:

The tango is a good dance,
That no one can resist...

'Eaglets! Little falcons! Darlings!' shouted out a closely shaven, drunken peasant in a jersey, slapping his sides with his hands, as if he were ruffling his wings.[1] 'Ah, my little Vasilii is going straight into the forces from the enlistment office. Oh, if only I could hold the train up! I need to have a little word with him.'

'As if you haven't been talking him to death for the last twenty years,' bellowed a fat woman. 'You'd do better to give him something to eat for the journey, you old prattler!'

'Give him something to eat! That's what you women do,' he remarked instructively, jumping from one foot to another. 'I want a heart to heart with him... about the whatsit... his service. I tell you, I've got to put him right,' he concluded severely.

'Do shut up, you old preacher,' said the woman, still not pacified. 'You shift from one foot to another like an inspector.'

'Old Semën!' someone shouted out from the crowd. 'Ask Sergunkov. Perhaps he'll hold up the train for you. Tell him it's important.'

'How can we – it's state property!' continued the crowd, and cackled loudly.

'So what? I'll have a go,' he said, coming to a sudden decision. 'He'll understand. I tell you, he's a sympathetic bloke, that boss of ours.'

'What a load of commotion...' thought Sania, grimly.

She glanced into the office, but there was no one in. 'Where are the station employees? I wonder if they are just having a break? Perhaps they have had too much to drink, like this lot...'

Sania followed the clean-shaven peasant in search of Sergunkov. She left her case in the duty hut.

Between the barracks it was pitch black and filthy. Sania tried to pick her way on the drier, lighter patches of ground, but kept on ending up in the mud. The peasant in the jumper who walked on ahead of her, opened the wooden barrack door and shouted joyfully, 'Little falcons! Darlings! Eagles!' and he quickly dived in through the door.

Sania went in after him. The building turned out to be the station buffet. The strip-light hanging above the counter dimly lit the soot-blackened, wooden walls. Two men were sitting on barrels, drinking vodka near the wooden shelves. One was a ginger-moustached sergeant major with a bag on his shoulder. The other, in front of whom the peasant in the jumper was politely trying to attract his attention, was a corpulent fellow with a puffy face, and cheeks in place of his eyes.

'Get on, Semën! On your way!' said the chubby fellow, waving him towards the door, through which the peasant had just come in. 'You can see I'm busy with this man's bags.'

---

[1] 'Eaglets' and 'falcons' were Soviet epithets for pilots: this indicates that the conscripts were to join the Soviet air force.

'You can talk! We're all busy,' Semën said. 'All I wanted to say was that I want the train holding up for fifteen minutes. I must have a talk with my young lad, Vasilii.'

'Are you Stationmaster Sergunkov?' Sania asked the chubby man.

'Well, possibly,' he replied, eyeing up Sania from head to toe. 'What do you want? Are we to have another government inspector? I'm not on duty this evening. Go and see Shilokhvostov and we'll have a chat tomorrow.'

'I'm not an inspector,' replied Sania. 'I have been sent here as the stationmistress.'

'Wha-a-t?' drawled Sergunkov, dumb-struck, looking at the sergeant and suddenly turning a deep red. 'And what's with your voice, darling? Did you catch a chill on the journey, or is it naturally like that?'

'You leave my voice out of it!' Sania plunged her hands sharply into her skirt pockets, stuck her elbows out, and looked incredibly like someone ready for battle, as if she had hidden some stones in her pockets, just in case.

Sergunkov scoffed.

'Get a load of you, you little devil! Well then, Comrade Stationmistress, get out there and hold the train up. Our visitor here requests it,' he said, nodding towards Semën.

'What I was just saying is...' he said, addressing Sania. 'Young Vasilii is going away on active service.'

Sergunkov and the sergeant burst out laughing.

'Stop playing the fool,' Sania said severely to the drunk.

'What for? Don't you like it?' prompted the officer, emboldened by Sergunkov's laughter. 'Why don't I give you a kiss? How about that, then?' he said, stretching towards her.

'Get away from me, you scum!' shouted Sania so unexpectedly and fiercely, that the two comics stopped short, and the barman, who had hitherto been standing silently by, came out from behind the bar. He grabbed Semën by the scruff of the neck and pushed him out of the door.

'Lout! Such a crowd of louts, these people. It's shameful!' said the barman in an apologetic tone, walking back. He wiped his hands on his jacket and introduced himself. 'By the way, I am Krakhmaliuk.'

'Not bad for a start,' remarked Sergunkov. 'Who are you going to chuck out next?!'

'You'll see – at the station,' answered Sania and walked out of the buffet.

Chapter Two

Sania spent the night at Nastasia Pavlovna's, the widow of the first stationmaster, and the only one whom people addressed formally, since everyone else was called either by their surname, or simply by a nickname. This elderly pleasant woman had come here about twenty years ago as a watchman at the station. Here, she brought up three children. Here, she had also buried her husband.

She spent the whole evening telling Sania about the surrounding area, about the locals, and about herself. She sighed often as she told her stories, and her unattractive face with her large, almost bulging lips, was preoccupied.

'You'll soon have more than your fair share of unhappiness here, my girl. The people here are difficult. Everyone wants to be his own boss. But you're young and seem hot-headed.'

'You just watch – they won't get the better of me,' Sania retorted.

'But life will,' said Nastasia Pavlovna, shaking her head. 'I too came here young and beautiful. But look at me now – I've lost some teeth.' She showed her teeth and pushed her finger in the gap. 'Some have just fallen out.'

While she talked, Nastasia Pavlovna was constantly busy: she either made scrambled eggs or pastry, or knitted a woollen jacket for her daughter who was a student – the rest of her children no longer needed anything. Listening to her tales, Sania soon came to know the whole story of Kasatkino Station and its numerous residents.

It was not a lively place. The railway, constructed at some time or other through the steppe towards the frontier, had more strategic than financial importance. For that reason, Kasatkino was simply a station halt with a watchman's hut and five log barracks, where the railway employees lived together with a defence platoon.

Recently the steppe had become populated along the railway line: **sovkhozes** had appeared, settlements had sprung up, and passenger trains ran along this so-called 'line of strategic importance'. Kasatkino railway halt was declared a third category station, and a former barrack became the station hall. There was neither lighting, nor a radio link here, and even drinking-water had to be brought from the town by locomotive.

'But isn't there at least a film on here from time to time?' asked Sania.

'The mobile cinema used to come round,' answered Nastasia Pavlovna, 'but it doesn't come anymore. We walk to the **sovkhoz**. It's not far away – one and a half kilometres. The young ones run off to Zvonarëvo, at the foot of the hill – it'll be about six **versts** away. There's a garrison there.'

Nastasia Pavlovna gave Sania her daughter's bed.

'This bed's been empty for five months now,' complained Nastasia Pavlovna. 'My daughter's gone off to college, to study. I still can't get used to being alone here.'

Sania laid down on the soft, fluffed-up featherbed, and delighted in pulling the blanket right up over herself on the clean, rather cold, cotton sheet, which smelt of cheap soap.

Nastasia Pavlovna sat at Sania's bedside with her knitting and kept on talking.

'Never mind. It's peaceful here. It's only when the collective farm workers get their **pay advance** that there's a rumpus. Everyone knows that the new recruits are a mad lot...'

'What kind of rumpus?' interrupted Sania.

'Oh, they get up to all sorts of mischief around the buffet. It's a ritual: they attend communion solidly for three days and nights, and end up nose-down in the puddles... And they brawl!'

'How do you mean "attend communion"?' questioned Sania.

'Fists fly – some get it in the chest, some in the head – they all get hurt in different ways,' laughed Nastasia Pavlovna. 'Just you wait, my girl, you'll see plenty of that.'

'And do our villagers drink as well?'

'Oh, our lot are too tight-fisted! Sergunkov is different from the rest – he drinks, but at the porters' expense.'

'He's let himself go. He's got as fat as a pig,' Sania said, disgusted with him.

'Don't judge him too hard, dearie. He's a kind man, but he's weak-willed. He gets it in the neck from all sides: both at work, and at home. Have you heard of the pointsman, who played the balalaika for him in the office? There's a bloke like that here. He brought all the cushions for Sergunkov's office, and some vodka, and some **pelmeni**. Kuzmich bought the station bathhouse from him for four hundred roubles and he built himself a house. Now he doesn't need Sergunkov anymore. It was he who played the balalaika for him... So that's how things are. And at home, his wife makes his life a misery. He keeps running off from her to hang himself. No, he's just weak – he could do with a bit of back-bone.'

The next day, all the station staff made for the duty hut on the occasion of the new stationmistress's arrival. Altogether, there were three duty clerks who worked shifts, three pointsmen, a cashier, a cleaning lady, and Krakhmaliuk, the snack-bar attendant, who was also responsible for being steward, stableman, and even manager of the shop. Krakhmaliuk was the first to arrive. He made himself quite at home behind the duty desk, grabbed the telephone and started shouting into it with all his might: 'Get me the **sovkhoz**! Eh? Who's going to supply the iron? Eh? And what about the potatoes? Eh?'

His 'eh?' was so resonant, that it made the electric bell quiver, and it almost rang.

Sania walked about the dirty, squeaking floorboards and felt something so heavy, so blunt rising within her breast that it pressed right into her throat. 'Don't anyone else come in here now,' she thought. 'I'm going to clip this buffet attendant's wings.' But fortunately, the door gradually opened, and a forty-year-old woman came in and stood in the doorway, strangely dressed in a long, canvas apron, which stone masons and tin-smiths might wear. She looked at Sania with her grey, child-like, naïve eyes, then she suddenly let out a quiet laugh, and covered her mouth with her hand. Sania shrugged her shoulders and asked the woman in the apron to sit down on the wooden bench.

'Oh, it's true that the boss is a young girl,' she said, laughing. 'I thought that they were having me on.'

'And what's so funny about that? Who might you be?' Sania asked.

'Just now, Shilokhvostov said that there'd be no control here with a girl in charge,' the woman continued on her own train of thought.

Sania listened with increasing incredulity.

'She's deaf,' Krakhmaliuk interrupted her from the telephone. 'It's Polia, Sergunkov's sister-in-law. She's the cleaner. His wife is officially registered to do the work, but she's the one who really does it.'

After Polia, Shilokhvostov himself came in: he was the one whom Sania had taken for a woman in the dark yesterday evening. Now, Sania thought he looked even smaller, although he had a large head and a long, spindly nose. He greeted her cautiously and, when he had removed his peaked cap, carefully smoothed his black hair, which was combed in a parting.

Then the pointsman, Kuzmich, came in, and, to her astonishment, Sania found out that he was not called Kuzmich at all, but Pëtr Ivanovich. He was a thick-set chap, very affable, but fidgety. He held out his strong, rectangular palm and bowed slightly.

Soon all were assembled, with the exception of the cashier. Deaf Polia, who had been sent to fetch her, told Sania that she had to milk her cow.

'What's going on,' she had asked, 'having a meeting at the crack of dawn?'

After this, Sergunkov remarked, 'She'll be here soon – she won't go far. Why don't we start?'

'I see,' thought Sania. What surprised her most of all was not that the cashier had not come, but that they all seemed indifferent towards this kind of behaviour, as if that was how things should be. Sania was even more amazed that no one was wearing their uniform. Such goings on!

'There's no need for me to say much,' said Sergunkov, casting his sunken eyes somewhere past their heads, towards the window. 'I've done my time. Now I can rest – retire, that is. So now it's over to you. It's your turn to speak,' he concluded, turning to Sania. He sat down.

First, Sania read out the official order appointing her; she also spoke little, but firmly, and everything went well until she came to her new orders.

'From tomorrow, you will turn up for duty only in uniform!'

'But, where are the uniforms?' asked Shilokhvostov. 'We only see it worn by employees on passing trains.'

'And why haven't you bought any?' asked Sania, glancing sidelong at Sergunkov.

'There's no one to send after them,' he answered, sharply. 'You won't get Krakhmaliuk to ride into town on his horse. In any case, it's voluntary whether we wear one or not.'

'Couldn't you at least find a red-topped peaked cap?' asked Sania.

'Oh, my dear,' replied Nastasia Pavlovna. 'I buried the last peaked cap with my husband.'

'All right then,' said Sania, not giving in. 'I'll leave mine in the duty hut. For the time being, you will all have to wear the same one.'

'Oh, Lord Almighty! What a great thing she's done – she's presented her peaked cap to us!' said Sergunkov, clasping his hands. 'We've got a roof full of holes, no lighting, and she's brightened our lives up with her cap!'

All the railway employees sitting on the wooden bench became restless, and a titter was even heard.

'And the duty office is no longer to be left unattended,' said Sania, raising her voice. 'There's the staff system in here, the points switch, telephone and...'

'You couldn't sell the staff system at the market if you wanted to. What use is it to anyone?' Sergunkov sarcastically remarked.

Someone again tittered, and this laugh felt like a whip to Sania.

'It certainly is no longer any use to you,' snapped Sania, plunging her hands sharply into her pockets, a gesture already familiar to Sergunkov.

At this moment, the cashier came in, dressed in her milking clothes: a green jersey, her skirt tucked up, and bareheaded.

'Who summoned me here?' she asked, looking inquisitively, eyeing Sania up and down. She was young with small, facial features and, in spite of her dress, she was quite pretty.

'Who is this woman?' asked Sania.

'The cashier,' Sergunkov replied, reluctantly.

'The cashier?' reiterated Sania sarcastically, at the end of her tether, and hardly stopping short of shouting at her. Speaking in her hoarse, high-pitched voice, she said, 'First of all, untuck your skirt, and don't forget to comb your hair next time. Then, Comrade Cashier, we will speak again. And now go. You have not come into a cow-shed! This is a duty office.'

The cashier looked astonished and her fine eyebrows arched, sliding up on to her forehead.

'Are *you* talking to *me*? We are educated people here! It is bad manners to talk to people like...' She did not finish her sentence, and left with an expression of sorrowful reproach.

'You can all go home now. Thank you for coming to meet me,' said Sania. 'There is nowhere I can get away from them,' she thought sadly, and then, she suddenly remembered Nastasia Pavlovna's words, 'Here, you need a bit of back-bone.'

Chapter Three

Sania moved in with Nastasia Pavlovna.

'Come and live at my place, my dear,' she said in a persuasive tone. 'The house is empty anyway. My husband built it himself for the family, but they've all flown the nest. I'll end up snuffing it in this nest, like an old hen!'

It was the beginning of September. Although the weather was hot with midday breezes and peaceful mosquito sunsets, everything announced the onset of autumn. On the distant hills, covered with sparse woodland, there were patches of euonymus, looking like red calico. The small larches of Zvonarëvo cemetery were turning brown, as if they had been covered with rust, and every evening wild ducks gathered, whistling as they passed over the station. But the steppe, which had drunk its fill of August downpours, did not want to surrender to the force of autumn, and under brown panicles of couch grass and bluegrass, at their very roots, grew feathery, luxuriant leaves. It felt good to walk in the steppe at this time of year. The grassy covering was so thick and springy that it resisted one's foot, as if it were made of rubber.

But in places, where this ancient, grassy covering had been removed, the disturbed, ploughed, bare earth was swollen and it greedily sucked at one's foot. Across the fields of the **sovkhoz**, Sania saw five tractors pulling out a combine harvester which stood on runners. How strange!

'Are you going to spend your whole life pulling out combine harvesters?' Sania asked an elderly **brigade leader** in an oilskin jacket.

'How do you mean, "my whole life"? Mother Earth will soon dry out and get into shape,' the foreman answered, winking gleefully. 'She's gone to pot, been neglected. It can't be much fun for you, can it, being neglected?'

'Where did you get that idea?' asked Sania, irritated.

'She whispered to me, real friendly,' he replied gravely. Then he suddenly burst out laughing.

Sania also visited Zvonarëvo, where the garrison was stationed. It turned out that they already knew about her there. As she walked past a two-storied, wooden house, she heard a subdued conversation among a couple of women sitting on the steps. 'That's the new boss. An upstart, I dare say. They say she's already been bossy.'

'Don't worry; she'll calm down,' lazily replied her collocutor.

'Have you noticed – she's got wild eyes?' repeated the first voice, persistently.

'Some fool will turn up and fall for her – probably someone like her,' said the second, good-humoured woman.

Sania found it difficult not to engage in an exchange of fire with them.

'Oh, I'll not win them all over,' she thought despondently. 'They can see every step I make. Well, let them sit in judgement.'

There was a small, round hillock near Zvonarëvo. The local Don Juans called it 'Lovers' Hill'. Sania climbed to its well-trodden summit and looked long at the surrounding area. The whole steppe spread before her and it had become even broader, more boundless. How much of it there was! You could see more and more, the further up you climbed. 'But why didn't everything in life seem so dependent on our own will? Surely things should be like that. Just like that,' thought Sania. The thought that life could be like that, if everybody wanted it to be, took her breath away.

From here, Kasatkino Station, which clung to the steel track, as infinite as the steppe itself, looked amusingly insignificant and unreal. But even here, an enlightened, joyous life had to be made, just as in the big city. But the people here brawled, got drunk, and they were lazy... Ah! How slow they were to develop! 'Who among them will be my friend? My support?' Sania speculated. 'I wonder who might come with me to this "Lover's Hill"? Where will he come from? An agronomist from the **sovkhoz**, or a soldier, perhaps? Anyway, all this is silly, girlish fantasy,' she suddenly said aloud, in her shrill, hoarse voice, and she went quickly home.

By the track, within the station rail enclosure, there stood a newly assembled wooden store hut. Sania had even noticed it previously, but with the fuss caused by her reception, she had forgotten to check the documentation on it. Whose it was, and who had given building permission, she hadn't a clue. And why hadn't Sergunkov mentioned it to her? What if it had been erected illegally? It would be her neck on the line. Now some workers were crawling about on its roof, covering it with tarred roofing felt.

Sania went up to the store hut and asked the nearest person, a curly-haired worker: 'Who's in charge here?'

The worker was holding some nails between his teeth, but he pointed to himself and happily winked at Sania.

'Don't act the fool!' Sania commanded severely.

The workman put the nails into his palm and asked, in an offended tone, 'Don't you believe me? I really am in charge.'

He jumped off the roof and, with the swagger of a self-assured man, he approached Sania.

He was wearing a grey suit and a shirt, fastened to the top. Sania saw that he was just bashing nails in, as if he had nothing better to do.

'And who would you be, Grey Eyes?' he asked politely, but condescendingly, stooping, as if addressing a little girl.

'The stationmistress.'

The young chap looked amazed and whistled.

'And did Sergunkov willingly surrender the throne to you?'

'I wasn't particularly interested in his "willingness".'

'That means we'll have to wait for the usual hanging session. Just like this – "Crrrr...."' He clenched his fingers around is neck, then pointed to the sky, and rolled his eyes amusingly.

Sania burst out laughing. He was a pleasant, humorous chap: he had curly black hair, thick eyebrows which met at the bridge of his nose, and strong, constantly bared teeth. He had a particular way of snapping his fingers with each phrase he spoke, and he smiled between the two rows of his clenched teeth.

'I'm sorry! I forgot to introduce myself, as they say. Valerii Kazachkov, a builder from the **sovkhoz**. Very pleased to meet you,' he concluded.

'Well, we are yet to see how pleased you'll be!' replied Sania. 'Let me have the building permit for this building.'

'Permit?!' drawled Kazachkov, amazed. 'Of course, there is one, but it's still there.'

'Where's "there"?' asked Sania, already getting annoyed.

'At head office. But don't you go thinking that I'm avoiding the issue,' Valerii pressed earnestly. 'Go and see Sergunkov – he'll explain everything to you.'

Sergunkov spoke slowly, as if every word was being squeezed out of him.

'I informed them over the phone. They're sending the papers on. They promised.'

'Who promised?' inquired Sania.

'Well, who do you think?! The railway boss.'

'I told you, didn't I?! said Kazachkov, happily.

'It's all above board. Do you know what?' he said quickly, leaning towards Sania. 'Our work force is going out for the day to the Amur. In fact, it's today, Saturday. Why don't you come along with us?'

Sania hesitated.

'Yes, why don't you go?' remarked Sergunkov kindly. 'Some of our folk will be going.'

'I will go, in fact, or they'll think that I'm afraid of them,' Sania decided. 'All right, call round for me,' she said to Kazachkov.

'That's the ticket!' Kazachkov exclaimed, opening his arms. 'Wherever the masses go, so should the bosses.'

Kazachkov went off very contented and he promised to drop by soon, in the lorry.

'What's that builder like?' Sania enquired of Nastasia Pavlovna.

'Kazachkov? Oh, he's an athletic type. He's from the town. Apparently he taught in the **FZO**. He came here last year with the bosses and he just stayed on. He says life is more free and easy here. Why do you ask? Do you fancy him?'

'Don't be silly!'

'He's all right. He's a good-looking bloke,' said Nastasia Pavlovna, and she gave a meaningful smile. 'There's a rumour that he fancies Verka, the cashier.'

Sania put on her black, lace blouse and took her grey jacket in case it turned chilly. Her sleeveless blouse revealed her thick arms and made her look more chubby and older. She put a gilt locket around her neck, but took it off at the last minute. 'He'll think that I've dolled myself up just for him,' she thought.

Kazachkov arrived in the lorry, as promised. He jumped out of the cab and, pleasantly surprised by Sania's appearance, asked her to take his place.

'I'll travel in the back,' said Sania refusing, and she climbed over the side with the greatest of ease.

The other passengers obligingly made her a small space on the bench and the vehicle moved off. Only Verka went from the station employees. She was wearing a white nylon blouse, through which her round, milk-white shoulders could be seen. She had this jacket, she said, since her marriage and she only wore it on special occasions, and she used this as an excuse to recall all her past, and, judging by her stories, it was a happy life. She sat opposite Sania, staidly pursing her thin, painted lips, and her small, round face wore a constant discontented expression. She started all her sentences with, 'We, the officers' wives...' 'We, the officers' wives, liked going to outdoor parties,' she continued. 'We called them "picnics" in officers' jargon.'

This affected, drawling voice of a person who had been everywhere and done everything, irritated Sania. Verka had convinced everyone that her husband had died in service in the air force. But Sania found out from Nastasia Pavlovna that he was not dead at all, and that he had run off somewhere. Now, every Sunday, the cashier was reduced to selling butter and sour cream at the garrison.

'She probably got her blouse by swapping butter for it,' thought Sania.

The lorry rolled along quickly. Small chips of gravel shot up and noisily hit the bodywork, and the road so crackled and crunched under the wheels, that it sounded like someone unstitching an old coat.

The people in the lorry were friendly and jolly. There were **sovkhoz** machine operators and combine harvester drivers, several elderly builders with their wives, and bosses from the town sewing factory.

They sang a great deal: '**Stenka Razin**', with all choruses, came off particularly well. A tall, long-nosed tractor driver stood with his back to the cab and amusingly used someone's sandal to conduct. At the end of the chorus he suddenly called out in a thin voice, 'What's happened to the girls?'

'We're right there, right there,' replied the seamstresses in unison.

After this, a young chap pulled a painful face and bellowed in his bass voice, 'And my Marfuta did a parachute jump.'

'Oooo..!' shouted the girls in a shrill voice, imitating the sound of a falling bomb. 'Bang!' shouted a young chap, banging on the cab roof with a lead cam. The driver slammed his brakes on and, leaning out of the cab, asked, 'What's up? Does someone want to get off, or what?'

Friendly laughter resounded in answer.

'I hope you lot get blown up!' he cursed.

The lorry moved off again and they started a new verse.

Sania laughed with them all, and even joined in the singing with the seamstresses. Only the cashier was discontented, and she made a point of just looking at the singers, because they had interrupted her story.

Finally, beyond the red-brown expanses of soya fields, wide stretches of river gradually showed their dim reflection through the willow foliage of the river banks.

The lorry went up to an ox-bow lake on the river and stopped.

'Hurrah! The Amur!' they shouted amicably in the back, and they all jumped up together. Then they all ran after one another to the water.

Sania had heard and read a great deal about the Amur, but she had never seen it. Now, together with Valerii in a boat, which it seemed had appeared from nowhere, she was floating along a river branch, marvelling at everything: over there stood a solitary, rounded willow bush, whose reflection went deep, deep down into the water. 'Look at you,' thought Sania. 'You're the size of a nettle, but from your reflection, you look like a great oak! And how many branch pools there are here, and island after island! You can't see the river itself. Wherever you look, there's just river banks. A lake – a huge lake and thousands of islands. That distant bank over there is so small, that the trees on it look as if they are growing straight out of the water. How strange!'

'What are those signs over there?' she asked Valerii, pointing to some posts with red boards on them, which looked like small flags from a distance.

'They're not signs – they're marker posts,' laughed Valerii.

He stared at Sania with screwed up eyes and powerfully, measuredly began to pull on the oars: they glided nimbly, like small palms, over the water and quietly splashed, just as if they were stroking, caressing the water. This gentle, happy splashing disturbed Sania. It was as if it were promising something, whispering something to her.

It was that particular time, just before sunset on a warm day, when everything limply and meekly submits to the approaching night. The wind had tired of blowing all day, grasses tired of whispering to each other, grasshoppers wearied of chirping, and even the sun had had its fill of warming this great, expansive steppe. The sunlight gradually cooled and crawled imperceptibly towards the distant hills, as if it wanted to hide behind them.

And how wonderful were the Amur branches at this time of year! What colours the waters make their play! Looking at the water straight in front of her, facing the sun, Sania could see nearby the most tender colour of bluish-green, but further away, towards the bank, everything looked rose-coloured, and the light emanated from the depths of the river, as if huge lights had been lit under the water. The further she looked along the bank towards the sunset, the redder and richer the colour became, until the water was as purple as blood, a mass of quivering, shimmering reflections... And how it made her heart quiver and rejoice! Why should that be?

On one of the islands, Valerii picked a martagon lily, a bright red one with black spots, and offered it to Sania.

'Just look, a wild lily! Autumn is coming, but it's still in flower,' marvelled Sania.

'There are no two flowers alike,' Valerii condescendingly explained. 'Some don't even manage to bloom, while others have already faded. But others flower right through their lives. That's just like people, by the way. That's life!'

Later, he took Sania's photograph with his own camera, a 'Zorkii'.

'I prefer to take a *half-provile* shot,' he said, showing Sania his profile. 'And then like this,' he added, turning full face towards her and looked meaningfully into her eyes.

'Profile,' thought Sania, wanting to correct him, but she was somewhat embarrassed to do so. 'Oh, it doesn't really matter,' she decided. 'The important thing is that I'm enjoying myself.'

In the twilight, dew fell, and it grew chilly. On the way back, Valerii sat in the back with Sania and shielded her with his grey jacket. All the way home, on the bench seat opposite, the cashier sat, aiming her penetrating gaze at them.

Chapter Four

That evening, Sergunkov ran off into the vegetable garden to hang himself. Earlier that morning, Stepanida had sent him packing out of the house, saying, 'Either go to the town, or settle down, or die off by the fence, like a dog!'

He returned from Zvonarëvo towards evening, drunk as a lord, and he knocked on the window pane so boldly that he broke the glass. Then he fell forwards, hitting his chest on the windowsill and, panting like a blacksmith's bellows, he tried to lift his bulky body through the window, but he was floored by the powerful hand of his wife. Then she soaked him with water.

Wet and humiliated, he solemnly pronounced a curse on his wife, his house, and Kasatkino Station. After that, he ran heavily and clumsily, just like an elephant, splashing through puddles, into the vegetable garden. There, he wound together some pumpkin tops around his neck and tried to hang himself on the wattle fence. Naturally, the leafy tops broke under the weight of his ample body, but his wife took fright and they made the peace.

The next morning, he came to Sania with a request: 'Take pity on an old man. Leave my daughter registered as the watchman and I'll do the job myself. I've got nothing to do any way.'

It must be noted that although Sergunkov's daughter was the official 'watchman', she did not actually work there. The whole family took turns in doing the job for her. Sergunkov's wife, somewhat worried about this job, had got her husband to have a word with the boss. Now, Sergunkov addressed Sania politely, screwing up his narrow eyes even more than usual, in a servile smile, and Sania felt sorry for this corpulent, elderly man.

'But look, Nikolai Petrovich, you yourself know that it's not allowed for one person to work and to pay another. Your sister-in-law is already working instead of your wife.'

'But my dear, what difference does it make?' he said with a forced, slightly hurried, laugh. 'It all goes into the same pot. Humour an old man, otherwise my life will be hell. My Stepanida isn't a wife – she's a tiger. I'd do the job myself, and then she could go to hell, but I can't – I'm on a full pension.'

'Very well, Nikolai Petrovich,' concluded Sania, annoyed at her own indecisiveness. 'But mind, this can't go on for too long. You'll have to come to some agreement with your wife and daughter.'

'Thanks, my dear.'

Looking at Sergunkov's broad back and pendulous shoulders as he walked away, Sania could not decide whether he was genuinely upset, or whether he was just crying the poor tale.

'In fact, what does he lack?' thought Sania. 'He's built his own house, retired on a decent pension, his son-in-law is chief storeman at the garrison, his wife gets Deaf Polia's pay, and he's even managed to set his daughter-in-law up in a job. No, I shall not put up with it for long. I'll send him packing, along with his daughter.'

At the beginning, there were generally many complaints from her subordinates: they complained about life, work, about each other, about their wives, and even about the weather. Listening to them, you would have thought that they had been used to living in heaven, and she couldn't imagine why they didn't go back there. Sania was not yet familiar with the sweet delusions and the reminiscences of lazy, day-dreaming people, for whom an imagined happy past is a hint of their self-imposed importance. 'There was a time when we too used to be at the front of things,' such people would say. It had not yet occurred to Sania that they were using their complaints to cover up for their own flattery and denunciations.

'I, as the people's deputy of the village council, draw your attention to the buffet attendant's singularly negligent attitude to his duties, as attendant and bursar,' said Shilokhvostov. Sania got the impression that his words rolled down his long, spindly nose, and as a result, they became longer, and somehow rather muddled. 'What do you think he gets up to? He comes straight out of the stables where, let's say, he's been combing horses, or God knows what else – messing around with dung, I suppose – and he goes straight to the buffet and sells bread, without even washing his hands.'

'Why don't you tell him about it yourself?' asked Sania, amazed. 'Why don't you bring him to order, as an official?'

'I did warn him myself,' affirmed Shilokhvostov hurriedly. 'On the other hand, you are the boss, and you should know all the negative shortcomings, as they say.'

The cashier tried several times to enlighten Sania about her former, happier life: 'We, the officers' wives, used to have a good time. We used to go to a shop, get a hundred grams each of one kind of sweet or another, and...'

'I haven't got time to listen to stories about sweets,' said Sania, interrupting her. 'I've heard enough of how well you all used to live.'

Even Kuzmich came to her to complain about Sergunkov. 'He hasn't paid me for ten glasses of black-currants, at one-and-a-half roubles a glass measure. It's all written here,' he said, giving Sania a quarter of a page, torn from an exercise book. 'You should take it out of his pension...'

'Even he wants his pound of flesh,' she thought. 'Very well,' Sania said. 'I'll pass your complaint on to the court.'

Kuzmich cast a suspicious, side-long glance at Sania and took back his invoice.

Sania neither liked nor understood their complaints. Her stern, hot-tempered character was alien to these complainers' submissiveness and self-abasement. 'You can see what's wrong for yourself – so put it right. I'll get them out of this pitiful habit of making complaints! I'll turn things upside down here. In the first place, we need a radio link, and in the second, we need lighting in the station. Oh! And wouldn't it be great to build a new station?! But the main thing is that, whatever I do, I must make them all happy.'[2]

She was like a young eaglet, which had looked out for the first time high over the steppe: its unbounded scope intoxicates it, as it throws itself headlong into the face of strong winds, and how is it to know, that the gusty steppe wind can break a wing, which has not yet grown strong, or has been badly presented to the air?

Sania had her first brush with the cashier. That night, Krakhmaliuk's wife fell ill. He ran to Nastasia Pavlovna's house, wearing only galoshes on his bare feet, and, almost in tears, he wailed in the darkness outside, 'Help me, help me! Riva is dying... She's delirious ... And the kiddies are crying.'

'What are you snivelling about?' snapped Nastasia Pavlovna rudely. 'You're supposed to be a man! Harness your horse. You'll have to go to Zvonarëvo for the doctor.'

Krakhmaliuk suddenly took a grip on himself, grabbed his galoshes, and rushed off headlong.

'And where are you going barefoot like that? You'll catch cold!' shouted Nastasia Pavlovna after him, but she did not manage to stop him, and, with a wave of her hand, she added, 'He's useless.'

Sania dressed quickly and, together with Nastasia Pavlovna, she went to Krakhmaliuk's house.

Riva lay in bed in a small room, under a kind of grey blanket. She was wearing her dress, lying straight on the flock mattress, without so much as a sheet.

She was a young, radiant woman, with full, podgy cheeks, and thick, flowing hair. She groaned quietly and regularly, with her eyes closed. By the bed, on the floor, sat two youngsters, dirty and trouserless, in short tops, and each screaming more penetratingly than the next.

'There, there, boys...!' exclaimed Nastasia Pavlovna, picking them up in her arms. 'Who's upset you two then, eh? The cat? Where's that cat? I'll give it what for when I catch it...'

In the dim light of a hanging lamp, which barely dispersed the shadows, Nastasia Pavlovna quickly found some children's clothes and, still cursing the offending cat, dressed the little boys, then she took them home with her. Sania stayed by the invalid.

'Where's the pain?' she asked, bending over Riva.

'Everywhere – it hurts all over,' she answered with difficulty, in the short pauses between her groans.

---

[2] Making complaints about other people and denouncing neighbours and work colleagues was endemic in the Soviet regime, especially when Stalin was in charge. In the worst years of the regime, during the time of the Purges (1934-38), a denunciation could actually cost the life of the person being denounced. In later years, the penalties were not as severe, but denouncing neighbours and colleagues to the authorities went on in varying degrees, and such denunciations were often motivated by self-interest and spite.

Krakhmaliuk brought the doctor – a young, broad-shouldered woman, who, in one abrupt movement threw back the blanket and, when she had felt her stomach, said in a deep voice, 'Send the patient to the town clinic on the morning train.'

'And what will I do about the tickets?' Krakhmaliuk asked Sania.

'We'll issue a ticket. You get your things together.'

The cashier, however, flatly refused to issue a ticket.

'Don't you know the rules?' she asked, surprised, when she met Sania and Krakhmaliuk. 'The railway doctor has to write out a permit to issue an invalid with a ticket, and not just any old village doctor. And even then, we can only issue a ticket for our line. Only the main junction station can issue a ticket to the regional capital.' Verka pursed her lips mockingly.

'I haven't got the money to keep on travelling there and back,' pleaded Krakhmaliuk.

'And do you think that I've got any money to spare?' asked the cashier.

'Enough! You can argue about who's got what later. Now, issue the ticket,' interrupted Sania, pulling rank.

'I will not defer my duties as cashier to you,' answered Verka, in a flash of temper.

'In that case, you'll have to be relieved of your duties,' warned Sania severely.

'Well, if it's going to be like that… Be my guest!' Verka threw the keys to the cash desk onto the table in front of Sania, and, swinging her shoulders provocatively, she left the office. On the door step, she said with a smile, 'We'll soon see. You'll be asking me back!'

Sania sealed the cash desk and then asked Nastasia Pavlovna to come to the office and, together, they wrote an official declaration regarding the unsealing and contents of the till.

'What's going to happen now, my dear?' asked Nastasia Pavlovna, sighing anxiously. 'You know that at the end of the month you've got to balance the books. Can you do that?'

'No, Aunt Nastasia,' answered Sania, gloomily. 'But I won't ask her back.'

'Of course. It wouldn't do,' agreed Nastasia Pavlovna, nodding her head. Seeing Sania's depressed face, she exclaimed cheerfully, 'What are you looking so glum about? We'll get by, between us. We used to have to do that kind of work. We'll remember how to do it.'

For almost a week, Sania sat over the paperwork with Nastasia Pavlovna. Sania was amazed how involved it all was: totals were kept for luggage, loads, and tickets, and then military tickets had to be noted separately. Local connections had to be kept separate from direct journeys. Waybills were to be kept separate… Just to mention a few. But, as all the multiplicity of transactions were coming to a close, not only did a severe reprimand come from head-office for the cashier, but also a bill for Sania to pay for the two illegally issued tickets.

'Well, now they've sat in judgement,' said Nastasia Pavlovna, with bitter sarcasm. 'There's rules for one, and rules for others.'

This first reprimand did not make Sania complain about people's unfairness. 'I don't give a damn that it cost me three hundred roubles – at least I saved a human life,' she reassured herself. But this act of kindness did not go unnoticed by her fellow workers, by the people whom Sania had thought were selfish and indifferent.

On one occasion, at lunch, while Nastasia Pavlovna was serving some strong smelling, well-stewed cabbage soup, which was claret-coloured from the tomatoes, she said to Sania:

'A little while ago, Kuzmich and Shilokhvostov came to me about a matter concerning you.'

'What about me,' asked Sania, pricking up her ears.

'"Well," they said. "It's not fair that the boss takes the rap for Krakhmaliuk all by herself. We all have to share the three hundred roubles."'

'There's nothing to discuss!' Sania snapped, displeased, and, leaning over her plate, she could feel her face blush. 'I've paid it, and that's the end of it.'

A short time later, recovering from her embarrassment, Sania suddenly burst out laughing.

'What's wrong with you?' asked Nastasia Pavlovna, staring at her.

'I could just imagine the expression on Kuzmich's face, when he had to cough up his share.'

'What's to imagine? He'd have paid up like the rest.'

'He'd hang himself for a **kopeck**. You know, he came to me to complain about Sergunkov, who hasn't paid him for ten measures of blackcurrants.' Sania sniggered again.

'There's nothing funny about that,' said Nastasia Pavlovna sternly. 'Sergunkov didn't just ask for the blackcurrants; he gave the impression that he was going to pay, but he just took them. That means that he's deceived him.'

'And Kuzmich hasn't deceived him over the bath-house?'

'Oh, my dear, where is the deception, when it was already falling down anyway? If Kuzmich hadn't got the bath-house, someone would have pinched the logs bit by bit. Everything needs an owner you know.'

'But Aunt Nastasia, you yourself criticised Kuzmich for getting Sergunkov drunk, and now, somehow, you're sticking up for him.'

'I'm not sticking up for anyone. It's nothing to do with Kuzmich. It's Sergunkov... If it hadn't been Kuzmich, someone else would have come along.'

'Perhaps. But I still won't take money from them.'

'You don't have to take it,' said Nastasia Pavlovna, touching her on the shoulder and sympathetically giving in to her. 'Use the opportunity, my girl. You see, people are coming round to you.'

'What can I get out of this?'

'Oh, aren't you the boss? And how much is there to do at the station? I don't think you'll get far by yourself. Do you remember how they greeted you?'

Sania put down her spoon.

'I don't know what you're getting at, Aunt Nastasia.'

'What's there to understand? You have to start small. Just take our school. There's a stove right in the middle of the classroom. The kids keep knocking their heads on it. It smokes. It's an absolute disgrace!'

'So?' said Sania, looking at her inquisitively.

'What about Kuzmich? He's a painter, decorator, carpenter, and he can also fix stoves. He can turn his hand to anything. He came to ask you a favour recently, now you go and ask him. You barter with him. Tell him that there's no money in it, but the stove needs shifting. After all, it's for the little kids.'

'Yes, but what will happen to their lessons? We can't close the school for a week.

'I've thought about that as well, but I don't know whether you'll agree...' Nastasia Pavlovna was silent for a moment. 'Your office is roomy... Perhaps you could turn it into a classroom for a while.'

'Aunty Nastasia, you're a real politician around here!'

Sania stood up and quickly kissed Nastasia Pavlovna.

'I'm off,' she said, heading towards the door.

'But, where are you going? Can't you wait? At least have some potatoes, for God's sake!'

'Later! Later!' Sania slammed the door and went outside.

The only classroom of the railway school was housed in one of the barrack huts. There were fifteen pupils altogether studying in the school, the majority of whom were railway repairmen's children, living about half a **verst** away from the station. The teacher also lived there – an elderly, unmarried woman. Sania recalled the teacher who, pulling in the corners of her plain, dark headscarf, complained on numerous occasions about the gap in the floor, which was draughty, about the broken windows, and about the stove.

Sania also thought that this troublesome stove, which was a relic from a former flat and stood in the middle of the classroom, was an eye-sore. Now she was on her way, with reserved hope, to Kuzmich. What would come of this first attempt? He would probably laugh and show her the door. Well, nothing ventured, nothing gained! But what if he agrees? It's not just a matter of a repair – it's a way through to a man's soul. Oh, Aunt Nastasia! You understand everything...

Sania went up to the wicker gate of Kuzmich's house, which stood apart from the rest. Somewhere, to one side, out of a thicket of corn, a shaggy, black dog rushed across her path and started to snarl threateningly, twisting madly on its chain. Kuzmich came out slowly from the doorway.

'Shut up! Don't you ever get tired?!' He quietened the dog and stared inquisitively at the stationmistress.

'I've come to see you,' said Sania and, almost by way of an apology, she added, 'to have a chat for a moment.'

'Go on into the house,' said Kuzmich with a gesture of largesse, pointing to the door, and he followed on after her.

The house was clean, fresh, and exuded a bitter, stupefying smell of geraniums standing in broken pots on the window-sills. By the door were his wife and two ten-year-old girls, sitting on a piece of oilcloth, which was spread out on the floor: they were removing kernels from corn cobs. A small bench covered with a tarpaulin was set next to the stove, and scraps of leather, wooden lasts, and unstitched boots, were strewn about. It was only then that Sania noticed that Kuzmich was wearing an apron. He pulled a stool up to the table for Sania, took off his apron and, when he had glanced at his hands, which were badly marked by waxed thread, he remarked with a careless grin, 'We're doing a bit of shoemaking.'

'They say that you can turn your hand to anything,' remarked Sania, remembering Nastasia Pavlovna's words.

Kuzmich, visibly flattered, hurried to brush off the compliment. 'Oh, we do what we can! We try a bit of this, and a bit of that. That's how it is with a house and a home.' He perched on the edge of the bench, opposite Sania.

'Talking of house keeping... Every time I walk past our school my heart aches. Winter is coming, but there are holes everywhere. The stove smokes and it even stands in the middle of the classroom.'

'Yes, yes, it does,' said Kuzmich, and he started nodding his head sympathetically.

'Don't mention that stove, my dear,' replied his wife from the floor. 'All last winter the poor little kids froze. And this year, you'll see, it won't be any better.'

'They've let the summer go by and now, you can't get in there to do the repairs,' said Kuzmich, as if justifying himself before his wife. 'You can't close the school.'

'Why close it? There is a way out,' remarked Sania. 'I've decided to turn my office into a school room, while the repairs are being carried out.'

Kuzmich quickly flashed his rust-coloured, nimble eyes at Sania.

'But what happens when someone arrives from head office? What will we do with them then? Won't they tell us off?'

'Perhaps they will, but what can we do? There's no other way out,' answered Sania, resignedly.

'That's right, that's right,' answered his wife from the floor.

Kuzmich cleared his throat and moved his bench nearer to Sania.

'So, I've decided to ask you, Pëtr Ivanovich, if you would perhaps agree to shift the stove.'

'Why shouldn't he agree?' his wife replied quickly, shaking the ears of corn. 'He'll shift the stove and patch up the holes. He'll do everything.'

'It's not complicated,' said Kuzmich, shrugging his shoulders.

'Only, there is just one problem,' said Sania, warily broaching the question of money. 'You see, we haven't a single **kopeck** to pay for the repair just yet.' She made a sudden move towards Kuzmich and pronounced warmly, 'but I will do all I can to settle up with you later.'

'Don't worry, don't worry,' said Kuzmich in answer to her promise. 'It's for the good of the community. How could I not do it? If you get some money – fine, if not, it's no loss.'

'Thank you! Thank you!' said Sania, offering her hand.

'My hands are covered in cobbler's wax,' said Kuzmich, embarrassed, and he cleared his throat again. 'Come on, Mother – get the samovar on! Let's have a drop of tea with some jam...'[3]

His wife raised her large body with unexpected ease and stared at Sania in readiness.

'No, no, thank you! Another time...' Sania left Kuzmich's house so light-hearted that she flew home, not even feeling her feet beneath her.

'Aunty Nastasia! Victory!' she shouted, tearing in, and when she had hugged Nastasia Pavlovna, she spun her around.

'Stop that! What the devil...?!' said Nastasia Pavlovna.

'It's a small start, Auntie,' said Sania, calming down. 'Now, all we need to do is install lighting and a radio in the station... Then, we can get down to work on the station itself.'

The next day, while Sania was making her report, Kopaev, the chairman of the railway himself, came on the telephone line.

'Well, how are things there? Have you settled in?' resounded his familiar, bass voice.

'I've settled in all right!' answered Sania cheerfully, and she even surprised herself by blurting out, 'We've decided to put lighting in the station.'

'Who's "we"?' asked the chairman, with ill-concealed irony.

'Well, the station employees. Using our own resources...'

'Your resources? This is all too good to be true!'

'Will you send us the cable?'

---

[3] Russians often eat a little jam with a cup of tea, especially if the jam is homemade, as it almost always is in the countryside. It is also common practice to put a spoon of jam into a glass of hot water or weak tea, as a beverage.

'Well, we'll see,' Kopaev said, hedging around the request.

Sania hung up and only then did she realize what she had done. Not only had Kopaev heard about the project, but all the stations around would hear. What would happen if nothing came of it? They would laugh at her. How could she have told him?

Chapter Five

For a whole week, Sania's spacious office was closely set out with school desks and her table was so ingrained with chalk dust that it was impossible either to wash or scratch off the white coating. Kuzmich kept his word, and the unpopular stove now stood modestly in the corner of the classroom. This happy event, however, went unnoticed by Sania. The one and the same thought pursued her everywhere: 'We need to install lighting in the station. It's a must. The main thing we need is telegraph poles. Where can we get them from?' For days on end she racked her brains over this. Valerii unexpectedly helped her.

After their walk by the Amur, he had taken to visiting the station. But, knowing how strict Sania was, he would always come on business. Once, he came to inquire about putting up a platform, another time to ask about the best place to unload sand or bricks. Only then would he move away from Sania's table and sit more comfortably in the deep, wicker chair, blackened by time – goodness knows how it had ended up in the stationmaster's office – and he would sit there for ages. His grey jacket, thrown about his shoulders, would slide off, baring his tight, knotty biceps, which were smooth and brightly polished by the summer sunlight and sweat, and they looked like cobblestones. Valerii would often smile and talk a great deal, but he did so through his clenched teeth, and from the side, it appeared that he was doing you a favour by talking to you at all.

'Although it looks as though you've come to the back of beyond, Alexandra Stepanovna, others might even envy you.' His low voice sounded condescending. 'It might all look as thought everything's gone to seed, but it's a station after all, and you are the boss. You have great possibilities, but the main thing is that you're independent. Autonomy. With the judicious use of comradely support,' (and here he stressed the 'a' of "comradely"), 'you can put things right. That's the ticket! Oh! I left my room in the city for this autonomy.'

'And where did you work before?' asked Sania.

'I taught in a **FZO**. I had a basic salary of seven hundred roubles and my whole life in front of me,' he sneered. 'I had prospects there, as they say, and promotion. By the time you're sixty, you could be principal, if you managed to respect the hierarchy. You'll get a pension and a plot of land out of town. But those kind of prospects are not for me. You have to wait too long and pay the price. But here, I'm my own boss.'

At the office doorway, he stood to one side and took Sania by the arms, just above the elbow, and led her over the door-step, as if helping her over a puddle. Sania felt the force of his gripping fingers and she tried to free her arms with a jerk, but Valerii seemed not to notice her protest and, with an affectionate smile, in the same condescending way, he said, 'Careful now! The porch is dilapidated and the steps are rickety, and you're in high-heels...' Sania's feelings for him were mixed: her decisive character could not help but take to Valerii's strength and agility, that particular self-assured way in which he acted and spoke to people. But that indolent condescension... Who could tell, could it be a mark of a hidden disrespect for her? Sania was wounded most readily of all by a lack of respect. When alone, she would often reflect over Valerii's words in her mind – 'Other flowers bloom right through their life, just like some people, by the way. That's the ticket!' 'You have great possibilities – autonomy. You need the support of your comrades...'

'What kind of man is he? He tells everyone what they should do. "That's how this is," and "that's how that is." He's set himself up as some kind of tin god. He tries to teach me, like a little girl,' thought Sania, beginning to get angry. 'Or is he trying to find out my real worth?... And does he like me?'

Then she remembered other moments... Valerii next to her, jumping up onto the bench in the back of the lorry, chilled to the bone by the wind, while she wore his grey jacket, and he, right next to her, his eyes not scowling condescendingly, but attentively wide-open, and with a bright, distinct, warm glint in them. Sania could not form any definite opinion of Valerii: her thoughts constantly strayed as she remembered the trip to the Amur. Sania imagined his tenacious, strong hands around the oars and she could almost physically feel their tight grip.

It was Sania's fate that, despite her twenty-three years, she had never managed to fall in love. She had had a difficult time when young due to family problems and squabbles. Her father had never come home from the war. Her mother worked in a barrel works and went into the town to buy the week's supply of food – wheat, oil, and bread. Sania got her allotted share: the flour was put into small sacks, and the oil divided into smaller bottles, and then put into her rucksack. Thus Sania would leave for the town to study with her week's rations on her back. She lived in a flat with other girls from the surrounding villages. They pooled everything – their broth, rent for the flat, and money to buy books. Sania had an elder brother who studied in Minsk, in a trade school, and he used to send his threadbare shirts home from there. Sania was brought up in these shirts: they were her working clothes, her student 'uniform', and her 'Sunday best'.

With her thin figure, her short-cropped hair, her darting eyes, and her oversized shirt, she did not think about the tender charms of love. She was simply called 'Sanka', just like a young lad. She thought that everyone looked at her mockingly, and she was ready, at a moment's notice, to stand up for herself. Her off-hand manner, which had evolved over the years, frightened off admirers, and even the station militia, once they had noticed this mannerism, kept a respectful distance from her.

And now Valerii had turned up. He had appeared as an unsolved mystery, frightening her with his attentive grasps and his attractive, powerful, masculine persistence.

One evening, he came straight into the duty office. Sania was sitting alone at the table. She had just seen a train off, jotted down its number in the log, and she was ringing in her report to the controller by telephone. 'You can't come in here!' Sania said imperiously, putting down the receiver and not answering Valerii's greeting.

'I've got something important to tell you!' Valerii sat up to the table. 'I think I've found some poles for you.'

'Really?' replied Sania joyfully. 'Good. We'll go in a moment. I've just got to switch the points and then we'll talk.'

'Just a moment,' said Valerii, stopping her. 'Let me at least have a glance at your secret work.'

He looked around the office, as if it were his own. He stood by the railway equipment and listened for a moment at the clicking of the relay.

'It's like a spinning wheel. My grandmother had one in her house. It was a funny old thing,' he said, pointing to the selector and winked cheerfully. 'You could make a marvellous proposal of marriage from this table.'

'Why?' asked Sania, puzzled.

'Because, with the switch in the right place, the whole station would hear, and there'd be no getting off the hook, no wriggling out of it.'

Sania burst out laughing.

'Let's go! I've got to switch the nearest point.'

They left. It was an overcast, dark night. The line was clear. The pointsman had gone far off into the steppe to a distant signal. The green light of his signal lamp shone, swinging, just like the eye of a wolf. Valerii held Sania firmly by the arm.

'It's less risky like this,' he said, making excuses. 'If one of us falls, the other can support.'

This little trick, for a second time, would have set Sania off laughing, and, with her usual abruptness, she might have said, 'Don't act daft! Get off!' But Sania, not understanding why, grew timid in the face of this man's persistence, and she felt ashamed that she allowed him to pay her attention while she was on duty. But Valerii, emboldened by her silence, stroked and squeezed her fingers.

'I've found some poles for you,' he said, becoming excited. 'Nothing to it! They wanted to build a bridge over the meadow road, over Kamenushka River, but they've put it off until the winter, since there's no sense in building it now. That's the ticket! Now we'll get started, and you'll soon have lighting, and a radio.'

Sania listened to him in silence and thought that Valerii was not so much interested in the poles, but in something quite different. She also caught herself thinking, that she was not so much interested in the poles, for which she had searched for such a long time, as in something she expected from him, and feared would happen.

When they came up to the points, Sania pushed Valerii aside and grasped the lever.

'Here, let me help you,' said Valerii, grabbing her arm.

'Get off and don't interfere!'

He caught her other arm and pulled Sania towards him. She flung back her head and limply met his kiss.

'Now go away!' Sania lowered herself onto the rail and buried her face in her hands.

Suddenly she felt ill at ease, she wanted to run off, to hide somewhere, as if she had become naked and someone was looking at her.

'What's wrong with you? Are you offended?' Valerii bent down towards her and put his arm around her shoulders.

'Will you go away?!' she shouted shrilly.

He recoiled, frightened, and quickly disappeared into the darkness.

She sat motionless for a few minutes and her feeling of resentment wore off. Now, she already wanted to see Valerii again, to talk with him and caress him. Surely he hadn't left. This thought suddenly frightened her. She jumped up anxiously, looked around, and spontaneously shouted, 'Valerii!'

He answered her so close by, appearing from a stack of wood, that he frightened her.

'You're here, then...' is all Sania could say.

'I knew you'd call.'

'How... clever you are.'

Sania submissively flung herself towards him.

Chapter Six

All that week Sania lived as if in a dream. That feeling, for which she had waited so long, suddenly overwhelmed her. It filled her heart like melt-water during the spring thaw, flowing over the ice, which had not yet broken up. There were no more doubts, nor anxious feelings of hesitation – all those sank to the bottom. But, in the same way that Sania did not know that, just as unbroken ice always resurfaces, so, with time, her doubts about love, about divergences of opinion and differences in personalities, about the contradictions in her conscience... they immersed, as they were, in waves of emotion, and they would undoubtedly rise again to the surface, and remind her that they had once existed.

Sania somehow took a grip on herself and transformed even outwardly: there were no more of those sudden movements, those fleeting, anxious looks. Her grey eyes, transparent as ice, took on a richer colour, became darker, softer. Valerii and Sania frequently met by day and in the evening, and they talked non-stop about the details of the forthcoming Sunday **voluntary work**, as if they would not just simply be putting up telegraph poles, but as if their very fate depended on it.

Sania came to an agreement with the commander of Zvonarëvo garrison, that a company of soldiers would be assigned to the **voluntary work**. The director of the **sovkhoz** promised transport to distribute the poles. Sania even managed to elicit two barrels of beer from the restaurant at the town station. 'Let everyone have a good time after a bout of honest work,' she said.

'Yes, yes. We must do everything we can to make it a day to remember,' said Valerii significantly.

Sunday started wonderfully: the warm, autumn sun hung softly, pellucid, with a tinge of cold green over the horizon, with a fine, silvery mesh strewn in the dizzy heights. What a boundless, clear expanse! And there was a hint of approaching frosts – that morning nip in the air, which you drink in, and it exudes an intoxicating aroma of watermelons.

Sania noticed neither the drooping brown grass, nor the withered leaves of the mournful bare hazels. Her soul rang with the music which originated in that pure, exultant sky, and the free, unbounded steppe wind sounded forth, announcing the arrival of a familiar, and yet enigmatic, new and invigorating time.

Very early in the morning, Sania called all her group leaders to remind them of the forthcoming Sunday **voluntary work**. 'We'll see how our bears respond. Let's just see if they crawl out of their dens,' she thought, referring to her station workers. But, contrary to her expectations, they were the first to assemble at the duty office.

'It looks as though we might have a bit of sun,' said Sergunkov, happily screwing up his eyes and shading them from the sun.

'It's also come out for Sunday work,' supported Kuzmich, also shading his eyes.

All of them, as a team, started looking up towards the sun, shielding their eyes with shovels, caps, and their hands.

All the station workers' families assembled here; the numerous members of Sergunkov's household, with the burly Stepanida at the forefront; Shilokhvostov with his decrepit, lisping wife, whom everyone called Fera; Krakhmaliuk, with his now healthy and just as carefree wife Riva; together with pointsmen and watchmen. Even Vera, the cashier, turned up with her shovel, in her calf-skin boots. She had not forgotten to paint her lips.

After the memorable trip to the Amur, the cashier would always appear carefully dressed, especially when Sania and Valerii were present. Sania responded to this challenge in silence and kept her strictly at an official arm's length. One could also not help but notice Verka's well-proportioned figure, her full, beautiful calves stretching down to her neat, thin shins. 'Well she's certainly got decked up to the nines. And she calls that her working gear!' remarked Sania inimically to herself. 'To hell with her! Let her try it on with the soldiers... But our people have turned out in their droves!' she said, cheering up and looking at her fellow workers. 'That's independent farm workers for you.' At the same time, she felt abashed that she had not believed in their enthusiasm, and she did not know where it had come from.

'Well boss, aren't you going to lead the way?' shouted Deaf Polia, with the widest of smiles. 'Or are we going to stand and warm up in the sunshine?'

'Anyone would think that you weren't happy at having an extra chance to warm up,' answered Sania, with a searching look at those who had gathered.

'That's enough,' shouted Sergunkov. 'They've warmed up enough. Winter's round the corner.'

'Look everyone! The soldiers!' shouted Shilokhvostov joyfully, standing on his tip-toes on a rail. 'Well done, Alexandra Stepanovna! You've won them over!'

On the hill, coming out of a dip, a neat column of soldiers appeared. On their shoulders were shovels in place of rifles. They sang a far-eastern song:

Always on our guard
To do our country's bidding...[4]

It soared up, along with clouds of dust from the road, over the emptiness of the yellow-brown steppe, rising higher and higher up to the heavens, where no larks or swifts remained, but only wisps of clouds hung like tracks left by flocks of departed white-winged swans.

The soldiers laid down their spades around the duty office and dispersed among the railway workers.

'You might at least give us each a girl per section... to keep and eye on things,' shouted one of them in a resonant tenor voice. An infectious chuckle rippled among the crowd of soldiers.

'Eh, Snub Nose!' said a sergeant with thick eyebrows, to Verka. 'Don't yer boots hurt yer knees? 'Ere, 'ave mine!' He pointed to his army boots.

'But I don't know how to wrap my feet in **footcloths**,' Verka answered, baring her thin, even teeth, as she smiled.

'Don't worry, darling, I'll show yer how to do it... This evening, when it gets a bit darker...'

Again, spontaneous laughter grew among the crowd, drowning the sergeant's last words.

'Perhaps you might, in fact, divide your people up among our gangs?' suggested the smart, well-groomed lieutenant, with his cap pushed back at an angle. 'It'll be easier for them, and we'll find it handier to keep an eye on things, if we're together...'

'No, Alexandra Stepanovna,' objected Sergunkov, standing near by. 'Our people want to work separately.'

'But will they work?' asked Sania, looking doubtfully askance at Sergunkov.

'Don't worry. It's a job that means a lot to them.'

Chebotarëv soon brought up a small group of maintenance workers. The maintenance workers, who lived one-and-a-half kilometres away, held themselves aloof from the rest, and they did not even want the water, which was brought in from the city, preferring to order some especially for themselves. Chebotarëv, the chairman of the local committee, was good-looking, but he was a bit of a ladies' man, whose wife was five years his senior and who jealously guarded him, not letting him anywhere out of her sight. So now, she came with him, crowding him out with her large belly, and demanded separate work for them from Sania.

'We don't want to work for anyone else – we'll do our own thing.' She moved her sloping shoulders and looked at her husband expressively.

---

[4] This is part of a song from the Soviet Far East, which was popular in the late 1930s, and it is typical of its era and genre. It was composed in 1938 as a marching song, and the text reflects the pioneering spirit of the Far East and the feverish campaign for rapid industrialization and economic expansion, conducted under Stalin. The words of the song pledge total obedience to the Soviet regime in a spirit of self-sacrifice, and a threat to all potential enemies not to hinder the relentless and inevitable progress of the Soviet people and industry.

'Yes, yes. We'd prefer to work separately,' affirmed Chebotarëv hurriedly, nodding his curly, fiery head.

'All right. You'll load the poles onto the lorry,' answered Sania. 'You can get there by lorry.'

Finally the **sovkhoz** workers arrived. Valerii sat in the cab of the first lorry. When he saw Sania, he stood up tall on the wing, took his cap off and started waving to greet her. Sania spontaneously ran to meet him. Valerii also sprang to meet her, excited and cheerful, squeezed her hands and said, flashing his teeth with a smile, 'Well then, has your army assembled? That's the ticket!'

The gusty wind made the open collar of his blue shirt flap.

'Do your collar up or you'll catch cold.' Sania herself started to fasten his collar when suddenly, noticing the inquisitive glances of the bystanders, she became very embarrassed and turned bright red.

'Silly girl,' Vasilii whispered to her. 'Why are you embarrassed?'

People were quickly divided into teams and they separated in single file along the route of the future electric cables, from the **sovkhoz** to the station, and work got into full swing.

The four nearest poles were to be put up by the station workers. This spot was low-lying and water appeared instantly. The sticky clay soil yielded, sinking under their feet, and sucked hard at their boots.

'Damn soil, it's just like dough!' grumbled Sergunkov, breathing heavily through his nose as he threw the liquid, oozing earth out of the hole with his spade. 'Girls, just pop home and get some buckets!'

Sergunkov's daughters were there: one was a schoolgirl, and the other, who was married, was near her term. The latter perched on the edge of the hole. The youngest jumped up and ran off home, her plaits sticking out at the side of her head. Stepanida dug the hole together with her husband, and their son-in-law waited for his turn.

'Nikolai Petrovich,' said Sania approaching. 'Let me have a go.'

'No, you join in with somebody else. This one will be ours, our family pole,' he said, giving her a mischievous wink with his puffy, little eye.

Verka, the cashier, was wading through the same sort of mud, together with Kuzmich at the second hole. Her little, calf-skin boots were filthy all the way up. The Shilokhvostovs and Krakhmaliuks were working around the third hole, just as diligently, filthy, but cheerful. Sania went from one group to another, taking a spade, spitting dashingly onto the palms of her hands, shovelling the soil, just like all the others, and waded around in the mud.

'That's what the bears can do! That's what independent workers are like,' she thought, constantly amazed at her fellow workers. 'They're not just digging the ground, they're devouring it... And they're all trying to out-do one another.'

'Nikolai Petrovich!' said Sania, addressing Sergunkov, who had just had a rest. She could not hide her joyful smile. 'Just look what our people are doing! If only we could always get on so well...'

But Sergunkov did not let her finish.

'They're doing it for themselves, my dear. And it's the right thing to do. It makes sense. Putting poles in, installing lighting.' He slowed down a little and, looking straight at Sania, added ironically, 'It's got nothing to do with a peaked cap with a red band!'

Sania again turned bright crimson, as she had done in Valerii's presence. She remembered the first meeting in the duty office, their expectant faces and her strict, bossy tone. How funny she must have looked in their eyes! And her schoolgirl idea about the uniform cap. 'I'll leave my uniform hat in the duty office... You'll all have to use the same one!' Sania remembered her own words. And how gravely they were spoken. She wanted to discipline them by a cap... 'I'm a fool, an idiot!'

'Deeds speak louder than uniforms, Alexandra Stepanovna,' said Sergunkov, as if he had guessed Sania's thoughts.

'And louder than vodka?' said Sania, scowling angrily.

'You're right there too,' agreed Sergunkov meekly.

Valerii often drove up and down the line in his lorry. Each time, he greeted Sania with a shout, but of all he said, she could only hear one thing clearly, 'That's the ticket!'

He spaced out the line of poles, distributed them, and, after midday, started to erect them. They arose one after another in the barren steppe, like exclamation marks. Sania knew that with every newly erected pole she was nearer to the moment when she would meet him and, who knows, that moment might change her whole life.

Now Sania saw Valerii in the steppe: to her, it looked as though he was not driving in his truck, but flying over the steppe, and his unbuttoned grey jacket opened out like wings.

Sergunkov's pole was the last to be erected. They did not manage to pack the water-logged soil around it sufficiently, so it lurched to one side. Jokes were made all around.

'Hey lads, Sergunkov must have managed to get the pole drunk! Look at it leaning!'

'You live with people till you get like them! Look, it can't even stand up straight!'

Laughter, squelching through the mud, trampling down the earth – everything merged into an unrestrained stream of sound.

This whole band of people were fuelled by work and sunshine, bubbling with jokes and they had all gone without food, yet all of them had invaded the railway line. The midday sun earnestly warmed the earth, as if it had forgotten about autumn, and it dried the grey clay, smeared all over their boots, hands, and faces.

'Water! Give us some water,' went up the shout from among the crowd.

Sania ordered Krakhmaliuk to open the spare tanker truck. 'I'll phone the depot today and have some more sent. Come on, open it up,' she said, nudging Krakhmaliuk. 'Then tell them about the beer...'

Krakhmaliuk opened up the tank, buckets rang out and everywhere there glistened a lavish fountain of spray with all seven colours of the rainbow. People washed, stripped to the waist, poured water over themselves, hooted, and shrieked. In a few minutes, the water was all finished.

'Comrades!' shouted Krakhmaliuk from the tanker. 'Stop splashing around! We have something a bit stronger than water. There's beer! Two barrels... Alexandra Stepanovna has arranged it all.'

'Give us the beer!'

'Let's lift up the boss!' bellowed the crowd, and rushed towards Sania.

But Valerii was near Sania. He grabbed her arm and led her off behind him, pushing people out of the way. They quickly ran to the station and hid in Sania's office.

'I'll hug you for everyone else,' he said, locking the door. 'Now then...' He led Sania solemnly to the desk and looked at her, as if he were looking at her for the first time, and solemnly said, 'I've decided to make an honest woman of you.'

Not a moment later, he was sitting at Sania's desk, as if it were his own, not waiting for her reply, which he obviously considered a superfluous formality.

'I've already thought about how we would set up home together,' he said, carried away by his idea, to Sania's amazement. 'Our first job is to turn your office into a flat.'

'Yes, but it's an office,' said Sania, attempting to object.

'So what? Today it's an office, tomorrow a flat. It's up to you to decide what it will be. You're the boss.'

'I'll tell you what. I'll talk to Nastasia Pavlovna. I think she'll probably let us have half her place. We can live there for the time being. In the mean time, we'll have a flat built – a little house.'

'But listen, Brain-Box!' said Valerii, getting excited. 'If we take over the office, they'll build a house sooner. Every inspector will be able to see that the boss is living in the office, because there's nowhere to house her. It stands to reason, they'll have to build you a house. It'll make them get a move on. You can't run a station without an office. That's the ticket!'

'It seems as though we're being underhand,' reasoned Sania, still unconvinced.

'Where's the deception?' asked Valerii, brushing the matter aside with disappointment. 'We simply have to live. You have to get everything you can out of your position. You're supposed to get a house, so go for it.'

'There are many things we're supposed to get. Look, we've no lighting, no radio.'

'That's completely different. Don't be difficult, please.' Valerii stood up and walked around the spacious office. 'I've already planned everything out. There, we'll have our bedroom, and here, a kind of living room. I'll make the partition from the materials I've already got – it won't cost much. I'll get one of our lads to make the curtain rails and get them to do all sorts of fixing up. Well, how about it?'

'I'll have to think about it and ask the railway boss.'

'Oh, you little coward! And yet, you seem so brave...'

'This is nothing to do with being brave.'

'All right, all right,' he said, putting his arm on her shoulder. 'You're a good girl, but you just don't know how to get on in life. But we can soon do something about that, with a little help, eh?' He laughed contentedly.

But Sania did not find it at all amusing: a disquieting, oppressive heaviness filled her breast, and she cautiously, anxiously listened to the sharp, loud beating of her heart. In the depths of her soul, she was unhappy with this conversation. But what could she do? Argue with him now? Object? That would offend him... No, she could not do that now. Sania avoided looking into Valerii's eyes.

Chapter Seven

Towards evening, Valerii and Sania went for a walk to Zvonarëvo. The **sovkhoz** workers walked around the station in groups. One group was hanging around beside the station wall, and six young lads were sitting on a piece of sacking, which one of them had brought with him. In the middle of them was a bucket of beer, and glasses were lying all around, along with empty vodka bottles. A black-moustached, young lad, who looked like a gypsy with his deeply tanned skin, in an unbuttoned canvass jacket, which he wore with nothing beneath, strummed his guitar strings with his short, fat fingers, and sang in a hoarse, but pleasant voice:

Burn, burn, my star...[5]

Sania stopped next to them and, shaking her head sternly, said, 'What are you doing here, making yourselves at home by the station? Come on, quick march!'

The young lad stopped singing and courteously asked:

'What? A march? With pleasure!' He started to play and sing:

---

[5] This song is a Russian romance (a song of love), composed by P. Bulakhov, lyrics by V. Chuevskii. Bulakhov was a popular opera singer, a tenor much loved by Moscow audiences in the early 1820s-30s. The song is about a star which burns in the night sky as a symbol of enduring love, which, unlike real love, is constant and, even when in the grave, the singer can rely on the star keeping watch over him.

My heart is gladdened by a jolly song...[6]

Valerii took Sania by the arm and firmly led her away from the happy gathering.

'You should know better than to get involved with drunks,' he said, cajoling her. 'Come on, let's go. This is nothing to do with us.'

'But they're up to no good. They might set the station on fire,' protested Sania weakly.

'People have got drunk there for years and nothing has happened. Do you think they're going to set it alight now?'

'God knows what possessed me to order the beer,' she remarked in a fit of pique.

'It's nothing to do with the beer,' objected Valerii. 'They would have got drunk on vodka anyway. They got their monthly **pay advance** today.'

'They work for a whole month and then drink it all in two or three days. What kind of people are they?' questioned Sania bitterly.

'But what have they got to save up for? They're here today and somewhere else tomorrow. They are new recruits, bachelors...' answered Valerii, cheerfully.

'It sounds that you'd like that too.'

'No, it's simply nothing to do with me.'

'But they work on your site!'

'So what? Good luck to them! They all get what they earn.'

'It's really all so simple!' remarked Sania sarcastically.

Sania was becoming increasingly ill-humoured. After such a day of radiant enthusiasm, when her whole soul should have rang out like a taught string, when now, all she wanted was tender, special words and passionate embraces, she had heard only the most mundane, official proposal, as ordinary as the **sovkhoz** workers getting their monthly advance. And then there was the conversation about living in the office...

---

[6] This is a line from a tremendously popular song of the 1930s, which became widely known through its inclusion in an early Soviet film entitled *Happy-Go-Lucky Guys* (1934). The film was one of the first musical comedy films, which starred the jazz band leader, Leonid Utesov. The music for the song, entitled 'March of the Happy-Go-Lucky Guys', was composed by I. Dunaevskii, who could be described as the 'king of Soviet song-writing', until his death in 1955. Dunaevskii wrote the music to some poetry which Mozhaev had written right at the outset of his literary career, and thus he turned his poetry into popular naval songs. The song quoted here is typical of the optimism and pioneering spirit of the early 1930s, and it expresses sentiments that everyone loves a song, which helps to make life happier and motivates the workers. It celebrates youth, calling young people 'masters of the earth', and pledges the conquering of the North Pole and the 'blue vault of heaven', i.e. space travel, which was but a dream at this point in history. As already noted in an earlier song, enemies are warned not to hinder the inevitable progress of the Soviet regime, or spoil their lives, which are offered and dedicated to the Motherland. The text of the song can be found in *Mass Culture in Soviet Russia*, edited by James von Geldern and Richard Stites (Bloomington and Indianapolis: Indiana University Press, 1995), pp.234-35.

But why should she, who was just starting out in life, have to fiddle things and deceive people? Why should her happiness depend on making a deal with her conscience? What kind of a life is that?!

All the way to Zvonarëvo, Sania was silent and became more and more morose.

'You really are down in the dumps! I know what will cheer you up. Let's go to the dance,' suggested Valerii.

The garrison dance area was a concrete enclosure, surrounded by a fence. All around the fence stood benches, which were set into the ground. People danced to the music of the **bayan** in their overcoats. The towering dark building of the club-house was closed – it was still being refurbished. The concrete dance surface was rough and the sand under foot made an unpleasant crunching sound. Valerii twice stood on Sania's foot.

'What's wrong with you?' he asked. 'You're not listening to the music at all.'

'I can't dance anymore,' she said, miserably. 'Let's leave.'

'Where shall we go?'

'Anywhere you like. I don't care.'

Valerii looked at Sania intently, and then hurriedly made his way towards the exit.

'Let's go to "Lovers' Hill". The breeze there will clear your head.' On the way he repeatedly said, 'You'll feel much better.'

While climbing the slope up the hill, once so matted with vegetation, but now bare, Sania looked over towards the station and her heart stood still. There, the long squat huts appeared dark against the thick, crimson sunset. Over one of the huts, long, knife-like, sharp flames leapt up and died down, alternately. Sparks swarmed thickly in spirals of black smoke and then dispersed far into the steppe, like fire-flies.

'What's that? Is it a fire?' asked Sania, anxiously gripping Valerii's right arm.

'Yes, I think the station is on fire,' he replied cautiously.

'We're on fire, we're burning,' was Sania's terrible, resonant cry, as she dashed headlong down the hill, and then through the steppe straight to the station.

Valerii ran after her, and, from time to time, he tried to hold her back.

'Calm down, Sania! You'll wear yourself out.'

'We're on fire, we're burning,' she replied in a frenzy, and did not even stop to catch her breath.

To her amazement, Sania saw a small crowd standing near the burning station. There were locals and a few maintenance workers standing around, muttering quietly, and, a little further away, near the fire engine, quietly stood the firemen and some people who had probably come from Zvonarëvo with them. None of the **sovkhoz** workers were there. The flames had already devoured the wooden roof, and they were now roaring and growling intensely inside the station, just like the sound water makes at the bottom of a well.

Everything around the burning building was bathed in an uneasy, flickering light, and there hung an unusual, eerie silence in the air.

Sania rushed up to the firemen.

'Why aren't you putting it out? Have you just come to gawp?'

'What? There's no water,' replied the moustached fireman, who was posing on the wing of the fire-engine.

'And why aren't you using boat hooks? Come on, pull! I order you to!' shouted Sania hysterically.

'What's the point in pulling the walls clear?' said the fireman, unmoved: he was obviously in charge. 'As soon as you touch it, the whole lot will collapse. It's all rotten.'

'So that's it! You refuse?' Sania ran to her fellow workers. 'And what are you all staring at? Do you think it's a free show, or something? Get some boat hooks and pull the walls free.'

'You are getting all worked up for nothing, my dear,' said the voice of someone in the crowd. Sania could not make out whose voice it was. 'The cash box has been taken out and it's safe. The rest of it is not worth bothering about. Let it burn!'

'How do you mean, "let it burn"?' asked Sania taken aback, almost crying with helplessness and rage.

Those who stood in front of her were not the same people who, that day, had so diligently dug holes, waded in mud, and heaved the poles around.

'Why are you getting upset? It's already done its job, and it's seen better days.'

'They'll build a new one now.'

'What's the point in getting mixed up with the flames?' spoke voices in the crowd. But Sania just became more and more furious.

Someone ran up to the crowd and shouted, 'Hey, everyone! Chebotarëv is running here with his scythe. He's drunk. He's looking for his wife. Mind that he doesn't cut you up!'

'Only when he's drunk can the poor fool get his own back on his witch of a wife,' said someone sympathetically.

'But in the morning, when he's sober, she'll give him what for,' pronounced another, gloating.

'Let's go, everyone! Run for your life...'

The crowd started to disperse quickly. This cut Sania to the quick.

'Run for your life! The station *is* my life! That's important to me! Are you going to let it burn?' she asked, trying to stop the crowd. No one listened to her.

'Come on, let's leave,' said Valerii, pulling her by the sleeve. 'Let's not look for more trouble. What they're saying is right. They'll have to build a new station now. That's the ticket!'

'Ah, you can follow the rest. I know that everything for you is just somebody else's... You only look after your own skin... That's your ticket!'

All that was seething in her heart, everything that had hurt her, due to the loathsome meanness of those around her, weighed heavily upon her – all this rose up like a sharp tongue of fire, gripped her throat, and caught her breath.

'Get away from me! Get away from here!'

'What's wrong? Have you gone mad?' Valerii recoiled from her, but when he saw Chebotarëv's fiery, red head, which looked just like a glowing ember, and the wide blade of the scythe behind his shoulder, reflecting the flames of the fire, he took to his heels. But Sania, shouting, 'Beat them! Beat them all! All of them!' pounced on Chebotarëv and slapped him about the cheeks, until she fell onto the ground in a helpless rage. Chebotarëv sobered up in a trice, threw down his scythe, and stood before her, perplexed.

'So that's how it is,' he mumbled. 'I'm sorry... I must have made a mistake.'

Sania was taken unconscious to Nastasia Pavlovna's. Then the militiaman came by bike from Zvonarëvo to fetch Chebotarëv and put him into the police station cellar, which had been fit out as the divisional sobering-up station.[7]

Chapter Eight

Sofron Mikhailovich Kosiak, the head of the personnel department, arrived to investigate the fire at Kasatkino. He was a respectable, over-polite man: he had large, reddish curls and greying temples, which lent him an artistic look. All his features were rounded – his wide, tapered chin, his rose-coloured cheeks, which looked like freshly baked pies, and his plump, glossy nose. He had been in the army for over twenty years and had risen to the rank of major. However, he had not got any higher than the position of instructor in the political department. When staffing was reduced for the very first time, he was made a reserve. He had worked on the railway for three years and had gained the reputation for being an objective and impartial man.

Sofon Mikhailovich, experienced in all manner of assignments, got straight down to the job. He decided to begin by questioning 'the opposition', that is those people with whom Sania had clashed at work.

'Objectivity, above all things,' he reasoned. 'But one must find it in disagreements.'

Therefore, he summoned the cashier first.

He received her in the buffet, which had been hastily set up as an office.

'Please take a seat, Vera Grigorevna,' invited Kosiak, softly. Verka affectedly pursed her lips and carefully sat on the edge of the chair.

---

[7] Drunks were regularly picked up by the police and taken to 'sobering-up stations', where they were 'given' a bed for the night, fined the next morning, and a report of the event was sent to their employer. Though punitive and intended as a deterrent, this 'service' was essential in the winter months, when the temperatures fall well below zero, and a drunken person is in danger of freezing to death outdoors. However, drunks often woke up the next morning to find their money and valuables had gone missing, and the arresting officers were frequently reputed to have helped themselves to the arrested person's valuables, which they saw as a perk of their job.

'What can you tell us about the circumstances of the fire?' Kosiak again smiled sweetly.

Verka shrugged her shoulders: 'How do you mean, "circumstances"?'

'Tell us, in other words, what went on before the fire.'

'What's there to tell? They put the poles up then wallowed around by the watchman's hut. They drank some beer. Then the **sovkhoz** workers came and started drinking heavily. But, when the firemen came to put the fire out, it turned out that there was no water.'

'Where had the water gone?'

'I've already told you. After work, they all splashed around in it and used it all up.'

'And who gave the order to use the water?'

'Our boss, Kurilova.'

'I see... Would it have been possible, let's say, to take people off somewhere into the steppe to wash their boots? There are marshes there, aren't there?'

The cashier looked intently at Kosiak and gave an agreeing smile: 'Dozens of them!'

'I see. That means that in this respect, Comrade Kurilova was thoughtless. Would you not agree?'

'Of course, I agree!' she said , happily catching on to Kosiak's drift.

'Good. That's what we'll note down.'

He suddenly approached Verka and quickly asked: 'Why did Kurilova sack you from your job?'

'She wanted me to issue an unofficial ticket, but I refused,' answered the cashier with dignity. 'She then wrote it out herself. She was made to pay the unauthorized ticket herself. But if we're being frank, I must say that the rules have been broken every step of the way.' She had finally understood what was being demanded of her and she lost all her inhibitions. 'Here, everything is done by deals made with Kurilova. She keeps the former stationmaster on as a watchman, but the money is paid to his daughter, because he's not entitled to earn anything as a pensioner. And, by the main line, the **sovkhoz** workers have built an unauthorized store hut. They don't have any papers to authorize the building. I know everything that goes on here! They bribed the former stationmaster with vodka, but Kurilova and the site foreman appear to be almost bride and groom. He arranged the poles for her – probably at a cost. He certainly wouldn't do it for free. But I am an honest person. I will not hide anything.'

Kosiak noted everything down quickly, nodding in agreement.

'Very interesting... Thank you, thank you,' he said, rubbing his hands. 'Could you possibly ask that builder from the **sovkhoz** to come and see me? Let's say, after work?'

'Why not? I'll tell him. He'll come.' Verka, pleased with herself, cheerfully got up from the table. 'Kurilova is thinking about marrying him! But between you and me, she's got no chance. Ah, yes! While the fire was burning she went hysterical. She called everyone names, and him as well, and she was spoiling for a fight... So undignified! He's tried to avoid her since then. I know everything, everything...'

'Well, well' nodded Kosiak, politely showing his visitor to the door.

Kosiak also summoned Krakhmaliuk, Shilokhvostov, Kuzmich, and even Deaf Polia, to his 'office'. But contrary to his expectations, he did not get any corroborative evidence from these people: they either replied unwillingly, using the same words, 'No, I didn't see...' or 'I can't talk about what I don't know...', or they kept completely quite.

Kuzmich even tried to prove that the station had caught fire due to a passing train. 'The sparks flew from the chimney and fell on the roof. The roof is very old – it's not like falling onto a splinter of wood. More like falling onto straw, and that's why it caught fire. How can you blame Kurilova for that? The station was old anyway – it's served its purpose... It wasn't worth a brass farthing.'

Kosiak gave him a stern telling-off for treating state property so irresponsibly, and, seeing him out, thought: 'She's already managed to work on her employees.'

Then he summoned Sania. He purposefully spread out on the table all the pages he had written and, greeting Sania, he said: 'Well now, Comrade Kurilova! Basically the situation is clear. Let's not beat about the bush. As far as discipline goes in work at this station, it's gone to pot. And where there is no discipline, something is bound to happen.' He made a significant pause and added, particularly affectionately: 'And even you, it must be said, have morally decomposed.'

'So, do I smell, then?' asked Sania, hoarsely.

'There's no point in looking for a confrontation,' remarked Kosiak, not even raising his voice. 'You are still young, you have a long life in front of you, so there's no point in complicating the issue...'

'Leave my youth out of it,' interrupted Sania. 'And I don't expect any favours from you.'

'There's no point in taking that tone with me.'

'We have nothing to say to each other. You've already got everything written down, based on the evidence... You have already come to the conclusion that I've let things go without even talking to me.'

'Well then, Comrade Kurilova, in that case, will you allow me to clarify one or two facts?'

'Please do.'

'Did you give permission for the water from the tanker to be used up?'

'I did.'

'Was the beer brought on your orders?'

'Yes, it was.'

'Good. And were you absent during the fire?'

'Yes.'

'And would you mind telling me where you were?'

'What?! Has someone not managed to tell you that?'

'Comrade Kurilova!'

'Don't shout! I'm not afraid of you. I was at a dance. Note it down, if you haven't already. And then finish the interrogation. You are not a prosecutor, and I am not the accused.'

Kosiak stood up.

'Fine. Show me the authorization for the store hut by the main line.'

'I have no such authorization.'

'Who built the hut?'

'The **sovkhoz** builders.'

'And did they also supply the telegraph poles?'

'What are you getting at?'

'Nothing in particular. I simply want to clarify, who allowed the hut to be built by the main line.'

'Verbal permission was granted to the previous stationmaster.'

'Is that what you think?'

Kosiak went to the door and called Sergunkov who was waiting nearby.

The latter came in, pounding over the creaking floor boards, sighed loudly, and sat near the table without looking at Sania.

'Are you in work, Comrade Sergunkov?'

'No, I'm retired,' he replied, not lifting his head.

'So, who is the night watchman?' Kosiak asked Sania.

'His daughter is registered, but he does the work,' Sania replied.

'With your permission?'

'Yes.'

'I see.'

Sergunkov shook his head, obviously wanting to say something, but neither paid any attention to him, and he sighed heavily again.

Verka came in without knocking and, having appraised Sania with her crushing glance, she loudly announced to Kosiak, with a kind of inner delight: 'Kazachkov has come from the state farm. Shall I call him in?'

'Yes, please do.'

Verka went out.

'There's only one more point to clarify.'

'I've had enough,' said Sania, standing up, and she went towards the door, but at that moment the door opened and Valerii appeared on the step. He carefully closed the door behind him and walked past Sania as if she were not there.

'Ah, so that's how it is!' thought Sania, plunging her hands sharply into her pockets and turned back to the table where Valerii stood. She was ready to confront him face to face, as if she were entering into a fight.

When they had exchanged greetings, Kosiak dryly asked: 'Have you the authorization for the hut by the main line?'

'No,' answered Valerii, cheerfully 'But I built it on the authorization of both stationmasters.'

'That means that the present stationmistress knew that you had no documents for the appropriation of land for the store?' asked Kosiak, with a satisfied smile.

'It stands to reason she knew,' Valerii answered, confidently. 'Here we help each other, you might say... I did not remain in her debt.'

Sania instantly coloured, her temples pounded as if they had been struck with a sledge hammer, and her ears rang...

'You villain!' she pronounced gravely, and left without closing the door behind her.

Sergunkov ran out after her.

'My dear girl, my dear!' he shouted after her. 'Forgive me, forgive an old sinner...'

'Go away, Nikolai Petrovich! Go away and don't add insult to injury!' answered Sania wearily and hoarsely.

'How has all this happened? Oh, my dear...' he halted and, stamping on the spot where he stood, shouted, 'I'll give her what for!' And he dashed home.

The Sergunkov family were all assembled at the kitchen table, drinking tea. He reared up in the doorway like an infuriated bull, huge and dark in the shaded light, puffing and panting heavily.

'What are you snorting for, as if you had carried a load on your back?' asked the unmoved Stepanida. She was sitting in the corner slurping her tea loudly from a saucer.

'And you would have been the one to put the harness on... Provided I brought the load home...'

He bore down on his wife like a storm cloud, and his voice, full of suppressed terror, got louder and louder.

'You've never, ever been content with just me! My blood has never been enough for you! Now you've started on others. You got Kurilova to break the rules!'

'Are you mad? Keep quiet!' roared Stepanida in a deep, threatening voice.

'No, I've had enough of keeping quiet!'

Sergunkov thumped sharply on the table right in front of Stepanida's nose. The samovar gave out a puff of steam, as if frightened, the crockery rattled, and the girls started crying. Stepanida, however, quickly grabbed the stool from under her and hit Sergunkov deftly on the back with the edge of it. He would have flung himself at her, but so great were the exclamations from the others around the table, that Sergunkov was dumb-struck, and he stepped back.

'Ah, so that's how it is! You're all against me, the lot of you... Very well!'

He ran out into the next room, took off his belt, quickly stood on a stool, tied the belt to a hook in the ceiling, which was used for the cradle, made a loop, slammed the door shut with his foot and pompously announced: 'A curse on you, you blood-sucker!'

He then heard people rushing to the door. He kicked over the stool with a groan, and it was only at that moment that he realised that the door had locked and that the key was on the inside.

'Save meee...' he shouted out, choking, and he began to struggle convulsively, hanging in the noose.

His son-in-law broke through the door with several blows and, grabbing the choking Sergunkov across the stomach, he lifted him up a little with an almighty effort. Stepanida, white as a sheet, and sobbing as if she had been scalded, ran around, saying: 'Oh my godfathers! What's going on here? For goodness' sake...! Oh, you're always causing me trouble...'

'Cut the belt! Cut it!' shouted the son-in-law at her, flushed with the strain.

Finally, they managed to cut the belt, and they laid the subdued Sergunkov onto the bed. He slowly began to turn pink and opened his eyes. Stepanida sat by him, still in tears, saying: 'What have you done, Old Man? Am I such an evil devil to you? I try and do all I can for the family's sake.'

'All right, that's enough,' replied the son-in-law, bored, and, having looked at his hand, he remarked disappointedly: 'He's broken his watch... Look, he's smashed the face. He can't half kick!'

He listened to the watch for a moment.

'It's stopped. You'll have to take it to the town for repair. What a shame!'

Chapter Nine

Four days after Kosiak had left, the guardsman of a passing train gave Sania a summons to appear before a **Comrades' Court**. As she read it, Sania recalled Valerii's phrase, 'You need the help of your comrades...' and she sneered. Leaving Sergunkov in her place as the order had bid her, she set off to the town. As she travelled on the main line, the boss of the neighbouring station, Vasiukov, joined her in the same compartment.

'Ah, my dear girl!' he said, cheerfully greeting her. 'What's made you turn so green?'

'You'd turn green, Uncle Vasia.'

'Don't you grieve! We'll stick up for you.'

He was a jovial man with a grey moustache and a large nose. On his small, withered head he wore an ample peaked-cap, which looked as thought it was hung on a stake, and his long neck, with prominent veins, protruded over the black collar of his overcoat, just like a potato shoot sticking up out of a cellar. There was something of the puppet figure Petrushka about him – cunning, kind-hearted, and very amusing.[8] Some time ago, Sania had taken a shine to him, and she simply called him 'Uncle Vasia'.

'So, your station's burnt down?'

'Yes, it has, Uncle Vasia.'

'Well, it serves it right.'

'The station is not the problem.'

'What is it, then?'

'I've had the inspector round.'

'Who?'

'Kosiak.'

'He gets around!'

'He cross-examined me. I got worked up.'

'Oh, no!' Vasiukov shook his head and tutted.

'And everything turned out against me, Uncle Vaska.'

Sania started telling him about how Kosiak had led the inquiry. Vasiukov reacted strongly: he took off his cap and then put it on again, then grabbed Sania's hand.

'Just you hang on! So, he even dragged your boyfriend into it?! Ah, the crafty devil!'

He got so involved in the tale and pronounced 'the crafty devil' with such relish, that Sania found it difficult to decide whether Vasiukov sympathised with her, or whether he was wholly on Kosiak's side.

'Kosiak has got a gift for cross-examining on the inquiry board,' concluded Vasiukov. 'Sanka, what happens is that people like him show their talent on idiots like us. Sometimes, they even get promoted.'

'I don't know what will happen to me now, Uncle Vasia,' said Sania sadly.

'Nothing will happen. They'll talk and talk, and leave it at that. You're not the first. We've all been before the court at some time or other.'

'Yes, but I don't believe that Kosiak will leave me alone that easily.'

'Just who does he think he is, this Kosiak?' said Vasiukov, getting ruffled, like a cockerel. 'And what about us? We weren't born yesterday!' He angrily pulled down his cap onto his ears. 'There's no way they can come to any decision without us.' Leaning his whole body forward, he announced grandly, 'You, Sania my dear, just rely on me. I

---

[8] Petrushka is a character from Russian folklore. He is also a puppet, who featured in performances given by travelling puppeteers, similar as a character to the English puppet 'Punch', as in 'Punch and Judy'.

won't leave you in a mess. I'll appear at the court. I'll show him!' Vasiukov shook his thin, wrinkled hand in the air.

It was already dark when they arrived in the town.

'So, they will hear our case at eight o'clock.' Vasiukov pulled a watch out by the strap from his deep pocket. 'That means that we've got over an hour to spare. Let's go straight to the buffet and have a little something hot.'

'Yes, let's,' Sania agreed willingly.

In the buffet, Vasiukov, sitting down at a table, coughed into his fist and casually remarked, 'There'd be no harm in having a little tipple.'

'I won't,' Sania refused. 'But perhaps I could order you a drink?'

'Yes, yes. I'll have a little glass of vodka. The standard measure. Ha, ha, ha!' Vasiukov's eyes glistened gaily. 'You know, I didn't think about bringing much money with me, but we know each other well... So don't you worry about the court. I'll try and do something.'

'Fine. Let's leave it at that,' said Sania, getting upset. She had already started to regret that she had divulged so much about the affair to Vasiukov.

'What's all the fuss about? It is written, brother for brother, and an eye for an eye. After all, aren't we all decent people?'

Vasiukov dragged his drink of vodka on and on, and quickly ate plate after plate of food, with great gusto. He had already finished, and Sania had already settled the bill, when he caught the waiter by the arm and asked for 'another little glass'.

'Uncle Vasia!' said Sania reproachfully.

He gave a guilty smile.

'I'll pay for this one. Dutch courage!'

'Do just as you wish, but I'm off.'

'Just a minute,' he called after her.

Kopaev himself met Sania by the right wing of the station, where the railway office was situated.

'Ah, there you are, you naughty girl! Well, come into the office.'

But in the office, the railway chairman immediately assumed a dry, official tone of voice, and Sania's heart sank.

'What have you caused there? I've read Kosiak's file. Things have gone to pieces! I can't believe it.' He stared straight at Sania with his dark, bulging eyes. He made an awesome impression with his heavy build and his broad shoulders. His jet-black, straight hair, and his ample, yellow, crow-like nose, and those eyes... they all simply hypnotised her. Sania, almost crumpling into a heap, meekly kept silent.

'And please do not remain silent,' he added, somewhat softer. 'Tell me everything, down to the last detail.'

Sania started her story. At first, it came out all confused and inconsistent, but then she got into her stride and told him everything – the squabble with the cashier, the unpleasantness which had occurred because of Sergunkov, the water tanker, the illegal store hut, and also all about how they put up the telegraph poles, all of which had been misunderstood as a deal. It was only about her unsuccessful love affair that she kept quiet.

'Is that everything?' asked Kopaev sternly, when she had finished her story.

Sania hung her head and quietly said, 'That's all.'

Kopaev stood up.

'Well now, off you go to the court. Keep a civil tongue in your head. I'll come without fail.'

Other stationmasters were there, along with traffic controllers of all three station groups, and section supervisors – they had all assembled in the **Red Room**. On the agenda were two matters; the results of this month's work and the disciplinary matter.

The head of traffic management led the production meeting. Sania took refuge right in the corner and was pleased nothing was said about her.

'It looks as though they've forgotten about me. I wish they would!' she thought, hoping that the meeting would go on and on, and never ever finish. She could hardly hear those who stood up to talk – it all seemed so far away, just like an illusion, but then a quiet, unpleasant sound started to bother her and it got louder and louder, growing to such proportions that finally it washed over her, like a hot wave. From time to time, Sania felt something hot breathing into her ear, as if it wanted to say something important, but could not decide whether to, or not. She shuddered, as if suffering from a chill, and unconsciously looked around.

'What's happening to me?' she wondered, burying her chin in the soft woollen jumper, which Nastasia Pavlovna had knitted. It was only when a mild, unrestrained drumming sound rushed over her whole body and she saw stars on the ceiling and walls, that she realised she had a fever.

'That's all I need,' she thought apprehensively, and she gripped the chair tightly to control her shivering. From the opposite corner, Vasiukov, sitting by the shiny black stove, kept winking at her diligently, saying: 'Hold on!'

It was obvious that the warmth from the stove completed his state of bliss, and the deep violet colour of his podgy, porous nose bore witness to this.

Kopaev came into the tribunal and sat side-ways towards the table. Three elected representatives remained at the table – the judge Serpokrylenko, the head of the regional office, a rather angular looking woman, who, despite of her fifty years, was very agile; and a juryman, the head of the locomotive division, a smart, foppish man, with a bushy, light-coloured moustache; and Kosiak, whom Sania knew all too well. All the members of the **Komsomol** group, who were formerly in Sania's care, came to the tribunal. They flocked around her and eyed her up with tense expectation.

Serpokrylenko rose from the table, wrapped on the water jug, and asked: 'Kurilova, do you have any objection to any of the members of the bench?'

'No,' replied Sania, hoarsely.

'In that case, I declare this **Comrades' Court** in session. Note that down,' she said to Kopaev's secretary. 'Comrade Kosiak will begin.'

Kosiak had already written out his speech, and he started reading it carefully and slowly. 'Comrades, just as in the world, there is nothing which cannot be explained. Everything is inter-related and inter-dependant, just as it is in life. There are reasons for the occurrence of all kinds of irregularities in the conduct of those in charge, in deviations from the norm, and from the rules of a socialist society.' Kosiak made a slight pause and first cast a cursory glance at the section head, who was gloomily sitting at the table, and then at the public, who had fallen silent with anticipation.

Then he continued, with some satisfaction. 'The cause and circumstances of the fire, Comrades, are unknown, but the reasons have been fully ascertained: the circumstances arose because of a lack of work discipline at Kasatkino station, and also because of the moral slackness of Kurilova. By way of evidence, I shall put several facts before you. Think them over, Comrades.'

Kosiak started to itemize all Sania's breeches of the rules, going into every detail of each one. There seemed to be an enormous number of them: breeches of state interests – the incident with Sergunkov; illegally issuing tickets; the irresponsible use of the water; then going off to the dance; and even, pandering to the base interests of the masses – the two barrels of beer.

Sania listened to him even more anxiously, holding in check the worsening chill and fresh bouts of shivering. At times, she saw stars in front of her eyes, and then Kosiak would fade away, diminish in stature, but his voice resounded clearly and dryly in Sania's ears, as in an exhaust pipe.

'She, Comrades, even struck up a deal with her suitor over telegraph poles, and, perhaps for other services rendered, she allowed a store hut to be built by the side of the main line.'

'You're lying, you're lying,' Sania shouted finally, unable to take anymore.

Serpokrylenko wrapped on the jug and upbraided Sania severely for contempt of court. Kosiak threw up his hands and waited contemptuously, and on his face he wore an expression as if to say, 'I am willing to suffer for the cause of the truth.' He concluded his speech with a request that Sania be demoted.

Judging by everyone's silence, Sania felt that Kosiak's request had had the desired effect, and she expected the worst.

Then Vasiukov asked to speak. As he got up, he knocked his chair over, then bent down to pick it up, and rattled around with it for some time.

'Will it take you much longer to put that chair straight,' asked Serpokrylenko, finally becoming impatient.

'Only a moment,' answered Vasiukov glibly. 'There we are. Now we can chat. Well now...' He leaned against the stove and a seraphic smile crept across his whole face.

Only then did Sania realise what an unexpected threat Vasiukov's speech might be for her, and she dreaded what he was going to say next.

'That's a good speech Kosiak gave. There's no denying that. And why?' Vasiukov shook and lowered his head, as if he wanted to butt someone. Laughter broke out in the room. 'Because everything has been noted down properly, just as it should be. It's just as we say, "A word is like a sparrow which flies off – you can't catch it". And why should we try and catch it? But, if we write it down, it won't go anywhere.'

'Keep to the point,' interrupted Serpokrylenko.

'I am keeping to the point,' continued Vasiukov, undeterred. 'It is said that you cannot add anything to a closed file, but Kosiak has said his bit because he understands the situation. What he has said about Kurilova is fitting and proper. I said to her recently, "Sania, don't worry, they'll sort it all out properly," I said. "I'll put in a good word for you." And why shouldn't I? Because she's a good, sincere person. So, we went to the buffet together... Why did I mention that?...'

Laughter increased in the room and Serpokrylenko tapped in vain on the jug.

'Listen, Vasiukov!' said Kopaev, drowning the noise of laughter. 'Perhaps you could just pop outside and have a breath of air, and then you might remember!'

'All right then, don't mind if I do! Why not have a breath of fresh air.' He hurried to the door, but tripped up against someone's chair. He was held by the arm and escorted through the door.

The commotion was calmed with some difficulty, and Serpokrylenko pronounced furiously, 'I am deeply disturbed by Kurilova's latest misdemeanour. Before the Comrades' Court, she took her so-called "defence colleague" for a drink at the buffet. It is quite obvious, Comrade Kurilova, that you have not come to this court with a clear conscience.'

'Go on, pile it on!' thought Sania bitterly. 'In for a penny, in for a pound!' When Kopaev's turn came to speak, her heart beat fast and hard, and her vision faded with another bout of fever. 'This one will finish me off,' was the thought that flashed through her mind.

'We have long known Kurilova to be a meticulous, well-disciplined worker.' He sternly turned his crow-like nose and angrily separated his wide, black eyebrows. 'How has it come about that within less than three months of working independently, a previously good worker managed to become so morally lax, if we are to believe Kosiak's findings?'

A muffled hum rippled thought the hall, like a sigh of relief. Serpokrylenko anxiously opened wide her colourless, little eyes with their whitish eyelashes, placed her hand on top of the jug, and froze in that position, just like a statue, and only the violet colour draining from her cheeks betrayed her anxiety.

'Let's suppose that, due to her inexperience, she drained the water tanker, forgetting about the possibility of a fire,' continued Kopaev. 'She even went off to the dance on that ill-fated evening. We may rightly censure her for that. But we must remember that she is not the head of a fire-station, or even the night watchman. We might reproach her, even punish her, for the misunderstanding over the official staffing of the station, but we have no grounds for thinking that it was done as a deal at the State's expense. In any case, regarding the telegraph poles, there is no question of making a deal. I have received a collective letter from the workers at Kasatkino station and, I must be honest, I feel that I am personally to blame, as is our department, for not helping to install lighting earlier at this station. Those workers did all they could. I shall read the letter out to you...'

Those were the last words Sania heard. Something heavy and soft overcame her, causing her to black out. She felt warm tears flowing down her cheeks, tickling her. At one moment she thought that they were not tears at all, but reflections of the sun, and she felt greatly comforted...

Chapter Ten

Sania spent two weeks in hospital with pneumonia. When she had already sufficiently recovered to start walking about the ward, she appeared to have a nervous disorder.

'Bear in mind that you must stick to a strict diet and regular sleeping times,' said the doctor, as she left the hospital, shaking Sania's emaciated hand with his silk-soft palm. 'Perhaps you might stay a little longer here?' He looked at her amusingly, over the top of his glasses.

'No, no, I can't.'

'As you wish! Here is a medical certificate for ten days, and if you need anything else, come and see me.'

Sania travelled, as she had done three months previously, on a goods train, but this time she rode in the locomotive. She saw the same, familiar steppe, which passed mournfully by, but now it was different, being lightly covered with a wet, whitish blanket of the first snow. On the horizon, here and there, small mounds appeared: they were once neat and looked tightly curled with vegetation, like young lambs, but now they were bare, appearing in the distance like grey, bristly hummocks. Sania tried to spot the familiar hillock, the one she had seen then, lit by the fiery twilight glow, but she did not manage to. They all stood under the lowering, dull sky, each one as gloomy as the next.

'Long, boring winter is coming,' thought Sania. 'I must get ready for it. New worries, new problems. And alone again...'

Then, Kasatkino appeared, and the squat barracks and houses rushed towards her. The place where the station had burnt down had been cleared and it was as if nothing had ever stood there. Next to it lay logs and new planks in piles...

'What's all this? Where have these come from?' And there is the log duty-hut...' Pouring out of it was a whole gang of people heading towards the line... 'Why have they gathered there?'

The train gave out three sharp whistles – the stopping signal – and it made a piercing screech as the brake blocks scraped on the wheels, as it shuddered to a halt.

Sania leaned out of the locomotive and immediately understood what was happening. In front of her stood all her fellow-workers, all in new uniform caps with a red band.

They shifted awkwardly from one foot to another in silence, slightly embarrassed, yet pleased.

Sania felt like rushing up to her charges in one jump from the train, but her hands were trembling from weakness and nervousness, and she spent some time searching for the step with her foot.

'There we are,' said Sergunkov, carefully supporting her, and noticing how glad she was to see them all. 'I asked Kopaev himself for the caps, to observe the rules. The boss has been. Have you seen these?' he asked, pointing to the logs. 'We're going to build a new station.'

'We're going to build a station,' came the joyful shout from all directions.

'How did you find out that I was coming?' asked Sania, unable to hide her surprised joy. 'I didn't tell anyone.'

'Vasiukov phoned us,' they answered, vying with each other to reply. '"She's coming," he said, "alive and kicking, hale and hearty".'

Sania noticed a buxom girl in a uniform and boots among the crowd.

'Valia Dunina,' said the girl, introducing herself.

'The new cashier.'

'She was sent to replace you know who.'

No one mentioned either the first name or surname of the former cashier.

When she was at home again, Nastasia Pavlovna told Sania:

'They got rid of her, straight off. Sergunkov and Shilokhvostov tried the hardest. After you went away, she took up with that Valerii. Like two peas in a pod... They decided they were going to move in here. God forgive them, they've no shame, nor conscience! She ran off to him and took her cow along with her on a bit of string. Oh, my dear girl! I look at you and think – how on earth did you manage to win them over? What spell did you use to bewitch them? Kuzmich has just brought round a jar of jam for your homecoming, and Riva – God help us..!' At this point Nastasia Pavlovna burst out laughing, '...has brought a pot of cabbage soup over. You're obviously a strong girl – you've got a backbone of steel!'

Snow fell at dusk. Sania looked long through the window and watched the dark, bare patches of earth being arrayed with snow, and the wide, limitless steppe appeared softer, cleaner...

1957.

Lively

Illustration 5. 'A Drive through a Snowstorm in the Famine-Stricken Districts of Russia', *The Graphic*, May 21 1892.

Foreword to Lively

This work is a tale of a **kolkhoz** 'serf', who has the temerity to ask his Soviet masters for his freedom, which he only gains by his wit and tenacity. He almost loses his life trying to provide a meagre living for himself and his family, and given the sheer weight of bureaucracy and official spite he has to endure, it is a wonder that he is still 'alive' or 'lively', at the end of the story. Fëdor Kuzkin, to give him his proper name, is the main protagonist of the story, but cleverly Mozhaev gave him the emotive nickname '*Zhivoi*', which in Russian means both 'alive' and 'lively'. The name is ironic and highly evocative, and it immediately alarmed **Tvardovskii**, the editor of the **thick journal**, *Novyi mir*, when Mozhaev gave him the manuscript of the story for his consideration to publish it. (See the Introduction, p.xxvi.) This story established Mozhaev as a talented, but controversial, writer. People stood in line for hours to buy a copy of the edition of *Novyi mir* in which it appeared.

Although Mozhaev spent a great deal of energy researching life on the **kolkhoz** and writing about how such farms might be reorganized and become more productive, he was never in a position to suggest the unthinkable, radical step of scrapping the whole system and letting rural folk set up their own independent farms. He could only express that conviction much later, in the latter years of the *glasnost* period, when Soviet ideology was rapidly crumbling. But, at the beginning of this story, Kuzkin has already given up trying to live on the **kolkhoz**: he wants out. This was not something many peasants had the temerity to request – for good reasons, as can be judged by the avalanche of bureaucratic spite such a demand brought down upon the head of the suppliant. Mozhaev fully understood what it meant to kick against the serfdom of the **kolkhoz** system: his own father had resisted getting involved with the **kolkhoz** in the first place, and he found himself dubbed an **'enemy of the people'**, an extremely dangerous epithet with which to be branded in the Stalinist 1930s, when millions of people perished in the GULags during the purges for much less than that.

The title of the story was not the only alarm bell which rang loud in **Tvardovskii's** ears. The very first line set off others: to leave the **kolkhoz** was unthinkable, but to decide to do it within the context of a religious feast day...! The Soviet regime had done much to beat religion out of the peasantry, who generally tended to be more religious than urban dwellers – their churches had been destroyed and desecrated before their very eyes, and their priests had been humiliated and exiled. As the peasant community was collectivized, which meant that their communes were disbanded and their livestock and equipment requisitioned for use on the **kolkhoz**, they felt that their whole life, as they had known it, was coming to an end. They saw these events in apocalyptic terms, as urban activists, who were atheists, invaded their villages and turned their lives upside down. But worse than that – they did so with such violence and malice. They condescendingly viewed the rural population as backward and uneducated, referring to them as 'dark people', and their faith as 'obscurantism'. The peasantry saw the activists and officials as the Anti-Christ, and the **kolkhoz** as a wile of Satan himself. This apocalyptic vision was fuelled by the local priests, who encouraged their parishioners to resist the Anti-Christ with all their might. In extreme cases, peasants took the law into their own hands: just as officials and activists made off with their property or 'dispossessed' them, it was not uncommon for peasants to retaliate by murdering the odd activist and official. Mozhaev did not shy away from linking life on the **kolkhoz** with hints at its Satanic origins, as the peasants saw it. More alarm bells for **Tvardovskii**!

Thus, the **kolkhoz** system was built on blood, tears, and violence. Those peasants who still refused to join the **kolkhoz** by the mid-1930s were simply taxed to the hilt as 'independent' farmers, until they submitted or ran off to the cities. By 1937, when collectivization was just about complete, there were six million fewer rural households than before the campaign started. The damage done to the rural community and agricultural development was incalculable. But it was also a story which remained largely untold until the latter years of the Soviet regime.

Tvardovskii cut a number of the most controversial passages out of the story and these passages are marked in this translation by italics. However, despite toning down the work in this way, Mozhaev was still attacked in the central Soviet press, and by the newspaper *Pravda*, in particular, in which the Secretary of the **Writers' Union**, the conservative Markov, called him a 'blackener of the Soviet countryside'. *Lively* was not reprinted for another six years, and Mozhaev found that he was *persona non grata* within the literary establishment. Scandal followed scandal, when, in 1968, Mozhaev was asked by Liubimov, the director of the Taganka Theatre, to adapt the story for the stage. It was banned on a regular basis until it was finally premièred on 23 February 1989. The play drew international attention and central newspapers praised the production, especially the content, which critics said was still as relevant then, as when it was first written, twenty-one years earlier.

Mozhaev's story shows Soviet officials and bureaucrats at their most vicious. Characteristically, they parade around in military garb, as opposed to wearing civilian clothes – a lead they took from people like Stalin and other prominent political leaders, who also preferred to wear military clothes. Much is made of the background of Motiakov in the story: he is typical of a group of poorly educated, party die-hards, who crop up in Mozhaev's *œuvre* time and time again. They were individually dubbed a '*vydvizhenets*', for which there is no single noun in English. In my translations, I have used the adjective 'fast-tracked'. These people were of proletarian origin, who had worked in factories, and the like, and in the absence of well-educated and politically literate activists, who could be relied upon by the new regime, these people were rapidly promoted within the party structure to high ranks and to posts of considerable responsibility and power. They were sent on courses, which had been specially shortened, in order to get them qualified quickly. Hence the use of the word 'fast-tracked'.

Many specialists and intellectuals, who had occupied important posts before the Revolution, were not trusted by the Bolsheviks because of their so-called 'bourgeois' background. Lenin and his fellow political activists were so unsure of the stability of the new regime, that they did not trust those who were truly well-trained specialists from former tsarist times, and every effort was made to promote those dedicated to the Bolshevik cause, despite their inferior qualifications. This meant that many ardent activists were promoted, who should never have been so. In fact, Lenin, even after just a few years of the Bolshevik regime, became worried by how 'diluted' had become the general standard of education and cultural development amongst those in charge. As Gooding has commented:

Party officials were increasingly appointed from above: elections, if they took place at all, became a formality. The tendency to concentrate unlimited power at the top was reinforced by massive expansion, which saw the party's numbers swell from 20,000 in early 1917 to 732,000 by March 1921. The newcomers who swamped the Old Bolsheviks (as pre-revolutionary members, especially those of intelligentsia background came to be known) were nearly all workers or peasants radicalized by Red Army Service. The educational and cultural level of most was little higher than that of the non-party masses. A party so composed needed, for practical and ideological reasons alike, to be ruled very firmly by the handful of initiates at its apex, and most of its members expected nothing else.[1]

Khruchëv comes in for criticism in this story. References are made to **kolkhoz** amalgamation and to closing regional main towns, or 'capitals'. This was all part of the Soviet penchant for 'big is beautiful', a concept which they saw as typical of the United States of America, whose sky-scrapers, huge cities, and massive farms, seemed to be the epitome of scientific progress and modernity. Stalin had been lured by the attraction of the grand project, believing that the bigger the obstacle to the project, the more heroic was the finished product: this 'proved' that Soviet man was master of his world and destiny, and that all was possible with determination. Khrushchëv, and others after him, were of the same mind-set, and the term 'gigantomania' was coined in Russian.

Mozhaev's character, the official, Guzënkov, loses his job in a regional reorganization exercise, which was instigated under Khrushchëv, as Robert Service has written:

> Khrushchëv also returned to one of his pet schemes by carrying out the amalgamation of **kolkhozes** into bigger units. The number of such farms consequently dropped from 125,000 to 36,000. Khrushchëv wanted the biggest possible units of agricultural production. He also strove to turn **kolkhozes** into **sovkhozes**, thereby increasing the number of peasants employed directly as state employees; and he severely reduced the area under cultivation in private plots.[2]

In this story, Kuzkin meets Guzënkov on a fishing trip, after he had lost his job. At that point he appears a much smaller, insignificant man, an image compounded by his casual dress – he is not in his customary suit. The ogre has been deflated in Kuzkin's eyes. It is also revealed that he fishes with a drag-net, the use of which he himself had forbidden throughout the region. This is indicative of his hypocrisy – a feature common among Mozhaev's bureaucrats.

Mozhaev's Lively is one of his most memorable characters, and his sharp tongue and wit come straight from his author's own heart. More than in any other work to date, Mozhaev shows himself to be a master of peasant speech and dialogue.

---

[1] John Gooding, '*Socialism in Russia: Lenin and his Legacy, 1890-1991*', (Basingstoke: Palgrave, 2002), p.78.
[2] Robert Service, '*A History of Twentieth-Century Russia*', (London: Penguin, 1997), p.350.

Illustration 6. SS Florus and Laurus. 15th century, Novgorod school.

Lively

Chapter One

Fëdor Fomich Kuzkin, known in the village by the nickname 'Lively', had to leave the **kolkhoz** on St Frolov's Day.[1] It had become a tradition in his family that all misfortunes happened to fall on St Frolov's Day. Whether one of his ancestors had committed a grave sin on that day, or whether his homestead had been built on a bad spot... Who could tell? But Lively was certainly unlucky on that saint's day. 'You'll have to change villages, mate,' Old Filat had once advised Lively. 'You're incomers to the village... You're not protected by our church. God has forgotten you on that day. But Satan is winding up his merry-go-round...'

But Lively hadn't the slightest intention of moving villages. He was born and bred in Prudki. It was his grandfather who was the incomer. He used to make quality **bast shoes**, and there were stacks of linden trees around there. His grandfather used to make the shoes and his grandmother used to weave the **footcloths** to go with them, and then they would sell them... That's how they scraped together the money to build their seven-**arshin** log house, in which Fomich now lived. Lively found it absolutely impossible to part with this house 'due to lack of funds', as he used to say. He didn't have a wage. His father and uncle might have got on their feet, had it not been for that cursed St Frolov's Day.

There were three brothers: Foma, Nikolakha and Emelia. They used to work away in the city from spring onwards, as street cobblers. They used to earn decent money. Once, on St Frolov's Day, they settled down for a real boozy session. They strung up a demijohn of vodka and poured it into earthenware mugs. As they drank, they got het-up. Nikolakha tried to cadge grandmother's plot of land from Foma, which she had inherited from some childless uncle. Nikolakha had a big family, but Foma had only one child. But since their grandmother lived at Foma's house, she refused to let Nikolakha have it.

'Why do you need somebody else's land when you don't even tend your own? Leave off, will you!'

Well, one thing led to another, and the brothers, Foma and Nikolakha, came to blows. Nikolakha was strong, so God help Foma!

---

[1] SS Florus and Laurus, to give them their original names, were stone-masons and twin brothers. They were building a temple in Illyria, on the Balkan Peninsula, when they converted to Christianity, whereupon they destroyed the pagan images they had made and turned the temple into a Christian church. As a punishment, the emperor had them drowned in a well, and thus they became martyrs. In Russia, this religious festival is celebrated on 18th August (Old Style). Apart from the religious significance, the day was also associated with an agricultural activity, as was common in rural Russia. Typical of the tradition, there are a number of sayings associated with this festive day, such as 'If, by St Frolov's Day, you don't finish your [winter] sowing, you'll have a mass of wild flowers and corn cockle [in your crops].' There is another phrase which expresses a superstition connected with St Frolov's Day: 'Don't plough with horses on SS Frolov and Laurus Day, or there will be cattle plague.' Hence, these festive days were religious, but they were also connected to traditional farming practices.

Once Nikolakha and Emelia went down to the river to fetch a tree brought down by a storm. They loaded the wood as high as the shaft-bow. But the sledge got stuck – so Nikolakha unharnessed it, saying, 'Let the horse get cold – then it will pull better.'

He bound the shafts with the saddle-straps and put the harness on himself.

'Emelia, you'll have to rock the sledge, or I'll never shift it from the spot.'

Emelia rocked it, Nikolakha dug his **bast shoes** into the snow, and the shafts creaked. But no sooner had the sledge moved forward, that he kept on pulling, right as far as Prudki, with the horse following on behind.

Well, they had a bust-up, Foma and Nikolakha. Nikolakha grabbed him just once and forced him down onto the bench. Foma just went quiet. He took to his bed for about a week, and then died. That's how Fëdor Fomich became an orphan. It's true that, at first, Emelia and his mother helped him. But not for long.

Nikolakha gave his eldest daughter's hand away in marriage. The wedding happened to be on St Frolov's Day. The brothers, Nikolakha and Emilia, got worked up again on this occasion: they got into an argument, this time, about who could drink the most. Nikolakha drank a total of sixteen tumblers of vodka. Emelia drank fifteen. But on the sixteenth, he fell under the table and died.

All these were major misfortunes. But there were minor ones too that happened on Frolov Day. In 1924, when Lively was just a teenager, he killed his own horse. On St Frolov's Day in Prudki, it was traditional to bless the horses with holy water and then a race was announced. There were prizes: a bucket of vodka, a sheep, or a set of wheels – all the menfolk clubbed together to buy them. They used to race on the cattle track – a wide pathway along which cattle were usually driven to pasture towards the forest. But that year, telegraph poles had been set up along the cattle track. People hadn't got used to them being there.

Fomich raced a pair of horses: he borrowed his neighbour's horse, and, when it had been blessed, he harnessed it to the other.

'If one starts to fall behind, the other will pull it along,' he thought.

He drove his pair hard and got really excited – the family spirit in him was plain to see. He urged the pair on with more cunning than the rest. He broke away from the pack and headed for the verge, thinking, 'I'll have a clear run there'. He gathered speed. Just how the telegraph pole reared up in front of him – he couldn't explain. He just remembered flying through the air straight at the pole. There was no way he could have turned to the side, because his horse, Bulanets, was pulling to the left, and the neighbour's, Pegach, was pulling to the right...[2] It was Pegach which pulled the hardest. Bulanets hit the pole head-on and Fomich went head over heels. When he came to, Bulanets lay lifeless by the pole...

Fomich remembered all this while sitting next to the window. His house was unusually empty. The kids had gone off to school and the youngest hung around with the

---

[2] The names 'Pegach' and 'Bulanets' have meanings in Russian, associated with the colours of horses: 'Pegach' is related to the word for 'skewbald' (irregular markings of white and brown or red), and 'Bulanets' means 'dun' (a dull, greyish brown colour).

neighbours' kids in the street – some were barefoot, others were even trouserless. They didn't seem to notice the fresh autumn breeze… His wife was winnowing buckwheat on some coarse cloth in front of the house.

The buckwheat had been delivered that day from the **kolkhoz** threshing-floor – all sixty-two kilograms of it. What kind of pay was that with seven mouths to feed? What were they going to eat for the rest of the year?

Yesterday evening the chairman had said, 'Don't expect any wheat. We can't even make our state quota…'

As a family, their allocation of rye had been delivered long ago and there was now just enough left for seed. 'And don't expect any spuds – they've all rotted.' Naturally, those who had grown them had made sure they were okay. Once again, the men had managed to get some extra hay in the meadows, and the womenfolk had done their bit, somehow or other. Lively worked as a kind of **kolkhoz** supply-man, and he was always on the move: on one occasion, he'd got hold of some sacks, then on another, some vats, a harness later on, and then some carts… Doesn't a farm always need something? He was credited sometimes with two, sometimes with three, **workday units**. They weren't too badly off with **workday unit**s – with his wife's efforts, they had clocked up eight hundred and forty units in all. But they had 'earned' just sixty-two kilograms of buckwheat. How can you live on that? 'Such generosity nowadays,' thought Fomich. 'They used to give everyone equal **workday unit**s… Now the **brigade leader** gets a salary of more than a thousand roubles a month, and tally clerks and all kinds of managers get proper wages, but those who work out in the fields, or people like me who run errands – we get sod all. We all have to fend for ourselves…'

A while back, he thought that the **workday unit** would be worthless and he thought about jacking in his job as a supply-man and getting one which would involve him closer with grain. But he dallied, weighing up the pros and cons… Now it was too late – he'd missed the boat. There'd be thin pickings until the next harvest.

But then, looking at it from another point of view, he wouldn't have too much trouble in getting some work that paid – but you needed to be strong and nifty. However, he had only two fingers left on his right hand, because of the war. It wasn't so much a hand, as a claw. Of course, he could manage to use it… if only to transport grain. Now, if you did that kind of work, you could pinch enough for lunch in your shirt, and then enough for the evening in your trouser pockets. Every little helps. But what was there to live on now? The sum of his livestock was a single goat. What could he do? So he came to the conclusion that he had to leave the **kolkhoz** – for ever.

Lively had had a hell of a time with the new **kolkhoz** chairman, Guzënkov. Last year their **kolkhoz** was amalgamated with the adjoining one, so the administrative offices were transferred to Svistunovo, and a new chairman was sent from the regional centre. He was a big noise of formidable proportions and famous throughout the whole region. Apparently, he'd been head of all regional departments in turn, one after the other. Guzënkov had been the chairman of the regional consumers' unions, the head of the meat procurement organization, and even the director of the consumer service establishment. He was addressed as Mikhail Mikhailovich… But everyone had forgotten the time when he was simply called 'Misha the Spark' in Tikhanovo. Where he'd come from – nobody knew.

In 1932, the old, smoky steam mill, which stood in the centre of Tikhanovo, was converted into an electricity station. Nothing of the dirty brick building changed externally, which looked like a large warehouse, only the iron chimney was rebuilt, thicker and taller. Instead of the frequent farting sounds and the heavy breathing of the flour-grinding steam engine, now this warehouse let out abrupt, shrill shrieks: 'Screeeeech! Screeeeeech!' It sounded like someone chopping logs with a hacking cough. And, keeping time with each 'hack', all the light bulbs in the village would flare up and grow dim, by turns. Misha the Spark turned up on the streets of Tikhanovo in an oily, thick cloth cap. He was soon promoted within the regional committee of the **Komsomol**, being a rare representative of the working class in Tikhanovo. Gradually, Misha the Spark vanished into thin air... A couple of years later, the old flour-grinding steam engine was working again, in place of the electricity station. And Mikhail Mikhailovich Guzënkov had become firmly established amidst the managerial ranks.

An incident caused Guzënkov and Fomich to clash during the first days of his chairmanship. Naturally, it was all Lively's fault, or, to be more precise, it was his tongue, that was to blame.

The first thing Guzënkov did was to put all managers, bookkeepers, and cattlemen on fixed salaries. And just to make sure they knew who was boss, he 'invited' them into his office, one by one, for an 'endurance test': he did not ask them to sit down, but he sat firing questions at them for ages, while they stood.

The men from Prudki arrived in Svistunovo like a gang and burst into Guzënkov's office *en masse*, some occupying the chairs, some just squatted down along the walls. That's what they used to do in Filka Samochenkov's time... Guzënkov eyed them up with curiosity for a long time, then he slapped his hand down on the desk and asked: 'What are you lot doing? Have you come to a pigsty or to the chairman's office? Quick march out of here! Come back in, strictly one by one... On my command.'

They emerged glum from his office and remarked to those who had gathered by the office porch: 'He sits there, but he makes you stand to attention... What a boss!'

'And why's that? It's because he graduated from the academy by the back door', quipped Lively. 'He passed through the corridors, but they wouldn't let him into the classes. He sniffed around the back door in the bins, which is where he picked up a thing or two. That's why he's so stroppy.'

Someone informed on him to Guzënkov. He took against Lively and he refused to put him on a fixed salary, leaving him on the **workday-unit** rate. Also, he told the bookkeeper to give him personally, as chairman, a special report of every trip Fomich made as a supply-man.

'You just watch, you son-of-a-bitch! You can stare till you're blue in the face, but you won't catch me out!' thought Fomich, angrily. He had never stolen – he was too smart for that. What awful laws there were! Who wants to go to prison? Money is not like rye: however you hide the traces, it can still be found. Korneich was a cunning bookkeeper, who could spot a trick a mile off in any document.

Lively had wanted to leave to be a bookkeeper on the farm. But again, Guzënkov wouldn't release him: he'd be freer and earn more money – even a salary! In a word, the chairman had got Lively cornered, like a hare before a fox. You can run all you like, but it comes down to the same thing – you'll end up knackered and fall flat on your face…

So once again, there's no way other than to leave the **kolkhoz** – but to do what? If they left the house for somewhere else, they'd not get on their feet, even with a salary. Anyway, they wouldn't let him go. What about asking for suitable paid work here? But whom could he ask? Who'd give him such a job? As soon as you leave the **kolkhoz**, there's no one to ask for work. But if you stayed on, you'd hit a blank wall. So the bottom line is – you're buggered. And all this fell on St Frolov's Day.

'Fate is testing me,' thought Lively.

So, once and for all, he decided to leave the **kolkhoz**. It might be a mistake, but somewhere he would find a job. Once he had finally decided, he felt relieved and happier. 'Fate has again put a full stop to my life on St Frolov's Day, but I've changed it to a comma…'

He even stood up, and he was about to take his balalaika to sing 'Bold Khaz-Bulat', when he remembered that his neighbour had arrived back from the regional main town.[3] He was afraid he might leave for the meadows and he could do with paying him a visit before he did… He might even treat him to a drink, on account of it being a saint's day.

Chapter Two

Lively's neighbour really knew how to receive a guest. The host, Andrei Spiridonovich Kirillov, who was simply known as Andriusha, had just had 'one for the road', and he was fixing his wooden leg to his stump. A cut-glass decanter, full of dullish-blue moonshine, was on the table next to a snowball berry pie, already cut in slices. By the fact that Andriusha was fixing his wooden leg to his stump, Lively could immediately tell that he was off to mow the meadow. Andriusha had two wooden legs: one he called 'Gun-Stock', and the other 'Hub'. 'Gun-Stock' had a highly polished side plank, which looked like an ironing board that went right up to his hip. Andriusha attached it to his hip with two straps and he lent on it with his hand. Andriusha would put this false leg on when he went out to work at the regional finance office, or when he simply wanted to take a stroll. Now, 'Gun-Stock' stood by the doorway, and Andriusha was fastening on 'Hub', a short false leg with a brass ring on the end. With 'Hub', Andriusha could mow, plough, or even dance.

Andriusha lived and worked in the main regional town and he used to come and help his mother with her homestead. The **kolkhoz** had assigned her one-and-a-quarter hectares of land in exchange for a calf she had handed over. It's true that peasants were only given what was left over, after mowing, for surrendering a calf. But that wasn't to be sneezed at. Otherwise, you'd have to drive your cow away from home to pasture.

'Are you getting ready to mow your meadow, Andrei Spiridonovich?' Fomich asked warmly, having greeted him.

'That's right,' he replied. 'But why are you not at work?'

---

[3] This is a traditional Russian romance – a song which has love as its theme, but its ending is frequently tragic. In this song, Khaz-Bulat, a warrior, is tempted with gifts of weapons and a horse, to surrender his wife. However, the deal is not worth pursuing when it is revealed that she lies in his tent, with a dagger in her heart.

'I've just done my last stroke... I've waved goodbye to my collective duties.'

'Come and join us at table, neighbour,' said Old Matrëna, Andriusha's mother, a stooping, but still sturdy old woman. 'Let's raise a glass to the saint's day.'

'To your good health, as they say.'

Lively went through to the table, poured himself out a full glass, drained it, broke off a slice of pie, sniffed it, and started eating it.

The pie was a little bitter – Old Matrëna had picked the berries a bit early. A smell of burnt rubber from the moonshine hit him. But Fomich drank it with pleasure and stuffed his face, while continuing to tell them how he had 'waved goodbye to his collective duties'.

Andriusha finally adjusted his wooden leg, took a few strides on it as if it were a boot, and jokingly said:

> *Happy is the man*
> *Who has a single leg.*
> *His trousers don't wear out*
> *And he's happy with one peg.*

Andriusha was a big chap, and when he walked, the floor boards creaked piteously.

'Well, he lives a good life,' thought Lively, looking at Andriusha's red neck and his powerful body, with his wide officer's strap across his belly.

'Aren't you worried about supplementary taxes?' asked Andriusha, sitting down at the table.

'What can they confiscate from me? An armful of rags?!' Fomich wriggled on his stool and hesitated. 'I haven't heard of supplementary taxes being given out recently.'

'But what if they exile you?'[4]

'Isn't there Soviet power there also?'

'There, it's the commandant's law.'

'So, I'll be the commandant's assistant...'

'So, what is it you're after?'

'I just want a little job, like yours. I'm fading away, I need to put on a bit of weight. A job a bit like yours.'

Andriusha burst out laughing, and even his chest shook.

'Where will you go? Just look at yourself, mate...'

Besides Andriusha, Lively looked like an old gelding next to a shire horse. Andriusha's skin was all white with a shining bald patch and a round, rosy face. Fomich

---

[4] Here, Andriusha is talking about the authorities sending peasants off to a distant prison camp for non-payment of taxes as a punishment.

had an almost slate-like, yellow pallor, which was very dark, with sunken, bony cheeks, and he had a dark moustache and dark hair, which made him look even thinner. He really did look like a horse ready for the knacker's yard. His collar bones stood out on his shoulders, and his spine was all knobbly, like a horse's. Only his brown eyes were animated, young, and really lively.

'I'm an invalid from the Civil War, but you were invalided in the Patriotic War...[5] There's the difference!' said Andriusha, with a smile. 'I was comfortable before the war. There weren't many of us invalids. They valued us.'

Andriusha poured the rest of the moonshine out into their glasses. They drank it in one.

'So, what are you going to do?' he asked Fomich.

'Well, I've just been sitting and thinking about that. No matter which way you turn, you're buggered. There's no grain. The kids' clothes and shoes are worn out. Can't buy any 'cause we've no money. There's only one way out: take to your coffin alive, as the song says. But hang on, I thought. There is a way out! When the market comes, I'll borrow some money and buy a cow. What does milk fetch these days? Three roubles a litre. If I manage to sell six litres of milk a day, I'll get the money back in five months. I'll pay the loan off in full. I really know how to choose a cow. The first thing you have to do is look how the hair spreads out. If it starts to fork on its shoulder blades, that means that the interval between milk-producing periods is up to four weeks. But if it forks on its back, it means that it will be dry for seven weeks before calving. In that case, the cow's a dead loss, a loafer. Then, you have to feel the depression – there's a kind of depression between its stomach its chest, the one just at the end of the vein. If you can push in your index finger up to the first joint, that means that she will produce a **pood** of milk a day. Then I also look at the tail: if you part the hair at the very end and there is a sort of excretion, it means its milk is creamy! Your milk can stand for a full day and night, and if you put a brass five-**kopeck** coin on the surface, it won't sink. That's the sort of cow I would choose!'

'Well, what's the hitch, then?' asked Andriusha, smiling.

'Nothing at all. I've decided to borrow the money – three thousand. I decided to approach my neighbours – you, that is. Can you let me have a thousand roubles and six months to pay it back? I'll give you an IOU. All above board.'

Andriusha roared with laughter.

'Your mother must have dropped you on your head at birth. Ah, Lively, you old bugger! You'll be the death of us! And I was all ears...'

'You haven't understood me at all!' said Lively, with a sigh of regret.

'Listen, come out with me and mow the hay! I'll give you a rouble for every **sotka** you cut... And a **pood** of millet on top. Is that all right with you, mother?' said Andriusha, turning round to the old woman.

---

[5] The Russian epithet for the Second World War is 'The **Great Patriotic War**'.

'Well, that's great!' sounded Old Matrĕna's voice from the stove.[6] 'I'd thought about hiring someone anyway. You had to go to the regional office. You're up to your neck in your own problems.'

Both Lively and Andriusha were pleased with their deal. They slapped hands together and set off for the meadows. Apart from his scythes and a whetstone, Andriusha also grabbed a half-litre of vodka, and Fomich took his gun.

'We'll have a little drink this evening, when we're tired of mowing,' said Andriusha.

The meadows were a long way off. The land they had been allotted in exchange for the calves was beyond the Luka, which used to be a long winding river and lake, but the bed was now dry. The best pasture land used to be around there and, on a number of occasions, the menfolk from Prudki had fought over them with the men from Brĕkhovo village, just over the other side of the water. But now, these lands had become overgrown with bushes of linden and snowball trees on the hillocks, and with alder in the dips. And in the places where the meadows remained, oak saplings grew. You couldn't get a tractor there – it would have broken the mowing blades. The **kolkhoz** had not managed to mow the hay there, and so it had been allotted to them, in exchange for their calves.

The road to the meadows followed the river Prokosha, which formed intricate loops here and there, as if out of sheer mischief. The gently sloping sandy banks, which were overgrown on the ridges with sharp-leaved willow, rose, and blackcurrant, alternated with bare, bluish-grey steep-sided banks of clay, which from afar looked like thick wedges of sliced hempseed-oil cake.

Andriusha and Lively sat down to rest at Kuziakov Ravine. The chilly morning breeze had finally died down and a clinging heat haze flickered, as in summer; it hung over the riverside willows, over the fresh, sappy greenery of the after-grass, and over the brownish-yellow, squat hayricks. The wide stretches of water shone bright, as if just for show, and they seemed to spread out even wider. The plain, adorned in bright green, seemed to disperse far off, right up to the blue edge of the wood, and the pure firmament, with its cool, greenish hue, soared up high, and everywhere was imbued with a kind of abundance and grandeur. But the brown hayricks, which had been permeated by the rain, cast pathetic figures. Perhaps this all looked sad because of a single, solitary kite which hovered in the sky, letting out a prolonged whistle, modulating its cry as it went: 'Pheww-liii-riuliuiuiu…' It seemed as though the kite was goading someone, making fun of them.

'Oh, Mother-nature!' sighed Lively. 'Just tell me why the earth is so giving, and man so grasping?'

'What are you on about?' asked Andriusha, sat on the edge of the ravine: he had removed his wooden leg, which caused some clay clods to fall into the water.

'Just take this Kuziakov Ravine. Do you know how many sheat-fish live down there?[7] Masses! But try as you may, you'll not catch them. The only chap who could catch them

---

[6] The stove in a peasant house was an extremely large brick or stone construction. It was designed so that food could be cooked in it, like an oven, but also a bed could be made on top of it. Because of the transference of heat through the bricks, it was always warm, though not hot, and traditionally the old folk and children used to sleep on top of it.

was Kuziak. But he died. What a mean bloke he was to die and not let on how he did it. He took his secret with him to the grave, curse his old bones!'

'Did you try to get it out of him?'

'Many a time! But he didn't let on... But who was he to me? He didn't even confide in his own son! I even repaired his nets and stood him some moonshine... No luck! What would it have cost him? He might have told me as a mark of respect for my large family. If only I knew his secret... Ah! Not a single **kolkhoz** would bother me then. I'd catch about four poods of sheat-fish and not have a care in the world.'

'I once went fishing with him for sheat-fish,' said Andriusha.

'Oh, yes? And what was the auspicious occasion?'

'I did him a favour on a little tax matter,' said Andriusha discreetly, cunningly screwing up his eyes. 'Do you know how to bait the hook?'

'Absolutely! I read it in my book... It gives a blow by blow account.'

'What oil do you fry the mussel in?'

'In vegetable oil.'

'And on what kind of line do you put the bait?'

'Just ordinary...'

Fomich though for a moment, then added, 'On woollen line.'

'Just you remember!.. The line should be made of pure flax.'

'Bloody hell! And was it him who told you that?'

'Yes.'

'Anything else?'

Lively stared at Andriusha.

'Did he get the sheat-fish to show?'

'He did... They came right up from the depths. They circled around the boat. One even jumped right out onto his oar.'

'And were they good ones?'

'Head as big as a horse's feeding bucket...'

'The bugger! How did he land it? Tell me, how on earth did he bait the line? There's not a single book that tells you that.'

'He put his arm into the water up to his elbow. He held it there for a moment, and then he said, "The sheat-fish is full... It'll eat no more bait, but spit it out".'

'Mother of God!'

---

[7] The sheat-fish is a large, fresh-water fish, which is common in the rivers of eastern Europe. Its zoological name is *Silurus glanis.*

Lively struck his knees in vexation. 'He was just having you on. No way! Would Kuziak ever tell anyone? He wasn't human – he had a heart of stone!'

Some ducks suddenly emerged from a bend. They closed ranks, keeping their distance so close to the water from the kite, so that when Lively took a shot at them, it was as if he had shot them from above. Two ducks flew head over heels, straight into the water, but a third duck got as far as the slope of the other bank. Suddenly, it let out a penetrating quack, and at that moment the kite struck it: it snapped, like a dry stick, with such force that its feathers flew everywhere. The kite carried it low, hiding in the willow undergrowth, as if it had turned the corner of a house.

'The villain!' exclaimed Lively after the kite. 'That's just how they live. Did you see how it got it? Without so much as a by your leave... Just as if I'd shot the duck for him.'

Fomich strained his neck for some time to see where the kite had gone. 'Eh, it's a shame I don't have a boat to go after it! I'd teach it to go after someone else's property.'

When Lively had fetched the ducks, he became fidgety, and said, 'Perhaps we shouldn't put things off till the evening. After all, ducks go off quickly! Let's put 'em on to cook now... And we'll have a drink! It's Frolov Day, after all. As for the mowing, I'll finish it on my own for you.'

Andriusha hesitated for politeness sake, and the moonshine they had already consumed left him jaded.

'Well, I'll bung you thirty roubles on top,' he agreed.

'We've got a couple of ducks, but only one bottle. Do you know what will happen? We've loads of food, but the vodka will run out. Give me the thirty roubles now and I'll stand you a bottle, as if it were my treat... My shout!'

'As you wish,' said Andriusha, pulling out a wallet from his pocket and handing over a thirty-rouble note to Lively.

'You get the fire going. I'll be back in a moment. It can't be more than three kilometres to Prudki. No further than that. And don't worry about the meadow. I'll mow it so short that you'll see a ten-**kopeck** piece at ten paces. What a turn up for the books! Imagine, this is the first time I've had any luck on Frolov Day.'

Lively happily trotted off to Prudki.

Chapter Three

The news that an independent mower had appeared in Prudki spread through the village like wild fire. The milkmaids, up to their ears in work at the farm, used to hire itinerant mowers, anyone from demobilized soldiers to moonlighters. Now, one of their own people was at hand. Fomich was inundated with requests – and even more numerous from hapless widows, than from the milkmaids. Anyone who didn't have millet to pay him offered potatoes or rye – Fomich would take anything. First, he took a deposit and, to ensure that no one else grabbed the job, at the edge of the owner's plot he cut a swathe as fine as a clipped sheep's back, and left his mark by leaving a pile of hay before going on to the next customer. 'Now anyone who takes my place will have to answer to me. This way, my mind is at rest,' thought Fomich.

But rivals did turn up. Old Filat was the first to come trotting along. Early one morning, when the dew around the bushes was still steaming and had not yet had time to subside on the grass, Fomich found him on Marishka Britaia's plot. The old man was sitting on a pile of hay right by Fomich's 'marker' pile. The wooden handle of a sharpening tool jutted out from the top of his kersey boot. The blade of his scythe, fixed to an oak shaft, hung above his head.

'What are you up to, Uncle Filat? Did you spend the night here?' asked Fomich.

'I might have well spent the night here, Fedia... I can't sleep. Day or night – it's all the same to me.'

'You should be lying on your stove. Why have you come here?'

'It's my niece's, Marishka's, plot.'

'So what?'

'How do you mean, "So what?" I've come to mow it.'

'What? Have you only just woken up? She gave the job to me. Where were you before?'

'Where I was is none of your business. Don't push me, Fedka! You're still a young 'un. We'll mow together and share the cash. Otherwise, I'll have nothing to patch my trousers with, not to mention getting an anorak before the cold weather comes.'

'No doubt you'll be mowing on all fours, Uncle Filat,' Lively remarked sarcastically.

'You whelp!' said Old Filat, turning puce. 'You start first, but mind I don't nick your heels.'

Old Filat was a wiry, slightly stooping old man with a sparse, straggly little beard and a slightly pock-marked, sheet-white, wrinkled face. Whether he got angry or laughed, he had the same expression on his strangely-stretched, immobile, grinning lips. Whoever saw this 'grin' for the first time thought that Old Filat was silently crying. He lived alone: both sons had perished in the war, and he had buried his old lady just after that... He didn't have a pension because he had been a **kolkhoz** farmer, as had his sons. Old Filat got by as best he could: in the winter he made toboggans, and in the summer he wove baskets and fishing nets – large, single-stitch nets, nicknamed 'sandpipers' in Prudki. He used to tan the nets himself with the juice from purple loosestrife.

'Set against mine, your nylon nets are like a reed compared to a willow,' Old Filat used to say. 'A stick will rot before my nets will – they're made to last.'

Despite the fact that Old Filat had never ever seen nylon – he'd only heard about it – his nets compared favourably with nylon ones, and people used them for years and they caught fish well.

But that summer, there was a campaign against poachers and skivers. Every village had to weed out its skivers. Officials came down on Old Filat like a ton of bricks. A cart came from the regional administrative offices with a couple of officials. Their own villager, Pashka Voronin, a **brigade leader** from Prudki, brought them. They filled a whole cart with these nets and confiscated every last inch of thread...

'You should be working on the **kolkhoz** instead of skiving,' preached an unfamiliar official, wearing a peaked cap bearing two oak leaves as an insignia.[8]

Old Filat compliantly fussed around the cart, helping them to pack up the nets.

'Pashka, you make sure to avoid those potholes: even a little sandpiper falling under the wheel is enough to break it,' he ordered the **brigade leader**.

'Fool!' said the official in the cap with the oak-leaf insignia. 'Do you think we're buying your nets? Or taking them for storage? We're confiscating them... Don't you understand?'

'What's there not to understand? You go ahead and take 'em,' muttered the old man impassively, looking long and hard after the cart from under his hand with his teeth bared, either crying or laughing...

Fomich understood Old Filat's position and he fell deeply pensive. It would have been the decent thing to share the job with the old man. But he had to look out for himself. He had a houseful of mouths to feed: every morning they opened up, saying, 'Give us something to eat!' But who would feed Fomich? He sat down next to the old man and lit up a roll-up.

'I dare say, Old Filat, that your sharpening tool dates from when you were an independent farmer.' Lively pulled the tarred handle out from the top of Old Filat's boot. 'It must be twenty years since anything like this was on sale.'

The sharpening tool was black and in very good nick, in fact, just like new.

'My eldest son got me a couple of these before the war, from abroad,' said Old Filat. 'I wore one out.'

'Let's have a go!' Lively steadied the blade of his scythe against the toe of his kersey boot, which looked every bit as tired as Old Filat's pair, and he set to sharpening the uneven tip. 'Scraaape, scraape...' it went, echoing on the other bank of the river. Then Fomich placed the scythe down on its shaft and, straining so much that his Adam's apple shot upwards, he finished sharpening the end.

'Wonderful! You can say what you like, it's a lot handier than sharpening it with a whetstone. My scythe is a pain in the neck: two swipes and it's already blunt. I bet yours is Viennese, isn't it?' Fomich looked enviously at the sharpened, narrow, snake-like blade of Old Filat's scythe.

'It's got two hallmarks,' said Old Filat proudly.

They were silent for a moment and looked beyond the lake at the hayricks, which had turned black from the rain...

'What a summer it's been! The hayricks are rotting,' remarked Fomich.

'Call those hayricks? They're just heaps of hay... They're not hayricks. There's just three forks-full in one of those ricks. The rain goes right through them. They rot on top and the rain collects at the foot. They put them here today, over there tomorrow... Phah!' The old man spat, threw away his fag-end and stood on it with his boot. 'All the

---

[8] The oak leaves indicate that the official was a representative of the forestry commission.

meadows have been "stained" like that. When we used to make hayricks, you'd not shift them in ten cartloads. They were real ricks... They were taller than oak trees! And we always put them in the same place.'

'That's true,' Fomich said in agreement. 'When our **kolkhoz** started, our team used to have me cap the hayrick.'

'You, cap the hayrick?! You were just a whelp. There was no one better in Prudki to cap a hayrick than Father Vasilii. And he assembled the foundation sheaves himself. He put all the sheaves arse downwards. He built one rick next to the other and they looked as though they'd been licked clean. They used to stand for a year intact. He was a real craftsman.'

'Yes... Voronok and I arrested him. Voronok was the chairman of the poor committee, and I was the secretary of the rural soviet...[9] "The authorities are here, Mother. Pack your bags!" he said. "No," we said. "We're only taking you to the rural soviet, Father Vasilii." "But they're waiting for us both there," said the priest. And he was dead right. The plenipotentiaries from the regional offices were there, waiting for him. He knew everything. He could suss anything out.'

'He was a bright spark,' Old Filat agreed. 'Well, Fedka, that's enough sitting around...'

Old Filat stood up, threw off his threadbare jumper, and grabbed his scythe by the shaft.

'I'll go ahead, as we agreed.'

'When did we agree anything?' Lively went slack-jawed in amazement.

But it was as if the old man had not heard. He took a couple of short swipes with his scythe in the corner, mowed a small patch, and he was off along the length of the plot. He mowed with amazing ease, steady on his feet, leaving neat little piles of grass.

'There's an uninvited work-mate for you! What am I to do with him? I can't just drag him off by his shirt,' thought Fomich. 'I suppose he needs to feed himself as well.'

Lively would have easily kept up with the old man, but in his row, as if on purpose, thick stems of false spirea and tall, reddish-brown tussocks of grass were everywhere. The grass had stood too long and the false spirea had wound its roots around it, like wire, and his scythe rang out as it hit it. You had to watch out, otherwise you'd cut your heels. You could strike about ten times, but the scythe wouldn't cut it – it just bruised the grass and that was it. Fomich had to keep stopping for a moment, take out his whetstone, and sharpened the scythe. But there was no stopping Old Filat – off he went, and his shirt even billowed!

'What sort of scythe is that?' thought Fomich. 'It's just like a snake. And the old man is still a wiry old boy! To look at him you'd think he'd fall over if you blew on him, but just look how he gets stuck in. Perhaps it's just as well he's turned up as a helper. The other day, when I'd finished mowing Andriusha's plot, I had still to rake up the hay and make a hayrick, but who had I to help me? I couldn't have put Dunia on top to cap the

---

[9] See Appendix II, p.441.

rick – she doesn't know how. [10] I had to do the lot – stack it, cap it, and press it. You climb up one hayrick after another till your tongue hangs out. But stick that old boy on top and the job's a good 'un. And he's got some good forks – four-pronged, proper hay-forks. You can't buy those nowadays.'

When Fomich had finished mowing his row, Old Filat was already getting his breath back.

'Well, Fedka, now eat your words! Didn't I tell you I'd be at your heels?'

Old Filat sat with his mouth open, like a goose in the midday heat, with his dark blue shirt looking even darker from sweat, as it stuck to his back and chest.

'Your scythe is worth its weight in gold!' said Fomich, wiping the sweat away with his sleeve. 'You didn't have to sharpen it once along a whole row. Honest to God, I wouldn't have believed it if someone had told me.'

'In times gone by, Fedka, I've mowed half of Russia with this scythe. I've been around the Don, the Kuban, even as far as the *Caspcasian* mountains.[11] Our **Riazan** mowers were highly rated. When I used to go to the Topknots' market, where they hired mowers, I used to write on my shoe, 'Fifty kopecks', and then go to sleep. Whoever wanted me could have me. I never accepted less than anyone else. If they didn't like it, to hell with them!' [12]

They mowed for ages, with occasional pauses, until the sun set behind the hill. Only then, as they were setting off for home, did Old Filat admit: 'I had to compete with someone else to work with you, Fedka.'

'Who else wanted to?' asked Fomich, pricking up his ears.

'Spiriak Voronok…'

'Why does he need the work?' said Fomich, frowning. 'He wants to get his hands on everything.'

'Yesterday, I was on my way to the cattle farm. He was pestering me like a lame devil, winking at me. "Let's get in on Fomich's moonlighting," he says.'

'I'll give him a share! He'll get my scythe right in his teeth,' said Fomich, boiling up.

'So I says, "And what happens if he don't agree? Then what?" "Then," he says, "I'll shop him to the chairman. I'll get nothing, but neither will he".'

'He tries to put the frighteners on me with the chairman!'

'You just mind – he'll be on you like a ton of bricks this evening.'

'I won't let that scrounger past my door,' said Fomich.

---

[10] 'Dunia' is an affectionate shortening of Lively's wife's full name, 'Avdotia'.

[11] The old man confuses the word for Caucasus Mountains and the Caspian Sea. The rendition here is an approximation of what he says in the original, to give a flavour of his muddled language.

[12] 'Topknot' is a slang word for Ukrainians, who traditionally shaved their heads, except for a single tuft of hair. The Ukraine was one of the most productive areas of the Russian empire and the former Soviet Union for wheat.

Chapter Four

That evening, while it was still light, Spiriak slipped into Lively's house without so much as a knock. Even though he was well beyond sixty, he was still known by his nickname Spiriak.[13] He was also called Voronok.[14] In former times, he had had some really good jobs. And even now, although he only worked as a cow-hand on the farm, in so far as his elder brother was a **brigade leader** in Prudki, Spiriak still had a lot of clout. He had a badger-like look about him: he had a pointed, blunt-nose face, with a black moustache, and a little white beard, a low, cropped forehead with strong, grey, bristle-like short hair, which looked as though it had been sleeked down. Spiriak's gait also had something badger-like about it – he came into the house as if he were darting into his burrow. You'd never hear him… He'd stand on the threshold and twist his head as if he were having a good sniff around. He greeted you in such as way that he stretched out his neck, as though intending to bite you.[15]

'Good evening all! Bread and salt to you all.'[16]

Fomich and Avdotia were eating millet gruel. The first shift of children, having eaten their fill, was already leaving the table and pottering about right there, on the floor.

'Come right in, now you've crossed the doorstep,' said the housewife. 'Don't stand by the door. We don't charge for standing.'

Fomich kept quiet.

Spiriak sat down at the corner of the table and unceremoniously looked into the pot.

'Is that millet gruel? I keep my millet for pancakes.'

'We don't keep any for pancakes, 'cause we don't even have any for gruel,' said Avdotia.

Fomich put down his spoon and looked sternly at Spiriak.

'What are you doing, playing the inspector? Isn't it enough that your brother is ripping off the **kolkhoz**?'

'My brother isn't even taking his **pood** of millet from the farm. It's only Father Vasilii who used to rake in money at that time,' sarcastically remarked Spiriak Voronok, smirking into his beard.

'You and Pashka even robbed the dead!'

'How did we rob the dead?'

'You removed the headstones from their graves… He did it for the foundations for his house, and you for your cellar.'

---

[13] The Russian original means 'Quibbler'.
[14] The Russian original means 'Little Raven'.
[15] The association of animals with humans is a feature of Russian folklore and fables, similar to those in French literature, exemplified by La Fontaine (1621-1695), and his Russian counterpart, Krylov (1769-1844). The association of people and animals is common in Russian culture, as can be seen in the modern period in the Eisenstein film *The Strike*, where human characters' heads transmogrify into animal heads.
[16] This is a traditional Russian greeting: bread and salt are the symbols of hospitality.

'They were religious things… crosses. We only touched the stone, nothing more. As for the millet, we only took a **pood** a head.'

'You've been making off with it by the cart-load,' shouted Fomich.

'You just catch us! Not caught – not guilty. We live by the law,' said Spiriak, constantly grinning into his beard. 'An honest man sleeps soundly. Stop causing trouble. What have you to fear? How do you mean "inspector"?' Spiriak changed his tone: 'Avdotia, out you go and take the kids with you. Me and Fomich need to have a talk.'

Avdotia had worked ten years on the farm while Spiriak Voronok had been a manager, and she was used to obeying his orders automatically, just as an old, well-trained cavalry horse did as it was told. Spiriak was no longer a boss, he was a mere water-carrier, and Avdotia was no longer a milkmaid – she had been a housewife for many years with her permanently swollen, distorted fingers, caused by some unknown illness – yet she still obeyed his orders. She stood up from the table and hurriedly tied her scarf.

'Where are you off to?' Fomich sullenly nodded towards the bench, and said, 'Sit down! What secrets could I possibly have with him?'

Nevertheless, he sent the kids packing.

'Go out and play!' Fomich pushed the children's backs and gently slapped the back of their necks – besides his own five, there were two of the neighbours' kids in the house. When the children's footsteps had rumbled through the porch and they had jumped onto the veranda, Fomich said, 'There's no point in starting. We've nothing to discuss.'

'Who told you I was coming? Filat, I suppose.'

'A sandpiper in the swamp.'

'This is what I'm driving at, Avdotia.' Spiriak purposefully now addressed the housewife. 'There's a plus side to everything. But he just doesn't see that.'

'I know where you're coming from… Wherever I can get rich quick, there am I in the thick!' snapped Fomich spitefully. 'Well, there's no need to slacken your belt here – we have nothing.'[17]

'I saw my brother yesterday,' said Spiriak, looking at Avdotia. 'He said, "We'll stop Fomich from being an independent mower and fine him for not working for the **kolkhoz**".'

'Oh, God, Fedia! What will become of us?'

'No one's asking you, so shut up!' he snapped at his wife.

'But, I said to Pashka,' continued Spiriak Voronok, in a gentle voice, '"Fomich has a large family and he also has to eat. Let's appoint a fellow worker for him to mow with and count this work officially as a social obligation, then it will all be above board".'

'You fucking rip-off merchant…' Fomich let out a stream of compound swear words.

---

[17] This is not a literal translation, but it close in meaning to the original Russian. Fomich's quip rhymes in the original, which is what the translation here attempts to convey. The reference to the belt is in the original text – it hints at him feeding off the 'fat' of others.

'There you go! I suggest a way out for him and he effs and blinds at me.' Spiriak Voronok looked at Avdotia, as if Fomich were not there at all.

'All right. Tell Pashka that I'll have Old Filat as a fellow worker,' said Fomich.

Voronok shuddered, as if an electric current had passed through him, but then he came clean: 'You'll mow with me and we'll split everything fifty-fifty... Do you understand? Or else...'

'Go fuck yourself... I've had my fill of working with you before.'

'How do you mean "before". My poor committee had a good reputation.'

'How many people did you exile? Vaska Salyga, for instance – what was that for?'

'He was a horse dealer.'

'He didn't deal, he swapped them, like a gypsy. He exchanged them til all he was left with was a single lame mare... I know why you exiled him...' Fomich in a frenzy pointed a threatening finger at him. 'You were afraid he might spill the beans on you.'

'What for?'

'Didn't you and Lysyi nick a load of horses from Brëkhovo in 1927?[18] And wasn't it Strashnoi who was your fence in Kasimov?'[19]

'Don't judge everyone by your own standards,' Spiriak Voronok remarked politely, but unperturbed. 'Who gave Pëtr Lizunin a travel permit? You! Was that a freebie?'

'But, as soon as Lizunin had gone, you cleared out all his trunks.[20] I bet that you are still using his canvas, aren't you? And I don't regret giving him a permit. Now look where he is! He's in **Gorky** in charge of the wharf. His children are working as engineers and doctors. You've got only one son, and he's in prison for thieving.'

Purple blotches started to appear on Spiriak Voronok's face and he stood up, menacingly pulled his cap right down onto his eyebrows, and said: 'You were a **kulak** sympathizer before... You got to be secretary of the rural council by deceit. And now you're a parasite.[21] We'll throw the book at you. We'll get the law on you!'

He left without so much as a goodbye, having slammed the door hard behind him.

'What will become of us now, Fedia?' asked Avdotia pitifully.

'Nothing... God won't betray us, and pigs won't devour us.'

---

[18] The nickname 'Lysyi' means 'Baldie', i.e. someone who is bald. Rural nicknames were often based on physical characteristics, character traits, or jobs.

[19] Strashnoi means 'fierce' or 'frightening'. Kasimov is an actual place: it is situated on the river Oka, about one hundred and sixty kilometres south-east of Moscow. Mozhaev often combines fictional places with real places, and he frequently cross-references his own fictional places and characters from one work to another, even though the works might have been written many years apart.

[20] Russian peasants kept their valuables in a trunk or trunks, which were made of wood with iron straps and they were often decorated with fine examples of folk art.

[21] Anyone who did not work was officially classified as a 'parasite', for which there were specific punishments. From time to time, the regime initiated a clamp-down on so-called 'parasites'. As with many terms coined during the Soviet regime, this was a catch-all term with wide definitions, so that it could be applied as a coercive device within the law. Dissident writers were sometimes called 'parasites', because, officially, they were not considered as professional writers by the regime.

Fomich realized that his short-lived good fortune would soon come to an end. 'Whatever happens, I'll not back down. There's no going back,' he thought.

The next day, towards lunch time, when Fomich and Old Filat were finishing off mowing Marishka Britaia's plot, the **kolkhoz** chairman's **drozhki** appeared high on the opposite bank of the lake. Mikhail Mikhailovich Guzënkov had turned up in person. He tied up the grey dappled trotter to a lime tree on the lakeside and looked at the mowers for a moment in silence, as if it was the first time in his life he had ever seen any. Fomich and Old Filat also stood on the bank, looking back at the chairman: their heads protruded on their skinny, crane-like necks above the reedy thicket, like two pots hanging on a peg. The chairman rose up on the lime-tree mound, his thick legs set wide apart in his yellow box-calf boots, his arms crossed across his protruding stomach, encased in an embroidered, white peasant shirt, and he wore a canvas peaked cap. Below him stood a mirror image of this powerful chairman in his cap, with his feet pointing outwards, and it looked like he, his reflection in the water, was the real chairman, and that he was supporting the whole lime-tree mound on his head.

'What are you staring at? Come over here!' beckoned both chairmen.

'We're fine here,' said Old Filat.

'What's the point of us coming over there?' responded Fomich.

'Come on over here... I'll explain things to you,' said Mikhail Mikhailovich, trying to persuade them calmly.

'You've got a horse, so you come over here,' said Fomich.

'Like I'd drive my horse for the sake of you two layabouts.'

'Well, on your way then, if we're just layabouts... We haven't time to make small talk with you.' Lively put his scythe over his shoulder and walked on.

Old Filat followed on after him.

'Where are you off?' roared Guzënkov, to such an extent that the horse threw back its head and shuffled its front legs. 'Halt, I say!'

'What are you shouting for?' asked Fomich, standing still.

Old Filat dived into the bushes.

'What are you – a **kolkhoz** worker or an anarchist?' asked Guzënkov, getting angry.

'I am no one.'

'How do you mean, "no one"?' asked the chairman, taken aback.

'I left the **kolkhoz** four days ago. I haven't yet been hired by highwaymen... So, who on earth am I?'

'Why are you skiving? Why aren't you going to work?'

'How much do you get? Two-and-a-half grand? Just give me a third of that, then I'll work on the **kolkhoz**.'[22]

'Quit fooling around! I'm telling you for your own good.'

'If you want to talk to me properly, then come over here. Let's sit by this bush and have a chat. But I'll not take you shouting at me from on high, on top of that hill. I've seen a lot of bosses on peaks. A lot more than you.'

'You've got some nerve! So, are you refusing to work?'

'What am I doing here? Mowing or having a kip?'

'You're playing the fool. We'll summons you to headquarters and then you'll change your tune.'

'I shall not turn up at any headquarters! I've told you, I've left the **kolkhoz**. For good!'

'No-o-o, matey! No one leaves the **kolkhoz** as easy as that. We'll clean you out, we'll slap supplementary taxes on you and chuck you out of the village, lock, stock, and barrel. We'll make an example of you... Do you understand?'

'I understand how the peasant tired the life out of his old lady,' quipped Fomich. 'Anyway, would you be turning my house into an office? If you did, I'd be **dekulakized**.'

'I'll teach you to laugh!' The chairman untied the trotter at a single stroke, got into the **drozhki** and, leaning back on the reins, he set off along the lake.

By the way the trotter bared its teeth and threw back its head, Guzënkov was pulling hard on the bit, and by the way that the chairman's body was held rock-solid, with its closely-cropped neck flushed crimson, one could conclude that he went off in a terrible huff.

'Well, Fedka, brace yourself,' said Old Filat, looking at the authoritarian chairman, shielding his eyes with his hand.

Chapter Five

Fomich's house suddenly started subsiding. Last year it appeared to stand in good order, but this spring, when Fomich was clearing away the heavy snowfall from the house, which almost reached the windows, he suddenly noticed that the lower row of logs was swollen, as if someone had pushed them out from the inside.

'Our house is bulging. For the time being, we'll have to fit a retaining belt to it at least,' Fomich gloomily reported to his wife.

But towards the autumn, the tie beam, blackened with age and soot, sagged noticeably, and at night, when the wind blew and the chimney wailed its melancholy accompaniment, the beam emitted dry creaks from time to time, groaning under the strain.

---

[22] At the time of writing, two-and-a-half thousand roubles per month would have been a huge salary, since the average wage for professional people was around two hundred and fifty roubles a month.

'Fedia, prop up that beam,' Avdotia would complain at such times. 'It'll come down on us and the kids, and we'll never crawl out.'

Avdotia and the kids slept on the stove, but Fomich slept in the wooden bed – if you could call it a bed. It was no longer than one-and-a-half metres, although it took up the full length of the partition wall, right up to the door, but the house couldn't take anything bigger – it was only a seven-**arshin** hut. You couldn't even stretch out on such a small bed. At night, he placed a stool next to it and he would rest his feet on that.

'Necessity is the mother of invention,' as Fomich loved to say.[23]

After the encounter with the chairman by the lake, Fomich was summoned to the **kolkhoz** headquarters at the farm centre in the neighbouring village of Svistunovo. But Fomich never turned up. A decision had been taken behind his back to exclude him from the **kolkhoz**, to be ratified at a general public meeting. It was ratified. The **kolkhoz** workers were forbidden to allow Kuzkin to mow the pasture land they used for their calves, and thus his unexpected source of income was cut off. However, Fomich joked: 'Never mind, Dunia! Now I'll have time to repair the house. Thanks to them, I'm free from work.'

Life had not indulged Fomich to any real extent. He'd had a difficult childhood as an orphan. As a young man, he had not had the chance to sow his wild oats before he was married. Everyone wore sheepskin coats on the way to the church on his wedding day, and they went in dressed as they were. Fomich wore his father's old sheepskin coat, in which he dragged himself up the church porch steps with the hems trailing behind him, and the collar hid his head to such an extent, that all that could be seen was his fur hat. 'He's just pint-sized,' sighed his mother, crest-fallen, following on behind him. 'It looks like the bride is taller than him.'

When the priest saw this timid wedding procession, huddled in the corner, he asked cheerily, 'Where is the bridegroom, my children?'

Apart from Fomich, the only other man there was Dunia's father – a strapping chap, with a thick, broad grey beard. Those who had come to gawp were suppressing their mirth behind the palms of their hands, making it look as though they were crossing themselves. His mother pushed Fomich in the back, pushing him gently forward. 'Here he his, Father. He might look pint-sized, but the lad's alive.'

The priest laughed out loud, and asked, 'Is that his name, "Lively"?'

'He's alive and Lively,' she blurted out in panic, to the general sound of suppressed chuckling.[24]

'If he's alive, then he'll grow up,' pronounced the priest cheerfully.

From that time, Fomich was known as Lively...

In fact, he did grow after the wedding – he shot up when he started working. He and his young wife hired out their labour to the butter-maker in Svistunovo, then they bought a cow and a horse, and they started off their own farm. These first years after their marriage were a protracted, but happy time of struggling to make ends meet.

---

[23] A literal translation of the Russian would be, 'If you want to live, learn how to take evasive action.'

[24] The joke here hinges on the fact that the Russian word for 'alive' and 'lively' is the same word – '*zhivoi*'.

'We were like a *troika*,' Fomich would say, when remembering those times. 'Lyska was the shaft horse, and me and Dunia were the outrunners!'[25]

Ah, Dunia, Dunia! Now you have become quick to sigh and close to tears... But previously, you used to be like a chaffinch, like a bell ringing from dawn till dusk – there was no one jollier than you...

They used to amaze the other villagers in Prudki, that even in their second and third year of marriage, they would still attend the spring singing sessions. The young people used to gather on Red Hill, by the church yard. Fomich would turn up with his accordion on his shoulder. Dunia would be in her yellow boots with the buttons down the side, wearing a colourful headscarf and a sleeveless, thin blouse. Lively would have a good look at the accordion player, to see whether he was a local or an outsider, but all the same, he would get his accordion ready, and put his ear to the bellows... Oh, how it sounded! The voice of one accordion would blend with the other into a single melody, and the two instruments played as one. And that was all Dunia was waiting for – you didn't have to ask her. She looked reticent to remove her headscarf and, lazily moving her shoulders, she would walk in a circle stomping, and only the drumming of her heels resounded:

> *Accordionist, accordionist,*
> *With your neck so narrow.*
> *Let your fingers play so well,*
> *And I will dance my sorrow.*

From a bench, Lively's soft, deep baritone voice responded:

> *Oh, migratory bird,*
> *Flying so high,*
> *Come down and see us,*
> *Just like a fly...*

'They're lively buggers!' muttered the old women on the hillock. 'It's time they were bringing up children, instead of courting.'

'We never had time to finish our courting before we were married. We're just taking what was due to us,' replied Fomich.

In the founding years of the **kolkhoz**, Dunia distinguished herself among the Sunday **voluntary workers**. She would go along the furrow, behind the plough, planting potatoes, and she never fell behind. She would follow on as if she were tethered to it, taking short steps, a basket strapped to her chest, and her hands darting to and fro from the basket to the furrow. She just took time out to refill the basket. The kids used to come and watch her planting the potatoes. Not a single woman on the **kolkhoz**, old or young, could keep up with her planting. Not for nothing did they call her 'Lively' as

---

[25] A *troika* is a Russian sleigh, drawn by three horses and it is derived from the Russian word for 'three'.

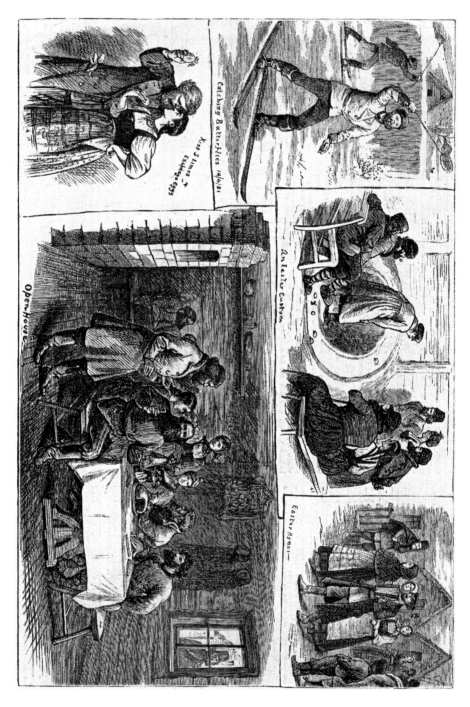

Illustration 7. 'Eastertide in Russia', *The Illustrated London News,* **April 14 1881.**

well. She looked like Fomich in her youth – her face was swarthy and she had darting, grey, sunken eyes. It was for that reason that Fomich's mother, a sharp-tongued old woman, called her a 'hollow-eyed wench'. When the children were born, they had the same hollow eyes. Then, all the responsibility for running the household – the 'watering and the feeding' – as Fomich called it, fell to Avdotia. Fomich himself soon moved on from **kolkhoz** business, being promoted along the managerial route, since he was from a landless background, from the 'poor class'.

This 'poor peasant' background did not work at all in his favour, in fact, it did quite the opposite – it dealt him a bad hand.

In those first, halcyon years on the **kolkhoz**, when the workers were given twelve **poods** per head as pay, Fomich was sent to the rural soviet as a secretary. They paid the bare minimum – you couldn't even stretch to cheap boots. You couldn't get kersey boots at that time – no one knew how to make them. Then things got worse: the rural council offices were closed down in Prudki, so Fomich went to work for the Svistunovo rural council. Each day he had to cover five **versts** each way.

'I'm just like a corncrake,' Fomich would say. 'It rushes off to its winter hide like I go off to work. All I need to do now is learn how to quack.'

'When winter comes, you'll quack all right,' replied his old lady. 'You've got nothing to wear. Your jacket is so ancient that when the wind blows, it will fall apart, just like a magpie's nest.'

'Happiness, Mother, doesn't lie in a jacket.'

'What's it in then?'

'Who knows?'

In fact, Fomich did not know wherein happiness lay. When he was little, he thought that happiness was a big house with a nice garden, like Father Vasilii had, which smelt of lilac and apple blossom in summer, and of pancakes in winter. When he grew up, he thought happiness would be to get married to Duniasha. But before he could tarry a while with his dreams, as he should, he found himself married to her. Then he dreamt of earning a lot of money, buying lots of horses and cows, and building a large farmstead, like Lizunin had. *But then came the kolkhoz. A fat lot of happiness could be had on the kolkhoz! Being rich was frowned upon. It was all 'revolutionary discipline' and 'work for the general good'. Fair enough! Perhaps such happiness was possible.* But by working as a secretary for the rural soviet, Fomich knew that, year on year, more produce *was being taken from the kolkhozes and they were getting poorer.*[26] Moreover, at first, enough grain was given to all **kolkhoz** workers so that there was no apparent shortage. Enough for each mouth to feed. And there was a bonus on top, for those who worked best. *But now **brigade leaders**, tractor drivers, and all sorts of clerks were well paid, but the rest got a pittance. So how could everyone live well on such a kolkhoz? He remembered Lizunin's words: 'I'll tell you what the kolkhoz is – the cunning get rich, the beautiful get all the loving they want, and the fool just buggers about.' Just prove that wasn't the truth! When the kolkhoz was founded Fomich thought, 'We'll set things up so*

---

[26] In the original *Novyi mir* edition, the tense was changed from 'they were getting poorer' to 'they had got poorer', i.e. the censor made it sound as though this was now all in the past and that things had been put right.

that everyone will live well'. But it turned out that there was no happiness for him on the **kolkhoz**.

In 1935, Fomich was fast-tracked onto a two-year law course. But even before the first year was up, the unqualified students were sent as chairmen to the **kolkhozes**. Fomich was sent to a forestry **kolkhoz** in the Meshchëra area. Fomich had spent all his life farming in the black earth areas and in meadow lands. And what kind of farm was he sent to? The depth of soil was less than a pig could carry on its snout! It was a **kolkhoz**, and a forest **kolkhoz** into the bargain... At that time, Fomich started to understand a thing or two – a good chairman was one who could keep well in with the bosses by supplying more than demanded by the **plan**, but at the same time, he could keep his farm workers well-fed. This required great versatility. The main thing was to have a good basis for farming, having either fertile soil, or a profitable trade. Then you could get by. But when Fomich got to the Meshchëra farm, he saw it was just podzol and swamp land.[27] When winter came, the farmers would tuck their pick behind their belts and go off to find work elsewhere. Their own land had never supported their families. What would Fomich manage to pull off there? On what basis could he develop the farm? When autumn came, he'd have to surrender grain to the state and dole out the farmers' share. What kind of versatility, what kind of imagination would you need for that? No, he'd not get far there. Fomich refused outright to become a chairman. So they threw him out of the Party and off the course, and he went to Prudki with a stained reputation: he was officially dubbed a '**secret element**' and a '**saboteur**'.

Disaster soon struck. In 1937, on the occasion of the first elections to the Supreme Soviet, there was a large meeting in the regional offices.[28] The deputy of the People's Commission for Finance attended in person. Peasant men turned up from all the regional villages because it was a market day, and the square was full to bursting. In the centre of the square was a wooden platform, on which the deputy stood, and the peasants noted perceptively that he was as tall as Vania Borodin, the tallest peasant in Svistunovo, and that the deputy's fur hat was made of beaver fur, and that he smoked cigarettes 'as thick as a frying pan handle'.

After the meeting, a promise was made that white rolls would be available at the hawkers' stands. However, it turned out that there were few of them and when Fomich's turn came round, they were all sold out. Fomich read out loud the sign over the stall which said 'Consumers' Association', but he remarked, 'No, it should read "Confusers' Association".'[29] This provoked laughter all round him. Then the chairman of the regional executive committee came up to Fomich and said, 'Please follow me.' Well, there was nothing written on his forehead to say that he was such a chairman, so Fomich told him to eff off. The chairman grabbed Fomich by the collar of his sheepskin coat... Lively would recklessly get into a fight. He grabbed the chairman's arm, dived under his armpit, and picked him up in such a way that his galoshes and box-calf boots flew off. Police whistles sounded and Fomich was arrested.

---

[27] Podzol is a sterile, greyish-white soil, which is deficient in salts and is of low fertility.

[28] Elections were instituted as part of the new constitution, which was introduced by Stalin in 1936.

[29] The original pun is actually a play on the Russian word for 'tatty' or 'shabby', but this translation gives a flavour of Fomich's quip. Making such comments in Stalinist times was very dangerous, as the story shows, and people were imprisoned for such remarks.

A trio of judges found him guilty *of 'anti-Soviet propaganda', all the more so since it occurred 'during the run-up to the elections'.* Then they dragged up the '**secret element**' and 'sabotage' incident, when he refused to be a **kolkhoz** chairman, *and his exclusion from the Party, and he was sent off to prison for five years as an **enemy of the people**.*

However, Fomich did not tarry long in prison. In 1939, many prisoners were released by volunteering as soldiers for the Finnish War.[30] Fomich applied. His file was examined and he was released. But whilst the commission sat and investigations were carried out here and there – 'Was he, or was he not, amongst the disenfranchised?'[31] 'Had he resisted collectivization, or not?' – and so on, and so forth... by the time he was released, the Finnish War had ended. However, Fomich had his fair share of fighting during the big war, and he came home with the Order of Glory and two medals – and a claw for a right hand.[32]

So how could Lively know where on earth happiness was to be found? Or even what it was? Considering the days and years of his life, he sorted them out like willow withies for the baskets he made: the thicker ones were for the framework, and the thinner ones were for the sides. None were rejected and everything was used for the job. *Nowadays it was said that happiness lies in toil. If that were the case, then Fomich was the happiest man in the world. Even at the most difficult times of his life, he had always managed to find some suitable work.* And even now, several nights running, he had managed to carry home some oak beams from the far side of the river Luka, he'd fixed the lower rotten beams, and, the most important thing of all, he'd repaired the tie beam, so that his wife would at least sleep peacefully in her bed.

Along with the winter chill, another anxiety knocked on Lively's door – a summons arrived ordering him to attend the regional executive committee 'with regard to his exclusion'.

Chapter Six

The next day turned out to be slushy: from morning onwards, wet snow alternated with rain. The ground, which had frozen the night before, had turned slimy and it stuck to the soles of one's boots. Fomich looked at his ancient box-calf boots and decided to attach some rubber soles with tanned leather belts. It was a long way to Tikhanovo – ten kilometres. In such weather, it would be silly to lose your soles on the way. He fastened his military belt across his coat – it'll be a bit warmer that way. And to keep the rain out above, he threw on a wide hay sack. That'll do as a raincoat! And he put on a hood and a kerchief on the top of his head. It looked just like a Budënnii cap.[33]

---

[30] Stalin wanted to push the Russo-Finnish boarder back northwards, at Finland's expense, but the resistance was unexpectedly strong and the Red Army was poorly co-ordinated. The incident cost the lives of 200,000 Soviet soldiers between the end of November 1939 and March 1940, when a settlement was agreed.

[31] Kulaks, priests and so-called '**enemies of the people**' were automatically deprived of the right to vote, until the new constitution in 1936, when voting rights were restored.

[32] This is a reference to World War II. The Order of Glory was instituted in 1943 for non-commissioned officers and rank and file soldiers.

[33] This was a piece of head-gear, which was made of cloth: it had ear flaps and came to a point at the top. It was worn during the Civil War (1918-20) in Russia by members of Budënnii's forces. He was a Red Army cavalry officer, who fought against the White Guard in the Caucasus, and he played a decisive role in defeating Polish rebels. He also took command of the south-west front during the Second World War, when Germany invaded Russia in 1941, though he fought with less success there.

'Well, I'm off!' he announced at the threshold.

As soon as Avdotia saw him in such 'combat vestments', she broke into a lamentation: 'For whom are you abandoning us, little ones and older ones? You are our wondrously beautiful provider! Oh, how evil is our fate... We are destined to wander the world, like poor little orphans!'[34]

'What are you wailing for, silly woman? I'm not in my coffin yet!'

'Oh, Fedia, my love, they'll arrest you and put you in prison... Oh, my poor old man! What shall I do with the little ones?' Avdotia sat at the table, rested her elbows on it and hurriedly lamented, crying out stridently. Shurka, the youngest, buried her head on her mother's knees and also started to howl.

'You've gone daft, Dunia...' said Fomich, as gently as he could. 'We're not in the 'thirties – it's fifty-three now.[35] There's a big difference! They can't play around with you as they used to... Even Beria's been arrested.[36] And you're in tears! You should be laughing!'

Lively thus dismissed his wife's weakness. He went outside. On the way he thought, 'Well, what's Semën Motiakov got in store for me this time?'

Motiakov, the chairman of the regional executive committee, was born in the same year as Fomich. They were once fast-tracked workers together – Motiakov took on the job of rural soviet chairman in Samodurovka. Then, they had studied on the law course together. They were both sent as **kolkhoz** chairmen at the same time. Only Fomich had refused his post, whereas Motiakov's career took off...

Lively knew well that you couldn't joke around with Motiakov: he was a nasty character to get involved with before, but after the war, when he had attended some courses, he became the scourge of the region. His favourite expression, 'We'll break some balls! Once and for all...', was well-known to every **kolkhoz brigade leader**.

'So what? I haven't any balls to break – they've already been broken. So I have nothing left to fear,' thought Fomich, trying to keep his spirits up.

At the executive committee offices, he decided that he would stand his ground. 'Let them do their worst with me. Let them send me off to prison? That would be a first! I'll get the trip at the state's expense. You get fed and watered, even if it's only skilly.'

Lively was soaked and frozen to the bone when he arrived in Tikhanovo. The regional executive committee was housed in a two-storey, brick building in the centre of the town,

---

[34] This dramatic outburst is typical of the Russian folkloric tradition of pronouncing lamentations (otherwise known as 'keening'), which was done not only at funerals, but even at weddings and other special, social occasions. Keening was the province of women, who extemporized on a theme, using set expressions and other linguistic devices, such as diminutive endings on nouns, etc., to express grief, self-pity, regret, and other similar emotions.

[35] The 1930s were difficult and dangerous times, especially 1934-38, when the Purges took place, during which time literally hundreds of thousands of innocent people were incarcerated and perished under Stalin, including many prominent political figures.

[36] Lavrenti Pavlovich Beria (1899-1953) became head of the secret police (then known as the **NKVD**) in 1938, which administered the vast network of labour camps, or GULags, throughout the USSR. He was arrested in June 1953 and shot after a secret trial in December of the same year.

the regional capital. He made no attempt to take off the sack and walked into reception just as he was.

'Who's the person who summoned me?'

'Where do you think you've come to?! A farm yard?' asked the young secretary, lacing straight into him. 'Take that sack off now! Not in here! Take it out of the room! Water is pouring off it... Take it out of here!'

Lively took the sack off, but he did not move from the spot.

'And what happens if it gets nicked? It's my last one...'

'Who on earth would want it? Out you go! Why are you standing in the doorway?'

Lively made for the chairman's office door.

'Aha! Don't think you're going in there with that sack. That would be the last straw!' The secretary got up from her desk and energetically showed Lively to the door. 'What dimwits these people are! You've left a great puddle. And who do you think I am, a charlady?'

A minute later, Lively came in without the sack, but he still dripped rain none the less.

'Have you been swimming in the pond or something?'

'Aha! I've been fishing with a dragnet. Then I thought, "Why not warm-up in the regional offices?" You've got such nice, soft furniture here.'

This time the secretary did not manage to get up in time before Lively unceremoniously went past her desk and flopped down on the sofa.

'There! Just like I said...'

'Who have you come to see?'

'Motiakov and the committee.'

'Are you from Prudki? Are you Kuzkin?'

'The very same.'

'What are you lounging around for?!' she said, just as if she had realized who he was, and she went for him with fresh vigour. 'Get up! All the officials have been waiting for you for a whole hour, and here you are, playing the fool.'

She quickly disappeared behind the door without waiting for a word of explanation from Fomich, then she came straight back.

'Get straight in there! Look how he's made himself comfortable!'

Lively went into the office. Motiakov himself was in the chairman's seat and next to the table stood Demin, the secretary of the regional party committee, in a dark-blue, expensive suit. Members of the executive committee were present: Lively recognised Guzënkov, and the chairman of the neighbouring **kolkhoz**, Petia Dolgii, and the chief doctor of the regional hospital, Umniashkin – they were sitting along the wall, smoking.

It was obvious that the executive committee had concluded its business from the masses of sheets of paper, full of writing, and pencils all over the long table.[37]

'Here he is – finally, our beloved friend! Let us rejoice!' Motiakov flashed his steely teeth as he followed Fomich from under his eyebrows.

Demin nodded to Lively to sit down on a chair, but before Fomich could take up his seat, Motiakov stopped him with a shout: 'What do you think you're doing? You'll stand... You haven't been invited to tea.' Motiakov stood up. He was wearing a military jacket and dark-blue officers' breeches. With his hands plunged in his pockets, he walked around Fomich like a cockerel, sarcastically saying, 'Wet chicken! Another act of rebellion.'

'So what's this place then, your roost? You look to be gathering in your chicks,' remarked Lively.

'We'll be having words!' Motiakov shouted at him again, then went over to Demin and whispered something in his ear.

Demin was so tall and lanky that Motiakov had to stand on his tiptoes, and his short, wide nose comically pointed upwards.

'It looks as though he's sniffing him,' thought Fomich, observing Motiakov, and he sneered.

Demin nodded his small, wizened head in assent to Motiakov, and the latter approached the table and banged his knuckles down on it.

'Let's start. Timoshkin, take your place!'

The rotund, agile secretary of the regional executive committee, Timoshkin, with his turnip-yellow face, took his place at the table to the right of Motiakov and compliantly fixed his bulging, crab-like eyes on him. Demin moved towards the wall and took his place with the other members of the committee.

'C'mon, Guzënkov! Make your report,' ordered Motiakov.

Mikhail Mikhailovich stood up and set his legs apart in his massive boots, as if he were checking out the floor-boards, wondering, 'Will they support me?' He took out a sheet of paper from his pad and began, keeping an eye on Motiakov.

'Well, after the September Plenum, the whole country, so to speak, is making strenuous attempts in the matter of developing the agricultural sector.[38] Each **kolkhoz** worker has a duty to respond to the historic resolutions of the Plenum by exercising selfless toil. But, there are still amongst us one type of **element** and another, who, during working hours, go out into the meadows with their gun and shoot ducks. As if that were not enough, they incite the biddable women of the farm to make all sorts of illegal deals, because they are too busy to finish off mowing their pasture plots. Others do the mowing instead of them, in exchange for millet and money. What does all this lead to? It is a

---

[37] This fictional character appears again in a number of Mozhaev's works, and in a later story in this collection. The character was inspired by a number of real **kolkhoz** chairmen whom Mozhaev knew and admired personally. The surname 'Dolgii' means 'long' or 'tall'.
[38] For 'September Plenum', see p.325.

relapse, a return to independent farming... We will not tolerate the unproductive **element** Kuzkin to undermine our **kolkhoz**. Let him either work on the **kolkhoz**, or let him leave our land. We request that the executive committee ratify the decision of our **kolkhoz** meeting to exclude Fëdor Fomich Kuzkin.'

Guzënkov sat down and Motiakov gloated maliciously over Fomich: 'Well, what do you have to say now? Doubtless you're going to start making excuses for yourself.'

'I'm not going to excuse anything. I don't thieve and it's not my snout that's in the public trough!' said Fomich.

'We'll have words!' shouted Motiakov.

'So why have you summoned me here? To keep quiet? If you have nothing to ask me, then decide what you like.'

'We're not asking for your advice. We're going to break your balls, once and for all,' said Motiakov, starting to laugh and baring his steely teeth.

'Comrade Kuzkin, why do you refuse to work for the **kolkhoz**?' Demin asked politely, in his quiet, rather hoarse, voice.

He gripped his knee with his long, white fingers and looked at Lively with his head tilted slightly back.

'Comrade Demin, I do not refuse to work. I've worked for a whole year and the **kolkhoz** has allotted me twenty-one grams of buckwheat per head, per day. But in the **kolkhoz** chicken shed, each chick gets fed forty grams of pure wheat per day.'

'Just listen to the wise guy! He's trying to teach us higher maths...' said Motiakov. 'But I'll jog your political mind. You should have worked harder. Do you understand? *You've let yourself go! A year ago you didn't make a squeak. You wanted your rights. I am reminding you of your obligations.*'

Demin turned to Motiakov and quietly, apologetically, said, 'Comrade Motiakov, you must stop using these methods. You won't get far by using them.'

'Oh, yes we will!' shouted Motiakov.

Demin perked up his head, as if in amazement, and, in a different tone, said 'Comrade Motiakov!'

'Well, well...' Motiakov muttered something indistinct under his breath and sank back behind the table.

'So, are you refusing to work?' Demin asked Kuzkin again, in an even tone.

'I do not refuse to work, Comrade Demin. I will simply not work for nothing. I have five children, and I myself am an invalid from the **Great Patriotic War**.'

'Get him! Now he's asking for a salary… We have before us the People's Commissar of the "Red Bast Shoe",' mocked Motiakov again.[39] 'First produce a good harvest, then ask for money. You scrounger!'

'And what kind of harvest do you produce?' asked Lively, getting angry. 'You neither reap nor sow – all you do is hold your pocket open!'

'We'll have words!' shouted Motiakov, banging his fist on the table.

'Semën Ivanovich! Calm down, for the last time!' Demin again stared long and hard at Motiakov.

Motiakov pouted and fell silent.

'But listen, Comrade Kuzkin. You are not the only **kolkhoz** worker, but you're the only one refusing to work!' observed Demin.

'That's a strange question!' replied Fomich. 'What if I were to say, for example, I don't want to die? Would you then tell me, "You're not the first, and you'll not be the last"?'

'You have a point,' grinned Demin. 'But, Comrade Kuzkin, we all have to sustain our **kolkhoz** together.'

'We do sustain it,' replied Kuzkin. 'But some of us sustain it in different ways. I sustain hunger cramps in my stomach, but Guzënkov there sustains a hang-over.'

'Let's not get personal! We have a critic in our midst!' said Motiakov, unable to keep quiet.

'Comrade Kuzkin, why is your **kolkhoz** so bad? Who is to blame?'

'The war is to blame,' said Motiakov.

Kuzkin stared at him, imitating Demin.

'The war's to blame…' he repeated, and turned towards Secretary Demin. 'Do you know, Comrade Demin, how our potatoes were ruined?'

'Which potatoes?' said Guzënkov, taking note.

'The seed potatoes!'

'Well?' asked Demin, taking great interest.

'They were being sorted out, when the workers went to lunch. When they got back, there were three cows scoffing them – they had smashed up the store and appeared out of nowhere… Their sides swelled up like this.'

'How did that happen?' asked Demin, looking at Guzënkov. The latter got all puffed up and just shook his head.

---

[39] A 'People's Commissar' in Soviet Russia was the head of a government department, equivalent to the position of minister within the British system of government. The title was changed to 'minister' in Russia in 1946.

'It was his work,' said Kuzkin. 'The store was made out of matchwood... He hired the joiners. He paid them a bonus and they feasted on the fatted calf. But the store was so badly cobbled together that a pig could push it over with its snout.'

'What happened to the potatoes then?' asked Demin.

'Guzënkov told us to take all the potatoes that were left to be stored in Voronin's, our **brigade leader**'s, cellar. When spring came he said, "There are no potatoes, they all got frozen".'

'And did you write anywhere, to the regional authorities about it?'

'I did. But what's the point? Writing to our regional authorities is like spitting at the moon.'

'Who did you write to?' asked Motiakov, raising his head.

'You, for example!'

'Me? I don't remember.' He turned to Timoshkin. 'Timoshkin, is that right?'

'It was not received,' he blurted out.

'And what's this? Is this not your signature?' asked Kuzkin, taking out a postcard from his pocket and handed it to Timoshkin. 'My letter has balls... err, I mean, weight. I know who I am dealing with.'

'My signature has still to be subjected to documentary verification. Perhaps your postcard is a forgery.'

'Let me see that.' Demin went up to the table and took the postcard. 'Comrade Motiakov, this matter has to be investigated.'

'That goes without saying.. We'll look into it. Whoever lost the letter and whoever falsified the facts... We'll find out and punish them.'

The door squeaked and the secretary came in.

'Comrade Demin, you are wanted on the telephone. It is the **oblast** office calling.'

'Very well!'

Demin placed the postcard in front of Motiakov.

'Sort this out!' he said, and left the room.

'There's no point in talking to him!' said Guzënkov, dismissively. 'He's a well-known **element**... A dyed-in-the-wool **element**.'

'I founded the **kolkhoz** in 1930, but you, Comrade Guzënkov, turned up at the ready when the job was already done. Who knows what you were up to in 1930?'

'It is we who have summoned you to account, and not the other way about!' said Motiakov, cutting Lively short. 'And we'll set you right, once and for all! Do you understand? Will you work for the **kolkhoz**?!'

'I shall not work for nothing.'

'What exactly is it you want, then?' asked Umniashkin.

'Give me a **passport**. I'll find a job.'

'We'll not give you a **passport** – you'll be issued a ticket to hell!' said Motiakov.[40]
'Go wait in reception. We'll call you when we need you.'

Lively left the room.

'What *are* we to do with him?' asked Umniashkin, a corpulent man of middle years, whose face constantly wore a gloomy, tired expression of despondent intensity, which afflicts many rural doctors who have served their time.

'Give him a fixed-penalty fine... in the form of a double supplementary tax,' said Motiakov. 'Then we'll see how he gets on.'

'But such taxes have been abolished!' Umniashkin objected.

'That's for **kolkhoz** workers. But now he's been excluded from the **kolkhoz**, we'll treat him like an independent farmer.'

'We'll tax him in meat, fleeces and eggs... Twice over!' chimed in Timoshkin.[41]

'Are we agreed?' asked Motiakov, turning to the members of the committee.

'This is not right,' said the chairman of the Brëkhovo **kolkhoz**, Zvonarëv, whose nickname was Petia Dolgii, on account of his great stature. 'He was not paid for his **workday unit**s. We must find a solution to this. It is a difficult situation.'

'It's as simple as two and two makes four,' said Motiakov, slapping his palm down on the table. 'Exclude him from the **kolkhoz** and issue a fixed-penalty fine, once and for all.'

'I would let him go,' objected Petia Dolgii. *'We should help him sort out a job.'*

'That's called liberalism,' said Motiakov. 'If we aid and abet every idler and fly-by-night, the whole **kolkhoz** system will collapse. He'll leave today, another will do the same tomorrow... Who will be left to work?'

'People don't leave our farm,' said Petia Dolgii.

'That's because your farm can stand on its own feet, but Guzënkov's is crawling on all fours... There's the difference! You don't understand dialectics, once and for all.'

'Absolutely right, Semën Ivanovich!' Timoshkin joined in. *'We must make an example of Kuzkin to teach people a lesson. A double fixed-penalty tax to be paid in meat and fleeces!'*

'That's just plain nasty,' said Umniashkin. 'You're skinning him twice.'

---

[40] What Motiakov says in the original is, 'We'll issue you with a "wolf's ticket".' A 'wolf's ticket' was pre-revolutionary slang for a tsarist internal passport, which indicated the political unreliability of the holder, meaning that the bearer could not gain access to government or academic jobs.

[41] Many local officials wielded an inordinate amount of power locally, especially in remote areas, where they ruled their districts and regions as their own fiefdoms. Frequently, there were flagrant breaches of legality, as here: such taxes as independent farmers had been abolished by this time, but these officials choose to punish Kuzkin's temerity for wanting to leave the **kolkhoz** by these trumped-up taxes, which were levied on independent farmers in the early 1930s, to force them into the **kolkhoz** system.
There is also a *double entendre* here: the Russian word for a 'fleece' is also the same word as human 'skin', and the word for 'eggs' is the slang word for testicles.

'So what?' responded Motiakov. 'Compulsory procurements require the surrender of a fleece. So let him give two. Timoshkin, note that down!'

'But he is a category three war invalid,' observed Umniashkin. 'At least take that into consideration.'

'So now three fingers aren't enough,' sneered Motiakov. 'You can see what he's like – he might look like a knackered horse, but he'll see us lot out. Let's put it to the vote: who is "for" exclusion? Let's have a show of hands!'

Motiakov, Guzënkov, and Timoshkin all voted for exclusion. Umniashkin and Petia Dolgii voted against.

'Majority "for",' remarked Motiakov triumphantly.

'Aha, the "majority"… all unanimous!' remarked Petia Dolgii sarcastically.

'I am unanimous!' said Motiakov, putting up a single finger. 'We've weighed our opinions – your voice and mine.'[42] Then he shouted towards the door: 'Get Kuzkin in here!'

This time Lively came in holding his sack. Motiakov suspiciously eyed the sack.

'I shouldn't be surprised if you'd brought some piglets in that sack!'

'That's right. I was in a rush to get rid of them before you took them away from me.'

'I'll teach you to talk like that! I'll beat the desire to talk out of you! Once and for all! Give me the report!' Motiakov took the sheet of paper from Timoshkin and started to read it aloud: "As a consequence of his exclusion from the **kolkhoz**, Fëdor Fomich Kuzkin, resident of the village of Prudki, in the administrative region of Tikhanovo, is now considered to be an independent peasant farmer, and as such he is liable to be taxed twofold, to wit the sum is to be calculated on the basis of his private plot of 0·25 hectares of land, in accordance with the tax, abolished by the most recent government decree, which is to be doubled. To wit, Fëdor Fomich Kuzkin is obliged to surrender within one month one thousand seven hundred roubles, eighty-eight kilograms of meat, one hundred and fifty eggs, six kilograms of wool, or two fleeces".'

'Semën Ivanovich, how about if I write down forty-four cubic metres of firewood as well? Let him get that together also,' suggested Timoshkin, leaning over towards the chairman.

'You get it together,' remarked Fomich. 'But the joke's on you – you won't get all that in your gob 'cause of your hangover.'

Timoshkin wryly distorted his mouth and said, 'Perhaps we could do without the *insultations*.[43] Otherwise you'll be answering also for your personal remarks.'

'I answered for you in the thirties when your father ran a salami shop.'[44]

---

[42] There is a play on words here, because the Russian for 'vote' and 'voice' is the same noun.

[43] Timoshkin gets the word ending wrong in the original Russian, indicating a lack of education.

[44] This is a reference to the ending of private trading at the end of the 1920s to the early 1930s, when a certain amount of private enterprise had been allowed again during the period called the New Economic Policy or NEP. See Appendix II, p.440. Timoshkin's father was obviously a private trader.

'Are there any questions?' Motiakov asked Fomich.

'I wonder, should I pay in instalments, or all at once?' asked Fomich, looking innocently at Motiakov.

Motiakov said, in a grave, official tone, 'You can bring it all now, if you like.'

'All of it?'

'Yes, everything. All of it!'

'I'll bring you the money... All of it, down to the last **kopeck**. I'll retrieve it from the eaves of my house. And I'll get you the meat – I'll buy a calf at the market. I'll also hand in the eggs... But, regarding the fleeces, please go easy on me. I've already found one.'

'Then find another where you found the first,' said Motiakov.

'Well, I'll fleece myself for the first one, but I can't take my wife's. We have equal rights now.'

One of the committee members spluttered with laughter. Umniashkin covered his mouth with his hand – only his eyes were visible, and they watered with laughter. Petia Dolgii looked as though he was pecking with his nose, and somehow uttered a deep, crane-like sound. But Motiakov bellowed, turned crimson, and bashed his fist so hard on the table that Timoshkin nearly jumped out of his skin with fright.

'Get out of here, once and for all!'

Outside, the rain drizzled, alternating with wet snow, as before. Fomich put the sack on his head and plodded along the muddy street. He felt sick to his stomach, having exhausted his supply of jauntiness and sarcasm in Motiakov's office. Just now, he felt like lying down in the middle of the filthy road and bawling. He would have had a few drinks, but he didn't have a single coin in his pocket...

At the edge of Tikhanovo, opposite the former church, now used as a granary, the ex-priest's house stood at a distance: the walls were faced with boards and it used to abound in a garden. On their way out of Tikhanovo, people would stop here on a hot summer's day and drink their fill at the well. Fomich suddenly felt a wave of exhaustion and his knees started to shake. 'Hell, I feel as though I'm carrying a load of sacks... That's down to your executive committee.' He leaned on the well hatch and looked at the priest's house. 'That looks like a confessional. I'd better pop in,' Fomich decided.

The former priest's house now accommodated the regional finance office. In the far corner office Andriusha sat counting on an abacus, and sticking out from under the table was his wooden 'Gun-Stock'.

'Greetings, neighbour!' he said, merrily welcoming Fomich. 'Why are you so wet and pale? You look as though you've been attacked by devils.'[45]

'Devils indeed!' Fomich sat down on the sofa covered in worn, black oilcloth and took a deep breath, as if he had just run a long race. 'I've come to confess to you, since you're here in the priest's house.'

---

[45] See Mozhaev's story *Shishigi*, translated in this volume.

Fomich told him all about what had happened at the executive committee. Andriusha maintained a long, concerned silence, occasionally moving counters on the abacus.

'This is what you should do: get a paper from them with the details of the supplementary taxes. Hide your gun and sell your goat. Don't bother about your bike – it's old anyway. Let them confiscate something. Then submit a complaint. It's absolutely essential that you get a certificate from the **kolkhoz** for all your **workday units**.'

'Who'll give me that?'

'You'll have to be cunning. Do a bit of wangling.'

'Won't they send me packing?'

'They could, under article thirty-five, because you've no specific job, like a tramp.'[46]

'But invalids aren't exiled, are they?'

'No, not invalids. But you are a category three, so you should work.'

'I'm not refusing to work. Let them issue me with a **passport** and I'll get a job.'

Andriusha simply held up his hands helplessly.

'That's not in our gift. Just remember this, when they come round to make their inventory – keep shtoom.[47] Do you understand? If they try to pick a quarrel, don't even think of being rude. Just knuckle under. Let them take what they want. You must keep mum. Just get a grip!'

Chapter Seven

The committee descended upon them in the snow, after the feast-days. Fomich managed both to sell his goat and hide his gun. He wrapped the gun in oil-soaked cloths and hid it in the eaves. His old Penza bike, which was pre-war, stood on the porch by the door, chipped like a mangy old horse, as if saying, 'Here I am – take me, if you want'.

The committee comprised five people, headed by the regional finance department boss of the Svistunovo section, Nastia Protasova, a big-nosed, ageing old maid, nicknamed Riabukha, behind whom came the **brigade leader**, Pashka Voronin, and another three deputies from the soviet – strapping tractor drivers from Svistunovo.[48] 'These three are here in case I kick up a fuss,' thought Fomich. He darted off into the store-room and pretended to be sleeping.

'May we come in?' sounded Nastia's voice at the door.

'Please do,' said Avdotia.

'Good day,' pronounced various voices at the doorstep. 'Where is the man of the house?'

---

[46] This is a reference to the law on 'parasitism'. See footnote № 21, p.101.

[47] The speaker actually uses the rather quaint expression, 'Behave quieter than water and lower than grass'.

[48] Nastia Protasova's nickname probably reflects her facial complexion, since the word means 'pock-marked'. At one stage in his career, Stalin bore the same nickname.

'He's over there, in the store-room on the bench.'

Nastia pulled back the curtain a little.

'What's wrong with you? Are you ill?'

Fomich got up from the bench and said, 'When your name's Lively, you're not allowed to be ill!'

The tractor drivers and Pashka Voronin sat round the table.

'Do please forgive us, dear guests. We've nothing to wine and dine you with,' said Fomich. 'Before you arrived, we had pancakes and turkey, but now we're all of a quiver... Why didn't you warn us you were coming?'

The tractor drivers laughed amicably, but Nastia went for Fomich: 'Stop playing the fool. You'd do better to tell us when you are thinking of paying the taxes.'

'Nastia, I just can't think at all. Officials think for us. All we do is keep going forward! There is no retreat. Pashka Voronin over there will think for me.'[49]

The tractor drivers burst out laughing again, but Pashka Voronin knit his straw-coloured, shaggy eyebrows and said, in a threatening voice, 'We haven't come here to listen to your tales. Do you understand?'

'You should be ashamed of yourself, Fëdor Fomich,' said Nastia, joining the offensive on him. 'You're a bright bloke, but you don't work! There are women who, for whole days, never leave the farm, and you're here, kipping on a bench.'

'He's just a malingerer!' said Pashka urging her on.

'Even worse! He's a parasite and an alien **element**, who used to mix with scroungers.'[50]

Nastia and Pashka were egging each other on against Fomich. In a trice, he grasped what was going on. He sat on a stool, crossed his arms across his chest and pronounced in such a meek voice, 'Oh, Nastia... And you, Pasha! Don't waste your fine language on me. I have turned to God. I used not to believe in God, nor in the Devil, not even in the poker. If people had a go at me, I used to give them back tenfold. If you just scratched me, I'd belt you on the ear. But now, I have read the Gospel – if you hit me on the right cheek, I shall offer you the left. So curse me as you will, and take what you wish.'

'Who tipped you off about us?' asked Nastia, point blank.

'A black raven in the forest. I went there this morning for some firewood. I saw it sitting on an oak tree. "Krrr! Nastia and Pashka are coming to visit you. See that you don't offend them".'

---

[49] The references to always going forward and never retreating are typical of the militaristic language of the early Soviet period, when all aspects of life were expressed in battle terminology, and workers were constantly urged to work hard to develop Soviet industry to improve life and the economy.

[50] These epithets are all 'sound bites' from Soviet propaganda of the era. Although it is not reflected here, she gets some of the expressions wrong, which show her lack of education and the fact that, as an official, she simply repeats the political and militaristic cant of the time. Such epithets were frequently applied to kulaks, independent traders, and priests, until all were eliminated in the 1930s.

'Why are we listening to this prattling? Let's make an inventory,' said Pashka, irritated.

Nastia took an official ledger out of her briefcase.

'Where's your gun?' asked Pashka.

'I sold it.'

'Don't lie. You've hidden it somewhere, haven't you?'

'Search for it.'

Pashka Voronin, straining the full length of his long body, looked at the stove, groped around behind the chimney, then went out onto the porch.

'Get a ladder and climb into the attic', said Nastia.

'I don't need a ladder! There is no attic, just a loft. I can reach there with my arm.'

In fact, Voronin stood on tiptoe and extended his neck, just like a crane.

'Hey, giraffe, don't make my house collapse, or you'll have to build me a new one,' said Fomich.

'I'll build you a monkey cage and send you off to a menagerie, you idler.'

Fomich suddenly remembered Pashka's brother, Voronok, rummaging around in Lizunin's house, after he had run off. The evening before, Voronok had ordered Fomich to impose a supplementary tax of one **centner** of carrot seed on Nester Lizunin. 'And make him pay up within twenty-four hours!' he had said. Voronok was the chairman of the rural soviet. His order was law for a secretary. Fomich issued the order. Towards evening, Nester came to see Fomich and asked, 'Fëdor, do you know how far so much seed would go?'

'How far?'

'It would be enough seed for the whole **raion**! Where could I get a quantity like that from?'

It was then that Fomich had written out a release warrant for Nester Lizunin and he cleared off that very night, with all his family.

Fomich now looked at Pashka and he could see in him the older Voronok, standing before him. What kind of jumped-up breed were these people? They're not satisfied with bread. All they want to do is order people around. Or confiscate things. They don't even look similar: one is red-haired, lanky, with a horse-like mug, the other – stocky, dark-haired in his youth, now like a dung-beetle. But they both had the kiss of death. They both followed the father... He was regularly sent to the GULag – he was the foremost thief of the whole region.

Pashka jumped down from the roof space, dusting his sleeves off.

'What's up there?' asked Nastia.

'Nothing but clay and dust. There isn't even any chaff up there. He must have scoffed it.'

'We fed it all to the **domovoi**. He's been eating only chaff all year.'

Again the tractor drivers let out a friendly laugh, as if on command.

'Where do you keep your valuables?' Nastia asked Avdotia.

'Can't you see them? We have tons of valuables – they're on the stove, on the bed…' Fomich replied once again.

'You just stop playing the fool! Where's your trunk?'

'Under the bed.'

Pashka pulled out from under the bed a green trunk bound with iron straps – it was Avdotia's trousseau.

'Have a look!' he said to Nastia, moving discreetly to join the tractor drivers at the table.

Nastia threw back the lid and suddenly, amongst Dunia's old rags, Fomich saw Dunia's purse with its small fasteners. 'Holy Mother! It's got all the money in it from the sale of the goat – three hundred roubles! All we've got in the world.' Fomich gasped when he saw Nastia grab the purse and opened the fasteners. His first thought was to snatch it from her. But what then? These wolf-hounds would have throttled him. He remembered Andriusha's advice: 'Don't curse! Let them take what they want.' Fomich clenched his teeth with vexation and got out of harm's way.

'Dunia!' shouted Nastia. 'Come over here, please.'

Fomich's wife came over to her from the stove.

'Look here!' she said to Dunia, leading her over towards the trunk. 'These **debentures** – you shouldn't keep them with your glad rags.' She thrust the purse with the money into the dumb-struck Avdotia's hand.

'Oh, my godfathers! It's a wonder the children didn't get hold of them,' exclaimed Avdotia, bursting into tears. 'Fedia, why did you throw them in here?' In the meantime, she hurriedly stuffed the purse down her bosom.

'You blame everything on me, you old nag!' Fomich feigned anger with Dunia, but deep-down he felt so relieved. 'Ah, dear old Nastia! Sweet Riabukha! A woman with a conscience! Just look at you. And I'd got you down as a sour old maid…'

'There's nothing to go on the inventory here – just a load of rags,' said Nastia from the trunk. 'Have you still got your goat?'

'We held its funeral ages ago,' said Fomich.

'What on earth are we going to take?'

'Let's take the bike,' said Pashka.

Nastia wrote out a receipt for the bike and handed it to Fomich. 'Here, sign that!'

Fomich signed it, then handed the bike over to Nastia, declaiming, '"Why the neighing, my ardent steed?" You have served me well and true. Now rest, and grant me repose.'[51]

Nastia handed over the bicycle, with its paint peeling off, to Pashka, and the confiscation committee left as a group.

'Fedia, now they'll sell your bike,' sighed Avdotia, following the procession, as she gazed from the window.

'Don't worry, Mother. Good people won't buy it, and bad people would just have pinched it anyway, because they begrudge the money. People have got used to taking things for nothing. Whoever takes it will bring it back to me...'

The next day, Fomich went to Svistunovo to the **kolkhoz** office and said to the book-keeper: 'Korneich, I've got one problem after another! Can't even catch my breath!'

'What's wrong?'

'I'm turning to you, because the regional social security have done me a bad turn. They say that I haven't clocked up the minimum **workday unit**s. So, they're holding back half my pension.'

'But that's against the law.'

'You just try and tell them that. Write out a certificate for me to say how many units I earned.'

'I can do that.'

Korneich wrote out a certificate confirming that, 'He and his family had accumulated eight hundred and forty **workday unit**s over the year'. He stamped the document with the official stamp.

Fomich carefully read it, folded it in four and said, contentedly, 'Now I've got you, my little darlings! I'll send this certificate off, not to the social security, but to the Central Committee itself!'[52]

'Give that back to me!' said Korneich, getting up aggressively, but Fomich gave him the 'V-sign' right under his nose. 'You weren't expecting that, were you?! And you can tell Guzënkov all about it.'

'I'll tell him you tricked it out of me.'

'Bye-bye!' said Fomich, waving his cap. 'Have a nice chat with Mikhail Mikhailovich!'

---

[51] Fomich is quoting the first line from a poem by Pushkin, entitled 'The Horse', written in 1834. His dramatic outburst is comic, particularly since the bike is old and in a poor condition.

[52] The Central Committee was founded by Lenin in 1912 to determine the broad policy objectives of the Bolsheviks, and in 1917 it established the Politburo (political bureau), which became a more important decision-making body. The Central Committee functioned as a quasi-parliamentary body, where policies were debated until the mid-1930s, when Stalin had most of its members executed in order to wield his power as a dictator. Thereafter, its standing and role in Soviet politics was diminished, though it continued to function and grew in size to over three hundred 'elected' members. Most of the members were ministers of major government departments. Both the Central Committee and the Politburo were disbanded upon the demise of the Soviet Union in December 1991.

When he got back home, he removed a double page from an exercise book and drew a large circle in ink over both pages. Around the edge of the circle he wrote, in capital letters, 'THE VICIOUS CIRCLE OF THE TIKHANOVO REGIONAL EXECUTIVE COMMITTEE', and in the centre of the circle he wrote: 'I, Fědor Fomich Kuzkin, excluded from the **kolkhoz** for having accumulated eight hundred and forty **workday units**, received for my whole hoard of seven people a total of sixty-two kilograms of buckwheat (including sparrow crap). I have one question: How are we to live off that?' Fomich enclosed his certificate for the **workday units** with this sketch, and a letter of complaint, stating how he was excluded from the **kolkhoz**, the supplementary taxes levied on him, and the confiscation of his bicycle. He wrote the complaint in a roundabout style, starting with: 'The elections are approaching and the Soviet people rejoice in the possibility of being able to elect their own government. My family will not be doing any voting…' Fomich put all these documents in a sealed envelope, wrote out the address of the **oblast** regional office, addressed it to the first secretary himself, Lavriukhin, and walked to the station to take a train to Pugasovo, forty kilometres away. He posted the letter there, in the station post box, saying to himself, 'They won't think of checking here.' And, pleased with his own artfulness, he drank to his personal success – he got a pint of beer and one hundred and fifty grams of vodka, and he mixed them together, which made a wonderful 'cocktail'.

Chapter Eight

Towards evening, Fomich was left in no doubt that his complaint had had the desired effect when, out of the blue, Pashka Voronin stopped by and, without even stooping through the doorway, shouted across the threshold, 'Go, fetch your bike. It's at the rural council in Svistunovo.'

'I have no right to do that,' Fomich answered humbly. 'He who took it, can bring it back.'

'Fine. It will be brought back. Sometime never!' Pashka slammed the door shut and left.

'Well, Mother. We can expect some more elevated guests!' remarked Fomich ponderously.

The next day, around midday, they suddenly descended. One of them was a very young chap, sharp-nosed, dressed simply in a half-length, dark-tanned leather coat, and wearing black, combed-woollen boots with galoshes. The other man wore a dark-blue overcoat with a grey astrakhan fur collar, and a similar tall, proud hat. The second man looked much more imposing and he had a pale, soft face and a respectful gaze. They came in, greeted everyone politely, took off their hats, and, having wiped their feet at the threshold, they approached the table.

'Did you write the complaint?' the more imposing of the two asked Fomich.

'I don't know,' replied Fomich, looking at them and playing for time.

Avdotia stood stock still by the stove with a handle in her hands – she had just moved a pot of potatoes to one side to cool a little for their lunch.

'We are representatives of the **oblast** committee,' said the younger man.

'I wouldn't know,' said Fomich, not turning a hair.

'Ah, I understand,' said the sharp-nosed man. 'Fëdor Ivanovich, show him the documents.'

The imposing man took out an envelope containing documents from his side pocket and offered it to Fomich. Lively took the envelope, checked to see that the documents were meant for him, but once again cagily said, 'I don't know… Who would you be?'

'Come now, Comrade Kuzkin. You're an old hand!' joked the sharp-nosed fellow. 'Here are our identity papers.' He offered Fomich his **oblast** committee I.D., and the distinguished man did the same.

Fomich unhurriedly perused their I.D., and only then did he invite them to sit at the table.

The kids came in, three of them together, and, with their schoolbags in their hands and not paying any attention to whom or what was at the table, they cried out, 'Mam, we want lunch!'

'You wait, you rowdy lot! You've only just come in. You're like a bunch of ravens. You can see we have visitors at the table.'

'No, no, please feed them!' said the younger man, quickly getting to his feet. 'We shall just sit and wait.'

Fomich brought a bench out from the store-room and invited the officials to sit down.

Avdotia poured out cups of thin buckwheat soup and served the cooked potatoes, which were as small as peas, in an aluminium dish. The kids unceremoniously eyed the guests and only then approached the table. They ate quickly and amiably, in silence, as if it were a race. They ate the potatoes in place of bread, dipping them in some salt before putting them into their mouths. Once they had finished the potatoes and slurped their cup of soup, they crawled onto the stove.

'Why haven't you served their main course?' the distinguished man asked Avdotia.[53]

'That's all there is,' replied Fomich. 'The cup of soup was their first course, and what was in the *luminium* dish was their main.'[54]

'Mam, what was for the main course?' asked the youngest, Shurka.

'Just a sign of the cross!' answered Avdotia.

'Cross yourself and then turn in. Isn't that right?' the distinguished man asked, smiling at Fomich.[55]

Fomich seized on the joke, remarking, 'And pull your stomach in!'

The distinguished man remarked, 'It looks as though your belts are already on the last hole.'

---

[53] Normally, the main course would be a meat or fish dish, but the family is so poor they have none.
[54] Kuzkin means, of course, 'aluminium'.
[55] It was believed that making the sign of the cross before going to bed protected the sleeper from evil spirits. This passage was cut because of its religious context.

'There is still a bit of slack,' joked Fomich, slapping his stomach.

The imposing man shot a quizzical glance at his younger colleague, who almost imperceptibly winked at Fomich and said, smiling, 'Please show us your food reserves.' To the distinguished man he said, 'Let's start with the cellar, Fëdor Ivanovich.'

'Of course. We must take a look,' agreed the imposing man, standing up and started to unbutton his coat.

Fomich took his heavy coat and put it on the bed.

'You'd better hang it up,' the distinguished man remarked, looking warily at the bed, covered in an old patchwork cover.

'The stuff on our coat stand is even tattier than that,' said Fomich. 'As you wish! I'll hang it up.'

But when the imposing man looked over to the coat stand and saw Fomich's ragged jersey and the children's shabby jackets, he stopped him, saying, 'No, no. Just leave it there. I didn't mean anything by it.'

The sharp-nosed man stretched his nimble, laughing lips wide across the full width of his face and gave Fomich's wife a friendly pat on the shoulder, saying, 'Never mind! Don't worry! All will be well.' He threw his own coat onto the bed next to the other, and said, 'Off we go, to the cellar!' He opened the hatch himself, jumped down first. Then he asked, 'Do you have any light?'

Fomich handed him a lit lamp.

'Well, Fëdor Ivanovich, are you coming down?' he asked from the cellar.

'Yes, I am.' Fëdor Ivanovich was wearing a fine black suit and boots. He carefully steadied himself on the hatch. 'It looks deep! I could do with a parachute! I need a foothold.'

'I'll get a stool for you,' said Fomich, handing them one.

Fëdor Ivanovich lowered himself into the cellar and instantly they looked round and saw a small pile of tiny potatoes.

'What's this here, your household potatoes?' asked Fëdor Ivanovich.[56]

'That's all we've got,' replied Fomich.

They climbed out of the cellar in silence.

'Do you have a pantry?'

'No.'

'But is that the sum total of your food reserves?' asked Fëdor Ivanovich, pointing his finger at the cellar.

'There's a tub of sauerkraut on the porch.'

---

[56] He means potatoes for eating, as opposed to seed potatoes, which were reserved for planting in the spring, for next year's crop.

They all went out onto the porch.

'How on earth do you manage to live?' asked Fëdor Ivanovich, visibly perplexed.

'Just like this,' answered Fomich.

'I said this would all be typical of his misrepresentation,' said the sharp-nosed man. 'Pure Motiakov antics!'

Fëdor Ivanovich turned grey and his face seemed to get longer. Without so much as a word, he went back into the house, hurriedly put on his coat and bid farewell to the hostess, his eyes downcast. 'Sorry for the intrusion,' he said. 'We'll try to help you.' Then he turned to Fomich and said, 'Come along with us.'

Their jeep was parked by the **brigade leader**'s house.

'Please get in!' Fëdor Ivanovich let Fomich take a rear seat along with the sharp-nosed young man and then issued an order to the driver: 'Sound your horn!'

At the sound of the horn, Pashka Voronin came running out of his house and Fëdor Ivanovich nodded to him. 'Get in!'

Pashka also got in the back, squeezed up close to Fomich, and they all set off. They turned off towards Svistunovo. They came to a halt in front of the main office.

'Let's go!' Fëdor Ivanovich went in first.

Guzënkov was not in the office. The bald Korneich popped his head out of the accounts office and obligingly said, 'Take a seat. I'll just run and fetch Guzënkov. I'll be back in a moment.'

'Don't bother!' Fëdor Ivanovich stopped him. 'And what is your position here?'

'I'm the bookkeeper.'

'Excellent. Do you know Kuzkin?'

'Yes, sir!' replied Korneich, in a military fashion.

'Tomorrow you are to assign a horse to Kuzkin. He will be going to the regional office.'

Korneich's moustache twitched, looking with disbelief, first at the official who had just arrived, and then at Pashka Voronin, who was standing behind him. Then he cautiously expressed his doubt: 'I shall, of course, inform Mikhail Mikhailovich. Only this man, Comrade Chief, is a loafer.' But he quickly added, 'I mean, the management has so defined him.'

'And what's this?' Fëdor Ivanovich asked, showing him the certificate. 'Who issued this? The management?'

Korneich simply looked and blurted out, 'Absolutely! It was me. But allow me to say, Comrade Chief, that he got this certificate out of me by deception.'

'How do you mean?'

'He asked me for it for the social security.'

'It doesn't matter who it was for. Is it true that he has accumulated so many **workday units**?'

'Absolutely!' Korneich stood to attention as before, and his heavy fists, with their bulging, blue veins, almost reached his knees.

'Fine. So tomorrow, give Fomich a horse.' And, turning to Fomich, he said, 'You come to the regional committee offices by nine o'clock.'

'Comrade Chief, I'd better go on foot,' said Fomich.

'Why?'

'I'm worried I'll freeze to death on the way. There is such a hard frost. And my clothes are like lace – the wind blows at the front and flies straight out the back.'

'Fine. Then give him a horse with a cart and a sheepskin,' said Fëdor Ivanovich.

'Will do!' barked Korneich.

'And you,' he said, turning to Pashka Voronin. 'Return the bicycle to Kuzkin today, without fail. Where is it now?'

'It's at the rural soviet.'

'That's fine.' Fëdor Ivanovich left the office without bidding farewell.

Fomich ran out after him.

'Get in!' he said to Fomich. 'We'll take you home. Just make sure you turn up on time tomorrow. And you must come by horse.'

Late that evening, Pashka Voronin brought the bike back. He left it on the porch and knocked on the windowpane. But, when Fomich went out, he could see neither hide nor hair of him.

Chapter Nine

Fomich decided against taking the horse – it was too much bother: he would have had to go to Svistunovo, cause hassle in the office, then get it back there, and then he'd have to trudge almost another five **versts** back home. What was the point of all that? If the horse had been kept at his homestead, or even in Prudki, it would have been different. But to make the round trip to Svistunovo was just as far as making a single journey to Tikhanovo. You couldn't make the trip without the fleece – you'd freeze to death. And there'd be more fuss and bother with the fleece: you couldn't take it into the regional committee offices, but you'd be uneasy about leaving it in the sleigh. What if got stolen? You'd never pay it off.

So, early in the morning frost, he set off at a light jog all the way to Tikhanovo, without stopping to catch his breath: the frost drove you on better than any whip.

'It's odd how our life has turned out,' thought Fomich along the way. 'The whole of Prudki had been left with only three horses – one was for Pashka Voronin, and the other two for the farm to fetch water. But for the peasant men and women, it was a case of "get about as best you can". You had no buses or cars. If you wanted to go to hospital, you had first to get to Svistunovo to the office, beg for a horse, and then *if* you were given one, you could go. But if you wanted to get to the station, to market, or even to the regional main town – don't even bother asking! Guzënkov had his car, Pashka – his horse and a motorbike, but the **kolkhoz** workers had only Shanks's pony. In times gone by, when you had your own transport in your yard – you just used to get it harnessed, then off you went, wherever you liked. Business or pleasure. Or you'd simply go for a spin around the village, especially after a few drinks – it was damn good fun! And taking the kids out for a ride was a sheer delight. Making a trip to the forest at night... It was so beautiful there! But now they spent days on end, dossing about like tramps in the meadows, with nothing to do. In the past, at winter time, only the lowest of the low went on foot to Tikhanovo. Like Ziuzia, the horse thief. But even he would get lucky and manage to ride on somebody else's horse...'

At Tikhanovo regional committee offices, Lively was greeted by the head of the social security section, Varvara Tsyplakova.

'Please come into my office, Fëdor Fomich,' she said courteously and chasséd ahead, filling the whole corridor with her body.

It was early in the day and the regional office was empty.

Fomich was taken aback by how politely she treated him and by the unexpected invitation to her office.[57] Usually, when pensioners gathered in the regional social security office, when it was exceptionally noisy as people thronged at the cashier's window, Varvara Tsyplakova would bawl from the adjoining office at the cashier in her booming voice: 'Egor, restrain your dependants! Otherwise, I'll chuck the lot of you out in the cold!'

But on this occasion, she opened the door personally for Fomich – the social security office was right next to the regional committee office – and she let him enter before her.

'Do please go in, Fëdor Fomich,' she said.

It was only half-past eight and Fomich was in no hurry. He took the more comfy seat – the oilskin sofa.

'Well, since you are being unimaginably polite, I'll show my gratitude to you,' thought Fomich.

He took out his tobacco-pouch, made a big, fat roll-up the size of his index finger, and blew strong-smelling smoke rings directly at the official.

'I've been wanting to chat things over with you for ages, Comrade Kuzkin. Ahem! Ahem! But you never drop in here. You're not to be found when you're out and about. Ahem! Ahem! What kind of tobacco is that? It's making my eyes water.'

'Just have a sniff of your own, Varvara Petrovna,' said Fomich, with a wink. 'Then it'll pass. What's sauce for the goose is sauce for the gander. Anyway, I bet your tobacco is even stronger.'

Varvara Petrovna took a pinch of her own snuff. Usually she kept this little weakness of hers from her visitors.

---

[57] Russian officials and bureaucrats were notoriously uncooperative and rude to those who approached them for their help. The fact that this woman is so polite is a sure sign that she has been 'lent on' by her superiors.

'Well, I just treat myself to a little, every now and then. All right, then. Perhaps I'll just have a little pinch to keep you company.' Varvara Petrovna smiled with embarrassment and took out from her desk drawer a large, round powder-compact with a black swan on the lid, sprinkled a pinch of snuff onto her index finger, and first put some up one nostril, and then up the other. Then she quietly let out a thin, little squeak, covered her eyes with her hand and, extending her lower lip, spasmodically gulping in air, she suddenly let out such a roar. Fomich was so startled that he choked on his own tobacco smoke and also started coughing.

'Atchoooo! Atcchhooo! Oh, my godfathers!' Varvara Petrovna exclaimed, smiling and wiping away the tears from her eyes, turning as red as the rising sun.

'Ha, ha, hhaaa! Bloody hell!' swore Fomich, blowing his nose and wiping away the tears in his eyes, along with Varvara Petrovna.

'You're a bad influence on me, Fëdor Fomich!' Varvara Petrovna put away the powder-compact with the swan decoration and got straight down to business. 'You have been behaving rather arrogantly, Comrade Kuzkin. Are you really hard up?'

'What can I say?' Fomich said evasively. 'In some ways I…'

'That's just the point. You should have come to see me, had a word, and written out a request for help. Otherwise, I'd have to do everything for you. There's only me working here, but there are countless numbers of you pensioners.'

'But we don't hold it against you,' Fomich replied, just to be on the safe side.

'My very point! Knock and the door will opened, as they say.[58] But we have to drag you lot in by the nose, like puppies. You never come on your own accord. So be it! So what if they lead us a pretty dance?!' Varvara Petrovna opened a grey file, took out the money lying on top of the papers, and offered it to Lively. 'Here's five hundred roubles. Take it! It's a one-off payment. And just sign here, in the ledger.'

Fomich took the money and started counting it slowly. While he was counting it, his brain went into overdrive: 'I wonder if I'm selling myself too cheap? Since she has entered it in the ledger, I can count on it as mine. But the question is – should I take it now? I never asked for this. That means she has been lent on by the bosses… So how will this all turn out? My case still hasn't been sorted out, but I'm expected to take the five hundred. If I do, they'll think I've kicked up all this fuss to get some money. No! That won't do…'

Fomich put the money in a neat pile and tapped it with his palm.

'Quite correct. There are five hundred roubles there,' he said, and placed the money back on the table.

'It's yours. A payment, like I said. Take it and sign.' Varvara Petrovna smiled while offering him the ledger.

---

[58] This is a Biblical reference. In Russia, even though priests had been exiled and churches closed, and religious belief was officially discouraged and actively repressed, older people still used Biblical expressions in everyday speech. This sentiment appears in Luke 13, vs.25 and Revelation 3, vs.20.

'But, why should I take it? I didn't apply or make a fuss for it. Then out of the blue – have some money! What money? Where from?'

'It's like I said – it's to help you out, a benefit.'

'We have to discuss benefits,' said Fomich. 'But if the regional committee has granted it, then that's a different matter.' Fomich made for the door and, turning round at the threshold, said, 'I thank you for your trouble, Varvara Petrovna!'

Varvara Petrovna sat dumb-struck and looked blank.

The reception in the regional committee office was full of people. Fomich's visitor from the previous day – the sharp-nosed young man in the black, half-length coat – was surrounded by several **kolkhoz** chairmen, amongst whom stood Guzënkov.

'Comrade Krylyshkin, will our region be sent any "thirty-thousanders"?' someone asked the sharp-nosed young man.[59]

'The committee has not yet met, but I think so.'

'Which **kolkhozes** will they be sent to?'

'Who will be sent, Comrade Krylyshkin?'

'That, I couldn't say.'

'Are you yourself not thinking of transferring to a **kolkhoz**?'

'Thinking is not enough – we must decide!' replied the sharp-nosed man.

'That's right! But who does actually think? Hee, hee…'

'Comrade Krylyshkin, come to my farm! We desperately need a vet.'

'There's bright! He'll take your seat and you'll be out on your ear…'

'No, I'll just shuffle to one side. We'll both get on the same chair!'

'Same chair as you?! Your arse is bigger than an armchair! Ha, ha!!'

'Fëdor Ivanovich is on his way!' shouted the receptionist from his desk, whereupon the noisy crowd of chairmen dispersed in a trice and fell silent.

Fëdor Ivanovich slowly climbed the stairs. He held his cap in his hands and only now did Lively notice that through the thinning, slicked-back hair on the top of his head, a large, pink bald patch shone through. Demin walked next to him, and behind him, in his military jacket and boots, Motiakov strode deliberately. The expression on his face was like that of an officer inspecting his guards on duty: whoever glanced at him now would have imagined that, what had silenced the noisy chairmen was his appearance, his, Motiakov's, and not that of some Fëdor Ivanovich, or other.

'Good day, Fëdor Ivanovich!' could be heard from all around at that moment.

---

[59] The 'thirty-thousanders' were a group of mainly young people, who were recruited through the Young Communist League (**Komsomol**) to be mobilized and work on farms as volunteers in new areas of '**Virgin Land**' in far-flung areas, such as Kazakhstan, eastern Siberia, and the **Volga** basin.

Fëdor Ivanovich politely replied to all: 'Good day, Comrades. Greetings!' he said, smiling.

As they looked at him, everyone else around was smiling, and Fomich also smiled, not really knowing why.

'Good day, Comrade Kuzkin!' he said, offering his hand to Lively, who, not in the least timidly, shook his soft, warm hand.

'Did you come by horse?' asked Fëdor Ivanovich.

'Not at all!' replied Lively, standing bolt upright, as if to the command '"Shun", like Korneich the day before.

'Why not? Did they not give you a horse?' asked Fëdor Ivanovich, looking severely at Guzënkov.

'It's cold, Fëdor Ivanovich,' replied Fomich, calling his former guest by his first name and patronymic for the first time.

'And what about the fleece?'

'You can't take a fleece into the regional offices. And if you left it in the sleigh, it would get pinched. Then Guzënkov would have got a third fleece from me. He's already got two out of me.'

Fëdor Ivanovich burst out laughing, aimiably endorsed by the rest.

'Motiakov, he's given you the finger', said Fëdor Ivanovich, laughing.[60] 'By the way, did you make your leather boots out of Kuzkin's skin?'

'His skin is not fit even for box-calf boots,' replied Motiakov gloomily, but looking at Lively as if to say, 'Just you wait, I'll teach you to give me the finger. You'll cry tears of blood.'

Fëdor Ivanovich took out a piece of paper from his pocket and showed it to Motiakov, asking, *'Who wrote out this supplementary tax?'*

'Timoshkin,' he replied, soldier-like.

'And who signed it?'

Motiakov looked at his signature for a second and finally admitted: 'I did.'

'We'll tan your hide for this supplementary tax.' Then, he told Demin in an official *tone, having nodded towards Lively, 'First we'll sort him out.'*

'Please go in, Comrade Kuzkin.'

Demin admitted Fomich into his office.

People poured in after them in their droves and sat along the walls. 'As if they've fallen into rank,' thought Lively. He was told to stand at the end of the long table

---

[60] This expression defies translation and it is a play on Kuzkin's name. The name 'Kuzkin' is very close to a Russian expression, which is a euphemism for 'fuck off': the literal translation would be something like, 'He's sent you to Kuzkin's mother', meaning, 'He tells you to go fuck your mother'. For the reference to 'skin', see footnote № 41, p.116.

covered with green baize. At the other end of the table, Fëdor Ivanovich sat down in the secretary's seat, and Demin sat next to him. Then Motiakov found a seat apart, and Fomich even threw him a challenging look.

'Well, Guzënkov, give us your report on Kuzkin,' said Fëdor Ivanovich.

Mikhail Mikhailovich coughed loudly to clear his throat and, standing where he was, announced: 'We excluded him as an alien **element**… Because he didn't work…'

'How do you mean, "He didn't work"?' asked Fëdor Ivanovich. 'What about the eight hundred and forty **workday units** credited to him?'

'He was moonlighting,' replied Guzënkov.

'So what were you doing on the **kolkhoz**, playing skittles? How do you mean, "moonlighting"?' asked Fëdor Ivanovich, raising his voice.

'Well, he was a supply-man. He got sacking here, timber there… Or he would get hold of a harness, or mechanical spare parts,' said Guzënkov, haltingly. 'That's how he notched up his **workday unit**s. He got lots. We failed to keep track of him.'

'So did he not do his job? Could he not get what you wanted?' asked Fëdor Ivanovich.

'As far as that was concerned and getting what we wanted, he proved to be resourceful.'

'All right! And what did you ask for, Kuzkin?' asked Fëdor Ivanovich, looking at Lively.

'In as far as they have not provided my family with food to live off through my work on the **kolkhoz**, I asked for a **passport**. I mean, I want to find a job elsewhere. I want to earn money.'

'I understand. And what did you do?' Fëdor Ivanovich asked Guzënkov.

'We refused… since we can't do that. And we excluded him from the **kolkhoz** for not going out to work.'

'Can you make use of him on the **kolkhoz**, or not?'

'If he won't work, why should we put up with a parasite?'

'Oh, what a chairman! How can you discard such a person? You yourself said that he got all that you wanted for the **kolkhoz**. And it's obvious that he's honest. Any other worker would have pocketed half of what he got for you. He could have lived the life of Riley. After all, he was dealing with lots of money! But his house is like the one **Baba Yaga** has, living in a swamp, and it's so rickety that a pig could push it over with its snout. The kids run around bare-foot and bare-arsed. He has nothing to eat himself. How has the **kolkhoz** helped him? Have you ever even visited him at home?'

Guzënkov turned the colour of red calico and finally muttered: 'No, I've not been there.'

'Just look at this little tin god! Never had the time? Or were you frightened of losing your status as a chairman? I found time to visit him from the **oblast** offices. But you didn't bother… How are we to interpret all this?'

Guzënkov's entire, voluminous face smouldered, but he maintained a painful silence.

'How much invalidity pension do you get?' Fëdor Ivanovich asked Fomich.

'One hundred and twenty roubles.'

'You don't get rich on that.'

'Social security gave him five hundred roubles... and he refused that!' announced Motiakov, sarcastically. 'Apparently, that's not enough!'

'How do you mean "refused" it? Why?' asked Fëdor Ivanovich.

'Invalids who crawl on all fours need that kind of benefit. I have hands and feet. I want work and earn a wage. And it's a bit suspicious that you give such a benefit.' Fomich turned to Motiakov and said, 'Twenty minutes before this meeting, I was enticed into the social security office and slipped some money. "Here, now keep shtoom!" Do you take me for a beggar?'

'That's just the point!' said Fëdor Ivanovich with a grin, picking up the point. 'You're such a tactical bunch, Motiakov. That's just it!' Fëdor Ivanovich hit his pencil on the table. 'There is no point in being devious. You couldn't keep Kuzkin on the **kolkhoz**. Let him go! But you, Guzënkov, and you, Motiakov, will be given a written warning. That will to teach you not to squander **kolkhoz** staff in future. *You must look after people. Improve their lives. It's high time you got out of using old methods, like the rod and knout. That's who you should learn from about dealing with staff,'* he said, *nodding towards Petia Ermolaevich Dolgii.*

'If Zvonarëv's **kolkhoz** is so good, why did he refuse to sow maize on his pasture land?' asked Motiakov.

'Why was that?' Fëdor Ivanovich asked.

'Because the land was too low – it would have just rotted,' answered Petia Dolgii.

'So, it would have rotted on your land, but not on Guzënkov's – is that it?!'

'On the contrary – it did rot for Guzënkov, but I simply didn't sow it.'

'So what did you do, Motiakov – just transfer Zvonarëv's quota for maize to Guzënkov?' asked Fëdor Ivanovich.

'Something like that... But he entices Guzënkov's staff to join his farm.'

'Ah-ha! Just you watch out Guzënkov that you don't let your **kolkhoz** go to pot, or you'll join the ranks of the ordinary farmer. And you won't be transferred to Zvonarëv's farm as a **brigade leader**.'

'We don't need brigade leaders,' Zvonarëv responded. 'But I could give you a job milking the cows!'

Everyone roared with laughter, but Guzënkov puffed himself up, yet he meekly cast his eyes down.

'Enough! Let's decide what we are to do with Kuzkin. Where shall we fix him up with a job?' Fëdor Ivanovich asked, wiping away his tears of laughter.

'Let's give him a **passport** and let him find work in the town,' suggested Demin.

'I cannot leave,' said Fomich.

'Why not?'

'On account of a total absence of an up-turn.'

'What's this, political economy Prudki-style?' asked Fëdor Ivanovich.

'It's nothing to do with political economy, it's utterly boring. I have five children and a son still in the army. You've seen my "wealth" for yourself. How on earth can I expect to be on the up with my horde?'

'He makes kids by the dozens with one stroke of his scythe,' muttered Motiakov.

'God made man and put no restrictions on him using his tool. So, I'm using mine!' shot back Fomich straight at him.

Fëdor Ivanovich once again roared with laughter, and everyone else joined in.

'Ah, Kuzkin, you're as sharp as a razor! You ought to have been a batman to an old general… You'd have entertained him for years with your jokes!'

'We have a retired colonel living with us in Prudki. But, apparently, he's all fixed up – there's no chance there. But Guzënkov sniffs around there day and night!' said Lively.[61]

Again, everyone burst out laughing.

'Okay, that's enough!' said Fëdor Ivanovich, taking out his handkerchief and wiping the tears from his eyes. 'Let's come to a decision. Quickly!'

'Could we give him the watchman's job at the pressing station?' Motiakov asked Demin.

'But we've got Ëlkin there, from Brëkhovo,' someone pointed out.

'He must be sacked,' said Motiakov glumly. 'It's been discovered he has relatives living abroad.'

'What sort of relatives?' asked Demin.

'A son. He's now turned up in America. He thought he was dead – he'd even had a wake for him.'[62]

'We ought not to rush into that', said Demin.

'I'll take him on,' said the thin, ungainly Zvonarëv, getting to his feet. He was the chairman of the neighbouring **kolkhoz**, just over the water from Prudki. 'I need a

---

[61] The joke here is based on the hierarchical concept of rank and being a servant, i.e. batman, to a person of superior rank. A general is above a colonel in rank and Kuzkin implies that Guzënkov is eager to serve anyone of rank, even if it means starting at a high rank and moving down the line until he eventually finds an officer, whom he can serve.

[62] At certain times in the Soviet regime, it was dangerous to have any contacts with foreigners for fear of being branded as a spy or foreign informer. Some Russians had emigrated before the Revolution of 1917, but many shunned any contact with former relatives abroad for fear of reprisals. Such contacts were particularly dangerous during Stalin's reign.

watchman for the winter to look after the timber yard. He'll get paid in money and bread.'

'Will you do that?' Fëdor Ivanovich asked Lively.

'I will. Only get Guzënkov to issue me with an authorization for leave. Then I'll get a **passport**.'

'Wait out there. We'll do that after the meeting', said Guzënkov.

The meeting went on right until the evening. When Fomich finally came home with the long-awaited release papers, his wife Avdotia said to him on the porch, 'Come on, Fedia. Come inside the house.'

In the middle of the living room, lit by – what seemed to Fomich's eyes – the blinding brightness of the electric light, lay side by side two sacks of flour and three of potatoes, and on top of them were two bundles. Fomich squeezed the sacks and he could feel that the flour was dry and the potatoes large. Then he unwrapped the bundles and looked at the contents in a paternal way: there were three children's jumpers, three grey school blouses, three pairs of boots with rubber soles, and three nice, new, grey school caps.

'Well, these aren't much use!' he said, taking hold of the caps. 'They can do without these at spring-time. Fur hats would have been more useful.'

Chapter Ten

Fomich lived carefree until the spring thaw: the flour had lasted almost all winter and he had bought some extra potatoes, so that there were enough to plant. Avdotia had even reared a piglet. Fomich had acquired some felt boots for himself and the kids, he had bought himself a half-length sheepskin coat and a cap with earflaps, made from dog fur. He went into the forest with his gun, like a sentry on duty.

One day in March, Old Filat called over to him from his **mound**, where he was warming himself in the sunshine.

'Fedka, is that really you?! Come over here!'

Fomich went over and they exchanged greetings.

'I looks over and thinks, "Who's the barge hauler? Or has some one turned up with an incomer?"' said Old Filat, looking at Fomich with his eyes screwed up. 'Look at you, dressed to the nines!'

'I am now a free Cossack... a kind of forester,' bragged Lively.[63]

'So I've heard,' said Old Filat, feeling the hem of Fomich's red-brown sheepskin coat. 'It's soft. I dare say it's a state one.'

'Yes, I bought it myself. And how are things with you, Old Filat?'

---

[63] Cossacks were noted for their independence and indomitability – indeed, their very name is derived from the Turkish, meaning 'free man' or 'adventurer'. They lived in the northern hinterlands of the Black and Caspian seas.

Illustration 8. 'Russian Serfs (from a drawing by Raffet)', *Illustrated Times***, April 17 1858.**

'Not bad. I'm having bother with my pension. The other day I went to Svistunovo, to the rural soviet. The chairman said, "Leave the **kolkhoz**. Then we can officially put you down as homeless. You'll get eighty-five roubles a month". So, I want to leave the **kolkhoz**. What d'you think, will they let me go?'

'They'll let you go. Make a fuss! They let me leave.' He threw his gun over his shoulder and off he went…

But Fomich did not swank around for long with his gun on his shoulder. As the flood waters on the river arrived, so his career as a forest watchman ended. The last loads of sawn timber were transported away through the crunchy April snow.

'Now what am I to do?' he asked Petia Dolgii. 'I'm not going back to Guzënkov!'

'Get a transfer to my **kolkhoz**. People don't work for nothing on our farm. You won't starve.'

'But where will I live? Can you provide me with a house?'

'No, you'd just be general staff.'

'Well, of course,' Fomich agreed. 'If I was some kind of valuable specialist, then that would be a different matter. But I'm not. So, like everyone else, I can shoot a gun or twist a cow's tail! The other **kolkhoz** workers wouldn't allow a house to be built for a "specialist" like me!'

'You could always go back to Prudki for the night.'

'It's eight **versts** to Prudki. And I'd have to cross the river... I'd drown at night. No, but thanks for the offer.' Lively was very downcast. 'Now Guzënkov will have me for breakfast!'

'Hang on a minute!' said Petia Dolgii, detaining him. 'The Raskidukha hydro-electric power-station sends timber down to us on the spring flood waters. They send telegraph poles for all the **kolkhozes** – throughout the whole region. Would you be a watchman for that wood?'

'Definitely!'

'Hang on a minute!' Petia Dolgii dialled the number. 'Is that Brëkhovo? Give me Raskidukha, please! Eh? Is that Raskidukha? Get me the boss, please! Comrade Koshkin? Greetings! This is Zvonarëv. Yes, yes. Listen, have you found a watchman yet, for your timber? You haven't? I've kept my eye out for you. Available to be hired, you say? Yes, he is. No, no, he's not a **kolkhoz** worker. Even more suitable. What? From Prudki. That's just where we've plans to set up a yard. Roads to Prudki? They're okay. Like everywhere else. Eh? Even better.'

Petia Dolgii hung up.

'That'll cost you a half-litre bottle,' he joked. 'Go to Raskidukha and put yourself down as their watchman. They're going to float the timber down to the area around Prudki. Work just falls into your hands. Off you go!' Petia Dolgii put his hand in his and wished Fomich luck. 'Don't miss the boat! Off you dash!'

In the meadows, the snow had almost fully thawed, leaving huge puddles of melt-water which flowed slowly into the bogs and lake, swelling the old, porous ice patches which were being eaten away by the sun. Fomich thought, 'The ice has not started to break up on the lakes yet, which means it will still probably hold me on the river. I'll go across on the ice!'

He returned to Prudki with a light heart – jammy devil! 'Now we're sitting pretty, right until harvest time. Then the new wheat will be in. Sparrows themselves shout at that time – "I can feed seven wives now." The main thing is to struggle through to the spring.'

In spring, the river came to his aid. How dear was the river Prokosha to his heart! How many times had it come to his rescue at the leanest times? They went through the winter of 1946 without so much as a crust of bread. The potatoes then didn't even come up. Even the cattle had to be slaughtered... It looked as if it was the end for Lively. But no! He and Old Filat had made nets, cut ice-holes all along the Prokosha and roped it off: they beat the ice with wooden mallets and stamped with their boots to frighten the fish. It didn't work well. But then, for the first time, some chemical poison was released into the Oka River. All the fish made for the Prokosha. Every cell of the net had a fish in it. Although they stank of paraffin, the whole village ate them without a second thought.

In 1933, from the onset of spring, there was no fish.[64] *There was such a famine and it was as if the fish had all died off or buried themselves at the bottom of the river. But then again the Prokosha saved all the inhabitants of Prudki: in the backwaters, a plant called a 'bollock cutter' grew thickly. It wasn't a reed or a grass, and there weren't really leaves or stems that stuck out of the water, but they grew tall, like triangular lances. If you got in the water with a drag-net, it would really scratch you between the legs, which is where it gets its name. It was looked upon as a complete pain! But suddenly... There you go! It turns out that this bollock cutter has edible roots. So, old and young people littered the banks of the backwaters and creeks, pulling on these black, hairy stems, washed them by the basket load, then dried them on their roofs and shoved them in their soups, and baked buns with them. They were all right... You could eat them... And they even smelt a bit like bread.*[65]

And now, once again, the Prokosha had provided him with work. 'A salary of four hundred roubles – we'll survive with that,' thought Fomich. It was also good that, from spring onwards, the local shop in Prudki started being supplied with bread, brought from the regional capital. Admittedly, it was delivered only once a week and they'd only let you have two loaves per homestead. But even then, it was a help. They used to bake

---

[64] 1932-33 was a disastrous year for Russia, as there was widespread famine, on which there was a total news and media blackout for many years. It cost the lives of millions of peasants and it was a taboo subject until the very last years of the Soviet regime, when *glasnost* and *perestroika* were introduced under Gorbachëv. The famine started late in 1932, as peasants killed their animals in an act of self-sabotage against the draconian methods used to requisition agricultural produce by the state. Many peasants fled to the cities and, in an effort to stem the tidal wave of migrating peasants, cordons and blockades were set up by the police and the armed forces. There are no official figures of those who died during this event, but some experts estimate casualties to be around six million. People turned to eating tree bark and anything they could find growing around them. There were even reports of cannibalism. Note that this passage was cut from the original *Novyi mir* edition, because of the reference to the famine. For more details see Robert Conquest, *The Harvest of Sorrow* (London: Pimlico, 2002).

[65] The plant here in question is rather difficult to identify because Mozhaev only gives this local (and rather singular!) name for it. Such local names proliferate in their scores, even though they might refer to the same plant, because of the isolated nature of communities in rural Russia. According to experts, the plant in question is most likely to be *Scirpus lacustris*, which is abundant in Russian lakes. This plant was mentioned as a famine food in a work by A. Maurizio, *Histoire de l'alimentation végétale* (Paris: Payot, 1932), p.177. When Mozhaev mentions that it was 'not a reed or a grass', he is merely describing the appearance of the plant, and not its true botanical classification: it is, in fact, a 'club rush', a member of the *Cyoeraceae* family. This passage was cut primarily because it refers to the famine, but the word 'bollock' was also regarded as being improper in Soviet times, and it almost never appeared in print.

potato cakes to go with these loaves, and together, they filled the kids up. 'Now we'll survive,' Fomich reassured himself. 'Now I've no reason to curse my fate.'

He approached the Prokosha by Bogoiavlensk Crossing.[66] The ice had risen up on the river and stood level with the banks. On the bank lay a black, unwieldy wooden ferry-boat, which resembled a flat iron. The water lapped at its enormously wide belly. Nearby, under the lee of the ferry-boat, sat the ferryman by a camp-fire: he was a withered, large-nosed old man in an oilcloth cape, worn over his jumper. In the area he was known by his nickname – Ivan Vesëlyi.[67] On the fire stood a pot of boiling water, cooking some potatoes.

'The water will carry your ark away,' said Fomich, sitting down at the fire.

'It will' agreed Ivan Vesëlyi. 'Those arse-holes wanted to drag it away by tractor in the autumn. They brought a drag-frame for it and pulled the ferry onto the bank... But then they couldn't load it onto the frame. So, they just left it on the bank...'

'So, do you live in it then?' Fomich asked, half standing up and looked in the ferry-boat: its hold, right up to the upper deck, was full of hay.

'I just watch over it. Just in case the flood water carries it right off to the Oka. What's it to them? They're going to knock together another log boat, bring it here, and dump it in the river. "'Ere y'are, Ivan. Get on with the job!" And I'm supposed to work with that. But what happens if it doesn't handle well? You can bust a gut, but they don't give a damn.'

'And does this handle well?' sneered Fomich. 'It looks more like a barn!'

'Don't say that! It handles beautiful on water. I can pilot it all by myself as far as Brëkhovo.'

'Well, I never! You'll get the boat to the village and the hay to your farm... You're no fool!'

'I gathered the hay myself. It was what was left from the hayricks. I'll use it for bedding...'

'Bedding?!' Fomich pulled a wisp of fine, aromatic hay from the hold. 'You could use this "bedding" to make tea. And there must be a full two cart-loads.'

'You just keep your nose out of what doesn't concern you!' snapped Ivan Vesëlyi. 'Aren't you the timber watchman? Then watch it! The meadows are someone else's job.'

'No, I was just saying...' said Fomich. Then he added glumly, 'Anyway, I'm no longer the timber watchman.'

'Oh, your contract finished, then?'

'Yes, it has, Ivan.'

Lively went down to the water's edge.

---

[66] Bogoiavlensk literally means 'Apparition of God'.
[67] Ivan is a very popular name in Russia and the word 'vesëlyi' means 'happy' or 'cheerful', which is ironic, since, as is obvious, the old man is anything, but cheerful.

'What do you reckon, Ivan? Will the ice get on the move this week?'

'Definitely! Last night it crackled by the bank. It's pulling away. If not today, then tomorrow it'll be on the move, without so much as a "kiss my arse".'

'Hey, let me have that staff!' Fomich took a light pine pole from the ferry and flung it to the ground.

'What d'you want that for?' asked Ivan Vesëlyi, surprised, his Adam's apple high in his throat.

'I've got to get to the other side.'

'Are you out of your mind? Well, kiss my arse! The river banks are flooded – it's like a lake over there. You'll drown.'

'I'll float to the surface. I turned to wood long ago, mate. People like me don't drown. Let me have that plank, as well!' He took a wide plank from the boat and went to the river.

'Hey, not so fast, you hothead!' shouted Ivan Vesëlyi.

'What?'

'Go along the bank. By Prudki there's a wide gap where the ice has melted. If you shout, they'll come over in a boat. You'll get a lift across.'

'But what if no one comes? Who will hear me? There's not a soul about by the river at this time of year.'

'Well, wait a day or two. When the ice flows, I'll take you over on the ferry.'

'I haven't the time to wait.'

Fomich threw his plank over the flooded bank: one end rested on the bank, the other just touched the edge of the spongy ice.

'Lord, bless me!' He advanced warily along the plank, leaning on the staff. The plank floundered in the water and slowly started to sink. Fomich rushed onto the ice with short, frequent jumps, splashing as he went. But suddenly, the edge of the ice-floe, on which the plank rested, broke off. One of his legs slipped into the water up to his knee and, with a push on the staff, he threw himself, at a stroke, on his belly, onto the ice-floe.

'Oh, you hot head! Well, kiss my arse!' swore Ivan Vesëlyi from the bank.

Fomich took off his boot, poured the water out of it, rewrapped his **footcloths**, and on he went, carrying the staff and plank. The ice in the middle of the river was solid. Fomich just avoided the ice puddles, fearing he might fall through an ice-hole. On the far side of the river, the ice went right up to the water's edge. Fomich did not even have to use the plank – he darted around, hanging on to his staff, and then he was there.

The next day, Fomich was already at Raskidukha hydro-electric station early in the morning. The power-station stood at the confluence of the Prokosha and Petliavka rivers. He had covered almost forty **versts** in twenty-four hours. He arrived just at the right time: the ice at Raskidukha had started to move and in the afternoon, rafts were being prepared to send the timber downriver to Prudki.

Three days later, right after Fomich had been registered as the timber watchman for the Raskidukha hydro-electric power station, his little cutter was towing along the Prokosha River three huge log rafts, which looked swollen and black, like a beetle. In fact, it looked nothing like the Prokosha, for, as far as the eye could see, it was a sea of flood water. Gone were the bends and banks of the river. You could stick to the river if you wanted, but there was nothing stopping you sailing straight over the meadows and bushes. The river banks were only marked by the tops of the waterside willow trees sticking out of the water, and by the occasional red and white marker pole, which looked like handkerchiefs dropped on to this sea. He came across not a single ferry or boat... only wind and waves. And in the midst of all this expanse, Fomich sat cooking gruel. It felt good! But Fomich regretted that this waterway was so devoid of life and that the riverbanks were hidden beneath the water. There were no solitary carts, no fishermen's tents, no mowers' cabins – otherwise people would have looked over at him, shielding their eyes with their hand, and shouted out, 'Eh, Fomich! Chuck us a log!' Shout all you like... They hadn't a hope! And Fomich didn't give a damn – he would just sit there on view to the world, eating his gruel.

The little cutter made deep groans and snorted like a horse as it pulled the rafts along, attached by a long cable. When Fomich had eaten, he huddled up in some hay in his tent, like a little god. He had been given the tent in the electricity station office and he had got hold of the hay himself.

Fomich slept and he had a happy dream: he felt as though he was sailing along the **Volga**, on a large, white steamer, standing on the top deck in a glass booth at the ship's wheel. He was looking out, not any old how, but through binoculars. 'Who is that on the bank? Who are those people gathered there?' he asked the officer on watch.

The officer shouted back to him through a loud-hailer, 'Prudki has come out to see you, Comrade Captain!'

'But what is Prudki?' Fomich demanded sternly, as if he had heard the word for the first time in his life.

'They want to come aboard,' replied the officer from the lower deck. 'Do we pull ashore or not?'

'Tell them that those who have not fulfilled the required quota of **workday units** will not be allowed on board!' shouted Fomich to the officer. 'I shall check on each one personally. Pull ashore!'

The steamer let out three blasts on its hooter, only instead of a horn, it turned out to be a siren which mooed. 'It sounds like a cow mooing,' thought Fomich. 'The horn has probably gone rusty. I must order it to be cleaned.' Fomich came down the ladder in his white naval tunic and white cap, his binoculars hanging round his neck. The horn kept on mooing.

'Bung its hole up!' Fomich ordered the officer, as he very much wanted to hear what the Prudki men and womenfolk would say, when they saw him in his captain's uniform. But suddenly, the officer shouted 'Foo-mm-ii-ch!' into his megaphone, followed by a string of effing and blinding, such that Lively woke up. He heard the cutter's siren sounding, and the petty officer stood at the stern, shouting into a megaphone: 'Foo-mm-ii-ch! What's wrong with you? Have you snuffed it in there?!'

Fomich got out of the tent.

'What's wrong?'

'What's up with your eyes?! Look! We're arriving at Prudki.'

Only then did Fomich come to from his dream, and he saw, right in front of him, his native Prudki, with its poplar hill where the church used to be, and Lizunin's former old wooden house, which was now covered in tin plate, having been reassembled there as a social club. Beyond that, he could see some white willow trees above the thatched roofs of Prudki houses, which thinned out towards the edge of the village, and, almost standing alone, the white-stoned building of the **kolkhoz** cow-shed, with its beautiful slate roof, arranged like a multi-coloured draught-board. He could see the farm yards in front of the grey walls of the Prudki houses, full of straw and woven fences, and the white walls of the cow-sheds, which towered like palaces.

The cutter entered the oxbow, on the banks of which stood Prudki. Back at the power-station, Fomich had been instructed to land the rafts in the oxbow, next to the social club. 'Then we'll send a tractor to pull them onto the bank,' said the boss. 'Just make sure they are firmly secured so they don't get carried away into the river!'

People had come out to greet him on the poplar mound in fewer numbers than in his dream – most of them were old women and children. It's true that Pashka Voronin would have come out, but, having seen who was on the boat, he went off into the social club. He had a booth with a telephone in it there. 'Now I bet he will be ringing Guzёnkov himself,' thought Fomich, not without a certain amount of satisfaction. 'I bet he's saying, "Kuzkin is hauling rafts on the river. What are your orders for him?"'

And Guzёnkov will say, 'Now he is untouchable.' And he'll eff and blind. 'Well, you curse to your heart's content. I couldn't give a damn,' thought Fomich, looking at the mound.

There, amongst the kids, he saw his own – they were all there running around the poplars, shouting, 'The steamer's come! The steamer's come!'

When Fomich had hauled the rafts to the river bank, he moored the last raft with a rope to a poplar, and with great pride, just like a cockerel, he climbed up the mound. But Marfa Nazarkina spoilt this momentous occasion for him. She mumbled, 'Fedka, you look as though you've tied a cow up in a meadow. Just you watch out that the kids don't nick your rafts.'

'I'll rip the head off anyone who tampers with them!' said Fomich in a loud and angry voice, but meanwhile, he said to the captain of the cutter, 'By rights, of course, I should drive some mooring spikes into the ground and secure the rafts with steel cables.'

'But when the water level falls, they'll look as though they've been strung up,' remarked the petty officer, angry at having been woken up so early in the morning, and he snorted through his red-haired, smoke-stained moustaches.

'Could you leave the tent for me? In case I need it for work?' asked Fomich.

'What, sleep in that? You'll sleep a lot better at home…'

The petty officer let out a blast on the hooter, which emitted a long, mooing sound, then the diesel engine roared, the water began to gurgle under the stern, and the cutter, having traced a huge arc in the river, sailed off, disappearing amidst the murky waters of the Prokosha.

Lively went home, crossing the entire village, his gun on his back and his mess-tin in his hand, as though he had just won a victory. In front of him skipped his herd of kids and, as soon as they saw the house from some way off, they shouted, 'Mam, Dad's brought some gruel home with him!'

Chapter Eleven

On the eve of May Day, a strong wind blew up during the night. Fomich was by the rafts. Waves started lapping at the logs around the sides of the rafts, then the water lapped over them and they became slippery. Then, by the bank, it looked as though the water was whirling and sections of raft started to pile up, one on top of the other. Lively would have tried to tie them to the poplars, but the rope either swung like a see-saw, or went taught and snapped with a crack, like the strings of a musical instrument. Fomich realized that here, at the foot of the hill, the rafts would not hold on such a stormy night. He would have to get them quickly to a more sheltered spot. But to move them now was rather frightening, and he would not be able to handle them on his own. The simplest thing to do would be to pull them aground on the bank, and when the water had calmed down, he could push them back in. But he would need a tractor for that. Fomich remembered that a tractor had been rumbling all day long on the farm, piling up manure. He would have to ask about it.

He ran off to Pashka Voronin's house and hastily knocked on the window. Pashka came out on to the porch, yawning, and when he saw it was Fomich, he did not even invite him in.

'What d'you want?'

'Listen, lend me that tractor, just for an hour – I want to beach the rafts. In case the river carries them away. Just look at the wind that's blown up.'

'How do you mean? Give you a tractor, without rhyme or reason! Who to? What for?'

'How do you mean, "What for?" To save the rafts! The timber is not for a house for me, it's for providing lighting for the **kolkhoz**...'

'So what? The tractor's not mine, clever dick – it belongs to the **MTS**. It depends on the tractor driver, and on the chairman in particular. Let Mikhail Mikhailovich decide what to do. Go and see him.'

'How can I see him and leave the rafts at a time like this?' Fomich pleaded. 'You give him a ring!'

'You need him, you ring him!' Pashka lazily replied, turning his long back to Fomich.

'What can I ring him on? Do I have to climb a telegraph pole?'

'What's it to me?'

'You parasite!' said Fomich, getting angry. 'I'll get witnesses. I'll let everyone know that you refused to save state property. You'll end up in court, you shit!'

'Don't you get worked up or I'll bash you on your conk, and then you'll ring all right!' replied Pashka in a cold voice. 'I've told you, I don't have any authority over the tractors. Take my horse, if you must.'

'What use is that to me? Ring Guzënkov! Do you hear? Without delay!'

Pashka did not reply and he disappeared into the darkness of his doorway. In a moment he came out in his outdoor clothes.

In the club telephone booth, Pashka turned the dial for ages before getting through.

'What's happened to them there? Have you all snuffed it?' he said, cursing. 'Get me Guzënkov's flat. Mikhail Mikhailovich? It's me, Voronin. Some rafts of timber are being blown away by the wind. Yes. Kuzkin is asking for a tractor to pull them onto the river bank. What should we do? We have one parked at the farm for the night. What? Yes. What? Yes. I understand.'

Pashka Voronin put down the receiver and looked at Fomich, sneering contentedly.

'Well?' asked Fomich impatiently.

'He asked me, "Who's responsible for the rafts – Kuzkin?" I says, "Yes". So he says that even if every last one of them burns to a crisp, he wouldn't dream of lifting a finger. D'you understand?'

'I understand,' Fomich pronounced slowly, and suddenly he could feel his hands beginning to shake with anger, and he felt like punching Pashka's impudent, smiling face. He thought of grabbing Pashka's nose and squeezing it hard between his fingers, like he would a tick, then twist it to one side.

'You won't forget this!' said Fomich, and he ran out of the club.

Outside it was so dark, you couldn't see a hand in front of your face. Fine, sharp rain lashed his face, biting like small shot from a gun, and it beat against his resonant, tanned sheepskin coat. 'I must get some men together to try and drag the rafts into a backwater, towards Sviatoi Lake.[68] It's quiet there. But who will turn out at this time?'

He stopped by Vaska Kotënok's house:[69] he was the farm shepherd and still a bachelor. 'If I can talk him into it, he'd go to hell and back for me,' thought Fomich, but he knew that talking to Vaska was about as much use as addressing the **kolkhoz** bull.

Vaska, despite his nickname, was as idle as a genuine, old cat. He remained in the village owing to his own indolence. When he came out of the army, his mother said to him, 'Vaska, go to **Gorky**. Half of Prudki is working there on the steamers.'

'Who haven't I seen there?'

He was offered training on machine driving courses.

---

[68] 'Sviatoi' literally means 'holy' or 'sacred'.
[69] His nickname, Kotënok, means 'kitten', which must be understood to appreciate Mozhaev's description of him in the next paragraph of the story. Vaska is one variant of a number of familiar forms of the name 'Vasilii' or Basil.

'Who don't I know among those drivers?' Vaska would answer in his own way.

He worked as a herdsman, but in three years he had never been able to plait a whip.

'When have I time to make a whip? In summer, I have to take the cows to pasture… And in the winter, what's the point in trying to learn? I might not carry on working with cows.' So he used to drive the cows with a stick.

Vaska had another little vice – he liked a drink. Fomich decided to play on this foible.

His pounding on the door went unanswered for some time. Then Vaska's round mug appeared at the window.

'Who d'yer want?'

'Vaska, it's me. Come out for a moment!'

'Is that really you, Uncle Fomich? What d'yer want?'

'Come out, quickly! I've got a little job for you.' Fomich was worried that Vaska might just close the window. In that case, he would never get through to him.

'What kind of work at this time of night?' Vaska did not close the window, but he did not show any real interest.

'The boss of the power-station phoned me. He's ordered me to get the rafts to Sviatoi Lake. He's promised there's fifty roubles each in it,' Fomich lied.

'Well, we'll move them tomorrow. Where is the boss anyway?'

'The boss is there, at the station. He's told me to make the payment.'

'What sort of money do you have? You haven't got a bean in your pocket.'

Vaska grabbed the window frame with the intention of slamming it shut in Fomich's face.

'Just hang on a minute, will you!' Fomich seized his arm. 'He also ordered me to stand you a litre of vodka after the work's done.'

Vaska perked up a little.

'Is that right?'

'What do you think? The boss ordered me to. A boss's word is law to a subordinate. You know that – you've been in the army.'

'Hang on a bit,' Vaska said briefly, slamming the window shut.

'Thanks be to God! I've persuaded at least one person,' said Fomich, breathing a sigh of relief. 'Now, who else? We need at least one person per section of raft…'

Vaska came out a minute later, doing up his coat as he walked.

'Uncle Fom, d'we need someone else?'

'Another person wouldn't hurt.'

'Hang on a bit.' Vaska ran over the road and knocked on the door of the Gubanov house. 'Grin, come out a sec!'

The man who came out was the very tractor driver, whom Fomich had tried to get hold of through the chairman. After exchanging a couple of words, Vaska came over to Fomich with Grinka.

'Uncle Fom, d'yer think we could pull the rafts along the bank with a tractor?'

'We could have a go,' said Fomich, indifferently. 'It's a poss.'

'We'll run and get the tractor and pull 'em out in a moment!' said Grinka.

'Only don't drive through the village,' said Fomich, pulling them up short. 'There's no point in disturbing people. Go along the river bank.'

'Fine by us. Let's go!' Grinka and Vaska disappeared into the darkness.

'There *is* a good God!' thought Fomich, smirking. 'He's got it all worked out. They didn't want to let me have the tractor to haul the rafts... Now I'll cover the **verst** to Sviatoi Lake. The rafts won't just be pulled into the shallows, but they'll be on dry land.'

By morning, all three rafts lay on the gently sloping bank of Sviatoi Lake, right next to the cow-sheds. Fomich was ecstatic: only now did he realise what a complete cock-up the office had made in ordering him to moor the rafts by the steep banks, next to the club. Had the water level fallen, he would still have had to drag them out from the lake by tractor. That would have been a month's work. And the tractor would have had to be driven over thirty kilometres. But here, when the water level drops, they'll all be on dry land. And access to them was good. You could drive up in any type of lorry, load up, and take them wherever you wanted. 'As it turns out, I've saved them several thousands roubles. I might even get a bonus. And all for a litre of vodka. That's what I call "flood water"!'

Spring flood time in Prudki was a time of joyous relaxation and short-lived, free booty. The kids shouted like rooks all day long on the poplar hill, some played skittles, others played bat and ball, some played blind-man's-buff, and others 'horsies', which meant that, if you lost, you had to carry your opponent on your back, from one end of the field to another. From first light, the old women would ascend their own **mounds** and sun themselves for hours, occasionally looking out from their shaded eyes at the murky, yellowish, boundless expanse of water, with the sunlight playing on it.

'Where does it all go?'

'What, the water?'

'Yeah!'

'They say it goes into the sea.'

'So, is the sea bottomless?'

'It has an abyss...'

'Oh, my godfathers!'

However, the old men did not sit gossiping at this time: along with the other peasant men, those who were not busy with their machinery would dart about in boats upon the flooded meadows, collecting floating logs and sawing off dead wood from trees, sticking out of the water, and they gathered it inside the boat. But those logs, which were far too

heavy to lift, were towed back on a rope. Everything had a use around the homestead…
You never knew what treasure the flood waters might produce. You'd be bringing back
some logs, but you always kept your gun at the ready: just keep your eye out for a duck
flying out of the forest, or a hare turning up on a patch of high ground that hadn't yet
been flooded. They 'tidied' it all up. Prudki people showed no mercy.

At this time the murky waters teemed with bream, wild carp, and pike. Around the
bushes by the banks, now hidden under the water in great pools, the local men set up a
multitude of single and double nets, and they also netted the mouths of the backwaters
and former dry riverbeds. Those who did not have a boat walked along the banks using a
casting net – a square net fixed to the end of a long, sharpened pole. Each to his own.
But it was a rare Prudki peasant man who would refuse a sale to any fresh fish lover, who
had come from some waterless Tikhanovo valley. 'Take as much as you like. It's a
tenner a kilo.'

'Can't you do it a bit cheaper?'

'What does millet cost nowadays? That's the point. We can't do it any cheaper. We
have to manage on what nature provides.'

The flood water this year was high – it came right up to the farm and it even poured
into the seed potato store, near the cowsheds. People had to transfer all the potatoes
quickly. Guzënkov ordered the whole of Prudki to turn up at the potato store. He arrived
in his jeep. Pashka Voronin went from door to door, drumming up support.

Fomich had finished his morning's fishing and was sitting on his porch, reading the
newspaper, when Voronin stopped by his house.

'The chairman has ordered everyone to report to the vegetable store. You're to turn up
there with your whole family to transfer the potatoes. D'you understand?'

Fomich, not even looking up from his paper, asked, 'Who is responsible for the seed
potatoes? Is it Guzënkov?'

'Yes, it's the chairman himself. And it's his order.'

'Then tell him that if every last potato sank to the bottom, I wouldn't even lift a
finger.'

'I'll pass it on. But you may well regret this. We'll get you sacked for this.'

'You've not got the clout!'

'We'll see about that.'

When Pashka told Guzënkov what he had said, he bawled so loudly at the potato store,
that Fomich even heard it from his porch. 'I'll hound him out!'

Avdotia took fright and gradually crept away from Fomich, via the vegetable garden,
and headed for the potato store. But Fomich was not so easily frightened, and besides, he
was expecting some kind of praise from his boss.

And he was not disappointed…

As soon as the flood waters had subsided, there was a phone call to Prudki from
Raskidukha. The village **reading-room** attendant, Minka Sladenkii, a little chap with a

large head, which rested precariously on his slender neck, like a flail on the end of its chain, came rushing up to Fomich.[70] 'Quick, you're wanted on the telephone!' he managed to gasp to Fomich, at his timber store. Fomich took the **reading-room** key from him like a baton in a relay race, and he ran off across the common.

'How are things there – is it dry?' asked the hydro-electric station boss.

'Tip top,' Fomich blurted out, catching his breath. 'The kids are playing bat and ball.'

'Are the rafts intact?'

'The whole lot, down to the last log.'

'Tomorrow, we'll send you a tractor to haul them out.'

'We won't need a tractor. They're all on the bank.'

'How do you mean, "On the bank"? Who pulled them out?'

'I did.'

'Do you have a magic wand, or something?'

'Come and see for yourself. All the logs are on the dry bank', Fomich answered modestly.

'But is there access to them by vehicle?'

'Absolutely! They are right by the farm.'

'Are you having us on? Be warned, we'll be there after lunch!'

The boss's white cutter flew through the water like a fish, parting the waves like watery wings, with its nose in the air. It looked as though it would take to the air at any moment and fly over the bank. Fomich waited for it on top of Kuziakov Ravine. He took off his cap and waved it above his head, as if fending off bees. They noticed him from the river, and the cutter swung in towards the bank and came aground on the sandy shore at speed. Fomich ran down to meet them.

There were three people in the cutter; the boss, a dapper young man who wore dark glasses; the skipper, who wore a leather jacket and a genuine naval cap with a crab insignia; and a fat man with a briefcase, who was head of the stores department – the one who had issued Fomich with his timber.[71]

'Where are your rafts?' asked the boss, on greeting him.

Fomich took them over to Sviatoi Lake, where the three rafts lay on the green grass. There was indeed a road which went right past the logs, only twenty paces away.

'Just look! You couldn't wish for a better spot!' exclaimed the boss. 'Why didn't we come up with this place? Eh?'

'You can only get to the lake from the river when the flood water is really high. How did we know it would be so high this year?' answered the head of stores.

---

[70] 'Sladenkii' is a diminutive form, derived from the adjective 'sweet'.

[71] The symbol of a crab on the peaked cap was part of a Soviet naval officer's uniform.

'How did you think of it?' the boss asked Fomich. 'Why did you tow the rafts here?'

'There was a storm. It caused havoc with them.'

'Well I never! Every cloud has a silver lining! In any case, well done! You've saved us over three thousand roubles. We'll give you an extra month's pay! Pupynin, hand me that briefcase!'

The fat man handed the briefcase to the boss, who opened it, took out some money, counted out four hundred and eighty-five roubles, and gave it to Fomich.

'Have this!'

Then, he gently took Fomich's arm and asked, 'Did you have to shell out a lot to get the rafts shifted?'

'A hundred roubles. And I personally stood them a litre of vodka.'

'Oh, Merchant Igolkin!' joked the boss.[72] 'You're leading the working class to drink! Okay, we'll pay you for the litre as well. Only in future, just watch out – no more of these merchant shenanigans!' He turned again to the fat man with the briefcase. 'Pokropych!' Give me your distribution break-down.'

The fat man took out a sheet of paper which bore an official stamp. The boss handed it to Fomich.

'You issue the timber to the **kolkhozes** according to this distribution order. Do you know how to calculate cubic metres?'

'That's not tricky.'

'Ah, you're so on the ball! You're a top man. Who said he wouldn't cope?!'

Fomich threw a challenging look at the fat man with the briefcase.

'I was only bothered what we were going to do with a storeman,' mumbled the fat man.

'And is he not every bit a storeman? That's settled, you can be our storeman – for the time being. We'll see how things go. Issue the timber according to this order. Stick to the list, of course. It tells you who gets how many poles... And who gets the perfect and imperfect ones. Get to it!' The boss shook Fomich's hand and jokingly jabbed him in the side. 'Good luck, Merchant Igolkin!'

Chapter Twelve

Fomich studied the distribution order at length – who was to be issued with what. He assigned a whole page in an exercise book to each **kolkhoz**, then measured each log about ten times and worked out the cubic meterage. Fomich had become familiar with

---

[72] Merchant Igolkin is a reference to a character from Russian classical literature, to a play by Nikolai Alexeevich Polevoi (1796-1846), who was a novelist, historiographer, critic, and translator. He wrote a play entitled *Merchant Igolkin* (1839). Pre-revolutionary Russian merchants, who bought and sold all manner of goods, frequently appeared as characters in Russian literature and they even formed a social class of their own. They were categorized into various guilds, which reflected the level of their assets, and thereby, their social standing.

the black art of *gonometry*, as he called it, when he was on the law course. He had not mastered the whole subject, but calculating the cubic meterage of timber, or determining how much hay was in a hayrick or a sheaf – that, he could cope with. The number of logs in the rafts was exact according to the order, but the cubic meterage figure had been a little inflated. The fat-bellied assistant director had done him out of exactly five cubic metres. However, since he was supposed to issue the timber not just in terms of cubic metres, but by individual poles, he was not too fussed: these five cubic metres could be 'absorbed' without anyone noticing.[73]

And so lorries were just about to arrive from the **kolkhozes** and Fomich would be in great demand and held in high esteem. 'Fëdor Fomich, sign this out to me, please!'

'Fëdor Fomich, can't we have some poles that are a bit straighter?'

'And where do you expect me to send the curved ones?!' Fomich would reply, severely. 'Shall I send it to Andriusha for a crutch?' No, you couldn't creep round Fomich – he was fair and straight with you in all his dealings, and he would give no quarter.

Whilst Fomich was in the thick of these business reveries, Timoshkin unexpectedly bowled up in his jeep, wearing a white embroidered shirt, white canvass shoes, and a straw hat: he walked around the timber like a goose, eyeing up every single log, then demanded the distribution order from Fomich.[74] Fomich knew that Timoshkin had been promoted – now he was assistant chairman to Motiakov. Bosses! Fomich took out the distribution order from the pocket of his army shirt and handed it to him. Timoshkin scanned the order with his round, yellow eyes, and said, 'Marvellous! All this wood is to be distributed in strict accordance with this document issued to you. This very day.'

'All today!' said Fomich, surprised. 'There's more than three hundred cubic metres here. It will take a month to distribute that.'

'That's nothing to do with you. You issue it all at once according to the order. To a third party. We shall find our own watchman, who will work for **workday units**. Understood? The timber is ours.'

'Give that 'ere!' Fomich snatched the distribution order from Timoshkin's hand, buried it in his pocket, then fastened on a safety pin. 'When I get a signed receipt from you, then the wood will be yours. Until then, it's mine.'

'*Your* wood. Get you! What have we here, a private **element**? Just look at him!' Timoshkin pointed at Fomich with his short, fat finger, and asked his driver: 'Do you see this boil? Who will pay for this wood? We will!' Timoshkin went closer to Fomich.

---

[73] Creative accounting, fiddling the books, goods falling off the back of a lorry, etc., were endemic and deeply ingrained within all areas of Soviet life – anything from beer being regularly watered down in 'drinking dens', to large-scale, organized theft. This was a major problem for Soviet industry and it cost the state dear, seriously damaging the economy. People who did not operate such scams were very much in the minority. Anything a worker could secure on the side was sold or swapped for other goods on the black market, which flourished in a regime, where virtually everything was constantly in short supply. With such behaviour being so prevalent within the old Soviet regime, it is not difficult to understand how easily a mafia culture arose in the 'new' Russia of today.

[74] There are a number of characters in Mozhaev's works who are described in exactly the same way as Timoshkin is here. It is likely this is a veiled reference to Khrushchëv himself, who was often to be seen dressed, as Timoshkin is described.

'We have no desire to pay you! D'you understand? Get out of here! Release the wood as a whole unit.'

'No way!'

'How do you mean, "No way"? And what if we take it? The **kolkhozes** will come and get their wood on our orders.'

'Just you try! I've got two barrels over there...' Fomich nodded towards his gun, propped up on the logs. 'Whoever sticks his nose in around here will get put in his place.'

'Do you know what you get for robbery?'

'I am looking after state property. Let the one who took me on sack me.'

'We've already made a deal with the boss of the hydro-electric station, clever clogs.'

'That can't be!'

'Let's go and phone him!'

Timoshkin led the way and Fomich walked on behind him, downcast, his gun at the ready.

'Why are you pointing that gun at my back?' asked Timoshkin, turning round. 'Who am I to you? Your prisoner? Walk next to me! And sling your "canon" over your back.'

At the club house, by the telephone booth, Pashka Voronin and the projectionist from Svistunovo sat astride a bench, playing draughts.

'As you were!' Timoshkin commanded with a regal gesture, putting them at ease.

In fact, they had not even thought about getting up – they just looked at him from under their brows.

'I need to use the telephone,' said Timoshkin.

'Go on, then', said Pashka, nodding towards the telephone and then looked back down at the draught board.

'Is that the exchange? Get me Tikhanovo! Is that Tikhanovo? Eh? It's Timoshkin speaking. Connect me to the hydro-electric station. Yes, the boss! Yes, his direct line. Comrade Koshkin? Ah! It's Timoshkin. We're here to pick up the wood. Yes, at Prudki. So, Kuzkin will go back to the **kolkhoz**! Okay, just as we agreed. Fine, I'll tell him. Good bye!' Timoshkin hung up.

'There, you see. The boss has no objections,' he said to Fomich, almost purring with satisfaction. 'Sign the timber over to us according to the order, then off you toddle to work on the **kolkhoz**.'

At these words, Pashka and the projectionist suddenly looked up, as if on command, then they stared at Timoshkin.

Fomich thought that there was something fishy about this telephone call – the fact that Timoshkin got through so quickly to Raskidukha, and this business of the 'direct line'... And most suspicious of all – how simply and brazenly they had got rid of him, Fomich.

What did the boss's recent visit mean then? Was this some kind of joke at his expense? Was his boss really so two-faced?

'Just step aside!' Fomich shoved Timoshkin out of the way and lifted the receiver. 'Svistunovo? Niura, it's Kuzkin here. I need to phone Raskidukha. The boss.'

'You'll have to wait ages, Uncle Fedia,' answered the operator.

'Now there's a thing! We've only just been put through to Raskidukha!'

'Not through me, you didn't. Perhaps it was via Tikhanovo.'

'Just do what you can. I'll hang on, in any case.'

Fomich pressed the receiver to his ear for ages, listening to the monotonous, drawling voice of the telephone operator. 'He-lll-ooo! Samodurovka, Samodurovka! He-ll-ooo! Brëkhovo! He-ll-oo! He-ll-oo!' Fomich felt as though he was listening to the babble of a horn-owl, sitting at the edge of a forest, saying, 'I'm sl-eee-pi-ing! Sl-eee-pii-iing! Brëkhovo! Sl-eee-piii-nn-gg!'

Brëkhovo finally answered and the operator's voice became animated. 'Brëkhovo, connect me to Raskidukha! What? Can you get the boss?'

Suddenly, Fomich heard the familiar voice of the director of the hydro-electric station: 'Hello!'

'This is Kuzkin speaking, from Prudki.'

'What's up? Are the **kolkhozes** coming for their wood?'

'Not yet. I've been told by the regional executive committee that you and them have agreed to…' Fomich's throat went dry and he swallowed some spit, and finally he said, '…sack me.'

'Yesterday, Motiakov had a word with me,' said the director, after a short delay. 'Listen, Comrade Kuzkin. It appears that you are a **kolkhoz** worker. We are not allowed to take on **kolkhoz** workers, particularly without the **kolkhoz's** agreement. So Motiakov complained that I've been poaching **kolkhoz** workers.'

'But, I've been released from the **kolkhoz**. I have a certificate of release and a **passport**!' shouted Fomich.

Pashka and the projectionist had long since suspended their game, and now they were listening intently to this conversation.

'They let me go. Do you understand, they released me?!' shouted Fomich down the phone with all his might.

'Don't you worry, Comrade Kuzkin,' the distant director answered, finally. 'I never said that we were sacking you. You'll finish the job, in any case. After that, we'll see.'

'Have you had a word with anyone here, just now?' he asked warily, glancing at Timoshkin.

'How do you mean "here"? Do you mean my "here", or your "here"?'

'Did anyone from the Tikhanovo region phone you just now?'

'No. What are you getting at?'

'It's just that, in front of me right now is standing a certain…' Fomich burned his eyes into Timoshkin: '…Twat in a hat! And a manager to boot!'

It dawned on Pashka and the projectionist what was going on, and they expectantly and cheekily looked at Timoshkin. The latter removed his hat and mopped his perspiring brow.

'What's going on?' the director asked Fomich.

'He told me that you had ordered me to be sacked, and that I had to issue all the timber to him, according to the order, but as a single unit.'

'What a load of crap! Don't listen to anyone. Just do your job, Comrade Kuzkin.'

'You'd better have a word with him. He's standing right here in front of me. I'll pass you over to him.' Fomich shoved the receiver at Timoshkin, but he shied away from it, as if it were a hot brand, and he was straight out of the door.

The deafening laughter of Pashka and the projectionist followed on after him.

From early the next day, people came out in their droves to Fomich from the **kolkhozes**, on horseback and on transport, and they formed an encampment near the farm.

Each one looked out for himself and wanted to get their order loaded up as quickly as possible. It was Fomich this, and Fomich that. But what about Fomich?! He only had one pair of hands! He was dashing around in a whirl…

He decided first to supply the carts, which had come from distant **kolkhozes**. The carts from Khokhlovo were loaded up, and all that was left to do was calculate the cubic meterage and put a signature to the document, when Avdotia came running up in tears. Fomich's heart stopped.

'What's happened? Is it the kids?'

'Fedia, they won't let us buy any bread in the shop.'

'How do you mean?'

It was a Tuesday – the day the bread was delivered, and Fomich could not understand why they would not let them have any.

'The shop assistant said that the regional office had forbidden it. Motiakov rang personally and said, "Don't let Kuzkin buy any bread!"' Avdotia wiped the tears from her eyes with her colourful headscarf, which was knotted in the form of an 'X'. 'What are we going to feed our lot with now? O Lord!'

'Stop your wailing! We'll find out and sort it all out.'

The Khokhlovo **kolkhoz** workers had already finished loading their carts when Fomich said, 'Don't go just yet. I'll be back in a moment!' He ran across the common, straight towards the shop.

A group of about fifteen people – mostly peasant and elderly women – milled around the ancient brick storehouse, the back wall of which had been removed, and out of the crevices grew thin, crooked birch saplings. It was the bread queue. Prudki's village shop was housed in the half-demolished former storehouse, which was a 'legacy' from Father Vasilii, the priest.

'What's the latest twist in this pack of lies?' asked Fomich, coming into the dark premises.

'I'm not the one to blame,' said the shop assistant, Shurka Kadykova. 'Guzënkov came... He said that the regional executive committee has forbidden us to sell you bread... Motiakov! I don't understand why.'

'What's there not to understand?' snapped Old Ma Marfa, her eyes flashing spitefully from under her speckled headscarf, which looked like it had been spattered with peas. 'The bread's ours, it's **kolkhoz** bread.'

'That's true... The numbers wanting it have grown a lot...'

'Yeah, but now they neither reap nor sow...' people bawled from the crowd.

'Your wheat is in the field', said Fomich, addressing the queue. 'But this bread here was sent to you by the Lord God, like manna from heaven.'

'Yeah, but we worked long and hard for this bread...'[75]

'And what was I doing? Picking pears?' Fomich gave up talking to them as a bad job. 'Why did I bother to get into an argument with those women?' he thought.

He ran to the club telephone and asked to be put through to Motiakov.

'What are you after?' he asked sourly, once he had heard Kuzkin's voice.

'Why have you ordered not to sell us any bread?'

'This bread is brought for the **kolkhoz** workers. Not only do you not work for the **kolkhoz**, you refused to help us out.'

'But I work for the Raskidukhina hydro-electric power station!'

'Well go to Raskidukha for your bread,' said Motiakov, and hung up.

'You son-of-a-bitch! Just you wait. We'll see who comes out on top.'

Fomich phoned the director of the electric station and reported the bread ban.

'I can't issue any timber, Comrade Director. I have to go to Pugasovo to buy bread.'

'Quite right! Don't give them any timber if they're such mean bastards! Send all the carts and lorries back home. And here's a thought. In Pugasovo, there's a journalist from the local paper. Pop and see him. He works in the editorial offices of "*Kolkhoz Life*". I'll phone him and tell him to expect you. If you get nowhere, get back to me.'

Fomich returned to his timber store in a foul, but determined, mood.

'Unload your carts!' he shouted to the Khokhlovo **kolkhoz** workers, while still some distance away.

---

[75] The conversation here revolves around the fact that the Russian words for 'wheat' and 'bread' are the same: they sound identical and are spelt the same.

'Have you gone mad? We set off in the dark this morning and we'll hardly get back by night. Do you expect us to go back empty-handed?!'

'And how would you feel if you had got up with an empty belly, sodded around here all day long, then went home to sleep with the same empty belly?'

'But how are we to blame?' asked the drivers and carters, gathering round him. 'Why declare war on us?'

'They started a war on me without any declaration,' said Fomich. 'I didn't start it, and I won't be responsible for it. Go see Motiakov. Two can play at that game.'

'Give us a break. We've already loaded up...' said the Khokhlovo **kolkhoz** workers, appealing to him.

'And who gives me a break? Do you have children? Supper time is coming and the children will go to their mother and say, "Give us some bread!" and she'll reply, "Go to bed without supper. Your father didn't bring any bread home – he didn't have the time. He spent all day long giving the Khokhlovo farmers a break." Is that what you want?'

The Khokhlovo farmers made for their carts, cursing Fomich, Motiakov, and, with even more vigour, some mythical authority.

'All right,' said Fomich, stopping them. 'Give me the delivery note, I'll sign it.'

The tall, round-shouldered Khokhlovo **brigade leader**, overgrown with a mass of grey bristles and hair, which looked like lichen on a dead tree, handed the delivery note to Fomich. He rested it on his exercise book on his knee and signed it.

'Thanks!' said the **brigade leader**, putting the delivery note away, and said, 'We have some bread. We brought it with us. Take it for your kiddies.'

'You can't do that! You've got a long hike yourselves til night.' Fomich shook his head and waved his arms. 'I'll probably get hold of some bread. And you lads, don't be mad at me,' he said to some drivers. 'I'll try and get back by evening. Wait for me, if you want to.'

'Don't worry, we're not paying for the fuel.'

Fomich gave Avdotia his gun.

'You stay here in my place.'

'Where are you going, Fedia?' asked Avdotia, taking the gun.

'To climb a mountain! I'm seeking justice!' When Fomich saw Avdotia's face getting longer, he did, nevertheless, explain: 'I'm going to Pugasovo for some bread.'

'But you won't get there till nightfall!' gasped Avdotia.

'Unless some kind person gives me a lift...' said Fomich, glancing at the crowd of drivers.

Eventually, a thick-set, young lad, with prominent cheekbones, in an army shirt, came up to Fomich and put his hand on his shoulder: 'Okay, mate... Come with us. We'll take you right to Pugasovo. Your little kids won't sit around hungry.'

Avdotia suddenly snatched her scarf from her head, buried her face in it and broke into a muffled sob: her sharp, thin shoulders under her cardigan, whose colour was neither grey nor blue, so faded was it from being worn and washed, heaved up and down.

'That'll do, Mother. That'll do... You're showing yourself up in public!' said Fomich, stroking her shoulders.

'I'll be all right in a minute. Just a minute,' she said hurriedly and guiltily, but then she sobbed again. 'For me, the most upsetting thing was, that it's our own village women who threw me out of the queue...'

In an hour, Fomich was already in Pugasovo... The first thing he did was to go to the baker's and half-filled his sack with bread, and after that he went to look up the journalist.

He was met by a friendly, youngish, but already greying man, who had started to go bald and fill out a bit.

'I'm already familiar with the facts, I'm in the know...' said the journalist, stopping Fomich as he started telling him his story. 'I'll just go and ring Motiakov. But I have a request of you: do help the **kolkhoz**.'

'But I've already got a job.'

'Well, help after work. In the evenings.'

'But I relax in the evenings, because I work again at night – I keep watch over the timber.'

'I understand, I understand... Nevertheless, promise you'll help the **kolkhoz**?' The journalist smiled as he spoke, but it sounded as though even he did not believe in this promise of help, and that he was just going through the motions.

'This looks like more games,' thought Fomich. 'It was like being a soldier: if you said the right password, they'd let you through, if you didn't – they'd not let you out.'

'Why doesn't anyone come and help me?' asked Fomich.

The journalist raised his eyebrows, then pouted as if he had been insulted in some way. 'That's a strange question! But isn't your village a **kolkhoz**?'

'Why should everybody have to help **kolkhozes**? In the past, people never used to help peasant-folk. But they sowed, ploughed and harvested – all at the right time.'

'You have got off the subject, Comrade, err... What was it? Fedkin?'

'No, Kuzkin.'

'Well, Comrade Kuzkin, do you promise to help the **kolkhoz**, or not?' The journalist now looked severe and all traces of his former smile had disappeared.

'He won't take "no" for an answer, just like a priest,' thought Fomich. 'I'd better watch out that I don't make things worse.'

'While I'm working, there's no way I can... But afterwards – that's another matter... We'll just have to see. Why shouldn't I help?' Fomich replied diplomatically.

'That's the ticket!' the journalist said, gladdened. 'Now, if you'd just like to go out for a moment while I make a telephone call…'

Fomich emerged from the office, but he left the door slightly ajar and, leaning on the door frame, he listened in. From inside the office he could hear him saying, 'Comrade Motiakov, remove the ban… I would advise you to! Yes, yes. Otherwise he'll go all the way up to Lavrukhin. He has children… Yes, yes! We've had a tip-off from a certain place. Ah, the working class! Well, nevertheless…'

Then the journalist himself came out of his office, shook Fomich by the hand and wished him a good journey home.

'Go on home. They'll let you have some bread.'

Fomich managed to get to Tikhanovo by evening and went straight to Motiakov's office. This time, even the irritable secretary did not detain him. Motiakov remained standing at the window and he did not even turn round, as if it was not Fomich who had come in, but a fly.

'What are your orders now? Will they sell me some bread or not?' asked Fomich from the door.

'They'll sell it to you.'

'I want it in writing. You can't believe a word people say these days.'

'Timoshkin will send you a note. You can go home now.'

'What can I take home with me? I've got hungry children waiting for me there.'

'Go downstairs to our shop and get a loaf.'

'And what can I do with a single loaf? Give them all a slice each? Each person got more than that during the Leningrad blockade.'[76]

'Well, just take as much as you want,' uttered Motiakov through clenched teeth, still not turning round, but he clenched his hands in a fist behind his back.

'Well, that's a different story… Good night to you!' Fomich even smiled as he left him.

There were three women standing in the regional committee bread shop. One of them was wearing a red hat, almost like a bowler, and a foreign, knitted woollen cardigan – it was Motiakov's wife.[77] Fomich immediately recognised her, but he did not let on, and,

---

[76] The Leningrad 'blockade', or siege, was a terrible event during World War II. The German army and all its forces advanced rapidly into the former Soviet Union, capturing Belorussia, Lithuania, Latvia, and Estonia. By the beginning of September 1941, Leningrad had all land routes cut off by the Wehrmacht and the city had to endure a 900-day siege, which ended in January 1944, resulting in terrible starvation and a huge loss of life. There were even reports of cannibalism. In 1942 alone, 650,000 Leningraders lost their lives through starvation, disease, and shelling from the German forces. Leningrad reverted to its original, pre-revolutionary name of St. Petersburg in 1991.

[77] Motiakov's wife's foreign clothing is a status symbol: it indicates that Motiakov is well-connected with a very small elite who were allowed to travel abroad during the Soviet era, when foreign travel was strictly regulated. Soviet citizens who were permitted to travel abroad, even to other socialist countries, let alone the West, meant that their status in Soviet society at that time was elevated. Foreign travel was just one of many privileges accorded to people in influential positions.

just as Motiakov had not looked at him earlier, he treated her in the same way, remarking to Nastënka Roshchina, the shop assistant, 'You have a right boss there, Nastënka! A real reptile!'

'What boss, Uncle Fedia?' She was from Svistunovo and she knew Fomich.

'That Motiakov! May God make him live for a hundred years, and another two hundred to crawl around on all fours!'

'What's happened?!' asked Nastënka, taking fright. The other women customers fell silent, but Motiakov's wife – Fomich could see her out of the corner of his eye – turned crimson, redder than her hat.

'What kind of vermin gives out orders that stops you feeding your kids? That parasite gave orders that no bread should be sold for my children.'

Motiakov's wife went out, slamming the door behind her, but Nastënka started waving her hands at Fomich.

'That was Motiakov's wife, Uncle Fomich!'

'Let her report back to her husband what ordinary people think of him.'

'You just keep quiet,' said Nastënka. 'You'll get us both carted off together…'

'Don't you be afraid! Like they say, we've got nothing to lose.'

Chapter Thirteen

The day before the apple trees were about to blossom and the potatoes planted, Pashka Voronin turned up at Fomich's timber store in new box-calf boots and a white shirt with a detachable collar. Pashka was chewing sunflower seeds. From his red, tousled forelock, his red nose, and his drowsy eyes, Fomich could immediately tell that he'd had a skin-full. Evening was falling. Old Filat and Vaska Kotënok were sunning themselves on some logs, after having just rounded up their herd, and four Mikheevo **kolkhoz** farmers had come to stay the night before collecting their poles, having come from distant parts beyond the river. They were having a good chin-wag, and Fomich, particularly, had a lot to say.

Pashka sat on the end of a log and quipped: 'I've come to help Fomich to save him having a sore arse from over-working.'

'Haaaaah! You've got to let him have that one!' said Vaska, throwing his head back, like a foal.

'Well, Pasha, you've just slaked your thirst in time. I really could do with a dog to help me guard the wood…,' replied Fomich.

By now, all the Mikheevo peasant men were laughing, and even Old Filat burst into a little, bird-like twitter.

Fomich thought, 'If you want to pit your wit against me, let's see who comes out on top!'

'A dog would get in your way,' said Pashka, with a sour smile. 'It's easier to kip by yourself.'

'Oh, no! I'm not alone here: I have God the Father, God the Son, and God the Holy Spirit.'

'That's a bit deep,' said Pashka.

'Why? God the Father – that's me. God the Son – that's my senior helper... Both just like me! But God the Spirit – that's my native wit, which always gets the upper hand over unclean forces.'

'What is this "unclean force" that they overcome?' asked Pashka.

'It's you Pashka, and Guzënkov.'[78]

'Hi-hi-he! That's one to Fomich,' said Vaska, throwing back his red, wind-tanned face.

'Ah, Fomich, you certainly know how to shut their gobs!' exclaimed the Mikheevo **kolkhoz** workers, holding their bellies.

'And that's just what that liar gets paid good money for,' said Pashka spitefully.

'And that's just the point!' said Fomich, seizing on his remark. 'What do I need money for? There's as much water as I want, and fish as well – there's a whole lake over there! And the air we breathe is free... And to boot... the **brigade leader** rolls up to entertain us. And why shouldn't we let our hair down with the bosses? And now, it's come back to me how our pay was increased on the **kolkhoz**...' Fomich took out his tobacco pouch and started to make a roll-up as fat as a goat's leg, looking constantly sideways at Pashka.

Vaska Kotënok, with the expectation of yet another funny tale, moved further forward, and Old Filat was sitting with his back bent, holding on to his knee, not so much laughing silently, as simply gaping, and the Mikheevo **kolkhoz** farmers kept a curious eye on Pashka, as if asking, 'Well, how much more can you take?' It was written all over their faces.

'And so, there we all were, the whole group of activists gathered at the executive office. The agronomist gets up and says, "Comrades, we must raise the salary of our chairman. After all, we have overfulfilled the **plan** for our grain quota. And who tried harder than anyone else? He did! Without our chairman, we would have lost our way, like blind people. He is our leader!" – "Quite right", said the bookkeeper. "I am all for adding another one thousand roubles on to the chairman's salary. Let's put it to the vote. Who is against?" – All for.[79] Fine. Then the chairman gets up, and he says, "No, comrades, I was not alone in my efforts. First, we ought to single out the agronomist. He looked after the fields. Were it not for the agronomist, the fields would have been overgrown with weeds. I suggest we give him a rise of five hundred roubles. Do you agree? Let's put it to the vote. Who is against? No one... Good!" – "But comrades",

---

[78] This incident here throws some light on a likely interpretation of Mozhaev's allegorical story *Shishigi*.

[79] Note that there is no vote taken 'for' the motion. In many of his works, Mozhaev criticised the mere veneer of democracy which operated in Soviet Russia, which used to boast that it was the most democratic and fair country in the world. It was common practice only to take a vote against a motion, thus singling out the dissenters for all to see. Abstentions were regarded as a 'sign of agreement', as pointed out many times by Mozhaev and other critics of the Soviet regime. The meeting, which Fomich describes here, was common practice within the Soviet system.

says the bookkeeper, getting to his feet. "We fulfilled our milk quota also. We also ought to raise the vet's salary. If it weren't for him, the cows would have gone unmilked." Fine! So they put up the vet's salary. – "And what about the bookkeeper?" says the vet. "He keeps all our accounts – debits and credits. And who gives us our salaries? Again, he does. Were it not for him, we wouldn't have any money at all. We have to increase the bookkeeper's salary." Fair enough, so they put up the bookkeeper's salary. – "And what about the **brigade leader**?" asked the agronomist. "Who organizes the **kolkhoz** workers' roster? The **brigade leader**. Were it not for him, no one would go out to work. We have to put the **brigade leader's** pay up as well..." Fine. And that's what they did. – "Comrades, we must not insult my driver," said the chairman. "If he doesn't get me around, we wouldn't fulfil the **plan**. We have to put his salary up as well." They put it up. – "And what about me?" asked the cattle-breeder. "I work in the mating area. If it weren't for my input, there'd be no calves. Then where would we get milk from?" "Quite right," they all said. "How on earth did we forget about the cattle-breeder?! Put his salary up too!" – "And what about me?" asked Matrëna. – "But what did you do?" – "How do you mean? I work. I do the mucking out." – "Well, get on with it then. Don't just muck out three cart loads a day – do twenty! Then you'll get a **pood** of bread, plus ten roubles. More than anyone else... So, why do you need a salary anyway?" – So, off goes Matrëna to muck out. She mucks out one cart load, then a second... At the third load, the horse stops dead. "Well?" It just stands there. "Come on!" It doesn't move a muscle. So she takes a knout and beats the horse on the side. The horse fell down on its other side. It had done all the carting it was going to do. She went to the stables. "Harness that strong horse there for me," she says to the stable-man. "Can't use that one," says the stableman. "That's the one Pashka, the **brigade leader**, uses." Spring comes and the manure hasn't been taken out. "Once again, they've been buggering around all winter!" swore the chairman. "I teach you lot a lesson!" So he rings for a bulldozer from the **MTS**... It took out all the farm manure and the driver also scooped up all the money that would have been Matrëna's. "That's where your pay's gone," the chairman says to Matrëna. "You should have worked better." Matrëna was so distraught that she got blind drunk on moonshine... In the morning, when it was time for work, she didn't get down from the stove... Then, along comes the **brigade leader**, after her...'

'That's enough,' shouted Pashka and stood up. 'I haven't come here to listen to your filthy anti-**kolkhoz** speeches... I came here to pass on the chairman's order to you, that tomorrow the **kolkhoz** will sow millet on your vegetable plot.'

'How come?' asked Fomich, getting to his feet. 'I am still in charge of my own plot.'

'You *were*! But last year you were excluded at a **kolkhoz** meeting and your plot was taken off you. That's what I came to tell you. It is a **kolkhoz** executive committee decision. D'you understand? Your plot is no longer yours... That's that!' Pashka burst out laughing in Fomich's face. 'That's wiped the smile off your face, hasn't it? Now entertain your mates...'

And off he went.

'Well there's a tale with an embellishment!' said Fomich, scratching the back of his neck.[80] 'What should I do now? What do you think, Old Filat? Will they take my plot away?'

'They are capable of anything. They took Mitka Gubanov's off him...'

Gubanov worked as a buoy keeper and he was deprived of his private plot, right from his porch onwards, so he gradually worked some land on Lunevo Island.[81] Fomich knew that the island belonged to the ferry company... But who would allow Fomich on there?

'Now, I am a member of the working class. As such, I am allowed to have a private plot of fifteen **sotki**. I'll look up that law and I'll even go to court...'

'Ah, Fedka! By the time the court gets round to your case, they'll have taken your plot and sown millet on it,' said Old Filat. 'If you'd have already planted your potatoes, then that would have been a different story.'

'What have I to plough on? Do I use the wife?! Now, I can't even approach them to borrow a horse.'

The Mikheevo **kolkhoz** farmers, who had kept quiet until now, exchanged glances, and the really old man, who looked almost like Old Filat in his black moleskin jacket, from under which the cuff of his overwashed, grey shirt protruded down to his palms, said to Fomich, 'How do you mean, "Nothing to plough on"? Hey, mate! We've got four horses over there. Over night, we'll get your plot ploughed and the spuds in... Just get a plough.'

'What are you waiting for, Fedka?' Old Filat continued. 'Take my plough and get to it. You show 'em this time!'

'But your ploughshare is rotten,' said Fomich.

'Dope! What d'you think I use?' said Old Filat, his beard turning up.

The ploughshare did, in fact, turn out to be strong. 'What a resourceful old boy he is!' thought Fomich in amazement, looking around his homestead. 'He looks as though he can hardly walk, and yet his farmyard is all under cover and his house walls are caulked... And he's even got a turkey cock gobbling around on his veranda.'[82]

Fomich managed to drag the ploughshare to his vegetable plot with the help of the old man from Mikheevo, and they harnessed a horse to it... Then the work started. They ploughed in relays – when one horse was tired, they harnessed another... Then all

---

[80] A major source of entertainment in rural Russia, especially on dark winter nights, was the telling of stories and folktales. There was always someone in a village or nearby, who was known for their prodigious memory and ability to tell vivid tales and stories. Often the stories were told in verse and included musical elements, such as songs. They were formulaic in terms of story lines, epithets, and characters, but the storyteller had a certain license or latitude to add flourishes and embellishments, and it is to this that Kuzkin refers here.

[81] The unofficial annexation or use of land in this manner was strictly forbidden, but it did go on. Mozhaev describes another character in a story called 'Duck Hunting', written in 1954, who cultivates a large area in the middle of the forest, although he is fully aware it is illegal.

[82] Russian peasant houses were made of whole logs placed one on top of the other, horizontally, and jointed only at the corners. To make the house weather-tight and for the purposes of insulation, moss and other materials were placed in the gaps between the logs as they lay on top of each other This material was called 'caulk', and it had to be renewed from time to time. Traditionally, this was done in the autumn, in preparation for the winter.

Fomich's kids came out with their mother in charge, and by eleven o'clock at night, when it was already dark, they had planted all the potatoes.

'Now that's what I call Stakhanovite workers!' exclaimed Fomich, wiping the sweat from his face with his shirt hem. 'That's what working on a collective basis really means. C'mon, let's go and relax.'[83]

Avdotia went round to her neighbour, Andriushka's mother, and brought back two bottles of moonshine. She put a pot of potatoes on the table and the Mikheevo workers produced some bacon fat, which they cut into pieces. In an instant, people felt merrier. Fomich poured a little drop of the moonshine into a saucer and lit it, and a tall, bluish flame began to dart around the saucer.[84]

'It burns like paraffin!' announced Fomich ceremoniously. 'It's made with a clear conscience!'

The Mikheevo old man sniffed the bottle: 'Smells like paraffin as well!'

'How do you mean? It's made with pure sugar. Andriusha brings the sugar back from the regional main town.'

Sanka, the youngest child, while dangling her head from the stove to see the flickering blue flames on the saucer, broke into a **chastushka**:

> *There is no sugar in our shop*
> *For us to make our moonshine.*
> *It burns our mouth to the last drop*
> *But still we have a good time.*

The Mikheevo people burst out laughing. The old chap cut a slice of unleavened bun, put a slice of the bacon fat on top, and handed it to her on the stove, saying, 'Here, eat this, little one!'

---

[83] During the early years of the Soviet Union, and especially in the 1930s, there were numerous campaigns to mobilize the work force to develop the industrial, manufacturing, and agricultural sectors of the economy. Russia was a rural country and it had not gone through an industrial revolution. Stalin and his colleagues wanted to develop the Soviet economy as quickly as possible and to this end, the propaganda machine went into overdrive to urge people to work tirelessly for their country. An atmosphere of feverish self-sacrifice and a pioneering spirit were promoted in political speeches, by all sectors of the media, and even in the performing arts and in literature, and those who took the message to heart were fêted as heroes and record-breakers. When it came to the attention of the authorities in the mid-1930s that a certain coal miner, Alexei Stakhanov, had broken all records for producing far more coal than expected, he was used as the impetus for a whole movement and media campaign, and thus, the 'Stakhanovite worker' was born. Workers who managed to break records in all areas of industry and agriculture had their photographs taken and enjoyed a great deal of publicity. They were even selected as delegates to attend conferences and make speeches to encourage people to become like themselves. However, as in many areas of Soviet life, all was not what it seemed: Stakhanovites were not just patriotic, selfless workers – they were given gifts and privileges not available to the ordinary worker, in a society where most goods were in terribly short supply. This was all part of a vast and complex system of rewards and privileges.

[84] There has been for many centuries a whole ritual connected with drinking strong spirit in Russia. Setting light to moonshine is part of the ritual: the fact that it could be ignited and that the flame was blue indicated that the alcohol content was high. Distilling at home has been strictly forbidden, but it is widespread. Such alcohol production is not just made for personal consumption – it is a kind of currency, used to pay people for jobs, favours, or services rendered.

'Mam, let's have some as well!' Instantly three more heads dangled down.

'I'll give you a bash on the head with my whisk!' Avdotia shouted from the table.

But the kind old man sliced up the whole loaf and gave it to the kids, saying, 'Eat, eat! We're eating, but what about them? Aren't they people too? In the Holy Book it is written, that children are the flowers of our life.'

'With the kind of life we live, children don't bring us joy,' sighed Avdotia, wiping the glasses. 'We should never have had any at all.'

'Don't say that,' objected the old man. 'Whatever life is like, it passes – the bad and the good. The main thing is to leave something of yourself in the world... As it is written in the Holy Book, "It is not good for man to be alone".[85] Otherwise, you die, and there's no one to remember you in their prayers.'

'Nowadays, we have nowhere to pray. Our church has been destroyed and God has abandoned us,' said Avdotia.

'Don't say that! God is in each one of us', said the old man, pointing his finger upwards. 'As it is written, "God is our refuge."'[86]

'Well, refuge comes in many different forms,' said Fomich, pouring a round of moonshine. 'A cat on the stove has its refuge, and so does a dog by the fence. If God is refuge, then why isn't there the same refuge for all?'

'That depends on what our destiny is,' the old man remarked gravely. 'Each of God's creatures has its own joy. Man included: as it is written, "Do not covet! Seek within yourself a kernel of joy and bliss."'[87]

'But that's how we've lived up to now – we've only got the clothes we stand up in... Whether you search or not... Who ever helps us with anything?' said Avdotia.

'You've got off the subject, Mother. He was speaking about me: that if a person has lost his faith in himself, God no longer helps him. Is that what you mean?' Fomich asked the old man.

'Absolutely right! Because it is written in the Holy Book, that the worst sin is despondency.'

'Ah, he'll make a good preacher... Father Sergei,' said one of the Mikheevo men, hesitating slightly, the one called Ivan Pavlovich.

He was about the same age as Fomich, and he had the same dark complexion and black hair, and a dried-up, wrinkled neck.

'I want some food! And a few drinks would be no sin,' said Ivan Pavlovich, nodding to the moonshine. 'Before it loses its taste...'

The rest of the Mikheevo workers were just young lads – it was obvious they had not yet done their national service.

---

[85] The old man is referring to Genesis chapter 2, vs. 18.
[86] Psalm 46, vs.1.
[87] The old man is quoting Exodus 20, vs. 17, one of the Ten Commandments and also possibly one of many other verses which deal with finding inner peace.

'Well, here goes!' Fomich raised his glass.

They all chinked glasses. They drank slowly, sucking the moonshine through their teeth, as if it were not spirit, but some kind of home-made brew, and they grimaced to the point where their eyes disappeared under the wrinkles. Finally, when they had drunk up, they breathed out noisily and sniffed some bread.[88]

'It's strong!'

'Yep, it is...'

'Lord have mercy!'

'So then, you work as a priest?' Fomich asked the old man.

'Yes, as an Orthodox priest,' said Father Sergei, nodding his dry head.

'So why don't you have long hair?'

Father Sergei's hair was not quite grey, but not whitish, and it was thinning and short.

'He's still an inexperienced priest yet. He's a novice,' said Ivan Pavlovich.

'A priest who comes to fetch logs... There's something there I don't understand,' said Fomich.

'He has not yet been ordained,' said Ivan Pavlovich. 'Our real priest started misbehaving. He was blind drunk at the altar. The old women rioted and sent him packing. But our Father Sergei here worked as a joiner. And he was our psalm-reader. And so people asked for him, they called for him, as a group. So now he conducts the services... But the **kolkhoz** chairman won't release him from his job, because he says he is not yet a real priest...'

'It's like a social obligation for him,' said one of the young lads, the vodka having given him some Dutch courage. 'A kind of amateur dramatics!'[89]

'Vaska!' snapped Ivan Pavlovich, to silence him.

But Father Sergei meekly remarked, 'We toil inasmuch as it has been given unto us...'[90]

After a second glass, Fomich took his balalaika down from where it hung on the wall. His accordion had long since gone. Avdotia had sold it while Fomich was still in prison: she had managed to send him two parcels with the money she got for it.

---

[88] When drinking vodka in Russia, it is customary to drink the glass in one, not leaving any for a further drink, as it is regarded as bad luck not to drain the glass. Usually the measure is quite small. Drinking is always accompanied by food, which are called 'snacks' (*zakuski*) – certainly bread, but often pickles and/or salted fish are offered. Traditionally the bread is at least sniffed, but then it is often eaten as a way of mitigating the burning effect of the drink.

[89] Many people, especially bosses and Party members, were expected to engage in some kind of social, political, or sporting activity outside working hours. This might be as varied as running a badminton club or helping with literacy lessons. Here, Vaska is equating running an amateur dramatics club to conducting a religious service.

[90] This rather archaic phrase is a reflection of the language of the Russian Bible – Old Church Slavonic, which sounds as dated to the modern Russian ear as the King James Version of the Bible in English. Many of the utterances this character makes smack of this kind of archaic language.

Illustration 9. 'Russian Sketches: A Moujik's Courtship', *The Illustrated London News*, April 24 1880.

'And now a bit livelier!' He broke out into song with a weak, but pleasant, baritone-like voice.

Fomich struck the strings and winked at Avdotia: 'C'mon, Dunia. What have you got to show for our seventeen years?'

Avdotia turned red, but she looked younger, and she stretched her arms out, shook her shoulders, and started to sing at top volume:

> *Play, my Fedia, play our song*
> *Of love and tribulation.*
> *I will tell of our love long,*
> *And sing with modulation.*

Then Fomich took up the refrain:

> *Don't forget what you were like,*
> *Before I ever met yer.*
> *To all the lads you were a bike,*
> *But that did not upset yer.*[91]

The Mikheevo workers broke out into amicable laughter and Ivan Pavlovich shouted: 'C'mon, let's have the **kamarinskaia!**'

Fomich quickly retuned his instrument to a different key, ran his fingers along the fingerboard, and one string sounded out the thin, doleful, intermittent, almost faltering melody.

'He's started well! As if out of nowhere…' remarked Ivan Pavlovich.

He walked out into the middle of the room, pointed upwards, and started beating time with the music by clicking his fingers and tapping his foot.

'Ah, you son-of-a-bitch kamarinskii peasant… Livelier!' shouted out Ivan Pavlovich again, quickly bending, slapping his knees and stamping his feet.

'Akkhhh!' Fomich struck the strings harder, making them even more resonant, and he twitched amusingly, shook his head, and sang in time to the music:

> *He runs along our very street,*
> *He runs, he darts, he dashes,*
> *And as he runs, he twists and turns,*
> *As to and fro he thrashes…*

Fomich gained more and more momentum with the song, and then he progressed to the **barynia**.

'Uoopi-uoop!' shouted out Ivan Pavlovich, jumping up and down, slapping his boots at the shin, then he squatted and deftly, in small jumps, moved around the house, piercing the air with his whistling.

---

[91] This is a loose translation, but it conveys both the spirit and content of the original text.

Fomich sang an accompaniment to the song, shuffling around on the bench, as if he was about to dart off to join in the dancing:

> *With a hop, and a skip,*
> *And a jump so far,*
> *I will get to the samovar…*

'Phew!' exclaimed Ivan Pavlovich, and straightened up, taking great gulps of air, then flopped down heavily onto the bench.

'Just look at our lot!'

'That's right, Pavlich, you're nimble!' said Avdotia. 'Like two peas in a pod with my husband.'

Then they sang quietly, in chorus, in close harmony:

> *Immured in a cell by a high prison wall,*
> *A young lad, a prisoner, lay dying.*
> *His head was now bent, he had once walked tall,*
> *His lips slowly moved, prayers asighing…*

Father Sergei gracefully introduced his tremulous tenor voice, throwing back his head, and in his bright eyes were tears, like tiny beads…

Chapter Fourteen

The next day Pashka Voronin reported to the chairman: 'Kuzkin has taken it upon himself to plant potatoes on his plot.'

'Who did the ploughing for him?'

'He hired outsiders. They say he got them drunk and tricked them.'

'I'll ram his plot down his throat! I'll teach him to respect Soviet law,' said Guzёnkov.

There and then, he rang Motiakov and wrote a colourful account of how Fёdor Kuzkin had seized land without authorization for a vegetable garden and planted potatoes in it. 'Then he held a knees-up to mark the event'. Motiakov ordered that an indictment be drawn up, an officer from the agricultural and procurement administration office to be summonsed, and the indictment signed and sent off to the public prosecutor's office.

'We'll have him in court! It'll be a show-trial. We'll knock out of people the desire to leave the **kolkhoz**. Once and for all!'

One day later, a subpoena arrived from the prosecutor's office by messenger, sent out from the rural soviet: he handed it in person to Lively and required his signature. It said that he was to attend the prosecutor's office in Tikhanovo, respectfully dressed, and failure to present himself would result in 'the above-mentioned citizen being brought in by members of the militia.'

The 'above-mentioned citizen' naturally turned up there himself. First of all, he went to the regional executive committee to the chairman's office. However, Motiakov refused to see him and he sent him to Timoshkin.

'Ah, Comrade Kuzkin! Hello, hello! How may I help you?' Timoshkin sat at his desk: he was amiable and welcoming, and his round, yellow eyes shone like polished metal buttons.

'I haven't come for your help,' said Fomich, glumly. 'I'd simply like to know, whether laws are observed in our country, or not?'

'In our country, Comrade Kuzkin, our laws are written for the toiling class, and not for parasites. And those who break the law will be brought in to line by the Soviet procuracy.'

'I am fully aware of that. But just explain to me: Under what law is a vegetable plot taken away from a worker?'

'Away from what worker?'

'Away from me, for example.'

'That's a crafty twist! Just look what kind of hostile **element** has turned up!' Timoshkin seemed as if he were addressing a third party for support, although there was only the two of them in the office. 'The vegetable plot was not issued to you as a worker, Comrade Kuzkin. Therefore, no one can take it away from you. It all hinges on another factor: you seized **kolkhoz** land without authorization for your own private plot. It is for that reason you will answer to the law.'

'But, as a worker I am allowed to hold a plot of fifteen **sotki**, and mine is only fourteen. What more do you want?'

'But the fact is, Comrade Kuzkin, that in Prudki, we have no state land – it all belongs to the **kolkhoz**. We have no right whatsoever to give you any land in Prudki.'

'What do you mean?' asked Fomich, looking at Timoshkin, nonplussed.

'We do have such land, but only in Gordeevo. We can give you a plot there. Take it if you want.'

'Are you making fun of me, or what?' Fomich even stood up in dismay. 'Gordeevo is twenty-five kilometres from Prudki! What do you want me to do? Fly there?!'

'Take it or leave it.' Timoshkin was unruffled. 'You must surrender your Prudki plot.'

'The plot is mine! I'll surrender it to no one,' said Fomich, making for the door.

'Then we'll take it back through the courts. And you'll go down,' Timoshkin shouted after him, raising his voice.

The young lawyer Fateev met Fomich in the prosecutor's office. He was wearing a white naval tunic, with epaulettes with a star, and his shiny black hair was slicked back in a parting, and sprinkled with eau-de-Cologne. He glanced at the subpoena and announced merrily, 'I've been expecting you. Please go through into the office.'

The young lawyer led Fomich into his office, the white door of which bore the inscription 'Investigator'. He sat him on the sofa and he himself sat opposite at his desk, looking at him and smiling, as if there were no other guest in the whole wide world more welcome than Fomich.

'It's as if I'd been invited for pancakes,' thought Fomich, looking at the fresh, smiling face of the investigator. 'But what has he got in store for me? That's the question…'

The young investigator considered himself to be a cultured person. He had long served in the political department of the **MTS**, but now he was studying in the **oblast** pedagogical institute on a correspondence course. Despite his forty years of age, he was still thin and prim, he played the accordion at amateur dramatic performances and sang **chastushki** of his own composition. Once, he had played for the **oblast**. He believed that the most important feature for a lawyer should be politeness at all times.

'You are a courageous man, Comrade Kuzkin,' said the young lawyer, smiling even more broadly. 'I'm simply a great admirer of yours.'

'What's there to admire? I'm dressed in a fairly normal way – I don't look anything like a mummer.'[92] Fomich looked at his own speckled, but badly-creased, jacket worn over his black, side-fastening shirt. 'What's funny about my dress?'

'Nothing at all. You have misunderstood me!' exclaimed Fateev. 'I'm not making fun of you. I just wanted to ask how you had the cheek to grab a chunk of **kolkhoz** land? You have acted completely against the collective… One person standing against the whole village! It's just that.'

'So who am I, then, someone who's joined the ranks of the **kulaks**? And I didn't grab anything. The plot is mine.'

'The plot belongs to the **kolkhoz**… but you grabbed it and now consider it your own,' stated the young lawyer, in a jolly tone.

'How did I grab it? My grandfather ploughed it. My mother and father established an orchard on it. I cut the apple trees down and ploughed it. I ploughed it after the war… I turned it over to potatoes.'

'You have an interesting point of view. So, do you consider that you have the plot by right of inheritance? Didn't we have a revolution in our country?'

'We did.'

'That's just the point, Comrade Kuzkin. The Revolution abolished the private ownership of land in our country. And you understand this perfectly, only you evade this charge by turning it all into a kind of game. It won't work, Comrade Kuzkin. I love a joke myself, only strictly out of office hours.'

'So what is it that you are accusing me of?'

---

[92] A 'mummer' is an old English term for a play actor who took part in groups of travelling players. They used to tour villages and towns, putting on entertainment for anyone who cared to watch. Such groups are portrayed in the novels of Thomas Hardy in English literature. They had an equivalent in Russia. Groups used to circulate from village to village, performing plays and scenes, often on set themes, and sometimes they wore masks. They were particularly popular at Shrove Tide and at other set times of the religious and secular calendar. They are also mentioned in Chekhov plays, such as in *The Three Sisters*.

'You are accused of unauthorized seizure of **kolkhoz** land. A **kolkhoz** general meeting forbade you to use your plot... That was when they excluded you from the **kolkhoz**. Do you know about that?'

'No. I did not attend the **kolkhoz** meeting.'

'How can you prove that?'

'So, do you think that each person leaves a notch on the wall every time he attends? Well, if that's what people do, you'll not find mine there!'

'But we have eye-witness accounts to say that you were there. Do you know these citizens?' Fateev took out a piece of paper from his file and read it: 'Nazarkin, Matvei Korneevich, **kolkhoz** bookkeeper, vice-chairman Stepushkin, **brigade leader** Voronin – they all attest to the fact that you were present at the meeting.'

'Well, if they say I was, let them answer for themselves.'

'You have an interesting way of putting it, Comrade Kuzkin! So, it wasn't you who was guilty of unauthorized seizure of **kolkhoz** land, but the **kolkhoz** management?'

'But what if they're lying?'

'But didn't **brigade leader** Voronin warn you?' he quickly interjected.

'A **brigade leader** does not have the right to take my plot away,' said Fomich, hesitating a little.

'That's just the point. The people's court will find out who is lying. We do everything scientifically. Just answer one more question: Where did you get the horse from to plough your plot and plant your potatoes?'

'Kind people came for their poles and they helped me – they ploughed my plot.'

'And did you inform them that you had unofficially seized the land? What **kolkhoz** are they from?'

Suddenly Fomich felt sick to his stomach and he wearily looked past the investigator out of the window: the linen blinds moved gently in the breeze which penetrated the open **fortochka**, and behind the blind stood some pots, wrapped in white paper, in which grew pot-plants, displaying panicles of vivid red flowers. 'I wonder who waters them. Surely, not this pernickety bugger?' thought Fomich, by the by.

'Do you know that you have turned these people into partners in crime?' said the voice of the prosecutor, somewhere from the periphery. 'Or did you just dupe them? Which **kolkhoz** are they from?'

'I wonder who will be the judge in my case – an old bloke or someone young?' suddenly thought Fomich.

'Comrade Kuzkin, are you listening to me?'

'I don't know which **kolkhoz** they are from. I didn't ask,' said Fomich, suddenly coming to.

'In that case, you're getting in deeper. Just sit there!'

The investigator took his glasses out of a green plastic case and wrote for ages, tortuously knitting his black eyebrows on the bridge of his nose. Then he unexpectedly asked: 'What is your surname?'

'You know my surname.'

'Please, just answer the questions!'

Fomich had to answer what his surname, first name, and patronymic were, he stated his date of birth, and in which village he was residing... Finally, the investigator issued his own instructions: 'Please, remain where you are for a moment.' Then he closed his desk drawer and went out with the two pieces of paper he had written on.

Then, his voice could be heard through the wooden partition: 'Crime Sheet.' Fomich shuddered and started to listen in. The prosecutor monotonously read his report, but reiterated all the particularly important twists and turns of the story. The typewriter rattled on, choking on the speed of his delivery: '...charging Kuzkin, Fëdor Fomich, according to Statute 90 of the Criminal Code of the Russian Soviet Federal Socialist Republics...'

The prosecutor carried on dictating who Kuzkin was, where he lived, and who he had been. Fomich didn't really listen to this part and kept on thinking, 'Who will be the judge, a young bloke or an old one?'

'... Disregarding the statutes for hiring and using land, and regarding his small holding as his allodium, Kuzkin appropriated the above-mentioned land without authorization. In addition to this, Kuzkin obtained a horse by deceit from a **kolkhoz**, without the express permission of the management, to plough his land, and he refused to name his conspirators...'

'If Old Judge Karpushkin sits in session, he'll give me the works, and then I'm done for,' thought Kuzkin. 'Innocent or not – it's all the same to him – an order was issued, so you go down. But if it's a young judge, then I might get off. If he's only just out of school, he won't have had time to put the law beyond his mind...'[93]

'... Having been summoned by the investigator, accused of the aforementioned deed, Kuzkin denied all culpability of the alleged acts, yet he could not produce any substantial justification for his actions. His attestation that he was unaware of the resolution of the general **kolkhoz** meeting was not supported by material witnesses' testimony...'

Despite what had gone on, Fateev returned in his customary smiling, welcoming manner, as if now, after signing these document, they would go off and have tea together.

Fomich read both the report of his interrogation and the indictment.

'...On the basis of Statute 21 of the law of the judicial system of the USSR, the present case is now entrusted to the scrutiny of the people's court of the Tikhanovo region.'

Then came the signature: 'The **oblast** junior investigator, A. Fateev'.

---

[93] This is a stunning thing for Mozhaev to have written at the time: he is actually suggesting that the longer a judge serves, the more corrupt he becomes and that he 'conveniently' forgets the law. Mozhaev is also suggesting that the law in the Soviet Union is flexible and that justice is not dispensed equally. Again, this flew in the face of all Soviet propaganda at the time.

'You will be tried by a circuit judge in Prudki itself,' Fateev kindly informed him.

'Fine by me!' Fomich said with a sneer. 'You've saved me a trip here again. Thank you for your consideration, at least as far as that's concerned.'

'I just don't know what else I am expected to do with you. I don't know whether to release you on bail or take you into custody right now.' The young lawyer looked at Fomich with some disquietude.

'Wherever you send me, the outcome will be the same – a fifteen **kopeck** requiem.'

'How do you mean a "requiem"?'

'There's an embellishment to a story. A priest got drunk. In the morning, he could hardly lift his head, when an old woman came rushing in, saying, "Father, you have to conduct a requiem." "There are various sorts of requiems", said the priest from his bed on the stove. "There's a five-rouble one, a rouble one, and a fifteen-**kopeck** one. And there's fuck all difference between them all!"'

'That's a bit obscure…'

'It will all become clear at the trial… So, can I go, or will you escort me to…?'

'Okay, let's take the middle road. You give a written undertaking not to leave your permanent place of residence.' Fateev handed him a piece of paper.

Fomich read that on the ninth of June he was bound by warrant and that from that time he would not move from his place of residence. Then he signed it.

'Who will be the judge? Karpushkin?

'I don't know.' Fateev took the document from him. 'You are free to roam within the boundaries indicated.'

Fomich's case was heard in the evening, so as not to detract the **kolkhoz** workers from their work. Tables were set up on the small club stage and they were covered with red cloth, and just a little to the side, a bench was supplied for the accused. Fomich sat his kids on it and Avdotia sat at the end. The lively, bright kids with their grey, deeply-sunken eyes, happily sat there, swinging their legs, and, with great curiosity, scrutinized the judges, who were sitting behind the red table.

'Why have you brought your children?' asked a judge, a rather young, tow-haired lad, wearing a checked jacket and a very narrow tie. 'We have assembled not for your children's sake, but for yours.'

'My children run around on **kolkhoz** land more than they do on mine,' replied Fomich. 'That means they are even more guilty than me. Anyway, let them get used to the law from their earliest years.'

Fomich had put on an old, stained soldier's shirt and he had pinned on to it his Order of Glory and two other medals. He had polished them using ash and now they shone like gold.

Avdotia sat bolt upright, as if she had swallowed a long measuring stick, with her hands flopped on her knees, showing her fat, nodular, distorted fingers.

'What's wrong with your hands...?' asked the judge, but he stammered and he could not pronounce the usual word 'defendant', so after a pause he said, 'missus?'

'I used to milk cows... It must be the cold that affected them,' answered Avdotia blushing.

'Did she work for you as a milkmaid, then?' the judge asked, addressing the chairman who was sitting in the front row.

'Don't know,' said Guzёnkov.

'Three years ago,' explained Fomich.

'I see!'

The judge stood up and announced the members of the bench. A policeman emerged from somewhere near the stage and stood behind Fomich.

'The accused – you don't have any objections to the members of the bench, do you?' the judge asked.

'No,' replied Lively.

Amongst the people's assessors sat the old chemistry teacher from Svistunovo secondary school, whose nickname was 'H₂S', and the head of the regional tea-room Stepanida Silkina, an elderly, yet still vigorous, black-haired beauty – she was a permanent member of the presidium at all regional sessions.[94]

The indictment was read by the acting prosecutor, the young lawyer Fateev. He was wearing a snow-white navy tunic, epaulettes, and dark-blue trousers with green piping. He read out the indictment, as required, from a platform placed opposite the accused. The platform had been brought over for the event from the Svistunovo club and it had been covered in red material.

Fateev read with expression, or, as they say in Prudki, he 'laid it on thick', and when he referred to articles of the Criminal Code, he paused and looked at the packed hall. At that point, the hall was particularly quiet. According to what he was saying, Kuzkin, apparently, despite having been a **kolkhoz** worker, had an inclination towards parasitism, which had not afforded him the 'full possibility of toiling for the good of our Motherland'. And that now, he had simply become an anti-social **element** in so far as he had declared himself to be a 'worker', but in fact, he had no permanent employment. And, as a consequence of this, he had sunk to the level of seizing **kolkhoz** land without authorization, duping the managerial sector.

'I call for,' announced Fateev, summing up, 'Kuzkin be isolated from society as a pernicious **element** for the crime he committed, as manifested in the unauthorized seizure of **kolkhoz** land, and to punish him severely by giving him one year's corrective labour in a place of imprisonment.'

Clapping broke out in the front row, but there was no particular support for it in the hall, and this feeble clapping soon faded, drowned out by amicable coughing, shuffling,

---

[94] H₂S is the chemical symbol for hydrogen sulphide, which is the gas which smells of bad eggs.

and finally – whispering. The thunder had sounded, and now the hall was humming animatedly.

The judge announced: 'Given that the accused has refused counsel for his defence, and that he has opted to conduct his own defence, he is given leave to address the bench.'

Fomich stood up and he glanced at the platform, but no one invited him to go over and stand on it: he shuffled indecisively where he stood, not knowing where to look – at the audience, or at the bench, and to whom he should address his remarks. So, not having solved this question, he made a half-turn, so that the judge was on his right, and the audience on his left.

'Comrade Citizens! In our Soviet Constitution it is written: we have the right to own land, but parasites cannot ever. And in the song, the "International", it mentions that. You might ask, "Who am I?" The prosecutor stood here and called me a parasite, a kind of sponger. But I have ploughed, built Soviet power, and I fought at the front.' Fomich, seemingly unintentionally, brushed the stumps of his fingers across the row of medals and they made a dull jingling sound. 'I was invalided… I have bent my back all my life to feed my little fledglings. However, with all the ups and downs, they have never had to go begging from door to door.' He turned to the audience and asked, 'Isn't that right?'

'Yes, but so what?'

'People are not so generous these days.'

'It's not like times past…' someone bawled out from the hall.

'So, doesn't it appear that I'm not a parasite-sponger?' Fomich asked again.

'We don't have beggars anymore!' shouted a woman's voice. 'So why are you talking a load of rot?'

In the audience, people started laughing and shouting 'shhhh'. The judge rang a little bell.

'Citizen Kuzkin! The accused is not permitted to address questions to the hall.'

'I haven't even any more questions to ask. People have said what I am. Now you judge me.' Fomich sat down.

'Defendant Kuzkin, were you aware of the decision of the **kolkhoz** general meeting, at which your right to use your plot was removed?' asked the judge.

'No, Comrade Judge.'

'You must answer, "Citizen Judge".'

'"Citizen", if you like… What's the difference?' agreed Fomich.

'Were you at that **kolkhoz** general meeting?'

'No, I wasn't.'

'Take your seat!.. I call the witness Nazarkin, Matvei Korneevich!'

'Here, Citizen Judge!' shouted Korneich, jumping up in the front row and shooting down his enormous fists to his sides.

'You should say, "Comrade Judge".'

'Yesssir!'

'Have you given evidence that Kuzkin was at that meeting?'

'Absolutely correct!' Korneich affirmed briskly.

'Listen, Korneich! Why are you making yourself guilty of slander?' asked Fomich, tackling him. 'Do you know what you get for perjury? Citizen Judge, warn him that according to the law, he can get two years' imprisonment for perjury. And I'll put you on this very bench!' said Fomich, pointing to his own seat.

'It's true that perjury requires two years' imprisonment,' confirmed the judge, gravely. 'Witness Nazarkin, I am warning you!'

Korneich stood there blinking and shuffling from one foot to another, like a tired horse.

'I repeat the question... Witness Nazarkin, was the accused Kuzkin at the **kolkhoz** general meeting on the twentieth of September last year?'

'He sort of was...' Korneich cast a guilty look in the direction of the **kolkhoz** chairman, but then looked up at the judge.

'Be more precise!'

Korneich twisted his head as if he were trying to struggle out of the wide collar of his dark smock...

'Well, I don't really remember,' he said at last, looking at his feet.

Guzënkov let out a kind of snarl and looked angrily at Korneich.

'Sit down!' said the judge. 'I call the witness Stepushkin!'

Guzënkov's assistant stood up in the front row. He was a grey-haired man with a brown, deeply-wrinkled neck, a Svistunovo **kolkhoz** worker, who had been the chairman's assistant since time began.

'Can you confirm that Kuzkin was at the general **kolkhoz** meeting of the twentieth of September?'

Stepushkin looked up towards the ceiling and his forehead became as furrowed with brown ruts as his neck.

'I think he was,' Stepushkin pronounced, eventually.

'Was he or wasn't he?'

'Kind of...'

'What do you think you are doing, playing games with the court?' asked the judge, raising his voice.

'I don't remember.' Stepushkin sat down.

'Who informed Kuzkin of the decision of the **kolkhoz** meeting?' asked the judge, looking at the chairman.

Guzënkov answered without bothering to stand up: 'The **brigade leader** passed on my order.'

Pashka Voronin stood up.

'Yes, I warned Kuzkin. He was sitting at the timber store just at even-time. I went over to him, I even sat with him for a while. Then I told him not to plant potatoes because the plot wasn't his, it belonged to the **kolkhoz**.'

'The accused, Kuzkin! Did he issue such a warning?'

'He most definitely did,' said Fomich.

'What more do you need?' shouted Guzënkov.

'But, Citizen Judge, may I say a word?' asked Fomich, addressing the judge.

'Please do.'

'Almost every day, Voronin tries to frighten the life out of me: one day he said that I was going to be exiled. Then he threatened me with prison. Then he threatened to take my plot away. He'd just come out with anything. So, I stopped believing everything he said. A decision of a **kolkhoz** general meeting is the law, I understand that, Citizen Judge.'

'Quite right!'

'A legal ruling should be conveyed in writing, by a document. It should have been written down and sent to me. Then I would have read it and signed it. That's the law!' said Kuzkin.

'Quite right! Did you put down the ruling of the meeting in writing for Kuzkin?' the judge asked Guzënkov.

'No,' replied Guzënkov blushing.

Now everyone was looking at him. Fomich chipped in: 'He's a dab hand at terrifying people with words…'

When the bench retired to deliberate, Guzënkov stood up and left the club, stomping heavily in his boots. Pashka Voronin followed after him. However, Korneich and Stepushkin sat downcast on the now empty bench, afraid to look round at the hall. The hall resounded with a hubbub of bawdy jokes aimed at the hapless witnesses. Everyone could see that Fomich had won the day. When the judge read out the 'Not Guilty' verdict, someone from the hall shouted:

'He would come out of water dry! "Lively", he really is alive…'

Chapter Fifteen

At the end of June, just as all the kolkhozes had managed to collect their timber, the boss rang from the hydro-electric power station: 'Kuzkin, are you having a nap there?'

'The geese won't let me. People have been breeding them like locusts. The meat procurement order has been changed. They are shouting for joy throughout the whole of Prudki.'[95]

'Well, I have found you a nice, quiet job, away from the geese. Do you want to work at the jetty?'

'What jetty?'

'There's one being built on the Prokosha River, not far from Prudki.'

'What would I do there?'

'Everything! From issuing orders to sweeping up. You'd be skipper and dispatcher. Both in one. Can you do both?'

'I'll give it a go!'

'Right. Tomorrow go down to the river site. It's here, near us.'

The Pugasovo small-river steamship line was based near Raskidukha, just beyond the lock which separated the Prokosha River from the Oka, one-and-a-half kilometres further on. The whole site consisted of two log barns which had been turned into warehouses, a large peasant dwelling which now housed a shop and a snack-bar, and two landing stages. One landing stage had been assigned to passenger cutters, and the second had been given over to administrative offices.

The boss of the site, a black-haired, squat Chuvash man, with the unusual name of Sadok Parfentevich – uncharacteristic for the area – greeted Fomich in a business-like way: 'The work's good, but the pay's poor, so think on! Altogether, it's four hundred and eighty-five roubles.'

'That'll do me', said Fomich.

'We only pay until December. We don't pay for the winter. So think on!'

'I make baskets in the winter.'

'Do what you like. You're no concern of ours in the winter.'

'I'll hibernate!' said Fomich joyfully.

'Do you understand the construction of pontoons?'

'Of course! Well, there's a hold underneath, and a deck on top. On top of them are built...'

'That's enough!' said Sadok Parfentevich, stopping him. 'If a pontoon starts to sink, what would you do?'

---

[95] In 1953, Malenkov had taken over agricultural reforms, and it was a pivotal year for Soviet agriculture. Both he and Khrushchëv realized that private plots produced a large proportion of the nation's milk, meat and vegetables, yet they taxed the plot holders almost out of existence. In August 1953, Malenkov proposed a reduction in taxes on private plots, and procurement prices for meat were raised, meaning that anyone selling meat to the state got a much higher price for it. The reforms were popular for a time, and it was said that peasants remarked that, 'Malenkov came by, and we ate some *blini* (pancakes)'. The reforms came into force in January 1954, and it is to these reforms that Kuzkin makes reference here.

'The first thing would be to inspect the hold. If there's water in it, then it would have to be pumped out.'

'You'd have to beach it. So think on!'

'That stands to reason,' Fomich agreed quickly. 'In times gone by, we used to make our own barges in Prudki. We'd set the ribs in place and then we put on the skin. Now that's what I call a hull…'

'Fine! Tomorrow go to Tiutiunino and collect the pontoon. But think on! It's taking in water.'

'We'll get it here!'

Tiutiunino was about forty kilometres away. Lively travelled there on the river ferry for free – the first time he'd ever done that in his life. And that made it all the more pleasurable. He sat on the little steamer in the open air on a white bench, just as he might in a square somewhere in **Gorky**… There weren't any such convenient benches in Pugasovo, that was a fact… When he'd had enough sun, he went below deck, where there, the benches were a bit longer. He put a sack under his head and stretched out, and it was forty winks until Tiutiunino itself. 'I can survive quite well now,' thought Fomich. 'If the bread doesn't get delivered to Prudki, I can go to Raskidukha on the river ferry. I could go there and back, and before you notice it – the day's gone. It would all seem like part of my job.'

The pontoon for Prudki turned out to be the most ordinary barge, the kind that Prudki peasant men used to make, only on deck, instead of a booth, there was a small office for the skipper, which had two windows and an awning for the passengers, and four benches, and a little table. The benches were just as neat and white as those on the river ferryboat, and in the skipper's office there was a small, round, cast-iron stove, a little white cupboard, just like the ones in a chemist's shop, a table, and a trestle-bed. 'This is like a holiday camp!' thought Fomich. But here was the catch: there was water in the hold right up to the scuppers, which is why the pontoon had been found shelter at the river side and why its belly lay on the sandy bottom.

'How will I get it there?' Fomich asked the captain of the river boat, perplexed.

'Wait for me, for my return trip. I'll bring a Cameron.'

'What on earth is a Cameron?'

'You call yourself a skipper and you don't know what a Cameron is! It's a pump!'

The pump turned up towards evening. Fomich did not get a wink of sleep all night for pumping out the water, and when at five in the morning the river shuttle arrived with a towing cable, the pontoon was already floating lightly upon the waves. 'The whole hull has risen up out of the water… Just you wait, it will fly along,' Fomich thought joyfully.

They arrived at their destination at eight o'clock in the morning, just as the bosses were arriving at work.

'Let's go to the office… We'll get the paper work done,' said the captain of the river shuttle, a perky, pleasant young man, dressed impeccably in a blue navy tunic with burnished buttons, gleaming like gold.

He led Fomich to the controller's office and merrily announced to a stern-looking woman in a man's peaked-cap with a crab insignia: 'Maria, here's your new skipper from Tiutiunino.'

The woman lifted her head sharply and the long red curls spilling out from under her cap started to sway, like the ends of mooring rope.

'You're not going to sink the pontoon, are you?' she asked Lively.

'How could I?! It's state property…'

'Get you! What political commitment!' grinned the woman in the peaked-cap. 'Well, sit down. I'll write you out a travel warrant.'

'Why shouldn't I take a seat?' thought Fomich happily. 'There's no sin in sitting when you're doing business. It's warm in here and the flies are not biting.' He liked the controller. 'She might be a bit stern, but despite her airs and graces, she's striking.'

Then the chairman of the local committee, who was also the head of personnel, sorted out his paperwork. Fomich liked everything in his office. Even though it was small, it was nice and clean, all white-washed, with blinds and little tablecloths without so much as an ink blot – it was obvious they had just been cleaned. It was more like a tiny sick-bay, than an office.

The head of personnel was a stooping, but still agile, old chap, dressed in a neatly-pressed white naval tunic and sporting a beard, as white and as freshly laundered as his tunic.

'I'd quite fancy a nice tunic like that one,' thought Fomich. 'And a peaked-cap with a crab insignia. Then I'd like to meet Motiakov.'

The old chap started a file on Fomich by getting a cardboard folder and filling out a form. Then he issued Lively with a genuine **work-record booklet** and shook his hand.

'I wish you well in your job.'

Fomich plucked up the courage to ask him, 'What about a tunic and peaked-cap? Do I get issued one at the state's expense? Or isn't that done for the first year?'

'Here, we don't issue sailor and skipper uniforms.'

'I see. Well, that's fair enough!' agreed Fomich.

Then he went off to the stores, almost skipping, where he was issued with chains, mooring ropes, a set of bed linen with two sheets, a pan, a kettle, a mess-tin, and some basins. He got a full set of household equipment.

Finally, when the long-awaited siren sounded and the cutter pulled away from the shore, towing the pontoon, Lively even crossed himself, probably for the first time in his life.

They moored the pontoon not far from Kuziakov Ravine, amidst the boundless meadows. And so began his life as a skipper, which flowed as unhurriedly and peacefully as the Prokosha River itself. 'I can rest easy now at least until the winter. We'll see what happens after that,' thought Fomich.

He could not recall such a kind and gentle summer. The rains came and went at the right time, as if to order – they were long and plentiful from spring onwards, but there were very few thunder-clouds at the frenetically busy harvest time. It was as if a strict, but reasonable, landlord had finally taken over in the heavens, who looked down upon the earth and threatened them, saying, 'Why are you tarrying over the harvest? You'll see, I'll chivvy you along a bit!' The hay lay around too long in rows after cutting, and you could see a storm-cloud turning round, heading for here, letting out such a rumble of thunder that the earth shuddered. But it was only a storm in a teacup! The rain didn't beat down for long, just enough as a warning, to stop people resting on their laurels.

The inhabitants of the village of Brëkhovo, on the other bank of the Prokosha, worked well and harmoniously. People said of them: 'That lot can share a quarter-litre bottle of vodka between five, and still have some left over for the next day.' Those people worked as artisans, descendants of famous carpenters. They were a co-operative, collective sort of people. They got good rates for their **workday unit**s and then, in the winter, they supplemented their income by working away from home.

They rode out *en masse* to the meadows, as a whole village, and they built their straw cabins on the river bank, right next to their herds of cows, so as to have milk at hand. They lived well and happily for two to three weeks at a time: they hung rosy-coloured hams on the river-side oak and lime trees, and in huge, blackened cauldrons they stewed whole half-mutton joints, and on the river bed along the banks stood vessels of milk, cooled by the cold spring water. All you had to do was pull on a string and drink as much as you wanted, until you felt the cold in your back.

However, the inhabitants of Prudki went out to the meadows on foot and by the time they had got ready and arrived there, it was already blazing hot. They lolled about long after lunch, scooping up water from the river by the jug-full and sipped it as they ate bits of bread. The inhabitants of Brëkhovo used to shout over from the other bank, teasing them: 'Hey, luv, drink! Sup it all up, till there's none left!' There is a story that two Prudki womenfolk took one raw egg to the meadows with them to share for lunch. They sat down to lunch, broke the egg into the lake at the water's edge – they had no crockery. But a gust of wind spattered the droplets of egg, which floated off all over the lake. The one whipped up the other, shouting, 'Hey, luv, drink! Sup it up, till there's none left!'

'Stingy buggers!' the Prudki folk would shout back in their defence. 'Tell us how you manage to share a quarter bottle between five!'

As if anyone could out-do Brëkhovo folk with insults!

Towards evening, the smell of fresh mutton soup and millet gruel, simmering on the camp-fire, wafted over the river from the other bank, and it particularly bothered Lively. But, as luck would have it, his pontoon was right opposite the Brëkhovo folk's camp. In fact, they would invite him over from time to time.

Once, Petia Dolgii arrived in his jeep on the opposite bank and, as he got out, he looked over to the pontoon, shielding his eyes from the sun with his hand.

'Is that you working as a captain, Kuzkin?'

'It's me all right!' shouted Fomich.

'Get over here!' shouted Petia Dolgii, with a wave of his hand. 'We'll drink to your promotion!'

Lively had a keep-net in which were three bream, an ide, and a sturgeon.[96] So he didn't arrive empty-handed!

More than once the smell of sturgeon fish soup wafting from the pontoon captivated the fastidious noses of the Brëkhovo gruel-makers.

'Hey, fisherman! D'you want to swap some mutton for some fish? Kilo for kilo...' they would shout.

'Swapping like for like is not worth the hike!' replied Lively.[97]

'So, what else do you want?'

'A pot of gruel, into the bargain.'

At such times, Fomich thought that life had taken a turn for the better. People livened up and lightened up that summer. It's no word of a lie – and all just because requisitions and taxes were abolished.[98] It was the first summer that they didn't have to take their milk every evening to the creamery, or add water to it, or fiddle things in some other way. Now, if you raised a cow, you could drink your fill of the milk yourself. And you didn't have to surrender the meat or the hide...

Lively bought another goat. And they reared a piglet to the size of a gluttonous sow. Avdotia cut all the nettles she could find around the village and stewed everything she could get her hands on for this insatiable beast, and at noon, when the pontoon was closed, Fomich would cross to the other side of the river, to the Brëkhovo side, and collect wild apples from the bushes.

Early in the morning and towards evening, folk gathered at the jetty from near and distant villages to meet guests from the cities and towns. People came home on leave from the **Volga**, from **Gorky**, and most people were from Dzerzhinsk.[99] Back in the 1930s, during the period of collectivization, half the population of Prudki had moved there, to the city formerly known as Rastiapino, to build heavy industrial plant. They left wearing **bast shoes** and carrying sacks on their backs... Now they returned with fibreboard suitcases and rucksacks full of bread rolls, and long strings threaded with white crackers, like necklaces, which they wore by the twos and threes, hanging from their shoulders.

---

[96] An 'ide' is a fish of the carp family.

[97] This kind of quip is typical of Russian native, and especially rural, wit. Such quips rhyme, and the translation here is approximate to the original, which literally means, 'Swapping one fig for another is a waste of time'. However, the 'fig' here is akin to the English expression 'to give someone the fig', i.e. to make the vulgar gesture of sticking the thumb through two closed fingers. In vulgar expressions involving the word 'fuck', 'fig' is used as a substitute noun, i.e. instead of saying 'fuck all', it is slightly more excusable to say, 'fig all'.

[98] See footnote № 95, p.178.

[99] The city of Rastiapino was renamed in 1929 to Dzerzhinsk, in honour of Felix Dzerzhinskii, the head of the Soviet secret police. The city lies along the Oka River, about fifty-one kilometres from Nizhnii Novgorod, about six hundred and thirty kilometres east of Moscow. In Soviet times, the city was an important centre for the production of chemicals and synthetic textiles. It was also the site of a weapons industry and access to it was strictly controlled. During Soviet Russia's rapid period of industrialization, from the late 1920s onwards, many peasants left their villages to work in the towns and cities.

'Nowadays the bread supply where we live has become very good,' said the passengers as they arrived. 'If you want a roll or a pretzel, just help yourself. And there are no queues. Life's not bad.'

'And the grass is good round our way too,' said the inhabitants of Prudki. 'Just one stroke of the scythe and you've got a whole haycock. But we're short of people. It's rumoured that people are going to be sent back to live in the countryside again.'

'Oh, no! People aren't that daft nowadays!' said the passengers.

'If a decree was issued, then I dare say you'd be back.'

'Where are such laws written that straight-jacket a working man like that?' asked Fomich, sticking his oar in.

In arguments, he now took the urban dwellers' side. When any one of the passengers asked him, 'How's life?' he would answer in some detail: 'I have now become proletarian through and through... Everyone knows how the working class lives.'

Fomich actually couldn't say with a clear conscience whether they were living well or badly. The main thing was that life was calm.

But frequently, at night, he would dream the very same unpleasant dream: on the river bank, by the jetty, a large crowd of black-marketeers gathered, sitting in silence, dangling their feet in their **bast shoes**, with empty sacks on their backs. 'Why are you sitting there?' Fomich asked. 'Come over here to the jetty!'

'We might get thrown out on our necks,' they replied. 'Anyway, what are you doing there? You'd be better off here with us!'

'No one will touch you. I'm the main boss around here.'

'How can we be sure?' replied the black-marketeers. 'You don't look like a boss... You could be tricking us. No, we're better off here. We don't like the look of over there...'

Old Filat interpreted the dream for Fomich: 'It's poverty calling you, Fedka. Winter is coming and you'll have hardship in abundance.'

Chapter Sixteen

However distant winter seemed, and however much he put it from his mind, it arrived. At first, the lime groves turned red and shed their leaves, and then suddenly, the willows curled up their leaves, which turned black and fell off, then the soft, green bank opposite suddenly turned a fiery red, and the sharp-leaved willows, with their bare twigs, turned to bristle.

On the sandy spits of the Prokosha, birds no longer twittered, the thin-legged, restless wagtails no longer raced each other, chub no longer splashed around in the shallows, and sandpipers no longer woke Fomich up at first light with their penetrating cries of 'Ferry me across! Take me across!' Passengers became fewer and fewer. Life on the Prokosha River became boring.

On the eve of the October Revolution celebrations,[100] when all along the banks of the Prokosha, brittle, needle-sharp sludge ice could be heard intermittently, a cutter arrived and towed the pontoon away. Fomich returned home from the site as the first, fresh snow fell. Winter really had set in.

Throughout November, Lively wove baskets, but they did not sell well, and even when they sold, it was at half-price. The season had passed – everyone's potato crop was already safely away in cellars or in stores, and there were no mushrooms to be had in the snow… So, who needed baskets?

Once, Petia Dolgii met Lively with his baskets at the market in Tikhanovo: 'Why are you weaving these little, round baskets? If you want to earn some cash, make me some large baskets to fit on a goods-sledge.[101] Even if you make fifty of them, I'll take the lot.'

Fomich needed long, top-quality withies to make this kind of basket – particularly for the bottom. All the best switches had been cut nearby. But Lively had kept his eye on a willow thicket on the bank of a secluded pool, near Bogoiavlensk Crossing.[102] However, he was waiting for a track to be made there by sledges across the Prokosha, because to go there on foot on soft snow without skis was difficult, and not without danger – you could fall into a bog.

But then a letter arrived from his eldest son: 'I've served my time. I'm coming home!' That meant new expenses… They would have to welcome their son properly, have a knees-up! And the lad could do with at least a month's rest. You couldn't chuck him out to work on the first day. 'Before he gets home, I should just manage to make three or four baskets and get rid of them to Petia Dolgii. Then I'll have money,' Fomich thought.

He started getting ready early the next morning: he fastened his coat a bit tighter, tucked his ice pick and machete behind his belt, then he put some rope in his pocket for tying up bundles of withies and switches.

'I'm off, Mother.'

'Don't go now, Fedia. Look outside, there's a swirling ground wind and there are clouds gathering from the Prokosha. A snow-storm might blow up.'

Lively looked out of the window and it was true that the sky beyond the Prokosha looked very dark.

'It shouldn't be a problem – the wind is blowing that way, it will disperse the clouds. Ah, Mother, it's worth the risk!' Fomich tapped his scrawny stomach and said, 'It won't blow through me!'

---

[100] The October Revolution, or Bolshevik Revolution, of 1917 took place on 24-25 October 1917 (Old Style), but at that time, Russia was still using the Julian calendar, which was about 10-14 days behind the Gregorian calendar, which different countries in Europe adopted at various times. Russia changed over to the Gregorian calendar shortly after the revolution, hence the October Revolution was subsequently celebrated on 6-7 November each year. However, the Russian Orthodox Church still celebrates its holy days according to the Julian calendar.

[101] The kind of sledge in question here is not for carrying people, but for transporting small loads of goods. These sledges were low and wide, to which baskets were fitted to transport firewood and other goods.

[102] See footnote № 66, p.140.

Fomich reached Kuziakov Ravine quickly: there, though the area was exposed and a brisk ground wind whipped up the snow, it had not settled. He virtually flew towards the Prokosha, over the steep meadow slopes which were red from the uncleared after-grass, stamping over the dense bristles of osier willow strewn about the low-lying areas, but grasping at the pointed mounds they had formed under the snowdrifts on the steep slopes of the ravine.

Beyond Luka River, amidst thickets of bushes, it was more sheltered, but the going was more difficult because the snow came up to his knees. Fomich twisted and turned, keeping mainly to the slopes, for fear that in the low-lying areas he might fall into a half-frozen bog. It was already lunch-time when he arrived at Bogoiavlensk Crossing. There was no one about on the banks of the Prokosha – Ivan Vesëlyi's ferry-boat had left in the autumn.

The Prokosha had frozen by the banks, but in the middle he could see mist billowing over a wide, black band of the river, which had not yet frozen. Fomich pulled out the axe from his belt, went up to the edge of the river and bashed the head of the axe against the ice.

'Thump!' – the blow resounded long, all around on the opposite bank.

Long cracks, like rays of light, scattered all through the ice: and at the spot where the axe blow had struck, the white patch gradually grew darker, as the water underneath began to seep through.

'The ice is weak,' said Fomich. 'I'll have to go along the bank.'

He turned onto an exposed hill-side and a sudden, strong wind took him by surprise. As Fomich wound his way amongst the bushes in the sheltered areas, the direction of the wind changed – now it was coming from the other side of the Prokosha. And over there, above the dark wall which was Brëkhovo Forest, a dark-blue storm-cloud descended, pulling down low the leaden, chilled sky, like the peak of a cap.

'Where did that come from?' said Fomich, again thinking out loud.

He felt chilled: a ripple of cold made him shudder and then it settled within him, coming to rest somewhere between his shoulder blades. The thought occurred to him, 'I wonder if I should set off back?'

But it wasn't far to the spot where the withies were: that small pool with the osier willow thicket almost adjoined the river bank. Actually, until recently, the pool had been a backwater which had been cut off from the river by a sandy bank.

The pool had frozen completely. Lively was able to cut the willow withies at ice level. The withies were all of the same thickness and length, flexible, but strong... all choice specimens.

'You could even tie knots with these, or you could even weave lace ...' said Fomich joyfully. 'They're like silk... I swear to God that there's enough here for four baskets.'

He cut without taking a breather, until he had worked up a sweat. Then, he threw off his half-length coat and, despite the piercing wind, he worked away just in his shirt, not feeling the cold. While he was already tying the withies in bunches, snowflakes started to fall, covering everything white, swirling above and below, so that he did not know where it was coming from the hardest. He couldn't see a hand in front of his face.

Lively hoisted the two huge bundles of withies across his back and almost collapsed with the unexpected weight of them. Then he got used to them – it was sort of manageable. He could walk like that.

He turned towards the river. 'Now I'll have to trudge along the river right to Kuziakov Ravine, perhaps even as far as the Prudki backwater,' thought Fomich. 'Otherwise, I'll lose my way.' But following the River Prokosha meant making a giant loop, particularly beyond Bogoiavlensk Crossing, where the river meanders, making one loop after another. But what else could he do? There was no other choice.

He went down a steep river bank. Here it was a bit more sheltered – at least the wind did not whistle with the same unpredictable force. However, the descent to the water's edge was steep and his feet kept slipping. Walking along the slope, especially with the bundles of withies, was just impossible. Once again, Fomich took out his axe and hit the ice hard by the river bank. But each time cracks appeared, and the water seeped through. Fomich couldn't decide whether to step on the ice and walk along it as it was, but he climbed back onto the bank.

On the high, precipitous ravines, the wind started to howl through his bunches of twigs and made the hem of his half-coat flap, and it so suddenly, so forcibly knocked him to one side that Fomich took a few steps backwards, then staggered sideways, as if drunk. He kept a safe distance from the slope, fearing he might fall down.

In the hollows, sheltered by bushes, it was calmer, but the wind swirled around, and snowflakes filled his nostrils, his eyes, and even collected around his collar, then it thawed in thin, cold trickles down his back. Fomich waded straight through the snowdrifts, sinking deep into the snow, like water, up to his waist. Soon his trousers above his felt boots were wet, then they turned as stiff as a board from the wind and cold, and they were soon thickly coated with sticky, frozen snow. 'Just like bandages,' thought Fomich glumly. His thighs were wet and at first they felt frozen and burned, but then they grew used to the cold. 'Oh, I should have put on some quilted, thicker trousers!' thought Fomich. 'Then I could have even spent the night in the snow. But I'll just have to keep going in these and keep warm with my own sweat.'

He walked headlong, stooping heavily forward, with his head pushed down low against the wind, and his arms hung heavily, almost touching the snow. The bundles of withies were now tied to his back with the string criss-crossed over his shoulders and chest. They cut deep into his coat and constricted his chest, bit into his shoulders, and caused his hands to go numb with pins and needles running through his fingers. From time to time, he stopped by a large snowdrift, fell on his back, and just lay there with his eyes closed and his arms outstretched, until he could once again wiggle his numb, frozen fingers. He got to his feet and walked on again, until he reached a new state of total exhaustion, then he collapsed on his back to catch his breath, and after that, he carried on further.

It was already dark when he got to Kuziakov Ravine. Here he decided to take final leave of the Prokosha and turn directly towards Prudki, following the path of the wind. Above the ravine hung snowdrifts, like peaked caps... Fomich realized too late that the slopes of the river-banks under these snowdrifts could be deceptive. Now he plodded along like a weary horse, with his head down and not looking to the sides. This was why he was taken by surprise when, before his very eyes, the leading edge of the ravine, now exposed and black, gave way as a huge snowdrift collapsed into the precipice, talking Fomich down with it. He struck his leg against something hard, rolled over several times and landed on his back. For about five minutes he lay motionless and he even felt a pleasant relief from the nagging rubbing between his shoulders and his fingers, that had gone to sleep, only he felt an intense burning in his right leg, as if a red-hot brick had been placed against it. Eventually, Fomich slowly rolled over on to his side, then he attempted to stand. A dazzling flash, like lightening, literally blinded Fomich, and a sharp, searing pain knocked him onto his back again. He groaned slightly, then stretched out his hand towards his right leg. What's wrong with it? Have I broken it, or is it dislocated? But it was difficult to feel much through the thickness of his felt boot, but he couldn't move his foot – his leg below his knee did not react.

Fomich decided to crawl back home. Initially, he intended to untie the bundles of switches and abandon them, but when he considered that he would be able to make out of them four splendid sledge baskets to flog to Petia Dolgii at eighty roubles a piece, he decided this was not an option.

'Abandon such excellent withies... Wouldn't it be like chucking away three hundred and twenty roubles? I'd be off my head,' thought Fomich. 'Uncle Nikolakha managed to pull a cartload of logs home from here. So, can't I carry home a few switches?! Am I not a Kuzkin? Oh, no, my old uncles – I won't give you the satisfaction...'

Fomich crawled up the side of the bank, gritting his teeth in pain, with the bundles of switches on his back, heading along the path of the wind. Soon he lost his mittens, which had been made from material from an old coat, and he tore at the snow with his bare, white fingers. He no longer felt the cold or the pain in his leg. He had little idea in which direction he was crawling. But he did know that he must not turn over on to his back because he feared he would not have the strength to get back on all fours. He was also afraid of lying down on his side and falling asleep. So now he took short rests in the position he was in – on all fours, with his nose pressed down into the snow. It was night, the snow raged about him, the wind wailed, but he kept crawling along, and, by some inexplicable, wolf-like sense, he choose the only correct direction in which Prudki lay, drowned in a vortex of snow.

He was found during the night by the farm. He had poked his head just through the gate – there was no crawling any further. They thought that he had frozen to death...

Fomich came round in the hospital. Avdotia was sitting next to his bed, her eyes red from crying. He looked at his bandaged hands and legs and instantly he remembered what had happened.

'Are my bundles of switches all right?' he asked.

'Yes, they are,' answered Avdotia dolefully.

'Has our Volodia got home yet?'

'We've just got a telegram from him today. He'll be home tomorrow.'

'Good…' Fomich thought for a moment, then said: 'Tell him he'll have to weave the baskets. But just make sure you don't let them go cheap! Don't take anything less than eighty roubles a piece… They'll be tip-top.'

Chapter Seventeen

Lively lolled about in hospital for more than a month until his anklebone had mended with the aid of a splint. He came back to Prudki and joked: 'They say that a thighbone takes half-year to knit together. Well, I was unlucky! Had it not been my anklebone, but my thighbone, I'd have lived the life of Riley! I could have stayed in hospital being fed for free until the spring!'

'Fedka, you really look to have put on a bit of weight!' said Old Filat, greeting him. 'Only your face is as red as a boiled crab.'

'I'm just shedding my skin for the spring. I got fed up going around in the old one. If you'd crawled around in the snow, Old Filat, you'd look younger, like me.'

'I'm told that you've lost your finger nails. Have they disappeared?'

'Ah, what's the point of them? You just have to paint them and show them off! Anyway, the doctor says you just get infections from them. The main thing is that my fingers are fine.'

He showed everyone his miraculously healed claw-hand and wiggled his fingers.

'I can use them. I've still got the wherewithal to grasp things. We'll live.'

His eldest son, Vladimir, had gone off early in the spring. He went to Sormovo to work on a building site. But they had to kit him out for the journey. You can't let him leave empty-handed. He had needed some clothes – he couldn't leave with only the clothes he stood up in. Fomich had a bit of a moan, but there was nothing for it. He slaughtered the pig and took it off to market. And there went his dream of buying a cow.

'Off you go, son. Build a life for yourself. And don't worry about us!'

Fomich bought some extra potatoes with the money that was left.

'We'll be fine, Mother. Now we'll get by til the summer. We won't starve to death.'

But his supplies didn't last through to the summer. In May, during the hungry period between the seasons, he remembered Varvara Tsyplakova, and so he decided to go to the social security office and ask her for assistance.

Then, the staggering news reached Prudki that Tikhanovo as a regional capital had been closed down. It wasn't that it had been closed down completely – it was still all there. But it was explained that the region had ceased to be economically viable in that people had gone off elsewhere, **kolkhozes** were amalgamated and enlarged, and consequently, the region also had to be rationalized. It was high time! One might have said, and with some justification, 'Look here, my dears, you've gone a bit overboard – forty-two offices to run ten **kolkhozes**! You've got to trim down!' But the people of Tikhanovo didn't want to trim down and they continued to believe that it was their region and that they were all needed to run it. For the most part, the offices were housed in two-storey buildings – both new and former **kulak** houses – the streets were paved with cobble-stones, and a wooden walkway had been laid from the tea-room to the clubhouse... How was this town worse than any other? But just imagine... One morning the inhabitants of Tikhanovo woke up and... no more regional capital! Not a single sign on any of the buildings: no 'regional fuels', no 'regional shop', no 'regional executive committee'... How were they going to live like this?

When Fomich heard about this, he felt depressed: 'You can't just nip over to Pugasovo... And Varvara Tsyplakova won't be there.'

The inhabitants of Tikhanovo were most put out by the fact that invalids and the very elderly had been accommodated in their white-stone, two-storied building, which used to house the regional committee. 'Never thought we'd see the day! We used to be a regional capital, now they've turned us into an almshouse.' Tikhanovo market on the common became deserted, house prices fell... Boarded-up windows started to appear...

Tikhanovo was thrown into a real turmoil: managers who had a specialist training were transferred to various departments – banking and postal services were moved to Pugasovo, and the police and lawyers made for the **oblast** centre. Demin was transferred to the **oblast** executive committee, Timoshkin found a job as a shop assistant in the village store, but nothing was found for Motiakov. The chairman of Pugasovo regional executive committee refused outright to take Motiakov as his assistant, saying that he didn't even have enough positions available for his own staff, who were also fast-tracked personnel. Besides, Motiakov had no specialist training – he had completely lost touch years ago with what ploughing was all about. In any case, you could hardly send him straight to the plough from the office. For the time being, there were no openings for him in economic or managerial sectors. So Motiakov just whiled away the time in the meadows – fishing. Fomich once ran into him.

Once, towards evening, Fomich was casting his nets by Kuziakov Ravine, fishing for some sterlet.[103] He found his bait right there: he took off his trousers, went into the water and, with a sharp tin scoop, dug down into the bluish-grey silt riverbed, where mosquito larvae were hidden.

A black, foreign car came to a halt right there at the ravine. Fomich recognised it immediately. 'It's the son-in-law of Colonel Agashin! They must have come from Moscow,' he thought.

However, Agashin himself came out of the car. He was a corpulent old man with a shaven head, sporting an ample, red nose and little, grey eyes, which peeped out from under his bristly, red eyebrows.

'Greetings, Fëdor!' said the Colonel from the top of the steep bank of the ravine. 'Are you well?'

'I'm well! And why shouldn't we be? There's as much water as you want and fish in it – choose your favourite! And there are all kinds of birds in the sky,' Fomich replied. 'When did you arrive in these parts?'

The Colonel was about ten years older than Fomich, a significant age-gap between people from the same village, and therefore Fomich addressed him formally, having

---

[103] Sterlet is a type of sturgeon.

acquired the habit in childhood. He was a big noise in the village. A Red Commander! Even the old people called him by his patronymic – Mikhal Nikolav.

'I arrived yesterday evening,' boomed the Colonel's voice from above. 'I'm not alone... Come up and join us!'

Fomich stood up in the water, covering his private parts with both hands, and simply said, out of politeness:

'Oh, I dare say there's quite a few of you.'

'Come on, c'mon. We've got some fine nets. We'll cast some dragnets into the Luka River. You know all the nicest places.'

'We could have a go with dragnets. But we could also use ordinary nets as well. I'm not so sure... They're forbidden!' said Fomich, undecided.

'Oh, come on! We're the ones who make the rules... Well, we used to!' joked the Colonel.

'You can cock a snook at the law. Then you just get in your car and leave, but I have to live here...' However, without further ado, and before the Colonel might think twice about the invitation, Fomich climbed out of the water, put on his trousers, and in a moment he was on top of the bank.

'Aha, you can still jump like a goat!' said the Colonel, leading Fomich over to the car. 'Get in!'

Fomich got into the car and found himself sitting right next to Motiakov.

'Good morning!' said Fomich, as if addressing everyone at once.

'Hi!' said the Colonel's son-in-law.

Motiakov didn't breathe a word.

The colonel's son-in-law was at the wheel. He was still a young man, but he had already put on weight and had a round face. He was very friendly. Fomich had already met him before and he knew that he, Robert Ivanovich, worked for the foreign trade department, and that he had even been to America several times, which is where he had got the car from: it was a Ford. The interior of the car was upholstered in real leather, which was beautifully dressed and quilted, like a vest. The roof above his head was covered in a material which Fomich did not recognise – it wasn't exactly treated silk (he ran his fingers over it – it was the first time he had ever been in such a car), and it wasn't some kind of red oilskin, and it was covered in tiny pimples. On the parcel shelf at the back, there was a load of illustrated colour magazines of young, naked women wearing dark glasses, with just two tiny bits of cloth, the size of Fomich's palm, to cover their shame. 'They probably put those glasses on because they're ashamed,' thought Fomich.

'D'you like the car?' asked Robert Ivanovich.

'I don't know... It's beautiful, but a bit impractical. I'd be afraid of dirtying it,' Fomich replied.

'Ha, ha, haa!' laughed the Colonel out loud.

They drove to the lake. They took two nylon nets out of the boot. Fomich had heard about such nets, but he had never seen any, and so he examined them: the thread was yellowish and twisted, but very fine.

'Incredibly fine thread! But won't it break?'

'Just pull it and try!' said the Colonel. 'Hold it! Well?' The Colonel thrust the net into Fomich's hands. 'Give it a good tug!'

Fomich stretched one cell so hard that the thread cut into his fingers.

'It's strong!' he pronounced, enchanted.

The dragnet was also good, and, though it was not made of nylon, it was new: the cells were small and the mouth was wide – a sheet-fish would get into the net, but it wouldn't get out. They lifted the net out of the boot.

'Surely you haven't brought this net from Moscow?' asked Fomich.

'No, it's his,' said the Colonel, nodding towards Motiakov.

This was the first time since after the War that Fomich had seen Motiakov in an ordinary white shirt, with his sleeves rolled up, and not in jodhpurs, but in ordinary, grey trousers. And now Fomich thought that he appeared no more strapping than he, Fomich, was himself – he was just as thin and bony as he. And even his wide, flaring nose, which usually pointed menacingly upwards, now seemed like an amusing blob.

'So, is that your dragnet, or did it used to belong to the regional committee?' Fomich asked Motiakov.

'Mine. So what?'

'Wasn't it you, who personally forbade fishing with a dragnet? So why did you hold onto it?'

'You just talk less and do as you are told!'

Fomich and the Colonel unfolded the nets.

'What's wrong, Semën, don't you like criticism from below?' the Colonel asked Motiakov. 'You'd better get used to it, mate… Everything's going democratic.'[104]

'If you're going to be a critic, you need to be educated, and not just some kind or fool and loafer,' said Motiakov, spitting with ire and starting to unfold the dragnet.

'You're right about the education bit, Semën,' Fomich chanced. 'Do you remember, we had a *gonometry* teacher? He used to say to us: "Remember – education puts an end to irrational zeal".'

'Did you study together then?' the Colonel asked, with a smile.

---

[104] This is a reference to the changes Khrushchëv made within the Soviet regime. Stalin had ruled the country as a dictator: he had silenced debate and discussion within the policy-making bodies of Soviet government, he had caused the purges to take place and, by the end of his rule, he had eliminated most of his close political colleagues and certainly those who even dared go against his policies. After Stalin's death in March 1953, a policy of de-Stalinization was gradually pursued, mainly under the auspices of Khrushchëv, who was no liberal himself, but he promoted greater democracy within Soviet politics and society.

'Yes, we graduated from the academy. Can't you tell from Motiakov's zeal?' asked Fomich.

'Prat!' Motiakov lifted up the net and dragged it to the water's edge.

The Colonel asked: 'Fëdor, I bet you have a boat or some kind of dug-out hidden around here, haven't you? We have an inflatable, but we don't fancy bringing it down here.'

'Yes, I have. How can anyone manage without a dug-out? I'll be back in a minute...'

Fomich stood up and went along the bank. He kept his dug-out boat hidden in the reeds. In the same hiding place he also kept some oars, some jars of worms, a double fishing net, made by Old Filat, and some fishing rods. Fomich grabbed his 'pusher' – a funnel-shaped piece of metal fixed to the end of a staff, which he used to push the fish into the net – and his long, double oars, and then he jumped into the dugout boat...

From his dugout, Fomich stretched his net right across the Luka. Then he 'pushed' for ages, frightening the fish into the net from one direction, and then from the other. The Colonel shouted orders from the top of the bank: 'Slop around by that bush over there! That's it... Now go round the back of the reeds! Something moved just there... It's probably a pike.'

Fomich cast his net with the opening facing upwards and with one stroke submerged it in the water. It made a deep gurgling sound which resounded over the lake.

'Just perfect! That's the way!' came the Colonel's voice from the bank. 'And now bring it up from that direction... Get 'em where it hurts!'

Motiakov and Robert Ivanovich extended the dragnet, but after one trawl of the lake they gave up. The water was deep, even by the banks – it came up to their heads, even just three metres out, and in the shallows, there were lots of waterside plants – flowering rush and waterweed.[105] You couldn't even drag your feet through them, let alone a dragnet. Having finished with the dragnet, they were now sitting topless on the bank, watching Fomich pulling the nets into the dugout.

He had caught two small pikes, about the length of his forearm, a small pike-perch about a kilo in weight, and a bream the size of a malt-shovel.

'How was this lazy bugger attracted to the net?' asked Fomich, disentangling the bream from the net. 'It must have darted into the net when half-awake. It took fright! So it's ended up in the cooking pot out of cowardice, the daft thing.'

The fish soup was fantastic – aromatic and creamy white, a 'fisherman's colour', as Fomich would say. He also put into it three large onions and some chopped, wild dill.

They took the fish out, put it on a chopping board and seasoned it liberally with natural salt, the grains of which were as large as beads. The colonel had passed him a packet of

---

[105] These plants are, respectively, some form of *Botomus* and *Elodia*. Mozhaev gives the popular name, not the botanical name, and such names differ enormously from region to region throughout the expanse of Russia.

ordinary salt, but Fomich put it to one side: 'You only use this kind of salt for *kissel* or for semolina.'[106]

Fomich took out a small pouch which he kept in an old, round pastel tin, secreted in his boot.

'Salt for fish is like pepper for meat,' said Fomich didactically. 'The one without the other is tasteless.'

'And where do you get such salt from? It's like ground glass,' asked Robert Ivanovich.

'We crush it ourselves from the salt-licks.'

'From what?!'

'From the blocks of salt we leave out for the cows to lick... It's as hard as stone. You can get it in the shops here.'

'And you actually eat that kind of salt?!' said Robert Ivanovich, shaking his head.

The Colonel dipped a wooden spoon into the steaming fish soup and smacked his lips while taking small sips.

'Well, Fëdor, "The National" compared to your soup – it's like comparing an ass with a Don thoroughbred...' he said.

'Goes without saying,' Fomich said willingly, not understanding what the 'The National' was.[107]

'You could wine and dine a marshal with such fish soup,' said the Colonel in raptures. 'Robert, get those two jars!'

'What do we need jars for?' thought Fomich. 'What good ever comes out of jars? Now a litre of vodka... That's a completely different kettle of fish!'

Robert Ivanovich dived deep into the rucksack and Fomich looked at him from the corner of his eye.

Fomich wanted to treat the Colonel to something else, so he said: 'Would you like a nice drop of tea after the fish? I'll make you such a deep-coloured tea that you could write with it!'

He went off and cut several shoots of dog-rose right at the root, pulled off the blossom from some blackberry bushes, broke off a small twig from a blackcurrant bush, together with the green berries, and put it all in a bucket, ladled in some water from the lake, and hung the whole lot over the camp fire to heat up.

'I hope you won't poison us with your concoction,' said the Colonel.

---

[106] *Kissel* is a kind of thick, jelly-like preparation which can be made out of a number of things, especially fruit and berries.
[107] This is a reference to 'The National Hotel' in the centre of Moscow, which had a restaurant with a reputation for good food in Soviet times. The Don area in the south of Russia is home to Cossacks who, for centuries, have had a fearsome reputation as horsemen and for breeding thoroughbred horses.

'If you die, not a single professor would be able to tell what caused it. I'll put it on to infuse and you'll not be able to get enough of it... The tea will be ready when we've finished the fish.'

They spread out a ground-sheet under an oak tree with a canopy like marquee: in the centre they placed the pot of steaming fish soup, the cooked fish on the board, and some cognac... As Fomich sipped the soup, like tea, he kept repeating: 'This has medicinal properties... You could have this in the evening when you have a chill. You could live for a hundred years on this stuff...'

Robert Ivanovich sat with his back resting on the oak tree, looking over to the other side of the ravine, and exclaimed: 'What a delight! What views! I've been all over the world, but I've never seen such gentle, understated beauty as this.'

Looking from there, from the high bank, you could understand just what he was saying: far away on the horizon, as far as the eye could see, some soft, round lime groves appeared blue at this evening hour, and just beyond the lake, single dark oaklings, about knee-high, had just dropped in and had taken up their position, standing ponderously here and there, amidst the variegated carpet of flowers and grasses, as if they had lost their way and now knew not how to find their way to the forest. They had come to a halt, at one with their solitude. The grasses, having strained the whole day long, struggling violently with the wind, were now also at peace. And the rushes, weary of bending day after day and rustling over the water, now stood straighter and taller, reflected in the calm, limpid water. Everything at this hour in nature was in harmony, acquiescent, and for that reason, it seemed touchingly melancholic. No breeze, not a breath of wind. And even the birds seemed to understand that it would be inappropriate to cry aloud, and somewhere on the other bank a quail hurriedly muttered it's message – 'It's time to sleep!' – and from the near-by bushes a yellow-hammer kept on emitting its weak cry, 'Cart the hay away, but don't shake it! Cart the hay away...!'

Fomich felt at once happy and sad from all this beauty, and he exclaimed with a sigh: 'What's the purpose of man's life on earth, I wonder? To admire beauty... To find the good in yourself and do good to others... Everything for happiness. But we snarl at each other like wild beasts. Dammit!' He took out his tobacco pouch, but then he glanced at the packet of 'Kazbek' cigarettes, lying next to the Colonel.

'You're not here to admire beauty, but to work. Once and for all!' said Motiakov.

'So why don't you work then?' Fomich was about to roll a fat cigarette, but then he put his tobacco pouch away and stretched out his hand towards the packet of cigarettes.

'Please, do help yourself!' said the Colonel, offering him the packet.

'That's not for you to worry about,' replied Motiakov.

'That's the very point... Have you, Mikhal Nikolav, ever happened to see a chicken boss a load of ducks around?' Fomich asked, turning towards the Colonel.

'Apparently, in Prudki, in times gone by, we used to have ducks themselves sitting on eggs,' replied the Colonel.

'Aha, but that was in times gone by. Nowadays, ducks have become very pernickety. They lay eggs all right, but they don't want to sit on them. They make chickens sit in their place. A chicken is stupider!' Lively inhaled on the cigarette and blew smoke rings, just like a river steamer. 'And so, the chicken leads the ducklings out on to the common, clucks at them, swaggers around and displays its tail feathers. And it issues orders all the time in its "chickeny" language, "Do this!" "Don't do that!" And so, they all arrive together at the lake and the ducklings go for a little swim. But the chicken stands on the bank, clucking away. It turns out, that the chicken can't swim. But she keeps on clucking out orders, "Do this!" "Don't do that!" That's just like certain of our bosses. They sit in their posts, doling out orders, "Do this like this, like that!" Bossing everyone around! But when you sack them, what can you do with them? It turns out that they don't know how to work.'

'Who are you referring to?' asked Motiakov, going crimson.

'That's enough, Semën! You have to understand jokes,' said the Colonel.

Fomich paid him no heed.

'He who has an ear, let him hear. And for anyone who doesn't understand, I'll tell him one more story. This is to do with your field, Robert Ivanovich.'

The latter was leaning back on his arm, laughing silently.

'You'll answer to me for your anti-Soviet jokes. Once and for all!' Motiakov interrupted him.

'They're not anti-Soviet, they're *anti-demoted*,' said Fomich.

'What?! Do you want to go for a swim?!' asked Motiakov, half standing up.

'I'm not a duck… Just you watch out that you don't prove to be a chicken that needs to be cooled down!' said Fomich, also rising to his knees.

'That'll do! That's enough!' The Colonel put his hands on their shoulders. 'Here we're supposed to be drinking, and joking… And we'll fine anyone who wants to settle old scores.'

'Aren't you afraid?' the Colonel asked Fomich. 'What happens if Motiakov suddenly becomes your boss again?'

'His song is sung,' said Fomich. After a moment he added, 'I have nothing to lose but my calloused hands.'

'How do you mean "nothing"? What about the pontoon? And your job?'

'The job paid just for my potatoes this winter. I'd have turned up my toes but for those potatoes. For farming, you need really good roots in the earth, Mikhal Nikolav. But all I have is what I stand up in and what I carry around with me. Not a penny to scratch my arse with.'

'So join the **kolkhoz**… Put your roots down there.'

'I'd like to get into heaven, but I'm a sinner.'

'What kind of sinner?'

'I've committed a lot of sins since I was young. I get rid of one, but there's another five to deal with.'

'Don't talk like that! The main thing is not to get depressed.'

The Colonel removed the pink-coloured cap from the cognac.

'To the unsinkable Battleship Prudki and its glorious skipper, Fëdor Fomich Kuzkin!'

Chapter Eighteen

One overcast day in June, a cutter moored at Prudki jetty. When it had collected its passengers, the captain said to Fomich: 'Here's a tow rope. Fix it to your pontoon, and pull up anchor... You've been ordered to bring your old tub to the docks.'

'How should I take that?' asked Fomich, disconcerted.

'Take it how you like.' The captain was an old man of few words.

'Is this for a refit or something?' Fomich inquired. 'Or are they closing me down?'

'You'll be told at the office.'

Throughout the whole journey to Raskidukha, Lively rushed about on his pontoon, like a hare trapped on an island, cut off by spring flood waters. All manner of alarming thoughts arose in his mind about being closed down, but he dismissed them and set his sights on the idea of a refit... Why am I so bothered about a refit? I'll just stick around the docks for a couple of weeks and caulk the hull... It's as simple as that. But it might be that they're going to give me a new pontoon. Technology has gone mad these days! You can't call my jetty a pontoon – it's more like an old tub. I bail out about a hundred buckets of water a day. What the hell am I anyway, a Cameron pump?

Lively remembered sending a memo to the office last autumn, requesting either another pontoon or an assistant to be appointed, because 'one person could not cope with the pumping out and we do not really have the right to keep my family there, doing it for nothing...' Sadok Parfentevich curtly replied: 'We shall re-tar it.' But not a month had gone by since spring, and it was taking on water again.

'I dare say their conscience has got the better of them. The board will look at my case and in no time, Dunia will be taken on as my assistant. Then life will be fine...'

In the end, Fomich wrote another memo about the refit on a piece of exercise paper in pencil. 'I wonder if that will do the trick?'

By the time he arrived at the office, he had calmed down.

'What do they want me for – a refit?' he asked the red-haired controller.

'The deputy personnel officer will explain everything,' she replied evasively.

'Who is he? Vladimir Valerianovich?'

'No. A new person been appointed. He is in Sadok Parfentevich's office.'

The door from the controller's office led straight into the boss's office.

'Well, I'll go in and ask!' said Fomich, grabbing the door handle.

'Wait!' replied the controller sternly. 'Can't you hear? He's busy.'

He could hear voices in the office. The door was thin – it was only plywood. Lively put his ear to the door and listened.

'I'm telling you that you have to fulfil your **plan**. The **plan**! It's in the interests of the state! And don't give me stories about your children and the slop you have to feed them on…' pronounced a familiar voice, in great irritation.

The other voice was muted and apologetic: 'How are our families to blame in all this?'

'Who asked you to bring them with you? Is this a place of work or a kindergarten? Eh? Or a **kolkhoz**?'

A familiar voice – all *too* familiar! Lively lent on the door and it gave a treacherous squeak.

'Comrade Kuzkin, go down to the riverside.' The controller stood up and accompanied Fomich to the door. 'You'll be called when you're needed.'

There was nothing more for it. Lively went down to the riverside.

A little further on from the office pontoon stood two wooden barges. Two women in jumpers and an unshaven, grey-haired peasant man in rubber boots and an oilskin jacket, sat by the barges. 'They look like barge sailors,' thought Fomich.

'What are you lot doing, sitting around like gypsies?' he asked the old man, taking out his tobacco pouch.

'We've been sacked… Without any warning,' replied the sailor, lighting up one of Fomich's cheap-tobacco roll-ups.

'How's that?'

'Just like that..' The sailor let rip with a load of effing and blinding. 'A new boss has turned up.'

'What about Sadok Parfentevich?'

'He's gone on leave. The assistant personnel officer stood in for him. Now they've sent a new chap… A real prickly bastard. Wouldn't touch him with a barge-pole.'

'Aha, so that's it.' Fomich now knew why he was not allowed into his office. 'He seems to be a stickler for form. I've also been removed from my job. He's taken against my pontoon for some reason. It's that one over there,' Fomich nodded towards his pontoon, which was moored to the bank. 'It's been towed back from Prudki.'

'Done away with it?'

'Well, that trick won't work. We know the law as well,' Fomich spat into the water. 'Where are you from?'

'Around Elatma.'

'That's a long way.'

'I'll say. We were hauling firewood by barge. But there was a load of stone somewhere on the Petliavka River that hadn't been shifted. The **plan** hasn't been met. So this new bloke collared our barges: "Unload!" he says. "How d'ye mean?" "Simple as that. Your barges will fetch the stone." "And what about us?" "You'll just have to sit ashore for a week. Nothing will happen to you." So we're just sitting here. To go home would be a fool's errand – it's a hundred **versts** away. And it's not great here. We've got kids…'

'Yes. Mr Know-It-All in there is obviously a fast-tracked worker,' remarked Fomich. 'I was going to go into his office, but he didn't let me through the door. We talked through the door… We had one like that before in our region. He was as thick as two planks, and if you walked into his office he wouldn't even look at you. And he, the parasite, just sat at his desk and kept you standing. And why was that? Because he's qualified from the academy through the back door. It's obvious that this new assistant personnel manager is the same kind of "graduate"…'

The old sailor dug his elbow into Fomich's side. Fomich turned round and froze. Before him, in a dark-blue navy tunic and a peaked-cap with a crab insignia, stood Motiakov. By the fact that he was accompanied by Vladimir Valerianovich and a bruiser of a lad in rubber boots and a jumper, who was obviously the second sailor from the barge, Lively instantly guessed that the new assistant personnel manager was none other than Motiakov himself.

He did not shout at Fomich, nor did he swear at him – he just flared his nostrils, as if he was having a good sniff around, and left without saying a word.

'Now you're in for it big time,' said the sailor in the oilskin jacket.

Fomich just spat and threw his tab end into the Prokosha…

He went back to the offices with a heavy heart. This time Motiakov did not make him wait outside the door. He nodded to Fomich to sit on the chair by the wall and he himself walked to and fro a few times in the office, with his hands in his pocket, as was his wont. At last, he sat down at his desk and looked long and hard at Lively, as if seeing him for the first time.

'I just want you to be quite clear about things, Comrade Kuzkin,' he said, looking at Fomich placidly, even very amiably. 'Your pontoon will not be going back to Prudki.'

'Where is it going to?' In a moment, Fomich's back was wet with perspiration.

'To Vysokoe, on the Petliavka River. It will be moored there as a hostel for lightermen. You leave tomorrow.'

'So, who'll go to Prudki?'

'The jetty at Prudki has been closed down for economic reasons.'

'But what about the passengers?'

'There are only ever two passengers a day. It's a complete waste of money.'

'Oh, that's the rationale! But what happens when we send a couple of blokes to the North? They're given a plane, and sweets, and chocolate for a whole year. How are our people worth less than them?'

'Cut out the political lecture, once and for all! We have been given a **plan** and we have to close two jetties. It's economics. Understood?'

'You won't make big savings by sacking two skippers.'

'Just in our section, that's true. But throughout the whole country... How many sections are there? Possibly a hundred thousand? You do the sums.'

'I don't know anything about the others. All I know is that there's no way I can go to Vysokoe. All my pay will go on living expenses. What will I have left to send home?'

'If you don't want to go, then just quit.'

Lively suddenly remembered his memo about the refit – he had kept it in his wallet, which he took out of his side pocket.

'Since my pontoon is in poor shape and it takes on water to the scuppers overnight, there's no way I can get it to Vysokoe alone. I have no family there to help me bail it out. Either assign me a sailor, or sign my wife up as my assistant. Please don't refuse my request.' Lively put the piece of paper on the desk in front of Motiakov.

Motiakov read the memo and turned his penetrating eyes on Lively.

'Did you think this one up by yourself?'

'Yes.'

'Just go to Vysokoe alone and stop messing about.'

'I can't... The pontoon takes on water. Right to the scuppers. Go see for yourself.'

'You've flooded it yourself, on purpose.'

'I don't know what you're talking about. How do you mean "on purpose"? Explain! You are in charge.'

'I know you. I know all about you, once and for all!' Motiakov raised a threatening finger at him. 'You beached it and filled it yourself.'

'How was that, then? With buckets, over the side?' Lively threw an ironic glance at him.

Motiakov knew that he had gone too far, but he couldn't let go:

'There are ways and means... You're a dab hand at shirking work. I know you.'

'So that's it!' Lively shook his head. 'There's the parable of the loose mother-in-law and the honourable daughter-in-law. The mother-in-law put herself about when she was young, and she didn't trust her daughter-in-law to be faithful to her husband. So, she instructed her son to beat her, thinking she would confess. That's just how you operate.'

'We'll have words!' said Motiakov, but not as fiercely as he had said it at the regional executive committee, but he still slapped his hand down on the table. 'Do the job if you want, but you'll do the bailing out yourself.'

'What do you think I am, a pump? I've only two fingers on this hand. I am a war invalid. Assign me an assistant!'

'Get this, clever clogs! We're cutting back. Either go to Vysokoe or quit, once and for all!'

Fomich came out of Motiakov's office as if drunk and tottered to one side. He popped in to the shop.

'Valia, let me have a half-litre of **pertsovka**.'

'Why are you looking so glum, Uncle Fedia?'

'You'd look glum...' Fomich said with a wave of his hand. 'My whole life has gone down the drain...'

Fomich ran into the old, unshaven sailor in the oilskin jacket.

'What did he say to you?'

'He's sending me to Vysokoe. I can't support myself there and send money home. All I'll get is four hundred and eighty-five roubles. How can I split that? What a calamity...' Fomich shook his head in total despair.

'Don't be so daft! You're hail and hearty and you have a good head on your shoulders! You'll survive! Things aren't like they used to be. Come and join us! We've got supper on the go. And we'll have a few drinks.'

On the bank of the Prokosha, on the former site of a rags store, stood an oilcloth tent. There was a blazing campfire just in front of it. Smoke, carried by the wind, enveloped the steep bank and rolled slowly down to the river. A large pot of food hanging from a tripod was bubbling away. The womenfolk spread sacks out in front of the tent and put out bread, cups and spoons. Children ran barefoot around the campfire.

'Be quiet, you noisy devils! And mind you don't fall into the fire... There'll be damn all to scoff if you do!' the women shouted at them.

The second sailor, the one who had appeared with Motiakov earlier, was now just in his shirt, his sleeves rolled up, and he was barefoot, all red from the fire, and he stirred the pot, taking frequent scoops from it with a wooden spoon, and blew hard on it, then made great slurping noises as he tried the hot broth.

'May the Lord help you!' said Lively, as he approached.

'Come have supper with us,' the women answered back.

'It's scalding hot broth... Put out a couple of bottles!' said the sailor from the campfire, eyeing up Lively's bulging pocket.

'Match this!' said Lively, putting his bottle of **pertsovka** down on the sacking.

'Now you're talking! Mania, bring a bottle over!' shouted the sailor from the fire.

Earlier, from a distance, the chap seemed quite young to Fomich, but now, without his cloth cap, he could see a wide bald patch, sparsely covered with reddish, curly down. He took hold of the pot with its steaming contents and shouted: 'Come and get it... Others will watch us eating with envy!'

They served the broth – single cups for the men and a cup for the women and children to share. Another bottle was produced with a piece of rag for a stopper. They strained the moonshine through their lips, wincing and cackling. It was good stuff.

'Surely you don't make this yourselves?' asked Fomich.

'It's not that complicated,' said the unshaven man.

'You need the right equipment.'

'My equipment is over there – just a saucer and a plate. Just pile on the sugar,' the unshaven man remarked, with a cunning wink.

'With that kind of equipment, you've always got the wind behind your back, and you don't fear the rain,' said Lively with a smile. 'My own tobacco does the same for me. Here, try it!'

He took out his tobacco pouch and passed it round. They all lit up.

'Rain right now is just what the grass needs,' said the old man after a moment's silence.

'Yes, the hay will be good this year,' confirmed the bald man.

'All the same, half the meadows won't be harvested. People won't manage to mow it all,' said Fomich.

'Last year, that wasn't the case round our way – they managed to get it all in. Old men and women went to mow and a third of it was given to the **kolkhoz** workers.'

'It's not like that round our way. It's all about cracking down on people... Oh, those bosses!' sighed Fomich.

'Necessity will make them do it in the end,' said the bald man.

'Necessity should have made them do it a long time ago!'

'Those with any brain at all have said good-bye to necessity,' said the old man. 'Our chairmen have had the great idea of growing onions on private plots. The state pays two roubles seventy kopecks a kilo for them. Now that's what I call money!'

'Now loans to buy a cow are even available. On some **kolkhozes** you can even raise a calf,' the bald man confirmed.

'Yes, I've heard that... Round our way, in Brëkhovo, they do that. There, they have an excellent chairman – my mate Petia Dolgii,' said Fomich, telling a white lie. 'He keeps on asking me to join them. By the way, have you thought of going back to the **kolkhoz**?'

'Ours isn't that great,' the old man replied. 'We'll wait a while and see how it does. We go home and help the **kolkhoz** in the autumn. We go halves with the potatoes we dig up. That way we get enough for ourselves and the pigs.'

'That's great! If you can get hold of hay, you can keep a cow. And if loans are being granted – then why not?' said Fomich. 'I'm a dab hand at knowing how to spot a good cow. I really am good at spotting a good one. The first thing you have to do is look how the hair spreads out. If it starts to fork on its shoulder blades, that means that the interval between milk-producing periods is up to four weeks... It's a good cow! Then you have to feel the depression... between its stomach and its chest. If you can push your index finger in it, up to the first joint, that means that she will give you a **pood** of milk a day... So, what next? I'll hire myself out to Petia Dolgii. It's better to go to Brëhovo than travel fifty **versts** to Vysokoe. First, I'll pay a visit to Prudki straight from work. That's no distance. It won't be the first time. I'm good on my feet. Then I'll get a cow…'

Fomich took long drags on his roll-up and smiled. He was thinking about how deftly he would give Motiakov the run-around, how he would go to his office and give him the 'V' sign, saying, 'You wanted to get rid of me to Vysokoe… Well here you are! Take that!' His head spun from the effects of the vodka. He felt fine and dandy!

'Nowadays, you can survive anywhere,' said the old man.

'That's true,' agreed Fomich. 'You can make a living.'

I wrote down this story in the village of Prudki from the very words of Fëdor Fomich Kuzkin himself in 1956. I finished the story, then put it to one side.

One day, while sorting through some old papers, I came across this notebook. The story seemed engaging. I made a trip to Prudki and gave the story to Fëdor Fomich to read, who is still hail and hearty up to now, and I asked him to correct anything that wasn't quite right.

'It's all correct to the letter,' said Fëdor Fomich. 'Only the ending is a bit boring. Do you want me to tell you what happened after that? Life got easier after that…'

I tried to continue the story, but it didn't seem to work. Then I worked out why: now we are entering a new era, new times. And the old times have past.

'That's absolutely right!' Fëdor Fomich confirmed. 'But don't you fret. You'll write more. Enough has gone on in my life for you to write a whole novel…'

1964-65

One and a Half Square Metres

Illustration 10. 'No Longer a Nobody?', *Budilnik*, **1866.**

Foreword to One-and-a-Half Square Metres

Mozhaev had finished writing *One-and-a-Half Square Metres* in 1970, but it was not published until 1982, when it appeared in the **thick journal**, *Druzhba narodov* (Friendship of Nations*)*, which had gained a reputation for publishing contentious works. The reputation of *Novyi mir* as Russia's most liberal journal had gradually declined since **Tvardovskii** had ceased to be its editor, and *Druzhba narodov* had, in part, assumed the mantle of liberalism, until the revival of the fortunes of the former, under the editorship of the writer Sergei Zalygin in August 1986. Both journals, along with others, were to play a vital role in publishing previously unpublished and unpublishable manuscripts in the Gorbachëv era of *perestroika* and *glasnost.*

Once published, the work was side-lined by literary critics, in order not to draw attention to the story. It was subjected to a critical black-out. It was a tremendously popular work, and copies of *Druzhba narodov* sold 'like hot cakes', as Mozhaev stated in an interview. There were also long queues for the relevant edition in public libraries. The only critical assessment printed about the story appeared in the West, two years after the story's publication in Russia, in the émigré journal *Grani*, which gave the work an extremely positive review. The author, Kira Sapgir, expressed great surprise that it had slipped through the Soviet censorship machinery, 'with all its stumbling blocks, both seen and unseen', as she said.[1] The work was adapted for the cinema, and the film was released in 1988, under the rather clumsy title of *What's with you, don't you like our power?!* Once again, the film enjoyed great critical acclaim, but by this time, reform and liberalization had already taken a firm grip upon the Soviet regime and the production of the film was not opposed.

The main protagonist of Mozhaev's satirical work *One-and-a-Half Square Metres*, is Pavel Semënovich Poluboiarinov, who is something of a 'free thinker'. However, for this, he is universally vilified by local officials in the fictional provincial town of Rozhnov, which is the setting of the story. This is one of the few works written by Mozhaev not set in the countryside or on the **kolkhoz**. Officials fall upon Poluboiarinov with astonishing spite, like a pack of dogs at a hunt falling upon their quarry, and in this sense they are all an extension of the Motiakov and Guzënkov 'Stalinists', who persecuted Kuzkin. Such officials look more and more like the *shishigi* in Mozhaev's story of that name. As a consequence, the Poluboiarinovs have to look increasingly further afield, even as far as Moscow, in their attempt to find justice, through the labyrinth of Soviet bureaucracy and the legal system. In the end, they attain their goal in some measure, but their victory is only partial, and it comes at a cost.

The impetus for the work is simple, but ingenious, and it is typical of Mozhaev's cheeky sense of humour and his penchant for the absurd. Notwithstanding the comedy, the mafia-like plotting by local officials to grind Pavel Semënovich into the ground is truly shocking. Bating and persecuting him become a local sport, and the coterie of officials is shown in its true light during a garden party, convened to declare the opening of the hunting season. The officials and local dignitaries compare notes as to how they have been upset by Pavel Semënovich, and their spite generates its own momentum, to

---

[1] K. Sapgir, *Grani*, 131 (1984), 294-98. Unfortunately, the interview has not been translated into English. The journal was not available officially in the Soviet Union.

the extent that, ironically, the officials declare open season upon the Poluboiarinovs at that very event.

However, Pavel Semënovich is not alone in ruffling local feathers: his wife, Maria Ivanovna, has also managed to upset her boss during the course of her duties as the chief bookkeeper at the local newspaper. She had objected to the editor, Feduleev, buying a radio with newspaper funds, when in essence he purloins it and keeps it for his sole, personal use. He also commits other acts, which are revealed as nothing other than blatant nepotism, and when challenged, he retaliates by forcing Mariia Ivanovna to retire, supported by those officials, who also make Pavel Semënovich's life a misery. Hence, all the local officials form a coterie of people who are protective of each other and their mutual interests, privileges, and status, within the community. They are totally self-serving.

All this illegality is treated with Mozhaev's characteristic sense of humour, but the story gradually becomes darker and less amusing as it develops. Some of the humour is subtle and revealed in small details: the name of the town in which the Poluboiarinovs live – Rozhnov – is significant, in that it is reminiscent of the Russian expression '*ne pri na rozhon*', rendered in English as, 'Don't kick against the pricks', or 'Don't swim against the tide'.

There is also comedy in Pavel Semënovich's surname, as the name 'Poluboiarinov' consists of '*polu*', which means 'half' or 'semi', and a root word, '*boiarin*', which means 'boyar'. Hence his name could be translated as 'Half-Boyar' or 'Semi-Boyar'. A boyar was a term for a member of the upper echelons of medieval Russian society, who were a class of rich landlords, who served the prince as counsellors or advisors. Officials in the story regard Pavel Semënovich as rather snooty or aloof, and it is his constant dispensing of advice, which really irritates them.

Pavel Semënovich is eccentric and a bit of a pedant, but above all, he questions what he sees going on around him. He makes suggestions and proposes schemes to improve their life and society, which emanate, not from selfish motives, but from a genuine desire to improve the quality of life in their community, by exploiting natural resources, which are plentiful and near to hand. However, there is a certain *naïveté* with which he constantly puts his head above the parapet, which officials interpret as having aspirations above his station, and hence they resolve to silence him. What they do not realise is that he is also a stubborn man, and he doggedly pursues a personal vindication and justice for the wrongs done to him.

The provincial microcosm, which Mozhaev describes, is typical of Soviet society anywhere, where personal allegiances change as friendships form and dissolve, and as favours are mutually accorded and repaid. Hence, when Pavel Semënovich and his wife resolve to make alterations to their flat, they need to get the administrator of the building, Ekaterina Timofeevna Funtikova, on their side, if the project is to succeed. They know that, within the Soviet system, it is vital to get her 'on board', in order that she might persuade the other members of the residents' committee to grant permission. Pavel Semënovich is not sure whether Funtikova will remember a favour he did her, because, clearly, he considers that it is 'pay-back time'. However, on entering her office, he can immediately tell by the reception he gets that the favour has not been forgotten, and the longed-for permission he seeks appears to be within his grasp. This is a perfect example of what in Russian is called '*blat*', or using connections to achieve a personal goal. In Soviet society, and still in Russia today, connections, i.e. people with influence in one sphere or another, are far more important than mere paper money. The rich lexicon of expressions in Russian to express this phenomenon of mutual 'help' attests to its widespread existence. The reader will see how true it is that, to use just one of these many expressions, 'one hand washes the other'.

As in a number of Mozhaev's stories, there are passing references in this story to Russia's dark history during the time of collectivization. Maria Ivanovna has a militant past – she played a limited role in the local campaign for full collectivization and **dekulakization**. And the anti-religious campaign, which took place alongside collectivization, has left its mark in the community: the church in the park has been turned into a flour mill and the miller tells the couple how much gold was removed from the roof, which now, sadly, leaks, due to its removal. There is further mindless destruction in evidence in the gardens, graveyard, and flower beds – the latter were regarded as being particularly 'bourgeois' by the Bolsheviks. All this leads to a discussion as to whether the Revolution had been a good thing or not, and there is even praise for a former **barin**, who, contrary to the Bolshevik stereotype of being a grasping, avaricious tyrant, had turned out to have a strong social conscience and a generous philanthropic nature. However, the conversation is cut short almost as soon as it begins to become interesting: Mozhaev had gone as far as he could on this theme at the time of writing the story, but it shows which themes were uppermost in his mind. All these themes are explored in greater depth and with much greater candour in his novel, *Peasant Folk*.

Another conversation which teeters on the edge of the permissible at this point in time, was the question which Pavel Semënovich raises: 'Can a person know for what purpose he lives?' – a question touched upon in *Lively*. The miller's answer is an expression of Christian faith, which, again, was a topic which could not be taken very far in discussions in officially published literature. The same question is raised again in the dream sequence in this story.

The miller advocates serving God and peace, and Pavel Semënovich latches on to the concept of peace and harmony amongst people in society. This was a goal far removed from the militancy of Soviet class warfare and ideological struggle, as discussed in *Old Mother Proshkina* and *A History of the Village of Brëkhovo*. But this ideology aside, it is also a far cry from the viciousness of the officials who torment the life out of the Poluboiarinovs. Ironically, the Bolsheviks claimed that the building of a harmonious and just society was at the very core of their communist cause and aims, though the means to achieve this would necessarily involve considerable struggle.

The offer of a harmonious and just society seems a mere utopian dream to Pavel Semënovich, and he rejects being forced to accept it unquestioningly: he likens it to sticking chewing gum forcibly into a child's mouth to keep him quiet. He even insists on his right to reject this promise of future happiness – a real act of rebellion, reminiscent of Ivan Karazamov in Dostoevsky's novel *Brothers Karamazov*.[2] This profound philosophical argument is only touched on in this work and it appears as a mere off-the-

---

[2] Dostoevsky, *Brothers Karamazov*, Vol.I, Part II, Book V, Chapter IV "Rebellion".

cuff remark, but when seen in the context of his novel *Peasant Folk*, which contains many dozen pages of deep, philosophical discussion, it is highly significant.

There was an extremely strong utopian ideal embedded within the Bolshevik vision of the future model of society under communism. As long philosophical discussions in his novel *Peasant Folk* attest, Mozhaev was very damning of such utopian dreaming, which he shows was inherited from a long tradition of ideal societies, described by philosophers from Plato and Campanella, to a whole plethora of early socialist thinkers, mainly from the French, nineteenth-century tradition, i.e. Blanqui, Babeuf, St. Simon, Cabet, *et alii*. The works of many of these philosophers were banned in tsarist times, but they found their way into Russian circles of radical thought, and their ideas were imbibed and made their own by influential Russian thinkers of the nineteenth century. Marx, Lenin, Herzen, Bakunin, and many other radical thinkers, were all *au fait* with such philosophical writings, and they became part of the Russian utopian ideal. All these radical thinkers were convinced that they had discovered the truth of how society should be structured, and they believed that the past had to be swept away before the new, brighter future of a fairer, more equitable society could be built. However, Mozhaev, taking his lead from Dostoevsky, questioned the right of the individual to reject their vision. He challenges the profound conviction of the radical thinkers, that theirs is the only truth possible, that truth is singular and revealed only to them. So convinced were these radical thinkers of the immutable veracity of their view that they were quite prepared to force their ideas upon a society which was resistant to change: they regarded any reluctance or opposition to them as a mark of intellectual and cultural backwardness, which they were prepared to eradicate forcibly, if necessary. Mozhaev insisted on the individual's right to spit out the chewing gum forced into the child's mouth, which, for him in this work, is a metaphor for rejecting the radicals' utopian dream.

In *One-and-a-Half*, the **oblast** executive committee is housed in former administrative offices, when the area used to be classified as a **guberniia**, and Pavel Semënovich notices that there is a plaque on the building, indicating that Saltykov-Shchedrin used to work there. Mikhail Evgrafovich Saltykov-Shchedrin (1826-89) is considered to be the greatest satirist of nineteenth-century Russia, and he was a writer Mozhaev much admired. He was a civil servant for many years, working in Mozhaev's native **Riazan oblast**. It is ironic that the Poluboiarinovs are involved in a bureaucratic wrangle fit for the pen of Saltykov-Shchedrin himself. There are also strong parallels to be drawn from Saltykov-Shchedrin's satire *The History of a Town* and Mozhaev's *A History of the Village of Brëkhovo*, discussed in a later section of this volume.

There is a dream sequence in *One-and-a-Half*, which is not unusual in Mozhaev's writing. Russians generally, but rural dwellers in particular, set great store by dreams and their interpretation.

In the dream sequence in this story, Pavel Semënovich gets an audience, not with an official, but with the Lord God of Sabaoth Himself, whereas in reality, he is palmed off to a mere secretary, who, by the end of the story, is promoted and, therefore, is too exalted to receive him. The dream is surreal and it represents the ideal, as one might hope to be received by an official, but it contrasts sharply with the reality the Poluboiarinovs experienced when they were last in the offices. Instead of the cold stare which they actually received, the militia man in the dream doffs his cap to Maria Ivanovna and greets the couple with the utmost civility. They are shown to the reception hall along a red carpet, which has the same symbolic welcome as in Western culture. They are admitted to an audience with God Himself, who turns out to be the all-powerful Lord Sabaoth. There's nothing like going to the top!

God in the dream accuses Pavel Scmёnovich of cheating patients out of gold fillings, skimping on their treatment, in order to collect enough gold for a filling for his daughter-in-law, Berta. And Berta is not just any old person – she is none other than a citizen of the German Democratic Republic (East Germany), and thereby, she is special. She is distinguished by her birthright, by simply having been born a foreigner, and as such, her name becomes a mantra or magic word for assisting the Poluboiarinovs to make the desired changes to their apartment. Berta is openly called their 'trump card', and her name and citizenship are evoked, whenever they try to achieve the impossible. Her name acts like a Soviet 'abracadabra' – terms which, amusingly, both open doors!

In an era when foreign tourism was important to the Soviet regime, to enable the state to accrue valuable, convertible foreign currency, great measures were taken to make sure that all foreign visitors, even those from so-called 'Soviet-friendly countries', formed the very best impression of life in the Soviet Union. Western visitors seldom had to queue, unlike ordinary Russian citizens: they went straight to the head of queues for museums, restaurants, and theatres, etc., by-passing Russians, who had often been queuing for some considerable time. There was also a chain of special shops for those foreign tourists who had convertible currency to spend. Pavel Semёnovich is shocked to find that even in heaven, the magical word 'Berta', as a citizen of the **GDR**, has had the desired effect, leading him to muse on the 'power in a foreign word'.

For all the farce and comedy one expects in a satirical work, there is also a much darker side to this story. When the narrator returns to visit the Poluboiarinovs at the end of the story, he finds that their life has now changed for the worse, and Pavel Semёnovich's health is failing. All this has been caused by the spite of local officials and people with influence. He is still pursuing a retraction in print of a libellous article, sanctioned by the editor of the local newspaper – a campaign which has now become the goal of his life. It has even put an end, albeit temporary (he thinks), to his research and proposing further schemes for the betterment of the local community.

Yet again, journalists and the press are shown to be duplicitous. The journalist who visits Pavel Semёnovich to elicit the facts of his situation plays the role of *agent provocateur*, only to libel him in his article. The journalist was sent by the editor of the newspaper expressly to entrap him and there is not a whiff of unbiased, investigative journalism. The very thought of printing a refutation of the libellous article is unthinkable, because, as it has appeared in the press, it is *ipso facto* fact, and therefore, it cannot be retracted. The editor of the newspaper is the very epitome of Soviet smugness and arrogance: he cannot even countenance being wrong or being incapable of seeing the truth, which for him is singular – there is only one possible view of reality and life.

For all his pedantry and eccentricities, Pavel Semёnovich shows the same kind of tenacity and determination as Kuzkin. Although not fighting for his very survival, like Kuzkin, Pavel Semёnovich nevertheless fights for something equally precious – his personal reputation and standing in the community. He remains undaunted at the end and there are still letters outstanding…

One-and-a-Half Square Metres

An Amusing Tale in Fourteen Sections with an Epilogue and a Dream

Chapter One

One morning, Pavel Semënovich Poluboiarinov, a dental mechanic and a member of the housing committee, awoke to find that he couldn't get out of his flat: his drunken neighbour, Chizhënok, was sleeping at the foot of his door. The door opened outwards, into the corridor.

'Mariia, Mariia!' Pavel Semënovich shouted.

'What d'you want?' shouted back Mariia Ivanovna – but not immediately, and from her hoarse, half-asleep, grudging response, Pavel Semënovich knew that he should not have called out to his wife, and that he could expect a telling off.

'Oh, it doesn't matter,' replied Pavel Semënovich, cowed.

'You're not getting off that lightly! Now you've woken me, tell me what you want!'

'Chizhënok is asleep at the foot of our door again.'

'To hell with him! He'll sleep it off and then get up.'

'But I need to… you know… I forgot and left the pot outside. I'm dying to go and I can't hold it any longer.'[1]

'Pee out of the window.'

'It's broad daylight! Haven't you noticed that?'

The bed springs broke into a piteous groan, and Mariia's voice replied: 'God Almighty! Well, I suppose it's time to get up anyway.'

She dangled her fat legs with their purple, bulging veins out of the bed, and she stretched out her powerful, bruiser hands sideways, and let out such a loud, shrill yawn that Pavel Semënovich gave a start.

He stood by the door in just his underpants, shifting slightly from one withered, vein-ridden leg to the other. One leg bore evidence of an injury at the shin, marked by faded red welts, and it was noticeably shorter than the other.

'Well, don't just stand there, dancing the **kamarinskaia**,' said Mariia Ivanovna, grumpily. 'Give the door a shove!'

'I've tried that… But he's got his head against it.'

Mariia Ivanovna went over to the door.

---

[1] Communal flats were (and still are) common in Russia. The occupier or family has their own room, but bathroom, and often cooking, facilities are communal. In this story, the Poluboiarinovs have their own kitchen, as will become apparent, but they share bathroom facilities with their neighbours.

'C'mon, now!'

She moved the door with one blow from her shoulder, and in the corridor there was a resounding thump, as if someone had rattled a whisk in an empty wooden mug. Then there was a growling sound, which soon turned into a long string of effing and blinding. Finally, a voice came from the corridor, asking: 'Who d'you want?'

'Get away from the door, you drunk!' shouted Mariia Ivanovna.

The reply was a song, bawled out plaintively, but it sounded more like the mooing of a cow that had swallowed something, which had gone down the wrong way:

> *There are folk who call us stingy,*
> *But we couldn't give a shit.*
> *We got drunk on our own money,*
> *Do we care? No, not a whit!*

'You're an idiot!' said Mariia Ivanovna.

'And you lot can go fuck your mother!'

'We'll call the police. Then you'll sing a different tune.'

'Sod the police! I'm lying in my own space.'

'But we need to get out,' said Pavel Semënovich, pathetically.

'If you want to come out, open the door inwards. Don't dare open it towards me... or I'll smash you to pieces!'

'Volodia, the door only opens one way, out into the corridor. Couldn't you just get up?' asked Pavel Semënovich, gently trying to persuade Chizhënok, sticking his nose out into the corridor.

'I'll give you "get up"!'

'I have to get out.'

'Sod you! You should have thought of that earlier.' And again he bellowed:

> *All day long, the hunter stalked the islands,*
> *Cursing himself for his lack of luck...*[2]

'What are we to do now?' asked Pavel Semënovich pitifully, turning towards his wife Mariia Ivanovna.

'You do this every time – *you're* dying to go and you ask what *we* should do? We should have altered the door long ago so that it opens into the flat, instead of outwards into the corridor, and then we wouldn't be dependent upon anyone. And how long will it

---

[2] This is a quotation from a poem 'About Danila' (Pro Danilu) (1937) by Alexander Trifonovich **Tvardovskii** (1910-1971), who was a prominent poet in his own right, as well as being the editor of *Novyi mir*. The poem, from which the lines are quoted here, is about an old peasant man, Danila, who has had a drink too many on a feast day, and he becomes gripped by a bout of melancholia.

be before there's a disaster? What happens if there's a sudden fire? What would we do then, dive out of the window?'

'We'll just have to put up with it?'

'That's it… Go on, try and console me.'

'We've no way out.'

'And there's no way out here! And what possessions could we save by dragging them out of the window? Tell me that! You'd break your legs. Look at how high it is… It's not a house we're living in – it's a rookery!'

Mariia Ivanovna threw open the window and looked down to the ground, as if she was, in fact, going to jump. It was a long way to the ground. For a start, the side of the house was six rows of logs high. Why had it been made so high? Four rows would have been ample. And then there were the foundations – no less than a metre high. So just you try diving out from there. One false step and you'd come a cropper…'

'The owner of this house was a total idiot. He was a real *provizor*!'

Such a phrase usually marked the end of the couple's disagreements, caused by how impractical the flat was. The building in which the Poluboiarinovs lived used to belong to a *provizor* long ago. No one knew exactly what a *provizor* actually did, but everyone knew that it was a bad word, a swear word, akin to an 'exploiter'.[3] For a while, this epithet had stuck to Pavel Semënovich himself, as a nickname, on account of his learning and his somewhat haughty air. And Pavel Semënovich was utterly amazed when Doctor Dolbezhov, the most senior member of their clinic, explained to him that the word *provizor* simply meant 'a fully-qualified pharmaceutical chemist'.[4] In times gone by, the expression 'to live like a *provizor*' meant 'to put a brave face on being poor'. Like the expression 'to hobnob with your betters'.[5] However, Pavel Semënovich saw nothing insulting at all in this nickname, and he didn't mind it. With time, it disappeared of its own accord, like a scab that falls from a healed sore.

Sometime in the past, the old *provizor's* house had been divided into four flats and occupied by new tenants, which is when the afore-mentioned inconvenience started. First, the new partitions let every single sound through into the neighbour's flat. Secondly, the communal corridor was a nuisance. There was no way of avoiding it, wherever you went. It was narrow, long, and it had an L-shaped passageway. You couldn't walk down it without bumping into something – you'd either bang your head on the washing trough, or stand on the cat's tail, or even kick over a slop bucket. But lately, the top end of the L-shaped corridor – a two-metre passageway which led to the Poluboiarinovs' flat – had been unofficially appropriated by their neighbour, Chizhënok.

---

[3] Various prosperous professional people who lived before the Revolution of 1917 were dubbed 'exploiters', meaning they exploited the working class or peasantry. Many such professionals were entrepreneurial and innovative, but the Bolshevik regime regarded them with the utmost suspicion.

[4] The doctor's name has strong associations with the Russian word meaning 'to swot', i.e. to work hard at one's studies.

[5] The literal translation is 'to take your pig's snout into the street where white bread is sold'. As a refined product, white bread was more expensive to produce and buy than the traditional whole-meal bread. The expressions used here means to desire to associate with a class or people above one's station.

When he came home drunk every night, his wife Zinka, wouldn't open their own door to him.

'Go back to where you got drunk!'

'You're talking a load of crap, wench! You'll open up when you go to work. I'll take out my sleepless night on you. I'll smash you to pieces!'

Chizhënok would lie down with his cheek on his cap and sleep the sleep of the dead, blocking the entrance to two flats. Fortunately for Zinka, her flat door opened *inwards*. She used to step over her husband with the greatest of ease and go off to work. However, the Poluboiarinovs' door opened *outwards*, into the corridor…

They would have quite happily altered the door, so that it opened into the flat, but a lintel, adjacent to a flue from their neighbours' stove, prevented it, making it necessary to move the door frame further along the L-shaped passageway by a metre and a half, which meant appropriating one-and-a-half square metres of communal territory. This would require permission from the town council.

'Pavlo! Sit down right now and write a request about the door,' said Mariia Ivanovna. 'What'll happen when Misha and Berta come? What an embarrassment! We can't even pop out to the loo. And after all, Berta is a former citizen of the **GDR**. That's what you should write on the application: "This has a whiff of foreign complication about it".'

'I'm not so sure about the "foreign complication" part, but I'm about to have a complication right now,' replied Pavel Semënovich, rushing from the door towards the window.

'What are you messing about for?' said Mariia Ivanovna, looking apprehensively at the floor. 'Use the window!'

'God bless me!' said Pavel Semënovich, taking a deep breath as if sobbing, and he started climbing out of the window.

Chapter Two

Their daughter-in-law Berta was a real trump card, but this card had to be played deftly. In such a game, if you sacrificed it too early – you'd be out-trumped. So, just bide your time – it would trump any hand.

It's true that, recently, Chizhënok had taken to sleeping more regularly in the corridor, and his effing and blinding could be heard throughout the whole house. But what guarantee was there that he wouldn't end up in prison again? Every year, during the autumn, he used to go to prison for petty larceny. Then he'd come back to Rozhnov in the spring. He'd say, 'I get bored in the autumn. I get a yearning for warmer climes. That's why I go on the rob.'

In fact, if he did end up inside, it would be bye-bye to the door refit. They had to get a move on: autumn was just round the corner. That's just what Pavel Semënovich was thinking as he went to visit Funtikova, the house manageress.

Ekaterina Timofeevna received him courteously. During the long course of her duties, she had taken to heart the foremost precept of an educator – that cultured behaviour was the first indication of a managerial member of staff. And she kept up her outward appearance also: she dyed her greying hair a flaxen colour, back-combed her quiff, and shaved the nape of her neck. This made her look younger than her fifty-five years.

'Ekaterina Timofeevna, you really ought to go in for photographic modelling,' said the carpenter Sudakov to her. 'The whole arrangement of your face is so imposing: your eyes are lively and your face is round.'

And there was a time when her image was publicly displayed, during her career as a **kolkhoz** chairwoman. Her name resounded throughout the whole **oblast**. She was a plucky gal... She tackled all official demands made of her in her stride, just as a good race horse would handle any fence before it... In the **raion** a celebrated sisterhood of **kolkhoz** chairwomen formed.[6] Funtikova's **kolkhoz** was famous. The lively eyes of Katka (as she was called then) would peer defiantly from hoardings and official statements: they would say, 'What are you thinking about? Just follow us with your trump card! You'll not come a cropper!'

In the **oblast** newspaper she was mentioned alongside none other than Comrade Ovsov, the chairman of the Rozhnov regional executive committee. He was a shaven-headed, bruiser of a man, who wore a military tunic cut on the diagonal, with an officer's belt fixed around his stomach.[7] He cut a fine figure. And how he loved discipline and good manners! When the administrative committee would convene – a fireman stood in the doorway wearing his brass helmet. The committee would be waiting for him, and then as soon as Ovsov appeared in the corridor, the fireman would shout: 'Attention! Comrade Ovsov is approaching...'

All stood to attention and held the pose.

'At ease, Comrades! Please be seated. It is not really obligatory to stand. After all, we're not in the army,' Ovsov would say with a smile.

And he had an eye for beauty... When Funtikova was accused of voluntarism on the **kolkhoz**, that is, when all the calves had been slaughtered in the abattoir, Ovsov transferred her to the cultural education section. He said, 'We appreciate members of staff with good manners. Our Katerina has it all – her very appearance alone brings out good manners in everyone.'

However, it was Ovsov who was the ruin of Funtikova. Once, a big-wig travelled though the **oblast** on his way south to the seaside. On the **oblast** border, a procurement secretary from the **oblast** committee and a chairman of the **oblast** executive committee got into his carriage. During the journey to Rozhnov, they wangled out of the official two fleets of combine harvesters from Moscow to help with the harvest. They left the carriage in Rozhnov as pleased as punch. Ovsov greeted them like his own kin. They

---

[6] **Kolkhoz** 'chairwomen' were rather rare: despite assurances of equal rights, the higher echelons of managerial and administrative staff were predominantly male. Peasant villages were extremely patriarchal before the Revolution, and in communes women did not have the right to vote, although they were permitted to attend meetings. The woman's role was seen as taking care of the home, children, and domestic animals, plus weeding and helping in the fields with agricultural work. It took many years for such attitudes to change, despite mass migration into the cities, and even late into the Soviet era, the home – cooking, cleaning and shopping – and the care of the children, were still widely regarded as women's work by men.

[7] The wearing of military uniforms and the militarization of Russian society went back as far as Peter the Great (1682-1725), but the penchant for wearing military garb in civil society was very common in the early years of the Bolshevik regime.

threw a banquet in the **sovkhoz** garden. Ovsov assigned Funtikova to hostess duties. It was said that she sat right on the chairman's knees in the car. Where they went off to – no one knows. Only, the next morning, the chairman phoned the regional committee offices and asked, 'Did I break anything while I was drunk?' He was told, 'No, everything is fine.' 'Well, in that case, do give my thanks to Funtikova...' So Ovsov issued an order to express official thanks to her for providing such a 'cultural service'. But she was ridiculed: people said that she'd been given a medal for offering 'domestic services'. Whether she had 'serviced' him or not, no one knew. However, when Ovsov was sacked for 'deviating from the official animal husbandry policy', the 'cultural services' incident with Funtikova resurfaced, and she was demoted to the position of house manageress.

Pavel Semënovich knew Funtikova from way back. While still a **kolkhoz** chairwoman, she had asked Pavel Semënovich to fix a gap in her front teeth, which made her lisp slightly. Pavel Semënovich had fixed a pure gold crown for her on to a healthy tooth. For this, Ekaterina Timofeevna had given him a flagon of buckwheat honey, weighing about three **poods**. And now, on entering her office, Pavel Semënovich was trying to ascertain whether she had remembered his act of largess or not.

Ekaterina Timofeevna herself came to greet him from her desk, and offered him a cupped hand – it might even be kissed. Her smile was so broad that the gold tooth was perfectly visible... Pavel Semënovich decided that she had indeed remembered.

'What is the nature of your business, dear, esteemed Pavel Semënovich? Please, do take a seat!' She tapped the arm of the settee.

Pavel Semënovich also sported his broadest smile and thought to himself, 'Should I start in a roundabout way or mention Berta right off? She's so terribly affectionate that she looks as though she would stroke my shoulder with a smile, and yet she could refuse in the twinkling of an eye.'

'How are we getting on? What's our problem?' said Ekaterina Timofeevna in a sing-song voice from her desk.

'In our work, tranquillity is of the utmost importance,' said Pavel Semënovich, taking the roundabout route. 'You yourself know that my work is fiddly. Teeth are such little things.'

'What *do* you mean, Pavel Semënovich?! They might not be substantial as a mere detail, but they're important, given their location. One's teeth are there for all to see – one cannot hide them. One must keep them in good order. That is why your work is so highly esteemed.'

'That's absolutely right,' agreed Pavel Semënovich meekly. 'Now, answer me this in all sincerity: Should I, in my position, have cause to fret?'

'You must not, Pavel Semënovich. Without a shadow of a doubt.'

'Recently, I have lost my composure.'

'Whatever misfortune has happened?'

'You know our neighbour, Chizhënok?'

'Aha?!'

'Practically every night, he lies down at the foot of our door in a drunken state. Not only can we not get out to go to work, but we cannot even go to the lavatory, if you'll pardon the expression. You see, our door opens outwards, into the corridor!'

'We'll fine him.'

'That won't help. He even drinks at other people's expense.'

'Well, we'll summon him to a **Comrades' Court**.'

'Ah! All his comrades are in prison. What does he care about such a court?'

'So, what do you suggest?'

'I request permission to have our door refit, so that it opens *into* our flat. Then we'll be able simply to step over him. And that's all there is to it.'

'That can easily be done.'

'Thank you for that. Now, in order for our door to open inwards, it will have to be re-sited further down the corridor by about one-and-a-half metres.'

'How do you mean "re-sited". Do you mean the seizure of one-and-a-half metres of communal territory?'

'It won't open inwards in any other way – there's a lintel in the way and our neighbour's flue is on the left.'

'Pavel Semënovich, you are an educated and cultured man,' observed Ekaterina Timofeevna, and she kind of slapped her hand down on the table, which usually indicated her utmost disappointment. 'Seizing communal space without the agreement of fellow residents would be an infringement of the law.'

'I am not against the law. But just think for a moment – you are also educated and are familiar with culture… Answer me this question: how will it be, when my daughter-in-law Berta comes to stay with me? She is, after all, a former citizen of the German Democratic Republic! And yet, in the morning she won't be able to get out of the flat to attend to her "needs", if you'll forgive the expression. That would get you and me involved in an international situation.'

'Of course, we must not allow things to get to an international situation,' said Ekaterina Timofeevna, becoming pensive. 'Otherwise, people will say that everything is interconnected.'

'Absolutely… Interconnected!' exclaimed Pavel Semënovich, happily seizing upon her phrase. 'People will ask, "How can they possibly live in their town of Rozhnov, when everything is interconnected?"'

'Don't be surprised, Pavel Semënovich!' said Funtikova, bitterly shaking her head. 'And what if foreign correspondents were to slander us?'

'Well, we haven't been accused of covering up for each other yet.'

'Ah! But give a dog a bad name…! Very well. In so far as this is an exceptional situation, I shall make a personal recommendation to the executive committee. Have you written a request?'

'Absolutely,' said Pavel Semënovich, hurriedly taking out a piece of exercise-book paper folded in quarters.

'When is your daughter-in-law due to arrive?'

'We're expecting her by the autumn.'

'We'll try to get a decision post-haste,' replied Ekaterina Timofeevna, offering her hand by way of farewell, in the same down-turned, cupped manner, with all her fingers together.

Chapter Three

When Chizhënok was not drinking, he worked as a sweeper in the central square of Rozhnov. By the way, there was only one square in the town and he was its only sweeper. He used to sweep it in the heat of the summer, but in cold weather, he went to prison, and so it got snow-bound.

People got used to such a seasonal sweeper in Rozhnov, and Chizhënok's job had been kept open for him for a number of years. It would have been a bit silly to hire just a winter sweeper. So, what should be done? Sweep the snow away from the steps and the entrances to the flats? Or else sweep away the snow from the pathways of the square that nobody used? In any case, the road and the car park in front of the House of Soviets were kept clear of snow by a bulldozer: the services of a 'Belorus' tractor were used.

Chizhënok would get up early when sober, even before dawn, and take his broom, rake, and refuse pail to work. He used to hide all his tools in the acacia bushes behind the board of honour, and he would return home, casting a furtive eye around, and climb through the window of his neighbour, Elena Alexandrovna.[8] She would quietly and languidly exclaim, as if she was asleep: 'Ah, you frightened me…'

Yet she never locked her windows. She said, 'I wondered whether it might be thieves.'

'I am a thief,' smirked Chizhënok, removing his boots.

'Volia, please don't "vulgarize"!'[9]

Elena Alexandrovna worked for the editorial office of the local newspaper as a proof-reader, and she loved altering people's names. She used to call her deceased husband

---

[8] The 'board of honour' was a large hoarding used to display the poster-size photographs of the best and most distinguished workers of a district or area of a town or city. Such workers were also fêted in newspapers and magazines, and on notice boards at their place of work. This kind of honour, used by the regime *pour encourager les autres*, was often accompanied by more tangible rewards, such as luxury goods, holidays, and access to exclusive shops and establishments. It was all part of a system which rewarded its most faithful 'sons' and 'daughters'.

[9] In an effort to show her extreme – exaggerated – refinement, she tells Chizhënok not to be vulgar. However, she makes up a verb meaning 'to be vulgar', derived from the adjective for 'vulgar'.

Solomon – an old, feeble hospital bookkeeper – by the more literary name Misius.[10] She called Volodka Chizhënok 'Volia', and Old Ma Urozhaikina – a gloomy old woman, who looked like an **Old Believers**' icon – 'Mother Mariia'.[11] Although in her fifties, Elena Alexandrovna still adored poetry and romantic songs: she painted her nails, lips, and even her eyelids. When she crooned '*I have adorned our corner with flowers...*' she would throw back her head and half-close her eyes, and the blue eyelids on her white, podgy face, with the edges of her elongated lips turned down, as if racked in pain, made her look like a resurrecting corpse.[12] Alënkin, the most educated pensioner in Rozhnov and former director of the House of People's Creative Art in the town, used to dedicate poems to her. However, apparently, they had a tiff. Alënkin, for some reason or other, became very thin, bought up all the pantokrin in the local pharmacy and, right until the first frosts, he used to wash himself down in the yard with cold water and run about the forest just in his underwear.[13]

At this difficult time in her life of solitude and tiffs, Volodka Chizhënok crossed Elena Alexandrovna's threshold. Well, to be more precise, it was her windowsill that he crossed, not her threshold.

Once, Chizhënok was on his way to work as usual. Suddenly a window opened and something fell from a windowsill. It was just before dawn – anyone would have thought, 'Hang on, just go over to see what that white thing is.' However, Chizhënok would have simply walked on by, had he not heard someone calling to him, 'Volia, please help me pick that up!'

Elena Alexandrovna was leaning out of the window – her hair was down and her shoulders were bare. Chizhënok came over and picked up that something white... It turned out to be a wide, lace-up belt with some rather tough ribs sewn into it. It smelt of perfume...

'Whatever is it of mine that's fallen?' asked Elena Alexandrovna.

'Looks like a swimming costume... But it's a bit tough.'

'It's a corset.'

'Where does that go then?'

'Why, just here... Look!'

---

[10] This name does not mean anything *per se*, but it has a classical ring about it, i.e. like the Roman name 'Cassius'.

[11] Volodka is a rather common-sounding variant of the proper name 'Vladimir', which is more often shortened to 'Volodia'. However, Elena Alexandrovna's variation of his name – 'Volia' – means 'Freedom'. This is ironic, when one considers he spends half the year in prison! 'Mother Mariia' is evocative of the Virgin Mary, and this old woman's real name, Urozhaikina, has its root in the Russian word for 'harvest' — *urozhai*. See the Glossary for a note on **Old Believers**.

[12] This line comes from the first verse of a four-stanza romantic song, called 'Little Corner', by V. Mazurkevich and S. Shteiman. The song is tragic and it is one of many of its type, which express unrequited love: a woman has adorned her room, or 'little corner', with flowers on a hot night, full of passion and the scent of flowers, in anticipation of her lover's arrival. The scent of lilac and the moonlight burn in her heart, as she anticipates her lover's kisses. However, he never appears, and she loses all hope of ever seeing him again.

[13] 'Pantokrin' is an alternative medicine preparation, derived from deer or caribou antlers. It is said to increase energy levels and stamina, reverse aging, and increase sexual libido.

Elena Alexandrovna placed the corset over her nightgown, just a little below her bosom.

'What's the laces for?' asked Chizhënok.

'You *are* funny, Volia… They're to tie up.'

'Where?'

'Just here.'

'Let's have a see!' Chizhënok grabbed her windowsill – his usual way of entering a property – and he was in her flat in a trice.

That's how they became pally…

Elena Alexandrovna would sing softly and read poetry to him. Chizhënok would just sit there in silence.

'Don't you like poetry?'

'No.'

'That's because you can't write poetry.'

'Yes I can. I once made one up in prison.'

'What about?'

'About our town.'

'Please recite it!'

Chizhënok hesitated for a moment and then said:

> *Rozhnov is a provincial town*
> *And people need it all aroun'.*
> *From it you can go far and wide,*
> *And buy anything you decide.*
> *Rozhnov of all the world is best,*
> *Of great Siberia, and the rest…*

Elena Alexandrovna burst out laughing: 'What kind of poetry is that?! It's just nonsense.'

'Why?'

'Because we don't live in Siberia.'

'So what?'

'What's Siberia got to do with it?'

'I felt like making up a verse about Siberia, so I did.'

'What nonsense! It's not true! You say we can buy what we like here. Where can we do that in Rozhnov?'

'I didn't *say* that. I just *wrote* that in the verse. Life's one thing, poetry's another.'

'But they should both reflect each other.'

'Why? It's all boring anyway.'[14]

Elena Alexandrovna herself did not know why everything described in verses should be like life, and she never spoke about this again to Chizhënok.

He always left her flat by the door. As soon as Zinka had disappeared behind the fence, Chizhënok would leave, as if he were coming out of his own flat, thanks to their doors being adjacent, and he would take the back routes, along Malinov Ravine, and emerged in a moment in the main square. As he left, he would grab a bottle of vodka or port – whatever Elena Alexandrovna had managed to get hold of for him – and, to Zinka's great vexation, he would return home blind drunk.

This well-organized source of supply for Chizhënok came to a totally unexpected end. That morning, Funtikova had summoned the technical surveyor Lomov, and the carpenter Sudakov, to the Poluboiarinovs'.[15] A real rumpus kicked off in the house: floorboards creaked, doors banged, and all the inhabitants came out into the corridor, as if gathering for a meeting. Even Elena Alexandrovna came out, having donned her colourful dressing-gown. Only Chizhënok remained in bed, as if caught in a trap.

Zinka made more fuss than anyone else: 'What's all this – daylight robbery? How can you do this? Seizing a communal corridor?! Do you know what this is? It's con-fis-cation! Who gave you the right?'

'Comrades, everything has been done according to the law,' said Funtikova trying to calm them down.

'This is nothing to do with the law, it's con-fis-cation!'

'What are you calling confiscation? The Constitution?' asked Funtikova, raising her voice.

'Don't you shove the law under our noses!' said Zinka, not backing down.

'It's not my law, it's everyone's law!'

'We know to what extent it's "everyone's"…'

'What are you hinting at? I could take you to court for that.'

'It'll be us taking you. You turn up here, lording it over us…'

Pavel Semënovich cowered in the doorway, which required repositioning: he was critically examining the dilapidated corridor walls which, in just about half-an-hour, would cease to be communal and become his very own. He thought about how they would need to be treated with stripper, then filled, and only then could they be painted. Mariia Ivanovna stood behind him, listening intently to the skirmish between Zinka and Funtikova, ready to rush into the affray at the drop of a hat. Old Ma Urozhaikina listened with great satisfaction, her arms ceremoniously folded on her bosom, and her face, which

---

[14] Here Mozhaev is having a swipe at official Soviet literature, in which so much of what was written and published about everyday life was radically different from reality.
[15] Again, there is humour in the names: Lomov's name is based on the Russian word for a 'crow-bar', and hence associated with demolition, and Sudakov's is based on a Russian noun for a type of fish, called a 'pike-perch'.

had assumed a younger appearance, radiated a provocative grin: 'They're swearing quite well... Not bad. But I could do better...'

'Of course, the interests of the collective come first, but you didn't even consult us,' said Elena Alexandrovna, unexpectedly supporting Zinka.

'Comrades, the decision made by the executive committee is not subject to discussion. That's all there is to it,' said Funtikova and left.

The technical surveyor Lomov followed her. Just the carpenter Sudakov remained, and he leisurely sharpened his pencil with his axe: 'It's all been sorted out. Has representation been made? Yes, it has. Now there's nothing more to argue about. Off you all go home.'

'No way! We also know the law,' said Zinka. 'They'll dance to our tune yet.'

She hastily got her younger son Sanka ready for the kindergarten (her elder son went under his own steam), then she angrily slammed the door shut, and left. Chizhënok followed her with his eyes, propped up on his elbow – but from a bed not his own: 'I wonder where she's dashing off to?'

'To work,' replied Elena Alexandrovna from behind the screen.

'No way! Zinka never walks to work that quickly. She's got a bee in her bonnet. She'll be off round the whole region complaining. She'd drive even the Devil to distraction.'

'And where are you off to, Volia?'

'Where can I go? I can't even poke my nose out of the window – at any moment, the whole neighbourhood will be out. They'll accuse me of robbing. Sudakov and Pavel Semënovich are running the show in the corridor. All I can do is lie low and not move a hair.'

But Chizhënok didn't have his lie-in. Having delivered her younger son Sanka to the kindergarten, Zinka went to the town square to tell her husband everything, and to seek his advice as to where she should best send her complaint about the corridor. Alas! He was nowhere to be found on the square. His bucket, rake, and broom were all there, sticking out of the acacia bushes, and the pathways were unswept. It looked as if Chizhënok had disappeared into thin air. 'He must be plying his trade somewhere else, from first thing this morning,' she thought. 'He'll come home drunk again.' Then suddenly Zinka remembered that, in her rush to leave the house, she had forgotten to lock the second lock on the front door, the key to which Chizhënok didn't have. 'The devil will blunder in drunk, find my wage, and it'll be gone with the wind...', she thought.

As she hurried home, she noticed something familiar through Elena Alexandrovna's window... She looked more closely. Yes, it was! On the back of her chair, she could see Chizhënok's trousers. She recognised them by the belt – an old Circassian belt with its silver ornamental plates – a present from Zinka.[16] It was her father's belt... Once, it had sported long pendants in the form of daggers. On festive occasions, her father used to put on a black sateen shirt and this belt. Chizhënok had removed these silver daggers

---

[16] Circassia is a region in the north Caucasus.

and drank his way through the proceeds. However, he still wore the belt on his trousers. And now this belt, attached to his trousers, was hanging on the back of the chair, right there in Elena Alexandrovna's window.

Zinka went up to the window and quietly climbed up to the window-ledge.

There, in the room, sat Chizhënok at the table with a cup of tea and a bread roll, just in his underpants. Elena Alexandrovna had gone out to work. The bed had been made and covered with a lace bedspread – all hunky-dory. Only Chizhënok's trousers, and his hair tousled here and there in tufts, revealed the innermost secret of his fall from grace.

'And what are you doing here?'

The bread roll, thickly spread with butter and topped with cherry jam, came to a grinding halt halfway towards Chizhënok's mouth. Before he could think of an answer, his head had started to sink into his shoulders – an act of submissive self-preservation that he had developed over time. Finally, he turned round…

It was not a dream – Zinka was actually sitting on the windowsill, her eyes turning green with malice.

'Did I not ask you a question? You loser!'

'Quiet! The neighbours will hear,' Chizhënok finally managed to utter hoarsely.

'And what are you thinking of? Are you trying to keep your hanky-panky a secret?' Zinka said, getting louder.

'Shut up, you fool!'

Chizhënok, seeing that Zinka had climbed through the window, started to retreat apprehensively towards the doorway.

'How d'you mean, "hanky-panky"? I just climbed in here… I was just cadging! So what?'

'But why did you take your trousers off? So you wouldn't get jam on them? Is that it?!'

'I was just… err… trying on Solomon's suit. I wanted a change of clothes.'

'So where is this suit, then?'

'In the wardrobe… It turned out to be a bit tight.'

'You shameless bastard! You might at least blush…' Zinka went over to the table and grabbed the steaming electric kettle. 'I'll make you blush with this boiling water.'

'Stop, you idiot!'

Chizhënok caught his backside on the door and thus undid the latch, and he ran off towards Malinov Ravine, in only his underwear. The kettle flew through the doorway after him. It crashed against the wall and in a trice the corridor became dark and stuffy, as everywhere became enveloped in dense clouds of steam.

'What's happened?' asked Pavel Semënovich, rushing towards Elena Alexandrovna's room.

Zinka was standing by the wooden door frame, crying: 'I'm a fool, I'm a fool… I took parcels to him in prison, like you would to any decent prisoner… I thought he was just a common thief… But it turns out, he's a lady's man…'

Chapter Four

All this misfortune had befallen them because of that cursed door, thought Elena Alexandrovna. Had the earlier rumpus not occurred, Chizhënok would have left her flat with the greatest of ease, and his visits would have been kept under wraps. But now, she would have to go and explain to everyone that there had been no intimate relations between her and Chizhënok. Who knows whose windows he climbs through? And so what, if he'd climbed in through the widow's window? Was it really necessary to allude to intimate goings-on? Just so people wouldn't think she'd taken offence at Zinka, who that very day had made a scene right there in the corridor, Elena Alexandrovna put her name to Zinka's petition against the Poluboiarinovs' re-positioning of the door.

Much to the joy of Pavel Semënovich, Old Ma Urozhaikina hadn't signed the petition. 'You picked the fight, so you sort it out,' she'd said. Nonetheless, Pavel Semënovich had become very perturbed: What if the objection were to be successful and the door had to be put back in its original position? It all depended on who would deal with the complaint. If it fell to Pavlinov, then he would sign it like a shot and impose a resolution… He would have his revenge on Pavel Semënovich.

Pavel Semënovich and Pavlinov, the chairman of the regional executive committee, had had a tiff many moons ago over the historical past of Rozhnov and its present prosperity.[17]

Pavlinov had once given a lecture on the subject of 'The Cultural Revolution in China'. Pavel Semënovich had asked the question, 'What kind of socialism exists in China?' to which Pavlinov had replied, 'The opportunistic kind.'

'But surely opportunism is a negation of socialism. So what kind of socialism did it have there?'

'The kind of socialism based solely on deviations. Fine, we'll discuss it after the lecture…'

They stood together in the operating-room, which doubled up as a reading room, a casualty ward, and a meeting room. Pavlinov lent his elbow on a thick pile of newspaper files, looking long and hard at Pavel Semënovich, staring him out. But Pavel Semënovich sat calmly on his chair – he didn't even wriggle or look down at his feet. Eventually Pavlinov solemnly pronounced: 'So you didn't understand anything, then.'

'What should I understand?'

'That you go in for compromises and discrediting…'

'Whom?'

'Not "whom", but "what". You consciously denigrate our achievements.'

---

[17] The name 'Pavlinov' is based on the Russian word for 'peacock'. This meaning is significant, as will become evident.

'In what way?'

'With your ill-considered utterances. And that's not all… We have evidence of your activities. I've wanted to have a word with you for some time. Did you not write to Moscow to complain about the railway?'

'Yes, I did.'

'And what did you write?'

'That bureaucrats from the Moscow Economic Council had closed the railway line through the Meshchëra region.'

'And what if it was economically unviable?'

'How do you mean "unviable"? That railway line linked two **oblasts**. It was laid in the lean year of 1892.[18] It was constructed in a hurry and that's why it's a narrow-gauge line. It was used to transport grain from us there, and timber was brought back from the Meshchëra. Are you now trying to tell me, that it's no longer viable? Nonsense! It's been closed down because there's no bridge over the river.'

'So, what do you make of that? You're a dental mechanic after all!'

'But I can still work out that the Moscow Economic Council doesn't give a damn about our **oblast**.'

'How have you come to that conclusion? Have you conducted a private assessment of the railway? Is that it?'

'That's not the only thing… We once had a particular breed of cow called the Red Meshchëra. But where is it now? And how many pigs did we used to have? And sheep? Geese, ducks… And we used to grow hemp – it even used to grow in Rozhnov gardens. Birds used to get fat on hemp seed. Now there are no birds or any hemp. We've all got to go hell for leather to grow maize, just because the Economic Council orders us to. And where are they? In Moscow! Need I say more?!'

'I repeat, your reasoning is downright *comprometizing*.[19] A load of vague words.'

'Vague words?! Well, let's get down to details! Take the pigs, to which I referred. They used to forage for days on end. Each village had herds of three hundred, even five hundred animals. They used to feed on grass, rummage through the silt, eat various types of mussels and freshwater creatures…'

---

[18] 'Alexander III's reign witnessed the first real wave of industrial expansion shaped by Alexander's two great ministers of finance. Ivan Alexeevich Vyshnegradsky (1831-95), appointed in 1886, pursued a policy of squeezing extra revenues from the peasantry by increased indirect taxes. But this left the peasants without reserves of food or money. Hundreds of thousands died from starvation when the harvest failed in 1891. Vyshnegradsky was forced to resign. He was replaced by Sergei Iulevich Witte (1849-1915), a young star from the railway department. His policies were based upon a stable rouble and increased grain exports to attract foreign capital for Russia's industries, especially her railways.' See *The Russian Chronicles*, (London: Century, 1990) pp.322-33, where there are also details and pictures of new railway projects around this time.

[19] The speaker mispronounces the word: he does, of course, mean 'compromising'. This expression is one of this speaker's catch-phrases, as is clear later in the story. Many of Mozhaev's characters have catch-phrases. The mispronunciation indicates the speaker's poor level of education.

'That's enough!' exclaimed Pavlinov, unable to take any more. 'You either take me for an idiot or make yourself out to be one. I'm warning you – if you make any more complaints of this kind, we shall take sanctions. You're barking up the wrong tree, Comrade Poluboiarinov.'

After that, Pavel Semënovich had clashed twice more with Pavlinov. About two years after this tiff, Pavel Semënovich had outlined a proposal as to how non-working Rozhnov housewives might best make use of their time. He had suggested they be made to boil up potatoes to make a starch 'milk', because the potatoes were going to waste.[20] On his plan, Pavlinov had inscribed: "The author is to be censured by the executive committee for *comprometizing* women." Pavel Semënovich was summoned and he was kept standing for a whole hour under cross-examination. He left there all sweaty and red, but undaunted. He even managed to get one over Pavlinov. Pavel Semënovich got an announcement published in the regional newspaper. It was entitled: 'Attention!' In it he had written: 'The gardens of Rozhnov supply so much fruit that the preserves factory, "The Red Torch", cannot cope with it all. It's got to such a state that single women pensioners allow the collective bull into their gardens to eat up all the windfalls. For this reason, the local population should be encouraged to boil up the fruit to make jams and jellies…' To which Pavlinov had apparently replied: 'This lover of the sweet life should be prescribed a bitter pill to bring him to his senses…'

This is why Pavel Semënovich felt somewhat perturbed over the door. The first thing to do, he thought, was to break up the cabal of complainants, in other words, to drive a wedge between Elena Alexandrovna and Zinka. While the two of them were complaining together, they were strong, because they looked like a representative group. And a group is always taken seriously. It would be quite another story with a solitary complaint. If Zinka were out on a limb… Who would bother listening to her?

And so, Pavel Semënovich decided to arrange a little *soirée* and invite Old Ma Urozhaikina and her brother, the carpenter Sudakov, the very person who had repositioned the door. Elena Alexandrovna could be invited almost casually, on the pretext that it was Medical Workers' Day, and that it was a fitting occasion for them all to get together.[21] They got together as a charming little group, all nice, cosy neighbours together… She would come alone – Chizhënok was in the dog-house. And then there was the carpenter Sudakov, a very respectable man. He was dapper – all his clothes had a touch of the military about them (his son was a lieutenant-colonel). His sister, Old Ma Urozhaikina, was a woman who called a spade a spade. She kept a tight grip on herself. So he hoped that Elena Alexandrovna would take the bait…

And she did…

'Ah, Pavel Semënovich, I am a collective sort of person. You are in the majority. Let it be just as you have all decided.'

---

[20] In some parts of Central and Eastern Europe, the extraction of starch from potatoes is a major industry. It can be extracted and dried, then used in many branches of the food industry.

[21] Medical Workers' Day was one of a myriad of festive days, which the Soviet regime instituted to replace the vast number of religious feast days in the Orthodox Church calendar. Medical Workers' Day falls on the 20 June. Other such bizarre festive days were Tank Drivers' Day, Cosmonauts' Day, Teachers' Day, etc., as well as the more traditional Mothers' Day and Fathers' Day.

She had turned up at the Poluboiarinovs' all in pink, like a vision of dawn, her high bosom heaving with waves of ruched material with a double row of coral-red stitching encompassing her white neck, and sporting a ring with a green stone, which cut into her podgy finger.

'Mother Mariia, you really are very naughty for not having acquainted me before now with your brother,' she trilled, having first greeted the hostess.

'He's old enough to look after himself,' said Old Ma Urozhaikina.

The carpenter Sudakov, dressed in his camouflage military tunic, was a bit of a dry old stick, with a hook-nose and a protruding lower lip: he offered his wide, bony hand, and hummed and hawed: 'One fears to call in on you, Lena Alexandrovna.'

'Why?' she asked, her eyebrows leaping up.

'You are an imposing person.'

'In what sense?'

'In every sense. You are dressed up like a general's wife. You yourself are very respectable and you have a good job.'

'And one could not take you for an ordinary person, Matvei Spiridonovich,' explained Elena Alexandrovna. 'In your military tunic, and with your profile… you look just like a retired colonel.'

'More like a pantomime colonel,' quipped Old Ma Urozhaikina with a sneer.[22]

'Why? The other day in the tram, a young woman said to me, "Comrade Colonel, please move over so I can sit down",' said Sudakov.

'Well, don't judge a book by its cover.[23] What can I get you, a little drop of white or red?' the hostess asked Elena Alexandrovna.

'I'll have what everyone else is having.'

She was seated next to Sudakov and she was offered a full shot of vodka, which she took with just two fingers and lingered long over it, with her eyes closed.

'So, does the vodka taste sweeter with your eyes closed?' asked Pavel Semënovich.

'I simply can't look at it,' answered Elena Alexandrovna shuddering, as if out in the cold.

'I can't stand looking at the damn stuff either,' said the hostess. 'I also wince when I drink it.'

'If you don't keep your eyes shut, they'll pop out,' replied Old Ma Urozhaikina.

---

[22] The literal translation of her utterance is, 'a colonel for whom a ladle would cry'. Although semantically this phrase does not make a great deal of sense, the Russian rhymes in the original, and it is a play on the words 'polkóvnik' (colonel) and 'upolóvnik' (ladle). This is typical of the kind of humorous quip for which Mozhaev, and many other admirers of original native humour, had a good ear.

[23] The original Russian saying literally means 'one cannot feed a nightingale on fables'. This expression is used in two situations: it is commonly said before inviting a guest to the table to eat, and, less frequently, it is used when a person wishes to express the need for a more serious conversation to be initiated, rather than talking about trivia. Cleverly, Mozhaev has managed to combine the two meanings here.

'Ah, the weaker sex,' sneered Sudakov and shook his head. 'When it comes to the big things in life, you haven't got the bottle.'

He himself drank with the greatest of ease: not a single muscle moved on his face, and, were it not for the fact that his Adam's apple quivered spasmodically in his wrinkled neck, one would have thought he wasn't even swallowing, but rather that the vodka found it own way to his belly, as if through a wide-bore hose.

'I've heard it said that you have a good voice, Matvei Spiridonovich,' said Elena Alexandrovna.

'Good or bad, I'll sing for you,' said Sudakov decisively.

'He'd give the shirt off his back to a friend,' remarked Pavel Semënovich, nodding affectionately towards him.[24]

Sudakov threw him a serious glance, knit his brow, then suddenly broke into song with his high, thin voice:

> *On a stormy, foul night,*
> *The moon hidden in cloud...*

Old Ma Urozhaikina's face instantly assumed a serious expression, and she awaited the next verse while looking down at the floor. She then shook her head and instantly coupled her voice with his, elongating the words, merging and modulating her thin, pure voice, which arose from a source unknown within the flat-chest of this gloomy old woman.

> *To a green, sweet grave,*
> *Came a beauty in tears...*[25]

At this moment, someone bashed hard on the door.

'What do you want?' asked Pavel Semënovich.

'That's enough! You've had your sing...' boomed the drunken voice of Chizhënok. 'Each one of you get on your way! I won't beat you up... Or do I have to smash through the door?'

He took out an axe from his shirt and made several incisions, with great force, into the covering. There was a dry sound of ripping leatherette.[26]

'Oh, don't let him in! Don't let him in! He'll hack me to pieces!' exclaimed Elena Alexandrovna, beating the air with her palms, as if she were repelling someone.

'Get away from the door, or I'll call the police,' said Pavel Semënovich.

---

[24] The original expression is a rather rare proverb in Russian, which translates, 'for a dear friend, you'd even give him the earring out of your ear'.
[25] The song is a romance: it is a tragic romantic song about love and lovers, and it is associated with the Urals.
[26] The entrance doors to Russian flats are frequently to be found covered in a padded leatherette material, usually brown in colour, as a means of sound proofing the accommodation, and possibly providing a little insulation.

'But I'm telling you all to go home!' There was another blow to the door and more ripping leatherette.

'I'll go out and calm him down,' said Sudakov, getting up from the table.

'He'll hack you to death, Matvei Spiridonovich!' cried Elena Alexandrovna, grabbing his arm.

'Hey, you loser! I hope you've plenty of money to spare,' shouted Mariia Ivanovna, approaching the door.

'I'll spend every penny I've got... on making your life hell! Go home, I tell you!' shouted Chizhënok.

Sudakov, nonetheless, opened the door and went out into the corridor.

'What are you doing, waving that axe around?'

Chizhënok, caught unawares, retreated by about two paces.

'Ah-ha! The happy pair of lovers... What if I whacked you on the neck with my axe? Eh?!'

'I'd grab the axe and do the same to you.'

'Just you try ! Go on, grab it!' Chizhënok approached Sudakov, but he held the axe behind his back.

'Just you try hitting me! Well?!' said Sudakov, getting furious.

Thus they stood for a minute, nose to nose, looking at each other with an expression of open disgust.

'You whelp,' said Sudakov.

'You old hound.'

After this, the door slammed shut again in Chizhënok's face and he aimed a few more blows of his axe at it, with belated ire.

'Ah, so that's how you want to play it! You'll have only yourself to blame!' Pavel Semënovich made straight for the telephone.

Chizhënok stood calmly behind the door, listening to the telephone jingling as the dial turned.

'Hello! Is that the police? The police? Give me the duty policeman! What? So where is he? Where should I ring? Oh, hell!' said Pavel Semënovich, getting all het up.

When the telephone dial jingled yet again, Chizhënok's voice boomed out with renewed vigour at the door: 'I told you to go home! You fucking lovers...'

Chapter Five

The duty police officer that night was Divisional Inspector Lieutenant Parfënov. Captain Stenin, the fire inspector, came to see him in the evening: 'Vasia, come round to the fire station after supper and we'll take a drag-net to the weir. It's a warm night.'

'Where did you get the drag-net from?'

'Deserter brought it.'

'Is he coming fishing as well?'

'What do you think?! You and I would just get into a tangle with the drag-net. His drag-net is as big as your sweep-net – the bag alone is ten metres.'[27]

'In that case, I'll come along.'

Deserter was considered to be the best fisherman in the whole area. He had acquired this skill by dint of circumstance. For many years, fishing at night was his main source of income.

In the first place, Deserter had disappeared without trace. In 1943, a wake had even been held for him. Then he showed up alive… twenty years later. He'd spent all these years in his own cellar. But he didn't just sit it out there – he worked at night, prepared his house and yard for winter, mowed hay, fished… He had a number of children. As time went on, he became bolder and started working away. It was a blessing that **kolkhoz** workers were not issued with **passports**. You passed for whoever you said you were. He joined a distant group of carpenters from Tuma and went round **kolkhozes** with them, building cowsheds, storehouses, and rural houses… He lived on a farm called Vyksa. Before the war, there were about ten homesteads there, but by 1960 only one remained. The womenfolk from distant villages would ask, somewhat distressed, 'What?! Is Nastasia Gunkina still living there? There are only forests and meadows all around. The lakes are infested with devils at night…' 'She has a pact with those devils. She brought home a third child from them in the hem of her skirt.'

Deserter gave himself up. His mother died. While her body was being washed and funeral rites were sung, he still sat it out in his cellar. But when her coffin was carried out to the cemetery, he could stand it no longer. Pale, and not wearing a hat or coat, – it was autumn and the wind was blowing – he followed on behind her coffin, muttering in a wooden voice, 'Forgive me, dear mother! Forgive me, kind people!' He cried the whole way.

He went straight from the cemetery to the police station in Rozhnov. Nastasia wailed more for him alive, than she did for his dead mother… 'You could have at least come home for your wake! You could have sat with the kids after all,' Nastasia kept saying to him. He remained mute.

As it happened, the divisional policeman on duty was Parfënov.

'Arrest me… I'm a deserter.'

Gunkin turned up dressed just as he was, without a hat or an overcoat, his cheeks covered in smudged tear-stains.

'What kind of a deserter are you? Where have you deserted from?' asked the young lieutenant. 'Are you a deserter from the working front? From the **Virgin Lands**?'

'No, from the real front… the German one.'

---

[27] The 'bag' ('bowl' or 'purse') is the central section of a fishing net. The terminology depends on what kind of net is being referred to and there are regional variations.

'What's up with you, mate? Are you drunk, or what?'

While documents on him were sent to the higher realms of power, and while they waited for orders as to what to do with this deserter and where he should be sent, Gunkin got to work with his axe and plane on the whole police station: he made good all the floors, fixed the doors, and replaced all the window-frames. He even managed to do up the Chief's flat.

'He's a hard worker, this deserter,' said the Chief. 'Only he never looks you straight in he eyes, and he mumbles like a mute. If he's pardoned, we'll have to find him a job.'

The pardon came through two months later. As the district plenipotentiary, Parfёnov took him along to the regional municipal finance department: 'This chap's been a bit of a drop-out... He needs help to find a job. He's all right, he's a quiet bloke. He's a hard worker...'

He was taken on. The police have a lot of influence. Gunkin moved to Rozhnov permanently, built himself a large house and embellished it with fretwork, and he settled down, living a life no worse than anyone else.[28] His background was soon forgotten, but the name 'Deserter' stuck, and it even passed on to his children. But doesn't everyone have a nickname in Rozhnov? You can try digging around to find out how someone gets a nickname. The only eccentricity that Deserter got stuck with was that he slept badly at night. However, he turned that to his advantage – he would go fishing.

Earlier that evening, he had brought his drag-net round to the fire department – he'd made it himself out of nylon twine, the colour of frog-spawn, so as to fool the fish. Captain Stenin tested it for strength. He grabbed the cells with two fingers and stretched it so hard that it dug deep into his skin: 'That's strong!'

'You could hang yourself with it – that thread wouldn't break,' Deserter replied. 'It's been treated with a chemical preparation.'

'What kind of preparation?'

'It's sold ready-made. It's a kind of tannin powder.'

'All his life, my dad used to dress leather with women's urine,' said the Captain.

'Women's urine makes it flexible,' agreed Deserter. 'Pieces of rotten wood do the same... But this chemical takes away its 'organicness'.[29] It removes all odours, whether it smells of cows or dogs.'

When Lieutenant Parfёnov arrived, Stenin gave him the net to test its strength as well.

'The cells are really small,' said Parfёnov unexpectedly. 'We'll catch all the tadpoles with this.'

'Why should that bother you?' asked Stenin.

---

[28] Traditional rural houses, which are made out of wooden logs, are often adorned by their owners with fretwork and carving around the window and door frames. This gives each house its own particular character and the fretwork is usually done during the long Russian winters, when there is little to do around the farm by way of cultivation. Sometimes the fretwork can be extremely ornate, depending on the skill and creativity of the owner, and much pride is taken in this traditional craft.

[29] This word is invented from the Russian word for 'organic'.

'It's sort of awkward. According to conservation law, the permitted cell size is fifteen by fifteen.'

'So what? Did you make that law?'

'It's sort of awkward. The other week a hunter and I confiscated a drag-net from people in Brëkhovo precisely because of the small cell size.'

'And now the hunter himself fishes with that drag-net,' laughed Stenin.

'I shouldn't wonder. What's the point of it not being used?'

Lieutenant Parfënov was dour and business-like, and he wore an expression of constant preoccupation – 'Did I do that correctly, or not?' Whereas Captain Stenin had a round, satisfied and carefree face: his attitude – 'Why dwell on things? Sod it! However you do things, it'll all turn out fine' – was written all over his face. But Deserter's face was dark and vapid – nothing could be read from it, nor had anything been inscribed on it, right from birth. While the Captain and the Lieutenant were arguing about the mesh size, he just sat on the doorstep, smoking calmly.

They arrived at the weir in the dark. The Captain carried an empty bucket, Parfënov and Deserter, the net. Two horses were grazing by the pond and a flock of ducks had hidden away from the dogs, right beside the bank. When the ducks saw people approaching, they quacked and swam away from the bank, and the horses raised their heads in turn, looking cautiously, and stood stock still like statues, then they resumed nibbling the grass and snorted.

'Whose are those horses?' asked Parfënov.

'Why do you want to know?' replied Stenin.

'Just in case anyone comes to attend to them and we're spotted. It'd be awkward.'

'What's wrong, are you afraid of Shinkarëv? He fishes at night himself.'

'But he's the owner,' said Parfënov.

'The director of the **sovkhoz** is a public figure. And fish are also public property,' Stenin reasoned, confidently. 'And we are all equal in society. Therefore, if the director has the right to fish here at night, so do we.'

'That's as may be. But if we're spotted, it'd be awkward.'

'It's not your neck on the line. I am senior by rank, and it'll be me who has to answer.'

They unfolded the net and marvelled at its length.

'What a splendid purse!' said Stenin, with great delight. 'It's that big you won't find the fish in it – it'll be like looking for a flea on the fly of an old boy's trousers.'

'If they're in there, we'll give 'em what for,' said Deserter.

The Lieutenant started taking off his tunic and trousers.

'Why are you taking your trousers off? It's cold,' said Stenin.

'But I'm on duty. What happens if I get called out?'

'Where will you get called out?'

'Anywhere… It'd be awkward running around in wet trousers.'

'"Awkward" is when you go into an alehouse with empty pockets…'

Deserter took hold of the strap and made straight for the deepest water, wading in in just what he was wearing – his shirt, trousers and boots.

'Oh, look what a diver he is! He does right! Come on, let's join in the sweep – the fish won't be afraid of you. You smell earthy anyway,' said Stenin, giving orders. 'And you, Vasia, move away from the bank. If anything happens, they'll bring the telephone out from the fire station, and I'll pass you the receiver.'

'Don't tempt fate!' Parfёnov kept his undershirt and pants on, having neatly folded his trousers and tunic, just like in a military barracks in preparation for reveille, and he'd also placed his uniform cap on top. He'd given his pistol and map-case to Stenin.

They had just waded right out into the water, when the duty fireman came running out from the fire station:

'Comrade Lieutenant, you're wanted urgently on the phone!'

'What's happened? Who's calling?' asked Stenin.

'Poluboiarinov, the dental mechanic…'

'Oh, that damn utopian scribbler! What's wrong with him – doesn't he know who to complain about next? Or has he thought up a new plan to make frog jam?'

'He says that Chizhёnok is causing a rumpus at their flats…'

'Fancy that! You can't smash windows with words,' declaimed Stenin. 'Tell him the police don't pull people in for what they say.[30] And you go on! Pull!' he shouted at Parfёnov, who was about to stand up straight in the water. 'Stop where you are!' said Stenin, stopping the fireman in his tracks. 'How does Poluboiarinov know that Parfёnov is with us?'

'The night watchman told him… What now?'

'And what about you?'

'What about me?'

'You didn't tell him we're fishing, did you?'

'But he asked…'

'You idiot! Go on, Gunkin, hold the strap lower! Hold it to the bottom!' he shouted, turning round to the fishermen.

'The water is up to my chin as it is,' said Deserter, spitting water out.

---

[30] Mozhaev is being ironic here and it is surprising that this comment slipped through the censor's net when the story was first published. The point is, in the Soviet Union, people *were* arrested for what they said, as the imprisoning of countless dissidents attested. During Stalin's purges of the late 1930s, a single, careless word uttered to the wrong person cost many people their lives because they were sent to the GULag or labour camp.

'Then stick your head in as well – you don't go to the **bania** as often as you should.'

'The water stinks.'

'Water's not like shit – it doesn't stick.'

Their first sweep was successful. In the huge purse, which was covered with slimy duckweed, some whippy carp wriggled.

'Gunkin, lift it out of the water! Close the purse!' shouted Stenin, scurrying around with the bucket. 'Vasia, do you hear me? Shake the net, will you! Otherwise we'll see damn all with all this slime…'

Parfënov and Deserter let go of the straps and, having dropped to their knees, they grabbed at the net feverishly, pressing the cold, slippery fish into the ground with the palms of their hands.

'That's a good 'un, but this is a duffer,' said Stenin, assessing the fish while crawling around on all fours, grabbing the quivering carp, which shone white in the darkness.

When the fish had been put in the bucket, and the drag-net cleaned of all duckweed and put aside ready for a second sweep, the fireman came running up again: 'Comrade Lieutenant, the phone's ringing again! They're asking for you and threatening…'

'So what? Why have you come here? Haven't you anything better to do?' snapped Stenin, lashing out at the fireman.

'I should go and see… It's awkward,' said Parfënov. 'What if something's happened over there?'

'What could happen? What's wrong with you, don't you know that muck-raker by now? C'mon, let's do another sweep.'

'No, I really must put my trousers on…'

'Sod him! Are you really going to abandon the fishing? Go to the phone in your underwear, tell him to fuck off, and come back…'

'All right then.'

So Parfënov went off to the phone in his wet underwear and vest.

'What's happened?' he asked sternly over the phone.

'To whom am I speaking?' came the voice from the other end of the phone.

'It's me, the local police officer, Parfënov.'

'Comrade Police Commissioner, while you are fishing in the pond, a murder is about to be committed over here.'

'What murder?'

'It's Chizhënok… He's got an axe in his hand and he's hacking through the door to my flat, that's the Poluboiarinov's…'

'How do you mean "hacking through"?'

'Just that… We're being threatened with an axe.'

'And has he damaged your door?'

'He's slashed the leatherette all over.'

'Has he hacked through the door itself?'

'No… But he says that as soon as he does, he'll cut off our heads.'

'Well, we can't pull him in for what he says. We'll fine him in the morning for damaging the leatherette. Just tell him that. If he hacks through the door itself, we'll put him away for a fortnight…'

'You come and arrest him!'

'No, I haven't the right to yet.'

'But when you do, it'll be too late.'

'Comrade Poluboiarinov, don't precipitate events and stop provoking the police. We know best what to do…'

When Lieutenant Parfĕnov came back to the water's edge, Captain Stenin had already got a campfire going and Deserter was cleaning the fish, in only his underwear. His trousers and shirt were arrayed on poles by the campfire.

Chapter Six

Early next morning, Pavel Semĕnovich submitted a complaint to the Chief Commissioner of Police:

'On the night of the 19-20 August, our neighbour Chizhĕnok, in a state of inebriation, and, at the instigation of his wife, started to threaten us and break into our flat by means of an axe. This whole event took place between eleven and three o'clock in the morning, when he fell asleep in the corridor.

'We repeatedly telephoned the police from our flat, but the duty policeman, Comrade Parfĕnov, was unwilling to come to our aid, and thereby he conducted himself in an irresponsible manner…'

Chief Police Commissioner Abramov summoned Captain Stenin and ordered him to get to the bottom of the events. But first of all, Stenin went to see Parfĕnov to get their stories straight.

'What shall I say, Vas?[31] Were you at the fire station or not?'

'I just haven't a clue what to say,' replied Parfĕnov.

'Say the watchman called you away. To the **sovkhoz** garden… We'll say there was an assault there.'

'Yes, but shouldn't we tip the watchman off, just in case they ask him? It's rather awkward.'

---

[31] This is a familiar, shortened variation of his name 'Vasia' or 'Vasilii', in full.

'Let's go round to the garden to see him… We'll warn him and come to an agreement. And I need the hair of the dog. Otherwise I'm going to have a headache all morning. By the way, this one's on you. You're the one to blame.'

They picked up a half-litre bottle of vodka and went over to the **sovkhoz** garden.

The garden was large – you couldn't shout to someone else from one side to the other. On two sides, there was a high, barbed-wire fence, which looked like a military stockade. But from the riverside and Malina Ravine, the fencing was old and full of gaps. Anyone who fancied climbed into the garden. The watchman, Old Ivan, whose nickname was Murei,[32] lived in a straw hut on a high riverbank with his black, shaggy dog, Polkan. At night, when Polkan barked in alarm, Murei would stick his gun out of his hut and fire into the air, 'Bang! Bang!' If Polkan fell silent, the old man would go back to bed. In fact, one might say that he slept day and night. He would say, 'Dreaming is a godly thing, 'cause it's only when asleep that man doesn't sin.' He was kind and welcomed all – whoever turned up during the day, he'd offer them apples and honey.

People used to ask him: 'Why do you shoot at night and entertain people during the day?'

'At night, I'm on duty, but during the day, I do my own thing.'

'Old Ivan, you're showing kindness at the state's expense,' would say an ardent enthusiast of state property.

But the old man would say: 'We're all owned by the state. Eat while you're alive, 'cause when you die, you get eaten yourself.'

During the day, a huge number of people who fancied wetting their whistle would drop in to see him in the garden, thanks to the availability of free nibbles and nice countryside. And why not have a drink? It was beautiful and tranquil there. During the day, even Polkan didn't bark as he lay next to the hut, looking blank, with his sleepy eyes, at visitors.

Stenin and Parfёnov did not find Old Ivan in the hut. At the head of the bed stood a trunk with iron strapping in which he kept his crockery and food, and above that hung his gun. On the bed were strewn some striped sackcloth and an overcoat in place of a blanket and pillow… Polkan lay on the bed and blinked his gloomy eyes.

'Where's the owner?' asked Stenin, glancing into the hut.

'Grrrrrrrrr…'

'Hey, you arrogant devil!' said Stenin, crawling back on all fours. 'Let's call for him.'

'Old Ivv-aa-nn!' they shouted in unison.

Silence.

'It looks like there's a wisp of smoke coming from the Peskarёvka River,' said Stenin, looking out towards the far side of the garden, which fell away into a narrow valley.

'Looks like it,' Parfёnov agreed.

---

[32] This nickname is based on a Russian word for 'nonsense' – *mura*.

'Let's go over there!'

They came across Old Ivan on the bank of the small river, a tributary of the Prokosha. He was sitting by a campfire along with the renowned trouble-maker Chizhënok. As soon as he caught sight of the strong arm of the law, Chizhënok quickly stood up and started gathering up something white by the fire. This 'something white' turned out to be chicken feathers, and there was a chicken cooking in the pot.

'I see,' said Stenin, glancing into the pot. 'An act of God has been set to rights.'

Old Ivan calmly smoked, looking at the campfire, but Chizhënok kept his fist tight around some feathers behind his back, looking shiftily at the 'brass'.

'What are you staring at?' Stenin asked him. 'Is it that long since you were our guest?'

'No, and I'm not missing you yet,' said Chizhënok grinning.

'And what did you get up to last night?' Parfënov questioned him sternly.

'Me? I slept and can't remember a thing.'

'And who ripped up the leatherette on the door?'

'On what door?'

'The Poluboiarinovs'.'

'Don't know.'

'And I suppose you don't know how that hen got in here either?' asked Stenin.

'Perhaps it's a cockerel, not a hen,' said Chizhënok.

'D'yer see that – he's got the gall to joke,' remarked Stenin, turning towards Parfënov.

'I'll write out a charge sheet and put him away for a fortnight,' said Parfënov.

'That would be on what grounds?'

'We'll sort you out. We'll find an article of the criminal code to suit you. Now go home and wait there,' Stenin ordered.

'Who shall I wait for?'

'We're going to investigate the circumstances... In the presence of witnesses,' said Parfënov. 'And tell the others to stick around as well.'

Chizhënok threw a longing glance at the chicken, breathed deeply through his nostrils, and shuffled off.

'Everyone wants a free lunch,' he muttered.

'And I'll have words with you later!' Stenin shouted after him.

Chizhënok arrived home hungry and in a foul mood.

Old Ma Urozhaikina and Elena Alexandrovna were standing by the stand-pipe with their buckets, prattling on about something. But as soon as they saw Chizhënok, they shut up.

'Why so sad, my beauties?' he asked, approaching them with a feline gait.[33] 'You were singing together… As a duet!'

'Go on! On your way!' said Elena Alexandrovna.

'Are you not going to invite me in for tea? Or have you run out of jam?'

'There are plenty of you sweet-toothed blokes around.'

'Aha… Plenty? So, am I just any Tom, Dick or Harry? Did I drop in on you by chance?'

'Perhaps you had an ulterior motive,' sneered Elena Alexandrovna.

'What "ulterior motive"? Surely not thieving?'

'You'd know better than me. I'm not an expert in that field.'

'Scandalmongers get beaten and are not allowed to cry,' said Chizhënok.

'Just you try… Try and touch me!'

'Fine, I'll have a go.'

Chizhënok rashly slapped her on the ear.

'Oh, oh, Mother Mary, Mother Mary!' cried out Elena Alexandrovna.

But Mother Mary instantly turned towards the stand-pipe and started rattling her buckets.

'You villain! You villain!' Elena Alexandrovna clutched her ear and ran off home. 'I'm going to get ready and go to the police!' she shouted out of her room. 'They'll find a room for you there.'

'Liar! But I'll make a cell for you myself…'

Chizhënok rushed indoors, got hold of a hammer and a pair of six-inch nails.

'You coaxed me in through the window, didn't you? Yes, you did!' he shouted in the corridor. 'Now it's your turn to jump out of the window.'

Expressing his satisfaction in a string of 'Ha-ha's', he took huge swings at each nail with his hammer and thus nailed up Elena Alexandrovna's door.

'He-elp! Please help me! Help me, neighbour!' she shouted, beating her fists on the dividing wall between her flat and the Poluboiarinovs'.

But not a single floorboard creaked in their flat.

'Pavel Semënovich! Pavel Semënovich, he-l-p me!'

Not a single reverberation or murmur…

'Oh, damn the lot of you! All this has happened because of you… Because of your door. I'll write a letter of complaint about the lot of you! About all of you!'

---

[33] The question he asks them is evocative of a poetic style of language commonly found in folklore.

When Chizhёnok had nailed up the door, he stood for a few moments with his hammer in his hand, wondering whether the Poluboiarinovs would come out. Then he shouted: 'Whoever comes near this door will get a hammer on their nut.'

Elena Alexandrovna darted about her room, waving her arms around, exclaiming: 'This is an outrage against a person's fate. I'd rather die than surrender.'

She threw open the window and looked down, as if into a well, and she heaved her weighty bosom onto the window ledge. Never before had *terra firma* seemed so terrifyingly distant. A cockerel sauntered under her very windows, as if on guard duty: it turned its head to one side and looked at her with its round, darting eye, as if winking to her, saying, 'Don't be afraid! Hop down here and join me!'

Elena Alexandrovna reckoned that she couldn't reach the ground, even if she let herself down and stood on her tiptoes. However, she might just make the ledge of the foundations, from where she could jump down.

She sat on the windowsill and dangled her legs – no, it was too high. She turned round, rolled over heavily onto her stomach, and started letting herself down gradually. But suddenly she felt her skirt and slip sliding upwards, towards her chin. It was only then that she realized that her hem had caught on the window clasp, so she tried to pull herself back up, but couldn't. She thrashed around with her feet to see whether it was far to the foundation ledge. But she couldn't reach it... Her skirt was forced into her thighs and it was pulled taught, like a drum skin – if it had been hit, it would have reverberated, like a drum. Elena Alexandrovna kind of sat down, pushing her backside down, and her skirt made a ripping sound, and she was relieved to find she was flying.

Elena Alexandrovna didn't feel the impact much. She jumped and collapsed in a heap on the ground with a cry, and she felt as though she'd been shot through her knee.

First, the ambulance came – Pavel Semёnovich had summoned it by telephone. However, Elena Alexandrovna refused outright to go to hospital until a member of the police force had made a report at the scene of the crime. Finally, Parfёnov arrived, and Zinka appeared out of the blue, as if she'd been lying in wait for him, and even Pavel Semёnovich came out onto the porch.

'First, he slapped me across the ear,' said Elena Alexandrovna, beginning her testimony to the representative of the law.

'And I'll give you one to match on the other!' shouted Zinka, forcing her way through the crowd of gawpers.

'I request you to keep order,' said Parfёnov.

'Don't you ask *me*!' shouted Zinka. 'That's the one to ask! Her!'

Elena Alexandrovna lay on the stretcher, like Cleopatra on her sofa, propping herself up on an elbow, with her head tilted slightly back and her eyes half-closed.

'She's always getting my husband blind drunk... Then she lures him into her bed,' said Zinka, throwing her cardigan open and flapping her arms, as if about to enter a fight. 'I'm a mother of two. What do you make of that?'

'Quiet, Citizeness! We'll sort it all out... Calmly.'

'No, Comrade Divisional Commissioned Policeman, there will be no calm!' solemnly pronounced the voice of Pavel Semënovich from the porch, as if addressing them from a podium. 'Were you not fishing all night, instead of being on duty?'

'What?'

'It's just as I say… We know it for a candid fact. Instead of responding to the call of honest citizens to curb the actions of an inveterate hooligan, you, Comrade Parfënov, were pandering to your personal gratification. This is what your *laissez-faire* attitude has led to… To mutilation!'

'Oh, cut the crap!'

'No! I shall not cease. I shall go through every authority and each person will get his just deserts. We have a democracy!' announced Pavel Semënovich ceremoniously, pointing his finger to the sky, then he left.

Parfënov merely shook his head and started writing his report.

Chapter Seven

The cream of the regional hunting club had gathered for the opening of the hunting season. As usual, the chosen venue for the gathering was Lime Hill, a dry, open place with an apiary in the lime-tree grove, on the banks of Long Lake, where clutches of ducklings lingered right until autumn in the reedy brakes.

The director of the **sovkhoz**, Shinkarëv, a tall, plump-chested man, had turned up in his jeep with a bucket full of eggs. The Fire Inspector, Captain Stenin, and the Divisional Inspector of Police, Parfënov, had arrived on motorcycles with an ordinary gun and a small-bore shotgun, for shooting distant, sitting ducks, should they not approach the lakeside. Pavlinov had brought Deserter's drag-net, which Captain Stenin had lent him. Pavlinov had set out in a **Volga**, together with Feduleev, the editor of the local newspaper. As they passed through the village of Timofeevka, the last settlement before the meadows, they had decided to make a detour to the **kolkhoz** poultry unit, reasoning that, 'We might bag a duck at the hunt – but it can be tricky. However, you can rely on domestic poultry…'

Just beyond Timofeevka they got stuck in the meadows while crossing a little bridge, right in front of the poultry unit. Actually, the 'bridge' consisted of four logs which had been thrown down over a drainage channel that now washed them on all sides with murky water. They sank in right up to the chassis, so deep that the wheel hubs could not be seen. They abandoned the car, the drag-net, and all sorts of home-made 'goodies', and simply took their guns and a couple of half-litre bottles each: then they tramped over the meadows until evening.

It was already getting dark when they finally climbed up Lime Hill. By the apiary, a campfire was blazing, and some hunters squatted around it, rubbing their hands.

'I'll stun this lot,' said Pavlinov.

He took his gun and suddenly let rip with both barrels at the tree tops, 'Bang! Bang!'

In a trice, people jumped up, dogs rushed off barking, and there was a sudden flapping of wings and an outbreak of cackling, as a flock of rooks took to the sky from the trees.

'All that noise, but no fighting?' bellowed Pavlinov, as he approached the illuminated clearing.

'Fucking hell!' exclaimed Shinkarëv, slapping his thighs.

'What are you doing, Semën, trying to frighten the evil spirits?' asked Stenin.

'Salutations, chaps! The hunting season is open… Take your seats,' announced Pavlinov, chuckling.

'You'll have to feel whether all the seats are dry… to see if anyone's pissed themselves with fright,' said a huntsman in a jersey, by the fire. Despite his youth, everyone addressed him respectfully as Nikolai Ivanich.

'Where's the drag-net? Where are the ducks?' asked Stenin.

'Our driver's using the drag-net to catch frogs in the canal, and the Peking ducks have flown off to the newspaper offices. He's the one to ask, the editor here,' joked Pavlinov, slapping Feduleev on the shoulder, and roared with laughter louder than all the rest.

'In that case, you're not one of us, and we're not your mates,' said Shinkarëv.

'Aha, in that case we'll shower you with grenades. Off you scatter!' Pavlinov grabbed the two half-litre bottles and held them up in the air, bottoms upwards, and opened his eyes wide in a terrifying stare.

Feduleev also pulled out his two half-litres: 'Well then, are we accepted?'

'With tackle like that, you're not only accepted by us, you could request entry into paradise!' said Captain Stenin.

'Ah, but hang on, chaps! What are you cooking?' Pavlinov glanced into the cooking pot and flared his nostrils.

'It's Pontiff Soup,' said Nikolai Ivanovich.

'What's it made from? Frogs or something?'

'We plucked the hunters' decoy ducks and made it out of that,' replied Stenin, roaring with laughter again.

'Where did you get the fish from?'

'From the lake.'

'What did you catch them with, your underpants?'

'Parfënov shot a load of pike with his small bore.'

'Or did he use his pistol?'

'My pistol is a regulation weapon. It is not permitted for such use,' replied Parfënov, standing silently to the side.

'Why are you standing there so lifeless, like a pike-perch in a swamp?' asked Pavlinov, turning towards him. 'Your sour look is *comprometizing* the hunting season.'

'He's had a ticking-off,' said Stenin. 'Poluboiarinov scribbled a denunciation on him.'

'Who's that? The tooth-puller?' asked Pavlinov.

'Who else?!'

'That bloke would!' said Feduleev. 'He plagued the life out of me with his notes. "Why don't we manufacture tiles anymore? We used to, but now we don't anymore." "Let's get some experts in from the **GDR**", he says. "They know what's what, when it comes to tiles…"'

'Aha! Order him an enema from America – we'll stuff it right up him!' said the huntsman.

'"We don't mine coal anymore" – that was another note,' Feduleev continued, after waiting for the laughter to subside. '"Ours is the cheapest," he says. "In our region, the mines have water in them, but in the Donbass," he says, "they're full of gas."'

'He's probably had a good whiff of gas from Mariia Ivanovna and gone off his head,' said Stenin.

'I'd stick this under his nose and ask him what it smells of,' added the huntsman, showing his fist.

'"Gas can explode," he says, "but water doesn't even burn,"' Feduleev quoted. '"It's the same in England," he says, "their mines have water. Coal is mined there, but not in our region. Why?" I said to him, "Pavel Semënovich, this is not our bag. We run a regional newspaper!" And he says to me, "You're avoiding the issue".'

'He's discrediting and *comprometizing* us,' said Pavlinov, lighting up.

'Just listen to this,' roared Shinkarëv. 'He lectured me how to get hold of some fertilizer. He said, "In our lakes we have a lot of silt, which is called sapropel. In times gone by, the land society used to dig it up from the bottom, like waste from toilets." He says to me, "You're turning your nose up at it."'

'He himself should be stuffed head-down into that sapropel and held by the legs – that'd knock the stupidity out of him,' said the huntsman from the cooking pot, slurping the hot fish soup from a spoon.

'Why did Parfënov get it in the neck?' asked Pavlinov.

'They've been playing silly buggers. The neighbours had a punch-up over the corridor. Parfënov was accused of not separating them in time,' said Stenin.

'You should give him a drubbing through the paper,' said Pavlinov, turning towards Feduleev. 'You could accuse him of being a trouble-maker and not letting people get on with their jobs.'

'It's tricky… His wife works for me as chief bookkeeper.'

'Ugh, she's not exactly a big noise,' sneered Shinkarëv.

'It's a bit awkward,' pronounced Parfënov. 'He's an invalid, after all.'

'What?!' asked the huntsman. 'He's supposed to be gimpy… But he doesn't even use a crutch. He does better than me or you.'

'You go around on a motorcycle, and even then it belongs to the state. But he has his own car,' observed Shinkarëv, raising his finger.

'Hang on! Apparently his neighbours made an official complaint about him, something to do with him illegally seizing part of a communal corridor,' said Stenin to Pavlinov. 'Tell him to put the door back.'

'That just the snag, he's done it all legally. That half-wit, Funtikova, managed to get it through the executive committee.'

'D'you mean Katka?'

'That's her. She's paying court to invalids in her old age.'

'She looks back to the good times she had with Ovsov.'

'Ha, ha, ha!'

'The fish soup's ready!'

'C'mon, lads, that's enough gabbing! Let's get down to business. Where are the mugs? Fedia, Kolia, call the beekeeper over! Tell him to bring some mead. And some wooden spoons... Otherwise we'll burn our mouths with metal ones.'

The next day, around noon, Feduleev called his colleague, Smorchkov, into his office and shoved the complaint signed by Zinka and Elena Alexandrovna over to him.[34]

"We, the undersigned, request that Poluboiarinov be curbed in so far as he has seized communal territory in the corridor by re-positioning his door by one-and-a-half metres..."

'But there's no decision noted here by Comrade Pavlinov. After all, the complaint is addressed to him,' said Smorchkov, when he had finished reading the complaint.

Feduleev, who was flushed and puffy from the previous day's hunting, shook his head and made a 'rrrr' sound, as if seized by a wave of nausea, then he looked angrily and incredulously at Smorchkov:

'Am I not your boss? Get this clear, this trouble-maker has to be brought to book!'

'I am not against that,' said the editor's colleague, flashing his light eyelashes.

'So?! Go and see him and carefully question him in a roundabout way, sympathetically. The more wide ranging, the better! What is he unhappy with? Who does he have any claims against? And so on... Then accuse him of seizing communal territory. Push him towards the one-and-a-half square metres. Slap his mug to the ground! D'you understand?'

'We'll put something together.'

Vitia Smorchkov was a creative, biddable person. He was sent on assignments when, out of a theft, swindling, or a punch-up, a lofty moral lesson had to be extracted about

---

[34] This name is based on the Russian word 'smorchok', which means both a 'shrimp', i.e. small, insignificant person, or 'morel' – a type of mushroom.

serving society… And from this lofty height, with a bitter reproof and an appeal to the conscience, the errant black sheep would be returned to the fold.

This lean, quiet person, covered in brown freckles and yellow down, bespectacled, and with ears that looked like burdock from the back, like a jerboa, himself evoked compassion. Any poor devil, any prankster, might ask him passively: 'What should I tell you, Four-Eyes?'

'You just tell me about yourself, about your past. Have you, by any chance, been offended?'

But who hasn't been offended in Russia? And who can resist crying into their beer? Vitia Smorchkov grumbled and griped, suffered, and was filled with indignation… In a word, he tuned in to the right wavelength, then extracted a moral lesson from it.

Pavel Semënovich greeted Vitia like his own brother.

'Do you feel aggrieved?'

'How can you ask that?! How else would things be? It's happened, and that's that…'

Mariia Ivanovna put out some cherry vodka and some marinated mushrooms – after all, he was her colleague, as she was the chief bookkeeper to the editor: 'Eat! Don't hold back… Who on earth put you up to coming to see us?' she asked, fussing around Vitia. 'You're one of us – we keep no secrets from you. Here it is, the door – do you see? It's been repositioned by a metre and a half. The flue got in the way. But the main thing is that Chizhënok was a pest.'

But Vitia showed little interest in the door. He homed in on the grievances. Dig deep into your memory and recall them! Pavel Semënovich remembered that in 1948 or '49, he was under threat of dismissal. First, the dental lab was transferred onto a profit-and-loss basis, then an additional technician was appointed. All Pavel Semënovich's equipment was arranged to suit him alone.

'You can see, I have only one leg and my left hand is not what it should be – my fingers don't bend. That is why I set up all the equipment so I could use it with one leg and one hand. Suddenly, the order comes for us to work in two shifts. What kind of healthy person would want to work alongside me? So, a wise guy turns up from the **oblast** health department and says, "We have to take a production-line approach to our dental work, but this Poluboiarinov is ruining our whole shift work. We can't assign him instruments as his own private property." And on those grounds, I was sacked. However, the Central Committee of the Trade Union of Medical Workers reinstated me and ordered me to be paid for my absence. I can show you the award, if you like.'

'There's no need. I *do* believe you…' Vitia put his hands to his chest and smiled so sweetly, just as if he had swallowed a spoonful of honey. 'What I am interested in, though, is your invalidity: Is it from the First or the Second World War?'

'Neither! I was only a kid in the First World War,' said Pavel Semënovich. 'I used to play out in the yard in 1920. I came across a rusty grenade. It grazed me here.'

'Ah, how awful!' said Vitia, shaking his head and making a note in his pad.

Then, he looked round the sitting room and the kitchen, and asked: 'Does the blue flame work, the gas, I mean? Any leaks anywhere? And what size is the flat?'[35] He felt the leatherette covering on the door and counted the number of tears in it.

'Have you any complaints? Or perhaps, any claims against anyone?' he asked, towards the end.

Mariia Ivanovna responded: 'None at all now, thank God. The policeman has been reprimanded. Chizhënok has been put away for a fortnight.'

'And have you not written anything else?' he asked Pavel Semënovich, turning towards him.

Pavel Semënovich became pensive: 'I did write to the newspaper *Izvestia* about the peat works.'[36]

'Did you now?! How interesting!'

'Our region has some of the richest peat deposits. The layer can be as thick as four metres. But they're not worked. Yet our electricity comes from as far away as Shatura.[37] Isn't that just sheer bungling?'

'In your view, who is to blame?'

'It's the Moscow Economic Council and its planners.'

'But it doesn't exist anymore. It's been wound up.'

'That makes no difference. Those people still remain.'

'That's quite right,' said Vitia.

They lingered long over parting: Pavel Semënovich shook Vitia's hand warmly, and Mariia Ivanovna tried to cajole him: 'It would be nice if you popped round one evening sometime. In the autumn, our son is coming to see us with Berta.'

'Thank you! I'll definitely take you up on that,' replied Vitia.

Towards the end of their meeting, Pavel Semënovich became very pally and he hugged Smorchkov by the shoulders. He let slip some of his ideas for future projects: 'I have an idea! Why don't we write an article together on how to revitalize Rozhnov? Why not transfer a shoe- or knitted-garment factory here from the Moscow **oblast**? To inject a proletarian ethos into it. Eh? And, you know, the mud in Pupkovo Swamp has medicinal

---

[35] In Russia, the size of a flat is expressed as a number of square metres of living space.

[36] Two of the most popular daily newspapers in the former Soviet Union were *Pravda* (Truth) and *Izvestia* (News). *Pravda* was founded by Lenin himself in 1912, and it was to become the organ of the Central Committee of the Communist Party of the Soviet Union. *Izvestia* was founded later, in 1917, and it was originally published in Petrograd (now St. Petersburg), but later transferred to Moscow. From 1923 onwards it became the organ of the Central Executive Committee. Hence *Pravda* was the official mouthpiece of the Communist Party and *Izvestia* was the organ of the Soviet government. Most international news was handled by the newspaper *Izvestia*, and many people found the newspaper more interesting and livelier than *Pravda*. With the demise of the Soviet Union and the Communist Party, the readership fell dramatically and *Pravda* ceased publication in July 1996, but *Izvestia* became an independent publication in 1991. *Pravda* was associated with a conservative-nationalist stance in the last few years of its existence, but *Izvestia* was frequently critical of such political persuasions, and it retained its reputation as a more lively publication.

[37] Shatura lies about 125 km east of Moscow, at 55° 33` N & 39° 21` E.

properties.[38] A treatment centre and hotel could be built there. Can you imagine, a spa in the central zone? It's not as expensive here as it is in the south… Just think of how much people would save on train fares alone! We'd retain our young people here… Or what about writing about phosphorites? They're the pink kind! In times gone by, pigs used to make them explode with their snouts… Just give me a hundred thousand roubles and a cylindrical grinding machine. But I'd want to be the boss. I mean, I'd want to do the hiring and firing, and introduce my own pay scale. In a month, I'd be producing superphosphate!'[39]

'Where do you get all this from? What ideas you have!' said Vitia, approvingly.

'Purely from boredom… From having nothing better to do. I have to stand for six hours in the office, and I don't know what to do with myself. So I read an encyclopaedia, the Brokhaus and Efron.'[40]

'Where on earth do you get hold of that from?'

'From Doctor Dolbezhov. He's a really clever man! He knows all the old boundaries of our **guberniia**. He says that we used to send three million **poods** of hay to Moscow from our meadows alone. All the tsar's stables in Petersburg used our hay. But now, he says that they've all been ploughed up, so what is there to eat?'

'So, does your doctor eat hay, then?' sneered Smorchkov.

'He's just citing an example. Don't read more into it than that. We live well now…' said Pavel Semënovich, emitting a weak little chuckle, which sounded like beads falling to the floor.

When Vitia Smorchkov had gone, Mariia Ivanovna grumbled at Pavel Semënovich: 'Cutting your tongue out wouldn't be enough. Why did you bring up the thing about the hay?'

'What's wrong? He's one of us.'

'That's as may be, but you just think on. He's still an official employee. And not just any old employee – he works for a state organ.'

Chapter Eight

The article appeared in the newspaper three days later. Mariia Ivanovna flew into Pavel Semënovich's office and shoved the folded newspaper under his nose.

---

[38] There is humour in this invented name: the word 'Pupkovo' is based on the Russian word for '*belly-button*'.

[39] Phosphorite is a rock with a high concentration of phosphates in them, which are used extensively in the manufacture of fertilizers. As with many other essential items, Russian agriculture suffered from the perennial problem of shortages in getting enough fertilizer for farming. The point that Poluboiarinov is making here is that, as a country, they are not making the best use of the resources which they have on their own doorstep: there was no initiative to develop local resources, since being entrepreneurial was generally frowned upon within the Soviet system, and this led those around Poluboiarinov to regard him as a crank.

[40] The Brokhaus and Efron Encyclopaedia (sometimes spelt 'Brockhaus') is a work of great scholarship. It was published in 1890-1907 in 86 volumes and contains articles written by famous academics and scientists, such as Mendeleev. It was richly illustrated with diagrams and maps.

'What did I tell you, you windbag? 'Ere, read that! You found someone to pour your heart out to,' she said, sitting down in the dentist's chair and put her hands to her temples. 'What are we to do? What shall we do?'

Pavel Semënovich put his glasses on and opened the newspaper *Red Rozhnov*. His fingers quivered a little at the sight of the large type, and he instantly realized it was about him.

WAR OVER A SQUARE METRE

> There is an avalanche of letters and complaints from the Poluboiarinov couple: either someone has offended them, or they are unhappy about something...

Pavel Semënovich felt a sudden tickle in his throat: he took the glass of water which was standing next to the spittoon on the dentist's chair and, when he had taken a few sips, he put the glass back into the metal holder, but it wouldn't go in. It crashed to the floor. It made Mariia Ivanovna jump and she cursed Pavel Semënovich. He didn't even flinch. He skimmed through the beginning of the article where the very core of the matter was described: how, and for what reason, and by what means, Pavel Semënovich had repositioned the door in the corridor, and how he had seized communal territory. Innocent people had suffered because of this, and Funtikova, unfortunately, had gone along with the acquisitive personal interests of the Poluboiarinovs, and she had personally led the executive committee of the deputies of the toiling class into error.

> But who are they, the Poluboiarinovs, these citizens who are not satisfied with their lot?

asked the author, and it was at this point that Pavel Semënovich realized this was the crux of the matter.

| The owner of the flat is in a special position – he is an invalid. An invalid relies on the | rightful attention of society. There have been wars and injuries sustained. Alas, | Pavel Semënovich did not get the chance to fight. He was playing out in the yard as a child |

where he came across a rusty grenade, and he started to take it apart... There was an explosion, and Pavel Semënovich was crippled. But what of that? In our society, such invalids are also enveloped with care. His comrades treated him sympathetically, the state gives him a pension of twenty-three roubles (once he had worked the mandatory period).

Poluboiarinov interpreted all this in his own way. He took exception to the fact that a young specialist was appointed in his dental laboratory, and he went to great lengths to oust him.

"I am an invalid," he claimed.

"I have special needs."

However, to his not inconsiderable dismay, the whole thing backfired on him – the young specialist was retained, and Poluboiarinov was sacked.

Soon, he was to discover once again, that in a socialist society a person is not left to his own devices and that he is not abandoned in his hour of need. The oblast authorities, to whom he had sent his complaint, rang the hospital up and requested that Poluboiarinov be reinstated in his job – note, the word is *requested*, not "demanded", since there were no grounds on which they could have insisted. He was reinstated.

Not for long was he silent. He was soon up to his old tricks. Under the guise of being a champion of truth, Poluboiarinov dashes off letters to all authorities, outlining his harebrained schemes, and thus he gets on civil servants' nerves. You see, he thinks a bridge is required over the river, or he'd like to see peat cutting, or meadows have been ploughed up in the wrong place, or a spa should be opened in Pupkovo Swamp for mud cures. He accuses us all, apparently, of not making good use of our resources. Listening to Comrade Poluboiarinov, you'd think that we were all living somewhere in darkest Africa. And yet, in Poluboiarinov's own flat, he has "the blue flame", that is "gas". What is more, the door to his flat, at his own instigation and contrary to current policy, was covered with leatherette, paid for by the residents' association. This might seem a trifle, but it speaks volumes.

Isn't it time for Comrade Poluboiarinov to open his eyes to the reality of our life and take a good look around?

> You, Comrade Poluboiarinov, sully everything...
>
> Your public persona and your aims are clear to all in the light of your having seized one-and-a-half square metres of other people's living space.
>
> **Victor Smorchkov**

'The scoundrel!' said Pavel Semënovich, stuffing the newspaper into his pocket.

'And you're a fool! It was Feduleev who sent him to us undercover, with an ulterior motive.'

'How do you know?'

'It's an open secret. He's getting back at me for the radio incident.'

It must be pointed out that three years ago, when Feduleev was spending a holiday on the Riga coast, he bought a 'Spidola' radio at the newspaper's expense.[41] But he kept it for himself. This summer, he brought the guarantee to the editorial offices and said that the radio had broken down and it was to be written off. The board was convened, a note was drawn up, and they all signed it. Feduleev approved it and passed it on to Mariia Ivanovna. 'Deduct it from the balance,' he said.

'I can't. It's not out of guarantee.'

'It's broken down.'

'Sorry, but you have to draw up a separate document about it breaking down. Then put the broken radio...'

Feduleev let out a long snort.

'Do you want me to save every bit of old crockery for you when something breaks?'

'But that's our established practice.'

'Is an order from me not "established practice"?'

---

[41] 'Spidola' radios were made in the Riga radio factory in Latvia in the second half of the 1960s: the full official name of the factory was the 'Riga Order of Lenin State Electronic Factory, Named after Lenin' or VEF – Valsts elektrotechniska fabrika. Latvian electronic goods had a good reputation within the former Soviet Union and, like many 'luxury' goods, they were in short supply. Hence, the chances of obtaining them were better at source, i.e. in Riga and the surrounding area, rather than far away in Moscow, which is why Feduleev has availed himself of the opportunity of getting hold of such a radio while on holiday. In a memoir about Boris Mozhaev, Milda Shnore, his wife, who is Latvian and whose family home was near Riga, wrote that a kindly local shopkeeper, who had a great admiration and affection for Mozhaev, had kept a Spidola radio for him to buy. Mozhaev wrote this work at Milda's family home, which they were restoring in the summer of 1970, and Mozhaev has obviously used this biographical incident and incorporated it into this story.

On that occasion Mariia Ivanovna gave in, but for a long time Feduleev was curt and short with her.

'Your Feduleev is a scoundrel,' said Pavel Semënovich.

'He wants to get hold of a motorbike in the same way. But rest assured, it won't wash this time.'

'To hell with your motorbike! I want to be exonerated, or I won't be able to live with myself.'

'But what do you think I'm on about?' said Mariia Ivanovna, jumping out of the chair. 'Go straight to the local trade union committee at work and ask them to give you an official refutation.'

The chairman of the hospital trade union committee was the elderly Doctor Dolbezhov. He held consultations in the out-patients' department.

'Nikolai Illarionovich, please help me! I have been slandered,' said Pavel Semënovich, as he entered the doctor's office.

'How come you're so surprised,' droned the deep base voice of Dolbezhov. 'A dog barks, and the wind carries it away.'

'It's not that simple – it's in the newspaper.'

'Your newspaper's nothing special! Where is it?'

Pavel Semënovich had underlined in pencil the part about his being sacked from the hospital. Dolbezhov read it:

'It's nothing out of the ordinary. Just the usual pack of lies.'

'Yes, but it's a pack of lies about me personally, Nikolai Illarionovich.'

'Ah, my friend! They can do a lot worse to us than just getting personal. It's all a load of hot air.'

'I didn't expect this from you!' said Pavel Semënovich, looking dumb-founded at the old doctor. 'Do you not want to help me?'

'How can I help you?' asked the old doctor, pained.

'What do you mean "how"? Let's go to the editor and tell him it's a pack of lies and demand a refutation.'

'And do you suppose he'll listen to us?'

'We'll prove it! We'll take documents with us. I implore you, Nikolai Illarionovich!'

The doctor gave a kind of woeful smile, took off his white coat, and put on a grey, linen jacket with creased lapels, an old-fashioned white peaked cap with a broad cap-band, and grabbed his knotty walking stick.

'Let's go!'

They took with them an old abstract from the resolution of the Central Committee of the Medical Workers' Trade Union, reinstating Poluboiarinov in his job, and made for the editor's office. The doctor frowned as he walked, with his peaked cap pulled down over his eyes: he placed his walking stick straight and firmly on the ground, and he stood tall, as if he had swallowed a measuring stick. A little further on and to one side, Pavel Semënovich limped on his left leg, his shoulders reeling, and he talked and talked incessantly: 'The point is, it's not the scale of the insult – small or large. It's a point of principle not to let them get away with it. If you see an injustice and condone it in your heart, you then become an accomplice in the injustice. It's a kind of sin: a sin is not terrible when done in God's sight, but it is when it goes unnoticed. Sin and sin again, but repent. Because a bad example is infectious. One person grabs a cudgel to threaten honest people, saying: "Step aside, or I'll shut you up for good!" In that case, every one should pounce on this dear chap in a scrum! And he should be dragged out into the open by the ear and told: "Well now, face the music in public. Why are you going over the top?" But things don't work out like that... He's grabbed a cudgel and we've run into the bushes. Another fan of the fray, who is witness to this riotous scene, will grab an even bigger cudgel and say, "You're shutting them up that way, but I can do it this way. And with knobs on..." But we just play barrack-room lawyers and say, "Oh, he's going too far." Oh, the general public!'

When Feduleev's secretary announced that Plica, (for that was Pavel Semënovich's nickname), had brought the doctor with him, he shouted angrily from behind the door, so that they could hear:[42] 'I didn't send for an ambulance. We're all hail and hearty here.'

However, he received them all the same.

Feduleev was seated at his desk, pretending to read a fresh column of print, with his head bent, showing his extensive bald patch. It was in this pose that he greeted them, as if he was unable to tear himself away, so that they felt he was busy with some important matter. Doctor Dolbezhov and Pavel Semënovich stood by the door and waited.

'What is your business?' Feduleev finally asked, raising an eyebrow: his dull, grey eye became round, while his other eye, partly covered by a somnolent lid, still squinted at the newspaper. Feduleev took pride in being able to cast an eye in this divergent way.

Dolbezhov held his peaked-cap in his half-crooked hand, as if it were a helmet: 'Our request of you will take some time,' he said, not wishing to talk from the doorway.

'Unfortunately, I am busy,' he replied, still not acceding to them.

'We can wait,' said the doctor submissively, yet firmly sticking to his guns.

Feduleev's second eye also opened wider and came to rest firmly on the doctor: 'Very well. Sit down.'

Feduleev pointed to the conventional, high-backed sofa covered in black leatherette. They sat down. Dolbezhov stood his walking stick between his knees and hung his cap on it. Pavel Semënovich somehow retracted his head into his shoulders and arched his back, as if a spring had been removed from it.

'You have my attention,' said Feduleev.

---

[42] Pavel Semënovich's nickname is derived from the Russian word for the medical condition 'plica polonica', which causes the hair to grow in a knotted and matted fashion.

'We have come to express our objection to an article published in today's edition of your newspaper,' the doctor began, clearly enunciating each word.

'Personal protestations are not considered,' said Feduleev, cutting him short.

'The article is entitled, "War Over a Square Metre", and it concerns a person who works in our hospital, namely Poluboiarinov.'

'And what has that to do with you personally,' asked Feduleev, trying to wrong-foot him.

'In the article, there is at least one place where there is a crude distortion of the truth. Here it is, underlined in pencil,' stated the doctor, placing the newspaper in front of Feduleev.

Feduleev glanced at the newspaper with one eye, but he didn't read it.

'It is a matter of a deliberate distortion of the facts, which is libel. Here is an extract from the ruling of the Medical Workers' Trade Union, which refutes this lie.' The doctor took out the abstract and placed it in front of Feduleev. 'On this basis you are obliged to give a refutation.'

The doctor placed both hands on the peaked-cap, which was hanging on the walking stick, raised his sharp chin, and fell silent.

Feduleev fumbled with the note, as if it was all Greek to him, then placed it at the edge of the desk.

'We'll look into it! Only, I don't understand, what this has to do with you personally. Why are you getting involved in all this?' he asked the doctor. He'd not even glanced at Pavel Semënovich.

'I am the chairman of the hospital trade union. Consider my request not as personal one, but as a collective one.'

'Collective? Who sanctioned you to convene a collective to investigate facts printed in the press?'

'We shall do our own sanctioning and ratifying in our own time.'

'You yourselves? You should concern yourselves with hospital matters. The press is a public matter. The newspaper is a regional organ. So, there's an office at the regional executive committee. Take the matter up with them. If necessary, they will convene and appoint such a board of enquiry. Whether you will be included or not, I wouldn't know.'

'Is that all that you have to say to us?' asked the doctor, standing up.

'The matter is concluded,' said Feduleev, immersing himself in his newspaper – his head and shoulders became one imposing mass, as if his neck did not exist, as if it were a totally superfluous detail.

The doctor pulled his peaked-cap right down over his ears and left, to the tapping of his walking stick.

Chapter Nine

The next day, Pavel Semënovich and Mariia Ivanovna went to the **oblast** capital. They set off while it was still dark so as to be at the **oblast** executive committee offices in the morning, and return to Rozhnov by the evening. They went by bus to Starodubovo to catch a small, local train, which folk called 'Malashka'.[43] It got into Vyshgorod in the morning, which was handy in that they wouldn't have to pay for a night's accommodation. Also, a ticket on the 'Malashka' was half the price of a ticket on the ordinary passenger train.

Each time they went to Starodubovo, as they hit the main road, they experienced a strange feeling of relief and bewilderment. It felt as if they had been tethered to a stake, like horses, but now they had broken free and had ended up god knows where, and they felt happy, but they didn't know what to do.

First of all, as was their wont, they admired the brick buildings of the old stables, with their high fretted towers placed at the corners, and their toothed cornice, and the quaint, oblate, ornamental little windows, with their sharply cut spires… What a marvel! It was every bit a palace… Why should the landowner want to build such mansions just to house horses? What an eccentric! It should have been opened up as a sanatorium.

They had supper in the tall, log tea room. There was a general hum of conversation from people sat at tables – mostly drivers dressed in black, oil-stained jackets and jumpers, drinking solely **pertsovka** – it didn't linger on the breath. Two motorcyclists with white helmets on their knees, wearing short jackets of imitation black leather, treated some curly-haired young girls to some red wine at a small table. The girls listened to them, spluttering to one side, then rocked back in their chairs with peals of laughter. Whenever this happened, the motorcyclists exchanged winks with each other.

'You stupid girls!' Mariia Ivanovna felt like saying to them. 'Can't you see what they're scheming?'

'Why don't *we* have a little drop?' asked Pavel Semënovich, who was also looking at these giddy young women.

Mariia Ivanovna even shuddered: 'Where's the money coming from? Why the sudden urge to celebrate anyway?'

'Eh, Masha! We only live once. Count your blessings, as they say. If you are in the right, then you ought to be happy. Whether you believe it or not, I feel happy at the moment!'

'The fool's been made a laughing-stock and he's happy!'

'But that's not the point… I am fighting my own corner, that's the important thing. While I'm standing up for my truth, I have self-respect.'

'We'll turn up at the authorities tomorrow, they'll sock you in the gob, then we'll see how happy you are.'

---

[43] This word is generally used as a term of endearment for people and it can be rendered as 'Sweetie' or 'Poppet' in English. The name of the place 'Starodubovo' means 'Old Oak'. In the following sentence, 'vysh' is part of the word meaning 'high' and 'gorod' is Russian for 'town' or 'city': hence, the name could be translated as 'High Town'.

'Here we go again! So what if they do? What then?'

'You'll just have to wipe the shit off yourself and that's that,' said Mariia Ivanovna, with a spiteful grin.

'Will my resolve be shaken? No way! I shall stiffen my resolve all the more… I shall go on further, higher! Just let them beat me… But on whose side is right? That's the thing.'

'Who needs your "right"?'

'I do. I need it myself.'

'Then you're a fool.'

'No, Masha, you really must understand me. You must. Truth needs to be believed in.'

Pavel Semënovich caught the waitress by the arm and asked for a quarter-litre bottle of vodka.

Initially Mariia Ivanovna refused to have a drink, saying, 'All I need is heartburn!' But once she'd drunk a shot, she became flushed and cheered up, saying, 'You must be thick-skinned. They beat him and he says, "That's nothing." It's not for nothing that you're called Plica.'

'What's that to me?! The main point is, Masha, the crux is: they will not beat anything out of me. I have always fought my corner, and I always will.' Pavel Semënovich threw his arm back in a grand gesture and raised a threatening finger.

'Let's go outside, otherwise you'll end up breaking the crockery.' Mariia Ivanovna linked her arm in his, and they hobbled towards the door.

It was a warm, calm evening when, well before sunset, that early, somnolent mist hangs in the air only at the beginning of autumn. The sky was still light, but the trees already appeared dark. In the middle of the age-old, sparsely planted park, at the very top of a hill, surrounded by four mutilated lime trees, stood a little church with five cupolas, covered with black ruberoid – their crosses missing.[44] From there came the hurried, dull tapping of a wheat-milling machine and the guttural din of a flock of jackdaws, flying above the lime trees.

'C'mon, Mother. Let's go and admire god's beauty,' said Pavel Semënovich.

'There's nothing to admire there. It's long since been ransacked.'

'We can have a sit on the grass and reminisce about our youth. We've nowhere else to go anyway. There's ages until the train.'

'That's true…' said Mariia Ivanovna, coming round to the idea.

---

[44] This is a roofing material composed of felt impregnated with bitumen. It was common in Soviet times to see churches closed by the state in an attempt to limit access to religious services, which were not approved of. A great deal of damage was done to church artefacts during the anti-religious campaigns of the early 1930s and again in the 1960s, during which time gold was removed from the surface of the cupolas. In this case, it has obviously been replaced by a cheap alternative to keep out rain from the church. Many churches were damaged to such an extent that they have become irreparable, but many have also now been restored.

'Good. Let's go, Mother!' He hugged her by the shoulders.

'What about popping into the House of Culture? I've heard an art gallery has opened there,' said Mariia Ivanovna, still a little indecisive.

'You won't paint a better picture than this,' said Pavel Semënovich, gesturing at the neglected park. 'There'll be a lot of people there, but here we are alone. I'm rather tired, Masha.'

'Come on, let's go then...' said Mariia Ivanovna, embracing the rather languid Pavel Semënovich by the waist, and she led him along an old, tree-lined avenue, full of gaps.

They sat by the church on a wooden bench, which had turned dark with time and rain, situated near a stunted, mutilated lilac bush. A wasteland in the form of a wide gully stretched before them, as far as the small river. Here, there were once ponds with waterfalls and boats... In the middle of each pond there used to be an island with an arbour, with a riot of blossoming lilac and jasmine.

Mariia Ivanovna recalled how, in 1930, she had come here as a member of the **Komsomol** to a mass rally of political and village **reading-room** activists. "Let's set the pace for collectivization!", "Remove the sting from the **kulaks**!" they all shouted, holding their hands in the air. Then they boated on the ponds and sang. They were given red armbands to wear and were fed in the canteen on production of a coupon... How long ago all this was!

Pavel Semënovich smoked and coughed a little. Then, having extinguished his cigarette on the sole of his shoe, he said: 'I was just thinking... our life's a bit of a farce. As if we've been playing some kind of game. We keep on waiting for something else. It's as if that rational life were just on our doorstep, as if it's about to knock on our door and enter.'

'You'll wait and wait, then you'll snuff it, waiting for it,' said Mariia Ivanovna. 'It's very likely that all this fuss and bother *is* our life. Probably no other one exists, Pasha.'

The flour-mill watchman came over to them. He was an ancient old chap in a neat, greyish, little jacket and a dark blue Russian shirt, fully buttoned down the side.

'You wouldn't have a cigarette would you, please?'

Pavel Semënovich took out a packet of 'Belomorkanal' cigarettes. The old man lit one and sat down on the bench.[45]

'Are you from far off?' he asked.

---

[45] These cigarettes were named after the White Sea-Baltic Canal which links the White Sea (Beloe more) with Lake Onega. It was one of the grand projects initiated at the beginning of the 1930s, during the years of the First Five Year **Plan** (1929-32). It followed an ancient route, which had long been known, and had even been used by Peter I. Building began at the end of 1930, and it was finished in an astonishing twenty months: it was 227 km in length. However, it was built by convict (GULag) labour, leading many thousands of people to their death through exhaustion and malnutrition. It was also a rather ill-conceived project, since the water was not deep enough to allow large ships through. The cigarettes were named after this canal, but they are not ordinary cigarettes, as we know them in the West. They are *papirosy*, which comprise a half-cigarette, half-cardboard tube, which is crimped before smoking. This type of cigarette was later to be regarded as rather coarse and unsophisticated, though people still smoke them, and this brand continued to be made after the fall of the Soviet Union.

'From Rozhnov,' replied Pavel Semënovich.

'Here on business, or have you come to visit relatives?'

'We're going to the **oblast** capital. We're waiting for the 'Malashka'. But we know these parts. We're just sitting and reminiscing about the ponds,' said Pavel Semënovich.

'What do you remember?!'

'We?' said Mariia Ivanovna, perking up. 'We even remember the islands. We remember on which island lilac grew, and on which – jasmine.'

'Yes, it was like that,' said the old man, nodding his head. 'Never mind about the ponds! There were fountains. White swans swimming... And what tree-lined avenues! They used to cross this way and that. And they were paved with brick. They were laid edge-on, the bricks.'

'And did you used to work in the garden?' asked Mariia Ivanovna.

'I did all sorts,' replied the old man evasively. 'The garden was luxu-urious. All sorts of foreign trees were planted. They happened to flower just as the snow began to fall.'

'Why did they start to flower at such a time?' asked Pavel Semënovich. 'The blossom would have frozen.'

'It's because they were foreign. The earth told them what to do. But they were out of sync with our climate. We valued them as a novelty.'

'You don't live here by any chance, do you?' asked Pavel Semënovich.

'Yes, I live here next to the church... the flour mill, that is. What of it?'

'We just feel thirsty.'

'Come with me.'

The old man took them to the rear of the church, where a brick watchman's lodge with two windows backed on to a white-marbled, tall, semicircular wall. They went into the lodge: way at the back there appeared to be another door – a forged, iron door leading into the church. The old man opened it and disappeared beyond a tall, hewn threshold.

'Come this way!' called the old man, as if from the depths of a well.

They came into a dark, vaulted room.

'This is the incense room,' said the old man. 'This is where the priest used to come to the altar,' he said, pointing to the marble stairs which wound their way around a mighty, circular column. On the staircase stood a cistern full of water and a mug. 'Drink! Help yourselves.'

The water was so cold it made their teeth ache.

'It's just like a cellar in here,' said Mariia Ivanovna.

'In the winter I live in the annex. I put a portable heater in there.'

They could hear the flour-milling machine rumbling and making a dull groan, as if it were coming from the cellar.

'Both the walls and the partitions are thick. Just look, people could work at one end and you wouldn't hear them at the other. What a church!' said Mariia Ivanovna.

'It was built to last for centuries! Believe it or not, fifteen **poods** of gold were removed from the cupolas alone. But now the roof leaks,' said the old man.[46]

They sat at the doorway of the watchman's lodge right until nightfall. The old man kept on telling them about the estate and shaking his head: 'Just here, there used to be a tree – it produced Azov nuts as big as your fist.[47] There used to be a club over there. Ah, it was a marvellous one! People came here from all four corners of the world to have a look. They would say that they had never seen such a building anywhere else.'

'What happened to it?'

'Peasants ransacked it. Never mind the club! They sawed through all the apple trees during collectivization, broke up all the benches… They even stole the iron railings from the graves.'

'And where did the landowner get all this stuff from?' asked Mariia Ivanovna, with unexpected hatred. 'He also stole it all!'

'Everyone knows that,' agreed the old man. 'But you just consider this: he personally was left alone. He married a teacher and worked right up to the time of collectivization. But his own wife renounced him.'[48]

'Where did he work under Soviet power?' asked Mariia Ivanovna, who was taking an increasing interest in this unusual landowner's fate.

'In Pronsk. He built a four-year grammar school and went off to teach there before the Revolution. He was very keen on that kind of thing. He was even a member of the Duma.[49] He once said there, "Why do we need so much land? Let's share it amongst the peasants." The other landowners there got so angry with him that they cast an iron hat and galoshes for him.'

'How droll,' sneered Mariia Ivanovna. 'I suppose you'd call him a bit of a revolutionary, this landowner of yours?'

---

[46] This would amount to almost 245 kg of gold.

[47] Azov is a town situated in south-western Russia, on the left bank of the River Don, near the Sea of Azov. It was formerly the Greek colony of Tanais which was founded in 6 BC, but it was captured by the Turks in the 15th century, and by Peter the Great in the 17th century. The climate there is continental and temperate. It is difficult to be sure which kind of nut the old man is referring to here, since there is no universally recognised nut called the 'Azov nut' – the old man is probably using a local name, but it is likely that he is referring to some form of walnut.

[48] It was not uncommon for people to renounce members of their own family just after the Revolution of 1917 and in the 1930s, because the Soviet regime operated a system of 'guilty by association': the regime condemned several categories of people as enemies and antagonists, whether they were actively so, or not. Such people as former landowners, rich peasants (or **kulaks**), priests and people with a bourgeois or intellectual background, offended the authorities just by being, and this stigma was frequently passed on to the children and even associates of the person concerned.

[49] The Duma or '[State] Assembly' was an old Russian institution dating back to the Middle Ages, but it was established in the form referred to here in 1906 by Nicholas II, as the first step towards a parliamentary assembly. It was abolished after the Revolution of 1917, but it was revived in 1993, after the collapse of the Soviet Union, as the lower house of the newly created Federal Assembly or Russian parliament. The name is derived from the Russian word to 'think'.

'Who knows? He was a kind of nasal little bloke, unpretentious, and a bit scrawny. His main steward was a prominent man. He asked him, "Why do you do all this building? You'll only have your interest to live off." But he replied, "And what will other people live off?"'

'Ah! Are you telling me that he cared about peasants?' again asked Mariia Ivanovna spitefully, doubting what he said.

'Obviously. Who else would he care for? For example, if your horse dropped down dead and you produced an official certificate from the **volost** authorities, he would give you the money for it. When the Revolution came and an inquiry was held to decide what to do with him – let him be or destroy him – all the locals came out in favour of him.'

'There's something I just can't understand here. Are you glad there was a revolution or not?' Mariia Ivanovna asked point-blank.

'Are you out of your mind, Mariia?' asked Pavel Semënovich, rather perturbed.

'Why shouldn't I be glad?' replied the old man, unperturbed. 'We were given land then. In the twenties life got better. Before, without land, I was counted as an idler, wasn't I? But as soon as I got land, I started to outstrip the rest.'

'Hang on, don't get excited!' said Pavel Semënovich, touching Mariia Ivanovna's shoulder, and he turned to the old man: 'Answer me this: Can a person know for what purpose he lives, or not?'

The old man's eyes, which had looked as wan as ancient printed calico, suddenly became animated, and a glint appeared in them: 'People used to say: "Don't ask. Serve God and clothe yourself in peace."'

'And what is God? Whom do *you* understand him to be?'

'God is living in harmony with love.'

'That's true!' exclaimed Pavel Semënovich, and he even slapped his knee. 'It's all about harmony. Some people invent happiness and ram it down your throat, like sticking chewing gum into a child's mouth. Here you are, chew on that and keep shtoom! But what if I don't want that kind of happiness? Then what?'

'That's enough from you! Why have you got so worked up?' said Mariia Ivanovna, calling Pavel Semënovich to order. 'Let's go! It's already late.'

'So, what then?' Pavel Semënovich asked again, getting up from the porch.

'The Lord will help you,' replied the old man, bidding them farewell.

Chapter Ten

In the morning they had a stroke of luck – they were the first to be seen.[50]

The **oblast** executive committee was housed in an old, grey building with tall, circular windows. People said that formerly the town authorities used to occupy this building,

---

[50] Queues to see Russian officials were notoriously long both in pre- and post-revolutionary times. It was by no means unusual to have to wait not only hours, but sometimes days, in order to be granted an audience with a bureaucrat.

and, in the building opposite, which was now the **oblast** committee offices, there used to be the **guberniia** authorities. There, next to the main door, was a brass plaque: 'In this building worked the great Russian satirical writer M.E. Saltykov-Shchedrin.' Whenever he passed by this building, Pavel Semënovich would never fail to stop and look at the plaque, and he would remark to himself in wonder: 'He was a vice-governor, a general! But how much criticism he offered!'

And now also, he instinctively tarried by this former **guberniia** office and said: 'Do you see that plaque, Mariia? He was a general, but he criticised things. And you bend *my* ear.'

'Well, your general was a fool! What did he want for?'

'But, do we criticise things for our own sakes?'

'Well, for whose sake would it be?'

'For society's, you dope! So that everyone has a good life.'

'Life will never be good for everyone.'

All this time, they were being sternly scrutinized through the open door by the duty policeman.

'Come along! C'mon! Why are you standing there gawping?' said Mariia Ivanovna, tugging at Pavel Semënovich's sleeve. 'You might end up in the wrong place.[51] You critic!'

In the entrance hall of the **oblast** executive committee offices there was also a policeman on duty, but he was of a lower rank and not as severe. They stopped at his small table and rummaged in their pockets for their **passports**. The policeman took them politely and said from under his peaked cap: 'Where do you need to be?'

'The chairman's office or any of his deputies.'

'Please go up the stairs to the first floor.'

The staircase was wide and made of white marble with ornate banisters, looking like two bottles set end to end.

When they got to the chairman's office reception, they were told that Alexander Timofeevich was not there to receive visitors that day. If they wanted, they could see his secretary Comrade Laptev, and he would sort things out.

Laptev, the secretary of the **oblast** executive committee, turned out to be an unusually cordial man. He was short, thick-set, and had an iron grip, but his face was round, pale and soft. He was dressed in a grey suit made of thick, expensive material, but the wide lapels, which were like those on a military overcoat, were rather worn and over-laundered. He sat Pavel Semënovich and Mariia Ivanovna near to his desk, smiling all the time, as if he had invited them in for a cup of tea.

'What can I do for you?' he asked, turning his tender gaze from one to the other.

---

[51] This is a reference to prison or a prison camp. Both the Poluboiarinovs would have lived through the purges and excesses of Stalin's Russia of the 1930s, when even mild criticism of the regime was enough to land the critic in prison, often in a distant prison camp with hard labour and dreadful deprivation.

'We have a trifling matter…' said Mariia Ivanovna.

'That depends how you look at it,' interrupted Pavel Semënovich. 'If we approach it from the point of view of a personal insult, then it smacks of litigation!' Pavel Semënovich raised his head, looking angrily at Mariia Ivanovna.

'So what has happened, then?' asked Laptev, evincing a little impatience.

'I have been publicly insulted in the press! The facts were twisted… And the paper won't issue a retraction.'

'Look, you haven't started in the right place. Shut up for a minute!' said Mariia Ivanovna, stopping him and turned towards Laptev. 'Our door is off a communal corridor… It opened outwards, because a lintel stopped it opening inwards. Our drunken neighbour, Chizhënok, used to sleep by it. And so…'

'I don't understand a thing,' said Laptev, shaking his head and spreading his arms helplessly.

'What's the door got to do with it?' asked Pavel Semënovich, irritated. 'The door was repositioned correctly, according to a legal ruling of the executive committee. So what? And in the article, no one contested that fact. This is all to do with twisting the facts, wilful slander.'

'You're an idiot!' flared up Mariia Ivanovna. 'Tomorrow the door will be put back to its original position, then Berta will arrive… And what shall we do?'

'Comrades, comrades, let's discuss this calmly!' said Laptev, holding up his hands and splaying his fingers. 'Have you any material evidence or documents with you?'

'We've got everything,' replied Mariia Ivanovna.

'Put them on the desk and we'll go through everything in order.'

They produced a copy of the executive committee's ruling regarding the resiting of the door, certified by Funtikova, a copy of the resolution of the Central Committee of the Medical Workers' Trade Union, and the newspaper *Red Rozhnov*, with passages of Vitia Smorchkov's article underlined.

Laptev put on his glasses and inclined his large forehead. His expression began to change – his cheeks went saggy, his nose first went red, then blossomed like a lilac bud. Before them sat a weary old man.

'All quite legal,' he said, having perused the papers. 'The door was correctly repositioned. No one has the right to make you put it back in its former position. Distortions of the facts have been made in the newspaper. You must seek a retraction.'

'It's easy to say "seek a retraction",' said Pavel Semënovich, shuffling on his chair. 'The chairman of the trade union and I tried to confront the editor, but he would hardly look at us.'

'Very well, I shall telephone Pavlinov. You go home.'

When they were outside, Pavel Semënovich burbled with satisfaction:

'Did you see that, Mariia?! See how everything has turned out, eh? Now I can give that Feduleev character the V-sign.'

'You'd better hold back the boasting. What else will Pavlinov say?'

'I couldn't give a damn about Pavlinov now.'

They got the express train home. In Starodubovo, they were lucky with the bus, so they were home just after lunch.

'You clear up here and I'll go to Pavlinov's office to gloat over how he's feeling,' said Pavel Semёnovich, with joyful anticipation.

He got washed, shaved, put on a clean shirt, and went off, as if he were going to a banquet.

Pavlinov greeted him without any particular surprise, or even indignation. 'That means Laptev has phoned and has given him a real earful,' observed Pavel Semёnovich.

Captain Stenin was lolling on the sofa in Pavlinov's office. He and Pavlinov were planning a hunting trip that evening, to put the wind up a few ducks, and they were in a rather equable mood. Pavlinov had dark eyebrows and a forelock, and he looked youthfully fit and tanned: with his white shirt sleeves rolled up and his collar undone (his jacket was hanging on the chair), he resembled a fitness instructor.

'It's good that you have come in person,' said Pavlinov, greeting Pavel Semёnovich, but not offering him his hand. 'That means you understand. Take a seat!' he said, pointing to the chair.

'What is it that I should understand?' asked Pavel Semёnovich, pricking up his ears.

'That the general public is indignant at your behaviour. That this has been reflected in the press. It's time to stop all this tale-telling and put the door back in its former position.'

'What?!' asked Pavel Semёnovich, taken aback.

'Simple as that. Then your neighbours will stop writing complaints and the press will hush up. And you'll have no reason to go gadding about the **oblast**. You've only yourself to blame.'

'First of all, the press published some libellous statements about us,' said Pavel Semёnovich, who began to stutter a little at this unexpected turnabout. 'F-fo-for which Comrades Smorchkov and Feduleev must answer. And it's not *my*, but *their* pronouncements, which must be considered fallacious. By way of support for my evidence, here is a copy of the resolution from the Central Committee of the Medical Workers' Trade Union, certified by Comrade Dolbezhov.' Pavel Semёnovich put the document right in front of Pavlinov and he even slapped it with the palm of his hand.

'Don't you go shoving your bits of medical papers in front of me! If we need to, we shall summon Dolbezhov personally and ask him what his ulterior motive is in trying to cover up for all manner of slanderers.' Pavlinov flung the document in such a way that it fell from the table.

'So, am I the slanderer then?' asked Pavel Semënovich, just as angrily, picking up the copy.

'Who else would it be? Stenin?' sneered Pavlinov.

Captain Stenin made the springs creak in the sofa and he also smiled.

'Are you aware of the **oblast** executive committee secretary's, Comrade Laptev's, opinion?' asked Pavel Semënovich in a sterner tone of voice, with a toss of his head.

'Go on, surprise me!' sneered Pavlinov again.

'Comrade Laptev assured me that the ruling from the executive committee regarding the repositioning of the door was in order… And that…'

'But I'm saying that Funtikova misled the executive committee,' Pavlinov said, interrupting him.

'And that the newspapers distorted the facts. Feduleev must publish a retraction. You yourself are fully aware of this, but you are just playing games with me,' said Pavel Semënovich, raising his voice.

'You are a past-master in all manner of anti-social games!' bawled Pavlinov. 'Who's the one who churns out hare-brained plans? Me? You've lost the plot!' Pavlinov stood up, scraped his chair as he pushed it back, and paced to and fro behind his desk in silence for a moment, to cool down. Then he said calmly, 'As for Laptev, he rang me and said only one thing: "Let Poluboiarinov take Smorchkov to court, if he thinks he's in the right." So, go ahead and do just that.'

'I haven't come to a court, but to you, so that you punish the guilty. It wasn't the court which allowed me to reposition the door.'

'Same old story!' Pavlinov sat down at his desk and began patiently to ram his point home to Poluboiarinov. 'Your behaviour is unbecoming. You send out your unsubstantiated information to all manner of authorities, disturbing the status quo. You led Funtikova astray, and she did the same to the executive committee. You used this to your advantage to seize half the corridor for yourself. A communal corridor! You live the life of Riley, with a living room and a separate kitchen – a whole flat for just two people… while other people live in cramped conditions, and even in cellars. Instead of acknowledging that, you blame every one else without exception, demanding punishment… almost to the point of going to court! You are shameless, Comrade Poluboiarinov.'

'Thank you for the homily. But you'd do better to address the lecture not to me, but to yourself, for your own unseemly behaviour. What about you, for example? When you came to Rozhnov from Starodubovo, you seized a three-roomed flat of fifty-three square metres from workers at the canning factory. And with all mod cons! All that, for a family of just four people. As if that weren't enough, you didn't surrender your old flat in Starodubovo. You moved your relatives into that one.'

Pavlinov looked at Stenin and turned scarlet: 'Did you see that? We have a public inspector in our midst…'

'What's the point in talking to him?' replied Stenin. 'He should be put on trial himself, for slander…'

'I have evidence,' said Pavel Semënovich, lunging at Stenin.

'That will do! Enough said…' said Pavlinov imperiously. 'It's obvious you're not the kind of person to be persuaded. Let's put it another way: you have just one week to put the door back in its original position. Do you understand?'

'No, I don't. The door will stay where it has been repositioned by the town executive committee.'

'Then I'll be round to see you personally. And I'll bring the police with me,' he said, nodding in Stenin's direction. 'I'll break your door down.'

'Just you try…'

'Semën Ermolaevich, I'll assign not only one policeman, but two,' said Stenin. 'So that he will have support. Just in case of any opposition.'

'He is capable of anything. He might even grab an axe,' said Pavlinov, with a wry smile.

'I should like to know on what grounds you will break the door down?' said Pavel Semënovich.

'Try this one!' said Pavlinov, looking at Stenin. 'On the grounds of fire safety regulations. You're impeding people's free access.'

'On the contrary! The lintel used to be a fire risk. Just you look. I have plans,' said Pavel Semënovich, taking out yet another document from his pocket.

However, Pavlinov merely made a sweeping gesture, as if he were clearing rubbish from his desk.

'All your documents are forgeries. I won't even look at them. I'm giving you one week's notice. Woe betide you, if you don't shift the door.'

'I wouldn't even think of it.'

'Off you go!'

Chapter Eleven

Pavel Semënovich was all covered in red blotches when he came home from Pavlinov's, and he barked in to Mariia Ivanovna's face: 'You can gloat now. There will be no retraction! They're all hand in glove… And you're in league with them.'

Mariia Ivanovna resolved that, since Feduleev had publicly attacked her, it was not right for her to hide behind the stooping back of her nearest and dearest.

'What are you bawling at me for?' she asked, turning towards him, her face filling with rage at her husband's calumny. 'Who do you think I am?'

'Your Smorchkov's colleague, that's who…'

'You're a wimp yourself.[52] Can't you stand up for the truth, eh? Just you watch how us grown-ups do it.'

She put on her best black hat, which looked more like a felt boot, grabbed her black umbrella with its bone handle and, despite the late hour, she set out for the editor's office.

Feduleev was sitting at his desk, proof-reading a page. Apart from him and his secretary Irochka, there was no one about. Mariia Ivanovna thought, 'It's a shame there are no colleagues about. His fancy-woman doesn't count. It's not so much fun kicking up a rumpus without an audience.'

She had the utmost contempt for his secretary because, some time ago – about four years back – she had caught her red-handed in the accounting office of the town water department. At that time, Mariia Ivanovna worked as an auditor for the regional finance department. Irochka stole receipts, altered them, then took the cash. She was found guilty under Article 92 (Section 2) for appropriating state funds. But at that time the newspapers were full of articles about rehabilitation... So Irochka was put on probation...

Irochka greeted Mariia Ivanovna with mocking civility, like a school-girl caught up to no good: 'Your working day has already finished. Or have you forgotten something?'

'I forgot to ask you whether I should work or take the day off.'

Mariia Ivanovna made straight for the editor's door covered in black leatherette.

'Pëtr Ivanovich is very busy!' said Irochka, leaping towards the door with feline agility.

'And d'you think I've come here to play the fool? Out of my way!'

No such luck. Irochka put her back against the door and continued the polite conversation: 'You're not an outsider here, Mariia Ivanovna. You know that Pëtr Ivanovich does his proof-reading at this time of the day. Why are you distracting him?'

'And I'm telling you to get away from the door! I have a more important matter – I have come to check out the law.'

The door opened from inside. Feduleev stood there in the doorway, with a satisfied air.

'Representatives of the law are always welcome here. Please, do come in, Mariia Ivanovna!' he said, even bending his bald head, almost bowing, but the expression on his face was one of near mirth.

Irochka assumed the same respectful, clownish pose, and drawled in her sing-song voice, like the editor: 'Pl-ee-ase enter! Only leave the umbrella outside. It doesn't rain in *our* office.'

'And how many are there of you in the editor's office?' asked Mariia Ivanovna, mocking her.

'You're just like a real inspector,' sneered Feduleev. 'What is your mandate?'

---

[52] See footnote № 34, p.242.

'I'm here as a state official and as a bookkeeper... And as member of the Party, and a communist into the bargain. Is that enough for you?'

'You are such an el—lev–aated person!' drawled Feduleev.

Mariia Ivanovna went through into his office, sat down in the chair, and put her umbrella onto the editor's desk.

Irochka left the door wide open and moved over to her small desk, on which stood a typewriter, but Feduleev began to pace about his office.

'Perhaps you might shut the door and hear me out?' said Mariia Ivanovna.

'Carry on, carry on. We have no secrets here. This is a public newspaper. Everything is upfront,' replied Feduleev, chirpily.

'Fine. Since it's public, it's public. So will you publish a retraction?'

'Mariia Ivanovna, you simply amaze me. How long have you been working here with us? Over two years? Tell me, have we ever, once, published a retraction? Never,' said Feduleev, enunciating every syllable. 'Because we are the press. And only substantiated facts appear in the press. Have you ever read a retraction?'

'Don't stick your press under my nose. I know what kind of truth we have in this editorial office.'

'What are you alluding to?'

'Just as I say... You infringe government decrees.'

'Which?'

'The decree of the Soviet of the People's Commissars of the Union of Soviet Socialist Republics of 21 December 1921, Section Two. Have you read it?'[53]

'Well?'

'I'll give you "Well?"... According to this decree, it is forbidden to employ direct relatives as subordinate staff at work. She's not just a direct relative, but none other than your very own wife, who's working here. She doesn't even meet the educational requirements for the job. That's your "truth".'

Feduleev turned round and glanced at Irochka, then he stopped dead in his tracks: 'She has qualifications on a par with a primary school teacher's.'

'How do you mean, "on a par"? She might have passed through the corridors, but did she attend any lectures?'

Feduleev sighed dolefully and sat down at his desk.

'Mariia Ivanovna, you've been working for us for over two years and you have never once even mentioned such a serious decree. I'll be quite frank with you, I'm not a lawyer, and I was unaware of the existence of such a decree. Furthermore, I am disappointed that a worker, appointed specifically to deal with financial matters, has not

[53] The Soviet or Council of People's Commissars existed between 1917 and 1946: in Russian the acronym is *Sovnarkom*. In 1946, this Council became the Council of Ministers of the USSR.

informed me of this fact. I am willing to accept that you made this blunder unintentionally. Perhaps, it slipped your memory. Well, that's not surprising, given your declining years. In fact, I think it's time you retired, Mariia Ivanovna. High time.'

'I'll wait until your wife goes.'

'You won't have to wait, Mariia Ivanovna... The editorial staff will not put up with this. You know the order of events: there's an initial reprimand, then a second. Finally, there's an order for dismissal, and that's your lot. So why go to the wire?'

'Well, thank God, I've never had a single reprimand.'

'Ah, but there is, there *is* one already,' said Feduleev, spreading his hands with such an expression of distress, as if it were he who was suffering the most from this reprimand. 'Irina, please bring the order ledger.'

Mariia Ivanovna hardly had time to catch her breath before the editorial orders ledger was already under her nose, open at the required page.

Order No. 44

Issued by the Editorial Board of Red Rozhnov

27 August

In view of not presenting herself for work on the 27 August of this year with a valid reason, the editorial bookkeeper Poluboiarinova, M. I., is deemed to have been absent without leave and will not be paid, and, for not appearing at work, she is issued with a reprimand.

Editor of the Red Rozhnov newspaper,

Feduleev.

'Ah, so that's it!' thought Mariia Ivanovna, putting two and two together. 'That's why they were so bold-faced about being nice to me.'

'It's a lie! A falsification!' said Mariia Ivanovna, slamming her hand down on the open book, as if she had swatted a fly.

'The orders ledger is nothing to do with this. Please conduct yourself politely.' Irochka took the register and slid out of the office.

'What kind of falsification?' asked Feduleev.

'A malicious one! I went to the **oblast** executive committee to complain about your libellous statements. I came into the press offices and checked the monthly statement... Are you putting me down as absent without leave?'

'People go to the **oblast** offices on official business. Is that not so?' asked Feduleev sternly.

'I've never recorded her as being on an official business trip,' sounded Irochka's voice from reception.

'Quite correct,' said Feduleev, with a nod of his head. '…because I didn't issue an order for you to go on an official business trip. You did not request to go off on an official business trip from me. Isn't that so, Mariia Ivanovna?'

'But I had an official business travel warrant!'

'So what? The warrant doesn't exempt you from the rules.'

'But this is not the first time I have travelled like this.'

'I wouldn't know… Perhaps you've been there before to make a complaint… I don't know anything about that,' said Feduleev, remaining unperturbed.

'This is all arbitrary!' exclaimed Mariia Ivanovna, not giving in.

'How do you mean "arbitrary"? I am just bringing to your attention that you have received a first reprimand, and a second is imminent.'

'Are you taking the micky? Or is this some kind of play-acting? What's all this about a second reprimand?'

'It is at the draft stage, as yet… Whether it materializes, or not, entirely depends on you. It's the twenty-seventh today, is it not? And when are royalties paid to freelance correspondents? During the last third of the month. Isn't that so?'

'That's when the account is in credit. When it's not, then we transfer payment to the beginning of the following month.'

'The current account *is* in credit.'

'But only by seventy-five roubles. We need a total of one hundred and ninety to pay the royalties.'

Feduleev again gave a pitiful sneer.

'You get your salary in two instalments every month… You get your **pay advance**. Yet you seem to think, that sending authors their royalties in instalments is too much bother. You are in breach of my instructions. That's not good.'

'But we've been doing it like that every month…'

'Well, it's not right that you've been doing it like that. You will be punished for withholding writers' fees.'

'You're a no-good piece of scum!' said Mariia Ivanovna, grabbing her umbrella: she struck it against the floor, then stood up. 'But just think on, you will not manage to blacken my name with the regional committee of the union. I am a member of the trade union.'

'You're making things worse for yourself,' said Feduleev, not raising his voice. 'Why did you insult me? And especially in the presence of the chairwoman of the local committee,' he said, nodding towards Irochka. 'Before we take your case to the regional committee of the union, we shall deal with it here, in the local committee... I'm telling you this out of sympathy for you: submit a request for retirement. Just leave of your own volition.'

'You swindlers! Do you just want me to lie down quietly in my grave?'

'Why on earth should you? Live long and well. You'll have a perfectly decent pension.'

'Anything for a quiet life, eh? Well, it won't work. I won't live a quiet life, and I'll make sure you don't either.'

'The choice is yours.'

Chapter Twelve

The next day, Pavlinov rang Feduleev.

'How's the "lady of property" over there? Has she grabbed an extra one-and-a-half square metres for her office yet?'

'She's planning another campaign with the book of complaints and suggestions,' Feduleev replied jauntily.[54]

'Who's she going to complain to this time?'

'She's asking for leave to go to Moscow.'

'Oh, is she now?! Well, you just send her home. Tell her there is a deputation on its way from the regional executive committee.'

'Who's going to visit her?'

'I'll go myself. I'll get Stenin to come along and talk to her along the lines of, "People in glass houses shouldn't throw stones."'[55]

'You could try. I also tried to reason with her yesterday. "Don't rock the boat, old girl," I said, "while you're up a certain creek without a paddle".'[56]

'And what did she say?'

'She said, "We're both in the same boat".'[57]

Pavlinov was silent for a moment: 'She's become slap-dash, you know. And what did you say?'

---

[54] Every Soviet institution, office, shop, and even each individual bus, had a 'book of complaints and suggestions', which could be demanded by a disgruntled customer, to write a comment in, particularly if the assistant or employee had been rude or off-hand. Some limited reprisals were taken by way of withholding bonuses by the authorities, if complaints proliferated.

[55] A literal translation of the text here is: 'Don't try poking [your nose] into heaven, Matrëna, when you're tail is wet'. 'Having one's tail wet' is a euphemism for being 'morally tarnished' or 'tainted'. The name 'Matrëna' is a colloquial form of the name Mariia and it has rural overtones.

[56] Again, this translation gives just a flavour of the Russian original: the literal translation would be 'don't kick up a fuss, old girl, while you have a sack over your head'.

[57] The original text states: 'I'll cover [your head] myself with the hem of my skirt'.

'I suggested she retire,' chuckled Feduleev.

'Quite right! And what did she say?'

'She's digging her heels in.'

'So, she doesn't want to go willingly? Fine, just slap a couple of reprimands on her…'

'We've already thought of that. But she's counting on support from the regional trade union.'

'What's the point in your getting involved with the union? Just put it to a meeting. Bear in mind that a decision made by a meeting is not subject to legal appeal.'

'Quite right!'

'Anyway, just send her home…'

Pavlinov and Captain Stenin graced the Poluboiarinovs with their presence at lunch time. Mariia Ivanovna and Pavel Semënovich were sitting in the kitchen waiting for them. They didn't feel like lunch. Mariia Ivanovna had served a bowl of soup each for them, but they had only taken a spoonful when they fell into a funk, like at a wake. The soup had gone cold.

A knock at the door brought them to their senses – Pavel Semënovich, his shoulders reeling, rushed to unlock the door, and Mariia Ivanovna threw the soup in the bowls back into the saucepan.

When he saw the used bowls on the table, Pavlinov sneered: 'Ah, an invitation to lunch… Well, that means at least one of us is lucky.'

'Would you like to sit at table, perhaps? We can also find something to drink,' said Mariia Ivanovna, with a rather pathetic smile.

'We're not here for a party,' replied Pavlinov, resolutely brushing aside all unscrupulous attempts at a reconciliation. 'And I should advise you against cheap stunts at trying to *comprometize* representatives of authority.'[58]

'Whom are we compromising?' snarled Pavel Semënovich. 'It's you who started with niceties.'

'That's enough talking,' said Pavlinov, cutting him short. 'Stenin, you go and examine the door as a fire hazard.'

First of all, Captain Stenin measured the wall from the kitchen flue to the door lintel, using the palm of his hand. Next, he opened the door and put his finger into the slashes in the leatherette. Then, he paced out the remaining store area of the corridor and said to Pavlinov: 'The communal corridor space has been curtailed by one-and-a-half square metres.'

'So?' said Pavlinov.

---

[58] Currying favour with officials by means of bribes, and especially with drink, was endemic within the Soviet system. It was so common that it was virtually second nature to most people to engage in this kind of activity.

'That means that, in case of evacuation, in the event of a fire, access will be restricted,' concluded the Captain.

'There we are,' concluded Pavlinov, gratified.

'How come?' asked Mariia Ivanovna. 'If there were to be a fire, would people come running into our flat, rather than straight outside?'

'Precisely!' said Pavel Semënovich, rejoicing in this conclusion. 'Our door is not an escape route for the neighbours!'

'And what if *you* had a fire?' asked Stenin, disconcerting them with his question.

'We'd be responsible for our own fire,' replied Mariia Ivanovna.

'Excuse me! It is we, above all, at regional level, who will answer for any fire. And that includes for you,' intervened Pavlinov.

'And so, why weren't you answerable, when the door stood right next to the flue? Or did you just turn a blind eye to that?' asked Mariia Ivanovna.

'The flue is plastered over. It has nothing to do with this. What you've got here is a store area where gas bottles are kept,' said Stenin.

'And what if that's a lie?'

'We have information to that effect…'

'And what if that's a lie?' repeated Pavel Semënovich.

'How can you prove it's a lie?' asked Stenin.

'What do you mean "how"? Where do you see any gas bottles? Well? There aren't any here.'

'So what?' said Pavlinov. 'You've cleared them away, because you were expecting us.'

'But that's not evidence of a fire risk,' said Pavel Semënovich.

'Ah, that might not be enough for you!' said Stenin. 'Good. Let's continue.'

He went on into the kitchen and, with a majestic gesture, pointed to the crockery shelf and the bread cupboard on the wall, over the cooker: 'And what's this?'

'How do you mean "this"? It's a kitchen shelf,' said Mariia Ivanovna.

'I'm asking about it from a fire-hazard point of view.'

'A shelf is a shelf.'

'No, I'm sorry… In the first place, it's wooden, and secondly, it's right over the gas stove. It could burst into flames.'

'From what?'

'From the gas.'

'Not only can the gas not reach it – you can't even touch it,' said Mariia Ivanovna.

'That's not the point. Since it's forbidden, it's forbidden. You'll have to put the shelf and the cupboard on the other wall, or cover them with tin-plate. I'll give you two days, otherwise I'll fine you. Right… Let's go on. Let me see where you keep your gas bottles.'

All four of them went outside.

'That's it, there,' said Pavel Semënovich, pointing at the long, black box, which looked like a coffin, set against the brick foundations.

'And why isn't it covered in tin-plate?' asked Captain Stenin, looking at Pavlinov in amazement.

'Everyone in Rozhnov has the same kind. Deserter knocked them together,' replied Pavel Semënovich.

'I'm not asking Deserter, I'm asking you!' said Stenin, sternly. 'Why is the box not covered in tin-plate?'

'Is the neighbours' one covered? Just take a look!'

'Don't put the blame on your neighbours. Their turn will come. I want to clarify one thing: Are you consciously evading fire safety regulations, or not?'

'I'm curious how you've decided that I'm doing that "consciously",' said Pavel Semënovich.

'Well, you make reference to Deserter, and to your neighbours. If you were not aware of the regulations, you'd simply have said, "I'm guilty".'

'But what am I guilty of?'

'Don't play the innocent with me,' said Pavlinov.

'And don't you threaten me!' said Pavel Semënovich, raising his voice.

'Keep your voice down, Comrade Poluboiarinov! We are addressing you politely, for the time being. Change this wooden box for a metal one,' said Stenin, tapping on the wooden planks. 'You must not use this box. I forbid it. I give you two days to change it.'

'This is all arbitrary!' shouted Mariia Ivanovna.

'How do you mean "arbitrary"? We shall draw up an official statement and sign it, and you shall sign it. It's all done scientifically. You can make a complaint,' said Stenin. 'But we'll cut off your gas… temporarily.'

'Perhaps you might want to close down our flat as well,' Pavel Semënovich sneered, nervously.

'And what's that over there?' asked Stenin, pointing to the wooden construction, attached to the woodshed at the side of the house.

'It's a garage.'

'A wooden garage, next to the house?' exclaimed Stenin, turning to Pavlinov in amazement. 'Well, I never!'

'Who gave you permission to build a wooden garage here?' asked Pavlinov, severely.

'How do you mean "who"? The town executive committee did,' said Pavel Semënovich, looking incredulously, first at Pavlinov, then at Stenin.

'I never gave such permission,' said Pavlinov.

'It was before your time... ten years ago.'

'Show me the building permit!'

'Where do I get that from now? When was it?' Pavel Semënovich broke out into a sweat, and his hands started to shake a little, and his eyes darted to the side, as if he wanted to make himself scarce.

'This is a serious matter. Unless you can produce documentary proof, we'll pull the garage down and punish you,' said Pavlinov.

'Khaldeev gave us permission,' Mariia Ivanovna added. 'He's still around, thank God, and living opposite us. Let's go to see him and sort this out.'

Pavlinov's whole body contorted, and he looked at Mariia Ivanovna as if he'd just been offered a fried frog to eat.

'What are you talking about? Do you mean to supplant a legal decree by a verbal agreement? Come now, Poluboiarinova! Who on earth keeps you in your job? And you claim to be a bookkeeper!'

'What's my being a bookkeeper got to do with it?'

'Would you incorporate verbal affirmations into your accounts?' Pavlinov turned towards Stenin and raised his eyebrows in amazement.

Captain Stenin burst out laughing: 'She's taking us for fools.'

'It's you who are making fools of us. And it won't work!'

'That's enough chat,' said Pavlinov imperiously. 'Here's the order: You have one week to remove the illegally constructed garage.'

'So where will I put my car?' asked Pavel Semënovich.

'You'll have to get permission from the town executive committee to build one legally.'

'So, you give me the permission! You're the chairman. Everyone kow-tows to you.'

'I have official office hours, by the way. Put yourself down on the list to be seen without a prior appointment. But I warn you in advance, we have a specific place outside the town reserved for the construction of garages, near Pupkovo Swamp.'[59]

'But I am disabled! Do you think I can hobble on one leg as far as Pupkovo Swamp?'

'That doesn't concern us.'

---

[59] See footnote № 38, p.245.

'I was given that car for free by the union of medical workers. For a disabled person like me, the car is my legs! Are you taking my garage away from me?'

'I'm giving you one week,' replied Pavlinov coldly.

'Excuse me, but I have to investigate this garage,' said Stenin. 'To see whether he can still use it for one more week.'

'Absolutely,' agreed Pavlinov. 'Open it up, please!'

Pavel Semënovich rummaged around in his pockets for ages, totally unable to find the key.

'It's open... The garage is open,' said Mariia Ivanovna.

'Oh, yes. I've just got back from work. The key is in the lock, over there, in the clasp,' replied Pavel Semënovich, mumbling woodenly, and they all walked over to look in the garage.

The doors, as if sensing their impending doom, let out a shrill screech.

'Some owner! Can't even grease his garage doors,' sneered Pavlinov.

'He's not greased them on purpose,' said Stenin. 'It's an anti-theft device. Whoever thinks of nicking the car would wake up the whole street. But get a load of this!' Stenin pointed to an oily rag lying next to a tarpaulin. 'An oily article next to a piece of material – that's an outrageous breach of regulations. And there's more! An open jar, full of oil, next to a wooden wall. No, I'm sorry, we're going to have to issue an official order.'

Stenin put his hand in his brief-case and pulled out an official order book.

'So, where shall we start?' He was about to rest the book on the brief-case, while leaning against the car, when he felt a new onset of joy. 'Would you just take a look at that wiring! A tangle of wires fixed straight onto wooden boards. No insulation, nor fire-resistant conduit! This is tantamount to a Bickford fuse on a powder keg,' he said, poking at the electrical wiring.[60]

'It's not even live,' said Pavel Semënovich. 'There's no lighting in the garage.'

'How do we know? You might have just turned it off before we got here. Eh? No, you really must be fined,' said Stenin, turning towards Pavlinov again.

'I think so too,' said Pavlinov nodding.

While Captain Stenin was writing out the official order, Pavel Semënovich cleared away the jar full of oil, the cloths, and the tarpaulin – he put them all into the concrete inspection pit, and muttered guiltily: 'Just look how this has all back-fired on me! They've always been kept in the inspection pit... that's concrete! I've only just hurried back from work and I didn't have time to clear up.'

---

[60] The Bickford Fuse was invented by the Englishman William Bickford (1774-1834) who lived in Cornwall. He witnessed many accidents with explosives in the tin mines in the 19th century, and in 1831 he invented a safety fuse, consisting of gun powder tightly wrapped in jute or fabric, which was subsequently waterproofed. The fuse he invented was reliable and consistent, in that a given length always burned at the same rate, to allow the user to retreat to a safe distance before the explosion.

'Why are you fussing around? Can't you see they've come here with an ulterior motive?' remarked Mariia Ivanovna.

'Quite right. There's no point in troubling yourself,' agreed Pavlinov. 'We're not going to allow you to use the garage in any case.'

'Here, sign this,' said Stenin, offering the official order to Pavel Semënovich.

'I'm guilty of nothing and I shall not sign.'

'If you sign the order and pay the fine, then you can use the garage for a week. If you don't sign, we'll seal the garage together with the car.' Stenin took out a box containing the official seal: the seal was attached to a chain and it also had a breloque, in the form of an enamelled marmoset. Whilst Pavel Semënovich was wiping his oily hands, Stenin played around with the seal and breloque.

Every one had fallen silent. Finally, Pavel Semënovich took out a pen and signed in the place where Stenin had indicated with his finger-nail. After this, he didn't even look at anyone, as if he were ashamed of something. He hurriedly opened the car bonnet and buried his head in the engine.

When Pavlinov and Stenin had gone, Mariia Ivanovna shouted over to him: 'What are you rummaging in there for? Let's go and have some lunch.'

Pavel Semënovich did not respond. Mariia Ivanovna came round from the bonnet and saw his shoulders quivering.

'What in God's name is wrong with you? What's wrong, my dear Pavel? Don't be like this. Just you wait. We'll go to Moscow. We'll get the better of them…'

She put an arm round his shoulders, and with the other she clasped his head to her bosom, like a child.

'I'm ashamed, Masha, that I put my own name to a false document. I didn't have the stamina to hold out,' sobbed Pavel Semënovich.

Chapter Thirteen

Pavel Semënovich had a wondrous dream, as if he had been granted an audience with the greatest god, the Lord God Sabaoth Himself.[61]

He had gone up to that same building on which the brass plaque was displayed, with the inscription about the writer Saltykov-Shchedrin. Pavel Semënovich didn't manage to stand and ponder the inscription, since the thick doors, with their bronze handles, parted right before him, and a militiaman (the same one who had stared at him and Mariia so sternly on their first trip) personally insisted that he enter. He took off his peaked-cap and bowed towards him across the door step, saying, 'Do come in, Pavel Semënovich. The top man has been expecting you for some time.'

Anyway… Pavel Semënovich entered the building, and before him appeared the secretary, Laptev, who took Pavel Semënovich by the elbow, with his stone-hard grip,

---

[61] The Lord God Sabaoth is one of the names of God from the Bible. This name stresses the omnipotence of God, and the fact that he is all-conquering in war and conflicts. See James 5 vs.4 and Romans 9 vs.29.

and led him up the wide, white marble staircase, covered in a red carpet. They went up as far as the first floor, where it was so teeming with people that you couldn't even shoot your way through with a cannon. Everyone sat respectfully along the walls, waiting their turn. There was silence all around, just as in church. Only there was no service going on. In the middle of the great hall was a desk at which sat the same old chap, the watchman from the flour mill in Starodubovo. As soon as he caught sight of Pavel Semënovich, he jumped up and dashed towards him. He took him by the other elbow and said: 'Please come this way, Pavel Semënovich. He Himself is expecting you.'

'For what reason?'

'He's granting you an audience without your having to queue!'

'Add his name to the general waiting list!' shouted those who were waiting, beginning to get het up.

'Comrades, comrades! He's not to go down on the general list,' said the old man. 'After all, he's got a daughter-in-law who is a former citizen of the German Democratic Republic. Don't make a fuss. If she turns up, things will be worse.'

'Why?' someone asked in a child-like voice.

'Because, just as we're a most special individual, so is she, as a citizen of the **GDR**. You can't just lump everyone together. It could cause tension due to linguistic difficulties.'

They all fell silent immediately, and the door to the next room opened of its own accord, and in the doorway there was no one – it was pitch-black. Pavel Semënovich felt scared and even came to a halt.

'Go along, go along... The Lord will help you,' said the old man, shutting the door behind him.

There was a sudden flash of light. This hall was even bigger than the one in which the petitioners were sitting. A massively long table stood in the centre of the hall, covered in green material, surrounded on all sides with chairs. At the far end, in an oak armchair, sat God Himself, who looked remarkably like the writer Saltykov-Shchedrin, with a beard and a bald patch: He sat there, looking sternly at Pavel Semënovich and he didn't even blink. Pavel Semënovich completely lost his nerve, his legs turned to jelly, and he would have looked at the chairs around the table, but no invitation to take a seat was forthcoming and he was afraid to take the initiative himself.

'Why have you come here?' asked God, in the voice of Doctor Dolbezhov.

'I wanted to ask you whether a person can know the purpose of life or not?'

'This is a great mystery...' God replied, again in Dolbezhov's voice. 'But why do you need to know that?'

'In order to act according to my conscience,' replied Pavel Semënovich. 'Suppose someone offended me. What should I do? Take revenge upon the offender? But then, I would have to not give a damn about my public duty, because such revenge would sap all my personal strength and time.'

'And for what purpose have you been granted strength and time?' inquired God.

'To be of service to others,' replied Pavel Semënovich.

'How are you of service?' asked God formidably, again in the voice of Dolbezhov. He raised his top lip and picked his teeth with his finger. 'Didn't you put a crown in for me? It wore down in just two years.'

'Nikolai Illarionovich, it was all without ulterior motive. The gold turned out to be of poor quality. Please forgive me,' said Pavel Semënovich, falling to his knees before him.

'You're lying! The gold was pure, it was twenty-four carat... You put too thin a layer on it. You cut corners! Whom are you trying to fool?'

'I'm a sinner, Nikolai Illarionovich... Forgive me! I didn't do it for myself, I didn't profit by it. I fixed a gap in Berta's teeth. I couldn't give her a poor quality crown.'

'Well, since you economized on gold for the sake of a foreigner, you can stand up. That means you didn't do it for yourself, but for one of your nearest and dearest.'

Pavel Semënovich was amazed that Berta's name had done the trick here too. Just think, what power lies in each foreign word! He plucked up courage and asked: 'So what is the purpose of man's life? To be of service to others, or to plough one's own furrow, I mean to stand up for the truth?' he asked.

'Don't ask. Serve God and clothe yourself in peace,' replied God grandiosely.

'And who is God?'

'What's wrong with you – have your eyes rolled back in your head? Or have you gone blind?' asked God, in the voice of Mariia Ivanovna.

Pavel Semënovich woke up with a fright.

Mariia Ivanovna was sleeping next to him, and she had neither a beard, nor a bald patch.

Pavel Semënovich shook her to wake her up, and told her all about his wondrous dream.

'It's a prophetic dream, my dear Pavel. We have to carry on knocking at the door, go to the very highest authorities. We will win, and we shall be clothed in peace.'

'It's easier said than done – to go to the highest authorities. What will it cost us in effort? And in time? You'll neglect your job.'

'To hell with that! Otherwise we shall be consumed by disappointment.'

Thus, Pavel Semënovich temporarily had to set aside his public projects and concentrate on his own affairs. He abandoned his scientific projects relating to peat cutting, starch 'milk', sapropel, lignite, and he even forgot about getting hold of tile specialists from the **GDR**. He did the rounds of the authorities in the pursuit of his narrow, naked truth, though, in the depths of his soul, he begrudged this temporary distraction from his struggle for universal happiness.

He was whisked away to the point of dizziness...

'It's like a sleigh ride in winter,' he confessed subsequently. 'It's like when you don't know where you're going, because the road has disappeared under the snow, and when, all around you, things are seething and whirling, and your face is assailed as if by a thousand devils up to no good, and you're being carried off into the darkness, and you can make nothing out, other than the horse's rear, and you don't have the strength to get out of the sleigh…'

Thus he dashed around in this foolhardy pursuit with the fury of a ravenous man, desperate to satisfy his thirst – to prove the veracity of his personal truth.

Here is an extract from Pavel Semënovich's complaint to the highest authorities:

In August of last year, we approached the residents' association, requesting permission to reposition the entrance door to our flat, so that it opened into the flat for our convenience, and for fire safety regulations.

The town executive committee granted permission for the alteration. Consequently, the repairs and building department, in accordance with the request from the residents' association, repositioned the door by one metre plus a clearance of 35 cm for a flue, which was insulated with felt.

However, Citizeness Chizhenok, who lives next door to us, objected in the strongest terms, claiming that she had nowhere to put her coal and ash bucket, stack her firewood, keep her floor cloths and paraffin stove in the summer (which she puts next to our door). The width of the corridor is one-and-a-half metres, and the length is seven metres, after the repositioning of the door.

Because of this, Citizeness Chizhenok started to write complaints and letters to Soviet and party organizations, demanding that the door be put back to its former position.

Instead of calling her to order, the chairman of Rozhnov regional executive committee, Comrade Pavlinov, for reasons unknown to us, took her side and set about finding ways and means to make us put the door back into its former position, which was dangerous vis-a-vis fire regulations.

In addition to this, Pavlinov threatened us with legal action and the police, and announced that, if he had the time, he'd come to our flat personally to supervise the breaking down of our door.

I, as a disabled person, have a car, which, until August of last year, was kept in a wooden garage built by me, and with permission from the town executive committee in 1958. In response to our refusal to reposition the door to our flat, Pavlinov ordered the fire inspector to seal our garage and forbid us its use, and then required the head of the town fire service to dismantle my garage. Pavlinov allotted me a plot to build a new brick garage in Pupkovo Swamp, beyond the town limits. I should like to know how I, a disabled person, am expected to hobble there on one leg. Might I, perhaps, fly? But, where would I get the wings?

This is the ultimatum Pavlinov has put before us. You may feel like laughing, you may feel like crying.

From 29 August to 1 September 196..., my wife and I were in Moscow, seeking an attorney to defend us. At this very time, having found out that we had gone away to make our complaint, Pavlinov ordered our flat door to be broken into and put back to its former position.

Hence, a criminal act was committed, infringing Article 128 of the law.

There was no court permission or lawyer's authorization to break down our door.

By the way, we put you on notice that the head of the residents' committee, Funtikova, on the order of that same Pavlinov, has taken us to court to order us to put the door back to its former position. But the court dismissed her case, since it was discovered that she, Funtikova, had arranged for our door to be repositioned in the first place.

Consequently, she explained to us the circumstances of our door being broken down: "We were summoned," she said, "to the town executive committee, and we sat and waited. And what do you know? Pavlinov turns up and takes his seat in the office and says: 'I shall sit here, until the door of these usurpers is broken down. Otherwise, I'll sack you.'"

Funtikova said to me, "I also need to earn my crust. So, I got hold of Sudakov and Deserter" (these are our carpenters from the regional communal housing department) "and set about breaking down the door." This is the basis on which the conscience of the head of the residents' committee operates. And as regards the other housebreakers, in what way are they any better than she? But now they are all keeping quiet.

Lieutenant Parfenov, that guardian of peace and order, who was among those who broke the door down, is also keeping quiet. And when the time came to make an inventory of our embezzled goods and money, he pusillanimously ran off. He said, "I am an experienced and seasoned person in such matters. I shall not sign the inventory and I advise others to do likewise."

As well as our own personal effects, we have, in our flat, property belonging to my son and daughter-in-law, a former citizen of the GDR. At the moment they are on a business trip abroad, and we ourselves still do not know which of their things are intact, and which are missing.

During the evening of the 31 August, we received a telephone call from friends, while we were in Moscow, alleging that our flat had been broken into, and that the door had been put back to its former position. We immediately phoned Funtikova, the head of the residents' committee in Rozhnov, to find out whether it was true, or not, that our door had been smashed in our absence. She confirmed it had been, and that Pavlinov had ordered it to be broken down.

The next day, 1 September that is, we went to a meeting with the oblast attorney. We told him that, while we were away, our door had been smashed and repositioned in its former place. His clerk could not believe what we told him. He

said, "Go to the scene and get to the bottom of
what has gone on. If that has really taken place,
address your complaint to the local authorities."

Then we went to the oblast newspaper
Zarechenskaia Pravda, and we told the whole story
to the head of the public correspondence section,
Comrade Syroezhkin. He was indignant over the
facts of this scandalous situation and did not
believe us. We inquired about our letter, which
we had written concerning the slanderous article
in the newspaper Red Rozhnov. As well as our
letter, we had sent off an official document from
the hospital trade union office, pointing out that
the newspaper article contained lies. Comrade
Syroezhkin stated that Feduleev had been informed
by telephone that he should make a verbal
apology in a personal discussion with us. We
expressed our dissatisfaction with that: since we
have been slandered in public, we insist that the
newspaper make a public declaration as to who is
right, and who is wrong.

Comrade Syroezhkin replied: "Our newspaper will
not stand against Feduleev. If you are
dissatisfied with his behaviour, you can take him
to court." Then he stressed that, "Just you
remember – he may well still get at you through
the newspaper again."

During the evening of 2 September, we arrived
back in Rozhnov. We did not go home, but spent
the night in a hotel, and in the morning we
submitted our complaint to Prosecutor Pyliaev. On
his orders, a deputation was assembled to admit us
into our flat. All those responsible for breaking
down our door were included in this deputation.
However, it took three hours to force these people
to convene where all this took place, that is, at
the scene of the crime.

Funtikova, the head of the residents' committee,
and policeman Lieutenant Parfenov, were
particularly unwilling to attend.

The Police Chief Commissioner, Abramov, argued long and hard with Prosecutor Pyliaev, and he agreed to send Parfenov only upon receipt of written orders from the prosecutor's office. However, Abramov had previously sent Parfenov to break the door down without the prosecutor's permission.

While the deputation was convening, a copy was made of the warrant to break our door down, and it was certified with a circular stamp. These are the people who attended the breaking down of our door:

The Head of the Residents' Committee, Funtikova.
The Technical Surveyor, Engineer Lomov.
Flat tenant, Chizhenok, Zinaida.
The local plenipotentiary police officer, Parfenov.
The carpenter, Gunkin (known also as "Deserter")

Please note: Funtikova told us at the same time that there were two carpenters, but the warrant only listed one, and there was only one signature.

It was evening before we gained access to our flat. The carpenter Gunkin (known also as "Deserter") sloped off on the way to the investigation of our building.

On arrival at our flat with the deputation, we discovered that the door had been put back in its former position, but upside down, that is, the bottom uppermost, and what is more, the door was inside out (see the attached photograph). The hinges were affixed to the outside, like straps on a dog kennel, and even then, with only one or two screws in each hinge. It was a simple matter to force them and enter the flat, without even unlocking the lock.

From the photo included, it is obvious that the door is of a stable door design. The French lock was ineffective, since it was fixed to the outside of the door, and the door opened in the opposite direction, and the catches and latches were all on the outside. However, it was impossible to open the door from the inside, without a key. The second lock, a padlock, was secured on two clasps, and each clasp was fixed with a single screw, which could easily be pulled out with one's bare fingers. These clasps were torn off the door when it was broken into, and after the door was turned upside down, the clasps were fixed in their old positions with a single screw, which was simply a joke.

Even in its "locked" state, the door could easily be forced, creating a ten-centimetres gap, allowing the whole flat to be seen. Have a look, choose what you fancy, and enter freely.

Short Addendum: when the door was put back in its former position, the door lintel, the kitchen partition, and the shelf in the kitchen, were all gratuitously smashed.

When we entered the flat, we instantly discovered that: two newly painted planks of wood had gone missing, which I had prepared to replace the shelf above the stove, that had been condemned by the fire inspector. By the way, Lieutenant Parfenov said, in amazement, "Where have they gone? I distinctly remember them being there in the kitchen when we repositioned the door."

Ninety roubles were missing from the pocket of a jacket, hanging in the wardrobe in the kitchen. This money had been made ready by my wife for our trip to Moscow, but it had been left behind by accident (she had put on another jacket). We remembered the money only when we were in Starodubovo. It was too much bother to go back home to get it. Instead, we borrowed fifty roubles from my wife's niece, Kostikovaia, Svetlana Evseevna. She can confirm this.

A woollen, dark-brown, Chinese sweater was missing.

A length of dark-blue, woollen cloth, three-and-a-half metres long, was missing.

Please Note: these items were all in the home-made chest of drawers in the bedroom.

It might be that other things belonging to our son are missing. However, we have not been able to clarify this as yet: I repeat, they are working on an extended business trip abroad.

Members of the deputation did not make an inventory of these outrages, apparently justifying this by saying that they were tired. My wife and I made the inventory. However, the members of the deputation refused to sign it. Parfenov pronounced his famous phrase: "I am an experienced and seasoned person in such matters. I shall not sign the inventory, and I advise others to do likewise. If they don't list the things on paper, then we'll see..."

That very same day I telephoned the regional prosecutor. Comrade Pyliaev said: "Why didn't you use force to make them sign. Sign it yourself, and add a clause to the effect that they refused to sign. Report your missing things and money immediately to the Chief of Police. And don't forget to request that the guilty are brought to trial."

We wrote the report straight away, and submitted it to the police, and to the prosecutor's office. We were even further advised by the oblast prosecutor's office to get support from work colleagues. We did just that. Our hospital radiologist, Orlov, and nurse Glukhova, came to see us. Comrade Orlov even took photographs of our door, locks, and hinges, from all angles. He used flashlight... These are the people who showed real concern for us.

Sensing that things might go awry, members of the deputation scattered to the four winds. It is true that Lieutenant Parfenov brought the carpenter Gunkin with him and ordered him to put the door right (in order to cover up the evidence). However, we did not allow the carpenter to set to work, saying: "Until the executive plenipotentiary comes and makes a record of the crime, we shall not allow the door to be touched."

This is what we were advised to do by telephone from an employee of the oblast prosecutor's office. Furthermore, he advised us: "Get them not only to take photographs, but also, possibly, take finger prints."

On the 5 September, we submitted a second request to the police, asking that an inspection of the door by the executive plenipotentiary be speeded up, so we could lock it and go off to work. Otherwise, we have to sit on guard in the flat by turns, as a consequence of which, my wife has experienced complications at work and she has had to take early retirement.

This second request was submitted to the Deputy Chief of Police, Comrade Pomozov, in the presence of witnesses – namely, my hospital colleagues, Glukhova and Orlov. Comrade Pomozov said, with some considerable displeasure: "You'd do better to do less travelling around, hiding from the authorities. You relied on your locks and look where it got you. If you'd left someone in the flat, there would have been no theft. There's no point in relying on locks."

I objected, saying that, not only had I relied on my locks, but on the police also, and that I hadn't taken into consideration that there were such police chiefs capable of sending their underlings to break down the door of my flat, without having the right to do so.

To this Pomozov replied: "The person who sent them will find the right."

He sent our request and his decision on to the executive plenipotentiary Zhulikov, who had sat on our first request for over two days.[62]

Finally, Comrade Zhulikov visited us at home, that is, at the scene of the crime, on the 15 September with Lomov, two witnesses, and a police photographer. Comrade Lomov, in the presence of the witnesses, confirmed that the door locks and hinges were in the same state as they had been left on the 29 August, that is, on the day of the break-in. It was also established that it was easy to gain access to the flat, even without breaking the door down.

A report should have been made, but Comrade Zhulikov said that he would do that later and that, in due course, we would be invited to sign it.

The photographer started to photograph the door. Surprisingly, he had no flash and it's dark in our corridor - there isn't even a light bulb in it. Evidently, they took us for simpletons and decided to stage a sham investigation. After this so-called "photographing", they wanted us to allow the door to be repaired, thus covering up the evidence of the crime.

I turned to my wife and remarked in a stage whisper: "Masha, these efficient workers have obviously never photographed anything in the dark before. Bring our photographs and let them compare them."

Mariia Ivanovna brought out Orlov's photographs and I gave them to Comrade Zhulikov. He remarked, discontentedly: "You take a great deal upon yourself. We have very sensitive film in our camera." However, he took my photographs with him.

An hour later that day, the carpenter, Gunkin, arrived, but we did not allow him to repair the

---

[62] Amusingly, this name – Zhulikov – is based on the Russian word *zhulik*, meaning 'crook'!

door. Thus we lived for another two weeks with an unlocked door. Finally, on the 2 October, Major Zhulikov invited me to sign the report. He may well have stretched this out even longer had we not telephoned him every day, six times a day – my wife rang in the morning, and I in the afternoon.

A day later, Savushkin came to see us from the oblast prosecutor's office. On questioning us, Savushkin turned his attention only to who had repositioned the door and how, but he swept aside the fact that the door had been forced open, and that things had gone missing from our flat.

We said to him: "This is very strange! Why are you treating this crime as two separate incidents regarding the repositioning of the door, yet you are ignoring the fact that it was broken into and our things were stolen?" He replied: "Let the police deal with the break-in and theft. Our job is to ascertain whether you repositioned the door according to the law, or not." "How come? The people who broke the door down and repositioned it are one and the same. And it's their fault the theft took place. Let them pay for it in full."

We told him that unless he wrote in his report of our cross-examination about the theft of our things, we would not sign it. He did, grudgingly, add our evidence of the theft of our things and the money, albeit right at the very end.

Three days later, the Chief of Police, Abramov, informed us of his refusal to initiate criminal proceedings regarding the breaking down of our door and the theft, and he handed us the decision personally, signed by Zhulikov.

This decision, sanctioned by Abramov himself, throws light on the arm of the law, that is, they are not interested in bringing their colleague to book, and they merely want to conceal evidence. For example, in his ruling, it is stated that the door was secured by two locks, and that it was not possible to get into the flat. However, Zhulikov

himself opened the door in our presence without
even touching the locks! And Lomov did the same
in the presence of witnesses. Why did he write
such nonsense?

And here is yet another hitch in this ruling:
"Witnesses - neighbours living along the corridor
- confirm that no one entered the Poluboiarinovs'
flat while they were away."

How very interesting! One of these witnesses is
Chizhenok, who, in December of the same year,
stole a length of velvet from the state farm shop
and drank away the proceeds. This crime was
discovered by the same police force. We do not
know in what way this matter was concluded.

This whole thing about the neighbours was pure
fabrication: when Comrade Zhulikov was here with
witnesses, he never even set eyes on our
neighbours.

We approached the Rozhnov regional prosecutor
with a request to change this ruling. However,
Comrade Pyliaev refused.

Since that time, wherever we have sent complaints,
they are always returned to us without any
results. Comrade Pyliaev told us, "That is how
this matter will drag on. We are unable to
proceed with this matter, and we do not understand
why the oblast prosecutor's office keeps on
forwarding your complaints to us. Until Pavlinov
is punished - and only the oblast prosecutor can
do this - there will be no progress with your
case."

"Are other people also not guilty?" we asked.

He replied, "Of course others are guilty, but
Pavlinov has coerced them over this matter."

Then he admitted quite candidly: "I myself am
amazed that, in your letters, you write about the
door being broken down and the theft of your
personal belongings, but they write back to you

about repairing and repositioning the door. They
are doing this with an ulterior motive."

We have been carrying on this pointless
correspondence for months. We cannot see an end to
it.

P. Poluboiarinov.

Chapter Fourteen

Then, out of the blue... one fine day, the Poluboiarinovs received two letters by courier, at the same time, one from the police, and the other from the prosecutor's office.

In one document it stated:

29 August, 196... a deputation from Rozhnov town
executive committee in the presence of the local
plenipotentiary, Parfenov, arranged for the
entrance door to your flat to be repositioned in
your absence.

Comrade Parfenov's presence was unwarranted, for
which he has been disciplined by me.

Chief of Rozhnov Town Police Department,

Police Lieutenant Colonel Abramov.

Did you hear that, Mariia? One of them has got it in the neck,' Pavel Semënovich exclaimed with joy.

'Just carry on reading!' Mariia Ivanovna ordered, angrily.

In the other document, the junior counsellor for justice, Pylaev, had written:

...You have already been informed verbally that
the person directly responsible for the breach in
security of your residence, local plenipotentiary
Parfenov, has been held to account...

'When were we informed of this?' asked Pavel Semënovich, raising his eyes in amazement.

'Do as I tell you and read on!' repeated his wife, threateningly.

'So, can't I even ask now?' asked Pavel Semënovich, offended, and he continued to read:

The Head of the Residents' Committee, Funtikova,
E.T., who allowed the deputation to enter your

```
apartment, has also been disciplined, according to
the prosecutor's ruling.
```

'Aha! She's also got what she deserves,' said Pavel Semënovich.

'Not so fast, my darlings! You're not going to brush me off that easily. Until Feduleev and Pavlinov are punished, I'll get no sleep and I'll make sure no one else does either. Let's go to the **oblast** executive committee! Right now!'

'Who's there that we haven't already seen?'

'You fool! This means that the reply to our complaint has gone there. Otherwise it wouldn't have had this immediate effect in two departments. Let's go! Let them hand over the resolution of the Supreme Soviet to us in person. Then we'll see who's dancing to whose tune...'[63]

Mariia Ivanovna turned out to be right, although she did not actually get her hands on the resolution from the Supreme Soviet.

At the reception office of the chairman of the **oblast** executive committee himself, they asked an attractive young woman:

'Is Alexander Timofeevich in his office or not?'

'What is your business?' the young woman dutifully asked.

'We wrote a letter of complaint to the Supreme Soviet, and we have been reliably informed that the answer to it is here,' said Mariia Ivanovna, firmly.

'What is your name?' asked the young woman very politely and even with a hint of fear in her voice.

'We are the Poluboiarinovs from Rozhnov.'

'Just a moment, please!' The young woman darted out from behind her desk and disappeared behind a door – not behind Alexander Timofeevich's, but that of the office opposite, on which was a plaque with the inscription "Deputy Chairman I.V. Akulinov". Akulinov himself appeared in a minute.

'What do you want?'

'First of all, I want to be made aware of the contents of the reply to my complaint from the Presidium of the Supreme Soviet, and in the second place, I very much want to be seen by the chairman himself, Alexander Timofeevich.'

Although Akulinov was a man of advanced years, he seemed rather shy.

'Alexander Timofeevich is not in his office, so I shall ask you to follow me to mine. Lësia!' he said to the secretary. 'Bring me the necessary file.'

---

[63] The literal translation of this sentence is: 'Then we'll see who's dancing the '**kamarinskaia**', and who's dancing [to] "All Along Piterskaia Street".' See Glossary for **kamarinskaia**. 'All Along Piterskaia Street' is also a folksong: it is the sad tale of a lover who leaves his girlfriend behind waiting for him, as he goes along Piterskaia Street, instead of meeting her, as arranged. The song says that he has written a farewell letter to her, not written in ink, but with his tears.

Lësia brought him the file and Akulinov opened it, flicked through it for a moment, then said: 'Comrade Poluboiarinov, where did you get the telephone number for the department of the Central Committee? And why have you been pestering them over this door business?' he asked sternly, though smiling at the same time.

'In our country, Comrade Akulinov, telephone numbers are not secret, and it is strange that you are not aware of that!' replied Pavel Semënovich. 'And I rang them not about my door, but about the fact that for six months my letters of complaint have not been dealt with, in which I have raised matters of great importance to me, namely an infringement of the law by way of a criminal act, personal attacks on me, and humiliation, carried out by so-called members of the Party, who even occupy responsible posts.'

'I would advise you to choose your words more carefully,' said Akulinov. He was smiling no longer.

'Or else what will happen?' asked Mariia Ivanovna.

'I shall inform wherever relevant.'

'I wonder, where that might be?' sneered Pavel Semënovich.

'Why have you come here? To sort out your complaint or to besmirch a host of executives?'

'Give me the ruling to read,' said Mariia Ivanovna.

'There is no ruling. There is a letter addressed to the executive committee.'

'Let me read that letter.'

'I do not have the right. It is merely an internal memo.'

'In that case, we want to see Alexander Timofeevich.'

'You've already been told he is very busy and is out of the office.'

Akulinov looked into the file while answering these questions, read a couple of points, said something, then squinted at the file again.

Mariia Ivanovna nudged Pavel Semënovich, who caught her drift, and so he started to move along the chairs to get nearer to the desk.

'Given that the complaint is ours, the answer should be read to us, and not to anyone else,' said Pavel Semënovich, moving along the chairs.

'Surely you ought to be satisfied that they have been punished?' said Akulinov, interrupting his reading.

'Who are "they"?'

'Parfënov and Funtikova.'

'But it's us that have been punished! My wife has lost her job,' said Pavel Semënovich. By now he was leaning his elbows on the desk, trying to look in the file. 'And loads of our things have gone missing!'

Akulinov shut the file right in front of Pavel Semënovich's nose, and said: 'We are often told of losses of much more valuable things. Even of gold watches. But we can't believe everyone.'

'We don't intend to profit by this,' replied Mariia Ivanovna. 'We didn't write down that we lost two hundred roubles for the fun of it! We lost what we lost. Let Pavlinov pay us out of his own pocket.'

'It's significant that you have eyes on someone else's pocket,' said Akulinov.

'And what about people who are after ours? Someone put his hand in and helped himself...'

'I advise you to consider this fact – you could ruin your health over this door business,' observed Akulinov, looking at them reprovingly. 'And don't write complaints above your station.'

Pavel Semënovich replied to this remark with dignity: 'All I know is this – any abuse of power, even the smallest breach of socialist legality, is inadmissible in our country. No one is allowed to break the law.'

'By the way, I put you on notice,' replied Akulinov, 'the town executive committee has the right to make a ruling about repositioning your door, without inviting you to attend the hearing...'

Pavel Semënovich stood up again, and leaning his hands on the desk, he said: 'Is that the law then? Or is that written in the reply?'

'Please calm down. It's just my personal opinion.'

'There are many opinions, but only one law. I spent money on the train here, my time, and my health... not to seek someone's opinion, but to find justice!' said Pavel Semënovich, getting worked up and banging his fist on the desk.

Mariia Ivanovna also stood up and started shouting: 'Pavel, calm down! Do you hear me? I'm telling you for your own good!'

Pavel Semënovich didn't even look at her, and said: 'Very well! If you think that the town executive committee can make a ruling to reposition my door behind my back and break it down, then put it in writing on that piece of paper. And put your own signature to it!'

'I cannot confirm such a law in writing, but I stand by what I said,' replied Akulinov, who was also red-faced, just as if he had been scalded.

'You can stick your words where it hurts most...'

'And you can shut your mouth, you bloody windbag!' shouted Mariia Ivanovna louder, breaking out in blotches with her nerves.

At this point, an unfamiliar fellow employee came into the office. When he witnessed Mariia Ivanovna, all flushed and waving her arms about, and making threatening gestures at the desk where sat Akulinov, just as red. He said sternly: 'You, Citizeness, don't try going in for hysterical scenes. You're not down at the market, but in an official institution. We've seen it all here. I've seen lots of your type before...'

'And don't you, Citizen, be so rude to an elderly person. She has grey-hair, jangled nerves, and high blood-pressure,' said Pavel Semënovich, rounding upon the employee who had just come in. 'And she has had an operation on her eye for a detached retina.'

'And what are you doing out of your seat?' said the employee, going for him. 'Lolling on a boss's desk! Get away from there! Sit down where you're supposed to... Over there!" he shouted, pointing to a chair by the door.

'Ivan, have you gone mad?' Akulinov asked him. 'He's an invalid.'

'So what? Give him a yard, and he'll take a mile.'

'Would you like me to pull up my trouser legs, so that I can show you I've one leg shorter than the other? I am leaning on the desk due to a combination of unfortunate circumstances...'

At this point, there was a crashing of chairs and Mariia Ivanovna fell flat on her back on the floor.

'Water!' shouted Pavel Semënovich.

'Quickly, get some water!' shouted Akulinov also, running round from the back of the desk. 'Ivan, go on!

'It's all well and good them having nerves, but we're supposed to have nerves of steel,' grumbled Ivan, leaving the room. 'He ought to try my job for size. I bet he'd soon change his tune...'

Lësia came running in with a carafe of water.

Pavel Semënovich started to pour the water on Mariia Ivanovna's temples and chest. At first, she breathed deeply, as if only half-awake, and Pavel Semënovich, afraid that she might start to a curse in her half-conscious state, tried to pre-empt this by saying: 'Masha, here's Comrade Akulinov, who's going to read out the whole resolution to us. You just gently get to your feet. Come on...!'

Mariia Ivanovna opened her eyes and looked with surprise at Lësia, and then at the carafe of water, and she realized what had happened. She grasped her unbuttoned collar with one hand, and she offered the other to Pavel Semënovich: 'C'mon then, help me!'

Pavel Semënovich lifted her a little and she stood up.

Akulinov had left the office and in his place sat the familiar secretary of the executive committee, Laptev, who politely invited them to come over to the desk.

'Mariia Ivanovna, Pavel Semënovich, please come over here, nearer to the desk...'

He held the same file, opened it, and said: 'Comrade Akulinov is not appraised of your case. You should have come to see me. The thing is that a resolution has been made about your complaint by a plenum of the executive committee,' he said, holding up a piece of paper. 'Here is a copy of the plenum's ruling. If you like, I'll read it out for you. So now, as regards the hearing of your complaint,' he mumbled, perusing the document. 'Ah, it's here! Look! The plenum decided that:

> In the first place, it is noted that Comrade
> Poluboiarinov acted correctly in submitting his

application to improve his living conditions.
Secondly, it is noted that Comrade Funtikova acted
inappropriately, taking it upon herself to
arrange the repair without asking the neighbours,
by which, she broke the law and the principle of
popular democracy. Thirdly, members of the
residents' association and other persons having to
do with the repositioning of the door acted in
accordance with the decision of the town executive
committee, in other words, they acted correctly. No
wrongful, punishable act has been committed.
Hence, the plenum has ruled that: First, to censure
the incorrect behaviour of members of the
residents' association, who did not ensure the
security of the Poluboiarinovs' flat. Second, the
town executive committee's ruling that Funtikova
and Lomov have been punished is noted. Third:
Prosecutor Pyliaev's declaration that acting
plenipotentiary Parfenov has been punished is
noted. Fourth: that the editor of the Red Rozhnov
newspaper, Feduleev, is to apologise to the
Poluboiarinovs in an acceptable form. And fifth:
the question of prosecuting Comrade Pavlinov is to
be put before the oblast executive committee when
he returns from study leave.

That's it… And here is my signature. It's a copy certified by me, Laptev. Please take it,' he said, offering the document to the Poluboiarinovs.

'And what about our missing things?' asked Mariia Ivanovna. 'Who will pay for them?'

'There is also a decision on that matter…' said Laptev, taking out yet another piece of paper. 'Here is a ruling from the **oblast** prosecutor.'

Money is to be deducted from Pavlinov's pay during
the course of one year, to the sum of three
hundred and eighty-nine roubles, in favour of
Citizen Poluboiarinov, Pavel Semenovich. This
decision is final and not subject to appeal.

'So this means that he's just got away with having to pay money,' remarked Mariia Ivanovna, unsatisfied.

'Comrades, as far as him being disciplined is concerned, have no fears. As soon as he gets back, he will get his just deserts.'

'And what about the retraction in the press?' asked Pavel Semënovich. 'I refer to an apology from the editor.'

'There's a note on that also. Here it is.'

Laptev put a further sheet of paper on the desk and Pavel Semënovich and Mariia Ivanovna read it:

> Comrade Poluboiarinov
>
> It has come to light that the editor's office of the newspaper, Red Rozhnov, has been misled in publishing material regarding your complaints. The writer of the piece took a partisan view by disregarding the fact that the regional executive committee had not investigated your complaint with sufficient attention to detail.
>
> As a consequence of this, the author of the piece, Smorchkov, has had appropriate measures taken against him. The editor's office offers you an apology for the incorrect publication of this material. As regards publishing a retraction in the press, upon which you insist, it would be assessed by us as new material on an issue which is now closed. We consider such a publication to be inexpedient, since, in this case, it would be necessary to return publicly to the unedifying story of your lawsuit with your neighbours.
>
> Yours respectfully,
>
> *Feduleev, editor.*

Epilogue

Last summer I was in Rozhnov and I popped in to see Pavel Semënovich. He had aged, developed a stoop, and walked with a stick. His 'Moskvich' car stood under his window in winter and summer alike, covered with a tarpaulin. Pavel Semënovich had no further cause to use it: he is now on a pension himself, and Mariia Ivanovna had already left in the spring to go to look after their grandchildren at their son's.

Where the garage stood, there was now an awning, open at the sides, under which there was a stack of firewood and a neat clamp of peat briquettes.

'Look, peat from Pupkovo Swamp,' Pavel Semënovich said to me. 'I've written loads about that, saying that we have peat near at hand, help yourself, don't be idle... But no one listened. Anyway, they've seen the light now.'

To Pavel Semënovich's delight, the bridge is finally being built over the Prokosha River. An asphalt road is even being laid to Rozhnov, and the hardcore is being brought by barge from Kasimov quarry, in a roundabout way: first it travels along the Oka River, then along the Prokosha as far as Sukhoi Shoal, where it is off-loaded onto the bank, from where it is taken by lorries through meadows for fifteen kilometres... but only if it's dry.[64] The meadows are impassable when it rains, and the roads are unusable. Pavel Semënovich could not resist writing out a plan entitled: 'On using the stone quarry on Lysyi Hill by the town of Rozhnov'. He sent it off to the **oblast** committee. It was returned to the Rozhnov regional committee with the instruction: 'To be investigated locally'.

'The first secretary invited me to see him. He's a young chap, well-mannered,' said Pavel Semënovich. 'I told him that we were bringing in hardcore from a hundred and fifty **versts** away, when right by the road we had a whole mountain of stone. The whole of Rozhnov is built of it. Just set to it with a breaker. There's enough hardcore there to lay a road into the depths of Siberia.'

'And what did he say?'

'"I agree, Pavel Semënovich", he says. "But you have to take into consideration", he says, "that the road is of republic significance, but the hardcore is local. There is no official **plan** for it. And we ourselves don't have the necessary funding or equipment. They wouldn't be keen on taking our hardcore: their estimates are based on Kasimov hardcore."'

Pavel Semënovich has got a whole file on the door incident: all the complaints and replies, photographs, reports – all have been carefully filed and numbered. Post office receipts have been kept, railway and bus tickets, telephone bills for conversations made in connection with the hearing of his complaints. On each reply to a complaint, Pavel Semënovich has noted, either in his own sprawling hand in red ink, 'agreed' or, in minute handwriting, a string of objections. For example, on Feduleev's reply, Pavel Semënovich has written:

I object. Seek a public retraction, and, furthermore, in print, in the newspaper.

He wrote his most recent complaint to the neighbouring **oblast**, where Pavlinov now works: 'What form of punishment has Pavlinov been given for his voluntarism, i.e. for his act of hooliganism in the town of Rozhnov?'

No reply to this complaint has been received to date.

1970.

---

[64] The name 'Sukhoi' means 'dry', i.e. Dry Bank/Shoal.

Old Mother Proshkina

Illustration 11. 'Vassilissa in the Forest', Ivan Bilibin (1876 – 1942).

Foreword to Old Mother Proshkina

The story *Old Mother Proshkina* (1966) is one in a cycle of stories to which Mozhaev gave the collective title *Old Stories*: he called them so because, as a collection, they languished in various editors' offices for a long time, because no one would dare publish them. Eventually, some individual stories were published in small groups of two or three, over a protracted period of time, but they did not appear as a complete cycle, as Mozhaev had intended them.

Of all the stories in the cycle, *Old Mother Proshkina* is the darkest. The tone is set by a rather fateful epigraph quoted from Avvakum, an **Old Believer** archpriest. The setting of the story is the vicinity of Kasimov, an area which is redolent of medieval Russian history, associated with old citadels and highwaymen, who were really runaway serfs. Mozhaev mentions two local, legendary heroes – Kudeiar and Staritsa Alëna. For the purposes of this story, Staritsa Alëna is of more interest to the reader, because it is quite clear from early remarks in the text that Mozhaev intends the central character of the story, Proshkina, to be closely associated with this historical character. Staritsa Alëna is reputed to have been a member of **Stenka Razin**'s insurgents from the Penza and Tambov regions, who conducted many raids, seizing and looting the houses of nobles and officials.

Alëna and Proshkina share the sobriquet of '*staritsa*', which in Russian means an 'elderly nun', a Mother Superior figure of a monastic order. According to historical sources, Staritsa Alëna did live in a convent before joining the band of insurgents led by **Stenka Razin**, whereas Proshkina simply lives like a nun. The narrator associates her solitary life with that of a hermit, or cave dweller, comparing her to 'Serafim the Cave-Dweller'. Like a nun, Proshkina also refers constantly to God during the course of her life story, admitting that she is a sinner before God, that God is punishing her, and she frequently invokes God's mercy upon herself. However, this religious and aesthetic approach to life sits ill with her communist and activist background, to say nothing of her earthy language.

Another definition of the word '*staritsa*' is that of a 'dry river bed', i.e. a place indicating where a river once ran. Hence, as with the persona of a nun, this second meaning is also associated with the concept of sterility. Her life was once full and productive, it had a purpose and a goal, and she had played an important role in society on both an ideological and practical level within the Bolshevik regime. But now, she spends her time alone, rowing with and cursing her neighbours, spying on them, and writing letters of denunciation. The world is her enemy, and she appears to take a sadistic delight in being hated. She is sure that her vision of her milieu is the right one, and only she really knows the truth about what is going on around her.

Like a nun, Proshkina has sacrificed her marriage in pursuit of a higher cause. She was married to an ideal, rather than to a husband, and she served that ideal to the exclusion of all other distractions. She lived an ordered, structured life as a party activist, in accordance with her calling. Like a good nun/activist she had dedicated her life selflessly to the cause, doing its bidding with no regard to her own happiness, living according to party rules, to the extent that her husband no longer felt as though he 'owned' her.

There is, however, another side to Proshkina, which is not at all nun-like, and it is more closely associated with Staritsa Alëna – that of witchcraft. This supernatural element is to be found in a number of stories within Mozhaev's cycle of *Old Stories*. Just as Staritsa Alëna was reputed to be a witch and caused battles to be won by her sorcery, so Proshkina is associated with witchcraft and the famous character from Russian folklore, Baba-Yaga. Like Baba-Yaga, her house is rather unusual, and it looks attractive from afar, but rather frightening close up. The horse's skull and dead birds hung on the fence – both features of Baba-Yaga's home – reinforce this association.

Another feature shared between Alëna and Proshkina is their masculine mannerisms. Legend has it that Alëna dressed as a man, at least while she was on the campaign with **Stenka Razin**. Proshkina also, we are told, wears men's clothing, and when she was on official duty and made a speech on the occasion of Kirov's murder, she stood in the town square and the locals were unsure as to which sex she was, owing to her short hair and military garb. Even a female friend Katka, whom she had taken in to live with her for a time, called Proshkina 'masculine'. When Proshkina was sent away to prison, Katka sold all her possessions on the basis that they had lived together like a married couple, which gave her the right to act as she did. This incident does not suggest that Proshkina was a lesbian – Mozhaev would never have countenanced such an idea – but both Katka and her neighbours were firmly convinced of her masculinity.

Another aspect of her manliness is her extreme aggression, as if she suffers from an excess of testosterone. There are other masculine epithets associated with her – 'Woman Hetman' and 'Battleaxe'. Expressed in modern vernacular, the woman is 'butch', and her masculine physical appearance, her demeanour, and her psychological profile are mentioned by Mozhaev on several occasions in the story. She also swears foully, like the proverbial trooper, which is very much a male province in Russian society.

Proshkina's practical skills are also exclusively masculine: she has built her own house, dug an enormous pond in her garden, taught women on the **kolkhoz** to mow with a scythe – traditionally, a male task – and in her early life, she was a skilful stove builder. She has also been 'chairman' of a **kolkhoz**, which, although not an exclusively male province, it was still a rather unusual post for a woman to occupy, and she would have risen to such a position of authority by being assertive, to say the least.

Proshkina is a product of female emancipation and social engineering brought about by the early Bolshevik regime. She straddles the pre-revolutionary period (which was extremely patriarchal), and the post-revolutionary period, when women were granted equal rights – at least in theory. With the Revolution came the dissolution of estates and the demise of her surrogate mother, leaving her orphaned for a second time. Perhaps the camaraderie she found in the Party became a substitute family for her, and the genuine optimism and missionary zeal, which she applied to her role in the Party, are concomitant with the enthusiastic application she had shown in her earlier work at the stove-building cooperative. It is small wonder that such an industrious and committed party worker should rise to the position of **kolkhoz** 'chairman' in 1931. However, she suffered the same fate as many of Mozhaev's **kolkhoz** managers – demotion, but this occurred for her at a particularly dangerous period in Russian history – the Stalinist thirties.

Proshkina is a product of Stalinism: she was totally caught up in the paranoia and messianic zeal of those years to root out '**enemies of the people**', a habit which she finds impossible to shake off, even in the modern era. However, she herself becomes a victim of such a witch-hunt, 'shopped' by her own friend, whose mind is deranged and who believes that the **kolkhoz** system is the work of the Anti-Christ. Proshkina's rationale for keeping up her vigil for **enemies of the people** is that she cannot believe that they have all disappeared – sentiments which the narrator Bulkin expresses in the story *A History of the Village of Brëkhovo*.

By the end of her tale, she is so paranoid that she even fears for her own life, being convinced that if people knew she was keeping detailed records of what she believes to be nefarious activities, they would kill her, as her activist colleagues had been killed in the 1930s. Yet, she is convinced the state has not forgotten her, and that her pension is a reward, in part, for her vigilance and efforts.

Proshkina has a prodigious memory. When the narrator comes to see her again, a full two years later, her mind is still exercised over a lorry load of potatoes, which she believes had been stolen. However, by this stage in the story, it is difficult for the reader to judge whether she is right in her assumptions, or whether there is a perfectly innocent explanation for what she interprets to be a crime. In this sense, Proshkina is a monster and she sends a shiver down the spine of the reader. Her vision of events around her shows her to be an unreformed Stalinist, whose mind had been poisoned by the paranoia of that era, which she cannot rid herself of in modern, more enlightened, times.

However, the question is, Was Old Mother Proshkina a victim of the regime that made her? Can she be blamed for being taken in by Bolshevik and Stalinist propaganda? Certainly she fails Mozhaev's critical test of being able to think for herself. And the whole issue of personal culpability and the role played by individuals who actively supported a repressive regime, which has either burnt itself out or has collapsed, is strikingly pertinent to our modern times.

Certainly, Proshkina is one of Mozhaev's most memorable female characters and, as an activist who played a direct role in collectivization, she prefigures similar characters in his novel *Peasant Folk*.

Old Mother Proshkina

'See, O Listener: Our misfortune is
unavoidable – one cannot get round it.'
Avvakum.

On the open bank of the small river Petravka, a tributary of the Oka River, just below Kasimov, stand some well-preserved earthen ramparts of an ancient citadel.[1] They are fairly steep and high, and when you climb to the top of them up the damp grass, your foot slips and you end up falling on your knees – it's difficult to keep your foothold without a stick. The citadel is so well sited in the area that nothing occludes the panoramic view, not even the dark pine forest lying beyond the small river, which, from there, looks like a shrubbery. Some people say that it is here, in this citadel, that the highwayman Kudeiar once lived,[2] others say that it was Old Mother Alëna... People said, 'And there used to be towers standing at the corners, stretching up into the clouds.' Anything was possible. The citadel could have been a safe hideaway for **Riazan** runaway serfs under Alëna's command, or for ordinary highwaymen – it was a well-chosen place for raids – the Oka River and the old highway were both near by. It was easy to get around.

The old highway had long since gone untrodden. In places, the roadbed had been eroded, in other places, bridges had been swept away in the raging seasonal floods, and in some spots, others had been built... And here and there, patches of the abandoned road remained on the steep-sided, sandy slopes... In places, green patches of arrow-shaped leaves of couch grass, which had forced its way through the stone sets, travelled-over for centuries, had appeared, and clumps of wild grasses too, which had thickly colonized the road edges, untouched by any human being.

A little way off from the citadel, on the highway, there once lay the rich village of Kustarëvka, of which only four brick houses now remained, along with some depressions where houses had once stood. But now they were overgrown with dense clumps of nettles, cotton thistle, and gnarled stumps of felled white-willow, the size of a double arm's width. There were also overgrown patches, colonized by grass and untouched by any form of transport, that were growing over the white stone, which had once been the road.

---

[1] Kasimov is a real town, situated on the banks of the River Oka, a navigable, fresh-water river in the **Riazan** administrative area, not far from Mozhaev's own native village of Pitelino. Mozhaev frequently combines real place names with fictional villages and towns, and he also refers to these places in several unconnected works of his own fiction, even when written many years apart. This area of Russia is densely forested and has many tributaries and waterways connecting with the Oka River. The town was founded in 1152 and it had strong links with the Tatars, who ha left their mark on the architecture of the town, which feature mosques, as well as Orthodox Christian Churches.

[2] Kudeiar is a legendary hero who lived on the Russian steppe in the Don area. He was reputed to be a relative, possibly a cousin, of Ivan the Terrible, and he is celebrated in songs and poetry in Russia. He was a tribal leader, an **ataman**, of Tatar origin, and he was one of several such heroes, like **Stenka Razin**, who rebelled against the establishment and state, and became folk heroes, similar to the English Robin Hood: they represented freedom and the overthrow of oppression. For **Stenka Razin** see Glossary.

Such abandoned, mysterious citadels were legion in this ancient wooded district: they were to be found along the rivers Oka, Moksha and Tsna – all of which constituted the fortified frontier of the **Riazan** principality.[3] However, if one were to believe the old people, in each one of these citadels there lived either highwayman Kudeiar, or Old Mother Alëna with her band of forest runaways. 'Not a single Muscovite warrior could capture her. They got **Stenka Razin** in the end, but they couldn't catch her.' But these were tender-hearted stories with a wished-for happy ending. Old Mother Alëna was captured, though she resisted long and hard, and the Muscovite warrior Dolgorukii had to be sent reinforcements by way of Count Volkonskii. However, folk tales are more powerful than real life. 'Old Mother was never captured, and that's that! She was routed by deception. Then she took to the forest. She built a nunnery. She did the brick laying herself, and she put up the cupola. May God rest her soul!'

It was here that, by this abandoned citadel, I learned of a tale which made me believe that 'Old Mother Alëna was never captured, and that's that!' And that 'she did the brick laying herself and put up the cupola'.

At the edge of the village of Kustarëvka, which comprises only four homesteads, right at the foot of an incline where the wetlands start, clung a strange peasant house which, from a distance, from the citadel ramparts, I noticed had an unusual chimney: it wasn't exactly a bucket protruding from the thatched roof, and not so much a tin bowl with a very wide bell-end pointing upwards, something like a megaphone or a loud-speaker, which can usually be seen fixed to a pole in holiday resorts. One could just imagine a witch flying out of such a tube on her broomstick with the greatest of ease. Who thought up such an absurd thing? What kind of crank was that person?

It was only when I got nearer to the house that I noticed that the inside of the chimney was made of brick, and that it was only encased with tin-plate on the outside and secured by a wire. Why was that?

By the way, the question 'Why was that?' came to my mind time and time again. On the lath fence around the curtilage of the homestead, which led into the yard, hung a dead crow. In the front garden, above antediluvian, conical-shaped beehives, made from hollowed-out logs, some white horse skulls hung on white willow trees.[4] But the most enigmatic of all was the peasant house. It was constructed of logs of the most varied gauges – at the foundations, the rows of beams were thick and quite ordinary, but as the walls went higher, the logs became thinner and thinner, so that finally, at the eves, they were virtually poles, which made the whole building look almost like a play thing – whimsical, as if it had been put together as a joke. From a distance, I also noticed the unusual fretwork of the veranda, which looked like a woven lath frame, like a chess-board panel of trellis. But close up, this trellis looked to be woven out of thin, white sticks: it was, in fact, made of stripped lime-tree withies. And once again, it struck me that it had been made as a joke. And the window frames were of the most varied sizes, some large, some small. Some of them, the smaller ones, were fixed vertically, but others, the longer ones, were set horizontally along the wall. It was an absolute marvel!

---

[3] Ancient Russia used to be divided into 'principalities' or areas of land under the control of feudal 'princes'.
[4] The scene Mozhaev paints here is reminiscent of the traditional portrayal of a Russian folkloric witch called **Baba-Yaga**. See Glossary.

But upon a closer look, I realised that it had all been constructed not without design: all these anomalies were created more out of need, than out of eccentricity. Necessity is the mother of invention. In fact, had the long window frames been placed vertically, they would not have cleared the eves. From out of the tin-plated bell-end, a flue poked out, which had been made out of half-bricks. If it hadn't been covered in tin plate and secured with a wire, it would have collapsed. Even though the logs in the framework were rather too thin, and the old ones had served their purpose, under the windows there was a row of new ones, good and thick, and the upper row under the rafters was also sound. The whole look of the house was a rather touching, yet vain, attempt at artistry – in place of window frames adorned with fretwork, some white sticks had been fixed in intricate patterns, and the eves sported those same trellis panels. At first glance, you'd think it had been made out of straw…

'From a distance it looks like lace, but close up it's scary. Don't you think so?' someone remarked behind my back, in a husky voice.

I jumped and turned round. An old woman was approaching me from behind, plodding and dragging her feet, shaking her large, closely cropped head. She was wearing an undershirt tucked into a grey skirt, covered in mud and ripped at the sides, which made it look like some kind of enormously wide pirate's trousers. As well as this, one could just glimpse some red, mud-caked trousers from beneath her unpicked hem. She wore galoshes, which were tied on with wire to her calloused, bare feet. Her large, dirty, masculine arms and hands, with their crooked fingers, hung right down to her knees in front of her: she looked as though she was carrying them like dumb-bells, suspended from her neck. And under her low-necked top, cut on the oblique, her emaciated breasts, partly covered by a brass cross, hung just as lifelessly as her arms.

'You lost in admiration, darling?' she asked, coming to a halt and looking at me with her wan eyes.

'I'm just looking at your house, at how interestingly it's been built,' I replied, feeling rather disconcerted by her prolonged, unblinking stare.

'I charge for looking. My place here is not a theatre or a market… So get on your way.' She started hobbling away from me, muttering to herself, 'They stick like flies to honey. There's no end to them, God save us! I can't leave the house for two minutes.'

It was only at this point that I noticed the cart that the old woman had left near the fence. It was loaded high with grass and its wooden shafts were stretched out in front. It was all in order, just as it should be, as if just pulled by a horse. The cart was not a large one and it had iron wheels which had once belonged to a plough, but even so, the grass was fresh and heavy, and the load was higher than the fence. Surely she hadn't really pulled that all by herself? Or had she used a cow, or a calf?

The old woman opened the gate in the fence, took hold of the shafts and she moved the cart forward with surprising ease and, walking backwards on her bow-legs, she pulled it into the yard. Now that's what I call a draught animal!

Her outhouses were simple – they were thatched, little edifices, resting on white willow poles, surrounding a stone storehouse on all sides. At one time, they had just been stout columns, or, to be more exact, willow stakes, but now they had filled out and developed into white willows, which bore the thatched roofs high on their boughs.

Behind these sheds lay a small garden, which had become overgrown with elder and nettles along the lath fence. At the end of the garden was a fairly large pond with recently levelled banks, surrounded by a dense thicket of white willow trees. Ducks swam on the pond. The pond was clean and well-kept. Who had dug it out? Surely not the old woman?

I sat down on a hummock near the pond and racked my brains as to how I might strike up a conversation with the old woman.

Suddenly, from behind a distant clump of elder by the old, abandoned road, I heard the clear sound of a whetstone against a scythe – scrape, scrape, scrape! At that moment the old woman came out from her yard.

'Hey, you scrounger! Get lost, or I'll cut your heels! You mother-f...!' The old woman gave an evil whistle and let out a long stream of foul effing and blinding...

A peasant woman with a scythe looked out from behind the clump and also started to swear foully:

'How about I stick some salt up your arse?'

'I'll grab that scythe and...'

'C'mon then, come here and grab it! I'll show you! I'll cut off those bloke's kegs of yours!'

'You thief! Who are you ripping off? An old woman, that's who!'

'It's **kolkhoz** grass. You've been forbidden to scythe here, so stop yer blathering.'

'I'll stir up my bees and that'll change the colour of your mug.'

The old woman began to hobble back towards her front garden, but I went over to the woman with the scythe. She looked no more than forty years old: she had a broad face and was short and stocky, and she wore an ample, white-speckled top and a long skirt down to her heels, and she was barefoot.

'What's the argument about?'

'Sod her! She's been forbidden to cut grass here, then she goes effing and blinding. I'm used to her...'

'Who's forbidden her?'

'The **kolkhoz**. She was given fifteen **sotki** of land, together with that pond and told to keep to it. This is our grass, **kolkhoz** grass.'

'And whose is the pond?'

'Hers. She dug it herself, out of stupidity. But she goes into the forest to get grass with her **tarantass** and effs and blinds at the **kolkhoz** workers.'

'Who is she?'

'She was once a **kolkhoz** chairwoman. She kicked up a rumpus all over the district... She's called Proshkina.'

'Anna Ivanovna?'

'Perhaps she is Anna Ivanovna. Who knows? Around here, people call her Old Mother Proshkina, because she's become a recluse. Anyway, how do you know what she's called?'

'I've just heard...'

Anna Ivanovna Proshkina. How did I not guess straight away? My aunt had even told me about her – she was an old friend of hers. I had even once seen her myself, when I was a child. She had worn a black, knee-length sheepskin coat, trimmed with grey lambskin, a grey **papakha**, set at a jaunty angle, and she made a speech in our village at a meeting on the day Kirov was murdered.[5] I remember the market square, chock-full of sleighs and horses tied up all along the wooden stalls, and the peasant men and womenfolk in their felt boots and **bast shoes**, wearing uncovered sheepskin coats and black, gathered, patent leather, or long brownish-grey Ukrainian coats, with their round, buttoned-up collars – a whole dark, mass of people seething, pushing each other, surrounding a half-ton lorry covered in red calico. In the back, as if on a rostrum, stood about ten people: two of them were carrying a banner made of red fabric fixed to white planed sticks, and along the fabric it read in whopping great letters – 'NO MERCY FOR **ENEMIES OF THE PEOPLE!**'

Of all the speakers, I remember one – a paramilitary in a grey, knee-length winter coat, wearing a Budënnii hat, and Proshkina...[6] When the band struck up the 'International' and someone shouted out 'Hats off!', the first person to take off her hat was Proshkina, revealing her straight, closely cropped hair and her fringe, which covered her temples, lending her a stubborn and pugnacious air.

'What a devil! She's had a bloke's haircut...' exclaimed someone in the crowd.

'Who knows, she might be a bloke?!'

'She's twin-harnessed!'

'Ho, ho, hee, hee!'

'Shush!'

Anna Ivanovna Proshkina. An **ataman**-woman. A battleaxe. And this was how she had remained. How could I recognise in this old woman that vociferous virago? Even though my aunt had just told me about her, she prevailed upon me to go and see her for myself... 'Now she lives like Father Seraphim the Hermit.[7] Honest to God, it's true! Go and see, you'll be amazed...'

---

[5] Sergei Mironovich Kirov (1886-1934) was head of the Communist Party in Leningrad and he was a firm supporter of Stalin. He was a major force in the push for rapid industrialization in the Leningrad region. He was shot in his office in December 1934, and this event sparked off a wave of searching out enemies of the regime and of recriminations: the net was cast wide and propaganda about hunting out **enemies of the people** was intensified. Stalin used the incident to grant yet more powers to the secret police, then the **NKVD**, which meant that people could be arrested, tried and shot at will. Few peasants had any sympathy for the death of any communist activist or leader.

[6] See footnote № 33, p.109.

[7] Seraphim (or Serafim) the Hermit or 'cave dweller' was not a particular person, but one of a type. 'Cave dwellers' or hermits of this type were part of a sect which sprang up in the 1860s, and they were people who wanted to retire from the world and lead an aesthetic life.

From the stories I'd heard, I thought that she lived somewhere in the woods, at the back of beyond. But here she is, living by the side of the old highway, just three **versts** away from the **kolkhoz** offices and the large village of Zheludëvka.

I went into her front garden and said: 'Hello, Anna Ivanovna. I'm here to see you about something,' I said, announcing my name, and saying that I had come from my aunt.

She lifted her head sharply and turned round from her beehive, staring at me again with that unblinking look.

'And how do you know her?'

'I'm her nephew.'

'Her nephew! Oh, dear God!' she said, clasping her hands. 'Why didn't you say so right away? I thought you'd come from the **kolkhoz** office, to make an inventory of the hay.'

'Not at all! I want to make a deal with you. My aunt asked me to leave you a deposit,' I lied.

'Oh, my dear God!' she said, slapping her thighs again. 'Well I never, my beautiful friend has not forgotten about me. How is she? Hale and hearty?'

'Fine, thank God.'

'But what are we doing standing out here? Come into the house. I'll give you some honey. And I'll put some tea on.' She hobbled over towards the veranda. 'It's true, I don't have a samovar. But I'll boil up some water in my iron pot and make a drop of tea – raspberry tea. Now, don't turn your nose up at it, darling.'

As I walked past the white willows with the horse's skull, I asked her: 'What's this thing for?'

She gave a cunning smile and stuck out her lower lip: 'It's an old charm. A horse's head keeps the bees from swarming.'

'Do you believe that?'

'Believe it if you like, don't if you don't want to. I won't speak of God, sinner that I am. But something tells us it's true.'

It was dark inside the house due to the low ceiling, which had been lined with tin-plate. Although the walls were plastered and had once been whitewashed, now they were black from smoke. The floor, which had been made out of lengths of wood from old vats, was warped, like waves. All the furniture in the house – the table, bench, the bed, and the chair – was all made out of pieces of birch. The white birch-bark lent a certain elegance, even an individual, decorative quality, to it.

'Who made the furniture for you?' I asked.

'Everything here, from the lowest row of beams to this stove here – it's all my own work.'

'But surely someone helped you?'

'No. No one.'

'And did you put up the roof timbers yourself?'

'Yes, I did. I marked them out on the ground, then cut them. Then I put them up myself.'

'And what about the framework?'

'I cut it all myself.'

'And did you put the roof on by yourself?'

'Yes, all by myself. First of all, I threw the timber up there, then I climbed up and forced them into place with my feet...' Suddenly she wiped away tears from her cheeks. 'Ah, Lord God Almighty! I've done my time living in a dug-out house, travelled around a lot, and I did a long stretch in prison...'

She turned away abruptly, sobbing profoundly, took down a dry log from the stove and started to pare off some spills.

She lit a fire in the hearth of the stove and put the cast iron pot of water onto the trivet.

'That's my samovar! You just sit either in the little chair, or on the bench.'

'Thanks! I'm still marvelling at how you managed to build this stove out of brick rubble.'

'I used mud. My mud here is as strong as cement. It doesn't crack with the heat. I got it from the pond.'

'You'd have to make bonding layers, then lay the hearth-stone, then the upper section. Did you do all that out of half-bricks?' I asked in amazement, examining the stove.

'Ah, my dear. I've built so many of these stoves in my life that you couldn't count them, like hairs on your head. It was through stoves like this that my life went all wrong.'

'Because of stoves?'

'Yes. I learned the craft when I was a child. Then in the village I became the best stove builder, going round all the homesteads. Everyone knew me. That's how I got on. People used to applaud me.'

She stood by the hearth, illuminated by the flickering fire, and looked somewhere down towards her feet. Her grey eyebrows, so high on her forehead that they looked as though they were glued on, lent to her face an expression of agonizing bewilderment.

'I was plucked away, like a starling-house from a tree, and thrown to the ground. I felt, and still feel, like an empty box.'

'How did all that happen?'

'Oh, it's too long a story.'

'Do you at least get a pension?'

'No.'

'Why not?'

'They say I don't warrant it.'

'Who says?'

'Tararyshkin, the chairman of the regional executive committee. He says I haven't worked enough to be awarded one.'

'And what about the **kolkhoz**?'

'The **kolkhoz** here is nearly broke. They haven't even the money to settle **workday units**, let alone pensions.'

'Let them pay you as a homeless person!'

'Tararyshkin says that they have limited numbers for the homeless category. He says, "Wait your turn".'

'So, what have you been offered?'

'The workhouse! And if you don't want that, then wait until the state gives pensions to **kolkhoz** workers.'

'Why don't you go to an invalid home?'

'You'd die of boredom and of nothing to do there. I'm my own boss here.'

She had a point, but she was like stone – you'd never move her. So I didn't press the point.

'What is your official status: worker, civil servant, **kolkhoz** worker?'

'Me? I'm no one.'

'But surely you must at least have some official documents?'

'And what documents would they be?! The Party refused me documents. In those days there were no **work-record booklets**. I've a certificate there to say I did my time in prison.' She opened a table drawer, which was crudely nailed together, and took out a bundle wrapped in a cloth, then handed it to me. 'Here,' she said.

I undid the cloth binding. In it there was indeed a certificate, issued from the N-skii Criminal Investigation Department, attesting to the fact that Citizen Proshkina really had completed her period of incarceration.[8] In addition, there were another two yellowish booklets with cardboard covers – one with a red cross on the cover, the second with an inscription in large letters – MOPR.[9] Both these booklets were made out to Proshkina as far back as 1928, and on the inside, tiny stamps were affixed to confirm that membership dues had been paid. Also in the bundle was a warrant from the regional land department, issued in June 1931. On it was written that the worker from the women's section,

---

[8] The 'N-skii' is merely a literary convention to indicate an anonymous or undisclosed region.
[9] This is a Russian acronym, which, translated into English means The International Organization for Aid to the Campaigners for the Revolution. It was founded in 1922 with the aim of providing moral and material support to international revolutionary causes, and it was also a producer of information and propaganda for the communist cause, in many languages. It ceased functioning as an organization in September 1939. It had as its insignia a large red cross, referred to in the story, which stood for 'International Red Assistance', the original name of the organization. Red was the colour associated with the communist cause.

Proshkina, Anna Ivanovna, was being sent to the village of Eremeevka with a recommendation from the chairman of the **kolkhoz**.

'How come you've kept all this?'

'It was your aunt who kept it all. When I was detained on trial, she would come and visit me, to bring me communications. And I gave her these papers. They went to her in the first place. Did she not tell you all about this?'

'Yes, she did…'

I recalled my aunt's story: 'One evening, there was a scratching at the door. What on earth is it, I thought? Is it a stray cat or chicken? I opened the door and there stood a beggar in a padded jacket with a tatty bag. "Now, I'll give you what for!" I said. But she replied: "Anna Ivanovna, surely you recognise me?" "Is that my name's sake?" "It's me, Aniuta…" And she cried, her tears streamed down her face… She lived with me for a week and then went off. "Mind how you go!" "Every sparrow has its own nest. And I have hands and legs, thank God." Then she left…'

'Could you tell me your own story, Anna Ivanovna?'

'I could tell you. Why shouldn't I? When we've nothing more to tell, we've become totally brutalized. Here, I talk only to the ducks and the turkeys – and I swear and curse at people.'

She put the cast-iron pot, which had just boiled, on the table, and from somewhere under the table she produced a couple of cut-glass tumblers. They were so dusty that they must have lain untouched for at least a year. First, she wiped them with her finger, then with a dirty oven glove which was hanging near the stove hearth, and finally, she blew hard into each one and put them on the table.

'I myself drink out of a mug. I don't have visitors, apart from your aunt, Anna Ivanovna, who comes once a year to buy hay. I've got some nice fresh honey, straight from the honey comb. You drink, darling, drink!'

She brought the honey over in an earthenware bowl, and on top were two small spatulas, which had been carved out of stripped lime wood. She didn't drink her own tea: she just stared with her wan, unblinking eyes, looking down at her feet. Her eyebrows were just as raised on her forehead, motionless, and the same expression of agonizing bewilderment was stamped all over her face.

'My father died in the Japanese War, and my mother died as well…[10] I was just eight years old. I remember as if it were yesterday – we were working for a **barynia**, Bekmuratova, gathering in the hay. It was a warm, calm day. We kids gathered up the sheaves of hay, and the menfolk made hayricks. The **barynia** ran a tight operation: a hayrick had to be made of ten cartloads. We used to pile it up as high as a bell-tower. When it was capped, the men would have to lift the last bundle in pairs, and if there was a breeze, they used to sway like drunks. What high hayricks they used to make! They put my mother up top to cap the rick. She used to do a good job trampling it down and making it nice and even on top. When they'd finished, it looked like it had been licked smooth. "Well, Fedora, you could have made a great peasant man!" they said, poking

---

[10] This is a reference to the Russo-Japanese War of 1904-5.

fun at her. But she paid for her skill with her own death... You see, that's what our fate was like. She finished the hayrick, and she was putting the marker on the top.[11] But she slipped... She grabbed hold of the marker and pulled it down with her, falling head first onto the ground. It was dry. The soil was rock-hard. People brought her some water from the pond and wetted her face, thinking she would come round. She just about opened her eyes and looked at me. I was there, kneeling beside her, howling. And her friend, Old Ma Uliana, was standing by me, crying. "Alënka," she said, "take my girl for your own..." And with those words, she passed away. She thrashed, then shuddered, and blood streamed from her mouth. And that's how I became an orphan.

'Alëna became my second mother. I used to call her "Mother Alëna". She was a dyed-in-the-wool landless peasant, without her own house, and she lived in the **barynia's** house. I stayed with her there. The **barynia** used to love birds – geese, ducks, and turkeys. There were meadows and lakes nearby. There was loads of open space. So, I started working with Uliana in the poultry house. We had a huge number of chickens alone – over a thousand. But the **barynia** was strict! She would turn up herself to feed them, or watch us feeding them. And the stuff we gave them to feed on! We gave them ground chalk and fish. The herrings alone arrived by the barrel load. We used to cook them in a cauldron and they stank the kitchen out. But, I was just young and silly. I once put some sand in the pot. The **barynia** stomped her feet and shouted at me: "Under that stove!" I crawled under the stove together with the chickens. That's how I got my nickname, Aniuta-Under-The-Stove. And Old Ma Uliana was sacked from the poultry house because of me. She got another job in a brick cooperative, mixing lime and fetching water. And I kneaded the clay for all the stove-makers. I got splattered with it up to my belly-button. "Hey, Under-The-Stove! The hem of your skirt is all wet again. Watch out, or you'll never get a husband!"[12] I was very nimble. As soon as we started kneading the clay, not a single bloke could overtake me, they'd be all kneaded out! I was happy doing that work. I had a go at stove-making as a kind of joke. I turned out to be a real 'under-the-stove' builder! I had no equal. I might have soon settled down to a family life, but the war came... Then the Revolution. The **barynia** ran away and the estate was pinched, bit by bit. During the famine, Uliana and I got jobs at the stables.[13] We were totally worn out by the work. Mother Uliana used to draw water for the horses. That's where she died, right by the well, with buckets in her hands. And I was all alone once again...'

A bee flew in through the open window, hovered over the cup with the honey in it, and it flew up to my head. It got caught up in my thick shock of hair and started thrashing around, making a high-pitched, pitiful buzzing. Proshkina instantly dashed to its call. She deftly extracted it from my hair with her crooked fingers, put it onto her palm and offered it up to her lips, repeating: 'What are you doing, you silly little thing, getting all

---

[11] When the hayrick was finished, a piece of wood was placed on the top as a marker to indicate that the work on it had been completed and no more hay needed to be added.

[12] This is a play on words: the verb here 'to wet' has a secondary meaning, as part of an expression used with words like 'reputation' or 'record', when it means 'to spoil', i.e. to spoil one's reputation, to blot one's record, etc. The man implies that if she had a 'stained reputation', her chances of marriage were slim.

[13] The First World War, which broke out in 1914, precipitated the abdication of the tsar Nicholas II in February 1917, which in turn led to the Bolsheviks seizing power in the October Revolution of 1917, and the subsequent formation of the Soviet Union. The Civil War, which ensued after the October Revolution, had a disastrous effect on Russia's economy and food supplies and there was widespread famine.

het-up? The Lord be with you! You're among friends here. Ah, you silly little thing! C'mon now, calm down.'

The bee did in fact calm down and, when it had crawled around for a moment on her chapped palm, it took off and flew out of the window.

'Three swarms arrived here recently. I would have looked after them, but I don't have the hives and I don't have anything to make them out of.'

'Where did they come from?'

'From the neighbouring village. Homestead owners are useless nowadays. Ah, those mother-f...' Once again, she swore like a trooper, just as she had recently done at the peasant woman. 'It's one thing to rear something, breed them – they're a gift from God, but they can't even hang on to them. People are always hankering after someone else's stuff. You should see just how many white willows have been left alone in Kustarëvka. They've all been sawn down. And they've got their eyes on mine. I used to be able to mow hay from around my house – I use to get two whole cartloads in a trice. It lasted me the whole winter. But now it's forbidden. At the beginning of spring, a whole **brigade** descended on me, with their scythes. Ah, it was a bit overcast that day, otherwise I would have set the bees onto them, the shits. The bees would have shown them what for, for cutting someone else's grass.'

'Why don't they let you mow here?'

'Out of spite. They just do it to needle me.'

'Who does?'

'Those mother-fuckers, the **kolkhoz** bosses...'

'Why?'

'Because I'm always on their backs. I make a note of all their swindling tricks and send complaints off to wherever necessary.' She lent towards me and said in a quieter, constrained, husky voice: 'They're all crooks. I know. They think I sleep at night. But I lock up and go off to Zheludëvka. I sneak and crawl around back yards and streets. I hang about barns and under windows.'

She stood up, went over to the foot of the stove and plunged her hand deep into it: she pulled out a bundle of papers wrapped up in a cloth and handed me a rolled-up exercise book.

'Look, I have everything written down in here.'

I opened the book and in it several leaves had been written on in indelible pencil in uneven letters – some thick-black, others spidery.

'Look, read here!' she said, pointing to a line and read it herself: "**Brigade leader** Semiglazov, on the night of 27 August 1961, arrived with five sacks of rye. He dragged the sacks into the storehouse himself and his wife held the light. On 30 January 1962, that same Semiglazov took a whole load of rye to market." A note of it is made here. The question is: Where did he get the rye from? He stole it from the threshing floor. And the beekeeper Kolobok brought a whole small barrel of honey to the chairman. It's all noted down here: "On the night of 10 July, the head of the sheep unit ate a **kolkhoz** sheep." That's what they get up to! And how many cows have snuffed it! In times past, we were had up for things like that. I write and write about this kind of thing, but it all rebounds on me.'

She rolled the exercise book up again, carefully wrapped it in the cloth, tied it firmly, and put it back under the stove.

'If they found out I'd noted all this down, they'd murder me at night.'

'Don't you worry. I won't tell a soul. But what do the authorities do about your letters?'

'An inspection team did come once. But they all made a deal. It was through that that I was forbidden to mow the grass around my house. So now I take my scythe and cart, and I go off into the woods. I mow there. I should dry it where I cut it, but I'm afraid they'll steal it. So I put the damp hay on the cart and bring it home. The grass is heavy. If you hit a sandy area, the wheels get stuck. I struggle and struggle and end up falling down. Then I cry my heart out,' she said, breaking into a sob and wiping away the tears. 'Oh, Lord! Oh My Lord! Why do you torment and try me so? Have I offended you in any way?'

'Anna Ivanovna, perhaps they are turning a blind eye to these petty crimes?'

'How do you mean "petty"? In times gone by, we used to be had up for a pocket full of ears of corn. But this is a whole load of rye! That's not "petty", it's sabotage. I know. I was a Party member from 1927. It's not for nothing that they taught us how to seek out **enemies of the people**. I shall expose them yet. There's no hiding the truth. No way..! Anyway, you drink, drink!' She poured me out another glass of raspberry tea.

The colour of it was bluish-grey, either from the raspberry leaves, or from the cast-iron pot, and it gave off a kind of astringent, iron smell. But the honey was fresh and aromatic.

'Anna Ivanovna, you said that Mother Uliana died. What happened then?'

'What next? I got married.' Once again, she looked long and hard down towards her feet. 'I used to work with him in the same co-operative workshop. He was a submissive bloke, puny, not really my type at all. But I'd been all over the place, like a drifter. I wasn't fussy. I moved in with him. He was part of a large family: apart from the old folk, there were his three brothers-in-law, two of them were of marrying age, and the third one, the eldest, had a tribe of kids. The house was poky. What kind of life is that for a young couple, to be cramped like that? I tried talking my husband round, saying, "Let's split and get our own place." But my father-in-law was such a strict man! "Go on," he says, "pack your bags and that'll be your lot!" I had put some money aside from my stove building and so we bought a house for seven hundred roubles. We had a house, but nothing else to call our own. But it was like they say, there's no shame in being poor. All the money we had went on the house. We rented out our land for horses to graze on, and we went around the farms, working. I was known throughout the whole district – I built a stove for some people, I helped in the field for others. I was elected to the poor committee. We worked by day, had meetings by night. I also attended literacy classes. One minute you're studying, next you're in a meeting. They started pulling my husband's leg because of me: "It's not you who owns your wife, but she who owns you."[14] He started to get jealous and followed me in the evenings. Once, the meeting went on until half-past midnight. I left with everyone else, with the other four blokes from the poor committee. But my husband came out to spy on me. We'd only just gone our separate ways when he set about me with a stick. But I beat him off so hard that he lay there till morning. He just about came to. We had to go to court – his family put him up to it. "What's your problem?" asked the bench. "She neither feeds nor waters me." "Where will you go?" "If I get my share, then I'll go to live at my father's." "Will you have him?" they asked the old man. "If he gets his share, then I will." So the judgement was to divide the house half-and-half. But what was there to divide? I didn't give a damn, and I left. I went down to the nearest station, to the depot. I went to fetch some bread for the workers and fed them all. I stayed there, working as the head of the local social security department. At that time, I finished my literacy course and became a member of the Party. But I had an awful time: my husband pestered me, along with his relatives. They used to follow me, they made one scene after another. So I decided to leave my native area and start all over again. I complained to the organiser of the women's association: "It's too awkward for me here. Let me go away, anywhere away from here." So she sent me off to Kaluga.[15] There, a two-year party school had been started in the old church-school building. That was the one I had graduated from. I went to the Moscow **oblast** committee offices to find out what job I would be given. "Where d'you want to go?" they asked. I looked at the map and chose a place nearest to water. That area once used to come under the Moscow **oblast** boundaries. We arrived at the regional offices, me and a friend, Feshka Sapogovaia. She was a women's association organiser and I was a cultural organiser. Feshka settled in her house, and I bunked down at Uraza's place. You might remember her.'

'I don't know your friend. But I remember Uraza well. That was her nickname.[16] She was a podgy old girl. As kids, we used to tease her and say, "Eriaperia has pointy little ears, Uraza has a pot belly".'

Proshkina broke out laughing.

'In our village everyone had a nickname. Feshka and I were called "The Magpies". We were young and we used to talk a lot. We often had to get up and make speeches. So that's why they called us that.'[17]

'So why did you come to our district?'

---

[14] In traditional peasant households, the wife was widely regarded as her husband's property and she was expected to be subservient to him: before the Revolution, women were not allowed to vote in village gatherings on rural matters. With the establishment of the new communist regime, women were eventually granted equal rights with their husbands and they could become independent members of the **kolkhoz** in their own right, irrespective of their husband's status or membership. Women gradually took on jobs and duties which they had not done before the Revolution, but the old patriarchal habits and ideas, traditionally held by the peasantry, took many years to change. As a political activist, and subsequently a **kolkhoz** 'chairwoman', Proshkina was very much in the minority, and she would have been viewed with a great deal of suspicion, disapproval, and even animosity by her peers.

[15] Kaluga is a large town situated on the Oka River, about 200 km to the south-west of Moscow, and it has also given its name to a whole **oblast**. Kaluga itself was first mentioned in records in 1371. During the Soviet era, it had a number of major, heavy industry plants.

[16] Uraza is a typical nickname given to a rural inhabitant: nicknames were usually based on physical characteristics or based on some defining feature of the person. This word denotes the act of fasting during the time of Ramadan for Muslims. Hence, the name would suggest that she is a Muslim herself.

[17] The magpie in Russian folklore has the reputation of talking a great deal and very quickly.

'There's forest all around, and rivers and lakes. I lived for a long time in the steppe and got fed up of it. And I love fishing anyway. I dug my own pond in the garden. Did you see it?'

'You can't have dug that out all by yourself!'

'All alone. It took me five years. I was looking for a seam of gold. I used to go off there and just dig. No one could see me, and I could see no one either. Ah, Lord God Almighty!'

'How did you come to be a **kolkhoz** chairwoman?'

'This is how it happened. Although I was officially a cultural organiser, more often than not I was entrusted with getting hold of grain.[18] I used to go round all the villages as a plenipotentiary. We got a new secretary, Savostin. He asked me to come and see him and said, "What is your job?" "Cultural organiser", I says. "What use is a cultural organiser?! Our culture now is grain. You go and be chairwoman of the **kolkhoz** at Eremeevka." A warrant was issued from the regional executive department and I was taken in a **tarantass** by the chairman of the regional executive committee to the village. Nowadays, chairmen are elected. But then, it was all a lot simpler. You arrived at the **kolkhoz** and off you went to work. No one bothered whether you were a chairman or a **brigade leader.**[19] When harvest time came, you grabbed your scythe and off you went into the fields. Everyone used to work. When I went mowing, I was one of the best. My scythe used to ring out – it had three crowns on it.[20] Just try to keep up with me when I get started! People used to call me "Peaked Cap".[21] The womenfolk used to grouch about me: "Have you ever heard the like, sending the womenfolk out to mow?" At that time women didn't used to do the mowing. They went out to reap, but not to mow. I taught them how to do it. But they thanked me for it later, when there were no blokes around. "Thanks to you, Peaked Cap, for teaching us to mow. At least now we can mow enough hay for our cattle." Ah, what haven't I done during my life, what haven't I turned my hand to...? It's just like they say, beggars can't be choosers.'

She fell silent and looked motionlessly, glumly, at her feet again, as she had done before.

'Anna Ivanovna?'

'Eh!' she gave a start as she emerged from her reverie and slowly shook her head, as she had done a little while before.

'How on earth did you end up in prison? What was that for?'

---

[18] A cultural organiser was entrusted with arranging talks on various topics, usually political, and many other forms of entertainment, such as mobile cinema shows and other forms of popular entertainment. Such activists dedicated to the communist cause were so few that they often had to fulfil more than one job, as here.

[19] During the late 1930s there was a movement to promote greater democracy within the Soviet system, especially at local levels, and elections were instituted to vote for local officials and kolkhoz chairmen and chairwomen. Many rural inhabitants viewed all this with a good deal of suspicion, and the officials themselves, who were used to being appointed by fiat, were not enamoured of such a change. Although such changes took place and elections were held with all pomp and circumstance, the democratic nature of the process was barely skin-deep, and many people were not taken in by it.

[20] The three crowns are a mark of quality, like a hall-mark.

[21] The peaked cap would invariably be worn by a man, and not by a woman.

'Same old story… Everyone hated me for exposing them. I'd followed everyone and written to the appropriate authorities. People say that there are no more **enemies of the people**. But where have they all disappeared?[22] They're the same today as they've always been. Every pilferer is an **enemy of the people**. We started flushing them out in thirty-five… after Kirov was murdered. I looked out for them myself. No one hides from me. Whoever stole anything – I knew every last one of them. I had a lot more trouble assessing people's opinions and catching anti-Soviet conversations. Well, who would talk to me openly? After all, I was a chairwoman and a party organiser. But I had a storeman, Gavrilkin, working for me – he was a dab hand at that kind of thing. He wrote to the authorities more than me. And then there was Pankov, the secretary of the rural soviet, and a **Komsomol** organiser to boot. He also knew who was saying what, and who was thinking what. They squealed on loads of people. But peasant men sussed him out. Gavrilkin disappeared into thin air. He was found a year later in the pond. He was pulled out with a drag-net. He was badly decayed. His hands were bound and he had a stone around his neck. And Pankov was killed. I remember him arriving with our pay – he gave it out, then said: "I'm going to Kustarëvka to hand out some **debentures**." It was getting on towards evening. I said to him, "Vania, wait on: I'll just finish off here and I'll go with you. I have to hold a cultural workshop over there." But he said he didn't have the time to wait, and off he went. It had hardly got dark when Vostrikov came running in: "Anna Ivanovna!" he says. "There's a bloke lying dead on the road to Kustarëvka. And I heard someone whistling in the bushes. I took fright and ran off without looking closely at who it was." Then it struck me. I went to the chairman of the rural council's office and said, "Trusa, Vostrikov's come running back… He says there's a dead man on the Kustarëvka road. Let's go!" So off we went… It was just as I thought… Pankov had been killed. He lay there, sprawled out, face down. The wind blew all the **debentures** around. The **NKVD** turned up. They found who did it by their tracks.'

'How do you mean "by their tracks"? Did they use sniffer dogs?'

'Nothing to do with dogs! They already had their eye on them. They were amongst those Pankov had reported. They found them, father and son, Artem and Mitia. Mitia even had a blood-stained finger. "Why's your finger got blood on it?" he was asked. "I've been squashing bed-bugs on the stove," he said. They were both arrested. They didn't make a full confession here, but they did in Moscow.'

'When were they arrested? That same evening?'

'Not at all! By the time we had rung up, and the investigator had arrived, it was already morning.'

'What was wrong with them? Didn't they wash their hands all night?'

'Who knows? But they confessed to everything… It's true though, that they got confused in court – one said they'd killed him with a crowbar, but the other one said they'd used an ice-pick.

---

[22] Bulkin makes a similar statement in the story *A History of the Village*.

The case was heard in Moscow.[23] It was a military tribunal. Trusha and I were called as witnesses. They were brought into the courtroom and they looked dreadful, barely recognisable. They were both shot. From then on, I couldn't work there any longer, I thought "I'm leaving, I'm leaving." I was transferred to the trade union section of the state farm at Verkhnii Perekat.[24] I became the bane of the life of the director and his little fraternity. They were all thieves and drunks. However much I wrote about them to the regional executive committee and to the regional offices, I got nowhere. I wrote to the **oblast** trade union, saying "Send an inspector!" The workers hadn't been paid for seven months. The food was appalling – it was all rotten stuff, already written off from the books. We had some cows on the farm with brucellosis, but they were mixed in with all the rest. The infected calves were slaughtered and the meat served up in the canteen. The director himself, Striuchkov, used to disappear night after night in the pasture, chasing after the milkmaids. They all used to have far too much to drink... The milkmaids used to dress him up in their glad rags... as a woman! How shameful! And the silage tower burnt down due to spontaneous combustion – they hadn't put the silage in properly. So the auditors came – all Striuchkov's buddies from the regional executive committee, along with Shikunov, from the regional finance department. The director made a gift of five pigs to this Shikunov. A pig for the autumn, then one for winter, and another one for Easter... They arrived, had a good laugh together, had a skin-full, then served me with an indictment. It was all a load of lies. They'd put one of the workers up to no good against me. They all did their damnedest – well, Striuchkov was like their own father to them. I was dragged off to the **NKVD** and they wanted to imprison me as an **enemy of the people.** "For wrecking amongst professional personnel." They didn't put me in prison that time, but I was expelled from the Party and I lost my job. Oh, Lord God Almighty!' Once again she sobbed and fell silent.

'So I moved here, to Kustarëvka. People were abandoning the village and the houses were going cheap. I bought myself a wooden house and I went to work in the **kolkhoz** poultry unit. The henhouse was on a hill. My house was on the edge of the village, close to it. It was handy. Well, I managed to get by. They'd brought me down to rock bottom and thought, "that'll shut her up!" No such luck! I doubled my efforts to expose them. I followed all of them – the chairman, the **brigade leaders,** and the policeman. I'd started to suffer from insomnia. I used to mooch around the village all through the night. They would never have caught me if my Katka hadn't betrayed me. An illegitimate beggar-woman moved in with me. She was a native of Ermilov. She'd been imprisoned in thirty-eight for taking some ears of corn. She was in for two years... But she never went back to the **kolkhoz** – she just roamed all over, after that. She always called me her sister. She'd say, "I have seen the light, Old Mother. A person must be free, once and for all, from all property. Whoever is naked, is blessed. It's not your body you should save, it's your soul. Whoever works for the Antichrist will never see the Blessed Land of Zion. Why don't we chuck in all this working and travel around the world, which is now opening up to us." I told her nothing is opening up to us and that we'd just die of hunger. But she says to me, "Without truth, bread will not enter your mouth." And I told her that

---

[23] Mozhaev implies here that a confession was forced out of them, probably under torture, though he would not have been able to write this at the time the work was written. The fact that the evidence of the son and father did not agree suggests some form of coercion. The statement that they were 'barely recognisable' indicates possible physical violence and the fact that a confession had been beaten out of them. What they had not been able to do locally, the **NKVD** had managed to do at their headquarters in Moscow.

[24] The name literally means 'Upper Shore'.

truth is not like a bear, which just wanders around the woods. It cannot be sought, but must be created with both hands. But she kept saying, "No, no, it's not. Truth cannot be made by hand. He who works at the present time is serving the Antichrist." She kept on and on, preaching at me, calling for me to go with her. Then she says, "I'll just stay a while with you and get my strength back. I'll just stay a little while." Help yourself! I said. There's no shortage of space. And it was nicer living together. She stayed the whole summer with me. Then she betrayed me... Ah, Lord God Almighty!' She shook her head and sobbed again. 'And you drink! C'mon!' Proshkina topped my glass up with the infusion. 'It's gone totally cold. Would you like me to warm it up?'

'No, no! You just carry on with your story, please.'

'But, haven't you had enough? My story is far from happy. As people say, he who's never lived, has never suffered. There is no escape from begging and prison, as they say. So you see, that's my fate. Fate has willed it. Oh, Lord God Almighty!'

This exclamation sounded strange coming from her: at first the 'Oh!' sounded high and protracted, then there was a short pause, and it seemed that she would now whistle with abandon, or let out a long stream of effing and blinding, like she had done at the woman with the scythe. But she just followed it with a quiet, husky mumble, 'Oh, Lord God Almighty'.

'I kept some ducks and turkeys. I do have a little weakness for turkeys. They prattle away all day long, especially the cock. Gobble-gobble-gobble! Gobble-gobble-gobble! Ah, you poor devil, I think to myself, you had everything, and now it's all gone. I feel happier when I'm with them. Sometimes I used to bring them home the sweepings from the threshing floor. A full load of grain used to be delivered and dumped by the henhouse. We would carry it on to the storeroom, but the sweepings – chaff and earth mixed together – we'd put in our pockets. The ducks at home would eat it all up. They're greedy birds. So Katka goes and shops me to a policeman: "Come on over," she says to him, "...this evening – she's bringing sweepings home with her." I get home from work and they're waiting for me. The policeman's there, and the chairman of the **kolkhoz**, and the secretary of the rural council. "Halt! What have you got in your pockets? Are you stealing grain?" What grain? I say, it's just sweepings. "Tell that to the court." They wrote a report on me and I got stuck with ten years for embezzling state property. Caught red-handed. Oh, Lord God Almighty! But there is justice. Even though I did my full ten-year stretch, here I am, hale and hearty. But some of them died a long time ago, some served their sentences for thieving. They've all faded into oblivion. That's the way it is.

'I got sent down, but Katka stayed in my house. She took to squandering all my things. People even asked her: "Why are you doing this? What right do you have?" She would say, "Proshkina is not a woman, she's a bloke. She lived with me, as if I were her wife. Now I'm the rightful mistress of the house." It suited some people to believe her and spread it all round the district. "Proshkina's not a dame, but a bloke," they said. "No wonder she never got wed. She's never had a husband. She cuts her hair short, like a bloke, and wears trousers." We have people round here who'll believe any old tale. Only, they'll never believe the truth. And everywhere, there was wholesale thieving going on. I write and write and I shop them – but it's all pointless. Oh, Lord God Almighty! Me – a bloke. How's that then? I do cut my hair short,' she said, turning towards me with her hair unevenly cut at the neck, which looked more gnawed, than cut. 'I cut my own hair. I grab a bunch like this with one hand, and the scissors in the other, and snip! – I just lop it off. What's good about hair? It just gets dirty and infested. And why the trousers? So that horse-flies don't crawl up my skirt. Clothing was given to man not for beauty, but for convenience. It's fine as long as it doesn't get in the way.

'Well, as people say, hunger drives the wolf from the woods. So I did my time and I came back from there an old woman. Even your aunt didn't recognise me. I came back here to Kustarëvka... When I got back, there wasn't a trace left of my house, not even the **mound**. I had pancakes and turkeys, and all that was left were women evildoers.[25] There was hardly anything left of Kustarëvka – just four homesteads. Where could I have gone? What work could I have done? I couldn't work on the **kolkhoz** any more – I didn't have the energy or the strength. I wanted to get a job as a watchman, but no one would take me on – I don't have the right work record. I had nowhere to live. I wept by my white willow trees. Anyhow, who would see my tears? Who needs them? I had to get myself sorted out. I made a dug-out dwelling, right in that hollow, where my cellar used to be. I wove wattle walls for it myself. I made a stove out of broken bricks. Now, I thought, I'll see the winter out here. And I thought I would get some potatoes planted. Otherwise I'd die from starvation in the winter. I put a sack on my back and went all around, looking for some seed potatoes. That's when people christened me "Old Mother". People said, "She's gone simple, living in a dug-out." Now, whoever I denounce, they just dismiss me. "It's Old Mother again! She's gone senile." Oh, Lord God Almighty!'

'How come you moved in here?'

'Kustarëvka used to belong to that **kolkhoz** where I was the chairwoman, in Eremeevka. Then it was transferred to Zheludëvka. It still had a storehouse here, set apart. They signed it over to me. So I started off in the storehouse. I installed a stove in it. Unfortunately, there was no proper wooden floor in it. And the walls were terribly damp. I reared cattle there as well, and laid out a garden. Bit by bit, I brought timber home on the cart. I sawed new beams and picked up old ones from here and there. It took me five years to build it. Oh, Lord God Almighty!'

I looked closely at her outhouses with their roofs set on white willow, and the log **heated bee house**, and the garden, and the pond which she dug for five years, "looking for a seam of gold", and I was in awe at the limitlessness of man's determination, born of his love for independence. Go on, Proshkina, go to the regional executive committee, tell them that you are homeless – and they would have sent her off to a care home as an old person without any family. But she did not go. She spent years living in the dug-out and then in the storehouse, which looked more like a stone sepulchre than a person's home. And she had never given in... I glanced into this storehouse... I don't know what kind of cave Father Seraphim lived in, but he would not have lasted long in that storehouse. The window was small and had iron bars, there was only an earth floor, and the walls

---

[25] What she actually says in Russian is an expression which rhymes. It is not a standard proverb, as such, but it is a saying. Such sayings often consist (as here) of two short statements which are metrically finely balanced, separated by a comma, and they rhyme. Mozhaev was a great collector of such sayings and he had a good memory for them.

were cold and damp. It was dark, musty, and humid. In the corner, in the half-light, I saw an icon on the icon shelf.[26]

'Anna Ivanovna, why on earth have you put an icon in here?'

'It's a damaged one. The paint has peeled off owing to the damp. It's an old one. It's a shame.'

I took down the icon, which had become dark with time and soot. In places, on the thick piece of wood on which it had been painted, there was still some gold leaf at the edges, and in others could be seen the deep folds of a dark-blue woman's veil. But there was no representation of the face. The Mother of God had not been able to endure the *life* of Old Mother Proshkina.[27]

We didn't have to haggle: she asked for a very low price for the hay for my aunt. But she took the deposit readily – she unfolded the ten-rouble note I had given her, and stared at it lovingly.

'That will do me for a long time. For bread.'

As we were saying good-bye, she beckoned to me and, with a meaningful wink, she led me to the hallway. Here, in the half-light, she produced a small key on a chain from somewhere at her belt and she raised it towards my face.

'D'you see this?'

On the chain swung a flat bronze key, with an inscription in bas-relief 'GAZ'.[28]

'What's that? Where's it from?'

'From a lorry...' She raised a finger and said in a hushed voice, 'During the night, a lorry stopped by the **brigade leader**'s house. I had a look at it – it was loaded up with potatoes. There was no one in the cab. Everyone was in the house, getting drunk. I crawled and crawled, stole up, and grabbed it. Then I went home. I carry it about my person. I'll not surrender it alive. I've written to the secretary. Now I'm waiting for him to turn up. There's your evidence!'

---

[26] In peasant houses, there is a corner – usually the eastern corner – traditionally set aside for icons. It might simply have a single shelf, or a complete icon stand, supporting a number of icons. Tradition demanded that three icons be displayed: one of the Saviour, one of the Virgin, and one of John the Baptist, although there were regional variations. A small oil lamp was also hung before the icons, and an embroidered cloth draped above them. Prayers are said in the morning and evening before the icon shelf or stand, and tradition demanded that one never sat with one's back towards the icons. In case of quarrelling or love making, the cloth was used to cover the icons so that "God should hear no cursing" and for modesty's sake.

[27] The Russian word used here for 'life' ('*zhitie*') is rich in meaning, but it is generally not in everyday use. It is a word with strong religious overtones, being of Old Church Slavonic origin. Basically, it means 'biography' or the 'life and times', usually of a saint. The epigram at the beginning of the story is quoted from *The Life of the Archpriest Avvakum by Himself*, which features this very word, used by Mozhaev here in his original text. In one sense, Proshkina has related her '*zhitie*', her 'life and times'. She has been something of an icon herself for the Soviet regime, i.e. a Party activist and that rare phenomenon – a female **kolkhoz** manager, yet, like the real icon drawn to the narrator's attention, she has lost face with the regime and been relegated to a solitary life, abandoned by virtually all. She has lost her power and influence, also like the icon, and in so far as the icon is faceless, it is an anachronism, a **hang-over from the past**, just like Proshkina's Stalinist denunciations and investigations into '**enemies of the people**'.

[28] These letters are the Russian acronym for the '**Gorky** Automobile Factory', which was a well-known manufacturer of lorries.

And, having seized me by the sleeve, with her hooked, dirty fingers, she prayerfully implored me: 'You go to the secretary of the regional committee, for God's sake. Tell him, "Proshkina has a secret." Get him to come here.'

On the porch, she stopped me once again and said, with a threatening finger: 'No-o, they won't take me without a fight. I'll expose them yet.'

Two years after this meeting, I lived for a whole summer in Tikhanovo. Once, while passing through the meadows in the regional committee lorry, I turned off to Kustarëvka. Proshkina greeted me as if we had met only yesterday.

'Did you speak to the secretary of the regional committee?' she asked.

'What about?' I asked, looking at her bewildered.

'Well really! I asked you to tell him to come. To say, "Proshkina's got something of interest for you." You forgot!' She waved her hand in disappointment. 'I've written to him three times. But no, he doesn't come or summon me to see him.'

'How are you doing, Anna Ivanovna?'

'Fine now, and why shouldn't I be? I get a pension of twelve roubles. That's enough for bread and sugar. I've got everything else I need. So there! However hard they tried to get shut of me, the state has not forgotten me. It's given them the finger. Now I get along fine, thanks be to God. You wouldn't be going via Zheludëvka, would you?' she asked, becoming animated with curiosity.

'Yes, I am.'

'Give me a lift through the village. Let those sods there see me. I'll look at them from the regional committee lorry.'

I sat her next to the driver and told him to drive slowly through the village. She sat there proud, bolt-upright, as if she had swallowed a measuring stick. As we were turning into a side street to leave the village, she grabbed the driver's arm and ordered imperiously: 'Drive by that end of the street! The **brigade leader** lives there,' and she gave me a sly wink.

We drove her past both the **brigade leader**'s house, and even past the house of the chairman himself. She fidgeted anxiously on her seat, twisting her head about, trying to see whether anyone had seen her or not. However, the street was empty. Right opposite the shop she grabbed the driver by the arm again: 'Halt! I'll get out here.'

The driver stopped the lorry. She opened the door in a trice and jumped down from the footboard with a spring uncommon in a woman of her age.

Some womenfolk were standing on a high concrete porch in front of the shop. She went towards them with the bearing of a company commander. She came to a halt on the very top step, as if having mounted a podium: she shot a stern look at her fellow villagers, turned round to us, smiled, and waved farewell.

1966.

The Saddler

Illustration 12. 'You are helping to liquidate illiteracy. Everyone join the "Down with Illiteracy"society.' Soviet poster, 1925.

Foreword to The Saddler

The Saddler (1965), was another of the fifteen stories which Mozhaev had intended to be published as a cycle, under the general title of *Old Stories*. As has already been pointed out, the cycle was never published as he had intended it. *The Saddler* first appeared as a single story in the newspaper *Trud* (Labour) in 1973, just a short time before it was published, with some other stories from the cycle, in *Novyi mir* in 1974.

Many of the stories in the cycle have points in common: they feature a narrator-journalist, who makes a trip to a remote rural setting – either a **kolkhoz** or a village, and there he meets with either a single a local person, or a group of locals, who tell(s) their story. The rural dweller expresses his views on life in general, and on life in the countryside in particular. The stories are full of rural charm, folklore, and the odd diversion into philosophy, as they put the world to rights.

The main protagonist of this story is the saddle-maker himself, Old Evsei, who is repairing a saddle for a younger lad, Vaska, the chief **kolkhoz** horseman. As the saddler works, he and Vaska chat, and the narrator is a mere witness – an eavesdropper.

In common with a number of protagonists in the cycle of stories, Old Evsei has had a chequered career: he has followed the usual path, working his way up from the bottom to the elevated post of **kolkhoz** chairman, only to be sacked and end up at what is perceived to be the bottom of the career ladder, as a humble saddler again. He has come full circle.

Many people in the West might not understand why this story was considered controversial or subversive. One might think, 'So what, if a person is incompetent and loses his job?' But, in common with many of such characters, who have had this cyclical career, their competence is not in question – it is simply that they have fallen victim to the vagaries of ideological change – one might go so far as to say the 'whims' of ideological fads. In carrying out their duties in line with official policy, as they knew they must, they were caught unawares in the quicksands of policy change.

An individual's promotion to a position of responsibility and authority, only to be dashed down again to the bottom of the career ladder, is a potentially sad story and certainly a personal tragedy for the person involved. However, Mozhaev's characters prove to be rather sanguine over the unpredictability of their lot – they almost expect to be demoted, because it was not at all unusual that people suffered such a fate. It is almost a case of 'if you play with fire, you'll get burned'. And Mozhaev injects an element of humour into the whole story, which also lightens the mood and exposes the absurdity of Soviet life, which has proved to be a very rich seam for satirists.

As apparently slight and glib as the story may appear at a first glance, Mozhaev shows himself to be a master of situational and verbal humour, which is richly imbued with biting satire on the Soviet regime.

Old Evsei is not a stupid man, but he is unschooled. He is a simple peasant man, skilled and strong, but he has not grasped the subtleties of Soviet politics, despite his protestations to the contrary. Hence, he confuses real 'elements', i.e. chemicals, with politically subversive '**elements**'. In fact, he only knows about political elements, and he is blissfully unaware of the chemical kind. This is indicative of a phenomenon, much commented on by many who know the system intimately, that everything is 'upside down' in Soviet life. Surely everyone knows about Mendeleev's Periodic Table of Elements – he was a Russian scientist, after all! But what does a peasant need to know about chemical elements? Ultimately, he can survive and do his job without those. But what are the chances of surviving the Soviet system without knowledge of what constitutes a political '**element**'?!

Mozhaev combines situational and verbal humour over the nebulous Soviet concept of 'opportunism', a word which Old Evsei cannot even pronounce properly, so far is it removed from his own milieu and language: the word is of European origin, and it is not an easy word for the Russian tongue to get round. Old Evsei explains to the young Vaska that, he 'fell into *apportunism* because of those chicken droppings' – an amusing juxtaposition of the real and the abstract, which produces an almost surreal image. Similarly, he tries to get to grips with the equally nebulous concept of a political 'tendency', or the 'course', or 'direction', a policy might take, all of which are covered by the single Russian word '*techenie*'. In a normal context, the word means the 'flowing', or 'current', of a body of water, and it is only in concrete terms that Old Evsei can explain to Vaska what '*techenie*' actually means. He thinks within the parameters of the natural environment in which he lives and with which he is familiar. It is also highly amusing that the abstract concept of opportunism is juxtaposed with excrement, i.e. chicken droppings.

Opportunism crops up again, along with its allied concept of 'deviation' – of both the 'Left' and the 'Right' varieties – in *A History of the Village of Brëkhovo*. Amusingly, to be guilty of 'Right Deviation' or 'Left Deviation' – two concepts germane to ideological debates over the direction policies should take in the mid- to late-1920s – is interpreted as having a gait, with an inclination to lurch to the right or the left, since the Russian word '*uklon*' is used to express both phenomena – both the abstract, political idea, and the physical disability.

Old Evsei gets the word 'opportunism' slightly wrong, as many of Mozhaev's peasants do in his stories. These political terms are based on foreign imports, and Mozhaev is making the point that, not only is the very sound of the word alien to the peasantry, but the concepts they express are also incomprehensible to them. The concept of 'opportunism' had its roots in the second half of the nineteenth century, when radical revolutionary thought was being hotly debated: at the more extreme, left end, of the spectrum was anarchism, as expressed in the writing of Bakunin (1814-76), whose argument with Marx split the revolutionary socialist movement. Bakunin was accused of 'left opportunism', as his thinking was deemed to be on the left wing of socialist thinking, whereas that of Marx, and later, of Lenin, were deemed to be the norm. Further arguments and debates about policies and their political direction were rife in the early Bolshevik regime, before Stalin literally 'killed off' all debate and their proponents over policies. Hence, Trotsky (1879-1940) was accused of being a 'left opportunist', guilty of 'left deviation', by those who disagreed with him. Those on the right wing of Marxist-Leninist thought, such as Bukharin, were dubbed 'right opportunists'. In essence, anyone disagreeing with official socialist/communist thinking, as dictated by the Soviet regime, could be dubbed an 'opportunist'. These concepts extended also to international politics. When relations between the Soviet Union and communist China deteriorated in the early 1960s, the Chinese regime was condemned by Khrushchëv for its 'dogmatism', which was seen as yet another manifestation of 'left opportunism'. The boundaries between 'left' and 'right' opportunism and deviation were not set in stone – they depended on the current policies of the time: one might be a 'left deviationist' at one time, but then, as a consequence of a major shift in policy, one might find oneself dubbed a 'right deviationist'. Being on the wrong wing of the political spectrum could also be dangerous, as people's past allegiances to either the left or right were remembered as part of their 'autobiography', and these former positions could be used against them later, as a pretext to oust them, as many prominent politicians found out to their cost under Stalin.

An incident which led to Old Evsei's further demotion is told by the narrator-journalist himself. He came to the village in his professional capacity as a journalist to write an article on village cultural life. The narrator tells us that the year was 1954, which is highly significant: it was the year when Khrushchëv had mobilized 300,000 **Komsomol** 'volunteers' from the towns and cities, to go into the villages and **kolkhozes** to lend a helping hand, and it was also a time of change for agriculture. The narrator specifically mentions the September Plenum, which was central to improving agriculture by raising procurement prices in order to help farms of both kinds, **kolkhozes** and **sovkhozes**, to become more profitable. As a journalist, he wanted to see what the cultural provisions were like in the village, and he found Old Evsei in charge of the village library or 'reading room'. The narrator considers Old Evsei's attitude to the library relaxed, to say the least: he is reluctant to open it up, and when the journalist finally gains access, he is disturbed by how badly it is run. The narrator's subsequent newspaper article reporting this chaos was the cause of Old Evsei being removed from his post yet again.

The journalist *per se* does not appear in a good light in any of Mozhaev's stories. Officially, journalists enjoyed a high status within Soviet society, but Mozhaev knew the industry well, having worked as a journalist in it, and he is quite clearly of the opinion that journalists are mere patsies of the regime. They write what is expected of them, just as editors publish what they know to be acceptable to the regime.

The young lad Vaska is curious about Old Evsei's education, which took place during the early years of the Bolshevik regime, just after the Revolution of 1917. Formerly, there was little rural education for people like Old Evsei. He talks about 'liquidating his illiteracy', the rather emotive, militant Bolshevik epithet for the campaign for universal literacy, and Vaska asks him if he had ever studied geography. Old Evsei tells him that they never had, and although he does not know why this subject was not on the curriculum, he amusingly speculates that, perhaps a knowledge of geography would have helped them to run away from the **kolkhoz**. This hilarious, but politically blasphemous, comment was cut by the censor when the story appeared in *Novyi mir*.

The narrator leaves and Old Evsei bids him farewell, reminding him again that, after his last 'flying visit', he was removed from his post in the village reading room. The irony is that the Russian word for a 'flying visit' can also mean a 'raid', as might be made by cavalry-men during the course of a battle. Hence, the journalist becomes associated with an enemy interloper!

However, there is no malice or rancour in Old Evsei's heart towards the narrator-journalist, or towards his own fate in life – he just accepts his lot. As a peasant, he has to accept the conditions and hardships which nature brings, and he seems to face political tumult and caprices with the same kind of equanimity.

The Saddler

We were sitting in the shade on a low, lopsided, little porch. Some horses were strolling around the enclosure in front of us. Some were picking at the scattered cut grass, snorting at it, blowing dust around, and they lazily nibbled at the bits of grass. Others dozed, impassive to all that was going on around them, with their heads lowered and their lower lip relaxed. It was scorching hot…

The damp smell of the earthen floor and the sharp, rather sweet, scent of mouldy saddlecloths wafted over us from the open door of the saddler's workshop.

Old Evsei was repairing a saddle. He was a plump-nosed, bald, but still strong, broad-chested old man, with bulbous, camel-like eyes, which he screwed up owing to his short-sightedness. He was sitting above us on the top step, as if on a throne, with his legs wide apart, poking a bodkin into the leather and pulling through the waxed thread with both hands. He wheezed from the strain, then, when he had tapped the bodkin handle along the seam, he directed a long, meaningful look at us, as if trying to remember something, or about to order us to do something: but then, having given a horse-like shake of his head, he plunged the bodkin back into the saddle, and again, with a wheeze and a whistle, which turned his flabby, puffy cheeks red, he pulled through the waxed thread.

Vaska, a dark-eyed, bony-shouldered teenager sat at his feet, motionless with reverence – the old man was mending the saddle for his trotter: Vaska was the chief **kolkhoz** horseman. He was too busy to read the book he was holding in his hands.

Old Evsei glanced suspiciously at his book several times, then asked: 'What kind of book is it that you've got there?'

Vaska grew perplexed and turned the book over in his hands.

'I've got exams very soon. Chemistry.'

'Aha, that means fertilizer,' concluded Old Evsei. 'That's chemistry. In times gone by, we were tested on chicken droppings.'

He tapped the bodkin handle again and gave me a stern glance.

'And I fell into *apportunism* because of those chicken droppings.'

'It's not "*apportunism*", it's "opportunism",' said Vaska, correcting him.

'Very likely,' agreed the saddler. 'I'm not all that good at grammar. But it's true, I know about current policy.'

'What is opportunism anyway?' asked Vaska.

'*Apportunism* is flowage. It comes from nowhere, you might say. A bit like our river over there, the Talovka. It comes up to a sparrow's knees, but the rains come over, and then – don't mess with it! It will whirl you around and carry you off to the devil-knows-where! Even as far as the Caspian Sea… That's the spitting image of *apportunism*. It all depends on what times you land up in.'

The saddler tapped the handle of his bodkin again, grunted, and came to the edifying conclusion: 'If you get into the wrong current, you end up an *apportunist.*'

Old Evsei was addressing his remarks to Vaska, although I suspected they were intended more for me, as an outsider, and all the more so since I was a journalist.[1] As if to say, 'This is what we're like... We weren't born yesterday.'

I already knew that Old Evsei had gone through the whole cycle of the rural managerial official: he'd been promoted from saddler to **brigade leader**, then to chairman of the rural council, and finally he made it to **kolkhoz** chairman. Then, he slid back down to **brigade leader**, then to village **reading-room** librarian, and now back again to saddler. He'd gone full circle.

Incidentally, I myself was involved in one of his demotions. It all happened in fifty-four. I had come on newspaper business to investigate village culture. It was a period when, for the first time in many years, urban people were attracted to rural life: some wanted to have a good look at rural life, at its free and easy life-style, to ask people about the tax changes and the loans which were being granted for building work. They asked: 'Is it really true that now you can keep as much livestock as you want?' Others came from the city on propaganda campaigns, to get rural inhabitants to work better because the September Plenum had removed all sorts of obstacles, solved the main problems, and had completely untied **kolkhoz** workers' hands, saying, 'Now it's all down to you, the **kolkhoz** workers'.[2]

I remember a political canvasser coming with me one day to Panshino, a chap from some Moscow institute, either the Institute of World History or World Literature. In the little, cramped house set aside for visitors, this guest from Moscow – a short, stout man with tight, rosy cheeks, wearing nice clean boots and a grey shaggy coat with the collar turned up (it was autumn and there was a frost), stood by the doorway and asked, in a rather pitiful, dismayed way: 'Excuse me, but where is the lavatory in here?'

'Other end of the village,' replied Old Evsei.

He was sitting at the table in the **dezhurnaia's** seat, reading the newspaper. The cleaning lady, who also worked as the **dezhurnaia** in the visitors' house, was his wife Praskovia Pavlovna, and she had gone home to milk her cow. Evsei Petrovich was standing in for her.

'How do you mean at the "other end of the village"?' asked the canvasser in disbelief.

---

[1] Journalists who came to visit villages and report on what they saw in newspapers and magazines were viewed with great suspicion, and even hostility, in the former Soviet Union. Some local people, resident in villages, were also encouraged to write for newspapers and magazines – so-called *selkory* – or 'rural correspondents'. In the early years of the collective farm, criticism of **kolkhoz** chairmen and local officials was also reported by rural journalists, but as the years went on, most rural news had to be 'good news'. The regime used all these people to proclaim the great achievements in agriculture, and stories of record harvests, the delivery of new machinery, and the general improvements in rural life and standard of living, frequently appeared as front-page news. However, such reports were just 'stories', and many people did not believe them – hence the suspicion with which journalists were viewed. A number of Mozhaev's stories feature journalists and generally he portrays them in a poor light.

[2] See footnote № 95, p.178.

'It's by the **MTS**... It's in the former regional committee office,' Evsei Petrovich explained. 'There's a toilet there. Our one here collapsed last year. The menfolk made off with the wooden planks for firewood.'

'Impossible!' exclaimed the canvasser, standing stock still by the doorway.

'Our regional offices have been closed down. Who'll rebuild it now?' said Evsei Petrovich, patiently hammering home his point to him.

'And is it far, this "other end"?'

'Oh, it'll be a couple of **versts**...'

Evsei Petrovich turned back to his newspaper.

I sat with him in the guest house for almost half a day. To all my requests about opening up the village library, he replied, 'It's not the right time yet.'

'Anyway, what do you need this library for?' he suddenly asked suspiciously.

'How do you mean "what for"? To read books. It should be open.'

'Each to his own... Do you have any documents?'

'Yes.'

'Well then, just sit and wait.'

'Why?'

'That's how we do things around here.'

I managed to get into his library, or, as they say in Panshino, the 'book room', only late in the evening, when Praskovia Pavlovna had finished milking her cow and had tidied up the house.

I was struck by the musty smell of mildew and dust, and the whiff of mice in there... Books were scattered chaotically on crudely knocked-up shelves and in old trunks covered in tin plate with their lids ripped off, and there were other books kicking around the floor in the corner. In the middle of the reading room was a table made of wooden planks with no cloth on it, and four stools around it. On the walls, thickly covered with fly droppings, hung posters and portraits, and the wooden ceiling was blackened by soot, emitted by a cast-iron heater.

'You might have at least whitewashed the walls,' I said.

'What's the point? The flies will just shit all over them.'

I showed him my press card. He showed not the slightest interest.

'You might have said straight off that you're from a paper. I'd have run home to get Paranka, and she'd have opened the book room earlier.[3] She likes messing around at home... She's a real, typical country woman.'

'The reading room shouldn't be opened for me, but for the people.'

---

[3] 'Paranka' is a familiar form of his wife's full name, 'Praskovia'.

'We know it's for the people,' he readily agreed. 'Who else would it be for?'

'Have you compiled your catalogue?'

'What?' he asked, bristling for the first time.

'You know, an inventory of your books.'

'Oh, an inventory! What's that for? I know them all, right down to the last book. I've read them myself.'

'But how do you keep track of them?'

'By the box... I know how many boxes and how many shelves there are. The rest are in the corner over there. What's the point in counting them?'

I remember a political lecture in the club-house. Evsei Petrovich was sitting in the front row, and, when the speaker had finished his lecture, he asked, 'Are there any questions?' Old Evsei got up and asked one.

'Tell me how things are in Indonesia.'

'How do you mean?' asked the speaker.

'Has order been established there? Is our help not needed...?'[4]

After my article in the newspaper, Evsei Petrovich was sacked. That's when people started calling him simply 'Old Evsei'. It was strange that he didn't take against me, or at least he didn't appear to. At each of my visits to Panshino, he purposefully sought me out, struck up a conversation with me about the book section, and, on parting, he would always refer to the same event: 'After your visit then, I got the sack. Yes, indeed...'

But this time, Old Evsei led me out of the office into the stable yard, and he treated me to some cold **kvass**, and, towards the end of my visit, he started up an intellectual conversation. I suspected that this was his own way of getting back at me, as if to say, 'This is the kind of person you got sacked. You did not rate me...'

Old Evsei talked about his former managerial work, as if it had been some kind of jolly, but not fully understood, game, with which, even now, he would not have been averse to playing along.

'I once got caught in the flowage... I was summoned,' said Old Evsei, tapping the bodkin handle against the leather. 'I was asked, "Have you got to grips with the chicken droppings?"'

'I have,' I replied.

'So what are you doing about it?'

---

[4] As part of their political education, all citizens were taught about issues concerning the communist cause, both at home and abroad. Obviously what was happening abroad was of little interest to many people, and of even less interest to peasants and **kolkhoz** workers, who had more pressing and immediate problems to deal with. Mozhaev exploits these kinds of meetings for comic purposes in a number of his works. There was a coup in Indonesia in September 1965 and, as part of the struggle, a huge number of communist party members were slaughtered, possibly up to one million, right across Indonesia. The Soviet Union kept a keen eye on communist activities in other countries and events such as these were reported in Russian newspapers.

'We're collecting it,' I replies.

'Just who's collecting it?' they asks.

'The managerial committee,' I replies. 'We're going round the homesteads.'

'Idiot! Your job is to pass this task further down the line. D'you understand? But you're gallivanting around homesteads, like a priest.'

'I thought I'd better agree with them… I didn't know, 'cause at that time I had no experience of managerial ways. So I blurted out, "A managerial person should lead by personal example." Oh, I got a real scolding for that…'

'Do you really think managers themselves should be thrown into chicken droppings? Eh?! Cart manure and plough the fields? Eh?! Or perhaps you think communism should be built just by managers' hands? This is breaking ranks with the masses, d'you understand? That's *apportunism*.'

'That's the very point,' said Old Evsei, tapping his bodkin, and then he fell silent…'

'That's what the flowage was like at that time. I might have come slap up against it for a final time. But fortunately, the people in charge of the regional office had their heads screwed on – they knew what was what. I was kept on as a chairman,' he said, throwing a glance in my direction, then he added, pointedly at me: 'So there.'

Vaska must have found this story boring, for he opened his book at the Mendeleev Periodic Table of Elements and put it on his knees.

'What language is that written in?' asked Old Evsei. 'In German, or something?'

'It's Mendeleev's Table,' replied Vaska.

'Mendeleev?' asked Old Evsei, puckering up his lips and thinking for a moment. 'No, don't think I've heard of him. I understand current policies, but not history.'

He sewed several stitches, tapped the saddle, then grunted: 'What's it been done for, this table? Multiplication or division?'

'Uncle, it's about elements… It's classification, d'you understand?'

'What's there not to understand?! Everyone knows about **elements**. There are all different kinds. There are those that women take on – then the bloke does a bunk, and wham! He's down as an **element**. And there were those **elements** who were kulaks and got dispossessed… That's a **hang-over** from capitalism, that is.'

Then he looked at me and asked: 'Has this Mendeleev written about foreign **elements**, or something like that?'

'Uncle, it's chemistry!' said Vaska, irritated, shifting on his step. '**Hang-overs** from capitalism belong to history. Surely you understand that?'

'And you just stop shifting around, or you'll get a splinter in your arse,' quipped Old Evsei, offended. 'Aren't you the smart one! It's for you I'm mending the saddle, you little fool. And he doesn't want to talk to me!'

'What are you on about, kind Uncle?' said Vaska, taking fright and hugging his knees again. 'It's just that… I'm sick of chemistry. What did you think I was on about?'

'You're stupid, Vaska. If I'd been like you, learnt my letters as a child, I'd now be God knows who! You wouldn't have seen me for dust.'

'So where did you go to school?' asked Vaska.

'I did my *litracy* course in twenty-two. That is, I liquidated my *il'teracy*. You couldn't do any other: on the one hand, we was oppressed by the **kulaks**, on the other, by ignorance. So we destroyed them both. Then we built the **kolkhoz**.'

'Hang on, Uncle Evsei!' Vaska tapped him on the knee. 'Where did you study for your literacy course? At school?'

'Where else?! In the morning, the kids used to study, and in the evening it was us, the old fools. We studied by the light of a storm-lamp, like little owls, goggling at the blackboard. By the time you got home, you'd forgotten your letters. And what did we have at home at that time? A spill! Because it was **War Communism**. And even now, when I've had a few drinks, I sing all about the spill:

Burn out, burn out, my spill...[5]

'By the way, some people have forgotten all about that...' Old Evsei again screwed up his camel-like eyes, and looked at me. 'What's it to them? They've never known grief, they came at the ready, that's why they criticise. Each to his own. You can't make everyone equal or speak about them in the same way. In a queue at a shop, a person is standing in line, but another person gets his stuff by passing it over other people's heads. So what? You can shout and scream, but you'll end up making a fool of yourself. That's just how things are. You need to understand that.'

'What subjects did you study, Uncle?' asked Vaska.

'Different ones... You were shown letters, then you had to write them on the blackboard... We mostly did reading. Then we copied things out in our exercise book. We wrote in la-ar-rge letters, like this, each one as big as a cigarette... Then we had political knowledge. When we started political knowledge, we instantly knew what was what. Our life was downtrodden. After that came the Revolution. Then people showed interest in life. And the **kolkhozes** were formed. It was the only possible way. We might even have got by with **kolkhozes**... Why shouldn't we? But then, along came the war. The Germans came upon us... And before the Germans we had Wrangel, Denikin, and twelve states against us – all agents of world bourgeoisie.[6] I won't even mention the

---

[5] This is the first line from a Russian folk song, which gives the song its title. The spill in the song is a symbol of life coming to an end. It is full of regret to the point of near suicide and it is reminiscent in tone of the poet Sergei Alexandrovich Esenin (1895-1925), who was born and lived for a while in the same province as Mozhaev. Esenin committed suicide by hanging himself in a Leningrad hotel on 28 December 1925. Also mentioned in the song is the Russian epithet for 'plenty' or abundance, which was a promise Bolshevik activists made to rural peasants during the campaign for full collectivization in the early 1930s. The song describes a sleigh going through the 'land flowing with milk and honey'.

[6] All these short phrases are sound bites from Bolshevik propaganda, which, when presented in a list like this, give a glib, potted history of the stages of development of the early Soviet regime.
Wrangel, Pëtr Nikolaievich, Baron (1878-1928) was a general who commanded the White forces (anti-Bolshevik soldiers) in the last phase of the Russian Civil War (1918-20).
Denikin, Anton Ivanovich (1872-1947), led the anti-Bolshevik (White) forces on the southern front during the Civil War. He served for a short time in the provisional government which overthrew the Romanov dynasty

Civil War, because neither of you will remember it. The War finished with a victory, and then we started to get back on our feet. That meant ploughing with cows.[7] At that time, chairmen changed all the time... But now our life is moving forwards...'

'Uncle, did you do geography?' asked Vaska.

'No, there was no geography. I couldn't tell you why not. Perhaps they were afraid we'd run off from the **kolkhoz**. I couldn't tell you in all honesty, but I never liked it, that geography. Everyone knows where each country is. But books – that's a different matter. I love books. Whichever one you read, it's about one thing in one, and about a different thing in another. And the main thing is, you don't know what's coming next. You just read through a book and think, "What's next?" But then, my cursed Paranka bawls out, right out of the blue, "Evsei, give the cow some water to drink! Evsei, chop some firewood!..." Bah! It's annoying.'

A lorry stopped by the stable yard. The **kolkhoz** chairman opened the door and waved to me. I came down from the porch. Old Evsei put the saddle to one side and accompanied me to the boundary edge. Here, he bowed to me respectfully, offered me his hand and, looking at me with his bulbous, screwed-up eyes, remarked:

'After your last flying visit, I got the sack. Yes, I did...'

1965.

---

after the February Revolution of 1917. He turned over his command to General Pëtr Nikolaievich Wrangel in 1920 and emigrated to France, where he wrote his memoirs.
The 'twelve states' or 'powers' were counties which intervened in Russia during the Civil War, one of which was Britain, which sent an 'expeditionary force' to Archangel and Murmansk. Among other countries which threatened to undermine the Revolution in Russia were France and Turkey.
[7] After the First World War, there was a dreadful shortage of horses, which had been requisitioned for the war. Peasants had to plough the land using cows and bulls, instead of horses, which they had traditionally used.

A History of the Village of Brëkhovo, Written by Pëtr Afanasievich Bulkin

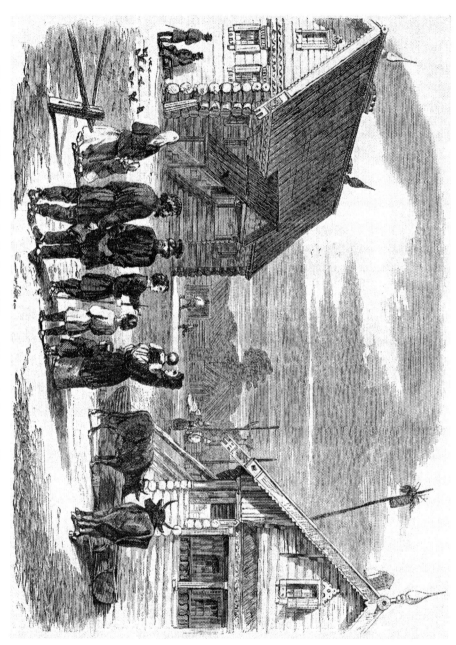

Illustration 13. 'Group of Russian Serfs, and Village of Goumnist, between Kostroma and Yaroslavl'.

Foreword to A History of the Village of Brëkhovo, Written by Pëtr Afanasievich Bulkin

Of all his works, Mozhaev's *A History of the Village of Brëkhovo, Written by Pëtr Afanasievich Bulkin* is the most bitingly satirical of the Soviet system. He had finished writing it by 1968, but it had to wait ten years before it was published.

The very title of the work instantly evokes two classical Russian authors: Nikolai Vasilevich Gogol (1809-1852) and Mikhail Evgrafovich Saltykov-Shchedrin (1826-1889). These two writers were satirists, whom Mozhaev often quoted, both directly and indirectly, in his own fiction and in his essays. Apart from the satirical content of his writing, Gogol had a penchant for giving absurdly long titles to some of his works, which in itself was a comic device. Saltykov-Shchedrin wrote a satire entitled *The History of a Town* (1869-70), which bears obvious affinities with Mozhaev's own title of this work. However, the similarities go far beyond the titles.

Both Saltykov-Shchedrin's and Mozhaev's works are fictional 'histories' of a small community. The word '*istoriia*', used in both titles in the original Russian, has a dual meaning: it can mean both 'history' and 'story', which, to the Western mind, are two very different concepts – 'history' is based on facts, whereas a 'story' is a product of a creative imagination. Of the two works, Saltykov-Shchedrin's work is more of a 'history' in the sense that it charts the policies and actions of a series of rulers or governors of a small town in provincial Russia. However, Mozhaev's work is more limited in scope, being set in a village, and it charts the activities, not of a governor general, but of **kolkhoz** chairmen and local officials, who are expected to do the bidding of distant rulers in Moscow. In Saltykov-Shchedrin's work, the only unifying factor between the series of governors who rule the town is that they are despots, and they regularly flog the inhabitants of the town of Glupov, whereas the unifying factor in the 'history' of the village of Brëkhovo is the **kolkhoz** and its dynasty of chairmen. For Mozhaev's narrator, Pëtr Afanasievich Bulkin, history only started in the Soviet period, before which, he claims, there was nothing of any note, except drunkenness, because, he says, there was no **kolkhoz**, and 'without a **kolkhoz**, how can there be any history?' The village is the **kolkhoz**, and the **kolkhoz** is the only form of history it has. Everything else is written off as a '**hang-over from the past**'. Bulkin conveys the arrogance, and to some extent, the ruthlessness, of Bolshevism, by insisting that very little of anything from the tsarist regime was worth preserving: historical tradition was supplanted by the new regime, and the past was jettisoned as the product of a dark, uneducated and unenlightened people. In essence, this was the thinking behind the campaign for the full collectivization of agriculture.

The name of Saltykov's town is 'Glupov', which is based on the Russian word for 'stupid' – '*glupyi*', and thus the name of the residents can be translated as the 'Stupids'. In Mozhaev's 'history', the name of the village is equally unflattering to its residents, as it is associated with the Russian word '*briukho*', which means 'belly' or 'paunch'. Whether the belly is swollen due to satiety, hunger, or pregnancy, is revealed in the narrative. Despite the narrator's protestations that, without the **kolkhoz** and politics, the 'history' would read like a string of disparate stories, the narrative is episodic and it is interspersed with amusing, parochial, and even inconsequential sections, such as 'Just

How Much can Paramon Drink?', which have nothing to do with real history, as it is universally understood.

Despite the varying lengths of the reigns of each of Saltykov's rulers, the policies of individual town-governors and their approach to their subjects show little variation: their sole aim was to suppress the Glupovites. In essence, this is exactly what the inhabitants of the village of Brëkhovo experience: the **kolkhoz** chairman may change, and the edicts as to which crops to grow may vary, but the local officials always maintain the party line, usually through the militaristic offices of officials like Motiakov, whom Mozhaev first introduced in his work *Lively*. His catch-phrase 'once and for all' is similar in spirit to the catch-phrase of Saltykov's governor Brudasty, who frequently says, 'I'll not have it!' They both attempt to rule by fiat and they resent their judgement being questioned.

In his satire, it is possible to identify some of Saltykov-Shchedrin's fictional despots as real historical personages, and scholars have speculated a great deal on this aspect of the work. In Mozhaev's history, one can also trace references to a real political leader. When Mozhaev's satire was published in book form in 1978, as part of his collection of *Old Stories*, he wrote, in the introduction to the volume, of the 'whims and caprices' of the Khrushchëv era. This criticism of the former Soviet leader was not officially resisted, because he had fallen from favour and he was subsequently *persona non grata*. Bulkin tells the reader that, were it not for the success of the **kolkhoz** under Dolgii's chairmanship, he would not have been able to refuse to plant Khrushchëv's maize and resist ploughing up their grazing lands (two themes on which Mozhaev wrote at length in his essays). In fact, Bulkin reports that Dolgii would have been put in prison for such non-compliance with official mandates. Hence, Mozhaev links his fictional satire firmly with a real historical character and a specific historical era.

Mozhaev's satire ranges far and wide, over many aspects of Soviet life – his satire is not confined solely to rural matters. At the beginning of the work, he takes a swipe at the literary establishment, enquiring into whether it is right that authors write about the countryside, when they know little about it – a swipe at Village Prose writers (see Appendix I). Then, his narrator Bulkin questions the whole issue of whether there exists an officially approved written style, which also governs the content and subject matter of a piece of literature: these are all matters concerning the state's control over writers and how they should write – a reference to the thorny problem of Socialist Realism (see Appendix I). Mozhaev also offers yet more criticism of the Soviet media and books in general, through remarks Bulkin makes about his wife's level of literacy. It is not that she cannot read, but, as Bulkin says, 'It's a shame that she can't read between the lines. I struggled for ages before managing to.' The reader may also wonder how Bulkin's awful doggerel on the October Revolution celebrations came to be published. What hope for literary taste?

Bulkin's literacy and level of political awareness are open to question from very early in the work. Along with many rural folk, Bulkin is confused over forms of address, whether to use 'comrade' or 'citizen'. When he addresses the children at the school, he uses – 'comrades' – which is just one in a whole series of *faux pas* evident during his speech. He mixes up set phrases of communist ideology with his own imperfect and simplistic logic, very much like the saddler, Old Evsei, in the story of that name. Bulkin's speech develops into a hotchpotch of Soviet cant and homespun wisdom, which show he has a smattering of knowledge and understanding, but overall it sounds like a political song sung slightly off key! The effect is hilarious.

Yet Bulkin's speech contains all the 'required' elements. In such official speeches, if they were to be truly instructional, comparing the 'then' with the 'now' was *de rigueur*, i.e. to explain how bad life had been before the Revolution of 1917, and how much progress had been made since. It was essential to convey the message that the present was incomparably better than the past. Any aspect of life before the socialist dawn, which had not yet been changed, was dubbed a '**hang-over** from the historical past', which was being dealt with at the present time. Bulkin shows his basic ignorance by making statements such as, 'formerly the regime was oppressed', not realising that, it was not the *regime* which was oppressed, but the *people* in it. It is through subtle comments such as these that Mozhaev injects much humour into the work.

Bulkin goes on to say that they 'now live better than under communism', but officially communism had not yet been achieved. Ideologically, the nearest Russia ever got to the attainment of the utopian state of communism was Khrushchëv's prediction that it would dawn in 1980. When it was clear that such a target would be missed, all future predictions were quietly forgotten about. Stalin had announced that they had achieved the milepost of socialism, but it was never claimed that communism had been reached. Bulkin goes on, quite rightly, to state: 'We get free health care and free education', but then he adds the illogical statement that, '… society must not stand still. It moves forward, just as the earth spins round.'

Again, Bulkin's narrative wanders off into the realms of the abstract, but conceptually he cannot deal in abstractions – he has to express his thought processes within the parameters of his own physical experience, just like the saddler. He tries to explain his concept of history and his historical method, but amusingly this is equated to a person's autobiography: he is talking not about a 'history' of the village, but a 'biography' of the village, which sounds as ridiculous in English as it does in the original Russian.

A person's background was germane to how that individual's career and whole life might develop, especially in the terrible 1930s in Russia. If one was a relative of a dispossessed **kulak**, priest, tsarist intellectual, or member of the former bourgeoisie, it was very difficult to enter higher education or get a job under the new Soviet regime. Such people were even disenfranchised until the new constitution of 1936, but the stigma of having such a blot on one's biography remained for much longer. During the Stalinist purges of the 1930s, one's background became even more of an issue in an atmosphere where saboteurs and '**enemies of the people**' were sought everywhere. Mozhaev's own father was dubbed an '**enemy of the people**' for refusing to join the **kolkhoz**, resulting in him being sent to a prison camp for a number of years. Many people lied about their background or kept it secret. People even made public denunciations of their own relatives in order to distance themselves from all taint and stigma of their family member. Some people moved from the countryside to the city, in an effort to start a new life and merge anonymously with the crowd – easier in the city and town, than in the stifling enclave of a rural community. Some people even managed to get false or new papers, such as an internal **passport**, which provided them with a sanitized, approved background, if they managed to lie convincingly, or bribe the appropriate bureaucrats.

Bulkin too thinks that a 'history' is as essential to a village and the **kolkhoz**, as a personal biography is for a person's work record, and this form of 'history' is essential for issuing official documents and even for receiving denunciations. The village also has its own Old Mother Proshkina figure, in the person of Old Makarevna, the midwife, who, we are told, would not balk at writing a denunciation on Jesus Christ himself!

Just as a person's fortunes change in line with current policy, so are street names and places altered. Like all towns and cities in the Soviet era, the village of Brëkhovo has been 'sovietized', by having its streets renamed after communist luminaries, iconic people, and significant historical events connected with the new order. Before this, the village streets were given rural epithets, reflecting their use or any particular activity which took place there, as is the case in many settlements. Hence, the village had streets called 'Straw Street', 'Horse Street' and 'Pottery Street'. But now, they have been renamed in a Soviet style, bearing names like 'Proletariat Street', '**Maksim Gorky Street**', and 'Lunacharsky Street'. This practice was widespread in Russia and it continued until and after the demise of the Soviet Union, whereupon names were changed back to their pre-revolutionary forms, as people reclaimed their cultural heritage and rejected the Bolshevik and Soviet paradigm.

Not only have the names of streets been changed, but the whole façade of the village has altered during the Soviet era. Bulkin reveals that during **NEP**, there used to be a comprehensive choice of tea rooms, canteens, bread shops, and many other outlets, which reflected the entrepreneurial spirit of the time. He puts this variety down to their lack of culture. But now, they have far less choice – they have one school, a club, and a single shop. Bulkin has been re-educated to regard choice as a lack of culture, and no choice, as progress. This is another example of normal values being turned 'upside down' within the Soviet system: it was a product of a topsy-turvy mode of thinking, when a failure or shortcoming instantly becomes, ipso facto, a success or a virtue.

In Saltykov's History, there is a great deal of inter-tribal rivalry before the Glupovites became a homogenous community, and they had all manner of amusing names: the Pot-Bellies, the Hash-Eaters, the Dunderheads, etc. Mozhaev's protagonists have similar comical names for other villagers, and there is a good deal of inter-village rivalry. Bulkin calls these inter-village rivalries and skirmishes a '**hang-over**' from the distant past. He sees this kind of normal rivalry as based on class struggle – an essential part of the Bolshevik vision of society. However, the skirmishes and fights which still occur even now, in enlightened Soviet times, are different: there is not a whiff of class tension in them – fights are now all fuelled by excessive drinking, which Bulkin sees as progress.

It is also clear that Bulkin has taken part in the campaign for full collectivization, since he took part in dispossessing a local miller and his family. Millers were common targets for **dekulakization**, as Mozhaev shows in his novel *Peasant Folk*. Owners of mills and butter-making establishments, or anyone who hired out agricultural machinery, were all deemed to be **kulaks**. However, the arbitrary nature and injustice of the whole campaign is exemplified in the case of the miller, whom Bulkin dispossessed. He describes the possessions he confiscated from the miller and his family, and it makes sorry reading: he could barely scrape together anything of value from this family of eleven children. Even their clock, which was commonly seen as a luxury item among activists and as a 'sure' sign of a **kulak** status, was not available for seizure, because it was at the repairer's. The absence of this token of luxury only emphasises arbitrary way in which activists treated the rural population during the campaign for full collectivization.

Bulkin notes with satisfaction the progress of the Soviet regime in many facets of village life. Before collectivization, times were austere: there was a shortage of grain and life was hard. Penalties for theft on the **kolkhoz** in the 1930s were extremely harsh, as has been seen in the story *Old Mother Proshkina*. But these times have passed and Bulkin notes encouraging signs of progress: grain now rots in the fields without anyone stealing it, because they can buy bread in the local shop, and even if a farmer wanted to feed his chickens on stolen grain, they need so little that it is hardly worth worrying about the theft. Bulkin notes, 'In a word, life has now got much easier'. Bulkin's optimistic affirmation is highly reminiscent of Stalin's 1935 declaration that, 'Life has become better, comrades, life has become happier'. This was said shortly before a great wave of terror, which sent millions of people to their deaths in the GULags.

When Bulkin trains as a tractor driver, his life-style bears witness to the extra perks such workers were accorded while working for the **MTSs**. This period of personal comfort also reveals his penchant for womanizing. He becomes embroiled in an amorous affair after being promoted, which in turn gives rise to a ruthless side to his character, common to many people in positions of power and influence. He uses his authority to further his own ends and cover over the tracks when his errant behaviour comes to light. He makes sure he gets off lightly, but his plans go awry when his wife discovers another of his little peccadilloes later in the *History*. Although amusing, Mozhaev was, in fact, exposing a serious problem of the early Bolshevik regime – that of men fathering children and abandoning their paternal responsibilities once a child came along. This phenomenon was the outcome of changing personal relationships within the early years of the Soviet regime, particularly since many people had taken up residence in towns and cities, where the strong moral codes of the former rural, patriarchal system no longer applied.

In a similar vein, he goes on a spree and charges cases of champagne to the **kolkhoz**, and he bribes mechanics to repair a **kolkhoz** vehicle – a common practice until the end of the Soviet regime. He has yet another affair, and he uses his authority to send the husband off to a place where he cannot get in the way of his amorous shenanigans. All in all, he is a typical **kolkhoz** chairman. And he is not the only official to have affairs in the story.

As in many of Mozhaev's other works, drinking to excess is endemic within the community. Although Bulkin admits that Paramon's story of drinking to excess is a diversion from the main narrative of the history of the village, it is, however, just one of a number of incidents where vast quantities of alcohol are consumed, giving lie to his earlier statement that all excessive drinking was part of pre-Soviet history and a 'hangover from the past'.

Different styles of kolkhoz management are also explored in Bulkin's History. He draws a clear distinction between Samochenkov's managerial style and Petia Dolgii's. Samochenkov follows his superiors' bidding to the letter and refuses all requests for anything out of the ordinary. He tries hard for the regime to prove himself, and his zeal is plain for all to see: he drinks like a maniac, 'as if it was not the vodka he was knocking back, but **enemies of the people**. That's why his whole life went pear-shaped.'

Samochenkov's fervour was such that, along with others, he started **dekulakization** a year early in Korabishino, but this meant that those who were not exiled got rich again, and they had to be dispossessed a second time. He set up a commune with the confiscated animals and he encouraged the communards to eat their fill on the basis that a full person works better than a hungry one. However, he had omitted to remove the former **kulaks'** beehives and the communards helped themselves to the honey, made mead out of it, and a period of total moral and organizational laxity ensued. Thieving was rife, and Samochenkov shot a thief who was trying to escape, but this led to him being brought to trial for his excessive zeal and his consequential discrediting of Soviet power. He ended up in an old monastery which was being used as a prison, but, unfortunately for him, the inmates were former **kulaks**, whom he had dispossessed and exiled, and he was beaten to within an inch of his life.

Within the historical context of the time, this bringing to book of Samochenkov was probably a direct result of Stalin's famous article '*Dizzy with Success*', published at the beginning of March 1930. Stalin blamed activists for exercising excessive zeal during the first wave of collectivization, and he reproached them for compelling peasants to join the **kolkhoz**, instead of persuading them. While apparently blaming such excesses on activists, Stalin agonized little over the consequences, and he certainly stopped short of condemning the vicious attacks on religious personnel, their buildings, artefacts, and the faithful.

Samochenkov's career is typical of Mozhaev's fictional chairmen: most of them fail in their jobs and are removed from their posts, as seen in his story *The Saddler*. Some are reinstated, but others take refuge in less demanding work. Many have personality flaws which mitigate against their success, i.e. most drink too much, or feel unable to stand up to administrative pressure from above and fall into a depression. Some just hide away to avoid officials and even their own farm workers, whose complaints and disputes can be rather petty, having their origins in their own despondency and chronic lack of self-fulfilment.

At the end of the account of Samochenkov's career, we catch him possibly at his lowest ebb. Significantly, he is working under Bulkin's supervision, shovelling horse manure into a cart to be taken away from the school yard. Bulkin asks him, 'Did you ever discover why you dragged the **kolkhoz** so slowly to a state of abundance?'

This concept of 'abundance' is highly emotive. It was one of the core promises of the campaign for full collectivization, because it was promised that, working on the **kolkhoz** would be much easier, since everyone would share the ups and downs of farming together. It was also stated that, owing to the reorganization of agriculture on a scientific, collective basis, and the adoption of new farming practices, which were also to be conducted along much more scientific and modern principles, there would be an abundance of produce beyond the peasants' wildest dreams. The lazy section of the peasantry swallowed this kind of propaganda all too readily, but the bulk of the hard-working peasants knew that Russia had never enjoyed such abundance. Generally, they had always managed to feed themselves and earn a passable living, but 'abundance' or 'plenty' never featured in their vocabulary.

As a chairman, Petia Dolgii has a completely different approach to his duties. He is enterprising, he stands up to officials who try to make him plant maize, he looks after his

kolkhoz workers and tries to keep them happy by paying them well, and he is flexible in all his dealings. But life is a struggle and a constant round of having to defend his position. Mozhaev based such a fictional character on several real **kolkhoz** chairmen, whom he had met and had written extensively about, and whose ideas featured large in his many essays. In this, Petia Dolgii is not an idealized character – he is firmly based in reality, though Mozhaev gives a quirky aspect to his character for comedic purposes. However, by including the descriptions of the careers of these two **kolkhoz** chairmen – Samochenkov and Dolgii, Mozhaev's criticism goes far beyond the confines of the **kolkhoz**: he directs his satire at all Soviet bureaucrats and officials, who carry out their duties without questioning their instructions. Samochenkov and Dolgii are two opposites of the bureaucratic mind-set.

The **kolkhoz** meeting is a rich vein for a satirist, and Mozhaev avails himself of yet another opportunity in this *History* to expose the absurdity of lecturing peasants on the international situation, amongst other issues. Bulkin, typical of his type, sees life both within and without the Soviet Union in terms of struggles, and he proclaims that, 'the troubadours of world imperialism are ever watchful'. This is a highly unconventional, but colourful, interpretation of capitalist enemies surrounding Russia, and it is typical of the tautology and paranoia which saturated Bolshevik ideology and outlook, although it is expressed in Bulkin's own inimitable way. Bulkin goes on to assess the international situation in his own terms, using another unconventional expression – 'the highway-robbery policy of world imperialism'. Again, this phrase is as unconventional as it is amusing.

Bulkin's vision of the future and the progress yet to be made by the regime is also given at the end of the *History*, and again, his vision has much to do with Soviet utopian dreaming, which was specifically reflected in Khrushchëv's *penchant* for gigantic, industrialized farms and scientifically planned cities, but also, more generally, as part of a much broader utopian fantasy, which was deeply ingrained in Bolshevism and the Soviet regime.

Mozhaev's satirical powers are at their very best in his *History*. It lampoons such a broad spectrum of Soviet life, making fun not only of its institutions, but also of the mind-set of those who had been taken in by official ideology, propaganda, and political cant. For all the farce and slapstick, narrated in the best classical tradition after Gogol and Saltykov-Shchedrin, he makes many profound and perceptive points.

A History of the Village of Brëkhovo
Written by Pëtr Afanasievich Bulkin

> On the ladder, along which man's reason has to descend towards the darkness of delusion, if we show something amusing and do good with a smile, then we shall be called blessed.
>
> A. Radishchev

Instead of a Foreword

Once Pëtr Afanasievich Bulkin, whom I knew very well, asked me to take his manuscript to any of the **thick journals**. I chose to approach Ivan Boborykin, the editor of the popular journal *The Red Seed*.

'How is he related to the Boborykin who wrote about China Town?' Pëtr Afanasievich asked me.[1]

'I think he's his grandson,' I replied.

'Then give it to him. That lot won't let us down – they are our people. He's from a good family.'

However, our famous literary critic, Boborykin, upset Pëtr Afanasievich. He wrote the following to him:

> Dear Comrade Bulkin,
>
> It is a little premature for you to take up the pen. You are not an educated person. I recommend that you register to study at a popular university and actively attend lectures on literature and art. First, you write only about what is already in the past, but we need writing about our current times. Secondly, your writing has neither a theme, nor characters, nor language. Your thinking is muddled, and the people will simply not accept or understand such a book. Take, for example, your use of the word "homopat".[2] Such a word does not exist in nature. There is a word "homeopath".

And so on, and so forth…

---

[1] 'China Town' ('Kitai gorod' in Russian) is an old district in the centre of Moscow.
[2] This word is entirely fictitious – it does not exist in Russian, any more than it does in English. It is an example of Bulkin getting the word wrong through his lack of education, despite his later protestations that there is such a word.

Pëtr Afanasievich wrote him a long letter by way of reply, in which his intellect, his repartee, and his literary knowledge are clear for all to see. Here is an extract from this letter:

> Much respected Comrade Boborykin,
>
> I will not take issue with you over education, or whether a writer needs your kind of education or not. I have seen writers (they have been to visit us in Brëkhovo), for example, who say "tis" and "countant", instead of "this" and "accontant".[3] So what? And, by the way, their writing is no worse than yours. And you yourself even publish their work. Now, did you not reproach me for writing without a theme? Do you know of the famous contemporary writer Vladilen Zolotushkin?[4] By the way, he wrote engagingly about how his name is derived, not from the word "zolotukha" — scrofula, the childhood illness — but from the gold fields which were to be excavated in his village on Piskarevka River, because a golden nugget was found in a goose turd there. It's true that, when the nugget was subjected to tests in the city, using acid, it fizzed, and it turned out to be a piece of old horse brass. But he wrote a book about it — and what a book! Have you read it? Has it got a theme? No. And it doesn't need one. Zolotushkin proved that the "theme" is a hang-over from the past.
>
> So now then, let us take the word "homopat". You write that the correct word is "homeopath". Perhaps that's how they say it where you come from. I won't argue with you. But why don't we look into the origin of this word? It is obvious that it is derived from the chemist's shop, from where the homopat prescribes his medicines. And what kind of chemist's shop is that from? It's from a homopatic one. That is, from a chemist's, just like the one you have in Moscow, which stands

---

[3] Bulkin still gets the word wrong: it should, of course, be 'accountant'.

[4] There is humour in this person's first name also. In the early days of the Soviet regime, a number of party faithful gave new, modern, invented names to their children. Zolotushkin's first name here is an amalgamation of the first part of the names 'Vladimir' and 'Lenin' making 'Vladi-Len'. Many, much more bizarre, names were coined, and this one here is by no means the strangest of its type.

on Kolkhoz Square. Surely you must have heard of
it?! Even we, here in Brekhovo, know of that
chemist's. Even my brother Levanid went there for
some medicine. So now then, explain to me what
grammatical correctness is and how one ought to
understand it.

It is a very strange question that you asked me,
about what day I should write about: should I
write about yesterday or today? How might I
write about today, when it isn't even over yet?
First, I'd have to wait til it was finished and
see what comes of it. Secondly, I would then have
to write about it... But you might spend not just
a day writing about it, but even more than a
year... Even Vladilen Zolotushkin has not managed
to write about the present day. It's not for
nothing that people read him and say, "Ah, that's
all old hat...".

Alas, dear reader! This interesting discussion remains unfinished: Pëtr Afanasievich is
no more. Last winter, he and his brother went to the meadows together to get some hay.
It was a long way... They hired the services of a driver who moonlighted from the local
forestry vehicle station, and they took some vodka with them, and disappeared into the
night. Unfortunately for them, a wind blew up and caused the road to be covered with
snow... They got stuck even before getting to the meadows. Where can you go at a time
like that? They drank the vodka and fell asleep. Pëtr Afanasievich slept right in the back
of the lorry, and the driver and Levanid in the cab. They were found in the morning...
Those in the cab had frost-bitten hands and feet, but Pëtr Afanasievich froze to death.
And so the bother of getting his manuscript published fell to me. I hardly altered it at all
– I just added some punctuation marks here and there. Despite all my admiration for Ivan
Boborykin, I cannot agree with his verdict that, 'Folk won't accept or understand this
book'. Whether they will accept it or not – I cannot say. But I am convinced that folk
will understand it.

How it all started

Yesterday I went to the new school with the **kolkhoz** chairman, Pëtr Ermolaevich Zvonarëv, known in the village by his nickname, as Petia Dolgii.[5] The school is so big and it has so many partitions that you could easily get lost in it. We goes into one room and on every table there's a little lamp with a coloured lamp-shade, sticking up like mushrooms. The floors were covered with some grey material which was called "*linolum*".[6] As you walk across it, your heels make a "splish-splash" sound, as if you're walking through water, only there are no splashes. There are bookcases all along the walls.

'What's this room for, then?' I ask.

'It's the reading room,' Petia Dolgii replies.

'Blimey!' I think. 'So now then, I could die in peace here.' I love reading books. One thing is written about in one book, another thing in another. And they're all different. A good book is always written so that it has a secret, just like a magic box. To discover the secret, you have to have a good head on your shoulders, and not just a boiled pumpkin. So, I looks at all these bookcases, and I says to Pëtr Ermolaevich: 'Believe it or not, my wife Maruska has never read a single book in her life.'

'What level of education does she have?' he asks.

'None at all. Zilch!'

'How on earth could she read if she's illiterate? She couldn't,' said Petia Dolgii.

But I replies: 'It's not a shame that she can't read, but it's a shame that she can't read between the lines.' I struggled for ages before managing to. No one taught me how. So now then, not only can I read, but I can also do creative writing. I have even had some poetry published in the regional newspaper about the Seventh of November celebrations:[7]

> *Leaves fall down from trees,*
> *Rain comes down in buckets.*
> *From the weather we are not surly*
> *'Cause we came out so early.*

I am a veteran and I receive a personal pension. I get a pension of sixty roubles from the **oblast**. Petia Dolgii invited me to address the school-children on the occasion of the celebrations, on the subject of how we used live and how we live now.

'Comrade **Pioneers**!' I said.[8] 'The social order used to be oppressed... We didn't go to school and we did not raise our education level. I myself, studied only for two winters.

---

[5] This character's nickname means 'long' or 'tall', i.e. Petia ('Peter the Long' or 'Tall'). An explanation as to how he was given this sobriquet is given later, on p.416. This character also features in Mozhaev's story, *Lively*, amongst others.

[6] He means, of course, 'linoleum'. This is another example of Bulkin mispronouncing a modern, foreign word.

[7] Regarding the October Revolution, see footnote № 100, p.184. Here Bulkin refers to the festival as the 'Seventh of November'. Many poems and songs were written to celebrate this occasion, one of the most important festivals of the communist calendar, but Bulkin's poem is apolitical in that it only mentions the weather, and not the victory of the revolution.

[8] Here again, Bulkin shows his political ignorance, since children were never addressed as 'Comrade'.

But how do I mean "study"? When the snow fell deep, I stayed at home. I had no felt boots, just down-at-heel shoes. And how far can you get in down-at-heel shoes in deep snow? But now, Comrade **Pioneers**, how can we not live well? We now live better than under communism. We get free health care and free education. But even so, society must not stand still. It moves forward, just as the earth spins round. But that is not what I wanted to say to you, Comrade **Pioneers**. You must obey your mother and father. Otherwise you will lose your way, like my Valka. All she thinks about is powdering her face and strutting around…'

My speech went down very well with everyone, and Petia Dolgii said to me: 'Would like to work at the school, Pëtr Afanasievich?'

'Work as what?'

'A kind of caretaker… At night you would watch over the building, and during the day you'd maintain order, and ring the school bell at the right times. The **kolkhoz** will pay you direct – fifty roubles a month.'

'And would I have to look after the horse?'

'We have a stableman for that. Your respectability is what we need here to maintain order.'

Well then, I thinks, I must make an effort for the sake of order. And the money's good. With the extra fifty roubles on top of my pension – I can live fine. Why not give it a go? I don't sleep at night in any case – I'm like a Korabishino owl. (Korabishino is a forestry settlement round here – I'll write about it later.)

I agreed. From my trunk, I took out my white, single-breasted naval tunic with a high collar, which I used to wear when I was a **kolkhoz** chairman, my dark-blue, diagonal-ribbed jodhpurs, and my calf-skin boots… I also got out my straw hat. That's how I kept watch. Not only the pupils, but the teachers themselves, stood stock still before me. And also Old Ma Sëmkina, the head of the regional department of people's enlightenment, took me for a military instructor due to her poor sight.

'Comrade Lieutenant-Colonel, why are you not at your lesson?' she asked.

'I am standing guard,' I replied.

I raised the bell to her ear and gave it a good bash. That made her drop a curtsey…

What's the point I am making? I tell you this, because it all started with this job. During the day, I dropped off a bit between bells, but as soon as night fell, I couldn't sleep and that was it – even if you'd poked my eyes out! At home, for want of anything better to do, I just argued with my Maruska. But here, it's quiet… Even lice would die of boredom. And books just fell from my hands because thoughts overwhelmed my mind. Then, I thought, 'Let's write a little book about our village of Brëkhovo? Others write books like that. How am I any worse than them?' A writer once accompanied me on a hunting trip. We got talking, and it turns out that he doesn't know what a '*wood*' is, the tool we use to drag hay off a cart with. So I says to him: 'How can you write books about the countryside when you don't know what a "*wood*" is?'

'Well,' he says. 'There's all kinds of wood: there's the oak, the ash, the asp… There are too many to remember.'

'But that's a "*wood*" on a root,' I replies. 'The one I'm on about is a tool. There's a big difference! Without this "*wood*" you'd not get the hay in. People of different nationalities give it different names. We call it a "*wood*", but the Tatars call it a "*bastard*". You see, the Tatars know about it, but you don't. And you've got the cheek to write books about peasant folk.'

Perhaps there are things I haven't learnt on an artistic level, so let critics not take too much against me for that. But for all that, I don't mix up '*wood*' on the root and '*wood*', the tool. But, I do know a lot of stories about Brëkhovo. So then, I starts to write them down. Every night that goes by, I writes another story. Just like *One Thousand and One Nights*. Only I am both the princess and the Persian Shah.

Why Our Village is Called Brëkhovo

The history of a village is exactly the same as a person's own autobiography. Just as a person needs a personal history for his working life, so a village needs a history for developing a **kolkhoz**, for regional official papers, and for making denunciations. But, to tell the truth, the real history of the village of Brëkhovo started only with Soviet power. Until the Revolution, what kind of history was there? Just drunken binges on religious feast days and going out to work on every weekday. And one must also take into account that there was no regional council, and no **kolkhoz**. What kind of collective history could there have been in the village? There could be no collective history because the village was divided up into single, independent homesteads. And, if you were to write about separate homesteads, all you would get is a load of separate histories, something like short stories. And that would be it – no politics. But real history is always closely connected with politics. Everyone has to understand that from the minute they start school.

So now then, I have to write about why our village is called Brëkhovo. If you ever came around our parts, you would notice our Brëkhovo hillock, even if you were from Prudki, or from Korabishino, or from Samodurovka.[9] The old folk tell how years ago, perhaps two hundred, perhaps even three hundred years ago, **barins** used to come here to hunt. On the slope of the hillock itself, there were kennels, which belonged to the landowner Briukhatov,[10] and there, his masters of the hounds also lived. Our villagers came from those masters of the hounds. Filipp Samochenkov told me that virgin house serfs would be brought there from Samodurovka as brides, and if someone, like the landowner himself, or one of his helpers, put one of them up the duff, they were sent on to Brëkhovo. First, the young woman was made to plant a lime tree, and then she was given in marriage to a huntsman. This is how a whole lime grove grew up around Brëkhovo. The grove was given the name 'Stray'.[11]

---

[9] The name 'Prudki' means 'ponds'; 'Korabishino' is evocative of the Russian word for a 'peddler' and other associated words; 'Samodurovka' is connected with the Russian for 'something done out of stupidity', or 'not thinking', and also for the Russian word for 'petty tyranny'. None of these names are exact in their meaning, (except Prudki), but their effect is comic.

[10] This name is linked to the Russian for 'paunchy'.

[11] The name of the village, 'Brëkhovo' is close to the Russian word for 'belly' or 'paunch', with obvious connections to the pregnant state. The name for the lime grove has strong overtones of the Russian for 'straying from the straight and narrow', or of a dog, which is ownerless and therefore 'stray'.

Ours is a large, trading village. Formerly, a market used to come from the regional main town of Tikhanovo, and even from the town of Pugasovo. All our streets used to be named after trading activities: Hay Street, Horse Street, Jug Street, and so on. During the NEP years, there were two inns, three tea-rooms, two bakeries, one salami sausage shop, and a dozen others. All this stemmed from our lack of culture. So now, not a trace of this **hang-over from the past** remains. Now we have a club, a shop, and a secondary school. All the streets are now called by modern names: Proletarian Street, **Maksim Gorky** Street, Lunacharsky Street – the latter is shortened to 'Lunchas', but this is strictly for unofficial conversations.[12]

We also have yet another **hang-over from the past** – villages feud with each other. For example, we call the inhabitants of Korabishino 'Lazy Buggers', and they call us 'Rock Cakes'. The swear word 'lazy bugger' doesn't mean anything in Russian. I found out from a visiting writer (the one who did not know the difference between '*wood*' on the root and '*wood*' – the tool'), that the expression 'lazy bugger' is a Latvian word, which in our language means an old 'incomer', or someone who has come from afar. Perhaps there is truth in that. Why? Because in Korabishino, it is said, unbaptized Latvians used to live there. Apparently, some prince lost them as a wager at cards and they were brought to us here, to live in the forest. The evidence for their non-Russian extraction can be seen in that, the residents of Korabishino build their peasant houses differently, without an entrance hall, so that the loft space is open to the house itself. They even kept their vat of fermenting **kvass** outside. We even used to tease them about this: 'Akulka, what's bubbling out there?'

'A vat full of fermenting grey-gelding p...' (The three full stops indicates an unprintable word.)[13]

The inhabitants of Prudki were called 'Goat Ringers', because they used a goat to sound the general alarm...[14]

A goat was tethered to graze in the church yard. A string from the fire bell hung low and was tied to a birch tree. Whoever saw signs of a fire would run along and pull on the string, the bell would ring, and people would all come out. But the goat got its horns caught in the string... It shook its head – 'Dong!' Then it went to one side and, once again – 'Dong!' Then it took fright and ran all over the place... The bell tower rang – 'Ding! Dong! Ding! Dong!' It's the alarm! The whole village came running out to join in the fun... From that time on they were called 'Goat Ringers'. The nickname was, in fact, coincidental, but it was entirely justified. The Prudki people are feckless, a perfect example of empty vessels making the most sound...

---

[12] For Maxim **Gorky** see Glossary. Anatoly Vasilievich Lunacharsky (1875-1933) was a close revolutionary associate of **Gorky's**: he was a writer himself and he was appointed the People's Commissar for Education in 1917. He promoted many theatrical productions and the preservation of works of art and historical buildings. In itself, 'Lunchas' does not mean anything, but it sounds ugly and ridiculous, and as such, it has a comic effect.

[13] The unprintable word is the Russian word for 'piss'.

[14] In pre-revolutionary times, before the churches were either destroyed or closed, the church bell would be rung as a tocsin, i.e. in cases of emergency, such as a fire, to summon the local people. Many church bells were taken down and smashed during the anti-religious campaigns of the revolution and during the campaign for full collectivization. Churches were often turned into storehouses or social clubs under the Soviet regime.

Why are we called 'Rock Cakes'? In former times, the inhabitants of Tikhanovo used to sell buckwheat biscuits, and our Brëkhovo folk used to sell buns and home-made pretzels. These were all called 'fancy bread'.

'Hot, freshly baked buckwheat biscuits! Come and get your hot biscuits!' the inhabitants of Tikhanovo would shout.

And our lot, Brëkhovo folk, would shout, vying with them:

'Fancy cakes! Come and get your fancy cakes!'

Some cheeky kid bought a fancy cake but couldn't get his teeth into it. He went behind the stall and chucked it at the back of the woman selling them. It almost took her breath away.

'Ouch! You Devil! Someone's chucked a bloody great stone at my back? It almost broke a rib.'

'It wasn't a "bloody great stone", it's one of your fancy cakes.'

From that time on we were known as 'Rock Cakes'.

But these are all things from the distant past. Now, we have an amateur choir and we perform **chastushki**, composed by ourselves. We performed at an amateur arts' festival, advertised as:

'The Brëkhovo Choir performing their own **chastushki**, music composed by Glukhovaia, the lyrics by Khamov' – our own local composer and writer.'[15]

We have a good **kolkhoz**. Pëtr Ermolaevich Zvonarëv, the last chairman, has a prestigious reputation – he is a people's deputy and a Hero of Socialist Work. The first chairman of our **kolkhoz** was Filipp Samochenkov, who now works with me as a stable hand at the school stables. I have also been a **kolkhoz** chairman in my time, but I shall write more about that later.

Our people are an industrious lot – they are artisans. They work well together. But if anyone nicks a barrel or, let's say, smashes a headlamp off a combine harvester out of sheer spite, you could beat people to death, but they would never nark on who'd done it. However, the inhabitants of Korabishino are just the opposite: if someone pinched so much as a chick from the hen-house, five of them would denounce him like a shot. And, by the way, that lot steal more than our lot. Our lot are quite harsh on narks – at haymaking time, they put a metal pot on their head and beat it with sticks until they go deaf. 'We are a musical lot,' they say. 'Let such narks remember our music! Troublemakers!' We also all have a nickname in the village – and with good reason. Ivan the Squinter even made up a poem about that. Back in 1929, at a meeting in the former inn, he proclaimed: 'So now then, I shall deliver a sermon to you...'

And he went right through the whole village.

'Pincers Drankin, Puffer Nazarkin, Lugovoi the Boar, Big Carp, Mikhail Dartabout, Timofei the Cricket, One-Eyed Alexei, Andrei Simpleton...' And so on.

---

[15] These two composers have rather comical names: 'glukhoi' in Russian means 'deaf', and 'kham' means 'lout'.

'Simpleton' is not his surname – it's his nickname. That's what we call all the idiots.
By the way, Andriusha Simpleton, whose real surname is Nails, recently died under the
following circumstances: he had just left the Cape of Good Hope (that's the name of one
of our villages around here), having had a real skin-full. He had been to one of their main
feast-days, Elijah's Day, or Local Church Day.[16] Andriusha knew every single patron
saint's day of every village to a tee, and he would always turn up for the celebration.

So then, he turned up and got blind drunk. People would give him chunks of food: he
had a bag hanging around his chest in front – that was for slices of pie, and another bag
on his back – that was for chunks of bread. He would amble along, swinging from one
feast day to the next, and whichever bag got the better of him, there he would fall, nose-
down, on the spot. He either ended up on his back or nose-down. And he fell asleep
right where he fell in the road. So, he was walking along on Elijah's Day and went to
sleep in the road.

But also at that very same hour, towards evening, Vaska Bondar was on his way to
Svistunovo in his tractor to get some vodka. The shop in Korabishino was not open. He
was also drunk. The Devil lured him onto the grassy verge…

At court he explained that the going was softer on the verge than on the road:

'Ivan and I were going along, drunk. Suddenly – bang! The tractor gave a jolt…
What's that? Perhaps we've hit a log? We took a look and it turned out to be
Andriusha…'

They had crushed him.

Do forgive me, I got side-tracked. Well… as I was saying, we all have a nickname in
the village. And they were all given for a good reason. Drankin was given the name
Pincers, for example. For his being tight and mean. Mishka Dartabout and Timoshka
Cricket stood out for being in the **Komsomol**. They were my secretaries. Filipp
Samochenkov would call us up and say, 'Well, Koms, once more into battle…' And
we'd set to our task.

Now, I'm writing these lines and I'm thinking to myself: What if Samochenkov were
now to give an order to Dartabout and Cricket? Dartabout is now the boss of the whole
oblast, and Cricket is a big noise in trading. He goes abroad and he spends a month or
more living over there. Now, that's what I call real Koms for you! ("Koms" is our old
name for "**Komsomol** Members".) It's simply astounding that even in those early years,
Timofei had already developed the ability to cope with going abroad. He read foreign
books and sang foreign songs:

---

[16] Traditional Russian rural life was rich in church festivals. Elijah's Day was celebrated on 2 August (20 July,
Old Style) and Local Church Day, which here coincides with Elijah's Day, was the day on which rural
inhabitants celebrated the dedication of their own, local church to God. Many of the religious holidays also
coincided with key agricultural events, such as sowing or mowing, and a number of them also had pagan beliefs
attached to them. Because of the way Elijah summoned fire from heaven, and the way he himself ascended into
heaven (as narrated in I Kings of the Old Testament), in a chariot pulled by horses amidst a whirlwind, he was
held in awe in popular mythology. On his festive day, peasants dare not work in the field or on their own plots
for fear of angering him. When lightening struck, it was said to emanate from Elijah, who was cleansing the
earth, and particularly the soil, from evil spirits.

> *Sail, O my gondola,*
> *Lit by the moon.*
> *Sing out, you bar corola,*
> *Over the sleepy wave...*[17]

'Gondola' means 'boat' in Italian, but 'bar corola', translated into Russian means the 'sounding out of guitar strings', so by now, you have probably guessed that 'corola' means 'guitar'.

By the way, my nickname in the village was 'Diudiun'.[18]

About Myself

I sat down to write about myself and I got to thinking... How amazing my life is! I constantly ridicule my wife, Maruska – she's pure ignorance! But what was I like myself? So now then, I have a private pension, and sometimes I stand in for the Party Organizer. I teach people to see sense and reason, and I am a creative writer. But what was I like in the past? Believe it or not, I had never been to the city before I was twenty. I had never seen the railway, never mind the city! I had never even seen a real clock. I had looked at the grandfather clock in the rural soviet office. But that was easy to get to grips with: a cuckoo popped out and cuckooed the right hour. All you had to do was count. But I had never seen real clocks with Roman numerals. And I couldn't read them.

Some people got lucky during the **dekulakization** campaign – they saw heaps of clocks, and gold rings to boot. But all we came across was flea-bitten **kulaks**, such as the psalm reader and Wet Vasiutka (she was a relative of the landowner Korneev), and the miller Galaktionov. The psalm reader's house was completely empty – all we could take from him was a samovar. Even then, while we were carrying it away, we broke the flue. From Wet Vasiutka we confiscated three baskets of gaudy wine-glasses and plates. She said she had already taken her clock away to be repaired in Pugasovo. Not only did the miller not have a clock, but he didn't even have any decent trousers. But he had a yard full of livestock and eleven kids. They'd had glasses, but they smashed them all, so all they had were tin mugs...

So, I never saw a proper clock until I went into the army. Because of that, a very funny story happened to me. I'll tell you about it now, and you will be able to judge for yourself who I was, and what I have become. However, first, for the sake of formality, I shall start with my background, and say who my father and mother were.

I am called Pëtr Afanasievich Bulkin. In my work record book it is written that I am the son of a victim who was killed by counterrevolutionaries in 1919.

But to tell the truth, Afanasii Bulkin was not my actual father – he was my stepfather. And he was no victim either. He was hired, together with a mate, to drive some cattle

---

[17] This extract is from a poem by Count Constantin Constantinovich Romanov (1858-1915), who was a member of the Romanov dynasty, which ruled Russia. Bulkin is wrong when he asserts that this is a foreign work, although the count did live abroad for a considerable time. Several of his poems were set to music by Tchaikovsky, Rachmaninov and Glazunov. Despite being married, he was known to be homosexual, which partly explains why his poetry was not better known in Russia, particularly under the Soviet regime, because homosexuality was illegal and a taboo subject.

[18] The name itself is meaningless, but it is evocative of a person who moans all the time.

from Kasimov to Pugasovo. On the way, they bashed a merchant's brains out with a bottle. They took his money and his revolver. But they were discovered and sent off into exile to do hard labour for life. My mother married another man and had me and my brother Levanid by him, out of wedlock. So now then, my father was called up to fight against the Germans in the war and he went missing in action. But after the Revolution, Afanasii Bulkin came home, claimed his wife and us two kids. Then, he started to play up – drinking and being violent. Someone sorted him out… It was that kind of time – lawless, but just you try to find out who did it.

So, my brother and I were alone with my mother, and we lived in a peasant house with three windows and a horse. I went out and found work looking after horses, and my brother Levanid looked after sheep.

I won't write in detail about our life at that time – it's boring, and the subject matter is dull. Then, I joined the **Komsomol** and became politically active: I liquidated my illiteracy, and that of others… On account of this political activity, I was drafted into the Red Army. Filipp Samochenkov, the **kolkhoz** chairman, gave me a prize to mark the occasion: I got ten canvasses, five towels with a cockerel design on them, and three gaudy homespun dresses.

So, we all got herded off to Pugasovo station. I kept thinking: 'What does the railway look like? It must be a 'way', covered in tin plate. You can travel along it without getting muddy.' So, we were herded to the station, but there was no tin plate. I looks and sees something crawling towards us. It wasn't exactly boxes, and they weren't really carts. But, it was on wheels… It came to a halt in front of us and the doors opened wide.

Someone shouted out the order, 'Get in!'

It turned out to be a goods train. We got in, but again it didn't seem like a train. It was more like a peasant hut inside – sleeping-benches and sitting-benches.[19] So, we settled down on the sleeping-benches and dropped off to sleep.

When we woke up, it was night. What's going on? We were being thrown from side to side, like on a road full of ruts. There was screeching and groaning… Someone shouted, 'We're off! We're on our way!'

We looks out of the window. We sees a narrow roadway and a deep ditch. Then we all gets frightened – what if we were to tip over?

But it was all right… We arrived safe and sound. We'd been taken to somewhere beyond Kiev. At Kiev Station, someone pointed out a clock to me: 'Look, Petro, at that clock! If you got your trousers caught on the hands, you'd hang in mid air.'

I looks and I looks, but I couldn't make it out. There's marks of some kind all round, in a circle, and two big arrows in the middle.

Fair enough. I was accepted in the cavalry school. I was given a horse… But of all the things to happen, I ended up getting eczema – in a most awkward place – in my crotch, if you'll pardon the expression.

---

[19] A 'sleeping-bench' is a high, raised platform in a Russian peasant hut, which is used for sleeping.

I went to sick-bay and the orderly looks at me suspiciously, and asks: 'Have you been bothering your mare or something?'

'No! I have a charger!'

'A male horse?!' he teased me. 'You dirty bugger!'

He sat down at the desk and noted something down in a book, then he says to me: 'Listen mate, you're going to have to go to the hospital in Dnepropetrovsk. When you get to the station there, ask for tram number four. It will take you straight to the hospital. Here's a five-**kopeck** piece for the fare.'

So, I'm sitting in the politics class and I'm thinking: 'But how will I get there? What do I do if I get arrested for being infectious?'

I couldn't remember the name of my illness for the life of me. 'If they're sending me so far away,' I thought, 'I must be really infectious. Once in Brëkhovo we had to shoot a horse that had malignant anthrax, and we buried it way beyond the village. What if I've got an awful disease like that...?'

Suddenly, a dispatch messenger comes into the class and shouts: 'Bulkin!'

'Right 'ere!'

'You should say, "Yes-sir"! You're wanted at headquarters.'

I was marched out, me in front, as if under escort. What could I do? I had to go. I'm marching and thinking, 'What's all this for?'

We go into some brick building. He opens a door and shoves me into an office. So, I looks around and sees that there's no iron grill and no armed guard. There's a nice, young, Red Army soldier sitting at a desk grinning, and asks me: 'What do you want, Comrade Red Army Soldier?'

'I don't know. I was brought here to you.'

'What's your name?'

'Bulkin.'

'Ah-ah! Here are your documents. Take them and go to Dnepropetrovsk.'

'And who will be guarding me?'

'No one. You're going alone.'

Well, I thinks, it's not that bad. The infection isn't that serious.

He gives me a whole wad of papers and says: 'Remember, the train leaves tonight at twelve o'clock midnight. Here's your ticket.'

I had supper. I wraps up a bit of bread and sugar in a small bundle and I puts it in my pocket. I sets off walking to the station, thinking: 'I wonder when it will be, this twelve o'clock?'

I arrives at the station as it's getting dark. I asks the bloke on duty: 'What time is it?'

'The clock's over there.'

He points to a clock on the wall. I looks at it – it's just like the one at Kiev Station – round, only the marks and hands are a bit smaller. I hangs around by it, blinking at it for a while, then I goes to the platform. There's some kind of train there. I thinks, I'd better ask where it's going. But I'd forgotten the name of where I had to be go to. I takes out my travel warrant, go over to the light and reads "Dnepropetrovsk". I walks away from the light and I forgets again. All right, so I get in the carriage. The train sets off... I look around – it's dark and there's not a soul about. Where are we going? I goes through to another carriage, and then to a third... Empty. What's going on? Surely it's not just me travelling...

The carriage lady comes along with a lamp, so I goes and asks her:

'Citizen Lady, can you tell me where I am going?'

'Where do you need to go?'

'Don't know.'

'How do you mean, you don't know?!' She shone her lamp in my face and, real strict, she says, 'Have you a ticket?'

'It's here in my pocket, but you can't see it here in the dark.'

Anyway, she reads it and says: 'That's fine. Dnepropetrovsk. Only, you'll have to change at Khmelnitsk. Mind you don't miss it.'

We gets to Khmelnitsk. I gets off and asks: 'What time's the train for Dnepropetrovsk?'

'Nine o'clock.'

I goes up to the clock, looks at it, and thinks: 'I wonder when those nine o'clocks will be?' Thankfully, a man and his wife turned up. Such nice, polite people having a nice little chat together... So I asks them: 'What time's the train for Dnepropetrovsk?'

'Nine o'clock.'

'I know that, but when's that?'

They exchanged a wary glance and almost backed away from me.

'Who are you? Where are you from?'

'Brëkhovo.'

They looked at each other again.

'Where on earth are you going?'

'To Dnepropetrovsk.'

'But how come you've no food with you?'

'I have... Here!' I took out my little bundle of bread and sugar and showed it to them.

They burst out laughing.

'Do you know how long you've got on the train?'

'No.'

'Two whole days.'

'Oh, what a calamity!' I just shook my head.

'Do you have any money? And documents?'

'I've only a five-**kopeck** piece. But I have documents.'

I offered them all my bits of paper. They read them and said: 'You nut-case! You have a food coupon here. You have a right to two days' food. You should have cashed it in.'

'Where?'

'At the stores.'

'Oh, what a calamity!'

Well, what could I do now? Anyway, the couple gave me some bread and herring. I took out my bit of sugar. So I had a bite to eat and I drank some tea, got onto the top bunk and slept for two whole days.

I wakes up and looks out of the window: it's Dnepro Station. Ah-ha! It's my stop. I jumps up, pulls on my boots, and dashes out of the carriage. On the platform I takes out my travel warrant and reads, "Dnepropetrovsk". It kind of doesn't match up. I ask a man on duty in a red peaked-cap:

'Is "Dnepro" Russian for "Dnepropetrovsk"?'

'No. Dnepropetrovsk is on the other side of the river.'

I looks and the train is already moving off. I run after it... I only just managed to catch the last carriage. I jumped, but my foot slipped. I nearly ended up under the train.

Okay. So now then, I gets to Dnepropetrovsk in the evening. The station is high and beautiful – I've never seen the like before. And on the clock, under the numbers, are all sorts of animal-type things, shining in brass. So I stands there, looking at it. Suddenly, behind me, someone says: 'What are you gawking at? D'you want to play with it?'

I turns round and it's a young bloke. His cap's pushed back on his neck and he's got a cheap cigarette in his mouth. Nice, cheerful, friendly bloke. Just like the one in the song, 'Andriushka, the lady-killer with the dark eyebrows...', the one that Katia the Shepherdess falls for.[20]

---

[20] This is a quotation from a popular romance or love song. It tells the tale of a handsome young man, Andriushka, who meets a shepherdess, Katia, in a village. He promises to buy her beautiful clothes and take her off to a better life in the city. However, after only a year, the young man abandons her and the child she has had by him, and she takes to drink on account of her depression. She wanders around the city looking for him, and when she does catch sight of him, he refuses to acknowledge her. She takes out a knife and, in an act of revenge, stabs him. The song is typical of popular songs which reflect the social problems of migration from the countryside into the cities and the break-up of the extended family: during the 1920s and '30s, men abandoning women was becoming an increasing social problem during this time of flux and large-scale social migration. Many young people believed that life in the city would be more exciting and offered more opportunities than staying in the village, however living conditions in the cities were cramped and grim, due to a chronic shortage of housing and accommodation, because demand far outstripped supply. It is rather ironic

'That's an interesting clock,' I says.

'Have you made a date to meet someone under the clock, or something?'

'No, I've just arrived. I have to go to the hospital. At eight o'clock in the morning.'

'So?'

'Well, I'm just trying to work out what little animals the hands will be pointing to when I have to go.'

'Oh, Vania, mate! You can't tell the time, can you?' said the bloke, bursting out laughing.[21]

Although I was ashamed, still I admitted it.

'Only, I'm not Vania, I'm called Petia.'

'Never mind!' He slapped me on the back. 'When do you need to go?'

'Eight in the morning.'

'I'll tell you when it's time tomorrow. Where are you from?'

I told him about myself. He was thrilled: 'What a fantastic uniform you have! Particularly your peaked-cap! And your overcoat is so stylish. Oh, I should join the Red Army, but I wouldn't know how to.'

'It's simple. Just fill in a form and they'll take you. Are you a son of the working people?'

'Goes without saying... Proletarian through and through.'

And that's how we got into conversation... We simply became friends. I lay down on a bench to have a kip and he even covered me with my overcoat.

'You have a kip,' he says. 'I'll wake you up at the right time.'

I woke up – it was light, morning. I look around and can't see my mate anywhere. And my coat's not on me, and my cap's gone... I run here and there, I ask around. He's nowhere to be found...

'What time is it?'

'Seven o'clock,' says the bloke on duty.

Oh, my word! I've got to get to the hospital. I go out of the station onto the square and I sees the number four tram right in front of me. That's good! I remembered what the medical orderly said: 'Get on the tram and it'll take you right to the hospital.'

So I ride and ride on this tram, waiting for the last stop at the hospital. But it keeps on going and going, and people get on and off. And I sits and sit. I looks out of the

---

that the young man Bulkin meets, who reminds him of Andriushka in the song, turns out to be just as unprincipled as him.
[21] 'Vania' is a familiar form of the popular Russian name 'Ivan'. It was also the name used in many jokes and amusing 'anecdotes', which feature a simple person, in a similar way to which 'Paddy' is used in jokes about Irish people, or 'Jock' is used about the Scots.

window, and ah!... It's the station again! Then the conductress comes up to me and says: 'Red Army Soldier, where do you need to go?'

'The hospital.'

'Why on earth didn't you say? I'd have told you where you needed to get off.'

Fair enough... I eventually found the hospital. I goes up to the gate and there's a kind of booth behind it. I looks and there's a bell, a little white button. Where did I learn, and who taught me, that you have to push that button? So now then, I couldn't tell you. I pressed it, but no one comes out. I press it again... Silence.

What's going on? I look through the gate and it seems the booth is empty and that it's even falling apart at the back. Oh, my word!

So I go up to some big doors. There's another door bell. I press it and I can hear running above. I hear footsteps. A man on duty in a military uniform appears: 'Who d'yer want?'

'The hospital.'

'Accident and emergency is round there,' and he waved his hand.

I goes in that direction. I sees an open door and steps going down. I went down and down them. I opens another door. What's going on? It's daylight, but the electric light is on. There's a massive stove blazing, belting out heat. Suddenly this grubby mug appears before me – all you could see was a mass of teeth.

'What d'yer want?'

'I need the hospital, for treatment.'

'Lie down over there,' he says, nodding to a pile of coal. 'I'll cure you with a bash of my shovel.'

'You miserable git!'

I went up the stairs, out of this inferno, and squatted by the door for a while. I thinks: 'You can all go to hell! I'm not going anywhere else.'

Suddenly, a nurse comes out: 'Where do you need to be?'

I stood up and explained what had happened.

'What's your illness?'

I stumbled... then I forgot again: 'It sounds something like "enema".'

She burst out laughing: 'Get away with you, "enema"! Let me have your papers, we'll sort it out.'

I reach into my trouser pockets and there were no documents, nor the five-**kopeck** piece. That friend at the station had cleaned me out... We had to ask my division for the details. It caused so much trouble... And all because of that clock.

Now, you might ask: How come the orderly had given me a five-**kopeck** piece for the tram, and I only remembered about it once I had got to the hospital? I have to admit in all honesty – I had forgotten to buy a ticket.

So now then, you judge for yourself what I was like. By the way, two years later, when I graduated from the cavalry school, I was awarded a watch for my stunts on horseback. At that time, I used to do three-hundred-and-sixty-degree turns. I was selected to take part in local horse shows. It's just like the saying: 'it's dogged as does it…'

About Manolis Glezos

At this point, I'll just take a little break from the history of the village. Yesterday we had a **kolkhoz** meeting about showing our support for Manolis Glezos.[22] What came out of that? Some members of the **kolkhoz** were far from understanding the difference between the international situation and the purely internal situation on the farm. So, it's too early to rest on our laurels and to let up on ideological educational work. The troubadours of world imperialism are ever watchful.[23]

So now then, we're sitting in the club-house, holding a **kolkhoz** meeting about showing support for Manolis Glezos. I was making a speech (the party organizer, Comrade Golovanchikov, had gone off to Moscow for some oakum – he was building a house for his mother-in-law), and Petia Dolgii was busy writing up some papers or other. Even though he was considered a good chairman, he still hadn't fully developed his managerial skills. Anyway, judge for yourself. We're all sitting there, on the platform, the table covered in red material, but he's adding up figures for pig feed (I noticed that later). How much hay to give them, where they are to be housed, where the piglets should go…

'Comrades!' I says. 'The highway-robbery policy of world imperialism, headed by the United Stated, by which I mean America, is in evidence everywhere. They couldn't give a damn that Vietnamese towns and villages are being burned with napalm, with bombs in other words, and not a damn about the blood of the patriot of black Africa, Patrice Lumumba…[24]

---

[22] Manolis Glezos (1922–) is a Greek communist activist, whose daring act of tearing down the Nazi flag upon the Acropolis in 1941 inspired guerrilla resistance to the Nazi occupation. He was condemned to death for treason in 1948 and he was imprisoned by the Greek regime on a number of occasions. He visited Russia several times and the USSR issued stamps in his honour in 1959, for his part in promoting the international communist cause. He is still an active political campaigner and recently he condemned the war in Afghanistan and Iraq. Even in remote villages, peasants were expected to take an interest in communist activity throughout the world, though many peasants and rural inhabitants felt this sort of issue was far removed from their sphere of interest.

[23] Bulkin's use of the word 'troubadours' here is comic – such a phrase was never used as one of the many set phrases of communist ideology.

[24] Bulkin refers, of course, to the Vietnam War (1955-75), which was a protracted and unsuccessful effort by South Vietnam and the USA to prevent the communists of North Vietnam from uniting South Vietnam with North Vietnam, under their leadership. Napalm was a type of petroleum-based incendiary bomb used during the conflict by the American forces. Patrice Lumumba (1925-61) was the first prime minister of the Democratic Republic of the Congo. He cultivated close ties with the Soviet Union which made many Western powers uneasy about the establishment of a stable regime in that part of Africa, in an atmosphere of Cold War between the Soviet Union and other foreign powers. Those countries around the Congo were concerned as to how the political situation would develop in the light of friendly relations with the Soviet Union, and many foreign powers viewed such a *rapprochement* as highly undesirable. Lumumba was murdered in suspicious circumstances in 1961. The Soviet Union offered student scholarships to many young people from the Congo to acquire a specialist education, which, of course, included a good measure of political 'education' for those taking part. An institute was set up in Moscow named after Patrice Lumumba.

So now then, they have started on Manolis Glezos. So now, they're oppressing Greece as well…[25]

And so on, and so forth.

When I had finished my speech, Petia Dolgii tore himself away from his papers about pig troughs and asks: 'Are there any questions from the floor?'

'I have a question!' says the carpenter Feduleev, Makar. 'It's about the cornices and skirting boards. We really *do* have to sort this out. Will you give us a decision or not?'

So I says to him, real serious-like: 'Comrade Feduleev, we are trying to come to a decision, but you are on about cornices and skirting boards…'

'So are we saying that cornices are not needed, then? The house won't stand up without them.'

'We know that. But we've all come together to discuss Manolis Glezos.'

'Yeah. You might know him, but we don't. So why have you asked us here?'

'The very reason you have been invited here is to come to a decision – we are standing up, with all our determination, in defence of Manolis Glezos.'

Then there was a shout from the floor: 'That was all decided in your speech. Now, let's decide about the cornices!'

I turned to the chairman for some kind of support. But he had buried his face in some papers and was laughing behind them. I decided to bring him to order, right there in public, and said: 'There is nothing to laugh about here. The chairman, Comrade Zvonarëv, will now have a word.'

He removed the sheet of paper from his face and said, as if nothing had happened: 'Well then, Comrades. Let's decide about the cornices. Who wants to say something?'

Feduleev stood up again, and then he started: 'What kind of situation do we have? We are paid the same price for fixing cornices and skirting boards. But just you fix a cornice first, and then a skirting board. The cornice is on top. First, you need to get some kind of support to stand on, either a barrel or a box, for example. So, you climb onto it and you lift your beard up towards it. You nail the cornice on, then you have to move the barrel a bit further on. Then you look at it from the side… Is it straight or crooked? Now, let's take the skirting board… You have to get down on your knees, you hammer – but not for long, and that's it. Because it's down below. So how can you equate the two jobs? You can't. We have to decide what to do.'

Feduleev sat down, and I say: 'Fine. Let's decide this at another general meeting.'

'No! Let's sort it out now!' came the shout from the floor.

At this point, Petia Dolgii gets up: 'We'll pay double-rate for the cornices. Is everyone agreed?'

'Agreed!' voted the whole hall.

---

[25] When a communist-controlled Provisional Democratic Government was established in Greece in December 1947, the USA provided support for anti-communist forces in order to defeat the communist cause there.

So, I says again: 'Comrades! Who would like to say a word about Manolis Glezos?'

'I would,' says Iakusha Vorobëv.[26] 'I propose, Comrade Collective Farmers, that we show our support for Manolis Glezos. Because, as someone who's been in prison myself, I know what it's like. So if there's any chance of us knocking off a bit of his sentence, then I think we should ask. There's no harm in asking, is there?'

'I suggest that my two **poods** of grain, which I surrendered last year to help Vietnam, should be redirected to Manolis Glezos. It never got sent to Vietnam anyway. What's the point in it just lying around in the **kolkhoz** storeroom?'

Then Marishka Drankina, our storeroom manageress, stood up and addressed him: 'But you took it back last year!'

'Just when did I collect it? When?'

'That's a bit rich! And who gave it to Galaktinov for milling? Who was it?'

'Are you suggesting *I* gave it to him?'

'It was you who ordered the grain to be given to Galaktinov!'

'For milling?'

'Yes, for milling!'

'How do you mean "for milling"? Do you call that milling? He chewed it for a tad, then spat it out. He's the one who should be fined for such milling, and not paid for it...'

Everyone laughed. But I rapped on the water carafe with my pencil and announced sternly: 'Comrades, we should be talking about politics, about observing rights and the Constitution. About the Law! Is there anyone who wants to talk about this? Please...'

Ivan Drankin stood up, Marishka's father-in-law: 'Just tell us, will there be a law or not?'

'What law?'

'Everyone knows which law... The one about cattle.'

'What's cattle got to do with all this?'

'How do you mean, "got to do with this"? Yesterday Shabykin's cow came into my farmyard and ate two **centners** of potatoes.'

'Don't tell lies! It couldn't eat two **centners** – it would burst!' shouted someone from the hall.

'That's just what I'm talking about. It nearly burst. It's sides were like this...' Drankin set his arms apart. 'It looked just like a barrel.'

'And what did you do with it?' shouted Shabykin.

'I just jabbed her and poked her right in that greedy side of hers...'

'I request that you write that down as evidence!' shouted Shabykin, again.

---

[26] His name means 'sparrow' in Russian.

'Just you hang on! You will answer for your own cow,' replied Drankin, turning towards him. Then, addressing the platform again, he said: 'So what happened? Shabykin took my cow and he won't give her back. So what I'm asking is, will we have a law or not?'

I turned to Petia Dolgii, who was chuckling into his papers again. Well, he was young, and he had no experience of education work. He was acting like a kid at school, when a pupil comes out with a load of rubbish. Then the stores woman, Marishka Drankina, takes to the floor again: 'And when will a decision be made about the seeds? Whether it's rye, or wheat, or barley – it's all put down on paper as one lot.'

'Comrades, these are all questions of purely internal disputes. We are discussing things on an international scale. You must understand...'

At this point, my comments were so forcefully made that even the Drankins were reduced to silence. I even put the kybosh on Marishka.

'Sit down! We're far too busy to talk about seeds. First, let's sort out the political issues. We must fulfil the orders of the regional committee.'

We put it to the vote. We made a resolution to support Manolis Glezos, and I thought for a moment, and then decided: 'I shall go to the regional committee without fail and ask for a lecture to be given on the differences between internal and international conflicts. They could even assign me to give the lecture. We must not slack in our education work with the masses.'

Filipp Samochenkov – Our First Brëkhovo Kolkhoz Chairman

I shall begin a description of the inhabitants of Brëkhovo with Filipp Samochenkov. In the first place, he lives on the edge of the village, and in the second, he was our first **kolkhoz** chairman. He has an engaging external appearance: he is thin, lithe, with a tendency to lean forwards, as if he is being pushed in the back. He walks with a bias to the front, and he minces, as if he's after someone. If you call over to him, he'll answer you, but he won't stop straight away – he'll carry on for another few steps, then swerve round towards you. It's as if he's kind of spring-operated: you wind him up and he rushes forwards. That's obviously why he's been thin all his life. He's held some good posts. Anyone else in his position would have acquired a belly and a fat neck. But Filipp was as gaunt as a blay in spring.[27] I don't know how his trousers managed to stay up. His most prominent feature was his large nose – it's as big as your elbow.

As far as Filipp being an historical character is concerned, I cannot resist saying a few words about history. In former times, all history was based on class struggle. So now we are told that there are no more classes and no more **enemies of the people**. Well, first of all, where have they all gone?[28] And secondly, if there are no classes, and no **enemies of the people**, where is the struggle? And what is history based on? That's the tricky question! So, don't give us any of your historical denials, Comrade Compromisers!

---

[27] A blay is a kind of carp.
[28] These are sentiments Old Mother Proshkina expresses in the story of that name. Mozhaev is drawing attention to the periodic changes of attitude and official policy which occurred within the Soviet regime.

And by the way, why should I be bothered about other people? I've got plenty of history to write about. There have been more struggles than enough in my lifetime.

I started writing about Filipp Samochenkov and I got to thinking: Why do people like me, and yet, not like him? Do you know what I will answer? Filipp Samochenkov had fervour in his managerial skills, or, as we say in Brëkhovo, "passionate overgrowth". He used to lead them to a full stop, but I used to slip in a comma – I took things easy myself, and I let others take a bit of a breather. He used to drink like a maniac, as if it was not the vodka he was knocking back, but **enemies of the people**. That's why his whole life went pear-shaped. But I can't drink a lot. The expression on my face changes and I find it embarrassing in front of my underlings. Although, if I had to, I could keep pace with Filipp Samochenkov.

In the forestry settlement of Korabishino, **dekulakization** was started a year earlier than everywhere else, that is, in 1928. All former **kulaks** were sent to the timber preparation station, mostly for concealing their grain or hiding their surpluses. But they were the kind of people that, in just a couple of years, got rich all over again. They had been proletarianized, and so the taboo was lifted. But they became wealthy again. We had to root them out for a second time. There were a lot of cattle from them in 1928. It was summertime. What could we do with the cattle? So we decided to set up a commune in Korabishino and give all the **kulak** livestock to them. Filipp Samochenkov was sent there as the chairman.

That's where our Filipp Samochenkov took a wrong turn. He said, 'The first thing we've got to do is feed the communards.' He even put out a slogan: 'Stuff your belly!' He reasoned that, a full person is more likely to obey a command. And work more conscientiously. All you get from a hungry person is meanness and grouchiness. So, fair enough. The communards ate to their heart's content and turned up willingly for work, and they built a communal canteen and a silage tower. But, unfortunately for Samochenkov, a lot of **kulak** beehives remained. And, before he knew it, all the honey was nicked for making mead and moonshine. Such drunkenness, such thieving broke out... Things got impossible. They nicked hives, piglets, sheep, pigs, and even went as far as nicking cows. Samochenkov spent the whole winter searching out the thieves. He came across a whole gang of them – they were sitting one night on some **kulak** land, drinking and singing songs. He was about to confront them when one of them flew at him on a horse from the compound, shouting, 'I'll crush you! You parasite!' Filipp fired his gun at him. The rider fell, injured. It turned out that he was the beekeeper.

Filipp was transferred back to Brëkhovo. Things were coming to a head there with **dekulakization** and exiling people. In a word, it was the dirty work of building a foundation for a new society. Samochenkov made a great effort and he fulfilled the instructions to the letter that he had received from on high. He even **dekulakized** the psalm-reader. We dispossessed that servant of religion, as I have already described, by taking his flueless samovar, and we took a sack of dried Caspian roach and a bucket of herrings from each of the **Volga** seasonal workers.

It was Samochenkov who liquidated our church. We founded a **kolkhoz** and we needed to build a pigsty, but we had no bricks. So Samochenkov says: 'What is the church built on? Let's liquidate the church and build a pigsty with the bricks.' That's how the priest came to curse him on the square. He says, 'He who builds a pigsty out of church bricks, God will turn into a pig!' We liquidated the priest as well, but Samochenkov was found guilty of going too far. About thirty people were called to give evidence at the court – they were all witnesses. The psalm-reader was there, and the **Volga** seasonal workers, and Wet Vasiutka... One of them shouted, 'He took my horse!', and another one shouted that his cow had been taken, and another accused him of screwing a loan out of him. They gave Filipp a real pasting. The judge asked him: 'What was your reason for doing all this, Filipp Samochenkov?'

'Citizen Judge,' he replied. 'Believe it or not, I did all this without malicious intent. It was my own zeal to blame, and that's all...'

He was given two years under Statue 109 for the Unlawful Use of Soviet Power and another two years under Statute 110 for Discrediting Soviet Power, and he was sent to Sviatogleb Monastery, where there were **kulak** inmates.[29] The first time he appeared in the exercise yard, he was beaten by **kulaks** to within an inch of his life. So he went to the guards. 'What are you doing? They're going to beat me to death...' Filipp was taken on as a stableman for the militia, but his daughter, Deaf Polia, used to pop round to him to steal oats. He was sent to a logging station for thieving oats. However, in 1935, Comrade Stalin changed the law: whoever was incarcerated under Articles 109 and 110 would be freed.[30]

Filipp returned and he was rehabilitated, but he was not given any managerial work. He worked for two years at the fat-rendering unit with Andriusha Gvozdikov, the very chap who had fallen asleep and was crushed on the road on St. Elijah's Day.[31] Then, as luck would have it for Filipp, a conspiracy of **enemies of the people** was discovered in Korabishino, and many **enemies of the people** were put in prison, including the **kolkhoz** chairman. Who should be sent to replace him? There was no proletarian thoroughbred in the region. Who, from the poorest ranks of the peasantry, could meet all the exacting requirements of the current policy at this historical moment? He, who had already shown his zeal in eradication. Filipp Samochenkov came to mind. At that time he was living on the edge of Brëkhovo, in his two-windowed little hut, and apart from Deaf Polia and the motley horse called Marsik, he had acquired nothing. So, he was sent back to Korabishino, as **kolkhoz** chairman...

I don't know how well he managed the farm there. Only, after the war, he was sacked for letting the farm go to rack and ruin and he was excluded from the Party. He came back to Brëkhovo, opened up the boarded-up windows of his house, let Deaf Polia settle

---

[29] Sviatogleb literally means 'Holy Gleb'. Boris and Gleb were medieval princes of the early Russian state and they are amongst the earliest canonized saints of the Russian Orthodox Church, having been slaughtered by Svyatopolk during some of the many campaigns over succession in early Russian history, in the 11th century. They became the epitome of Russian meekness and the passive acceptance of suffering, and the event and circumstances of their deaths are recorded in early Kievan chronicles. For a translation of part of the text and an illustration of one of the many icons painted in honour of Boris and Gleb, see *The Russian Chronicles*, numerous editors, foreword by Norman Stone (London: Random Century, 1990), pp.66-68. See also footnote № 41, p.381.
[30] In 1935 Stalin announced that, 'Life has become better, life has become more cheerful', a remark which heralded a relaxation of some of the harsher policies of the regime. Certain '**enemies of the people**' were rehabilitated and a new constitution was brought out in 1936, which gave a number of former 'enemies' the right to vote again. However, this was only a lull before a very vicious storm: the Great Purges of 1937-38 did to the urban population what collectivization had done to the rural community.
[31] His name 'Gvozdikov' means 'small nail' or 'tack'.

in there, and he himself went off to work in a quarry in Kasimov, as far away from sight and shame as possible…

But bashing stones was not like working at the fat-rendering unit. He just couldn't get used to it. He went into the local executive committee offices to find out about the availability of any kind of junior managerial work. He said: 'It's my fault, I'm the only one to blame.'

'Blame for what?'

'Because I was expelled from the Party in Korabishino.'

'Ah, but their decision was never ratified.'

'So what should I do now?'

'You could go to Brëkhovo as the deputy chairman of the **kolkhoz**.'

So he went there. But the chairman himself upped and died, and that left the whole **kolkhoz**, once again, to Filipp Samochenkov. It was a time when everything was expected from the **kolkhoz**: grain, timber, animals. Just do all you can to supply the goods. Filipp Samochenkov even managed to be among the top suppliers in some ways. He started out well, but he could not keep up the pace. His reserves ran low… Then they were on his back again: they lent hard on him, then removed him from his post as a wrecker, and he was threatened with criminal proceedings…

I was sent to replace him. The secretary of the regional executive committee came with me. He gave him an ear-bashing until the early hours of the morning: 'Well, what are we to do with you?'

'It's up to you – you make the rules,' replied Filipp.

'Okay, you will be transferred to the regional executive committee. Find a job for yourself there.'

'No way,' replied Samochenkov. 'I'm not moving anywhere else. The regional executive committee might hand me over to the militia. I've been through all that once before…'

So, he ended up as a stableman at the school stables.

I took his post as **kolkhoz** chairman and I thought: 'Let's just have a little look in his file and find out where's the flea in the ointment.' I have this rule – if you want to get to the bottom of a person, just look in his file, as it is written: 'The file is the mirror of the soul'. And if any notes on you still exist, your whole experience is passed on to posterity, into history, that is. So now then, it is said – 'A word is like a sparrow, once it's flown, you can't catch it.' Well, why should we catch it? It's better captured in reports, and file it in a personal file, hide it in a safe, and it won't go anywhere.[32]

So I started to read Samochenkov's notes, and the stack of requests, and his resolutions – and I understood the whole lot: Filipp is not an economic planner, but he was a manager of the first water. In other words, in all his dealings, he kept to the managerial line. He kept on message! He stuck to it with singular enthusiasm, as they say!

---

[32] Similar sentiments are expressed in the story *Sania*, see p.75.

I will produce, by way of example, one **kolkhoz** managerial committee report:

Agenda

Fulfilling the plan of the harvesting group.

On this first point, the following people spoke:

Comrade N. Glukhov (the brigade leader of the first brigade), who reported that progress with the haymaking was very slow. In the first place, the kolkhoz workers had all gone home: and in the second place, the machinery had broken down. There were no spare parts. They were reaping, but not milling, because it was damp.

Comrade Svidenkov (the brigade leader of the second brigade) said that, we are not mowing the hay, because the tractor has broken down and there are no spare parts to repair it. Only a small fraction of the rye had been harvested because the weeds clog up the combine harvester.

Comrade N. Dementev (the brigade leader of the third brigade) said that, the harvesting was going very slowly because there was a poor turn-out for work. Besides all this, people would not take orders. The grain was not milled because the machine had broken down and the grain was damp. Some cogs in the tractor are broken, but there are no spare parts...

The following made a statement:

Comrade Samochenkov (chairman). Comrades, surely don't the kolkhoz workers know that they get paid for their work-units in grain? But why don't we mill the grain? It is our own grain. Surely the kolkhoz workers have realized that we must strive for a cultured and prosperous life? We must tackle the following problems, Comrades... There are kolkhoz workers who have not a single gram of grain and still they sit doing nothing. Such people understand nothing and look out only for

their own property, and care not a jot for
anything communal. Comrades, these kind of
kolkhoz workers must be told off and deprived of
their hay and draught animals. Haven't I given
all you brigade leaders a task to do? So what's
going on?

Let's take, for example, Brigade leader Dementev –
he neither sows nor reaps, but he's always riding
around on horseback, always on the common, where
there is a constant, general booze-up. But
Dementev, instead of mowing and stacking the hay,
submits exaggerated figures, by which he deceives
the whole husbandry section of the kolkhoz and
the state. And what is worse, he does not check
the sheaved hay, and it's probably all being used
for cattle feed.

What is going on today? We have failed to meet
the plan for haymaking, and for the wheat
harvest also. And the reason for this failure is
wholly down to those in charge. Where is the
work discipline in Dementev's team? There is none.
And let's take the leaders Glukhov and Svinenkov.
All they do is cause trouble in the
administrative office and then they go out to get
drunk. I believe that the management of the
kolkhoz is to take decisive actions to address the
irresponsibility of those persons already
mentioned.

These are the resolutions:

Comrade Brigade leaders Glukhov, Svidenkov and
Dementev should be issued with an official warning.

As we see from this report, Filipp had not determined why the wheat was damp and
why the combine harvester had broken down. He had relied totally upon their political
awareness and on his ability to use impassioned managerial words. Samochenkov really
knew how to talk to them, you can't deny that. But he lacked flexibility.

Judge for yourself. Here is a request from Sysoev, Pëtr Semenovich:

I ask you to review my memo concerning the fact that, due to illness, I stabbed my cow to death. Please, let me have a cow in calf for meat.

Samochenkov's decision:

Please make a ruling on my memo concerning the fact that my husband has been taken on by the FZO and I am left behind. I want to go and join him, and he wants me to. Please, release me from the kolkhoz.

All best,

Smorchkova, Klavdia

I have three untreated sheepskins.

Please, treat them. Khamov.

Two substandard sheepskins to be given in exchange.

Samochenkov.

I request that I am released from work as the bookkeeper, on account of my semi-illiteracy and my poor health, or to be precise, my poor sight and my poorly guts.

N. Smorchkov.

I request that the managerial board of the "Sunrise Kolkhoz" sort out my application for me to leave the kolkhoz, since I joined it freely, of my own accord, and I want to leave freely, of my own accord. I am now living in the village of Sshibi-Kolpachek and I am now married.[33]

All best, Dementev, V.

Request Denied

As regards these decisions, you might think that Filipp Samochenkov is a heartless man and takes no pity on anyone. That is not the case. The secret is that he chose to stick to the managerial line, to official policy, that is, which consists of refusing everything – and that's that. Perhaps a particular directive had been forced on him and he strictly enforced it until there was a new change in policy. There is ample evidence to prove that Filipp Samochenkov was not a nasty person in the **kolkhoz** records. I shall cite a few consecutive examples, just so that you don't think I have specially selected them.

> It is noted that, on this day, Malantev, Svelii
> Ivanovich, brought in some youths who were of
> pre-military training age. Instead of making his
> own family go out to work, he used the volunteer
> help of others, leaving Dementev, A., and Dementev,
> V. at home doing nothing, and because of them, it
> was necessary to ride a kolkhoz horse at full
> tilt. This incident is duly noted here.

Malantev is to be given an official warning.

Samochenkov.'

> The following is noted, that on 28 February 1949,
> drivers Cherpenikov, Ivan, and Glukhov, Matvei,
> took it upon themselves to go to the stables by
> night, harness some horses, and they used them to
> fetch their own personal firewood. This left no
> one to get feed for the cows. They mooed all day
> long...

The drivers are to be given an official warning.

Samochenkov.

---

[33] This is an invented name and it has an amusing meaning: the first part of the name – 'sshibi', is the Russian imperative to 'knock off', and a 'kolpachok' (a slight variation of the second part of the name) is a 'cap' or 'top', like the plastic cover for a biro or pen.

Illustration 14. 'Let Us Go towards Abundance', Stalin.

As you can see, the managerial line was as clear as day in these decisions. From this, we can boldly conclude that Filipp Samochenkov liked the managerial line and never deviated from it. However, this mistake in no way came from a lack of moral qualities, because moral qualities are subject to fluctuations and even U-turns. Here, the line, the policy, that is, has not been deviated from. He must have had that kind of managerial mind-set. And everything is powerless before such a managerial mind-set – science and medicine included. Because the mind-set given to a person remains the same, from the cradle to the grave.

Filipp and I once got into conversation after lessons had finished (he was mucking out the school stables), and I asked him:

'Did you ever discover why you dragged the **kolkhoz** so slowly to a state of abundance?'

And he said to me: 'Well, we were treading an unexplored path…'

We both fell into deep contemplation.

Just How Much Can Paramon Drink?

Well, I must say that to drag out one story and read it is rather boring… History is history, and it's all in the past, as we say… For that reason, we must link it with contemporary times. And we should view it from the heights of the current path we have taken, from the sidelines, so to speak.

After all, where is the interest in history? It is interesting in so far as we are forging ahead, just as it keeps receding. So, when describing the past, you should point out current achievements. And what is more, even our shortcomings should highlight our historical progress.

Just take, for the sake of argument, binge drinking. Who used to be a real drinker in our village of Brëkhovo? The miller – because for doing his job, he use to take a cut in money and flour. But, whoever wanted to jump the queue, and have his grain milled straight away, used to stand him a half-litre bottle. Iurusov the carpenter and Dumb Mitia the cobbler both used to drink heavily.[34] These two used to get blind drunk every day. Everyone else used to get drunk only on high days and holidays. So now then, what? Now, one might say, everyone to the last man drinks a lot. If one looks at this from a moral point of view, one might well censure it. But what if we were to look at it from an historical perspective? It's an achievement. Because people drink when they have the wherewithal to drink. I dare say, no one drank during the War. And when we were picking the country off its knees, we couldn't even think about drinking. It wasn't that we didn't want to drink, but there wasn't a single spare grain of wheat to make it with. The state took every last grain from the **kolkhozes**. So binge drinking is a true sign of historical progress, evidence of the improvements in our living conditions. I cite that same Filipp Samochenkov as an example. When he lived well, he drank well. But now he never touches a drop. And herein lies the riddle of man's character: Why has Paramon Drankin drunk heavily at all times? And just how much can he take? No one can answer this question – not even Paramon himself.

Once, I invited him to my house to butcher a pig. We hadn't even finished skinning it when my wife Maruska brings in a half-litre. Having eyed this 'gear', Paramon says with a note of disappointment: 'Ah, you won't get through all that…'

He lit a cigarette and fell into a state of reverie.

---

[34] Cobblers were the archetypal drunks of Russia. There is a phrase in Russian 'to drink like a cobbler', which is the equivalent to the English expression, 'to drink like a fish'.

'I remember one time, Pëtr Afanasievich,' he said, 'drinking to my heart's content. But one question troubles me: How much can one drink in one sitting?'

'You'd have to have a suitable occasion to carry out such an experiment,' I replied. 'It's just like singing on stage: it's one thing to sing to a packed hall, and quite another to sing to rows of empty seats. It's the same thing – if you drink to prove a point, you wouldn't get much down. You could just drink, but it wouldn't have any effect. Take Mishka Kaban: he drank ten slim glasses, but on the eleventh he fell down and wailed till he could wail no more. But at a wedding, I have been known to drink twelve glasses... and carry on! On occasions, you could drink more, but the vodka always runs out. So, it's a case of right time, right place.'

'That's just the pity. I once was in a position to do just that. I had the opportunity, but I didn't take it. I regret not doing it to this day.'

And so, Paramon told me about this lamentable occasion.

'I was working with Senka Kurman as a state procurement officer for the village stores. It was the eve of the feast of Winter Mikola.[35] It started snowing – you couldn't see a hand in front of your face. As it happened, we had just bought a sheep for the village stores. But how could we get it there? The road was covered with snow. If you went on horseback and strayed from the road, you'd freeze to death. We've got vehicles now, but what did we have then? So, we're sitting in the wooden watchman's booth by the shop. The sheep's there with us. We sits and we thinks... "Semën," I says. "It's going to snuff it anyway. And worse than that – it's going to lose weight. We're going to lose money on it. Where are we going to find feed at this time of year? Why don't we slaughter it?"

'"Let's do it – we won't get home now anyway. It's a hell of a snow storm out there!"'

'While I got the stove going and fetched some water from the river, Semën butchered the sheep.

'"We'll save the carcass and offal for the womenfolk, lock, stock and barrel," he says. "We'll cook the rear for us and keep the front bit to sell, for the sake of the accounts."

'So, we sits there, cooking... The snow falls and falls. "Ah!" we thinks. "Wouldn't it be nice to have at least a half-litre to go with it. We've got such tasty food..."'

---

[35] Winter Mikola is a variant name for the standard Nikola (or Nikolai/Nicholas) Day, an Orthodox Christian feast day, which has two official days for celebration: one is in May (Vernal Nikola) which falls on 22 May (9 May, Old Style), and Winter Nikola, which falls on 19 December (6 December, Old Style). Nikola is reputed to have lived between 3–4 A.D. He is said to have been born in the ancient Lycian seaport city of Patara, and he rose to the position of bishop of Myra, now in modern Turkey. He is reported to have performed miracles for the poor and orphaned, and he became the patron saint of Russia and Greece. However, there is little historical evidence for his existence. In the West, he has been transformed into Santa Claus. In Russia, young girls on the point of marrying, traditionally turn to St. Nicholas/Nikola/Nikolai for a blessing to ensure a happy marriage, addressing him as, 'Nicholas the Most Gracious', which reflects his reputation for generosity. As is usual in the Russian tradition, the religious aspect is concomitant with a more practical, agricultural activity: St. Nicholas/Nikola is the patron saint of the harvest, fertility and hence, of cattle, and he was 'beloved of Mother Damp-Earth', the epithet given to moist, fertile soil which nourishes the crops and produces a plentiful harvest. The Spring Mikola denoted the *end* of spring sowing, but in the areas where the climate was harsher, it marked the *beginning* of spring sowing.

'But we've got no money and Polka Lugovaia, our shop assistant, had gone off to the regional capital. So we sits and thinks. How we can get some vodka? Semën says, "When you've no money, you have to play the respect card. Because it costs nothing to honour a person, but you get a big pay-back. You'll be trusted for a loan, and you'll even get it interest free." He says, "I got the 'George' in the war. And shall I tell you why? If I'm absolutely honest, it was entirely for boot-licking."'[36]

'So we sits there, telling funny stories. Suddenly, a light shines through the shutters. It sounded like some kind of vehicle. We run out and sure enough – it's a lorry. It ran straight into the gate. It was loaded higher than the cab with boxes, and through the gaps in the wooden laths we could see bottle necks. The oilskin covering had been pulled back by the wind and was flapping, like trousers on a washing-line.'

'"What village is this?" asked the driver from the cab.'

'I looks at these cases of booze and, believe me or not, I went numb with anticipation.'

'But Senka fussed around the driver like a devil. "Don't you worry your little head about what village this is, mate. Don't matter where's here – we've warmth and cheer.[37] Come on down and get warmed up. Our stove is heated and our pot is cooking."

'We goes into the hut. The driver's nostrils were enticed: "What's smelling here?"'

'"Food and booze", says Semën, giving a wink. "Where were you coming from?"'

'"From Pugasovo to Ermish."'

'"But you've landed up in Brëkhovo."'

'"Oh, you don't say! I didn't even turn off. How on earth have I ended up here?"'

'"Devils have tricked you. That's us, actually," said Semën.'

'He took the mutton stew off the fire and removed the lid, so the smell wafted towards the driver.'

'"Sit down," we says. "Spend the evening with us."'

'He didn't take much persuading. "Hang on, lads," he says. "I'll be back in a sec."'

'And he brings back a full half-litre. Well, you'd become a convert after that. We'd only just been dreaming about vodka and suddenly it falls right into our hands. You might ask, "Is it sorcery?" But no, it was Senka's smooth tongue, or rather, his boot-licking. Simple as that.'

'We poured out the vodka between us three. The driver says: "I can't drink. I've got to drive to Ermish."'

'"Where on earth are you going now? Can you really turn up this kind of treat?" asked Senka, tipping out the meat from the pot.'

'Our driver's breath was taken away. He says: "It's a crying shame to knock back one bottle between three with such wonderful food."'

---

[36] The 'George' refers to the medal of St. George and he is talking about World War II.

[37] This is an attempt to translate a humorous quip, so typical of peasant speech, which frequently rhymes in Russian. A literal translation of the Russian is, 'It's not a matter of which village it is, but of warmth'.

'So off he goes and gets another bottle. So we unsealed that one and drank it instead of the broth, and we ate the meat with it.'

'"Where there's a second, there's a third," said the driver, and brought yet another bottle.'

'"Well, Semën," I says. "What have we here? There's lots of vodka, but little to eat. Let's cook the other piece of mutton."'

'I ran down to the river for some more water... We cooked more meat. We poured out that bottle and finished it off.'

'"What have we here?" asks Semën. "We've got lots of food, but the vodka's run out."'

'The driver brought another bottle and we finished that one.

'"Well lads," he says, "I'd better be off."'

'He got up from the pot and managed to walk to the doorway. That's fine – it means he'll get there! It's true, he swayed a bit on the doorstep. He carried off the door lintel on his shoulders and fell down in the snow.'

'So, I says, "Semën, let's get some broth down him."'

'Senka gives him a mug of broth and we pours it down his mouth. He came round. And Semën bungs a warm bundle of meat into his hands.

'"'Ere," he says. "If you stray from the road, you'll keep warm, if nothing else."'

'"Hey, lads," he says. "I won't forget your kindness in a hundred years. Take a crate of vodka to remember me by."'

'So I thinks, Why not? But then I thinks, what if anything happens to you? People spotted you here with us. They could say that we stole it. We'll be the ones who'd be carted away. No, we mustn't.'

'"It's easy for you to say "'Ere, take this", I says. But how would we explain having a whole crate of vodka?"'

'"You could just say that I had a spare one. Emergency supplies. Only there was no emergency."'

'"An emergency is one thing," I thinks to myself. "But you get in your lorry and off you go. But what happens if they come for me for some reason or other?"'

'And there was the pity – I had no one to take advice from. Senka had already fallen nose-down in a snow drift. What kind of advisor was he? And I was plagued with doubts. So I refused the crate. But I stuck two half-litre bottles in each pocket.'

'I pulled the tarpaulin over the load and shoved the driver into the cab. He slumped onto the steering wheel, then drove off.'

'I turned my attention to Semën: I shook him, got him to his feet, but he was like cotton wool – he fell down again as soon as I let go of him.'

'"Semën," says I. "Let's go and drink the hair of the dog."'

'At this point, he opened one eye: "Are you having me on? Let's feel."'

'I bunged him a bottle and he had a feel, and, believe it or not, he stood up all by himself. We drank through these two bottles together and fell asleep.'

'But from that time onwards, wherever I went, and whatever happiness I endured, my finger twitches at the very thought: What would have happened if me and Semën had knocked back that case of vodka? I would not have held any grudge against my fate. I would have drunk it… I once knocked back four bottles of red wine in a canteen, and I could feel my legs getting heavy…'

'"What's going on? Have my heels stuck to the floor from the red wine?"'

'But a mate of mine says: "It's bison weed! There's a bull on the label."'

'But God only knows why it has a bull on it. Weed by name and weed by nature![38] But I still wonder, what would have happened if me and Semën had seen off that whole case?'

At this point, Paramon shook his head and began to relive the misfortune, expressing himself in unprintable words. And I just thinks, that's a typical Russian man – he forgets everything… He forgets his own date of birth, the day he got married, when he was injured… (Paramon has two wounds and a contusion, as the poet says.) But when and where fate smiled on his drinking – he will take that to his grave and never forget. What more can I say? Take me, for example: the most interesting moment of my life was when I drank a whole case of champagne to myself. But that's a story for another time.

How I Rose in the Ranks

So now then, I'll tell you about how I was fast-tracked in life, that is, how I made it from a country bumpkin to a manager.

The most important thing for getting on in life is a work autobiography. Your character must also be appropriate. You know my autobiography, and I never suffered from an inappropriate character. I never succumbed to any drifting, by which I mean, I was never a deviationist. If the **kolkhoz** chairman sent us out to work in the fields, I always went – I did not deviate.

When I came back home from the army, we had to plough using cows. I couldn't say who was responsible for allowing the **kolkhoz** to get into that state: whether it was Filipp Samochenkov, who ended up in prison, or whether it was due to exiled **kulak** wreckers, or the famine of thirty-three. Perhaps it was due to the feverish wrecking that went on – the masses at that time were a politically backward lot, and they expressed themselves in that kind of activity. Nowadays, you couldn't shake anyone up in that way: you could leave a whole stack of grain in the middle of a field, and it would simply stand there and rot – no one would touch a single sheaf. But in former times, people used to pinch single ears of corn. It's true that if you put out a pile of hay, even today people would pinch it, because you can't just feed your livestock on bread alone. People also nick fuel. If you leave a barrel around, they'd have it away. Because they needed it. Now that you can

---

[38] 'Bison weed vodka' or 'Zubrovka' (also spelt 'zubrowka') is so called because it contains a grass, variously called 'bison weed', 'sweet grass' or 'buffalo grass' – the botanical name of which is *Hierochloe*. The grass gives the vodka a yellowish tint, and it is highly aromatic, with a bitter after-taste.

buy bread in the shops, all interest in it has vanished. You just take some sheaves and thresh them – but then, what are you going to do with the grain? In the whole area there is only one mill left. And they would know straight away where the grain came from. Is it really for feeding your chickens? Do you need a lot of grain to feed chickens? You can get enough grain to feed chickens in your pocket, straight from the threshing floor, from under the winnowing machine. No one will search you. People used to get searched, so that they had to steal at night – sheaves, ears of corn, and chaff. In a word, life has now got much easier.

Anyway, at that time we had to plough using cows. People's personal cows were requisitioned for sowing. The womenfolk came running out to the fields to milk their cows. We'd take the traces off them and their withers would be pinched and bleeding. The women would cry and shout, 'Give me back my cow!' But who on earth would give it back? Not until the end of sowing... We ploughed on a collective basis. Individual wishes could not be countenanced. We had put the collective interest first and foremost, and only then could we consider individual interests. It was Filipp Samochenkov who drummed this commandment into me. And I stuck rigidly to it – I didn't let a single cow away from the sowing. Not even if it crawled on all fours along the furrow. I was a strict **brigade leader**. And I was the first to finish sowing. But those who lost their nerve and let the cows be taken back didn't get the sowing done. Then the management beat them and the women cursed them: they've kept back half of the cows! But I got the job finished and then let them all go home at once. Now what do you have to say about that, you silly women? Who was right? And what happened to your cows? So what, if they couldn't even stand up?! They can loll around at home. The main thing was, we got the job done on time.

For this kind of accelerated tempo in sowing, I was sent to be trained as a tractor driver. That was my first promotion in life, which I earned in my own way.[39]

Six months later I finished the tractor-driver's course and I was given a nice new KhTZ tractor and sent to the forestry settlement of Korabishino.[40] I drove the tractor there and the whole village came running out to stare. I sat there on my seat, which looked like an iron plate with holes in it, holding the steering wheel, and I really thought I was the bee's knees. I had some nice new boots on and my red shirt billowed, and my whole physiognomy was round with delight...

For a while, I lived amongst the first batch of tractor drivers! I had a whole entourage: a water-carrier, a petrol attendant, a bookkeeper, and a personal cook, called Pasha Samokhina. I ate a whole pot of stew a day! I used to drive the tractor back to the camp for lunch: the pot would already be bubbling, and Pasha would be lolling on the bed. I'd pull her off the bed, give her one next to the stew-pot, then get down to lunch.

Unfortunately for me, she got pregnant. Perhaps it was by me, but perhaps it wasn't. Well, I had a whole staff around me. I went out to plough, leaving my staff around the

---

[39] Being selected to train as a tractor and combine harvester driver was seen as a step up the career ladder: such drivers received a regular salary, and often bonuses and bribes, which meant that their pay was not subject to the vagaries of poor harvests and other unpredictable factors, which made the average **kolkhoz** worker's pay fluctuate so widely.
[40] KhTZ is the acronym for a type of tractor made in a famous factory in Kharkov, called the **Kharkovskii Traktornyi Zavod**, or The Kharkov Tractor Factory.

stew-pot. Maksik, the bookkeeper, was always hanging around near her. It was he who taught her to give evidence in a cultured way. I denied everything in court, and she says: 'How do you mean, Petia? Surely you remember "associating with me" by the stew-pot? And also on the Kasianova dried-up riverbed.'

So, she goes on like that. So, now I ends up with a judgement and having to pay maintenance, but I don't pay up. So the judge summons me: 'You so-and-so, I'll put you in prison! Give her the money today!'

Fair enough. So I goes to Pasha and counts out a hundred and eighty roubles – that's a whole year's maintenance.

'Check it', I says. She counts it. 'Is it right?'

'It's right.'

'Now, give it 'ere!' I snatch the money out of her hand and sticks it in my side pocket, and I slaps the pocket. 'It's safer in my pocket than in yours,' I says. 'When you need money, I'll give it to you.'

I get summoned to the investigator again. Blimey! So I goes to Old Ma Makarevna, who was her midwife, and says to her: 'You go tell the investigator that she has named Maksik as the father. If you do that, I'll pay you in soap.'

I must point out that soap was difficult to get hold of at that time. But I used to get loads of coupons for it, supposedly for washing. But I've never used soap in my life. I go down to the pond, get into it, rub myself all over with sand, and all's well and good. So I had a stack of soap and didn't know what to do with it. Well, for such a treasure, Old Ma Makarevna would not only name Maksik, but she'd write a denunciation on Jesus Christ! I got my own back on Maksik for his cultural administrations... That threw the investigator into a real quandary. He dragged the case out longer and longer, until he and the public prosecutor ended up in prison themselves, as wreckers. And I got transferred to the **MTS**.

At this point, I took this whole Maksik business into my own hands and said to him: 'The post of bookkeeper at the **MTS** is the first step towards a managerial position. However, Comrade Maksik, you have a blot on your autobiography with this Pasha Samokhina. Either you eliminate it, or we will have to take a good look at your personal file.'

He ran around to Old Ma Makarevna, and he got taken on at a peat works in Shatura. Then, Pasha Samokhina went off and joined him there. I don't know what happened to them after that.

Just before the War, I was appointed manager of the regional butter-dairy, and I moved to Tikhanovo. I must say that there I transformed myself into my final transformation, in accordance with all external and internal requirements of party lines. My Brëkhovan nickname Diudiun was forgotten. However, in Tikhanovo I gained a new one – **Centner**.

One's external appearance as a manager is one and the same thing as a harness is for a trotter. However high-spirited it might appear, it still has to prove itself. The horse brasses hang around its neck for all to see, straps with silver ends hanging from the headstall, reins with brass rings, and a bitless bridle with black tracery in the silver... But what can one say? You judge a bird by its flight, as they say. And that was the same for me. First of all, I got myself a khaki service jacket and some jodhpurs with a dark-blue stripe. And a straw hat...

I wasn't just accepted by the regional managers as one of their own... When I was called up into the army, I stood out among the masses of the bald-headed and shaven rank and file. We arrived at the garrison.

'And what was your line of work?' the lieutenant-colonel asked me in the assignment office.

'Economic,' I answer.

'Right, Pëtr Afanasievich. Please take charge of this group of people.'

Then I was appointed sergeant-major in charge of supplies. I rode around on the field kitchen, just like you would on your own cart. Not only did infantry soldiers make way for me, but so did tanks.

Only on just one, single occasion did my managerial appearance misfire. I got injured in the groin. I couldn't even move a leg. So, I'm lying there and I looks up – there's two blokes bending over me. 'Should we take this one then?' They huffed and puffed, and one of them says: 'What a hog! Hell will freeze over before we get this one back!'

'He must be at least a hundred **poods**, honest to God!'

'Let's take that skinny one over there instead.'

'But that one is a rank and file soldier, and this one is a sergeant-major.'

'Sod him! He should eat less. Let him lie there until a horse gets here.'

So I was abandoned right on the battle field. I'm lying there looking at the sky. I couldn't move my tongue, but my thoughts were clear, and I could move my hands. I felt my crotch and it was covered in blood. 'Ah!' I thought. 'My grenade's flown off. It's shot its last.'

When I came round in the military hospital, the first thing I did was ask the doctor: 'How are things down below? Have I had a good weeding? Have I been gelded?'

'Your weed's all okay,' he says. 'It'll still stand tall.'

Well that's fine – life goes on. I comes home and goes back to my old job in the factory, as manager. I got better, and everything got back on an even footing. And why shouldn't it? A buttery-dairy is not a **kolkhoz**. It's not so much me being accountable to other people, as they to me. They make their personal reports to me. **Kolkhoz** chairmen bring me their milk, and I give them back skimmed milk and curd cheese. And it's they who thank me. Well, of course, I don't give them curd cheese just for a 'thank you'.. In exchange for the curd cheese I get meat, grain and honey. Each person gives what he can... So why shouldn't I have lived well?

So there you have it! Nineteen fifty came along and they started to amalgamate **kolkhozes**. I was summoned to the regional committee offices. Then the first secretary was Semën Motiakov. You can't mess him around.

'Bulkin,' he says. 'Hand over the dairy!'

'How do you mean "hand it over"? What for? What wrong have I done?'

'You're being promoted. You'll be the new chairman of an amalgamated farm in Brëkhovo.'

'But, Filipp Samochenkov's working there.'

'He's ruined the **kolkhoz**. And he's taken to drink.'

Blimey! What should I do? I didn't get a wink of sleep and I turned blind with worry. I was going to go to hospital… But Motiakov's only got one answer: 'You're just a malingerer! Don't you want to go to the **kolkhoz**? Are you going against the policy of the top management? I know what I'll do with you… I'll stick you in the monastery. In the Sviatogleb!!'[41]

Well, in a word, I was grabbed by the scruff of the neck, elected as chairman in the office, and taken off to the **oblast** office for confirmation in the post. Motiakov stood behind the door while I stammered in front of the first secretary: 'I'm not up to the job… because of my lack of education…'

'Where on earth has this numbskull come from?' asked the secretary.

A member of the committee at the desk said: 'From the butter-dairy. He was the manager there.'

'Aha, so that's it! He's got used to scoffing butter there. So, he doesn't want to go to the **kolkhoz**? Throw him out of the Party!'

At this point, Motiakov could contain himself no longer: he burst into the office and said, straight from the doorway:

'Quite right, Comrades! He loves scoffing butter. Look how round he's got. Only, about the exclusion – let's wait a bit. We'll bring him to a state of political consciousness.'

So, we set off home with him 'effing and blinding' at me, all the way back. It was 'eff this', and 'eff that', every step of the way home. But what could I do? In the end, I agreed.

My Maruska said: 'Why are you looking so glum? Don't let it get to you! If you end up in prison, I go back to my own house. We'd best not sell it.'

We boarded up the house windows and moved to Brëkhovo. We said farewell to the regional capital for ever. What bad luck!

Jet-Black Horses

So now then, I must tell you quite honestly that I should never have feared the **kolkhoz** chairmanship. Everything went along swimmingly… Furthermore, we lived better than we did at the butter-dairy.

---

[41] See footnote № 29, p.366.

I had a salary of two thousand roubles and a yard full of livestock: twenty sheep, two pigs, a cow, and a year-old calf. Maruska didn't sit around. I took full part in all operations. I didn't hide myself away.

And the horses I had... Absolute beasts! It was just like in the song:

> *I shall spread carpets upon the sleigh,*
> *I shall adorn the horses' manes with ribbons...* [42]

They were black as pitch. The whole collection of accessories was black and red – the sweat-cloths, felt cloths, horse blankets... The head horse had large silver bells on its collar. It had to be held on a tight rein. We used to harness the horses at cockcrow...

'Sashka,' I would say. 'We'll be in Tikhanovo by nightfall!'

'Definitely by nightfall!'

I had a spirited driver. He would sit up front on one knee, the other leg dangling free in the air, just like a motorcyclist's. I would snuggle under a black fleece in the back, and lie back, fully covered up against the snow kicked up by the horses' hooves.

Hey, it's like taking the Tsar out for a ride!

Off we go! Ah, you couldn't see us for dust!

We used go by the cocks' crowing... We heard the first cocks crowing in Brëkhovo, and caught the second lot in Bogoiavlensk, and the third 'dawn' group, in Tikhanovo. We covered thirty-five **versts** in an hour. We used to go to Bogoiavlensk Crossing with the horses in single file – the road was narrow, and there were snowdrifts... But as soon as we were over the river, then the horses were harnessed in tandem and off we went along the road marked with posts... The metal plates on the posts flashed as we passed them by. [43]

I once got into a real mess because of those horses.

I was summoned to the regional office after sowing time. What have you done with the seed? Why is the germination rate so poor? And so on, and so forth... The plenipotentiary for the committee for state procurements turned up and created a hell of a stink. He was very much his own man and he deferred to no one. He was very powerful – if he wanted to, he would rifle through everything, down to the very last grain of corn. He would dart about from one granary to the next, and all you could do was follow on behind him and keep shtoom.

Anyway. I puts on my glad rags: my box-calf boots, my tunic of coarse yellow silk, and my straw hat at a rakish angle. And off we flew!

---

[42] This song is part of a traditional Russian romance entitled *Love for a Highwayman*, and it tells the story of a young couple escaping from the authorities on a sleigh, pulled at speed through the snow by jet-black horses, running away from a former life in pursuit of a happy, but probably illicit, life together. It is the words 'jet-black horses' from the song which lend this section its title.

[43] Tall posts marked where the road was: without them, travelling in the snow could be dangerous. Such posts are still to be seen in areas which regularly have heavy falls of snow.

We arrived at the crossing point and – Stop! There was a lorry driver we knew from Vyselki.'

'Where you off to?'

'The regional centre.'

'So am I.'

We did a deal with him. He took out a half-litre.

'C'mon,' he says. 'Let's crack this one open for a start, and freshen up with a drop of river water. We'll get down to some serious drinking in the regional centre.'

We polished off this bottle between the three of us, and I says to Sashka: 'What's the point of you going to Tikhanovo. You stay here with the horses and I'll go with him in the cab.'

We got into the lorry and off we went. Well I never! We didn't get as far as Svistunovo, when the lorry came to a grinding halt. It made a noise like a shot going off three times, as if the cross-beam of a cart had cracked, and we stopped. What's going on?

'It's probable that a spark plug's burnt out. We'll sort it out in a moment,' he says.

The driver opened the bonnet, peered into the engine, as if into a well, with only his backside showing, and he fell silent. I just stood there, waiting and waiting, and not a move from him.

'What *are* you doing? You having me on here? I'm in a hurry to get to a meeting and you're just messing around, as if you're preparing to take my photograph. I haven't got the time to stand here admiring your arse.'

'Just a minute, just a minute…'

Then he started running round the lorry: he ran from the front and looks and looks, slaps his thighs with his hands, like a cockerel flapping its wings, then he runs back to the front, and looks again.

'Well, what's going on?'

'Can't work out what's wrong,' he says.

Then he calms down, gets back into the cab and says, even with some satisfaction: 'I've finally worked it out.'

'And?'

'We're completely out of petrol.'

Blimey! What should I do? Run back to the horses? I wouldn't manage it even in an hour. Run on ahead? It was still fifteen kilometres – I wouldn't get there by lunchtime. The meeting has already started on time.

'You bloody murderer! What do you think I should do now?'

'There's a load of hay in the back. You just have a lie down, Afanaseich. As soon as a passing car comes along, I'll give you a shout. I'll just have a nap at the wheel. This often happens.'

How could I sleep? I could just picture the meeting at the offices of the regional committee and Comrade Motiakov giving his report – even lice would die from fear. What was I to do?

So, I stood there, like a gofer by the side of the road, waiting. I was so upset, I was on the point of whistling. But then, suddenly, a lorry comes along. There's a woman sitting in the cab next to the driver, and on the back, there was a table and a cow. I stop them:

'Give us some petrol!'

'Can't. We've only just got enough ourselves to get to Tikhanovo.'

'Could you give me a lift, then?'

'If you like, but you'll have to ride in the back.'

So, up I gets, next to the table and the cow. I sat on the table and grabbed the cow's horns. Off we go! On we go, but there was constant dust from the road – I couldn't even see the cow! I got so dusty that the yellow tunic turned grey. All you could see of my face was my eyes.

I turned up at the office looking like that. Oh, Motiakov gave me hell for that! Although by this time, he had been demoted to the head of the regional land department, he still had a lot of clout.

'Here he is! Take a good look! A miller straight from the mill… He's squandered the seed reserves and he couldn't give a damn about the committee members.'

'I've just had to hitch a lift in a lorry,' I says.

'Nothing to do with us. You got our telegram telling you to be on time.'

I got a right telling-off. I popped in to the canteen (in the Tikhanovo regional offices there was a direct link with the canteen, like a sort of tunnel), I drank some dilute vodka and just couldn't feel the effect of it.[44] So, I thumbs a lift to the crossing place, and when I gets there, I sees Sashka and my horses, which were tethered to a stake, nibbling at the grass. A mate of mine greets me, One-Armed Lenka Zalivaev, a mounted patrol man. He's got a gun on his shoulder, a dog at his heels, and a couple of ducks hanging from his belt. Despite having only his left arm, he can shoot a bird on the wing better than any bloke with two hands: before anyone else could even raise a gun to his shoulder, Lenka would already have bagged another bird with his second barrel.

'Why are you so knackered? Has the heat finished you off?' he asks.

---

[44] Alcoholic drinks, such as beer and vodka, were frequently diluted by canteen and bar-staff as a form of fiddling: they would steal a quantity of drink for themselves and top up the stock with water, as if the full quantity were still intact. Most people tacitly accepted this practice as the norm and only got angry when it was done to excess! This was just one of the myriad of fiddles Soviet shop assistants, waiters, canteen cooks, and many others operated to provide themselves with goods on the side, and they often sold their 'surpluses' to friends, family and neighbours.

'In my time, I've been on stoves that would fry your brains,' I says. 'So, it's not external heat, but internal, that bothers me.'

'There's a medicine for that,' says Lenka, with a wink. 'It takes a thief to catch a thief! And here's the right food to go with it,' he said, holding up the ducks.

'Well, what are we waiting for? Sashka, harness the horses! We'll take the cure at Bogoiavlensk!' I says.

'There's a quarantine cordon there,' says Sashka. 'They won't let us through.'

'What's the point in going there?' says One-Armed Lenka. 'I'll be back in a minute. We'll park ourselves here. In the open air.'

'But d'you know just how much we're going to need?' I asks Lenka.

'Let's add it up…'

'You'll underestimate, all the same. When a person is hell-bent on drinking, you'll never guess how much will be needed, not in all your born days. Let's go to it ourselves.'

So, we goes to the canteen – no vodka. Then on to the shop – no vodka! Only champagne… So, what should we do? 'You'll have to take the sour stuff,' they say. The only effect you'll get is a bloated belly – it never reaches your head because all its strength disappears with the bubbles. But Lenka makes one point by way of a reply: 'We'll trap it in our guts,' he says. 'And it can kick up a storm, like in a good barrel.'

Fine. So we gets the sour stuff, or the sweet stuff, I really can't remember which.[45] We took a grenade each… The corks flew out, right up to the ceiling – 'Bang, bang, bang!' It was just like shooting ducks – it even gave off smoke at the end of the 'barrel'. We polished it off… We were as sober as a judge. So we each grabbed another bottle… No effect! So I went back to the shop: I put the door on the latch and I says to Lenka, our salesgirl: 'Write out an invoice for the Brëkhovo shop. I'll settle it there.'

'What invoice, Pëtr Afanasievich?'

'For a case of champagne,' says I.

So she wrote it out. I put the invoice in my pocket and we carried the case to the shipping office canteen, put it under the table, and then the shooting started.

We saw off forty bottles! We drank them ourselves, and gave some to others. If we fancied some company at our table, we fired corks at them, then put the bottles on the table. Drink, lads, to a happy **kolkhoz** life! One-Armed Lenka kept aiming at the canteen lady, the shit! If he managed to hit her with a cork, he gave her the bottle. All she said was, 'Hi-hi-hi!' and 'Ha-ha-ha!' while she hid one bottle after another under the counter.

There's just one problem with champagne – one time, you might just get a bit of smoke out of the bottle, another time, a whole fountain gushes out, wetting you all over your mug. We came out of the canteen looking as though we'd just been in a **bania**. The horses just sniffed to find the way home, and they just bolted.

---

[45] Soviet 'champagne' was available in both dry and sweet forms of sparkling wine.

'Pëtr Afanasievich!' shouts Sashka. 'There's a barrier across the road.'

'Go through the barrier!' I orders.

Sashka stood tall on the sleigh, pulled on the reins, and shouts: 'Eh, it's like we'd given the Tsar a ride!'

Illustration 15. 'Champagne and Shells: Officers' Conviviality Interrupted at Port Arthur',
***The Illustrated London News*, January 21 1905.**

One-Armed Lenka sits up on one knee and grabs a bottle of champagne from his pocket. Nodding towards the sentries, he shouts: 'I'll catch those horse-doctors with a grenade!'

I reclined in the **tarantass** and happily thought to myself: 'Just try and stop us now...'

'Hey, Chaps! Move! Get out of the way!'

I remember the barrier snapping and the bottle clinking, – it was Lenka hitting the sentry's gun. Vets shouted something out. We flew through the air like tiddlywinks.[46]

On and on we went... I grabbed my head – no hat. I came to, and it seemed to be getting light. We had fallen asleep in the **tarantass**, and the horses were grazing in the oat field.

I turns up to my shop in the morning and hands over the invoice, saying: 'Here's a bill for a crate of champagne.'

'Please, bring it in, Pëtr Afanasievich.'

'I've already brought it in... In my belly. Never mind, Iakov Ivanovich will settle it with honey.'

Iakov Ivanovich was the **kolkhoz** accountant. He was a sharp man. He kept the accounts in such a way that he could get anything past any audit panel. You could ransack half the **kolkhoz**, and he could justify everything.

However, I got a real dressing down for breaking the barrier. That was my second reprimand of the day. But every cloud has a silver lining. The vets confiscated my horses for forty days and nights. But for me, that was the start of a period of relaxation because I couldn't set foot in the regional centre for over a month. They called me up on the phone and sent telegrams to summon me. 'Can't go! I don't have the right! My horses have been impounded!' And a vet is not like an investigator – you can't order him to release a prisoner! When it comes to livestock, the law is more strictly observed.[47]

My Brother, Levanid

As you already know, my brother Levanid once worked as a vet. Then he was transferred to Korabishino as a medical orderly. But since there was no paramedic there, Levanid treated everyone – both livestock and people. He treated every medical condition with the same substance – pure tar. He prescribed each patient a teaspoon of tar, three times a day.

---

[46] The original expression refers to a children's game called *chizhiki* in Russian, which was played in a circle: the object of the game was to hit a single sharpened stick with an individual stick held by each player until it had completed the circle. Hence, the translation here is an approximation to the original, but the sense is very close.

[47] The quarantine had been broken by Bulkin by going into the infected area when he broke the barrier, and therefore, in the interests of not spreading disease any further, his horses had to be impounded on the authority of the vets. Mozhaev states that rules and regulations are to be observed strictly when dealing with livestock, but by the same token he implies that legality and due process can be got round when dealing with people! The exact nature of the disease is not stated, but it is probably something like foot and mouth disease, which is highly contagious.

'Take it, and then wait a year and a half,' he would say. 'The illness will gradually come out from inside.'

And the amazing thing is – it helped a lot of people. People still come to him for advice. The other day, I was sitting having a drink with him. A neighbour turns up with her daughter who was ill with something, either eczema or psoriasis.

'I want to take my Lenka to a health resort, but I'm afraid to,' she says.

'So don't take her, then,' replies Levanid.

'But the health resort would bring the illness outside, wouldn't it?'

'But what if it pushes it in... even deeper...? What then?'

The neighbour was then thrown into a state of doubt.

'The doctor says "go", but the *homopat* says "don't".'

'The *homopat* knows everything.'

She didn't go. Levanid sent her to Korabishino, to a former colleague at the veterinary centre, Old Ma Kochabarikha. She pronounced an incantation over her with hempseed oil and stirred something into it... It was as if all the sores had been wiped away.

Levanid now lives on a personal pension. He also gets sixty-five roubles, but it's paid to him as a war pension. He went off to war as the commander of a section, but came home a *batlion* commander.[48] Strictly between you and me, he's fibbing a bit. He never made it to *batlion* commander, but he did make company commander... that's for sure. He still has a head wound from the war. Right on the crown, on the top of his skull, he has a dip – you could put a chicken's egg on it. Straight up! When Levanid has had a few drinks, he separates, I mean, parts his curls, shows his skull and shouts: 'So, you don't believe me that I've only half a skull? Go on! Stick an egg on it!'

I've done it more than once. The egg doesn't move![49]

'Levanid,' I asks. 'How come that, with your officer's rank, you couldn't manage to get into loads of hospitals to have that gap filled in?'

'Aha!' he says. 'We had some strange doctors. There I was in hospital, in Groznyi. The surgeon comes up to me and says, "Let's take out one of your ribs and fix the bone into your head".'

'What on earth..?'

'I refused.'

'Why?'

'You dope! How the hell can a man live without a rib?'

Do you think that's funny? Well, let's think this one through. With our rural work, ribs are more important than your head. If you go to mow in tall grass, you count its

---

[48] Bulkin means 'battalion', but he gets the word wrong, just as he does with the word '*homopat*'.
[49] Elsewhere, Mozhaev has described his own uncle as doing just the same, owing to a wound sustained in action during World War II.

height along your ribs, one after the other – the whole thing hinges on your ribs. But if you had one missing, you'd be all at sea. And what kind of mower would you make?

By the way, my brother Levanid still makes hayricks and mows on the **kolkhoz** – he's in charge of all the pensioners.

He also takes part in community work: he collects scrap metal, he addresses **Pioneer** groups, he tells them all about our cursed past, and he asks questions at lectures on the international situation, and so on...

On the occasion of the twentieth anniversary celebration of Victory Day, my brother led the Brëkhovan veterans' parade in Tikhanovo. The parade was announced for the 9th of May and, 'Those with medals and decorations are to go to the regional main town for the parade!' Senka Kurman comes running up to the office and says: 'Comrade Chairman! What should I do? My medal's got lost and now there's only this whatsit hanging here!' He pointed to the metal bar pinned on his jacket to which the medal had been attached.

'Do you have documents regarding your medal?' asked Petia Dolgii.

'What documents? I don't even have a **passport**!'

What a joke! By the way, my brother Levanid also had a funny story to tell in connection with his last decoration. So I must make a digression here.

Last autumn, there was a 'meat jam'. Loads of cattle had been raised, but there was nowhere to send them. The state slaughter houses wouldn't take them – the meat processing factories were overloaded with work. If you took cattle to the market, you couldn't sell them. The meadows had caught fire before any hay could be harvested. Who on earth would buy a cow for the winter? So Fenia, Levanid's wife, says to my brother: 'Let's sell the cow and buy a calf. The cow's in fine shape at the moment. In fact, it's not so much a cow, as a Saranpal.[50] She'll eat us out of house and home this winter.'

So, Levanid went to the state procurement offices and to the regional main town... He went up hill and down dale, through trials and tribulations, and drew a blank. At that time, the Brëkhovo composers Glukhova and Khamov had made up the following **chastushka**:

> *Old Ma Tania had some cows*
> *That drove her mad in autumn.*
> *'Keep and scoff the meat yourself,*
> *'Cause we just cannot slaught'r 'em.*

Then suddenly, a warrant came from Brëkhovo rural council:

---

[50] The speaker gets the name slightly wrong: she really means 'Sardanapal', which is the Russian name for Sardanapalus, who was a legendary king of Assyria. He was the last of thirty Assyrian kings, who exceeded all those who had gone before him in his sybaritic way of life, and he is reputed to have been responsible for the downfall of Assyria. This legendary character was also the inspiration for one of Byron's tragedies, entitled *Sardanapalus*, written in 1821. Sardanapalus had a reputation for living the good life, being very well fed, but being expensive to keep, like Levanid's cow!

'Accept two cows.'

So, Levanid goes to the rural council. The usual moves. Nevertheless, he did have a certain pull. He managed to wangle an allocation document. He brought it home in his inside pocket, as pleased as punch, as if he'd got a holiday voucher for a health resort.

Anyway. They drive the cow to the abattoir, as per his allocation document. But there he is told: 'We aren't even taking our own cows. They've all got to be vaccinated against foot-and-mouth disease, and then kept for two weeks.'

So, they did the jab. The two weeks go by, then they drove it back again to the abattoir. He gets told: 'We're taking no more. Our quota is up. Take your cow to the abattoir at Pugasovo.'

Blimey! Forty **versts** on a fool's errand! What else could they do? They tied some string to the cow's horns, stuck a loaf of bread under their coat, and off they went. One of them pulls from the front on the string, the other drives it from behind. They huffed and puffed for a whole day. Now, here's a thing: when they gets to the abattoir, they're told: 'Why didn't you come earlier? Our quota is whatsit... all *combeated.*[51] Come back at the end of the month.'

So, when the end of the month arrived, three of them clubbed together and hired a lorry to transport their cows, because the first snow had already fallen. They got the cows onto the back of the lorry, but the sides were low. What d'you know?! The lorry moves off, the cows started mooing and end up jumping over the sides. Levanid's cow fell on its head and broke a horn. What can you do? It looked wretched like that. Anyway, after a lot of chasing around they found a military truck with high sides. They made a deal. They were just about to load the cows when an errand boy comes running up: 'Uncle Leontii, you're wanted at the rural council offices.'

'Why?'

'Don't know. They just ordered you to turn up quickly.'

Levanid arrives at the rural council offices and he sees a lieutenant-colonel sitting there.

'Are you Bulkin, Leonid Afanasievich?'

'I am. What's this about?'

'I have your medals,' he says. 'We have been looking for you for twenty-three years to give you these decorations. Now you've finally turned up.'

'I've haven't been in hiding since I was born,' replies Levanid.

'No one suspects you have. It's just that your papers have been doing the rounds for ages. Well, you have been awarded the Order of the Patriotic War, first division, and the Order of the Red Star.'

'Thank you,' says Levanid.

---

[51] Again, the word is mispronounced because it is based on a foreign, Western word, and not on a native Russian word. He means, of course, 'completed'.

'You should reply, "I serve the Soviet Union!"'

'Oh, yeah! I forgot that bit. I am serving my old lady and a cow right now. So then, give me the medals.'

'I can't give you them both. There been a slip-up. Is your patronymic Afanasievich?'

'Yes, that's right.'

'Look. On one document they've written "Afanasievich", but on the other "Affonievich".'

'Oh, perhaps it's not mine then?'

'Well, by all accounts, it's yours. Your date and place of birth are right... but it's just this Affonievich thing. We'll send the Order of the Red Star back to Moscow with an accompanying letter, indicating that you're not Affonievich, but Afanasievich. Then they'll correct it and send it back. Is that okay?'

'That's fine. Can I go now?'

'But, there's the other medal! We can let you have that one!'

'Okay. Give it here!' said Levanid, holding out his hand.

'We can't just hand over a medal from one hand to another. We have to get official representatives together. We have to create a ceremonial atmosphere. Then we'll present you with the medal.'

'I haven't time to wait for a ceremonial atmosphere,' says Levanid. 'I've got to get my cow loaded.'

'You can put your cow off.'

'No way! I've been waiting two months.'

'Well, what shall we do? I have to go to the region... I'll tell you what!' said the lieutenant-colonel, having thought for a moment. 'Put a red cloth on this table, and I'll present the medal over the table and shake your hand.'

Our rural council chairman Topyrin got hold of a red cloth with a slogan on it from a trunk. He covered the table with it, slogan side down, and the lieutenant-colonel presented the order to Levanid.

I goes to see him the next day and the order is lying there on the table.

'What have you got this out for?' I asks. 'Are you sitting admiring it?'

'I was checking it out. I've always thought that a first category medal would be made out of gold. But I had a good look at it and bit it... It's just ordinary metal.'

Then he started telling me about how they got the cow to the abattoir and how much weight it had lost over the last two months: 'The cow was as big as a stove. But, by the time we handed it over, you could hear its bones clattering.'

About My Personal Life

The work record of a Soviet person is sometimes complicated by his personal life. For example, if you've got drunk and kicked up a rumpus, like break some windows, or given someone a good belting, or possibly had a bit on the side and in your free time, you've neglected to fulfil your family duties – all that is called your 'personal life'. Your personal life is picked over at the local party office, or, if you're not a member of the Party, then by the **kolkhoz** management board, or at a **Comrades' Court**. The outcome of all this is that your personal life is regarded as an ulcer on the body of society, a **hangover from the past**.

Well, I succumbed to one of these ulcers – unintentionally, you might say. I wouldn't have felt so much grief, had it not been for the fact that I loved my Maruska so. And, although she is prone to hysterical outbursts, she keeps the house and home on an even keel, she waters and feeds me on time, and puts me to bed. So, I wouldn't swap my Maruska for any other personal life. It must have been weariness that led me to neglect my family duties. That spring started out full of problems…

I was working late in my office, alone. The lady beekeeper turns up from the distant Korabishino apiary, and hands me a formal statement. I reads: 'This formal statement below has been drawn up due to the following, in that yesterday, during the daytime, the chief security officer Khamov, Leontii, and his brother, Mikhail, came to visit me in the apiary, apparently to check for dubious beehives. Leontii went round the apiary bashing on the hives with his whip, in order to discover any dubious hives. He claimed he'd found one. They opened the hive, took out the honey and threw the hive down, uncovered. And some other bees pitched in and ruined the whole swarm…'

So, as I'm reading, I'm looking not so much at the paper, but at the beekeeper herself: she wore box-calf boots and the boot-tops so gripped her calves, like rubber bands, that they made her legs look like fulsome, white loaves of bread. Her green cardigan was undone, and her pink blouse was so fine I could see her bra straps. Her hair was done up in a bun on the nape of her neck, standing tall, like one of your own haycocks, and her black eyebrows were outlined with a flourish, and looked like the wings of a swift… Blimey! My mouth went as dry as a bone, and all I could hear was a whooshing sound in my ears 'Wusssh! Wusssh! Wusssh!' And I remembered how I used to do my three-hundred-and-sixty-degree turns in the army… I pushed back my shoulders and I looked at her, besotted. And she stands there… one hip thrust forward and her hand resting on it, and in the other hand she had a stick, with which she whipped her boot-tops. 'Swish! Swish!' This is what led me into deviation…[52]

'Katerina Ivanovna,' I asks her. 'What is your opinion of the chairman here, that is, of me? Do you really think you should have to stand in my presence? That would be so disrespectful of me. Please, sit down on the couch.'

And she says to me, laughing: 'And what if I'm lonely on the couch by myself?'

'It would be futile for you to worry about that,' I says. 'You'll never have a dull moment with me.'

---

[52] Clearly, Bulkin is not talking about political deviation here, but moral deviation, and that is the source of the comedy: he is using a political term to express his lusting after this woman.

'Well, onwards and upwards…'

Her husband was a **brigade leader**, a puny little chap. He'd got long, withered legs, which were like sticks in his trousers, a nose like a potato, tiny little eyes, and a cap pulled right down onto his ears, just like an allotment scarecrow. But when he ran, you'd never catch him, even on horseback. Everyone called him 'Fidget'.

The first thing I did was to send him off to a distant logging station, well out of sight and mind. And I changed horses part way, so there wouldn't be any witnesses…

In the evenings, I used to tighten the belly-band and off I went! My saddle was decorated with silver tooling, and the pommel was low – you could ride for a hundred **versts** and not feel tired. So, as soon as I gets to the edge of the forest, I can see her there, waiting for me, my little darling. I scooped her up with one arm and sat her straight on the saddle, on my knees. Then I carries her off to wherever I fancy.

We made a kind of hayloft in the **heated bee house**: we made a bed right under the roof on some aromatic straw and put up a canopy. We'd strip right off, snuggle under the canopy, like diving under a river wave, and we fooled around all night long. 'I love you, Petia,' she would say, 'because after spending the night with you, I lie around all the next day like a wet rag.' And I must confess, I loved her too – I promoted her to the ranks of the foremost beekeepers, presented her with a wrist watch, and gave her an honorary certificate.[53]

All would have been well… But, you never see misfortune coming, and you can't hide from it, just as you can't hide from local officials. So, they rings me up from the regional offices: 'Don't go off anywhere – there's a plenipotentiary on his way to you.'

That means 'get a barrel of mead ready'. I sent for the mead from Dunka Siva and I sits in the office and waits.

He arrives, and he turns out to be a journalist with a camera – he wants to photograph the prize-winning workers. So I thinks: I'll cheer up my little Katerina Ivanovna. He'll take her photo and put it in the local paper. I trusted the bloke – we drank together more than once. We polished off the barrel of mead together, then off we goes to Katiusha, to the apiary.

She had loads of dresses in her trunk, which she kept in the **heated bee house**. She'll get all decked up, I thought, and she'll really look the part.

And that's what happened. She was so pleased… She provided us with more mead and she tried on one dress, then another. She came out to show us – the very Queen of Diamonds! She would make her neck look swan-like, then turn her nice little hand to look the same… She really turned me on.

---

[53] A great deal was done to encourage workers to excel themselves in work, especially during the 1930s in the Soviet Union, when the regime was rapidly developing its industry. All manner of rewards, prizes, and privileges were given to workers who excelled in their jobs: these rewards often took the form of gifts of goods, which were hard to come by, such as watches, sewing machines, etc., as well as documentary recognition of the honour by way of certificates and notes made in one's personal work record. Huge hoardings were frequently seen in towns and city districts featuring large photographs of such successful workers and officials, and these people were often fêted in local newspapers. As is obvious from this incident, such honours were sometimes awarded to those who had managed to curry favour with superiors and those in a position to promote and advance the careers of selected workers.

'C'mon, Katiusha, let's do the tent scene!'

In the **heated bee house** there was a wall-hanging, painted in oils: it was a picture of **Stenka Razin** carrying the Persian princess into a red tent. She had a lacy night-shirt on, through which could be seen her bare breast, and **Stenka** wore scarlet *sharovary* and a blue belt.[54] I gave her this wall-hanging as a present – I swapped some mead for it at Pugasovo market.

She got drunk as well... We took out the canopy from the **heated bee house** and spread it out in the meadow, and folded it in two, to make it look like a bed. She stripped off, down to her shirt, and her breasts poked out to the side, just like the Persian princess's did. I just stripped off, down to my underpants. I tied a thin, transparent scarf across my belly-button. The spitting image of **Stenka Razin**!

I lifted her up in my arms, and she put hers around my neck, and we say: 'Now, take our photo!'

He took our photograph from lots of different poses: right in front of the tent, in the tent, as if she was lying on cushions, holding out her hands towards me, and me, as if I was leaning over her. Then, he photographed her taking off her dress, and us both lying on the bed together... And so on, and so forth... We had a wonderful time.

At that time, we were assigned a new car. I took some milk to the regional centre and popped into the editor's office to see my friend, the journalist. He gave me a whole stack of those photographs, with '**Stenka Razin** and the Persian Princess' written on the envelope. I stuffed them into my pocket and, by way of a celebration, we had a drink at every stall we came across. I got home and downed another glass, and then I fell asleep.

Some peasant men from the **kolkhoz** came to the house to drink to getting the new car. Iakov Ivanovich, the bookkeeper, found he had run out of cigarettes. The idiot went into my pocket to get some smokes. I was spark out on the bed. He took out the stack of photos. Maruska noticed him and says, straight off: 'Where d'you get that from? What's that you've taken out? C'mon, give it 'ere.'

As soon as she saw the scenes, right there and then, in the presence of everyone, she set up her own re-enactment of the Tatar carnage.[55] My blokes took fright and ran off in all directions...

I woke up in the morning... What's going on? I couldn't move my neck at all. My right eye was all puffed up and my lip had swollen up higher than my nose...

'Get up, **Stepan Razin, Ataman** of the Don!'

Maruska was sitting at the table in a new dress, wearing a gossamer-thin shawl on her shoulders. That was a bad omen – if she tarts herself up in the morning, that means we're

---

[54] *Sharovary* are loose-fitting, wide trousers, similar to those worn in the East.

[55] The Tatars invaded Kiev and many other Russian principalities in 1237–40 and thus ensued a period which Russian historians call the 'Tatar-Mongol Yoke', by which they mean that they dominated the early Russian state for some two hundred years, forcing Russian princes to pay tributes to the Khanate of the Golden Horde. The word 'Tatar' became synonymous with cruelty and slaughter. Many of the battles and records of the time were recorded in various chronicles and ancient texts. It was not until 1480, when Ivan III (Ivan the Great) formally renounced his allegiance to the khan and, after a battle, the Tatars withdrew, and their dominance over Russia finally ended.

in for a real scandal. I try to recall – what did I do yesterday when I was drunk? Did I smash any windows, or crash into a pole? I felt something wasn't quite right, but I didn't let on. So I asks: 'What are you all dolled up for? What's the special occasion?'

'I've decided to become a believer,' she says. 'So I've dressed up for confession.'

Her voice was all smarmy and she pursed her lips. This usually happens just before the plates start flying. What the hell had I done?

'Do sit down, Petia. Perhaps you might like to take communion?'

So I sits and I glances at her. 'What are you going to give me for communion?'

And she harps on in the same way: 'Perhaps you like the hair of the dog?'

She brought me a little glass and I drained it...

'Did you, by any chance, pop by the Drozdovyi place in the car yesterday?'

'Which Drozdovyi?'

'The beekeeper, in Korabishino?'

'What for?'

'It looks as though you've got something of theirs.'

Now, I thinks, this is where my private life gets underway. Hadn't my physiognomy already suffered from it? But that aside, you always deny your personal life right from the off. So I put on an offended look.

'Are you accusing me of being a thief?' says I. 'I never take other people's things.'

'I'm not talking about thieves, Petia. I'm on about highwaymen... **Stenka Razin**!'

'I haven't the slightest clue what your "Cossack highwaymen game" has to do with me.'

'Really? Well try to remember. Why *did* you go there?'

'I've never set foot there in my life before... Well, perhaps I have, before the War. Honest to God, I can't even remember the way there.'

'Aha, so that's it! You had your photograph taken there before the War, then.'

It was then that she pulled out the photographs of me posing as **Stenka Razin** in my underpants, and she asks: 'D'you recognise these?'

'I've never seen them before in my life,' says I, and I even turned my face away, as if they were nothing to do with me.

Now that's where I made a gross tactical error – I had let the enemy out of my field of vision. She'd already made ready a heavy, clay basin under the table. She caught me on the left flank with this basin, straight on the ear...

I came round on the floor. I'm lying there all wet, because she had soaked me with cold water, straight from the well... I raised my head a little, and there, right under my nose, that famous story of **Stenka Razin** and the Persian Princess was burning up. There was a pile of ash from all my photographs.

Katerina's husband, Fidget, was a bit more underhand. He got a small barrel of mead and turned up at the regional editor's office to see the journalist: 'Pëtr Afanasievich has sent you this mead,' he says. 'He really liked your photos. He'd like some copies, if you could manage to send some.'

'Help yourself – they're in that pile over there, on the table.' Fidget himself chose the most interesting ones. He took them off to the regional committee offices, together with a written statement: 'On how the chairman is having relations with my wife, while he exiled me to the logging station…'

Semën Motiakov summoned me to the office. The traces of my domestic disagreement had not yet healed on my face. So I turns up, and Semën Motiakov says to me: 'Here he is, the trouserless **Stenka Razin**! There's no point in asking him any questions. The whole of his private life is written large on his physiognomy.'

Well, the bosses are not like your wife. Here, the tactic of an outright denial simply will not work. They simply won't even listen to you. For that reason, I put the whole thing down to productivity relations.

'What's my private life got to do with it? I was associating with a prize-winning beekeeper without any ulterior motive.'

'I'll have you! I'll knock out of you both your ulterior and anterior motives! Call in the victim,' ordered Motiakov.

And in she came… Pink dress, high-heel shoes, and even a fancy handbag in her hand – a kind of large, pouch-like wallet, with knobbly bits on. She stands there, swinging her little bag.

'I'm all ears, Semën Ivanovich,' she says.

Motiakov even cackled with delight at such manners.

'Do you have any "*greevinces*" against this citizen?' he asks, pointing at me.[56]

'What grievances could there be?' says Katiusha, breaking into a smile. 'We were simply play acting, just like on stage…'

'I'm sure you're right,' says Motiakov, also kind of smiling. 'Now, about your production figures… Just pop into my office after this meeting.'

'With the very greatest of pleasure…'

I got a good telling off, but Katiusha was transferred to the regional centre as a sales assistant. Fidget was sent off to Pugasovo as a dispatcher at the supply base. I once met him by chance in Pugasovo, in the canteen. He was three sheets to the wind.

'So, you denounced me then,' I said to him. 'What did you gain by that? You were at the logging station just fifteen **versts** away, but now you've been sent forty-five kilometres away.'

'That's not the bother of it, Pëtr Afanasievich,' he says. 'I simply got caught up in someone else's private life.'

---

[56] Motiakov gets the word wrong: he means, of course, 'grievances'.

Who Are "Opportunists"?

One evening, we were sitting around on some logs – me, Filipp Samochenkov, and Petia Dolgii – all three of us **kolkhoz** chairmen. A decision had been taken that the whole **kolkhoz** would build a new house for Samochenkov. So he asked us round for a drink. It would have been awkward to have refused. So we have some drinks and starts chatting…

'When a person gets old, his brain turns to soup,' said Filipp.

Petia Dolgii burst out laughing, but I asked: 'Who d'you have in mind?'

'Well, I just mentioned it by the way. It's just my old age, and nothing more. I used to be strong and not easily moved to tears. But, when the decision was made to build me a house, I just broke down. Tears just flowed from both eyes… I remembered Semën Motiakov.'

'Where's he now?' asked Petia Dolgii.

'In Kasimov, working on a river jetty as a lighterman,' replied Filipp.

'But, wasn't he in a managerial position before?'

'Yes, but they sacked him for getting drunk,' I said. 'I was in Kasimov the other day. I went down to the jetty. Oh, look! It's Motiakov. His horse and cart had got stuck. He was shouting and screaming along the whole riverbank, and belting his horse with whatever came to hand. He's such a fiend – he was aiming right between its ears.'

'That's just the point,' said Filipp. 'He always went for your sore spot. How many years I spent working with him! "Semën Ivanovich," I used to say, "I'd like a house building." But all he used to say was, "The state will provide you a house in your old age. In any case, it's a dead cert that you'll always have your hand in the till." Did he really think I was working to get rich? I just used to make sure that I kept to the official line.'

'What do you understand "the official line" to be?' asked Petia Dolgii.

'Since when did I have time to think about official policies?' asked Filipp in amazement. 'Life isn't based on thinking. I was up to my neck in work. You used to have to be in the regional main town in the morning, then back home for lunch. After lunch you asked, "Where's Pëtr Ermolaevich?" You'd be told, "He's gone off to the regional offices." You'd be running all around the **kolkhoz** until evening. But sometimes, I'd go off to the regional offices in the morning and sit through meetings, and I wouldn't get back til the next day, only to find that there was a telegram waiting for me, calling me back. "Sashka, get the horses harnessed! We're off again…" We'd get to the bottom of one problem, then they'd give us another. You would just go from one problem to another, like marker posts along the highway. There was no understanding anything. Just stick to the official line. When I was appointed **kolkhoz** chairman, I was scared stiff: "How will I cope? I'm poorly educated." "Don't worry," people said. "Everything's decided for you." It was true, everything was decided jointly. How are bonuses paid out these days? Whoever does more mowing than required, or more ploughing, just bung 'em three roubles. Same idea for group-raking the hay – two roubles apiece. "Sashka, settle up!" Sashka would just take out the pay-roll and right there and then, leaning on the '**Volga**', jot it all down and pay up. But how did it used to be? If you wanted to pay out a bonus, you had to go through the **kolkhoz** committee, then get approval from the executive committee, and then have it sanctioned by the regional executive committee. And then, it had to be presented officially – you had to get the whole **kolkhoz** together, an official would turn up and present the award and certificate.'

Petia Dolgii burst out laughing, but I said: 'Filipp, you are confusing the practical with the theoretical.'

'No way! What I'm saying is that nowadays, life goes along arbitrarily.'

'That's true,' I says. 'In times gone by, the regime was a lot stricter. Semën Motiakov used to get us all together and ask us: "Well, what are we growing at the present *momentum*?"[57] For example, when we had the offensive on growing clover...[58] And on deep ploughing in the spring... Anyone caught ploughing at a depth of less than twenty-two centimetres was called an "opportunist".'

Petia Dolgii merely chuckled and turned his head towards me: 'You might find it funny,' said Filipp, 'but I almost paid for that kind of "opportunism" with my Party card. And it was all over political education sessions. The eve of the Festival of the Holy Veil would come around and lectures on politics were announced.[59] What kind of trick was that to pull? On that day, everyone just gets blind drunk, pours out into the street, rolls around in the mud – but they had to arrange a political education session! And that's not all. You're also expected to invite questions from the floor. And if there were no questions, it meant that people hadn't grasped what had been taught.'[60]

---

[57] Again, this is an attempt to convey the fact that Motiakov gets the word wrong, which is indicative of his poor educational level. He actually means 'moment'.

[58] Under the Soviet regime, agricultural practice in Russia was extremely backward, partly due to the conservatism of the Russian peasant, but mainly due to the great upheavals to which the Russian countryside had been subjected. Farms were frequently forced to carry out the latest fads or policies dictated centrally, by Moscow, which often turned out to be totally unsuitable for local conditions. The Russian climate and soil conditions varied enormously throughout the former Soviet Union, but policy decisions about what to grow, when and how, were constantly being handed down from central planners to local officials (many of whom understood little about agriculture), who would insist on instructions being carried out to the letter. Frequently these instructions turned out to be totally impracticable and counter-productive, often leaving farmers and agronomists who did know what they were doing, frustrated and depressed at having to work by fiat, rather than by exercising their own judgement and experience.

[59] The Festival of the Holy Veil, fell on 14 October (1 October, Old Style) in celebration of the appearance of the Virgin Mary in Constantinople in the tenth century and it became an official festive day in Russian in about 1164. The appearance was supposed to have taken place in a church where the vestments of the Virgin herself were kept. She is said to have appeared with an angelic throng to a group of besieged people who were praying for deliverance, and she spread out her veil above the assembled faithful by way of a blessing. For the working peasantry, it represented the end of agricultural work in the fields for the year, which in turn heralded the arrival of winter. It also had a superstition about the weather attached to it: people believed that the oncoming winter would be as mild or as severe as the weather on this day, and there is an old saying that, 'What the weather is like on Holy Veil Day, so will the winter be.' Young, unmarried girls also used to divine whether they would soon find a husband on this day also.

[60] It was part of the **kolkhoz** chairman's job, along with other officials from the rural council, to make sure farm workers went through a prescribed and on-going course of political education. This involved lectures on both internal and international issues, as has already been seen earlier in the story. Despite strenuous efforts to persuade the peasantry to abandon their traditional, religious feast days, by supplanting them with secular, newly invented Soviet festive days, many rural inhabitants were strongly attached to their traditional

'I also copped it 'cause of those questions,' I interjected. 'We were holding our first political education session just like that, either on the Festival of the Holy Veil, or on Mikola Day.[61] "Any questions from the floor?" Paramon stands up and asks, "I should like to know if serfdom has been abolished yet?" "I see... Any more questions?" The speaker looked at us gloomily. No one says a word. "Serfdom was abolished in 1861. D'you understand?" "Yeah ..." And off he went. The next day the plenipotentiary rolls up: "Comrade Bulkin! How's all this stuff about serfdom cropped up here?" "I'm sorry about that," says I. "We're at the highest stage of development, I mean, we're going towards communism at full pelt." "So what's with the provocative questions, then?" "It's simply a misunderstanding," I says. "Because every year we start studying politics from the topic of serfdom onwards. The political instructor himself got confused and started with another topic. That's why that question was asked..." Anyway, we drank a small barrel of mead together and parted on good terms.'

'You got off light,' said Filipp. 'Things turned out quite differently for me. As it happened, the political instructor from the regional committee arrived on the eve of the Feast of the Holy Veil. "Where's the party organizer?" "He's gone off to get some firewood for his mother-in-law." "In that case, *you* call people to a meeting, then. We'll quickly whip through a chapter." Okay, short and sweet. So I sent the school assistant off to help, and I went from house to house myself. We managed to get everyone we found to the meeting – Communist Party members and non-members. I thought everything would be fine. Anyway. We got sat down as night was falling. He gets his nose into his exercise book, but folk started snoring. He talks on and on – two whole hours. Then he asks, "Any questions from the floor?" Well, what questions would there be on a feast day? Some people woke up and just sat there, looking at the floor, others yawned. So I thinks, someone's got to ask a question, or he'll just say that we're not up to the mark. So, I raise my hand and asks, "Who are 'opportunists'?" He looked sternly at me for a moment, as if he'd never seen me before, and said, as if talking to himself: "Fine." And he noted something down in his exercise book. Then he asks, "Are there any more questions?" Who on earth did he think would ask another question? If he noted me down in his book, he'd note someone else down as well. Then you'd be called up to explain yourself. Everyone kept silent. "Okay," he says. "For the last two hours I've been telling you about opportunists and then you ask questions about them! Fine!" He slams his book shut and off he goes. Wouldn't you know it, the next day I gets summoned to the regional executive committee. I asks the bookkeeper, Iakov Ivanovich, "Do they, perhaps, require some figures from me?" "No," he says. "No figures required. You are ordered to come in person." There's trouble ahead, I thought. When they call you in without any figures, and in person, you know it's not going to be for the best.

'Sashka drove me over, but I gets so cold, my teeth are chattering. So, I had a drink in Bogoiavlensk, thinking, I'll warm up. No luck! I'm shaking, like I had a fever. What am I being summoned for? All the way, I kept changing my mind. Believe me, I imagined I was a criminal five times over. Was it, perhaps, because the corn had rotted in its stack? Or was it because the flax had been sown in the low-lying virgin land and it had just rotted off? Only the devil knows...

---

celebrations. New, special celebrations were purposefully put on the same day as traditional religious festivals in the hope that the new would supplant the old.

[61] For Mikola – see footnote № 35, p. 374.

'It was late when we arrived in Tikhanovo. Usual trouble over lodgings. We'd got meat and mead with us. The landlord gave us a half-litre of vodka. You drink, but it doesn't hit the spot. You sleep, but you don't feel rested.

'The next day, I gets to the regional committee offices first thing – deserted. There was no one else around. Never mind spotting a chairman, I didn't even see a dog. There's trouble brewing! So I pops into the reception. Would you believe it, there's Tuzikov, the policeman in front of me… He's standing there, like on guard duty. I almost went to pieces. It was a bad omen. They've called the police in advance. I shifted from one foot to another for a bit, and said, half asking, half excusing myself: Have I been summoned?

'"If you've been summoned, then go in…"'

'He doesn't even look at me. I knock on the door, but no one replies. I open the door, and beyond, there's yet another one. Oh, I thinks, now I'm really off my trolley. I'd forgotten about the anteroom, it's a bit like in a **bania**. It's probably been made that way so that you can catch your breath.

'I goes into the office.

'Greetings all!'

'"Sit down!"'

'I sits down. I looks around – there's no one else, just them. There's a sheet of paper in front of each one of them. All I can hear is pencils scratching. And there's Motiakov, not wearing his boots, walking to and fro, just in his socks, spitting in… What's those things called? You know, the things brought to the school the other day, for spitting in… They look like stools.

'"Urns", prompted Petia Dolgii.'

'That's it! He had two of them in his office – one in one corner, and one in the other. So he's walking from one to the other, just in his stocking feet, spitting.

'Trouble's brewing, I thinks. If he'd wanted to say something, he would have said it by now. But he's pondering. He doesn't seem to want to say what he's thinking. He just walks up and down, and suddenly, out of the blue he says: "Why have you been asking provocative questions?"

'I stood there dumb-struck.'

'Semën Ivanovich, who did I ask a provocative question to?'

'"Don't play the idiot! Who asked our political instructor about opportunists?"'

'I only asked that for the sake of convention.'

'At that point, all the others guffawed. But Motiakov came up to me and bellowed: "Quit fooling about! I'll beat out of you the desire to play the fool, once and for all. What's wrong with you? D'you really not know what opportunists are?"

'This pulled me up sharp.

'I do know, Comrade Members of the regional committee! I really do know.

'They all burst out laughing again, but I felt insulted: 'Comrades, don't take me for an idiot.'

'"Well, don't make out that you are one. C'mon, tell us why you asked the question." Motiakov stood in front of me, rocking to and fro on his tiptoes, just in his stocking feet.

'Sëmkin, the assistant secretary, who was a curly-haired, sharp kind of bloke, says: "Semën Ivanovich, honest to God, he did it without malicious intent. Would you allow me to ask him a question?"

'"Go on, then."

'"Tell us, Filipp Samochenkov. Who are opportunists?"

'Everyone chuckled again.

'You and I, we are all opportunists,' I replies.

"What? Am I an opportunist as well?" asked Motiakov, thrusting his head upwards, but all the others fell silent.

'No, not you Semën Ivanovich. But all the rest of us are.'

'"How come?"

'Because we don't fulfil the **plan** we are given.

'And yet again, they all tittered.

'"You fool!" says Motiakov. "Opportunism is a tendency. D'you understand, once and for all?"

'Well, I thinks, now they've got me. If they think I've got a tendency, I'm done for. I knew there'd been a tendency in the Party… I just stand there as if I'd just taken a gulp of water. And the rest of them just laughed. Even Motiakov spluttered a couple of times.

'"Okay," he says. "We've had our little joke. Why haven't you delivered your quota of grain?"

'We've got nothing, Semën Ivanovich. Except for millet.'

'"And how much millet do you have?"

'About sixteen **poods** are left. Comrade Members of the committee, rest assured! Tomorrow I'll deliver it all…'

'They all burst out laughing again. Even Motiakov couldn't hold back.

'"Ha, ha, ha! Well, Samochenkov, now you'll remember what opportunism is. And make sure that the millet is at the collection point tomorrow."

'So I paid my way out of opportunism with millet.'

Well, we all had a good laugh too. But Petia Dolgii asks: 'Who are opportunists, in fact?'

'Who the hell knows?' said Filipp. 'Perhaps it's those parasites who are now being sent to far-away places.'

'No, it's not,' says I. 'Opportunists are people who don't keep to the official line. That's why we need to be on their backs.'

'Good Old Bulkin!' says Petia Dolgii. 'You retired far too early. You could still be very useful somewhere or other.'

'Who knows? That's very possible... Perhaps I might yet be...'

About Highwaymen, Hooliganism and About How Everything Has Taken a Turn for the Better

Matvei Kadushkin, a gardener from the village of Malye Bochagi, has a map of the European part of the Soviet Union on his wall with lines drawn across it in black pencil, and right at the spot where the lines cross, a bold circle has been drawn. That's Malye Bochagi.[62] It's the belly-button of the earth. It's thirty **vests** from Brëkhovo and five kilometres from Tikhanovo. Therefore, our region occupies a central position – a showpiece for all to see. For that reason, we used to have a lot of tramps, pilgrims, all sorts of cripples, passers-by, and thieves. People say that the tsar and the tsarina came through our region (formally an **uezd**) on their way to Sarov on a pilgrimage.[63] We cleansed the place of the first mob, I mean, we wiped them all out, but the thieving still carried on, as a '**hang-over from the past**'. And the hooliganism made it worse. Now, here's the explanation why: our people used to be oppressed by landowners and bourgeois people passing through – I mean, merchants. And that's why we had a lot of highwaymen.

Near the village of Zheludëvo, we have a small town, which is an ancient citadel with man-made ramparts. People say that the highwayman Kudeiar and his gang used to live there.[64] Further along the Prokosha River, there were even more settlements, whole villages of highwaymen – Sleznëvo and Bogomolovo, for instance.[65] The river between them becomes much narrower, forming rapids. It was in these shallows that the highwaymen worked – they used to 'greet' the merchants there. Merchants used to turn up to the upper village of Sleznëvo in tears. They used to negotiate the rapids successfully and come out into the expanses of Bogomolovo, where they prayed. It was safe there – you couldn't be pursued by boat.

Apparently, Petia Dolgii had read somewhere in a book that the womenfolk were the worst 'highwaymen' in our district. We even had an argument about it, because now, as far as I can make out, womenfolk (that's 'women' as we say nowadays) do all the work, while the menfolk get drunk and turn to hooliganism. But Petia Dolgii showed me a

---

[62] The literal meaning of the name 'Malye Bochagi' is 'Little Pools'.

[63] In Soviet times, Sarov never appeared on any maps because it was a centre of nuclear weapons and research into that field: the eminent scientist and human rights campaigner Sakharov worked there for a number of years. It also has an ancient monastery, where the Venerable Serafim lived, a miracle-worker in the Orthodox Church, which is why it became a place of pilgrimage. The town is situated south of the Nizhnii Novgorod region.

[64] See Mozhaev's short story 'Old Mother Proshkina' for a similar description and reference to this highwayman.

[65] The name 'Bogomolovo' is based on the Russian words meaning 'praying to God'.

book written by the bourgeois Tambov historian Dubasov.[66] And I read all about how the womenfolk really did used to be 'highwaymen'.

I even copied out one incident, so that you can judge for yourself. There was a certain landowner called Vedeniapin, who was travelling from Elatma to his estate in Zuevo, and he spent the night at a widow's house, who was also a landowner.[67] This is what the bourgeois historian wrote from the very words of the landowner, Vedeniapin, himself. I'll put it in quotes:

> *'On such and such a date, at midnight, a certain woman, M. A. Etalycheva came to the widow's house like a thief in the night, with her mob, and with some women from Matka, along with the priest, Semën Akimov, and the church-goer Silia Semënov, and, having tied me up, beat the living daylights out of me, and took seventy roubles of mine, and my horse, and my bay gelding, and made off with them.'*

And here's another historical example (I copied this from the local newspaper, from the neighbouring town of Kadom):[68]

> *'The merchant, Zalivaev, from Kadom, got a gang of highwaymen together and attacked the house of the merchant Lytin, at night in the town. Armed with rifles and maces, the highwaymen broke the porch door and burst into the house. Moreover, they violated two young maidens, and returned home safe and sound at dawn…'*

And so on, and so forth…

At this point we might say: 'Aha! This might be highway robbery, but this incident has a class element about it. It is the fruit of class antagonism. I mean, there is a touch of the irreconcilable here. So now, when we have a punch-up, it's just amongst ourselves, and even then it's because we're boozed. There's not a hint of ideological antagonism – it's just pure stupidity, one might say. Thieving happens more often than not from accumulated public goods. And even then, it's carried out without an element of antagonism. Escalations occur, of course, and people even end up in court. Particularly after the decree on hooliganism and the intensification of the struggle against it had been declared. Well, we just couldn't carry on without it. Judge for yourselves. Just take this one case…

---

[66] Tambov is situated on the River Tsna, 480 km to the south-east of Moscow. It was founded in 1636 as a fortress town to protect the Russian empire against Crimean and Tatar invaders. It has strong links to **Stenka Razin** (See Glossary).
The historian referred to is a real person: he lived and worked in pre-revolutionary Russia, which is why he is called 'bourgeois' by Bulkin. Ivan Ivanovich Dubasov (1843-1913) was an expert and noted archivist on the local history of the Tambov region, and he wrote a number of books on its history. He also taught history in an institute in Tambov, the regional capital of the area, to which the town also gives its name.

[67] Elatma is in the Kasimov region and the first mention of it is in 1381 when Dmitri Donskoi bought the settlement from Prince Alexander Ukovich. Peter the Great also passed through it in 1722, when the settlement comprised around 3,000 inhabitants. At the turn of the twentieth century there were fourteen churches and a couple of mosques. Zuevo is now called Orekhovo-Zuevo and the town is known for its weaving.

[68] Kadom is a settlement on the Moksha River, a tributary of the great river Oka, in the **Riazan** region.

Our regional capital was reopened only last year – it had been closed ten years before. I went to Tikhanovo about my pension. I settled in at a boarding house. Agafia Ivanovna happened to be on duty. 'Hello!' 'Hello!' 'How are you?' 'And how are you?! We haven't seen each other for ages,' she says. In my time as a chairman, I used to take chickens, geese, and honey to her… We go back a long way, as they say.

'We got our lives back,' says Agafia Ivanovna. 'We've got bread and sugar in the shops again. What else could we want? The only hitch is, I've been elected as a juror. We're in session every day.'

'Why are you in session every day? D'you not have anything better to do?'

'We keep sitting in judgement. It's the new declaration on hooliganism. Yesterday we had Valerka Klokov in the dock. The driver from Provotarov.

'What for?'

'He broke up a **kolkhoz** meeting.'

'Ivan Svinenkov is the chairman there.'

'He was the one it was all about. He was promoted to chairman from the consumers' association. Well! That was when they closed the regional capital… But now it's been reopened, the **kolkhoz** workers say, "Take him back". What use is he? He works for them over there, but he himself lives in Tikhanovo. He's even appointed a deputy from Tikhanovo. And they get their mates in from Provotarov. The **kolkhoz** workers grumbled and grumbled about him. But who listens to them? And then, suddenly, the annual general meeting comes round. People gathered at the offices and the chairman was there with his deputy. Now, here's a thing: Valerka drives up in his tipper truck, drunk. He stands on the porch and says to the **kolkhoz** workers, "What are you doing whispering in corners? Tie up Svinenkov and his deputy, and chuck 'em in the back of my truck. I'll take 'em off to the tip in Tikhanovo."

'Everyone burst out laughing. But Svinenkov shouted out, "Arrest him!" The deputy made a dash for him. Valerka makes for the truck. He had a load of logs on it. The deputy climbed up on the tyre. Valerka bashed him over the head with a log. He keeled over. Then Valerka jumped out of the back, but the chairman of the rural council jumps on him. Valerii grabs a pump from the cab and calms him down with that… Svinenkov ran off. But Valerka gets on his cab, like onto a platform, and says, "The meeting is over." Well, everyone had a good laugh and went off. He got three years for that yesterday. He broke down in tears… He's got three kids.'

'Let him cry,' says I. 'We shouldn't humour such people. Fear is a great teacher. Otherwise the dictatorship will get weaker.'

'I'm not at all against that,' said Agafia Ivanovna. 'So, we're in session again today.'

'Who are you doing today?'

'Some chaps from the brick factory. They climbed the chimney.'

'What chimney?'

'The factory chimney. That one, sticking out over there, like the Devil's finger.'

I took a look out of the window – the chimney was right opposite us… God, it was so tall!

'It must be fifty metres tall,' says I.

'Fifty-four.'

'What did they climb that for?'

'For a dare. After work, Vanka Salazkin says: "Eh, you load of whimps! I'm going to climb that chimney and fasten a jumper to the lightening conductor. If anyone of you dares take it down, I'll stand you a half-litre of vodka. If you don't take it down, you pay me a full litre. The **brigade leader** wasn't for letting him go up there. But he just shook his head, saying, "Keep your nose out of it!" So he climbs up there and fixes the jumper to the lightening conductor… Look, you can see – it's bent to one side.'

I looked out of the window, and she was right – the lightening conductor was bent.

'Who took the jumper down?'

'Vitka Buzinov. "What the hell," he says. "It's a piece of piss! All you did was hang a jumper on the lightening conductor." He took his accordion, strapped it over his shoulder, and up he went. He gets up the chimney and unties the jumper. He even spun it around over his head and let it go. Then, he sat on the edge, at the top of the chimney and played a sad song, "*Oh, bird of passage, come fly down to me, like a fly…*" Then, he threw down his accordion too. He stood up and even walked around on the top of the chimney… He even waved his cap. He started to make his way down and grabbed on to a clamp, but it came loose, together with the brick. He flew through the air.'

'Did he get smashed up?'

'No, he's alive… So today we've got him in the dock.'

'But what for? All because he fell?'

'No, we're not trying Vitka, but Vanka Salazkin. The one who put the jumper up there. He belted the **brigade leader**. Raised his hand to him.'

'Well, he deserves it,' says I. 'You shouldn't raise your hand to anyone.'

I went to see the brick factory. I've just got to take a look, I thinks. What kind of a miracle is that? He fell fifty-four metres and didn't come a cropper.

I rolls up. They're all sitting in the **Red Corner**, waiting for the judge. He'd got held up in **Riazan**.

'What were you doing, climbing up the chimney?' I says.

'What else is there to do? Work finishes at five o'clock now.'

'Oh, for the mass cultural activities,' I says.[69]

'What's all that for? Is it for playing dominoes? They might as well have broken off our hands.'

'How on earth did he not come a cropper?' I asks. 'Is he some kind of saint?'

'There's an awning there, just by the chimney: it's got a slate roof. It covers the hoist. That's where he landed. It had a slope. He smashed it to smithereens. Vitka went straight through the roof, right onto the wire mesh, just above the electric motor... The mesh held him.'

'Was he out cold for long?'

'You must be joking! He got straight up on his own feet. He walked to the hospital. Apparently, he pissed blood for a couple of days in the hospital. That's all.'

'Where is he now?'

'In the tea room, drinking vodka.'

I looked around at the broken awning and the metal mesh, bent like a cradle... I went over to the tea room. Svinenkov, the chairman from Provotarovo, happened to be there. 'Greetings!' 'Greetings!' We sat down and got a bottle of 'regional' (it was **pertsovka** – that's what we call it) and poured out a round. I mentioned about the miracle and the chimney, and he says to me: 'There he is, the hero, Vitka Buzinov.'

He was walking around like a real hero, wearing a striped sweater and a colourful scarf on top. He had a drink at one table, then moved on to the next.

'Vitka, over here!' Svinenkov shouted over to him.

He comes over, takes my glass, and downs it in one.

'Greetings, Svinenkov!' he says.

He offers me his hand, just like a cosmonaut: 'Victor Buzinov.'

I also give my name: 'Bulkin, Pëtr Afanasievich, from Brëkhovo.'

'Oh-oh!' he exclaims. 'News got as far as there, then?'

'Vitia,' I asks him. 'Did you fly for a long time from the chimney?'

'Yes. For ages.'

'Did anything go through your mind?'

'Yeah!'

'What came into your mind, while you were in the air?'

---

[69] Workers in all aspects of Soviet industry and bureaucracy were urged to engage in a whole range of physical and cultural activities, based at the work-place, usually after working hours. These activities were to promote health and vigour, which were intended to have knock-on effects in productivity, but they were also heavily imbued with ideology. In the 1960s, each institution, factory, and bureaucratic institution was given a quota of hours and number of people to fulfil prescribed activities.

He had another drink and said: 'I'm there, flying through the air from the chimney, and I thinks: "Bugger! This will cause more trouble at home..."'

So here, as you see, everything comes right down to domestic troubles. There is no irreconcilability here.[70] A problem on a larger scale was the misunderstanding at the **kolkhoz** level, what happened in the incident with Svinenkov and the driver from Provotarovo. But, once again, that's a simple, local conflict. In fact, everything was put to rights: the chairman kept his job, and so did his deputy. And the **kolkhoz** workers, society, that is, does not suffer from such hooliganism. And if society does not suffer, then that means there is no antagonism at play. It's just a matter of stupidity – it's as simple as that.

How I nearly ended up in court

I got my fingers burnt over a trifling matter – Semën Motiakov took umbrage at me over the head of the regional department of health, Stepanida Piatova.

She was an educated woman, so whenever it was icy weather she used to wear, not knee-length felt boots, but short, ankle-high, white boots, which she used to clean either with chalk, or tooth powder. Once, she and Motiakov made a pre-election tour of the region to meet the voters.[71]

We got a phone call from the regional centre. We came out to meet them *en masse*, the whole **kolkhoz**. We stood there at the edge of the village, all along the road, and we waited and waited, but there was no sign of them. It was already getting dark. The menfolk got into a bit of an argument: one lot said that a 'deputy' was coming, others claimed he was a 'candidate'. But Paramon Drankin says: 'Fools! It's neither the one nor the other... The one who's coming to us is a deputy-candidate.'[72]

Finally, they turned up... They drove a pair of horses with bells on their harness. They were bashing out songs – they were drunk. We gives it, 'Hurrah! Hurrah!' and

---

[70] Again, Bulkin is using political and ideological terminology to describe and explain personal relationships. There is a set expression in Russian which refers to 'class irreconcilability', that is, the enmity caused between the working class and the peasantry, or the working class and the upper, or educated, classes. Communist theoreticians claimed that in Soviet society, this 'class irreconcilability' had been eliminated fairly early on in the regime. Bulkin uses this concept of 'irreconcilability' to explain domestic disputes and hostility. The concept of 'irreconcilability' was also extended to the area of international relations *vis-à-vis* non-communist regimes.

[71] A new constitution was drawn up in 1936, which assured all Soviet citizens equal rights, irrespective of their background, and hence, voting rights were restored to former **kulaks**, priests and others, whom the regime had regarded as enemies. In the following year, preparations were made to democratize local and central government and to institute a secret ballot. There was talk of introducing multi-candidate lists and allowing non-party members to stand for election. However, this was all a façade and a sham: rather than granting greater democracy, Stalin merely tightened his grip on power. Elections did take place, often with official pomp and ceremony, but little real democratization had been achieved in reality, and this remained the status quo until Gorbachëv's *perestroika* or 'restructuring' in the mid-1980s onwards. The behaviour of the officials and the political canvasser in this section of the story implies that they too regarded the elections as something of a mere ritual, rather than an expression of real democracy.

[72] The peasants here show their ignorance of the electoral system and the terminology in which it is expressed. The whole system was rather alien to them, as were its representatives, who were usually from the towns and cities. The term 'candidate' was used to indicate a person up for election, but not yet elected: once elected, the candidate then became a 'deputy' or 'delegate'. The correct term here should be 'candidate for deputy', but amusingly, Paramon gets the expression back to front, implying that he is elected even before being voted for.

chuck our hats in the air. They just galloped on straight past us... They turned off towards my house. So I runs on.

My Maruska had already got the stove going and when I got there, she was rubbing Stepanida's feet by the fire. She said they'd gone numb 'cause of the steam. The boots were lying around on the floor, just like a couple of wooden shoe-trees. Motiakov was walking around the room in his bare feet, the deputy had not turned up, and Smirnov, the political canvasser, was leaning on the table with his elbows, and it looked as though he had gone to sleep.

'Petka!' says Motiakov to me. 'Have you assembled the working people?'

'You saw them yourself. You went right past them.'

'That was just for our drive past... And how about for our political discussion?'

'They've all gone to the clubhouse.'

'Good. Give the canvasser a shake. Take him to the people...'

I only had to touch his shoulder and he stood bolt upright, as if on command.

'Which direction are we to take?' he says, holding onto the chair.[73]

'Don't you think we should put it off til the morning?' I asks Motiakov.

'Take him over there! He's a man of habit.'

He was indeed a man of habit... While I took him to the clubhouse, he hung on to me all the way there. But as soon as he saw the lectern on the stage, he immediately perked up, pushed me to one side, got there under his own steam, embraced it with both hands, and started talking, just as if he were resuming after a short break.

'Comrades! As you and I all know, our achievements are plain for all to see...'

And so on, and so forth. He talked about the rise in the people's standard of living, about the scheming of international agents of imperialism, about the twelve powers who fought against us in the civil war, about internal counterrevolutionary activity on the **kolkhoz** front, and about the path towards abundance. In a word, he mentioned all stages of our historical development. He concluded by offering good wishes to all as he was supposed to. It all went off nicely...

This meant that the true official line had been maintained! Even a child knew where you were expected to start, and at which point you had to finish. And which historical stages had to be dwelt upon... and rehearsed in the right order... That was the main thing. Nowadays, some people say that in any official speech, the main thing is its 'intrinsic content'. But allow me to ask: What's more important – the correct order or intrinsic content? It is, of course, order, because it is formulated once and for all, and it is passed down from on high. You can keep an eye on it and it's handy for the purposes of control. But how could you control 'intrinsic content'? For a start off, anyone who fancies can make it up, and secondly, it takes various forms. That's why *I* say: You can

---

[73] This question has a double meaning: first, it could mean quite simply, 'Where are we going?', but secondly, it can also be interpreted in a political sense, meaning, 'In which political direction are we moving?'

only have one thing – either order and discipline, or intrinsic content. And who knows where we'll end up with that? It's as simple as that.

So there we are, we got home with the political canvasser. I'd also asked along Iakov Ivanovich the bookkeeper. My Maruska had made a load of **pelmeni**, and there was plenty of vodka to go round. Have a drink, it's the people's celebration!

When we gets home, I find Maruska sitting alone at the table.

'What's going on? Where are the others?'

'They're in the *gornitsa*, warming each other up…'[74]

I burst in on them. Blimey! There was Semën Ivanovich 'administering' to her, right there on the bed. We stood there in the doorway, rooted to the spot, speechless. And Semën Ivanovich just says over his shoulder: 'What are you doing? Trying to set me up in your own house?'[75]

'The **pelmeni** are ready…'

'You can stuff your **pelmeni**! Shut the door!'

I pulled the door to, and in the *gornitsa* the fun and games started up again. There's going to be all hell to pay! My bookkeeper downed a glass of vodka, wiped his mouth and couldn't be seen for dust. The political canvasser started snoring on the sofa, and Maruska and I sat opposite each other, nose to nose, like two cuckoos on an antique clock, just waiting to cuckoo the hour.

Finally, they emerged from the room, dressed. Stepanida took her boots down from the stove and started to put them on. She pulled and pulled, then stamped her feet into them, as if stamping on me and Maruska. We just sat there flinching.

'Have the horses harnessed,' Motiakov ordered me.

I hailed the driver, who'd been put up in the next house. He harnessed the horses in a trice. He brought them round. Motiakov didn't even look at me.

'Are the horses ready?' he asked.

'Yes, all ready,' I replies.

He glanced at Smirnov. He was snoring away.

'Bring him with you tomorrow morning to Svistunovo on your own horses… And don't even think of blathering what went on in there. If you do, I'll cut your tongue out!'

And he left. The next morning the canvasser got up and asked: 'When are we going to hold the public meeting?'

'You've already done it,' I says.

---

[74] In a rural or peasant house, the *gornitsa* was a room which did not have a stove in it. This fact is essential to understand the humour here!

[75] The original Russian literally means 'to arrange provocation', meaning to set somebody up in a compromising position. This was one of the many tactics used by the internal security forces or secret police (KGB) in the Soviet Union, for the purposes of entrapment. Frequently, such tactics took the form of a sexual snare, which is what Motiakov fears here.

'When?'

'Yesterday evening.'

'Get away! Can't remember for the life of me. What did I say?'

'You gave a good speech. Word for word, as if you were reading a script.'

'Did I sit down to it?'

'No,' says I. 'You held on firm to the lectern.'

'Oh, thanks, Bulkin. You've got things set up nicely round here.'

I should have kept my mouth shut, fool that I am, but I was pleased with that bit of praise, and I said: 'You should tell that to Semën Ivanovich – he left in a huff. He had to leave on official business.'

'What's with him? Wasn't there enough vodka for him?'

'He had a disturbed night... The cocks crowed, and the dogs barked. That's the countryside for you!'

'Don't worry... I'll smooth his feathers.'

What d'you know – the week wasn't yet up and Motiakov summoned me. He was sitting alone in his office and didn't even offer me his hand. I was about to sit on the chair by the door, but he beckoned to me: 'Come on over to the table. I want to look at you.'

I comes up to him at the table: in front of him is an order for timber to be supplied by the **kolkhozes**. He gives me a good telling-off and I just stands there, reading which **kolkhoz** has got to deliver how many cubic metres, according to the **plan**.

'I could have understood,' he says, 'if you'd put a foot wrong, let's say. If you'd probed into somebody else's private life. But to spill the beans to the canvasser! I'll never, ever, forgive you for that.'

He harps on and on, then he says: 'Go to the meeting with the chairman of the regional executive committee. In the mean time, I'll reflect on your behaviour. I'll decide how to deal with you.'

Now he's going to have me for breakfast, I thought. I go to the regional executive committee meeting, but I am at a complete loss what to think. What kind of meeting could it be when Motiakov has got you by the seat of your trousers? What will I do if he chucks me out into the world, naked as the day I was born?

So, there we all are, **kolkhoz** chairmen together in a meeting. What d'you know, Semën Ivanovich himself comes along, holding that same timber order. He sits down at the table next to the regional executive committee chairman and says: 'Comrade **Kolkhoz** Chairmen! We have asked you to come here to consult with you. What I'm saying is, it's all down to your conscience... Which **kolkhoz** can provide how much timber? You yourselves understand what the situation requires. Our neighbours have accepted great undertakings. Surely we won't lag behind them?'

So, we decided to push for a high figure ourselves. It all appeared to be kind of voluntary… We'd exceed the basic figure on the order. I should have kept my mouth shut, but I blurted out without thinking: 'But you have the quota there… All worked out on that paper.'

Motiakov suddenly jumped up and said: 'Who authorized you to speak for the regional executive Party? Who do you think you are? You have been allowed to approach the sacred table of the secretary of the regional committee, and you had the cheek to read his documents!? You don't yet have the maturity to be amongst managerial staff…'

I got a right telling off. Then the plenipotentiaries stuck their oar in. The first one to come down on us was the secretary for animal husbandry. He'd seen off a whole barrel of mead. He turned all red, his eyes bulged, and he kept looking out for something to find fault with. As he walked, he set his legs apart, as if his crotch were exploding. Our stableman came to meet him as he rode through the village on a stallion, forcing him to slacken his pace from a gallop to a trot… That's when the secretary started carping.

'Who gave him the right to gallivant on a breeding horse?' he asks me.

'He's not gallivanting. He's breaking it in.'

'Who the hell breaks a horse in by galloping?'

'What galloping? It was a trot!'

'It's not a trot, it's a gallop!'

'D'you, perhaps, think ambling is galloping?'

And so on, and so forth. We go into my office, and he says to me: 'Not only can you not be trusted to manage people, but we can't trust you with the breeding horse either. Surrender your files!'

Well, something inside me exploded – I'd also drunk a small barrel of mead. I grabbed my official stamp, charged it with ink, and slapped it right in his mush, saying: 'Here you are – you do the job!'

His cheeks were puffy and fleshy. My stamp smudged and ran down his cheek in rivulets.

'So, that's how it is!' He grabbed the ink-pot and chucked it at me.

I stopped it in mid-flight with my palm, so all the splashes ended up on him again. He grabs the telephone and rings up the public prosecutor: 'I request that you arrest Bulkin,' he says. 'He has raised his hand to a regional official – to me, in fact.'

The prosecutor asked him if the case had been investigated by his office. 'No? In that case, we'll wait until then…'

And so I was summoned to the office. I intentionally put on that same tunic which I wore when I had the run-in with the secretary for animal husbandry – when he chucked the ink-pot at me, 'cause the sleeve was stained.

'How is it,' he asks, 'that I'm supposed to have beaten him up with an ink-pot, but I'm the one who ended up with the ink all over me.'

'And by whose authority did you put an official stamp on a manager's face?' asked Motiakov.

I was going to mention the incident about the breeding horse, but they had no intention of listening to me.

'This is nothing to do with the stallion,' he says. 'It's political... Give him a good telling off!'

So I got my twelfth official reprimand. They resolved to check out my slush fund and take me to court. Well, who didn't have a slush fund at that time?

The evening before this meeting, an accident happened. We got a new GAZ-51 lorry in exchange for our milk. But we had no driver. As it happened, at that time, the nephew of our bookkeeper Smorchkov arrived in the village from the army.

'I have a driving licence,' he says.

So we summoned him to the office and decided to give him the new lorry. It turned out that he had nicked the licence from somewhere or other and faked it. He went to the town the next day and collided with a MAZ.[76] I received a phone call from there: 'Come and collect your old wreck!' Sashka and I went to the regional capital on horseback. We covered two hundred kilometres in a night and a day. I turns up at the repair shop.

'Write out a warrant for the repair,' they said.

'When will the vehicle be repaired?'

'In six months.'

'Blimey! And how are we going to deliver the harvest?'

'That's nothing to do with us...'

'C'mon, Sashka. Let's go to Pugasovo...'

We got a barrel of mead and a sack of flour. The usual way of doing things... First of all, we popped in to Tikhanovo with some flagons of mead – forty litres each for the Chief of Police, Zmeëv, and for the Chief Prosecutor, Abramkin.[77] They both accepted it... Well, that means the brakes were on.[78] Now, put your foot down to get to the turn-off – the barrier was open.

We called in to the repair shop in Pugasovo and showed our booty to the right people... Well, what's the problem? For such goods, not only would they repair the lorry – they'd even fit you up with a new set of guts! Just a week later, my lorry was rattling along the road, with chickens flying out of its way.

---

[76] The GAZ and MAZ are both types of lorries, so called because they were made in different vehicle factories. The former was made in the **Gorky** Car Factory (Gorkovskii avtomobilnyi zavod – GAZ), and the latter in the Minsk Car Factory (Minskii avtomobilnyi zavod).

[77] The name 'Zmeëv' is based on the Russian word for 'snake'!

[78] What he means here is that no further action would be taken against the driver: he had made sure that the situation would not develop into anything more serious.

We deducted the mead and flour from the slush fund, putting it down to expenses for the repair. But this latest bout of 'deliveries' made people come running to us like mice...

None other than the Chief of Police, Zmeëv, came to see me in person: 'Pëtr Afanasievich, I've come to see you on a matter of investigating an act of hooliganism. The Khamov and Drankin brothers got into a fight.'

'What's there to investigate? Arrest both lots of them. They're all guilty.'

'That's as may be, but nonetheless we are in charge. We can't just arrest them indiscriminately. We have to show them up, each in turn.'

'Well, go ahead, expose them.'

He settled in at my place. He eats and drinks, and don't so much as sticks his nose outside. Well, I don't begrudge him that. Go on, have a good time! I want for nothing. I'd got twenty sheep alone, and two pigs. C'mon, Zmeëv, eat, drink! And I behave as if I don't notice anything. But he pops into the accounts office from time to time. He picked out documents which referred to the mead and the flour, and left with them. As he left, he said to Iakov Ivanovich: 'Now look here, not a word to Bulkin, otherwise you'll come a cropper with him.'

But Iakov Ivanovich got drunk round at my place and spilt the beans.

'I'm a bastard, a treacherous Judas!' he says. 'And what's worse is, that I'm your colleague. He got me on his side. Go on, if you want, spit in my mug right now, or do it later, if you like. Even so, I really respect you...' He confessed, in tears. We'd both had an absolute skinful.

The next day, I went to the regional capital. I popped into a shop and Zmeëv happened to be there. 'Greetings!' he said. 'Where are you staying?'

'At a mate's.'

'You mustn't! Come stay with me. Make yourself at home.'

'Where would that be, then?' I asks. 'In a prison cell?'

He stood there, mortified.

'Thanks a lot, Zmeëv,' says I, 'for not balking at my hospitality.' And off I goes.

But he comes after me, saying, 'How dare you say that to me?! Just you wait, you'll be singing another tune.'

I didn't even get to my mate's house before Tuzikov, the policeman, caught up with me: 'Pëtr Afanasievich, go immediately to Zmeëv's office.'

I gets there. He invites me, with a nice smile, to sit down at the table, all respectful, as if we'd only just met. So I sits down.

'The prosecutor has ordered your arrest for theft and its consequences.'

'You must do as you see best,' says I. 'You people have to fulfil your duties.'

'Comrade Bulkin, please write down an explanation. What did you do with the barrel of mead?'

I wrote down that one hundred and twenty litres went on paying for the repair, and that Comrade Zmeëv, the Chief of Police, took forty litres, as did Prosecutor Abramkin. I hands it to him, also with a nice smile, and treat him all respectful, just as if we were strangers.

'It's all written here, Comrade Chief.'

He read it and pointed to his own name: 'What's with this? Cross my name out. I came to see you in all sincerity, to give you a tip-off.'

'Thanks for your concern, but I can't cross your name out.'

'You'll have to prove it. I took nothing from you.'

'Quite correct,' says I. 'I did not give it to you personally. Your wife accepted it from my driver. We also know how things are done.'

'You swindler! What if I were to put you in prison?'

'You would be carrying out your duty.'

So, he'd sniffed and sniffed around me, but he daren't arrest me.

Then something happened: Motiakov was replaced by a new secretary, Demin. And I fell foul of a campaign: whoever amongst the chairmen had not graduated from a CPS, SRY, or at least from a SCOS, was sacked.[79] The new secretary Demin sent Petia Dolgii to Brëkhovo to replace me. The fact that I got sacked worked to my advantage, because it at least covered up the embezzled mead.

Footnote: for those readers who are not familiar with the acronyms above, I shall explain. The CPS means 'commune parish school', and SRY is a 'school for rural youth', and SCOS means a 'School for Cutting Out and Sewing'.

---

[79] These are all acronyms for various types of educational institutions, which I have anglicised in this translation. CPS usually means Central Party School and likewise, SRY normally means School for Rural Youth; both these are familiar acronyms, which are instantly recognisable to Russians. However, the comedy here lies in the fact that Mozhaev gives these *common* acronyms rather *uncommon* names, and he includes a rather rare acronym – the SCOS, which he then explains in the text, in his footnote. The original Russian acronym for School for Rural Youth is ambiguous: it could equally mean 'School for **Kolkhoz** Youth', since the Russia words for 'rural' (*krestianskaia*) and '**kolkhoz**' (*kolkhoznaia*) begin with the same letter. The School for Rural Youth was an actual type of school, which was established in 1923: the period of study was three years, and such schools combined lessons in basic literacy with teaching in matters relating to agricultural practice. These schools were renamed in 1930, in line with the campaign for full collectivization of agriculture, to 'School for **Kolkhoz** Youth'. In 1934 these schools were transformed into 'seven-year' secondary schools, which were a shortened form of the full Soviet secondary educational course – the usual secondary school education in towns and cities lasted ten years. 'Schools for Cutting Out and Sewing' is something of a joke by Mozhaev: such schools did not actually exist, although individual courses in these skills were common. There were many courses in tailoring and dress-making skills organised as night-school courses, both in rural and urban locations, and the popular newspaper *The Peasant Woman* (*Krestianka*), whose contributors featured Lenin's wife Krupskaia, frequently carried items on dress-making. One wonders how well following a course in 'cutting out and sewing' would equip a person to run a **kolkhoz**, but the early Soviet regime was desperate to engage anyone in a managerial position with even the most basic education: this situation changed as more people became educated and acquired more skills.

Petia Dolgii

I've been trying to fathom out logically why Petia Dolgii made a success of the **kolkhoz**. My brother Levanid came up with the answer: he who says that he wants to build communism by his own hand is a fool. We have to build it together, and that includes using our enemies' manpower. And then I try to fathom out logically why we have managers who, not only don't use our enemies' efforts for the cause of building the bright future, but don't even trust the peasants either. But never mind the peasants! They don't even trust their own father.

I remember the next day after I'd been sacked, Petia Dolgii said: 'Pëtr Afanasievich, could you perhaps take on the livestock farm?'

'It's a lost cause,' I say. 'No one does any work there anyway.'

'Well, ask them to.'

'I've already done that.'

'Who've you asked?'

'Everyone.'

'But who have you asked personally? Who have you visited at home?'

'To tell the truth – no one. All the same, I know they're all parasites and they won't turn out to work.'

'Comrade Bulkin, you ought to take, not an administrative approach, but a military one. You'd better get a transfer to the rural council, before it's too late. Otherwise you might get arrested.'

And he was right. At that time there were rumours that, apparently, material had been written against me again. Nonetheless, he helped me get a job as chairman of the rural council. Any other official would have cast me adrift and let me end up as an **enemy of the people**.

I ask you not to confuse an ordinary enemy with an **enemy of the people**. An ordinary enemy is one who temporarily does not fully appreciate our country's advantages, as if he had merely strayed. Such a person needs to be re-educated and prevailed upon to work. But an **enemy of the people** understands everything. He is in our midst and wrecks things on account of his impotence. He needs to be unmasked, isolated from society, and brought to strict account, that is, to be repressed in prison.

So now then, I shall describe Petia Dolgii for you. He's still a young man, though married, and he has children. He started the job as a really young man – he was under thirty. He's a tall chap – tall enough to stride over horses. His fists are like sledge hammers. However, his facial expression is subdued, he's tow-haired, and he looks weak-sighted, because he's always screwing his eyes up.

He arrived in our village with just a suitcase, just like a student, in a white suit and barefoot. I fixed him up at Old Ma Bukhriachikha's. After a week had gone by, I asked her: 'Well now, Old Ma Vasiuta, is he not a drinker then, our new chairman?'

'He's no drinker at all, Old Man. I've offered him a good volume, and a drop of moonshine… Didn't touch a drop. The only thing is, he walks around the place in his drawers. And his boots are all tatty at the sides – they're just held together with straps. He recently asked me, "Granny, do they sell underpants in the shop here?" No, I says, we haven't yet sunk to such shame. "What shall I do?" he asks. "I haven't brought any underwear with me." So, I says, joking like, "I have some of Vaniushka's drawers. 'Ere y'are." He took 'em. Put them on and they're up round his knees. He's as tall as a telegraph pole.'

From that time on, he's been called Petia Dolgii. And it went all round the village: 'That's what the chairman's like! He's walking around in Vaniushka's drawers.'

'He's worn his own out on the way here, the poor devil.'

'He'll cut his teeth on our farm. The job pays well.'

'Listen, Chaps! Don't trust him. He's crafty. He's got money. He's one of those thirty-thousanders. One way or another, they'll have bunged him thirty-thousand for something or other.'[80]

'We all know why… He's going to try to get us to work for those thousands.'

And so, the first thing he did was to announce: 'From New Year onwards, we're going to pay you, not by **workday units**, but in real money.'

Kornei Ivanovich Nazarkin replies to him: 'Pigs might fly…'

But Petia Dolgii insists: 'From January, all **kolkhoz** workers will receive a wage. And you'll get your **pay advance** every month.'

The **kolkhoz** meeting was held in the school: people turned out in their droves and stood in the classroom, the corridor, and on the porch.

'And if there's no income, how will you pay us then?' asked Paramon.

'Even if we have to sell off the pig unit, you'll get your pay,' replied Petia Dolgii. 'A storm might flatten the wheat, or rain might drown the maize, but you'll still get your wages… just like the rest of the working class.'

'And what about the minimum?' they asked him.

'The minimum is cancelled,' he replied.

At this point, the peasants really did not believe him at all. They just laughed. What was it like with **workday units**? There was a minimum of one hundred and thirty-five

---

[80] At various times during the Soviet regime, there were massive recruitment drives, conducted principally through the **Komsomol**, to provide extra man-power for specific projects. Twenty-five thousand people were mobilized to assist in the campaign for the full collectivization of agriculture from late 1929 onwards, and these people were called the 'twenty-five-thousanders'. There was also a similar recruitment drive during the spring and summer of 1954 to provide assistance with the **Virgin Land** Programme, and on this occasion, three hundred thousand volunteers were recruited from the **Komsomol**. The speaker is probably referring to the recruitment drive carried out during the campaign for collectivization, but he erroneously believes that Petia Dolgii, as one of the new recruits, has actually been paid an enormous sum of money, rather than him being one of a huge cohort of helpers: he confuses their total number with a payment in roubles of the same magnitude. The speaker's mistrust of Petia Dolgii is typical of the wariness with which the peasantry regarded such outside, urban help.

units. Once you'd notched them up, you could do what you liked. For instance, you could go to the timber processing plant, or to the brick factory in Tikhanovo. But if you hadn't clocked up the minimum, you lived as a dependant of the farm: for a start, you couldn't get permission to earn money anywhere else, and in the second place, they'd slap a double tax on you to the tune of one thousand seven hundred roubles, as an independent farmer.[81] Taxes used to be levied on your cow, sheep, and you'd even have to hand in goat hair. Whether it gave wool or not – you'd have to give some in. You had to get it wherever you could. Whatever you sowed, you paid a tax on every **sotka** of land you worked. And if you hadn't clocked up your minimum, you had to pay a double tax. That's why the peasants just laughed: 'How can that be? If you abolish the minimum, everyone will go and work away.'

On the other hand, what if he really does pay up? But, with what? There wasn't a single penny in the current account – just a load of debts. And when you do get income, it all goes to offset debts or into the capital fund, to the state, that is.[82]

'I tell you this, chaps,' said Kornei Ivanovich, winking. 'Those thirty-thousands, which he was given in the city, he's making them available. I bet you that he's spent half of it on the journey here and on food. And he'll give us the other half. Who'll check up on him? He can just up and off. But our cows will be taken from us. No, we shouldn't take this money.'

He was a stubborn old stick, this Kornei Ivanovich. In January, when they actually got paid for a **workday unit**, he sent his grandson, Maksimka, off to the office: 'Pop in and see how they're paying us,' he said. 'See if they're paying us in bonds.'

It's a tricky question as to how Petia Dolgii managed to wangle the whole matter of payment. If I told you the truth – you wouldn't believe me.

The truth was like this. At the timber processing plant, we had planks of wood ready for a new pigsty. He made these planks available. He got the circular saw operators together and said: 'Saw all these planks again for use as fencing.'

'Your wish is our command...'

They sawed them all up again. Would you believe it...? He puts out an announcement on the radio: 'Whoever needs fencing laths, come along to the office and buy them, cash in hand.'

People turned up in their droves at the office. After the era of the independent farmer had come to an end, people didn't fence off their private plots because everything was kept on an equal, collective basis. While we were increasing working tempos, the womenfolk would rear the goats: we had hoof and horn, but no milk. Cattle and vegetable gardens don't mix: they'll ponce off you and cause a lot of damage. A dog couldn't get through a gap, but a cow can. Stupid womenfolk! They didn't understand the down side. Then it all ends up in tears.

---

[81] One way of making sure that peasants joined the **kolkhoz** was to tax them into joining, i.e. if a farmer decided to farm independently, local officials levied all manner of taxes upon them as a means of coercion.
[82] The 'capital fund' (literally the 'indivisible fund') was money held in a separate account, which the state allowed the **kolkhoz** to keep to invest or spend on projects of its own choosing. There was strict control over what a **kolkhoz** chairman could and could not do with the money it held.

So, the womenfolk flew down to the office for the fencing, like hens after millet. And they raised such a hullabaloo, climbing over each other, trampling on each other. They were afraid that there wouldn't be enough to go round. Then Petia Dolgii comes out to them and says: 'Calm down, Dear Housewives! We've enough fencing for all. If you want a complete new fence, put yourself down on Iakov Ivanovich's list. We'll form a **brigade** of workers and fence in all your vegetable plots for you. You'll have to pay for them immediately at the rate of five roubles a linear metre.'

It was child's play forming such a team of workers. Who wasn't keen on his own vegetable plot?

Petia Dolgii himself planned the whole layout. He hadn't managed the final check, when – what do you know?! – a jeep approaches. It's a plenipotentiary from the regional committee.

'A fine chairman you are!' he shouts from the cab. 'We've an election campaign on, and you're mucking around.[83] You should be engaged in outright political activism.'

But Petia Dolgii says to him: 'I *am* engaged in outright political activism.'

'Come off it! We'll show you what outright political activism is... over at the office!'

'You can do that later, but I'll show you some now.'

Petia Dolgii went up to the jeep and showed him a bunch of fives in the direction of the road out of the village: 'You see that road? Take it, before it's too late.'

'I came to help,' shouted the plenipotentiary.

'In that case, get out of the cab, grab a hammer and nails, and build a fence.'

'Are you making fun of me? Fair enough...'

You couldn't see our plenipotentiary for dust.

'Well now, Pëtr Ermolaevich,' the peasant men said to him. 'They'll put you away behind a fence yourself.'

'Let's get a move on and get the fences done. Full pelt, all together, and let's see if we can make others envious,' joked Petia Dolgii.

And he did manage to get the fences done! Towards the end of the month, the **kolkhoz** workers paid up for their fencing. Petia Dolgii settled their wages with this money.

'What do we make of this, chaps?' asked Kornei Ivanovich. 'We've brought home the bacon, and he's chucked it back in our mugs.'

Well I never...! The **kolkhoz** farmers went out to work in February... They had summoned up the enthusiasm for it. But more than that – they wanted to see how he would pull it off a second time. The end of month was approaching and he called in the bookkeeper: 'Iakov Ivanovich, how much revenue have we from the sale of milk and meat?'

---

[83] The original Russian expression for 'mucking around' is literally 'to fence in a vegetable garden': more usually this expression means 'to mess about', but here the literal translation is also apt.

'About a hundred and thirty thousand roubles.'

'Go to the bank and draw it all out.'

'How do you mean "all"? What for?'

'We'll pay the **kolkhoz** workers' wages…'

'All the money on wages? What about the capital fund?'

'We'll have lots of income in the autumn, so we'll transfer it to the capital fund then. It can wait for the time being.'

'Fine… But we'll have to get it agreed.'

'We'll call a meeting and get everyone's approval…'

'Absolutely not! We need to clear it with the regional office.'

'Iakov Ivanovich, we are our own bosses.'

'Yes, sir!'

He got away with it this time. But when Petia Dolgii went round to the pig unit in spring, Semën Ivanovich Motiakov turned up this time. An activist group had been assembled and they laid into Petia Dolgii.

'You're just courting cheap popularity!' shouted Motiakov. 'You're throwing down crumbs from the master's table… Paying them a salary indeed! This all stems from a nonchalant attitude to theory.'

But Petia Dolgii replied, with a grin: 'Quite right! And Marx was a nonchalant man. He also said, "If a producer is not given the wherewithal to live, he will get it by any other means."'

Motiakov merely shook his head and continued in his own way: 'Is it our job to flirt with **kolkhoz** workers? To be waving a salary under their noses? Political canvassing for the **kolkhoz** has long since finished. They need to get down to work, once and for all!'

'We *are* working,' replied Petia Dolgii.

'No, you're wrecking the **kolkhoz**! You're selling off the pig unit.'

'Yes, but we're expanding the dairy. I have water-meadows and you're telling me to keep pigs. What's the point?'[84]

'The point is they are part of the **plan**. The **plan** is a state assignment,' Motiakov insisted.

---

[84] This is one of Mozhaev's hobby-horses, about which he has written many essays. He is making the point that local conditions and circumstances should dictate agricultural activity and enterprise, and not distant planners in Moscow, who are ignorant of particular, local conditions. The water-meadows provide rich grasslands on which cows can graze, however, such damp conditions are wholly unsuitable for rearing pigs. He is making the point that the **kolkhoz** chairman and his farmers are in the best position to judge what they could most profitably and efficiently produce. Motiakov is a mere functionary who sticks rigidly to the rules, and he cannot find it in himself to make rational judgements. Within the planned economy of the former USSR, there was little room for personal initiative: the **plan** was paramount, sacred, and it had to be adhered to at all costs.

'But it's you who draws up the **plan**, and you're not the state.'

'But I'll put a stop to your anti-state antics!' Motiakov drank a glass of water, grabbed his briefcase, and left.

This time, everyone thought that our Petia Dolgii would be sacked. But sowing time was fast approaching and folk came out to work in their droves. The **kolkhoz** forged ahead…

How could you sack a chairman at that time?! True enough, they gave him a good telling-off. Hopefully, he'll think again, they said.

But he carried on in his old ways. 'A wheat farmer,' he says, 'lives amongst wheat. He shouldn't worry about his grain. Let's give him all the grain he needs.'

And this was what the management decided: if you work out in the field twenty-three days a month, you'll get your pay, plus a **pood** of grain per family member at the sale price to the state, which was almost nothing. And if you're a widow, you'll get the grain for all your family free of charge. Too good to be true! But that cheered people up. They didn't just go out to work, they danced and sang. They made up their own songs: the music was by Glukhova, the lyrics by Khamov, and so on.[85]

But the grain hadn't even ripened when – bang! A new directive from the region: supply three **plans**. Blimey! That was eighteen thousand **centners** of grain! We worked it out – we would have to surrender everything we harvested, grain for grain, to the state. Plus the sweepings-up. Petia Dolgii dug his heels in: 'We'll give half,' he says, 'and the rest will be for the **kolkhoz** workers and for seed.' Now here, I must say, he showed a lack of political awareness. How should a real communist act? You can feel for the **kolkhoz** workers, but you must fully supply all that the state requires of you. Motiakov was quite right to say to him: 'You're putting the **kolkhoz** workers in first place, and the state in second place. We'll dismiss you!'

A group of three officials came to the **kolkhoz**, headed by Motiakov: 'Assemble the masses! We need to talk.'

Fair enough, a meeting was called…

'Comrades!' proclaimed Motiakov. 'You know that we are all experiencing the usual difficulties… There's drought and crop failure.'

'This is some bloody funny kind of drought,' say the peasant men. 'Just over the way, in Prudki, there's a drought, but we don't have one here. It looks like the heavenly chancery is watching over us.'

'We're all under the same heavens, but our prayers are different,' someone shouted out, to general laughter.

'Comrades, let's not refer to unbiased difficulties. Your harvest is the best, and you should show an example. Let's rise to the Party's call – let's surrender twenty thousand **centners** of grain to the state!'

---

[85] See footnote № 15, p.352 for the meanings of these two surnames.

Someone from the hall shouted out: 'Why just twenty thousand? Let's deliver thirty! That's how we do things round here.'

'Quite right!' said Motiakov, and he even rubbed his hands. 'There's no place for the feint-hearted and sceptics who refuse,' he said, throwing a sidelong glance at Petia Dolgii. 'No matter. The toiling masses will put them in their place, once and for all.'

But Petia Dolgii stood up and, completely by the by, said: 'Well then, Comrade **Kolkhoz** Workers. Let's count up our harvest.'

They all counted up in chorus – they all knew every single field they had, and Motiakov made a note. They counted, and counted, but they could not get to twenty thousand.

'Forgive us,' they said to Motiakov. 'We can't do what we can't do. You've added it all up yourself.'

'What are you doing? Trying to make me a laughing stock?!' he shouted. 'I wouldn't if I were you.'

He stormed out of the meeting without even saying goodbye. The next day, Petia Dolgii was summoned to the office. They came down on him like a ton of bricks, saying: 'What have you been doing?! Have you been manipulating people? This is sabotage! Ask for forgiveness! Get down on your knees!'

But Petia Dolgii said: 'Those who can't work or have no qualifications can fall to their knees before you. I'm an academy graduate. I'll always find work.'

They proposed a resolution – sack him! But apparently, First Secretary Demin stuck up for him: 'We have no right to sack him without a **kolkhoz** meeting.' He told them that they now had whatsit… er… democracy.

Fair enough… Democracy is all well and good, but they still arrived at the **kolkhoz** meeting with the Prosecutor and the Chief of Police. Even Tuzikov, the policeman, turned up. It's true that they didn't let him into the hall – he stood at the entrance.

Motiakov sat on the presidium. He sat the Chief of Police Zmeëv on his right, and Prosecutor Abramkin on his left.

'So, who will speak?'

Our lot put him through one of our typical Brëkhovo long-drawn-out meetings. As I've already mentioned, we're a friendly crowd. If anyone nicks anything, you could kill them, but they wouldn't grass… So, Motiakov insisted on discussing Petia Dolgii, but the stableman, our own Matvei Glukhov, stood up and said: 'I want to say something about a harness. What's becoming of it? The sweat blanket is ruined, but it's down on paper as being new. Not only is it no longer fit to use with harnessed horses, you couldn't even use it to sole a boot.'

Motiakov got irritated: 'Do me a favour, quit this talk about fusty old saddlecloths, once and for all! We need to discuss the management of the farm.'

'That's just what I'm on about. How many fusty saddlecloths have been written off by our chairman?! And now, let's consider the old horse collars. On some of them, it's not only the edging that's damaged, the fasteners are split... And with all this, are we thinking about changing the chairman?!'

And so on, and so forth... They all trotted out this kind of trivia, as if by design. They prattled on until midnight. Abramkin and Zmeëv couldn't stand it any longer and whispered to Motiakov, 'Put it to a vote, or we'll all peg out with hunger.'

I was also on the presidium. What's the point of a vote? It was as clear as day – they were all for Petia Dolgii. There wasn't a single objection – I had refused outright. It was easy to follow in the footsteps of Filka Samochenkov. But just try following Petia Dolgii! You'd come a cropper... You'd end up with tar on your gate, or they'd stick a cooking pot on your head if they got drunk. Our people are a reckless lot. So Motiakov went off, having achieved nothing.

In the autumn, our **kolkhoz** came out amongst the best – we supplied more grain than any other. And we got the harvest in before the rest. Consequently, Petia Dolgii got a lot of kudos and went straight to the top. He might have been taken down a peg or two when everyone was being forced to grow maize and plough up the meadows. But for some reason or other, our region was disbanded, and Motiakov was transferred to work in the river section, and our village came under Pugasovo.

We ended up on the margins. It was good for some, but disastrous for others. Our **kolkhoz** is now worth millions. Although, in all conscience, I have to admit, that in many ways we break the rules. Our chairman has a lot of clout: he has two cars, and he has risen to the status of a member of the Chamber of Deputies. He's simply his own boss...

My last managerial job with a salary was taken from me. The rural soviet was amalgamated and a new chairman was sent from the town. Our local staff fell from favour for good. It was a time when Varangians came into fashion.[86]

And on this historical note my writing has come to an end. The **kolkhoz** stood back on its feet. So its entire history has now drawn to a close. Because history is all based on struggle. And the struggle has been transferred to another sphere. History now lies in an ideological struggle on the literary front. We need to make this absolutely clear, and show great vigilance.

About How To Establish Total Order

Although I wrote at the very beginning that we have begun to live even better than under communism, nevertheless, we still have to establish total order. And this has to be done on the national level, as well as on the international.

---

[86] The Varangians or Vikings/Norsemen, were a people of Scandinavian origin who were warrior princes: they first settled in Old Russia (Rus) in the ninth century and they helped turn Russia into a trading nation, establishing trading routes along Russia's great rivers to the south, towards Central Asia and Byzantium. They are recorded in ancient chronicles, but how much influence they had on forming the early Russian state is a controversial question: some more nationalistic historians have made little of the Viking influence, preferring to attribute Russia's roots to more native, Slavonic sources. As with Bulkin's rather unorthodox reference to the 'troubadours of world imperialism' (see p.361 above), he is using the word Varangians here with little knowledge of who they really were. The term has come to mean an 'interloper', someone brought in from outside, even from abroad, and given special privileges. Bulkin's remark here shows the extreme parochial nature of his thinking and his general lack of education.

We must never forget that society is divided into classes, by which I mean, into supporters and opponents of labour. Supporters recognise the dire necessity of labour, but opponents prefer to heap this dire necessity upon the shoulders of their very own neighbours. And so, in accordance with this division of society into classes, we observe the consequential conflict of nature: now, everyone loves freedom in all their personal actions, by which, I mean independence, autonomy, and so on. From the point of view of the individual person, personal freedom might even be the ideal. But if we look at this ideal from the point of view of society, we see that in it lies a very great evil. It is a truism, that even a thief loves freedom. So, go ahead, give freedom to everyone. What will become of it? First of all, people will run off in all directions. And in the second place, they'll run away and settle where life is best… Moreover, the politically backward might even go to live abroad. And who would there be to work in the fields then? So, we may conclude that the strength of mankind lies in the unity of all actions, and that the autonomy of individual members of society and their personal freedom lead to anarchy. For that reason, we must close ranks and build the bright future not only in theory, but also in practice. And let's tackle this project in an organized fashion. Let's nominate a nice little place where we can build the city of the future, strictly along scientific principles. On the basis of this example, we shall be able to judge what we need to do for the general construction of such cities. And let's start to attract people to build it. Legally![87]

After we have built this city, then we'll clearly show what the man of the future will be like. We could take foreign delegations there to appreciate once and for all the advantages of our social structure. For my part, I would suggest building such a city on our very own hill, here in Brëkhovo. It's a beautiful spot and it can be seen from afar.

Such a city would serve as a beacon by which one could monitor the direction of our core policies. For what happens in our country, more often than not? The better we live, the more inclined we are to deviate. You just have to look at the following fact: all **kolkhozes** are waiting in a queue for building materials in short supply – for slate, cement, iron, equipment, and so on. But our chairman, Petia Dolgii, got everything on the side, by making good use of his personal influence and connections. Having jumped the queue, he built a mechanized fattening unit for six hundred head of cattle, and an

---

[87] The building of a city along scientific lines was a feature of utopian thinking from Plato onwards. Some of the most notable models of such socialist utopian thinking are *The City of the Sun* (1602), written by Tommaso Campanella (1568-1639), and *Voyage en Icarie* (1840) by Etienne Cabet (1788-1856). There were other influential utopian works set, not in a city, but in a rural environment, which featured the ideal commune, such as 'phalanges' or '*phalanstères*', as described by Charles Fourier (1772-1837). These utopian works were known to radical, nineteenth-century Russian thinkers, although the books were banned by the tsar, and they had an influence on the early socialist theories of Marx and Lenin. These utopian works are discussed at length by rural intellectuals in Mozhaev's epic novel about collectivization, *Peasant Folk*, in which they compare the **kolkhoz** to the fanciful notions and utopian aspirations of these early socialist thinkers. However, Khrushchëv himself was not untouched by such utopian notions: he had promoted the building of a whole city in Siberia, dedicated to scientific research. It was called 'Akademgorodok', or 'Academic City'. Its construction was started in the late 1950s and it appealed to the pioneering spirit of the Russians at the time – an attitude which Bulkin clearly evinces here. Like Campanella's 'City of the Sun', it was dedicated to science. It was situated 2,900 kilometres from Moscow by the river Ob. It attracted tens of thousands of scientists and academics and their families, and it was from there that massive schemes for diverting several of the great rivers of Siberia emanated: their plans were big and bold, requiring almost superhuman feats of engineering, but had they been realized, they would have wreaked ecological havoc. The schemes were rooted in the belief that man is master of his environment and of his destiny. Hence, Bulkin's seemingly lunatic idea of building an ideal city is a satirical swipe, not only at Khrushchëv, but also at the utopianism of communist thinking in general.

irrigation system covering a thousand hectares. And what's more, he had an asphalt road laid on the **kolkhoz**.

Let's look at this from the state's point of view – is it a good thing, or a bad thing? Metalled roads should first be laid along the most used routes: first of all, along routes of **oblast** importance, then regional routes, and finally along local routes. But Petia Dolgii found a bunch of Georgian 'wide boys', who sold him some bitumen, so he did it in reverse. There's an example for you of a *petit bourgeois*, crony, nationalistic approach to building the bright future.

The aim of my life is to establish total order on this earth, by which I mean, to turn this hell into a heaven on earth, for the supporters of labour.

But, in our way stand all manner of wheelers and dealers, nationalists, doubters and cynics, by which I mean revisionists, who try to detach their 'I' from our communal 'we'. We have to fight decisively against them on two fronts, for they are not only our enemies, but also enemies of our people, and consequently, they are enemies of themselves.

1968

Shishigi

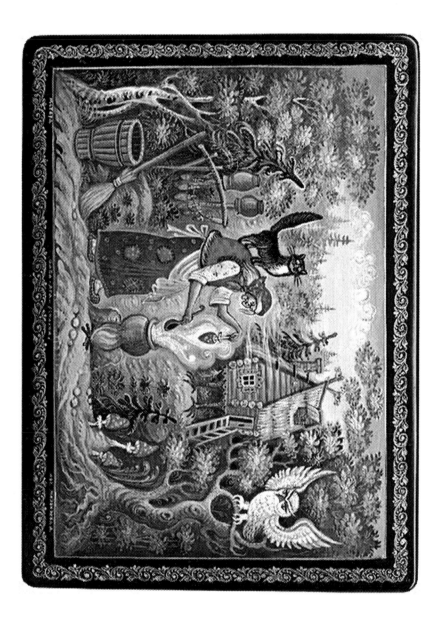

Illustration 16. BabaYaga on Palekh Box.

Foreword to Shishigi

A *shishiga* (with the stress on the penultimate syllable) is an evil spirit or demon, with which Russian folklore is replete. The plural form is *shishigi*, who feature in this rather curious tale. By their orthography alone, they are feminine, as are virtually all nouns which end in an 'a' in Russian. In fact, the majority of evil spirits in Russian folklore are female generically, as well as grammatically.

This is a story with a modern twist, because such spirits are generally confined to the countryside and they are especially associated with forests and other dark, frightening places. However, in Mozhaev's story, they migrate to an urban setting, and they are given a further contemporary twist – they use telephones. No doubt they would now use mobile phones, were Mozhaev to have written the story in even more modern times!

There are many spirits in Russian folklore whose mission in life is to lure the unsuspecting human into perilous situations, and even unto death. Many of these spirits are associated with natural phenomena, such as the Rusalka, a female spirit who lures men, by singing, to their deaths in fast-flowing streams or other watery graves. There are others who lead people into swamps and bogs, where their victims also usually perish.

Reference has already been made to the **Domovoi**, a little house goblin or sprite, who lives under the family stove in a peasant house. Whilst not mortally dangerous, this spirit indulges in making mischief unless regularly placated by small offerings of food. There are other similar spirits whose residence is the **bania**, who become active only at night.

Many Russian writers have found inspiration in folkloric and supernatural elements and have included them in their writing. In classical literature, the most notable of these was Gogol, who wrote a whole cycle of supernatural stories – some of them quite frightening. In the modern period, Mikhail Bulgakov (1891-1940) included a plethora of supernatural activity in his Moscow-based, satirical novel, *The Master and Margarita* (written between 1928 and 1940, but published posthumously in 1966-67, though in a heavily censored edition).

Mozhaev's spirits in this story follow Bulgakov's demons – they are active in the city. Claims are made that they encouraged people to behave in an aggressive way towards each other in the Moscow underground, that they encourage officials to take a much more severe line with employees, and that they operate nearer to their traditional home, in the countryside, by pushing people to say things which get them in trouble at **kolkhoz** meetings.

The most frightening aspect of the *shishigi* is that they work collectively: they communicate with each other, but it takes only one of them to single out an individual as their target, whereupon they all pounce on their victim and do their worst. All the other *shishigi* follow the instigator unquestioningly, and the impetus to act like this can be given by any single *shishiga* of their multitude – they do not need a leader. Unanimity is their mantra.

The only way to ward off the attacks of the *shishigi* is to be fearless. Once they sense fear, they are encouraged to take their attack further.

Clearly, Mozhaev intends this little story to be an allegory and it is more profound than it appears at first sight. Mozhaev has written extensively on one of the most unpleasant aspects of the Soviet system – the evil of unanimity. This unanimity, or unity of thought, can be expressed in one of two ways: either (i) by simply following along with the crowd, going with the majority decision, which, in Mozhaev's view, is to take the easy way out; or (ii) by not voicing one's opposition, despite disagreeing deep-down with what is going on. It is not only Mozhaev who has pointed out that, within the Soviet system, 'keeping quite is a mark of assent'. Those who did not make waves, did best within the regime. As the former Soviet *chansonnier* or bard, Galich, has remarked – 'Silence is golden'.

Kuzkin, in the story *Lively*, has clearly discovered that to have no fear of evil spirits is the way to survive their onslaught, as he tells the spiteful Pashka, who is only too willing to swoop down on Kuzkin, like a *shishiga*. Kuzkin believes that he is protected by God, which is tantamount to crossing oneself, as described in the story *Shishigi*. The courage that this belief gives him banishes fear from his soul. Pashka asks him:

'What is this "unclean force" [...]?' asked Pashka.

'It's you Pashka, and Guzënkov.'[1]

The contemporary devils and evil spirits are mindless officials, and Mozhaev urges the reader to take a strong, fearless stand against them, otherwise they will get the better of us all. During his career as a writer, Mozhaev's certainly did stand fearlessly in the face of the *shishigi* of the Soviet regime, and he made his own voice clearly heard amongst the crowd.

---

[1] See p.160.

Shishigi

Once, on a fishing trip, sitting by the river in the meadows, I noticed my mate, the skipper Fedot, moving away from the bank warily.

'What are you doing that for, Fedot Ivanych?' I asked.

'I'm afraid,' he replied with a shiver. 'It's getting dark. It's a dodgy time – the *shishigi* go on the rampage.'

'What *shishigi*?'

'Everyone knows which ones… The ones people call "unclean forces".'

'Have you seen any?'

'Of course I have! They've all got ugly mugs, some are hump-backed, others pot-bellied. But they've all got cold, little hands. If you bend over the river, a *shishiga* will grab you by the collar and pull you into the water. There are some deep spots here… A whirlpool! If you get stuck in that, you've had it.'

'Well, don't bend over the water, then.'

'But they nudge you, you dope! You sit there, minding your own business, and up come the *shishigi* and scream in your ears, saying, "You're just sitting around, but there's a fish right there, it's come right up to the bank, it's just waiting for you to pick it out." And you're daft enough to believe that you can actually see it. But just you try and grab it! You'll end up at the bottom…'

'Get away with you! And there was I, not knowing how dangerous sitting by the water is!'

'They don't just get up to no good by the water… You can come across them in woods, but also in open, empty places, and where there's people. They surround you, start screaming, and lead you so far into the back of beyond, that you'll never get out. And they lead you off the road. In the summer, you'll see a dusty guide-post, you turn onto the verge. It's a *shishiga* celebrating a wedding. If you don't turn onto the verge, they throw dust into your eyes and ears. Or they give your horse the plague. Also, they lure you off course. In winter, in a snow storm, they specially rage against you – they start tugging you, surround you, and you go mad, then you rush headlong to your own ruination. You imagine you can hear a bell. You go towards its muffled tolling. But you don't realize, that it's the death knoll for your own soul.'

'That's all old hat! Whoever travels on horseback nowadays? Especially roaming around the open countryside in a snow storm?'

'Makes no difference. *Shishigi* overpower people even in the city.'

'Where? Where abouts?'

'Even in the underground. I've been there several times and sensed them. You get tired out going around offices or shops all day long, and you just want to get home, back to your flat, so you go to the underground. And you're carried downwards, along the escalator, straight into the human caviar that is people's heads. Blimey! A mysterious force grabs you, squeezes you, sucks at you, until you can't even catch your breath. Your heart stands still with fright, and you feel something clearly whispering: "So, are you rushing home, then? To a nice, warm bed? Well, I'm taking you into the underworld. You come with me like a child. And not a squeak out of you! Fly away!" That's them, the *shishigi*, whispering to you.'

'Rubbish, Fedot Ivanych! You're just afraid of crowds. You've been brought up in wide open spaces and the underground just seems like the underworld to you.'

'There you go again! I'm telling you – the *shishigi* are everywhere. For example, have you ever been at one of our **kolkhoz** meetings? Have you ever been bawled out for not turning up to work?'

'So who bawls you out, the *shishigi*?'

'You get bawled out by the management. But it's the *shishigi* who egg them on and fill you with terror. D'you understand?'

'So that's what you're on about!' I just shook my head.

Fedot lit a "Prima" cigarette, made a pause for effect, and finally pronounced: 'The main weapon against them is – stop! Take stock, and cross yourself. Then look back and curse.'

'Does that help?'

'Not half! The main thing is to banish fear. If there is no fear in your soul, the *shishiga* won't approach you.'

'But where do they come from, these *shishigi*?'

'How do you mean, "Where from?" From the historical past, just as described in books nowadays.' Fedot thought for a moment and said, 'And also from our own stupidity, from our fear. Because those *shishigi*, they love companionship. I'll give you an example: I'm sitting down here, having a chat, and suddenly, some passing *shishiga*, for some reason, doesn't like what I'm saying. The *shishiga* gives a signal on their women's telephone: it says, we've got a hooligan-unbeliever who is defaming us, honest, decent *shishigi*. Into the whirlpool with him! And they fly in from all directions. The *shishigi* can hear from far off, with their women's telephone. For example, if one flies in from beyond the forest confines and cannot get home in time for the witches' Sabbath, she can let them know: drown him, the obstinate backslider!

I couldn't help sneering.

'What pushes them to do this?'

'Well, these *shishigi* live by their own dog-eat-dog laws: they'll all attack the same person, whoever is singled out. And if one of them cannot dupe someone, or doesn't feel like it, they'll still respond and say, "I'm with you!".'

'But, what do they do this for?'

'How do you mean, "What for?" They are carrying out the orders of Satan himself, maintaining unanimity. If they didn't pester and play dirty tricks on people, no one would remember about unclean forces. They would just die out of their own accord. And who the hell wants to die out? Even though they're an unclean force, they still don't want to end up in oblivion, so they hang on to life.'

Those meadows, in which Fedot and I fished, have long since disappeared – they have been ploughed up to grow maize, and my old mate has died, but this curious tale of the unclean forces, which he told me, comes back to mind from time to time, as night falls.

It's then that I can hear the voice of my kind, old, skipper friend: 'First of all, take stock... Look back, cross yourself, and curse as necessary, to banish all fear. If there is no fear in your soul, the *shishigi* won't come near you.'

1970.

Appendix I

The Politics of Soviet Literature: Soviet Realism, the 'Thaws', and Village Prose

The Soviet authorities wanted to control every aspect of life under the new regime and one of the most powerful tools in their armoury was literature. They soon realized that writers and their output would play a key role in educating people and spreading the communist cause. However, those in power also knew that the propaganda they wished to convey had to be of the right kind – it had to be 'on message'. Hence, writers, they thought, needed to be controlled and supervised. This supervision extended not only to the content, but also to the style of writing.

When Mozhaev started his writing career, writers were still being constrained to write according to the tenets of Soviet socialist realism, which was introduced in the early 1930s. This was a formula to which all writers were expected to adhere, and it governed not only their written style, but the content and the tone of a work. As time went on and the ideological climate changed, the constraints were gradually relaxed and writers became freer to experiment, to be more creative in their art. Socialist realism did not only affect writers – all types of art, including music and the fine arts, were all supposed to conform to the basic principles of the system, and the various literary and artistic unions were there to see that no one stepped out of line. Critics were all too ready to pounce on artists who dared to go beyond the boundaries of the officially 'acceptable'. Any writer who did not adhere to the methodology of Socialist Realism could not expect to be published in the **thick journals**, and subsequently, in books. That said, many writers and other artists did push the boundaries of what was acceptable, and brave editors gradually and subtly risked their jobs and reputation to publish works, which were innovative and did not conform to the strictures of socialist realism. Many writers had to resort to making the subtlest of hints to express what they really wanted to say in the hope that they would be missed by the censor, but not by an educated reading public: the perceptive reader became adept at reading between the lines, a phenomenon which was dubbed 'Aesopian language'.

Officially, the demands of socialist realism meant that a work of fiction had to convey the following concepts to be acceptable for publication:

1. 'party-mindedness', possibly better translated as 'party spirit', that is, the work should reflect the aspirations of the Communist Party of the Soviet Union and the building of a communist society, which was its ultimate goal through socialism

2. a positive hero, who in Soviet literature became the indefatigable toiler for the socialist/communist cause, a figure to admire and emulate. The positive hero frequently progresses from a state of immaturity to a more mature state of political consciousness and knowledge

3. an optimistic ending, expressing certainty that the obstacles to realizing a goal, whether in society or when trying to overcome natural impediments, had been overcome, and that a bright future could be anticipated. All obstacles

were surmountable, particularly natural obstacles, and Soviet literature gloried in the grand project, accomplished in record time and by almost super-human effort and grit

4. the language used to express all these features had to be accessible to the masses – dialect, quaint turns of speech, vulgarity – all were shunned in favour of standard Russian, which in practice meant Russian stripped of its individuality and full of political cant.

These were just some of the precepts the writer was expected to conform to in their work, whether it be prose, poetry, a play, or a film scenario. This 'blueprint' for writing sounds terribly prescriptive and dull, and indeed it was, but as with many phenomena in the former Soviet Union, many talented and creative people saw such constraints merely as a challenge to be circumvented, and there was a surprising variety of quality writing published even within such a straight-jacket. Officially, these tenets were in existence until the collapse of the Soviet Union in 1991, but in practice, after the 1940s, these prescriptive elements were being gradually eroded, as more and more variation crept into official Soviet literature. Indeed, many works by conformist writers, who received state prizes for literature and who adhered to these tenets, were printed in their hundreds of thousands, but frequently they languished unread on the shelves of bookshops, stacked to the gunnels with works of literature which nobody wanted to read, let alone buy. The reading public and the intelligentsia had a nose for the unusual, the critical, and the innovative.

After Stalin's death in March 1953, Khrushchëv denounced him in a Secret Speech in February 1956 before a Communist Party delegates-only session – even journalists were banned from attending. Then, there followed a subsequent public denunciation of Stalin a few years later, which led to a general liberalization of the regime, but with the occasional reversions to the near *status-quo*. Thus the prescriptive straight-jacket of Soviet socialist realism began to be loosened, as writers, with the help of editors like **Tvardovskii**, began to push the boundaries of the ideologically and aesthetically impossible towards a compromise: editors often negotiated between writer, editorial board, and sometimes Khrushchëv himself, frequently making textual changes by way of compromise – to produce a startling, even shocking, new work. This constant chipping away at the ideological nostrums of socialist realism gradually reduced it to nothing more than a shadow of its former self, to which few writers paid little more than lip-service – if even that. During this process, there were periodic backlashes from conservative literary critics and ideologues alike, but gradually ground was gained by the liberals in a cultural war of attrition, which side-lined socialist realism as a prerequisite to publishing. There were periods of considerable liberalization, which lasted for varying periods of time: these became known as 'thaws'.

Certainly the efforts and courage of the editor **Tvardovskii**, who was adept at negotiating with both officials and writers, raised the profile of the journal *Novyi mir*, placing it in the vanguard of all the **thick journal**s. The journal was frequently at the centre of fierce ideological debate, all initiated by the publication of innovative writing. **Tvardovskii** was dismissed from his post in a counterattack by conservatives against him and his journal, but he was reinstated in 1958.

The first period of ideological relaxation, or 'thaw', occurred in 1953-54. Although this 'thaw' was defeated by conservative elements, another one followed in 1956, when more works of a controversial nature were permitted, only to be followed by another 'freeze' in 1957, engendered partly by the political situation in Hungary. Political unrest broke out in Hungary, as a group of workers and intellectuals campaigned for fundamental reforms, followed by popular disturbance in November 1956. The Soviet Army was ordered by Khrushchëv to confront the rebels, which, obviously, was no match for them. Khrushchëv took fright of further reform and the ideological belt was tightened for a time. Mozhaev's short story, *The Power of the Taiga*, was published in the journal *Oktiabr* (October) in August 1957, but critics complained, that there 'was not enough socialism in it'. Another 'thaw' occurred in the early 1960s, when the truly amazing work by Solzhenitsyn – *One Day in the Life of Ivan Denisovich* – was published, followed shortly by Mozhaev's own *From the Life of Fëdor Kuzkin*, or *Lively*, as Mozhaev preferred to call the work. In addition, there were always works which contained contentious elements which slipped through the censor's net from time to time, even during the 'freeze' periods.

In the same year as Mozhaev's *The Power of the Taiga* was published, a *cause célèbre* occurred: Boris Pasternak's novel *Doctor Zhivago* was published abroad in Italy in November 1957, in an atmosphere of huge controversy in Russia. The details are described here, not because Mozhaev himself was involved in the events, but to illustrate how the state tried to control literature and writers.

The manuscript of *Doctor Zhivago* was being prepared for publication in Russia, and some poems from the end of the novel had already been published in a '**thick journal**' in the autumn of 1956. Severe doubts were expressed about the novel's suitability for publication on ideological and stylistic grounds. However, the manuscript had been smuggled out of Russia, and preparations were under way to publish the work in Italy – a fact that became known to the literary and political establishment. In August 1957, Pasternak himself was summoned to the Central Committee of the Communist Party, and he was requested to stop the publication of the novel in Italy. The novel came out in an Italian translation in November 1957, and, in October 1958, Pasternak was awarded the Nobel Prize for Literature, which he was forced by the state to decline. There ensued a campaign of vilification of Pasternak in the literary and daily central press. However, just before this event, **Tvardovskii** had two private meetings with Khrushchëv and he had spoken to the latter about matters of literature, defending the writers Margarita Aliger and Vladimir Dudintsev, whom Khrushchëv had publicly berated a short time previously. Khrushchëv struck **Tvardovskii** as being a reasonable man, who found everything he said interesting, but Khrushchëv had to watch his back as he had narrowly survived a personal coup against him in June 1957, and the **Writers' Union** and most of the literary '**thick journal**s' were still controlled by conservatives. Later, Khrushchëv admitted to never having read Pasternak's novel and he regretted that he did not give his permission for it to be published, but he was a man of limited education and, by his own admission, he had read little and understood almost nothing about literature.

During the 1950s, the 'sketch', or essay, experienced a revival as a short form of prose, combining a factual or semi-fictional event with a journalistic style, in which personal opinion features strongly in a form of literary *reportage*, a genre which Mozhaev took very seriously and which comprises a large proportion of his *œuvre*. A number of writers turned their attention away from writing about city life and war themes, and began to explore rural themes, a much neglected aspect of Russian life in literature, particularly given the fact that a large proportion of the Russian population lived in villages and small settlements. These writers' works caught the imagination and interest of the reading public and their works became known as 'Village Prose'. Village Prose developed into a loosely knit school of writing, polarized around rural themes. By the very nature and content of such writing, writers were moving away from the tenets of socialist realism: gone was the clarity and boring uniformity of standard speech and politically correct language accessible to the masses, and in came quirky regional dialects and colourful sayings, that many city dwellers were hearing for the first time. Gone was the hero struggling against all odds to build factories and heavy industrial plants, and in came the simple, toiling peasant, who frequently found it difficult to make ends meet, but whose seemingly dull life was full of traditional Russian feast days, belief in local folklore, and even in God, despite having been subjected to a vicious anti-religious campaign. The peasants portrayed in this new genre of literature were a repository of rural wisdom, far removed from urbane concerns and political ideology. The difference in the tone and style of writing in Village Prose could not have been more stark, when set against the officially approved novels of socialist realist writers.

Despite literary critics describing the movement of Village Prose as a 'school', it was, in fact, a broad church. As a literary movement, it comprised a very diverse group of writers, some of whom were extremely critical of the writing of their so-called 'fellow' Village Prose writers. As a phenomenon, Village Prose lasted from about the mid-1950s to the early 1980s, but some of the exponents of the school continued to write and publish after 1980. Mozhaev was critical of those who sought to categorize literature into such schools and movements, and he was also critical of a number of writers, whom he thought idealized the countryside or had a poor knowledge of it. He rejected the label of 'Village Prose writer' for himself, though the vast majority of his writing is to do with rural life. Some Village Prose writers, such as Soloukhin and Rasputin, felt that village life was fast becoming extinct, as younger people born in the countryside left for a very different life in the cities. Soloukhin and Rasputin believed that an essential mission of their writing was to portray a way of life that would not exist beyond one or two future generations. Hence, in some ways, they regarded their works as a repository for recording for posterity vanishing rural customs, beliefs, and life-style. Their works are full of the minutiae of rural life, and as such, they are extremely interesting, especially for the ethnologist, but they are also replete with apocalyptic doom that we are witnessing the death of a centuries-long tradition, an essential part of Russian life that will soon be no more.

Generally, in Mozhaev's writing, there is little of this doom, although the ending of Book II of his novel *Peasant Folk* is very bleak. His characters are very much alive and are to be greatly admired for their tenacity and indomitable spirit, which he saw as the essence of the Russian peasant, who survived, despite all the repressive measures brought to bear by the state. They survive the onslaughts of distant Moscow bureaucrats, who impose ridiculous and unrealistic quotas upon them, and demagogic local officials who, pressured by those in power above them, pressurize those below them, for fear they might be sacked from their post. The rural folk in Mozhaev's works are portrayed as independent and knowing their own mind, they are witty, and they are steeped in a rural tradition, yet their folklore, beliefs, and their way of life are never recorded merely for posterity. Unlike most Village Prose writers, Mozhaev offered practical solutions to the ills which beset Soviet agriculture, setting out the problems with clarity and precision, as one would expect from a person who had studied marine engineering. In all his works, common sense and a detailed knowledge of agricultural practice, amply demonstrated in the peasant characters in his stories, always set the rural folk at odds with ignorant, narrow-minded bureaucrats and officials. And rather than portraying the peasant as politically ignorant and unsophisticated, which so many writers had done, especially where politics and current ideology were concerned, Mozhaev ridiculed the regime and showed the absurdity of attempts to re-educate and reprogramme the minds of rural folk, who prove to be deceptively shrewd.

Another characteristic feature of Village Prose writing was a concern for the natural environment and environmental issues. The Soviet Union was ruthless in exploiting its vast natural resources, and it did so with scant regard for renewing them and polluting the environment, to say nothing of the equally ruthless way it treated its workforce, frequently exposing them to danger and primitive, harsh living conditions. Mozhaev offered some biting criticism of many aspects of Soviet industry, especially those of the timber and hunting sectors. In this way, writers, and Village Prose writers in particular, led the way towards founding a 'green movement' in Soviet society.

Appendix II

Brief Survey of the Soviet Farming System

It was in the early 1960s that Mozhaev openly expressed his views that farm workers on **kolkhozes** ought to be much freer from bureaucratic control, the **Plan**, and from being dictated to by **kolkhoz** chairmen. This plea for independence, and the conviction that direct control merely reduced the agricultural worker to the status of a modern serf, are central to virtually all Mozhaev's writing, both his essays and his works of fiction, and throughout his career he held fast to this view. His criticism of the **kolkhoz** system was severe, but it was all based on observation and long conversations with **kolkhoz** chairmen. To understand the points he is making, it is essential that the reader understand some basic facts about how rural workers ended up so disadvantaged on Soviet farms in the first place, and how agriculture was run and organized.

The Russian peasant was unique in the European developed world in that, as late as 1861, he was a slave within a feudal system, the like of which had long been abandoned by all other countries. The peasant was actually owned, body and soul, by the landowner, who had total power and control over him and his family: he could be bought and sold, kept in captivity or liberated at the whim of his owner, he had to work for his owner, the '*pomeshchik*', and pay him tithes. The landowner could even arrange his marriage, and he had the right of life and death over him. Such ownership of another human being and the archaic practice of farming on isolated strips of land, instead of on a normal field or enclosure arrangement, had long disappeared in the rest of Europe and the developed world by the late nineteenth century. The existence of such feudalism in Russia is one of the reasons the country had gained a reputation for backwardness.

In February 1861, a decree was passed which gave the peasantry their personal freedom, and thus the era of feudalism and serfdom in Russia had come to an end – at least in theory. However, there were many problems to be solved and agricultural organization and practice remain huge problems, even up to the present day. After the Emancipation Act of 1861, some land passed to the peasant communes through which it was bought, and the commune became the mainstay of rural peasant organization in Russia, with its own form of justice, traditions, democracy (of a sort), and land distribution. However, a large proportion of land was still owned by the *pomeshchiki* and there were many tensions and problems between them and the communes, which remained unsolved until the Revolution of 1917. Many peasants found themselves more in debt and poorer in terms of land after the Emancipation Act, than before it, so there was an urgent need to solve the land question. Land reforms were entrusted to Pëtr Stolypin (1862–1911), the last tsar's minister for Internal Affairs, from 1906 onwards. Stolypin saw the commune as a backward institution and he tried, with very limited success, to encourage the establishment of independent farming households, free from the constraints of periodic land redistribution by the communes. Various political parties representing peasant interests sprung up in the late nineteenth and early twentieth centuries, and they all had their input into the political melting pot of Russia's burgeoning and fragmented society: the land question and rural reorganization was a major topic, which divided and defined the growing number of political parties. Most Russian peasants were extremely cautious of new ideas and radical change. They were very attached to their communes, and so entrenched were they in the Russian rural structure, that even Lenin baulked at their total destruction. Hence, they became a major feature of his New Economic Policy, implemented in 1921, after the Revolution. Their total destruction was left to Stalin and his policy of collectivization.

All land remaining in the hands of the landowners was confiscated during the Revolution of 1917 and it was given over to the communes in the absence of any other organization or structure. Lenin was no lover of the commune, but village 'soviets' (councils) had not yet been set up by the Bolsheviks, who were, in any case, an urban party of whom the peasants were very suspicious and mistrustful. Civil War raged throughout Russia between 1918 and 1921 and, as is only to be expected under such circumstances, the infrastructure of Russia, including agricultural production, collapsed. Human casualties were very high during the Civil War and this devastating situation was compounded by a terrible famine in 1921-22. The Bolsheviks instituted a period of terror and coercion, known as **War Communism**, to confiscate and requisition surplus grain from peasants, thus alienating them still further. When the scale of the devastation and lack of food production became clear, Lenin retreated and instituted a period of calm, which was known as the New Economic Policy, having realised that the war of attrition with the peasantry could only lead to more famine. For a few short years, the peasantry was wooed back to produce food, and the policy of total state control over all forms of agricultural and manufacturing production was relaxed, from which the food supply and the economy benefited considerably.

The NEP period lasted from 1921 until the introduction of the First Five-Year **Plan** in 1928-32. The introduction of NEP was hotly debated: hard-liners amongst the party faithful saw this as a retreat from true communist ideology, regarding it as a step backwards towards the capitalism they had fought so hard to destroy. But Lenin, ever the pragmatist, saw this as the only way out. The peasantry responded, as did many other sectors of the economy, and the grain harvest increased slowly, back towards pre-revolutionary levels. There was also a resurgence of small workshops and cooperatives, which proved to be quite successful. Lenin had stated that NEP should be quite a long and protracted period, but upon his death in 1924, and Stalin's subsequent rise to power, the policy was cut short. During the era of *glasnost*, when these sensitive historical topics could be debated once again, many economists discussed whether NEP should have gone on for longer, as Lenin had wanted, and whether it would have made a suitable alternative to what Stalin put in place. However, those in favour of continuing NEP at the time were all ousted by Stalin, who put Russia onto a radically different course, as collectivization and rapid industrialization were forced upon the population. These policies were also accompanied by augmenting police powers and centralizing state control over all areas of life.

Stalin broke with the consensus of political leaders and economists around him over collectivization. Many thought that it should be conducted gradually, over a considerably long period – a view which Lenin himself had favoured. Stalin went out on a limb and set the wheels in motion to collectivize agriculture at a single stroke, whether the peasantry resisted it or not. The campaign for the full collectivization of agriculture got under way at the end of 1929. The Soviet government enlisted the help of **Komsomol** activists, along with many other 'enthusiasts', to spread the word and force people into the **kolkhoz** system. The media played a vital role in preaching the advantages of collective agriculture, as opposed to allowing communes or independent farmers to function. Activists and propagandists were despatched into rural communities to lecture the peasantry on collectivized agriculture, and, when they showed little interest in even attending such meetings, coercion was used again. A number of peasants had done rather well under NEP and they saw no reason why they should surrender their own equipment and livestock to found collective farms, and to work alongside certain other peasants, whom they knew to be lazy and would not work as hard as they had.

The regime came up with the idea of wooing over to their side the poorest stratum of the rural community – the landless peasant or *batrak* – who hired out his labour to other, wealthier peasants in return for payment, either in money or in kind. To this end, officials divided the whole rural community into three broad (and rather crude) categories. The wealthiest peasants were called '**kulaks**', the *bête noire* of the Bolsheviks, who were demonized before the Revolution as grasping, avaricious rural capitalists. In fact, most of the real **kulaks** had been destroyed before and during the Civil War. The next category was called the *seredniak* or 'middle peasant', who was productive and managed to feed his own family, with some produce left to sell on the open market. The third group was the *bednota* or 'poor group', who had no land of their own and they merely worked for others. Many peasants of the other two groups regarded the *bednota* as feckless drunks, who were lazy and poorly educated. It was this group that the regime tried to lure to support their campaign for full collectivization and many gave their support willingly – after all, of the three groups, they had the most to gain by joining the **kolkhoz** system. So-called 'poor committees' were set up, consisting of 'poor peasants', who played a direct role in deciding who of their neighbours was in which category. Needless to say, this was an ideal opportunity for old scores and grudges to be settled, and it did much to divide the community and cause a great deal of acrimony.

How to judge who fell into which category was never clearly stated – there were no definite criteria – and much was left to the whim of local officials and activists. The more spiteful officials saw this as an ideal opportunity to silence the dissenters, i.e. those who expressed their opposition to the **kolkhoz** system. Those peasants who were classified as **kulaks**, whether they were wealthy or not, meant that all their goods and chattels were confiscated by the state to be used on the new **kolkhoz**. The ire and spite against the **kulaks** was cranked up a notch when Stalin announced, that the **kulaks** were to be 'liquidated as a class', which, in effect, offered *carte blanche* to officials and activists to do with this group of people as they pleased. Many were sent off to Siberian labour camps or exiled elsewhere, but in so doing, the regime was destroying one of the most productive sectors of the rural community, at a time when food was in terribly short supply. However, so arbitrary were the criteria by which a peasant was categorized as a **kulak**, that many productive peasants from the 'middle group' were also caught up in the maelstrom of **dekulakization** and dispossession.

Forced collectivization was disastrous. It was a Pyrrhic victory. It caused widespread famine, loss of human life, and the whole policy set Soviet agriculture back by many decades. Even now, the cost of the campaign in terms of human life is not known, and there were many reports of cannibalism in the countryside. It was one of Russia's greatest modern tragedies, and it was kept secret and remained a taboo subject until the closing years of the Soviet regime. The whole campaign was the subject matter of Mozhaev's moving novel, *Peasant Folk*, which is his greatest work, written on a truly Dostoevskian scale – it is almost a thousand pages long.

When it became clear that the campaign for full collectivization of agriculture had caused more damage than it had brought benefits, Stalin took his foot off the accelerator and, true to form, he shifted the blame from himself onto local officials and activists, claiming that they had shown excessive zeal, and the pace to collectivize was slowed a little, but nevertheless, it continued until completed by the mid- to late-1930s. Rather than let the **kolkhoz** have their equipment and livestock, many peasants destroyed it, or ate it. Peasants who resisted joining the **kolkhoz**, like Mozhaev's own father, were taxed so heavily as 'independent' farmers, that they had no choice either to join, or run off to the cities. Even after joining the **kolkhoz**, many peasants, who still resented being entrapped within the system, committed acts of vandalism. The rural community had been further alienated by the vicious campaign against religious belief which ran alongside the campaign for full collectivization: peasants witnessed their churches being desecrated and their priests exiled and incarcerated in the **GULags**. The little goodwill that existed between the rural community and the state was destroyed at a stroke.

Life on the **kolkhoz** was deeply resented by many peasants. They had lost their independence and they were now told what to sow, when, and where. They were paid a wage – sometimes – and they had to work alongside other 'farmers' who did not pull their weight. They were at the mercy of a **kolkhoz** chairman, who often was poorly educated and knew little about farming, and whose own post was precarious in that, if he did not make the quotas set by the state (known as the **Plan**), he could be sacked. During Stalinist times, especially in the late 1930s, not meeting the quotas was enough to earn officials a sentence in the **GULag**. Theft and vandalism were also rife on the farms, and peasants developed the attitude that, since everything was the property of a faceless institution, i.e. the state, no one really owned it, and so stealing from it was not like stealing from one's neighbour.

The most constricting and crippling of all aspects of the Soviet economic system was the **Plan**. Economic Councils were the chief means of planning and controlling industry and economic development at regional and national levels throughout the Soviet Union. Economic planning took place in Moscow in various 'ministries' (though the name changed from time to time), each being responsible for a specific branch of the economy and economic development, from where edicts were issued to a whole network of regional and local offices. The autonomous republics had their own branches. Economic planning was overseen by 'Gosplan' or the State Planning Commission. The whole organization became far too bureaucratic and unwieldy, and radical reorganization took place in the 1960s under Khrushchëv, who had a passion for reorganization, and more reforms were attempted in 1974, but with limited improvement. All these interventions were no more than tinkering at the edges of a very serious problem. Major efforts were made to put greater emphasis on agricultural development during Khrushchëv's premiership, and there is no doubt that, while the lot of rural workers improved, there were still major problems in meeting consumer demands, both in food and goods. It was not until Gorbachëv's leadership (1987-90), that radical rethinking was undertaken to try to address the serious problems of Soviet industry and agriculture, under his programme of *perestroika*, or 'restructuring'. At the heart of this restructuring was the loosening of the stranglehold of central planning to give factory managers and farms a greater degree of autonomy, and to stimulate initiative and enterprise. However, the whole central planning system collapsed when the Soviet Union fell in 1991. Mozhaev wrote many essays on the problems of agricultural production and supply, which appeared regularly in popular publications during the Soviet era: his constant plea was for independence for Russian agricultural workers and for far less interference from Gosplan and central planners. Many of his articles caused heated debate, but they were based on a detailed knowledge of the problems farmers faced in reality, because he travelled extensively around farms and talked at length with **kolkhoz** chairmen and **sovkhoz** directors. He refused to write articles about bumper harvests and happy **kolkhoz** workers, which was the standard fare of most journalists' reporting on rural issues, and he campaigned tirelessly for living conditions to be improved in the countryside, in terms of housing provision, heath care, road building, and the supply of basic building materials, amongst other things.

The agricultural workers on the **sovkhozes**, or 'state farms', were paid a wage, just like a factory worker in the cities, but their counterparts on the **kolkhozes** were paid on a system known as the '**workday unit**'. The rate at which **kolkhoz** workers were remunerated varied: sometimes they might be paid in actual money, but other times they were paid in kind, such as in potatoes and/or grain and other produce. The **kolkhoz** 'workers' – not farmers in the traditional sense – also had the right to cultivate a plot of land, which was strictly regulated in size, and they also had the right to rear a limited number of animals for their own food. What they could and could not do on their private plots was tightly controlled, and policies and regulations changed from time to time, in tune with ideological thinking. Some leaders, like Khrushchëv, were fundamentally against private plots, because they saw them as a form of private enterprise, a step back towards capitalism and private ownership, of which he and many others had an absolute horror. They also saw them as a distraction from real work on the **kolkhoz**. It was natural for the worker and his family to spend as much time and effort on their own plot as possible, because any surplus produce could be sold for high prices at **kolkhoz** markets in the cities and towns, in a society where food was in constant short supply. Again, all this troubled ideological purists, who saw such trading as a form of capitalism, at best to be merely tolerated, but attempts were often made to restrict these practices or even wipe them out – chiefly through taxation. However, it had to be admitted that this kind of private production was not really a 'surplus' at all – it made a major contribution to the total supply of food for the nation. Attempts were also made, for similar reasons, to stop migrant rural workers from taking up seasonal employment elsewhere in the towns and cities – a practice they had engaged in even under the tsars.

The fact that the state refused to grant an internal **passport** to rural dwellers and farm workers also reinforced their status as modern serfs within the Soviet system. The 'internal **passport**', as it was officially called, was, in effect, no more than an official identity card. It could not be used for foreign travel, which was available to a very small, privileged group of party faithful. Internal passports were issued in tsarist times and the documents were hated by many as a symbol of despotism. They were abolished by the Bolsheviks after they came to power, but then they were re-introduced in December 1932 in response to the massive migration of the rural population into the cities, in the midst of famine in the countryside. The internal **passport** introduced by the Soviets copied the same format as the tsarist model, in that the document not only contained information such as name, date of birth, and sex, but also nationality: this meant that if one were Jewish, it was recorded as such in the **passport**, rather than simply stating 'Russian'. The **passport** also contained a residence permit to live in towns and cities and it was thus used to control the movement of the population. One could not simply choose to settle in large cities and get accommodation and a job without specific permission to be in the city in the first place. Passports were issued to residents of Moscow and Leningrad (now St. Petersburg) at the beginning of 1933, and the issuing of them was gradually, but inevitably, extended to all major towns and cities. Certain categories of people were not eligible to hold a **passport** – former **kulaks**, priests, gypsies, prostitutes, members of the tsarist bourgeoisie, etc., and others deemed by the regime to be unsuitable, due to their political and social backgrounds. Internal **passports** were issued only exceptionally to rural inhabitants in order to stop widespread migration into the big cities. It was not until 1976 that the staged issuing of internal **passports** to rural dwellers was introduced, allowing them the legal right, at least in theory, to internal mobility. Permission to reside in large, important cities, such as Moscow and Leningrad, was very hard to come by, and, predictably, there were many scams for getting such permission, such as false or arranged marriages for money to a person who already had a residence permit. The internal **passport** was everything to the holder: without it, no job, housing, education, or anything legal could be accomplished.

Rural dwellers were also discriminated against over pensions. Pensions were introduced gradually for urban workers as early as 1928 for certain workers in factories and heavy industry, and by 1937 all urban workers had a right to a pension. However, it was not until 1964 that these rights were extended to collective farm workers, and even then, their level of pension was set lower than that for urban dwellers. Other rights accorded to urban workers, but not to collective farm workers, were health insurance, paid holidays, and minimum wage levels. For collective farm workers, the guaranteed minimum wage was not introduced until 1966.

Kolkhoz workers were also the last in line to be paid for their work. The state took their quota of produce first, in line with the **Plan**. After the state had taken its cut, any contracts with the local Machine Tractor Stations had to be settled. The next group of people to be paid were **kolkhoz** staff – the chairman, bookkeepers, vets and other experts and specialists, who all received a salary, irrespective of how productive the **kolkhoz** had been in any given year. It was only then, when all these debts had been cleared, that the **kolkhoz** workers were remunerated: it was very much a case of being cast crumbs from their masters' table.

One of the greatest problems which troubled the whole of the Soviet agricultural system was technical support. Soviet tractors and other big machinery were notoriously unreliable and spare parts were very hard to come by. In the late 1920s, heavy equipment, such as tractors, were concentrated in strategically located units called Machine Tractor Stations, or **MTS**. They maintained and repaired their own equipment, trained their own drivers and operators, and they hired their services out on a contractual basis to the **kolkhozes**. Needless to say, it was in the individual **kolkhoz** chairman's interest to keep well in with those in charge of the **MTSs** and their drivers, so that whenever there was a conflict of interests, i.e. when one farm wanted their grain to be harvested at the same time as that on other farms, any 'kindnesses' and favours shown would be 'remembered'. This kind of wheeling and dealing was the very essence of the chairman's job in dealing with all local officials and the **MTS**.

As well as having to work on the **kolkhoz**, workers were expected to attend meetings to discuss **kolkhoz** business and, in this sense, they had some say in how the farm was run and managed. Initially the **kolkhoz** chairman was simply appointed, but later, as part of the (rather thin) veneer of democracy, the **kolkhoz** members could elect their own chairman or chairwoman. Few women rose to the rank of chairwoman, but women agronomists and other specialists were not uncommon. As well as attending meetings to discuss **kolkhoz** business, workers were expected to attend lectures on politics, like all other Soviet workers. Such lectures were often deeply resented by the rural population, who felt that such issues were far removed from their own reality. Mozhaev uses these meetings as a rich source of comedy in his stories, when the proceedings often degenerate into clowning around.

Life on the farm was hard for the average **kolkhoz** worker: there was little infrastructure – roads were few and often impassable for long periods due to weather conditions. Public and private transport was extremely rare, unless the **kolkhoz** was near to a railway station or on a bus route, medical services were sparse, and there was little to do by way of entertainment – a travelling cinema might come around from time to time, and efforts were made to provide a rudimentary social club. Some enterprising peasants set up their own cottage industry making baskets, weaving cloth, or some other form of craft, but this was generally frowned upon because it was regarded as a distraction from official duties on the farm. Drunkenness was endemic, particularly amongst males, and bouts of heavy drinking often led to fights and domestic violence, which came under the general category of 'hooliganism', for which penalties could be quite severe. Most of these social problems went unacknowledged by the media, except during periodic official campaigns to clamp down on these social ills.

Apart from **kolkhoz** workers being told what to plant and where by the chairman, the chairmen were also ordered what to plant and cultivate by central planners in Moscow. In keeping with the ethos of the time, Soviet leaders and ministers were always looking for the 'quick fix', i.e. a 'one-size-fits-all' solution to major problems in Russian industry and agriculture. Stalin and his successors were all anxious to develop their industry and economy at full tilt, in order to make up for Russia's backwardness. As hated ideologically as it was, both Stalin and Khrushchëv looked to America as the gold standard to be achieved – they saw it as a horn of plenty when it came to food supplies, especially meat. Before rising to the position of First Secretary of the Communist Party and also the Premier of the Soviet Union, Khrushchëv became heavily involved in agricultural production and planning from the late 1940s onwards, and even as First Secretary and Premier of the Soviet Union, he maintained a lively interest in agriculture, though he was by no means an expert. He convinced himself that growing maize was the panacea for all Soviet agriculture's ills, after having made a trip to the United States of America. Consequently, with little real scientific examination and consultation with experts, he ordered vast swathes of land to be planted with maize. Some of this land included water-meadows around Mozhaev's own village, which had to be drained before it could be sown with maize. However, this caused huge ecological damage, and Mozhaev wrote numerous passionate articles against this policy, which he saw as an act of sheer vandalism. Khrushchëv's plan to sow maize was celebrated in the Soviet media and his association with maize was so strong that he was given the nickname of 'Uncle Maize' (Diadia Kukuruznik). His photograph appeared on many occasions in newspapers and magazines with fists full of maize to promote its cultivation. Like many 'quick fixes' and grand projects attempted in Russia, they were promoted by leaders and officials whose knowledge was poor. Such projects were typical of the utopian dreaming which gripped many prominent Soviet politicians and leaders, and **kolkhoz** chairmen and workers had little option but to obey instructions passed on from on high, irrespective of whether they believed the project would be successful or not. The experiment was not a success and it caused great environmental damage in Mozhaev's own region and elsewhere.

Another similar project, also initiated by Khrushchёv, was his **Virgin Lands** programme. Russia had struggled to feed itself throughout the Soviet era and, in an effort to increase grain yields, new land had to be found. For various reasons, Khrushchёv decided on using virgin land in Kazakhstan, eastern Siberia and the Volga basin, and an initial area of some 30 million hectares were set aside. In Kazakhstan the soil was extremely fertile – it was of the *chernozem*, or 'black earth', type, which was rich in fertility and of a good structure. Many millions of hectares of virgin land were ploughed up for sowing crops, but in the process, the plan destroyed the traditional life of the nomadic Kazakh people, who protested. True to form, the Soviet regime rode roughshod over such objections, claiming that the end justified the means, or, to use a Russian expression, 'when wood is chopped, chips fly'. A campaign was launched in 1954, with direct appeals made particularly to the **Komsomol**, and three hundred thousand volunteers were recruited to work on hundreds of newly founded farms. The plan was successful in some respects, but there were constant problems with supplies of machinery and fertilizers. Newspapers and magazines made much of the recruiting campaign and whenever the yields were good, and reports of the scheme were championed with all the enthusiasm of Wild West pioneers. For the first couple of years, yields of corn were good, but the soil quickly became depleted of minerals and nutrients, and soil erosion by the wind led to yet another ecological disaster. Also, Soviet industry could not keep up with the production of combine harvesters to cope with harvesting the crop, and grain left unharvested in the field was not uncommon, though it was rarely reported in the press.

As the Soviet Union disintegrated during the last years of the regime, the **kolkhoz** system also fell apart. A great deal of former **kolkhoz** land was sold to independent farmers cheaply, and gradually, but very slowly, small independent farms started to appear, as people saw the possibility of making a living by working the land once again, as truly independent farmers. Ironically, those who returned to their rural roots, or discovered them for the first time, were actually farming in a way that Mozhaev had advocated all along. He did not claim he was any kind of guru or visionary – he simply felt that what he had said was just plain, common sense.

The story of agricultural organization and practice in Russia has been a complex and painful tale. Even as late as 2006, when a national agricultural census was announced – the first of its kind for eighty-five years – a central Russian newspaper reported the planned census under the title 'No one will be dekulakized'.[1] The title of the article is highly significant: the Russian state, and particularly the Bolsheviks, had dealt with the rural population with a very harsh and unjust hand, and memories of the horrors of collectivization and its concomitant policies are still fresh and painful, even decades later. Rural farmers were still deeply suspicious of the motivation behind the census and the inventory to be taken on the size of individual farms, and what was being produced on them. Obviously, farmers were not in fear of their lives, but they thought that the

---

[1] *Moskovskie novosti*, 'Nikogo ne raskulachat', No.19, 2006. Unfortunately, this article has not been translated into English. I am grateful to the *Information Digest* (Autumn 2006) of the Society for Co-operation in Russian and Soviet Studies for drawing my attention to this article.

information would be used to levy even greater taxes upon them. Such is the mistrust in Russia which still exists between the farmer and the state today.

Investment in the Russian domestic agro-industry is very low for the size of Russia and the number of people who have to be fed. Even now, there is no national food policy in Russia. The crisis goes on…

Glossary

arshin
An old Russian measurement, roughly equal to 71 cm.

ataman
An ataman (or 'hetman') was the title given to male leaders of groups of Cossacks, who were known for their horsemanship, swordsmanship, and bravery in battle.

Baba Yaga
A witch from Russian folklore, who lives in a broken-down hut, which stands, and even revolves, on chickens' feet. Traditionally, she is said to surround her house with a fence on which she places skulls and she gets around using a mortar and pestle, though some stories have her using the traditional witch's broomstick. She is said to capture children and eat them in her house, which is to be found in the depths of the forest. She is also associated with the onset of winter and has the ability to turn living things into stone. This folkloric character features in Mussorgsky's piano suite *Pictures from an Exhibition* (1874).

bania
A Russian version of the sauna. It was housed in a separate building, usually some distance from the main dwelling, because fires were not uncommon as the **bania** or sauna was heated to a high temperature. There were also a number of superstitions and folklore associated with the **bania**, such as the **bania** should not be frequented at night because evil spirits tended to gather there.

barin
A landowner in pre-revolutionary Russia.

barynia
Usually a female landowner, or a landowner's wife, but the term can also refer to a popular type of folk song, accompanied by a dance, which has as it's subject matter a **barynia**.

bast shoes
These were traditionally worn by peasants. They were woven from strips of bark from the linden or lime tree, and coarsely plaited.

bayan
A kind of accordion.

brigade/brigade leader
The Soviet workforce was organized along militaristic lines and groups of workers were called 'brigades', who were under the control of a '**brigade leader**'.

centner
A centner is a measurement, equivalent to a hundred kilograms.

chastushka
(plural *chastushki*) A popular form of verse, sometimes translated as 'ditty'. It is a four-line, rhyming verse, which is invented extempore. Such verses often provide an element of entertainment at bouts of heavy drinking and they offer an amusing commentary on everyday life, and even politics. If overheard by the wrong person, such verses might even have caused a person to end up in a prison camp in the 1930s, during the purges, as they were deemed to be 'anti-Soviet'.

Comrades' Court

A mechanism to deal with petty incidents of breaches in discipline and personal behaviour. They were convened in places of work, or similar venues, with the agreement of other workers and people in authority. Members of a **Comrades' Court** were elected for a period of membership of up to two years, but the numbers sitting in the 'court' depended on the size of the establishment it represented. Any minor matter of absenteeism or drunkenness at work, black-marketeering, petty crime, or repeated failure to fulfil one's duties, would be considered at the **Comrades' Court**. Fines of up to fifty roubles could be imposed. (This was quite a high percentage of a worker's monthly wage.) In addition to a fine, public confessions and personal humiliation were a staple feature of such 'courts', and they had the power to recommend that the matter be taken further and considered in a legal court of law.

debentures

These were official documents issued by the state, with which, on production, the holder had the right to receive a fixed rate of interest. They were a form of premium bond sold in favour of the state at savings banks, for which a small interest was paid.

dekulakization

The Bolshevik policy of destroying the **kulaks**, or so-called 'rich' farmers, as a class. Officials and activists confiscated the property and animals of these peasants, and exiled them (sometimes with their family), to far-off, inhospitable areas of Russia, or to prison camps, depending on the severity of the campaign at the time. Their property and livestock were taken for use on the new **kolkhoz**.

dezhurnaia

In Soviet Russia, there was a whole army of *dezhurnye* (the plural form) or 'women on duty', who sat in vestibules, entrance halls, hotel corridors, and in every room of museums, etc. There job was to keep an eye on visitors and passers-by, or tell people, in no uncertain terms, not to touch museum exhibits. Generally, it was women who performed such menial duties and it was partly due to these people that the Soviet Union could brag that it had full employment. However, they were very lowly paid.

domovoi

A 'house demon' or 'sprite' from Russian folk mythology. Traditionally, he has the appearance of a wizened old man and he lives beneath the stove. Periodically, he had to be placated with gifts of food or the owner risked him getting up to mischief. If the family moved, he had to be coaxed into a shoe to be transported to a new house.

drozhki

A light, four-wheeled carriage.

element/elements

The word '**element**' was an essential part of Soviet political cant, churned out in newspapers and speeches, particularly, but by no means exclusively, in the 1930s, to refer to deviants or dissenters of every kind. Those found guilty of hooliganism, drunkenness, and even fathers who abandoned their families to avoid paying maintenance to them – a common social phenomenon in the 1930s – were all hotly pursued as '**elements**'. See also under '**enemy/enemies of the people**'.

enemy/enemies of the people

The official Bolshevik/Soviet epithet for anyone deemed to be against the regime, especially during the early years of the Bolshevik regime and Stalinist times. A person might not have shown any animosity towards the regime at all, but they could be dubbed 'enemies' just by having the 'wrong' background. Priests, intellectuals, gypsies, homosexuals, prostitutes, dispossessed **kulaks**, etc., were all viewed as being **enemies of the people**. Nor did such people have to do anything against the regime – anyone harbouring opinions critical of the Soviet regime was enough to be classified as 'an **enemy of the people**' or as a '**secret element**', or '**saboteur**'. Even genuine mistakes at work, especially those made by people in managerial positions, were dubbed as 'acts of sabotage'. Once such allegations had been made, it was very difficult, if not impossible, to clear one's name, and such a person became a social outcast, making it problematic to get further employment and even access to education and other social services. The stigma of such a 'stained background' was even inherited by children from their parent(s).

footcloths

These were pieces of cloth which were wrapped around the feet, instead of wearing socks, before slipping the foot into a **bast shoe**, which laced up the wearer's leg.

fortochka

A 'ventilation window'. It is a small window set within a larger window frame. It can be opened to let a little fresh air in, rather than opening the entire window.

FZO

A Russian acronym for a form of technical college, providing courses of a practical nature, plus a general education. Russia was desperately short of well-trained personnel for its rapidly expanding industrialization projects, and many rural inhabitants saw getting a specialist education as a way to a better, more comfortable life in the city. Many people in the 1930s underwent intensive courses in such institutions, including people like Khrushchëv and Brezhnev, and they subsequently rose to prominent positions in the Soviet hierarchy. In fact, many people trained in this way were not terribly well-educated, as Khrushchëv felt and admitted in his memoirs.

GDR

The acronym for German Democratic Republic, or East Germany, as it was better known in the West.

Gorky (city)

Gorky is an ancient Russian town, originally called Nizhnii Novgorod, which was re-named under the Soviets in 1932, and remained so until 1990. The Soviet writer Maxim **Gorky**, much fêted by the regime, was born there, and the town was renamed in his honour. Until the Revolution of 1917, Nizhnii Novgorod was host to the largest market in Russia. The annual fair, established in 1817, used to attract traders from afar, from Europe and Asia. During the Soviet period, many industrial complexes of a military nature were built and operated there and, for this reason, the city was officially categorized as a 'closed city', i.e. foreigners and even many Russian citizens were not allowed to visit or take up residence there without special permission.

Gorky, Maksim (writer)

Maxim **Gorky** (1868-1936) was a writer from a humble background, who wrote stories, plays and novels about working-class people. He became a Marxist and he enjoyed considerable popularity and influence within the new Soviet regime, though he often found himself at odds with Lenin. His greatest literary achievement is his autobiographical trilogy, written towards the end of his life, which vividly portrays the harsh working conditions of ordinary people. He became the first chairman of the Soviet **Writers' Union**, when it was founded in 1934, an organization created to control writers in terms of both the content and style of their writing. For more information on the Writers' Union, see Appendix I.

Great Patriotic War

A common epithet for the Second World War.

guberniia

The largest division of land for administrative purposes, founded in the eighteenth century by Peter the Great. The Soviet government brought in new divisions and terminology for administrative areas and delineations in 1924-29, during which time, the term **guberniia** was abandoned.

hang-over from the past

A set expression redolent of Soviet political cant. When the Bolsheviks seized power in 1917, many things from the so-called former 'bourgeois regime', or from tsarist times, were disparagingly called a 'hang-over from the past'. Almost anything from a way of dressing and speaking, to attitudes towards politics, literature, etc., were condemned and disapproved of, and great efforts were made to re-educate people into the new, Soviet way of thinking.

heated bee house

A heated structure used to over-winter bees in the harsh Russian winter climate.

kamarinskaia

A Russian folk song, which is traditionally accompanied with a dance. It is a quick, lively dance.

kolkhoz

A collective farm.

Komsomol

Komsomol means The Young Communist League, or, to give it its full title, 'The All-Union Lenin Communist Union of Youth'. Founded in 1918, it was primarily a political organization in the former Soviet Union for young people from the age of fourteen to twenty-eight. Its purpose was to promote political awareness and knowledge among young people, but it also organized social events. Although membership was voluntary in theory, young people were expected to join, and its members were frequently favoured over non-members in schools, universities and in the work place. Its aid and activists were enlisted for a whole range of campaigns and propagandistic efforts, to help in the everyday organization of mundane activities, from 'educational' to social events, but also in large-scale projects, such as the full collectivization of agriculture. In the early years of the Soviet regime, membership was regarded as a privilege, but with time it became *de rigueur*, even for admission to university. Hence, many people joined, even though they shared little enthusiasm for the communist cause. Admission to full membership of the Communist Party was not automatic after being a member of the **Komsomol**, though it helped, and it was even expected.

kopeck

A hundredth part of a rouble. It has now fallen out of use, but it was possible, during most of the Soviet era, to buy things for just a few kopecks – for example, for many years an unrestricted ride on the Moscow underground system used to cost just five kopecks, and a telephone call within the city, from a public telephone booth, use to cost only two kopecks, irrespective of the length of the call.

krai
A large administrative division of the former Soviet Union, similar to an **oblast**.

kulak
One of three broad Soviet classifications of peasants, this one being the wealthiest and most productive. Because **kulaks** often employed other peasants to work for them, they were regarded as capitalists and as such they were hated by the early Bolsheviks.

kvass
A type of home-made beer.

Literaturnaia gazeta
A weekly publication of great influence in the former Soviet Union. It had a long history, dating back to pre-revolutionary times, but from 1934 until the demise of the Soviet Union, it was the official organ of the **Writers' Union**. It contained short stories, extracts of fiction, reviews, critical essays on literary topics, as well as publicistic material, i.e. essays on important political, social and environmental issues. Mozhaev contributed many essays and articles to this publication. It still exists today, though it is now independent of the state.

mound
In some regions of Russia, peasant houses were built of logs, as was usual, but after their construction, a **mound** of earth was placed on the side of the prevailing wind to provide protection from the severe weather.

MTS
A Russian acronym for 'Machine Tractor Station'. These were centres which were set up during the First Five Year **Plan** (1928-32), which promised 100,000 tractors by the end of the **plan** period. They were centralized facilities, providing agricultural machinery, such as tractors and combine harvesters, and the drivers to operate them. The drivers and those working for the **MTS** were very well paid for their services by contrast with the **kolkhoz** farmers themselves, who were last in line to be remunerated for their work, after the state, **MTS** staff, and other 'specialists' (such as agronomists, vets, etc.) had been paid in full. They also serviced their own equipment. One such station would serve a number of **kolkhozes** and they leased their work to the **kolkhoz** on a contract basis, which paid them directly for their services. The **MTSs** were beset by various problems, not least of which was getting spare parts for agricultural machinery, and many stood idle or worked very inefficiently. They were disbanded by a government reform in 1958 onwards, under Khrushchëv, and the impoverished **kolkhozes** were forced to buy the machinery, which led them yet further into debt.

NKVD
The Russian acronym for the People's Commissariat of Internal Affairs, which was the Soviet secret police, the precursor of the more famous KGB, an organization which went though several changes of name, though their activities remained essentially the same.

Novyi mir
One of the **thick journals** to appear monthly, published in Moscow from 1925 onwards, as the organ of the **Writers' Union**. The title means 'New World', which

reflects the utopian optimism of early Bolshevism. The fortunes and reputation of the publication as a liberal, progressive journal have fluctuated enormously, but its most brilliant period was under the editorship of Alexander **Tvardovskii**, from 1950-54 and 1958-70. It regained a reputation for being in the vanguard of reform and liberalization during the Gorbachëv era of *glasnost*, and for a number of years after that, when many works, which had been written with no hope of publication, appeared in it. The journal published a number of Solzhenitsyn's works in the mid-1990s.

oblast
An administrative classification of land, which varies in size according to the region, or *raion*, within which it falls. It can easily be as large as a whole province or region. It is akin to an English county, or larger.

okrug
A small administrative division of land.

Old Believer
The **Old Believers** were a sect of the Russian Orthodox Church. In 1666, a number of reforms were proposed which would change some aspects of Orthodox liturgy and practice. A number of believers did not agree with these changes and they broke away from the Orthodox Church, preferring to continue in the tradition they had always known. From this time onwards, this break-away group became known as '**Old Believers**'.

papakha
A Caucasian fur hat.

passport
Also known as an 'internal **passport**', this document was, in effect, no more than an official identity card. These documents were essential for obtaining residence permits and work, but they were denied to rural inhabitants until 1976 onwards. For more details, see Appendix II, p.443.

pay advance
In the former Soviet Union, workers were paid monthly, but they were given a proportion of their salary halfway through the month: this was called an 'advance'.

pelmeni
A form of pasta with a filling inside, very similar to Italian ravioli.

pertsovka
This is one of many flavoured vodkas available. This variety of vodka is flavoured with pepper or *capsicum*, which is called '*perets*' in Russian, whence its name is derived.

Pioneers
The '**Pioneers**' was the communist youth organization for children between the ages of 10-15. It was founded in 1922 and in many ways it was an organization similar to the Scouts, but with a strong propagandistic element: it organised camps and activities for young people. In fact, it was based on the British scout movement, being called 'Red Scouts', but it was subsequently renamed 'Red Pathfinders'. The movement underwent further changes and became the Pioneer Organization.

plan
A production quota handed down from central planners to all forms of Soviet industry, including farms. Planners in Moscow worked out how much of a certain commodity needed to be produced on a national level, then this quantity was

broken down into **oblast, raion**, and **krai** levels, and entrusted to local officials to demand a set quota from each factory or farm in their area, town, or district. This whole process was subject to a good deal of negotiation and bartering at local level, and a local official could satisfy all manner of former favours or personal grudges against individuals in charge of production units. The **plan** was sacrosanct and the quota had to be met, but it was preferable that the target should be exceeded, or 'overfulfilled'. Failure to meet the quotas often meant managers and officials were sacked. Within the Soviet system, not 'overfulfilling the **plan**' could indicate a serious lack of enthusiasm or effort on the part of those in charge.

pood

An old Russian measurement of weight, equal to 16·38 kg.

raion

A region or area. It is a designation of an administrative area, the next category down from an **oblast**.

reading-room

The reading room was usually a peasant house, often confiscated from a former **kulak**, but sometimes purpose-built, which kept a small library and daily newspapers for the use of the villagers. They sported propaganda posters and large portraits of Soviet leaders, especially Lenin, along with books on politics and other subjects. Literacy was promoted from such **reading rooms**, but it was heavily imbued with political and propagandistic material, as the state propaganda machine was keen to promote universal literacy, along with a political education. See Mozhaev's story 'The Saddler', included in this volume.

Red Room or **Red Corner**

Most institutions and offices, including schools, universities, and colleges, had a **Red Room**, or **Red Corner**. This was an area dedicated to communist propaganda and it featured Lenin and other icons of communism. Red was the chosen colour of the communist cause and all official banners and flags were of that colour, and Soviet young people were regularly told at school that it was the colour of blood, split by brave fighters for the cause.

Riazan

The main city of the **Riazan oblast** or area. **Riazan** (or Ryazan) is a real place and it is situated on the Oka River, about 193 km to the south-east of Moscow. It is also the city which has lent its name to the whole administrative region around it, and it is the regional capital or principal town. It was Mozhaev's own native region. Today, it has a population of around 515,000 people and its principal industries are engineering, petrochemical and oil-refining. It is, in fact, a very ancient town, whose earliest recorded history goes back to 1095 and it was destroyed in 1237 by the Mongols. It was sacked by the Tatars in 1372 and 1378, and it became the seat of the **Riazan** princedom in the fifteenth century. It has an ancient citadel, or *kremlin*, and the Russian nineteenth-century satirist, Mikhail Egrafovich Saltykov-Shchedrin (1826-89), worked there. Mozhaev was a great admirer of Saltykov-Shchedrin and he quotes him in a number of his works.

saboteur

See under **enemy of the people**.

secret element

See under **enemy of the people**.

sotka

(plural *sotki*) A measurement based on a hundred part, i.e. a hundredth part of a field. A worker was allowed to hold a private plot of fifteen *sotki*, or fifteen hundredth parts, which is equivalent to about 1,500 square metres.

sovkhoz

A 'state farm', as opposed to a '**kolkhoz**', which was a 'collective farm'. On the **sovkhoz**, the workers received a standard wage, just like a factory worker, and all produce went straight to the state. A **kolkhoz** worker's pay depended on how productive the farm was, and its produce was sold to the state at negotiated prices, and any surplus could be sold privately. **Sovkhoz** workers also did not have the same rights to private plots, which were much valued by **kolkhoz** workers.

Stenka Razin

A Russian folk hero, who epitomized freedom and a pioneering spirit. He was born in 1630 of a rather wealthy Don Cossack family and he became the chief, or **hetman**, of a band of runaway serfs from Poland and Russia. The band carried out raids on Russian and Persian settlements – they even captured a whole town and a flotilla of boats carrying goods owned by the tsar. Thus, the band acquired great wealth and fame, and the ranks of his group swelled to over 20,000 men. This personal army was a constant source of trouble to the tsar, who despatched his own forces to fight against them, and they were eventually overcome. Razin was captured and executed – he was hung, drawn, and quartered in Red Square, in Moscow, in December 1671.

tarantass

A type of Russian carriage without springs.

thick journals

The Soviet Union used to produce a huge number of journals of various kinds, a tradition inherited from tsarist times. Some of the most popular and prestigious were literary journals, which usually came out every month and featured works of fiction, plus essays on topical subjects, and literary criticism. Each journal had its own particular slant, reflecting the views of the editor-in-chief and writers accepted for publication by him or her. Amongst the most prestigious of these journals were *Novyi mir* (New World), *Nash sovremennik* (Our Contemporary), *Oktiabr* (October), and many more. These were available throughout the Soviet Union, especially in libraries. There were also regional journals, which promoted the writing of less well-known writers and favoured those whose native area they represented. Often regional journals managed to print more contentious works because they were not as closely scrutinized by censorship closer to Moscow. It was usual publishing practice for an author's work to appear in a **thick journal** before being subsequently printed in book form. Some of these Soviet journals have survived after the collapse of the Soviet Union and they are now operating independently from the state.

Tvardovskii

Tvardovskii, Alexander Trifonovich (1910-71) was the courageous editor of one of Russia's most prestigious journals, *Novyi mir* (New World), which published Solzhenitsyn's *One Day in the Life of Ivan Denisovich*. It was also under **Tvardovskii** that Mozhaev's controversial story *From the Life of Fëdor Kuzkin* or *Lively*, as Mozhaev preferred it to be called, was published, which also had to be sanctioned by the highest authorities before its publication.

uezd
> A small, pre-revolutionary administrative division of land, which fell within a **guberniia**.

verst
> An old Russian measurement of distance, roughly equivalent to 1·06 kilometres.

Virgin Lands
> The **Virgin Lands** programme was one of Khrushchëv's schemes to try and increase grain production rapidly in the Soviet Union. Virgin land in Kazakhstan, eastern Siberia, and the **Volga** basin, was selected to be ploughed up and planted with corn. The **Komsomol** and three hundred thousand volunteers were recruited to work on hundreds of newly founded farms. The result was an ecological disaster.

Volga
> As well as being the name of the great River **Volga**, there was a car called a **Volga**, which was widely used by Soviet officials and politicians. The car was large and black, and they could often be seen in Soviet times with curtains at the windows, ferrying officials around at high speeds in dedicated traffic lanes along the wide boulevards of Moscow and other cities. All other traffic and drivers were expected to pull out of the way of these cars, as they conveyed VIPs on official business, which, in Moscow, almost invariably meant the Kremlin and other ministries.

volost
> The smallest administrative division of tsarist Russia.

voluntary work
> In the former Soviet Union, workers of every description, including school children and university students, were 'requested' to take part in some form of **voluntary work** on Saturdays and/or Sundays. This could range from anything from picking up litter, to communal gardening, or some similar type of community work. Technically, they were all recruited on a voluntary basis, but most people felt they could not refuse, due to pressure from their peers and bosses.

War Communism
> The period called 'War Communism' (1918-21) refers to the early years of trying to establish firmly the Soviet regime, which was beset by all manner of opponents, such as the White Guards and the majority of the peasantry, who viewed Bolshevism with great suspicion and hostility. All economic activity was seized and controlled by the state, and placed under centralized control. This led to unprecedented material deprivation, which further alienated the peasantry and many others. By 1921 Lenin realized that things could not carry on as they were, and it was then that controls were relaxed, amidst great political and philosophical debate, and the New Economic Policy was instituted, which many saw as a step backwards towards capitalism, since it allowed again a degree of private enterprise.

workday unit
> A system of remuneration for **kolkhoz** workers, until the pay structure was changed in the mid-1950s. Each task or job on the **kolkhoz** was attributed a value in terms of a '**workday unit**', and workers were paid according to how many units they had amassed by the end of the agricultural season.

work-record booklet
> All urban workers and employees had a **work-record booklet** in which all their personal and professional details were noted, including any special prizes or bonuses awarded for distinguishing themselves at work. However, the converse

was also true – any disciplinary action taken against workers for 'breaches in work discipline', as it was officially called, was also noted. Every time a worker changed his or her job, the booklet had to be shown. It was also on the basis of this work record that a worker's pension was granted. However, **kolkhoz** workers or farmers had no internal **passport** or **work-record booklet** until well into the 1970s. As such, rural workers were treated very much as second-class citizens.

Writers' Union

An exclusive organization to which an author had to belong to publish his or her works officially. It was not a trade union in the normal sense of the word: it was more akin to an exclusive club, which had in its gift a whole raft of privileges and perks, which could be granted or withdrawn at any time, depending on whether a writer toed the official line or not.

Suggested Further Reading

There is a vast library of books on Russian politics, history, cultural studies, and sociology, etc., to choose from. Below is a list of just a few of the books which seem most relevant to understanding the history of modern Russia and the ethos of the Soviet Union, with a slant towards understanding rural life and the issues that Mozhaev raises, in particular. The choice is almost endless, but it is hoped that the interested reading, who wants to find out more about these issues, will find the following list useful.

Books and Articles Specifically on Mozhaev

D. Gillespie, 'History, Politics, and the Russian Peasant: Boris Mozhaev and the Collectivization of Agriculture', *Slavonic and Eastern European* Review, 67, No.2 (1989), 183-210

D.M. Holohan, *Collectivization and the Utopian Ideal in the Works of Boris Andreevich Mozhaev* (Unpublished PhD thesis, The University of Bath, 1994)

D.M. Holohan, writer entry and entry on *Peasant Folk* in *Reference Guide to Russian Literature*, ed. by Neil Cornwell (Fitzroy Dearborn: London/Chicago, 1998)

D.M. Holohan, 'Boris Mozhaev: One of Russia's Troublesome Writers "In Residence"', *The Salisbury Review*, 25, No.2 (Winter 2006), 24-26

K.F. Parthé, *Russian Village Prose: The Radiant Past* (Princeton: Princeton University Press, 1992)

L. Saraskina, 'People of the Resistance', *Moscow News*, 31 July (1988), p.10

Books with Passing References to Mozhaev

Birgit Beumers, *Yury Lyubimov at the Taganka Theatre, 1964-1994* (Northampton, U.K.: Harwood Academic Publishers, 1997)

D. Brown, *The Last Years of Soviet Russian Literature: Prose Fiction 1975-1991* (Cambridge: Cambridge University Press, 1993)

D. Gillespie, 'Ironies and Legacies: Village Prose and Glasnost'', *Forum for Modern Language Studies*, xxvii, No.1 (1991)

D. Gillespie, 'Russian Writers Confront the Past: History, Memory and Literature, 1953-1991, *World Literature Today: Literary Quarterly of the University of Oklahoma* (Winter 1993), 74-79

R. Marsh, *History and Literature in Contemporary Russia*, (Oxford: Macmillan, 1995)

A. Nove, *Glasnost' in Action: Cultural Renaissance in Russia* (London: Unwin Hyman, 1989)

A.I. Solzhenitsyn, *Invisible Allies*, translated from the Russian by Alexis Klimoff and Michael Nicholson, (London: The Harvill Press, 1997), 158-59

A.I. Solzhenitsyn, *The Calf and the Oak: Sketches of Literary Life in the Soviet Union*, translated by H. Willetts (New York: Harper and Row, 1980)

Books on Rural Life, Collectivization and the Peasantry

R. Conquest, *The Harvest of Sorrow: Soviet Collectivisation and the Terror-Famine* (London: Pimlico, 2002)

B. Eklof and S.P. Frank, (eds.), *The World of the Russian Peasant: Post-Emancipation Culture and Society* (Boston: Unwin Hayman, 1990)

S. Fitzpatrick, *Stalin's Peasants: Resistance and Survival in the Russian Village After Collectivization* (New York: Oxford University Press, 1994)

O. Litvinenko, *Memories of the Dispossessed. Descendents of Kulak Families Tell their Stories. Personal Histories*, translated and edited by James Riordan (Bramcote Press, 1998)

D.J. Male, *Russian Peasant Organisation before Collectivisation: A Study of Commune and Gathering 1925-1930* (Cambridge: Cambridge University Press, 1971)

L. Viola, *Peasant Rebels Under Stalin: Collectivization and the Culture of Peasant Resistance* (New York: Oxford University Press, 1996)

General Books on Russian History

R. Pipes, *Russia under the Old Regime*, 2nd edn, (London: Penguin, 1995)

R. Service, *A History of Twentieth Century Russia* (London: Penguin, 1998)

R. Service, *Russia: Experiment with a People. From 1991 to the Present* (London: Macmillan, 2002)

D. Volkogonov, *The Rise and Fall of the Soviet Empire: Political Leaders from Lenin to Gorbachev* (London: Harper Collins, 1999)

The Russian Chronicles, foreword by Norman Stone, numerous editors (London: Century, 1990)

Other Works of Interest

R. Conquest, *Stalin: Breaker of Nations* (London: Weidenfeld and Nicolson, 1991)

S. Fitzpatrick, *The Cultural Front: Power and Culture in Revolutionary Russia* (Ithaca: Cornell University Press, 1992)

S. Fitzpatrick, *Everyday Stalinism: Ordinary Life in Extraordinary Times: Soviet Russia in the 1930s* (New York: Oxford University Press, 1999)

J. von Geldern and R. Stites (eds.) *Mass Culture in Soviet Russia: Tales, Poems, Songs, Movies, Plays, and Folklore 1917-1953* (Bloomington: Indiana University Press, 1995)

J. Gooding, *Socialism in Russia: Lenin and his Legacy, 1890-1991* (Basinstoke, Hampshire: Palgrave, 2002)

G.A. Hosking, 'The Russian Peasant Rediscovered: "Village Prose" of the 1960s', *Slavic Review*, 4 (1973), 705-24

G.A. Hosking, *Beyond Socialist Realism – Soviet Fiction Since Ivan Denisovich* (London: Elek, 1980)

R.A. Medvedev and Z.A. Medvedev, *Khrushchev: The Years in Power* (New York: Norton, 1978)

R. Medvedev, *Let History Judge: The Origins and Consequences of Stalinism* (Oxford: Oxford University Press, 1989)

Z.A. Medvedev, *Soviet Agriculture* (New York: Norton, 1987)

M.E. Saltykov-Shchedrin, *The History of a Town*, translated by I.P. Foote (Oxford: Willem A. Meeuws, 1980)

R. Stites, *Russian Popular Culture: Entertainment and Society since 1900* (Cambridge Soviet Paperbacks, 1992)

R. Stites, *Revolutionary Dreams: Utopian Vision and Experimental Life in the Russian Revolution* (New York: Oxford University Press, 1989)

W. Taubman, *Khrushchev: The Man and His Era* (London: Free Press, 2003)

S.K. Wegren, *Agriculture and the State in Soviet and Post-Soviet Russia* (Pittsburgh: University of Pittsburgh Press, 1998)

Printed in the United Kingdom
by Lightning Source UK Ltd.
119041UK00002B/24